920
LOM

Lomask, Milton.

12356

**Great lives :
invention and
technology.**

$19.51

DATE DUE	BORROWER'S NAME	ROOM NO.

920
LOM

Lomask, Milton.

12356

**Great lives :
invention and
technology.**

INDIAN PLAINS SCHOOL
DISTRICT 204

GREAT LIVES

Invention and Technology

6 3684

Invention and Technology

GREAT LIVES

Milton Lomask

Charles Scribner's Sons · New York
Maxwell Macmillan Canada · Toronto
Maxwell Macmillan International
New York · Oxford · Singapore · Sydney

Charles Scribner's Sons Books for Young Readers
Macmillan Publishing Company · 866 Third Avenue, New York, NY 10022

Maxwell Macmillan Canada, Inc.
1200 Eglinton Avenue East, Suite 200, Don Mills, Ontario M3C 3N1

Macmillan Publishing Company is part of the Maxwell Communication Group of Companies.

First edition   10 9 8 7 6 5 4 3 2 1
Printed in the United States of America
Cover illustration copyright © 1991 by Stephen Marchesi. All rights reserved.
Library of Congress Cataloging-in-Publication Data
Lomask, Milton.
  Great lives : invention and technology / Milton Lomask.
  — 1st ed.   p.   cm.   Includes bibliographical references and index.
  Summary: Brief life stories of twenty-seven persons whose inventions or discoveries have altered the environment to a marked degree. Includes a list of important dates in the history of invention and technology.
  ISBN 0–684–19106–7
1. Inventors—Biography—Juvenile literature.
2. Inventions—Juvenile literature.
[1. Inventors.   2. Inventions.]   I. Title.
T39.L64 1991   609.2′2—dc20   [B] [920]   90–27619

For Ray Neville
with thanks

Contents

Foreword

Mankind inventing or mankind discovering the techniques that make inventions possible would seem to be mankind at his most human. Other animals must take their environment as they find it. Only *homo sapiens*, "thinking man," can change his environment, sometimes by bringing into existence new things and new ways of doing things, sometimes by enlarging his understanding of the world around him.

The pages that follow offer brief life stories of twenty-seven persons whose inventions or discoveries have altered the environment to a marked degree. Supplementing these biographical sketches is a list of important dates in the history of invention and technology, aimed at providing the reader with the names of some of the many other laborers in these fields.

Although, according to an ancient saying, necessity is the mother of invention, most of the stories in this book seem to support the often-expressed contention that the opposite is true—that invention is the mother of necessity.

A case in point is what happened in the wake of Alexander Graham Bell's invention of the telephone in 1876. Today most of us find it hard to imagine life without Bell's ingenious gadget, but at least twenty years went by after its appearance before very many people realized that they needed it. In 1880 the famous British author Herbert Spencer noted that in London, the capital of his country, "the telephone is scarcely used at all and it is unknown in the other English cities."

In America, during the administrations of presidents Grover Cleveland and Benjamin Harrison, a twelve-year period ending in 1897, the White House, in Washington, D.C., boasted only one telephone, and we are told that nobody but the servants used it.

What moved Bell to create the speaking telegraph, as the telephone was first called, was his desire as a teacher of the deaf to help his students. He believed that, having found a way to "make a deaf-mute talk," he could use his knowledge of electricity and materials "to make metal talk."

New information first, then invention: thus has much of what we call progress come about. In 1859 an American discovered—or, rather, rediscovered—how to bring a deeply buried substance called oil to the surface of the earth, and a few years later a group of German engineers began building successful internal combustion engines and putting the age of the automobile underway. In the 1870s and 1880s a Scottish physicist predicted and then a German physicist confirmed the presence in the atmosphere of electromagnetic or radio waves. In the 1890s an Italian physicist, building on these scientific findings, gave us the wireless telegraph, forerunner of the radio.

If this book, dealing as it does with an array of highly different individuals, can be said to have a central theme, it is this: that discovery is the true begetter of most new products and new processes. It is as our knowledge of the universe grows that inventions multiply.

M. L.

Charles Babbage

1791–1871   English mathematician; a pioneer in the development
of the modern computer

For sixty-six years following the death
of Charles Babbage in the fall of 1871
he was the forgotten man of English
science and invention.

Visitors to the Science Museum in
London, England, paid scant attention
to a machine he had constructed, a device known as the Difference Engine,
which still stands in the exhibit halls
of that institution. Unexamined for the
most part was the large collection of
his papers, the notebooks and engineering drawings that one of his sons had
presented to the museum. Almost
wholly ignored were the twelve books
and over seventy articles published by
Babbage during his lifetime.

Not until 1937 did all this change.
Then, thanks to a mounting interest in
the experiments that have given us to-

day's electronic digital computer, Babbage was rediscovered. Soon scientists
and engineers were scrutinizing his
notebooks and drawings. Computer-
minded persons all over the world were
searching for copies of his published
works. What they learned was that Babbage, in the words of his biographer
Anthony Hyman, was "the great ancestral figure of computing," the dean of
its early pioneers.

Designs among his papers at the Science Museum show that what Babbage
called his Analytical Engine, a successor
to his Difference Engine, boasted practically all of the main features of today's
computers. He was the first person to
devise a mechanism for the storage of
the data put into a computer, what we
now call its "memory." He was the first

1

to create a unit capable of performing a wide variety of mathematical calculations. He was the first to create the means by which a computer can be told what to do and then do it, the first to devise a way of printing out what the machine has produced.

He was born on December 26, 1791, in what is now Southwark, a borough of London, flanking the southern banks of the Thames. His parents, Benjamin Babbage and Elizabeth Plumleigh Teape Babbage, were natives of Devon, a county in the southwest of England. It was to be close to a London bank partly owned by Benjamin Babbage that they had moved to Southwark. Here their children were born: first Charles, then two boys who died in infancy, and finally a girl named Mary-Anne.

Like most children of the English gentry, Charles was brought up largely by nurses. One gathers, however, that his mother was attentive and caring. Not so his father. "Stern, inflexible and reserved," a "tyrant" with a "temper the most horrible to be conceived": So Charles, in a letter penned in his early manhood, described Benjamin Babbage. "Can such a man be loved?" he asked. "It is *impossible*."

He was in his twelfth year when his father retired and moved the family back to Devon. Here Charles passed the remainder of his childhood, first in Totnes, his parents' hometown, then on a hilltop estate overlooking the port city of Teignmouth on the shores of the English Channel.

It was during these years that Charles attempted his first scientific experiment. Inspired by his reading of the Bible, he fashioned a contraption that he was sure would let him walk on the waters of a local river—an exploit that came close to taking his life.

Off and on he attended the public schools of Devon. Then his parents sent him north, first to a boys' school near London, then to the home of a tutor living near Cambridge, seat of the ancient university of that name. Enrolling in Cambridge's Trinity College in October, 1810, he spent the next four years acquiring the foundation for what were to be brilliant careers in mathematics, astronomy, and political economics.

During one of his vacations in Devon he met and fell in love with a bright and lovely looking young woman. Her name was Georgiana Whitmore. Once Charles had completed his courses at Cambridge, the two were married, on July 2, 1814. By the fall of the following year they were living in a small house at 5 Devonshire Street, Portland Place, London. Of the at least eight children born to their union, only three, all boys, lived long enough to become adults.

At 5 Devonshire Street Charles plunged into what was to be his lifelong pursuit of the sciences that fascinated him. In 1815 he delivered a series of lectures on astronomy before an important London group. On March 14, 1816, he was elected to the Royal Society, his country's foremost scientific organization. Books and articles dealing with higher mathematics flowed from his pen.

From Devon his father watched these activities with distaste. He repeatedly urged his only son to abandon his books and seek a paying job, preferably a post with the British government.

Never could Charles bring himself to love his cantankerous parent. Never, however, could he altogether free himself from a deep-seated longing for the older man's approval. He looked for jobs, only to discover that for the time being the leaders of His Majesty's government had no work for a man whose political inclinations were known to be against the government in power.

In Great Britain at this time, the nation's political power was shifting from the land-owning aristocracy to the middle class. Those who favored these reforms were called liberals; those who did not were conservatives, or Tories. The day was near when, with the passage of the Great Reform Act of 1832, many of the changes sought by the liberals would take effect. Meanwhile, in the upper reaches of the Tory government of England, there were no open-

A daguerreotype of Charles Babbage taken around 1850. *National Portrait Gallery, London.*

ings for so outspoken a liberal as Charles Babbage.

With a sigh of relief he went back to his research. Fortunately he had a modest yearly income, and the death of Georgiana's father in 1816 had made additional funds available. There was enough for the Charles Babbages to live happily in their small house: enough to bring up the children, to hire a couple of servants, to go on occasional trips; enough for Charles to continue with his studies.

Indeed, for Georgiana there was more than enough. She enjoyed the simple life. When on February 22, 1827, Benjamin Babbage died in Devon and Charles came into his inheritance, she voiced alarm at the sharp improvement in their fortunes. She told a friend that she had learned how to be "a proper wife to a poor man." She was afraid that Charles would find her ill equipped to be the wife of a rich one.

She need not have worried. Charles adored her. When in August of the same year a sudden illness ended her life, his grief was so intense that he could no longer live in the house the two of them had shared. Lodging the children with relatives, he headed for the continent of Europe.

For a year he traveled from country to country, meeting the leading scientists of Europe and obtaining from them vast amounts of scientific information. On his return to London he purchased a house at 1 Dorset Street, Manchester Square, and continued his studies.

A few years before Georgiana's death he had begun work on his Difference Engine. This was a calculating machine, a device that could be used to rapidly carry out the extensive mathematical operations so vital to the navigation of a ship or the running of a factory. Other men in earlier times had fabricated such machines. But these calculators had to be operated by hand, a circumstance that made them prone to error. Bab-

bage's Difference Engine was the first mechanical calculator to be automated. Driven by steam—the use of electricity and electronics as dependable sources of power lay in the future—it ran on its own.

It took Babbage several years to design his Difference Engine, so called, according to his biographer Hyman, because it was intended "to compute tables of numbers according to the method of finite differences and then automatically to print the tables as they were computed." It took several more years to begin the actual construction of a few versions.

The work called for the creation of special tools. It called for the services of a skilled engineer and a crew of workmen. It called for space—enough to shelter the lathes and other machines used in the construction of the engines. To take care of this need, Babbage knocked down the coach house and stables behind his home. He replaced them with a two-story workshop, fifty feet long by some twenty-five wide and roofed with glass.

All these things required expenditures far beyond even Babbage's now ample means. Happily for him, the government realized that his invention could be of value to British industry. For almost two decades it financed his efforts. Then in 1842, irked to find the

A small portion of Charles Babbage's Difference Engine, No. 1 (calculating machine). *Culver Pictures*.

work still unfinished, the government withdrew its support and Babbage had to discontinue the project. By this time only a portion of one of the Difference Engines had been assembled and put into working order. It is this contraption that now stands in the Science Museum in London.

In 1843 Babbage began work on his Analytical Engine, the invention that today is regarded as the forerunner of the modern computer. This time the government refused to fund his work. All he could afford to do was make plans. Gradually, in the years that followed, he turned out over a hundred drawings of this second calculator. During this same period he filled over five hundred large sheets of paper with notes describing how it was to be built and the many functions it could perform.

By the time these labors began he had found a brilliant assistant and collaborator in the person of Augusta Ada, countess of Lovelace. Beautiful, charming, and aristocratic, Ada was the daughter of the great English poet Lord Byron. She was herself an accomplished mathematician. She helped Babbage solve many of the problems posed by his work. It was she who pointed out that a few changes in his machine would enable it to create musical compositions. Notes written by Ada for one of Babbage's articles remain the clearest

explanation we have of what went into the design of the Analytical Engine.

It would be a mistake to picture Charles Babbage as devoting all of his time to his mechanical calculators. He was a man of many talents and many interests.

He produced an array of inventions that are still around. Among them were the flashing beam later used by lighthouses and the recording device now known as a black box carried on nearly all commercial and military aircraft. For years he was active in the movement leading to the passage of the Great Reform Act of 1832. This law gave the vote to thousands of Britons who had not enjoyed it before. His writings on economic matters would greatly influence the work of later thinkers in that field.

Today nearly every large manufacturing corporation maintains a laboratory in which scientists and engineers create new products and new ways of making the old ones. In books and articles Babbage urged his country's industries to make more use of the findings of its scientists and engineers. He battled for the introduction of more scientific and engineering courses into Great Britain's universities and lower schools.

He delved into the mysteries of philosophy. The man who in his boyhood tried to walk on water was fascinated by miracles, those happenings that seem to defy the laws of nature. From his work with computers he came up with a possible explanation of these strange events. From the very beginning, he noted, a computer can be programmed to work now in one manner and then in another. Perhaps at the very beginning of time, he wrote, the Maker of the universe so programmed the course of history as to permit the occasional occurrence of what we call miracles.

Babbage was a social creature. He loved a party. Personable and witty, he was a frequent guest at the dinner tables of the rich and famous. For many years his own Saturday evening soirees were a feature of the London social season. His circle of friends included Charles Dickens, the famous novelist, and the duke of Wellington, the English general whose victory in 1815 at Waterloo in Belgium had ended the attempt by Napoleon Bonaparte to bring all of Europe—England included—under his rule.

His meeting in the early 1830s with Lord Byron's daughter was one of the high points of his life. Their long working association was precious to him.

Like her father, Ada wrote poetry. Like him, she died at the age of thirty-six.

This was in 1852. Babbage was sixty-one, and the remaining years of his life can be described, in the words of Shakespeare, as having a "dying fall." He found Ada's death almost as unbearable as he had found that of his wife. He had outlived most of the noted scientists and political figures who had once been his companions. A new generation of scientists and statesmen had no interest in a man whose Difference Engine remained unfinished and whose Analytical Engine had not been built. His three sons had gone to live in foreign countries. In his handsome house on Dorset Street, Babbage was lonely.

Death came quietly on October 18, 1871. His son Henry, recently returned from India, was with him at the time. Henry made the arrangements for the funeral, which was but sparsely attended. As his biographer Hyman tells us, there was only one carriage, that of an aging duchess, in the procession that followed the body of Charles Babbage to Kensal Green cemetery. It was an inadequate farewell, certainly, to the man whose inventions pointed the way to today's multipurpose computers.

Alexander Graham Bell

1847–1922   Scottish-born American scientist and teacher of the deaf; inventor of the telephone

Born in Edinburgh, Scotland, on March 3, 1847, the inventor of the telephone was christened Alexander Bell. But at some time during his boyhood Alec, as he was known to family and friends, was seized with a desire for an additional name, one that would set him apart from his father, Alexander Melville Bell, and his grandfather, Alexander Bell, both of whom had made names for themselves as teachers of speech, specializing in the correction of stuttering and other vocal handicaps. It so happened that in the spring of 1858 a genial young Canadian named Alexander Graham stayed for a while with the Bells in their tall stone house overlooking Edinburgh's fashionable Charlotte Square. Alec took a liking to young Graham. On his eleventh birthday, with the blessing of his parents, he became Alexander Graham Bell.

To be set apart, to go his own way—those longings shaped Alec's thinking and directed many of his activities throughout a long and eventful life. "A man's *own* judgment," he wrote in one of his diarylike notebooks, "should be the final appeal in all that *relates to himself*. Many men . . . do this or that because *someone else* has thought it right."

But doing what he thought right for himself was not always easy for a shy and reserved boy, growing up in a family of strong-minded individuals. There were times when Alec felt almost overwhelmed by his bright and talented mother, Eliza Symonds Bell, and by his popular and impressive-looking father.

His mother was an accomplished portrait painter and, although unable to hear without an ear trumpet, an equally accomplished pianist. Under her training Alec's younger brother, Ted (for Edward Charles), and his older brother, Melly (for Melville James), became reasonably adept at the keyboard. Alec so far excelled them both that it has been said that had he chosen a career as a concert pianist he would have enjoyed great success.

As a rule he and his mother got along well. Such was not the case where his father was concerned. For many years the relationship between Alec and Melville, as most people addressed the older Bell, was a strained one. Melville Bell was one of those brilliant men who easily forget that remarks that strike an adult as funny often strike a sensitive child as sarcastic and can be hurtful. In the guidance of his second son, there was a good deal of "Father knows best." Only seven years before Alec's creation of the telephone made him one of the most respected men in the world, the older Bell was telling people that his then twenty-two-year-old son was still "a perfect baby" who had to "be told when to wrap up on going out, when to change coats or wet clothes, et cetera, et cetera."

Big-brother Melly, a born charmer, was warm and outgoing, fond of social gatherings and the life of every party he attended. Not Alec. He had a passion for solitude, for getting away by himself to think and dream. Not far from the Bells' house stood one of Edinburgh's landmarks, Corstorphine Hill. On its heather-covered uplands, in an area called Rest-and-be-thankful, he would lie for hours, staring at the birds overhead and wondering what mysterious mechanism kept them aloft. This abiding curiosity would years later prompt him to invent a man-bearing kite and build an unusual airplane.

Not that he gave all his time to lonely rambles in the hills. He and his chum Ben Herdman played hide-and-seek and other games in the flour mill run by Ben's father on one of the Scottish capital's many streams, the Water of Leith. It was in these dusty, machinery-filled interiors that Alec achieved what he later called his first invention.

Noting the frequent presence of the boys on the premises, Ben's father suggested that they try doing "something useful." When asked what that might be, Mr. Herdman scooped up a handful of grain. "If you could only take the husks off this wheat," he said, "you would be of some help."

It was Alec who suggested that the attachment of brushes to a small device used in the plant for other purposes might provide them with a machine for removing the husks. To the delight and surprise of Mr. Herdman, the gadget worked and for some time was employed throughout the mill.

Science was very much in the air of the Edinburgh of Alec's day. At Edinburgh University, where his father taught, the faculty roster was studded with the names of world-famous physicists and other students of nature. Alec thought of botany, only to drop the idea on learning that a botanist must memorize the Latin names of thousands of plants. He turned next to biology. He and some of his playmates organized the Society for the Promotion of Fine Arts among Boys. Each member was designated a professor of some field of science. Alec was the professor of anatomy. He was too tenderhearted to even think of using a live animal for research purposes, but during one of his lectures to the gang he thrust a dissecting knife into the body of a dead pig. As air rushed from the animal with what seemed like a ghostly groan, the attic room where the boys had gathered emptied abruptly, all the members of the club stampeding down the stairs on the heels of a frightened Professor Bell. That ended the biology phase, and little by little Alec began turning his attention to the profession of his father

and grandfather: phonetics, the study of sounds of speech.

Like his brothers he received his early education at home from his mother. Only when Eliza Bell concluded that she had carried her sons as far as her capacities permitted did she send them first to a local academy and then to the Edinburgh Royal High School. At both places Alec's grades were low, and it would appear from incomplete records that at the high school he finished only four of the six years required.

The summer of 1862 brought a letter from Grandfather Alexander Bell, who, after a career as an actor on the Scottish stage, had moved to London and set himself up as a teacher of speech. The second of his wives had recently died, and he was lonely in his eleven-room house at 18 Harrington Square in the vicinity of Regents Park. He suggested that Alec pay him an extended visit.

Half a century later Alec described his year with Grandfather Bell as "the turning point" of his life. A wish for company was not the old man's only reason for wanting his fifteen-year-old grandson underfoot. He realized that Alec often felt shunted aside in a household dominated by the powerful personalities of his parents and his engaging and spirited brother Melly.

Alec, his grandfather reasoned, needed some close attention.

Alec's parents bought him new clothes for his journey south, and his father escorted him to 18 Harrington Square. No sooner had Melville Bell begun his return journey than Grandfather Bell announced that Alec's new duds might be all right for provincial Edinburgh, but they would never do in elegant London. A tailor was summoned, and Alec was fitted for an Eton jacket, kid gloves, a silk top hat, and a small cane.

Having refurbished the boy's exterior, Grandfather Bell began working on his mind. Alec was forbidden to read "light" or solely entertaining books. He and the old man pored over the works of Shakespeare, and Alec committed to memory speeches from *Hamlet, Macbeth, Julius Caesar,* and some of the other plays.

During Alec's stay in London his father gave him a modest allowance. Spend it any way you like, his grandfather said. Don't tell me what you're doing with it. You're old enough to manage your own affairs.

The old man's health was failing. Off and on Alec, turned medical attendant, knew the twofold joy of being in charge and of being needed by another human being.

When in the summer of 1863 Melville Bell returned to London to take his son home, even that critical gentleman was impressed with the change in Alec. The awkward and withdrawn boy had become a confident young man; the ugly duckling had turned swan.

During Melville's short stay in the British capital he and his son called on Sir Charles Wheatstone, one of England's foremost scientists. Wheatstone showed them his "speaking machine." It was a contraption capable of the mechanical imitation of the human voice. Back home in Edinburgh, Melville ordered Alec and Melly to fabricate a similar device. Eventually they did so, but only after a series of setbacks that taught Alec that success comes only after many and sometimes crushing failures. It was a lesson that would stand him in good stead when, a few years later, he embarked on the even longer and more grueling experiments that brought into existence that marvelous contraption, the telephone.

With their speaking machine finished, the two boys were restless at home. Both yearned to get away. For a time Alec considered running off to sea. Then one day he spotted in the newspaper an advertisement inserted by Weston House, a boarding school in Elgin on the northern coast of Scotland. Weston House had openings for what it called pupil-teachers in music and elocution.

Both boys applied, giving as a reference their father, the professor of elocution at Edinburgh University. When Melville Bell learned of this action, he reluctantly agreed to an arrangement whereby Alec was to spend one year at Weston House, after which he was to return home and Melly was to take over his teaching position.

At Weston House Alec reveled in the freedom of being his own boss. Some of his students were older than himself. But the year with his grandfather had given him the controlled bearing of an adult, and he was careful to keep his age—sixteen—a secret.

When in the summer of 1864 he returned to Edinburgh, it was to live there for another year only. On April 23, 1865, death came to Grandfather Bell, and soon thereafter the Melville Bells, accompanied by Alec and his brother Ted, moved to London to reside in the old man's Harrington Square house.

For Alec the next few years were busy, if not always happy, ones. He spent another year at Weston House, this time as a full-fledged teacher. He undertook his first original research into a problem in phonetics, only to learn that the process that came out of it had already been developed by another sci-

entist. He took courses at the University of London. He taught deaf children at a school in the South Kensington section of the city. He tried to set up as a teacher of the deaf on his own, only to see his plans squashed by his father, still convinced that his second son was not yet mature enough to function independently.

Melville Bell had published a book called *Visible Speech: The Science of Universal Alphabetics.* It was an attempt to give the world a universal alphabet. Pictures in the book showed the reader where to place the tongue and lips so as to produce practically every sound the human voice can utter. Using the pictures, Alec became adept at talking in Arabic, Hindu, Persian, Urdu, American Indian, and a dozen other languages, none of which he could speak on his own. It was while helping his father promote and demonstrate *Visible Speech* that Alec began formulating the methods for teaching the deaf to speak that in later years he would put into practice with much success.

Tragedy twice invaded the family fold: In 1867 brother Ted died, and in 1870 Melly died, both of tuberculosis. The loss of his brothers made more difficult than ever Alec's efforts to get out from under the direction of his father. Melville Bell had come home from a lecture tour in the United States and

Canada, impressed by the need for speech teachers in those countries. When in the summer of 1870 he decided to move what remained of his family to Canada, Alec saw the opportunity he was waiting for. One night he walked the streets of London for hours, dreaming up ways of persuading his father to leave him behind. But when the next morning he faced his parents and saw the sad expression in their eyes, an expression that said, "Look, you're all we have left," he caved in and went with them.

Happily for the young man, the freedom he longed for awaited him in the New World, where in the fall of 1870 the Bells found a home for themselves in Brantford, Ontario, Canada. A few months later Alec was teaching at a school for deaf-mutes in Boston, Massachusetts, and by the fall of 1873 he had taken on several private pupils and had begun his long service as a professor of vocal physiology and elocution in the newly established School of Oratory at Boston University.

Helping the deaf to communicate had become his life work, and it was out of this endeavor that the speaking telegraph, as the telephone was sometimes called, emerged. "If I can make a deaf-mute talk," Bell said, "I can make metal talk."

For almost five years, beginning in 1872, he experimented with a variety of materials in an effort to make a metal disk that, vibrating in response to sound, could reproduce those sounds and send them over an electrified wire. These were hard and often discouraging years. His earnings as a teacher were small. The equipment his creative labors demanded was expensive. Debts piled up, bringing from his mother a letter urging him to save his money and to "dissipate no part of it in mere experiments." There were times, Bell confessed to a friend, when the "cares and anxieties of being an inventor seemed more than flesh and blood can stand."

He brought to his exertions many of the attributes common to successful inventors. He was not afraid of hard work. Nor did he shrink from the long hours of study required to acquire the scientific information he had to have. During a visit to Washington, D.C., he called on Joseph Henry, first secretary and director of the Smithsonian Institution. Born in Albany, New York, and a longtime professor of physics at Princeton University, Henry was one of the handful of scientists who had made those discoveries regarding the behavior of electricity without which no one could have constructed a telephone.

Bell outlined for him the ideas he had assembled for developing that instrument. He asked Henry what he should do about his ideas. Should he simply publish them and let someone else perfect the telephone? Or should he try doing it himself? When Henry suggested that he do it himself, Bell asserted that he lacked the necessary knowledge of electricity. To this admission, Henry's answer was brief and pointed. "Get it," he said.

Bell got it. When a year later he obtained a patent for the telephone, the people at the Patent Office in Washington credited him with knowing more about electricity than all the other inventors they knew put together.

Another of Bell's qualities was what seems to have been a sharp eye for character and competence in others. In Massachusetts-born Thomas A. Watson, whom he selected to help him with the mechanical aspects of his task, he found an assistant who was at once able and loyal. The two men met for the first time in 1874, and in a book published years later Watson described the Alexander Graham Bell he saw that day as a "tall, slender, quick-motioned young man with a pale face, black side whiskers and drooping mustache, big nose, and high, sloping forehead crowned with bushy jet-black hair."

For Bell and Watson the climax of their struggles came on Friday, March 10, 1876. That morning, at Bell's quar-

ters in Boston's Exeter Place, they strung a wire from Bell's laboratory to his bedroom at the far end of a hall blocked by two closed doors. That afternoon Bell stationed himself in the laboratory at the transmitting end of the apparatus he had contrived, with Watson in the bedroom at the receiving end. Then Bell, bending over the mouthpiece, uttered a sentence that in subsequent years schoolchildren around the world would learn by heart.

"Mr. Watson, come here. I want to see you!" he said. To Bell's delight, as he wrote in his laboratory notebook, Watson came at once, saying that "he had heard and understood what I said. . . . We then changed places and I listened . . . [at the receiving end] while Mr. Watson read a few pages of a book into the mouthpiece." So the telephone was born. And in the years ahead other inventors, Thomas Alva Edison among them, would provide the improvements that have given us the implement we use today.

The tribulations of invention did not separate Bell from his work as a teacher of the deaf. Among his private students in the fall of 1873 was Mabel Hubbard, the sixteen-year-old daughter of Gardiner Greene Hubbard, a wealthy Boston lawyer. Mabel had grown up in Cambridge, site of Harvard University, across the Charles River from Boston.

In her fifth year an attack of scarlet fever had left her totally deaf. Since then her father had sent her to various teachers. They had taught her to read lips, and they had taught her to speak, though not well. It was Gardiner Hubbard's hope that Bell, whom he had met some months earlier, could improve on their work.

He did, greatly, but his relationship with Mabel was destined to be more than that of instructor to pupil. One gathers that he was smitten with her at once, with her gentle manner and puckish face. Her first reactions to him, however, were anything but romantic. "I did not like him," she wrote later. "He was tall . . . with jet-black hair and eyes, but dressed badly and carelessly in an old-fashioned suit of black broadcloth . . . and altogether, to one accustomed to the dainty neatness of Harvard students, he seemed hardly a gentleman."

Time rapidly softened this impression, and Mabel became more than a little fond of her teacher. In June, 1874, Alec wrote to her mother, saying that his "interest in my dear pupil . . . has ripened into a far deeper feeling. . . . I have learned to love her." During the following months Mabel's father began to help Bell in a financial way with his work on the telephone. Both he and Mabel's mother admired the young man

In 1876, using a liquid telephone that resembled a tall glass sitting on a stand, Bell spoke the historic words, "Mr. Watson, come here. I want to see you!" *AT&T Archives.*

from Scotland. But both were worried about their daughter's youthfulness. At seventeen she seemed to them still a girl. Their answer to twenty-seven-year-old Bell was that for one year he must not even mention his intentions to Mabel. At first he agreed to this request, but within a few months he was telling the Hubbards that he was too much in love to remain silent any longer. At this point the Hubbards relented, and Alec and Mabel became engaged, with the understanding that they would delay getting married until the young Scot was in a position to support a wife.

His invention of the telephone early in 1876 took care of that. Almost overnight Alec was rich. On July 9, 1877, the Bell Telephone Company, ancestor of today's American Telephone and Telegraph Company (AT&T), was founded to distribute telephone service throughout the nation, with Gardiner Hubbard as its president and Bell as its technical director, with the title of electrician. On July 11 Alec and Mabel were married, and on August 4 they left America to spend over a year in Europe, where their first child, Elsie May, was born in a rented house in London on the evening of May 8, 1878.

On their return from Europe, Alec confronted what he later termed the worst ordeal of his life. Ohio-born Elisha Gray had produced a telephone similar to his, and the mammoth Western Union Telegraph Company, using devices made by Gray and other inventors, had gone into the telephone business.

On September 12, 1878, the Bell Company requested the courts to stop Western Union from renting telephone apparatus. For the next eighteen years some 600 cases dealing with telephone-patent rights came and went in the courts, with Alec frequently summoned to give evidence from the witness stand. In the course of this long industrial controversy, two important matters were settled. In 1879 Western Union agreed to give up its telephone business in return for a share of the Bell Company's profits, and in 1888 the Supreme Court of the United States ruled that the underlying principle of the telephone had first been developed by Alexander Graham Bell, making him its inventor.

Bell was only twenty-nine when that triumph made him world famous. Though never again did he create an object so vital to mankind, he continued during the rest of his life to turn out inventions. Among them were several useful devices: a vacuum jacket for administering artificial respiration, which is now regarded as the forerunner of the iron lung so important to victims of poliomyelitis; a telescopic probe for detecting bullets buried in the human body, which was widely employed by doctors until the coming of the X-ray machine; some improvements in the phonograph invented by Thomas Edison, which helped make that technological marvel available to larger numbers of people; a tetrahedral cell that brought to the building of bridges and other structures a combination of relatively little weight and great strength.

Alexander Graham Bell at the New York end of the circuit to Chicago as this line was opened on October 18, 1892. *AT&T Archives*.

Early telephone operators on the job. *Brown Brothers.*

He continued to help the deaf, driven by a keen consciousness of the loneliness and sense of isolation the hard of hearing must endure. After all, the two most important women in his life, his wife and his mother, were deaf. He carried on a successful struggle for government financing of schools for the deaf and conducted for a few years a private school of his own. He produced a full-scale study of the degree to which deafness is passed on from parents to their offspring. He founded the American Association to Promote the Teaching of Speech to the Deaf. He wanted deaf children to learn sign language, but he also wanted as many of them as possible to learn to talk. He reasoned that the gift of speech would make it easier for them to live in a hearing world. When in 1902 the famous blind deaf-mute Helen Keller dedicated her autobiography to Alexander Graham Bell, it was her way of thanking him for having provided her with the services of the woman who taught her to speak, Annie Sullivan, better known to moviegoers as "The Miracle Worker."

His wife was once heard to remark that she hoped whoever wrote the biography of her husband would not present him as perfect. He had his faults, she said—and she loved him for them. One of them, in her eyes, was his practice of working all night and sleeping all morning. She fussed at him about it. She would have preferred a husband who lived as other men did. Occasionally, to please her, he tried working by day—only to return to his nocturnal habits. The man who in his boyhood spent hours alone in Edinburgh's heathery hills still reveled in what to him were the luxuries of silence and solitude.

The two of them had no trouble in communicating with one another. For one thing, they had learned to recognize many little pressures of the hand, signals that they alone understood. For another, Mabel read lips so adeptly that many people who knew her only in a casual way never realized that she couldn't hear. When she and Alec went to the theater he silently repeated to her all that was said on the stage.

Three more children were born to them: in 1880 a girl christened Marian but always addressed as Daisy and, in 1881 and 1883, two boys, both of whom died soon after birth.

Invention, the teaching of the deaf, and the promotion of science in all its forms—these interests kept Alexander Graham Bell busy. He helped endow the magazine *Science*, now the official organ of the American Association for the Advancement of Science. He participated with his father-in-law, Gardiner Hubbard, in the founding of the National Geographic Society and helped popularize its magazine, the *National Geographic*, over which one of his descendants, as president of the society, presides to this day. With the proceeds from the French government's Volta Prize, awarded him for the telephone, he established in Washington, D.C., the Volta Bureau for research into all facets of deafness.

In 1882 he became an American citizen and settled with his family in Washington, D.C., where he built at 1331 Connecticut Avenue the spacious structure that was their main home from then on. For some time Mabel's parents, the Gardiner Hubbards, had been living in the national capital. So had Alec's parents, the Melville Bells. The strain between Alec and his father had long since evaporated. Now when they got together it was no longer father preaching to son but equal talking with equal. The younger man's accomplishments, it would seem, had at long last won the older man's respect.

In 1885 Alec and Mabel acquired on Canada's Cape Breton Island a fifty-six-acre estate, to which they gave the name Beinn Bhreagh, a Gaelic phrase pronounced "ben vree-ah." Here for the next thirty-seven years they passed their summers, and here, on the evening of August 2, 1922, Alexander Graham Bell died after a long bout with diabetes.

Mabel's assertion a few days later that she could not live without him proved to be a valid prediction. Five months later, on January 3, 1923, she, too, was dead. Today she rests beside her husband in a grave blasted out of the rock atop Beinn Bhreagh, which means "Beautiful Mountain."

Carl Benz

1844–1929   German engineer; builder of the first automobile powered by an internal combustion engine

In the thirteenth century the great English philosopher-scientist Roger Bacon enhanced his reputation as "a wizard in league with the devil" by predicting that someday people would ride about in "chariots . . . that will move with incredible rapidity without the help of animals."

Not until five centuries later, in 1769, did the first such chariot appear. Built in Paris by Nicolas Joseph Cugnot, it was a three-wheeled carriage driven by steam power. It had a boiler in front and achieved a speed of about three miles per hour.

Word of Cugnot's contraption passed quickly to England. There, by the opening of the nineteenth century, so many steam-powered carriages were belching along city streets and country lanes that people were becoming alarmed by them and Parliament was passing laws restricting their use. Under one of these laws no self-propelled vehicle could take to the roads unless it was preceded by a man carrying a red flag by day and a red lantern by night.

With the passage of these laws in England interest in horseless travel diminished. By November 24, 1844, when Carl Benz was born in the village of Pfaffenrot in Germany's Black Forest, few self-propelled vehicles were anywhere in use. The story of Carl Benz is the story of how a few individuals, speedily changing all this, ushered in the age of the automobile and the traffic jam.

Carl was the only child of Johann-Georg and Josephine Benz. When Carl was two his father, a blacksmith by trade who worked as an engineer on the railroad, died of pneumonia. A short time later his mother moved to the nearby city of Karlsruhe. There she used her skills as a cook to supplement a small pension. In this manner she managed to send her bright and talented boy to the Karlsruhe lyceum, or high school.

At the lyceum Carl excelled in physics and chemistry. Fascinating to him was the recently developed process for making a type of photograph called a daguerreotype, after its French inventor, Louis Daguerre. Also fascinating to him were the workings of clocks and watches. During his vacations he contributed to the family finances by tramping the Black Forest, taking pictures of persons for a price and repairing timepieces.

Upon his graduation from the lyceum his mother increased her services as a cook and took in boarders so that Carl could continue his education at the Karlsruhe Polytechnikum, the local technical academy. From here he was graduated in the summer of 1864.

A series of jobs as a mechanic and draftsman followed. He was building bridges in the town of Pforzheim when, in the early spring of 1870, his mother died.

She was the first of the two women who can be described as especially help-ful in the shaping of his career. A few months after her death he met the second one, twenty-year-old Bertha Ringer. Plucky and lively minded, Bertha was the daughter of a Pforzheim building contractor. Her spirited manner and ready laugh dazzled Carl. Quitting his job in Pforzheim, he traveled to Vienna in the hope that the glamour of the gay and culture-loving capital of Austria would appeal to the woman he was now determined to marry. But Vienna had no jobs for an engineer of his limited experience.

Meanwhile August Ritter, a friend living in the German industrial city of Mannheim, had offered to put up the capital for a machinists' shop that he and Benz would jointly run. When Carl returned to Pforzheim his first words to Bertha were, in effect, a proposal of marriage. As Vienna's doors were closed to him, would she settle for living in Mannheim?

Not only did she "settle," but when August Ritter got cold feet and threatened to remove himself and his money from the machinists' shop, she coaxed her father into giving her the dowry, the money put aside for her impending marriage. With this Benz purchased Ritter's share in the shop, thus making it his own, and on July 20, 1872, he and Bertha became husband and wife.

In later times Bertha spoke of the

A portrait of Carl Benz. *Mercedes-Benz of North America.*

first seven years of their marriage as "awful days." An economic depression that began in Austria had spread to Germany. There were few buyers for the bending and metal-forming devices Benz made in his shop.

Obtaining a loan from a friend, he developed a hydraulic press for baling tobacco. But for that, too, there were few buyers, and his friend, growing impatient, got a court order that obliged Benz to repay the loan immediately. Only the value of his shop as real estate kept him from losing his business.

What should he do to pull himself out of this mess? What could he make that people would buy?

Gradually the answer came to him: He would endeavor to build a better internal combustion engine. This is a type of engine in which heat energy is transformed into mechanical energy as a result of the combustion of gasoline or some other fuel within the cylinder of the engine. Attempts to construct this kind of engine had been going on for almost two hundred years, but only in recent years had a German engineer named Nikolas August Otto succeeded in producing a workable one.

Benz was aware of the risks involved in an effort to improve upon Otto's design, especially if he were to change it enough to make it his own. As he explained to his wife in the opening days of 1879, never before had he at-

tempted anything as difficult. Did Bertha think he should go ahead with his plans? Though Bertha knew little about machinery, she urged him to do so.

He did. But a year later the engine he had long since completed was still not working. On New Year's Eve Bertha suggested that the two of them go to the shop for another try. That night the engine roared to life. The racket was earsplitting, but to their ears, as Benz said later, it sounded sweeter than the "magic flute" made famous by the Austrian composer Wolfgang Amadeus Mozart in the opera of that name.

Since owners of shops like his were beginning to use internal combustion engines to power the machines that turned out the products their customers wanted, Benz now had something he could sell—*if he could make copies of it*. But that took money, and what little money remained after his recent misfortunes had gone into the development of his engine.

Such was his situation—an ironic and frustrating one—until one day in 1882 a wealthy photographer came into the shop to purchase a needed item. His eyes fell on the corner where the engine stood. How did it operate? he asked. Benz showed him, and on the spot the photographer offered him enough money to establish a company for its manufacture and distribution.

Now with his financial woes behind

him, Benz could concentrate on an idea that he had been turning over in his head for some time. Could the internal combustion engine be used to drive a vehicle that could run "on its own power like a locomotive, not on tracks but like a wagon, simply on any street"?

At this point he thought of the velocipede (a forerunner of the bicycle), which of recent years had become a common sight on the roads of Germany. If he were to combine his internal combustion engine and a velocipede, what would he have? As time eventually demonstrated, he would have what today we call the automobile.

But fabricating an automobile was far from being a case of no sooner said than done. For one thing, it took time. In 1882 no one had ever heard of spark plugs, and as the ignition system Benz had in mind called for these devices he had to invent them. For another thing, the members of the board of directors of his company considered his ideas crazy. Discouraged by this reaction, Benz resigned and, a few months later, with funds provided by a couple of businessmen, established another company, Benz & Cie, Rheinische Gas-motoren-Fabrik.

His new partners were as enthusiastic about his ideas as he was, and in the fall of 1885 the world's first practical automobile rolled into the courtyard fronting the shop of Benz and Company in Mannheim.

By modern standards it didn't look like much. The tubular bicyclelike frame carrying the engine rested on three wire-spoke wheels—two big ones behind, a small one in front. Benz would have preferred four wheels, but it would be some years before he found a way of constructing a mechanism capable of steering that many. The steering apparatus was controlled by a tiller, like the levers used to guide certain boats.

The 580-pound Benz, as the car was named, had its limitations. It would not go backward on its own. When that became necessary, the driver had to hop out and push. It could not go very fast: about seven and a half miles an hour at the most. Nor could it be driven very far without breaking down.

It obviously needed work, and for the next several months Benz tinkered with it. Bertha helped, frequently pedaling on her sewing machine to charge the accumulator, a component of the ignition system.

By early 1886 Benz had introduced so many changes for the better that Bertha was urging him to put the car on the market. Carl shook his head. The Benz, in his opinion, was not yet ready to be offered for sale. Bertha cast about in her mind for a way to convince him otherwise, and in the fall the

With an unidentified companion, Benz (*right*) drives his original, chain-driven three-wheeler. *Mercedes-Benz of North America.*

opportunity she was looking for arose.

For some time she and two of her five children, fourteen-year-old Richard and fifteen-year-old Eugen, had been planning to visit Bertha's mother in Pforzheim. It was Eugen who suggested that instead of taking the train they make the journey in one of the two existing cars. Bertha snapped at the proposal. Surely if her husband's invention could get them the fifty miles to Pforzheim and back, he would see that the time had come to put it on the market.

Bertha and her sons were out of the house before daybreak. To keep from awakening Carl they pushed the Benz down the road a short distance before starting the engine—with Bertha at the tiller and about to become the first person in the world to drive an automobile a significant distance.

At Heidelberg, one of the towns along the way, they stopped for lunch. At Wiesloch they filled the radiator and purchased from a pharmacy a petroleum distillate used as a solvent for the fuel tank.

The town of Bretten presented them with their first big hill. The Benz could not climb it. So Richard took the tiller, and Bertha and Eugen got out and pushed. They surmounted subsequent hills the same way.

Other problems gave birth to other remedies. Bertha used her hatpin to remove an obstruction in the fuel line. She concocted an insulator out of one of her garters when an ignition wire short-circuited.

Night was falling when they neared Pforzheim, and the car had no lights. Happily, the last few miles were downhill. Soon Bertha was announcing their safe arrival in a telegram to her husband. In his telegraphed reply, Carl asked her to mail him the car's driving chains. He wanted to install them in a third version of the Benz that he was building for an upcoming engineering exhibition in Munich, Germany.

His wife's scheme had worked. Carl now pronounced his car ready for sale. But this decision proved easier to make than to carry out. Even the receipt of a gold medal at the Munich Engineering Exposition in September, 1888, along with lavish praise for his invention in the press, brought no buyers. The only person to order a Benz in Munich, Carl joked later, was "carted off to a lunatic asylum" before the sale could be concluded.

In 1889 Paris was the site of a world's fair organized to celebrate the centennial of the French Revolution. At this exposition, attended by 24 million people, Carl's three-wheeler was not the only automobile on display. Standing near it in one of the exhibition halls was a four-wheeled car called the Daimler that another German engineer, Gottlieb Daimler, had built in the fall of 1886.

Though Benz and Daimler were born in towns only sixty miles apart, neither became aware of the other until Benz's automobile attracted the attention of newspapers during the Munich exposition. If the two men ever met— and on this the record is unclear—it was many years later, and then only briefly.

Like Benz, Daimler had spent years dreaming up ways of using the gas engine to power vehicles. At about the time the first automobile rolled into the courtyard of Benz and Company in Mannheim, Daimler and his friend Wilhelm Maybach were completing the world's first motorcycle in Cannstatt, a suburb of the German city of Stuttgart. After this came their creation of the first boat to be driven by an internal combustion engine and, finally, the automobile exhibited in Paris. In Benz's original car, power was transmitted from engine to wheels by a driving belt. Daimler's original model was the first to employ a four-speed transmission that in the near future all automobiles would have.

By the end of 1892 both the Benz and the Daimler were selling fairly well. Toward the end of 1893 Benz produced his second model, a four-wheeler known as the Victoria.

This was selling briskly when the ministry of Baden, Benz's section of Germany, passed a law that threatened to hurt his business substantially. Baden's new law limited the speed of a self-propelled vehicle to twelve kilometers (about seven and a half miles) per hour in the country and to no more than six kilometers "around sharp corners" and in town.

Benz was appalled. His little three-wheeler could do twelve kilometers and his Victoria twenty. When he learned that the Baden minister of the interior was about to visit Mannheim, he invited him for a ride in the Victoria, during which he staged a trick that in a matter of minutes eliminated the new speed limits.

What Carl did was hire a local milkman to drive his horse-drawn wagon alongside the Victoria as one of Carl's workmen drove the minister from the railroad station. As the milkman's horse trotted past the Victoria, which was dawdling along at six kilometers an hour, the milkman laughed and yelled, "Get a horse!"

This infuriated the minister. He directed the driver to speed up. The driver reminded him of the law. The minister barked something to the effect that the law was hereby repealed. Then the Victoria spurted forward, reaching its destination well in advance of the milk wagon, with the minister shouting with glee.

In Mannheim in 1895, the world's first truck lumbered out of one of the shops at Benz and Company. Over the years Carl had become adroit at publicizing his products. To show what this one could do, he had the truck pick up some material at the railroad station that a merchant friend had ordered for his store. He said nothing of this to his friend, and when the truck reached the store the merchant refused to accept its contents.

What it had brought was a sack of oats. The merchant feared that he would lose the patronage of the city's coachmen if they learned that the oats for their horses had been delivered in a motorized vehicle.

In 1896 in the United States, William Jennings Bryan carried on a portion of his unsuccessful campaign for the presidency in a Benz car—and in industrial nations around the world the age of the automobile was in full swing.

Soon Benz and Company was selling over 3,000 cars a year. Daimler-Motoren-Gesellschaft, the company founded by Daimler in Cannstatt, was doing almost as well, and other car makers were setting up their own companies. In both Europe and America, races among competing cars were becoming frequent, festive, and widely attended events.

Gottlieb Daimler, who died on March 6, 1900, did not live to see his company construct the first model of what some years later became the greatly admired Mercedes-Benz, a product of the corporation growing out of a merger of the Daimler and Benz companies.

To Carl Benz, as to many another inventor, success was nowhere near as much fun as the long struggle to achieve it had been. As improved and speedier models appeared every year, Benz lost interest in tinkering with cars.

Why, he was heard to mutter, did people insist on moving faster and faster? What good did it do them? And to the end of his life in 1929, at the age of eighty-four, he continued to tool about in his original automobile, the chain-driven, twelve-kilometers-per-hour three-wheeler.

George Washington Carver

1864?–1943 American agricultural chemist, educator, and botanist; discoverer of new uses for certain plants and soils, deviser of processes helpful to small farmers, and a pioneer in the development of the philosophy underlying today's environmental movement

The date of George Washington Carver's birth is unknown. He himself sometimes described it as occurring "near the end" of the Civil War, and one of his biographers, Linda O. McMurry, places it in the spring of 1865.

His mother, Mary, was a slave girl belonging to Moses and Susan Carver, owners of a 240-acre farm near the town of Diamond Grove, in southwest Missouri. At the time of George's birth, Mary was also the mother of another boy, named Jim, and some students of her second son's life believe there were other children as well. If so, their names have not come down to us. Nor has that of their father or fathers.

In the region in which George Washington Carver began life the years be-fore and during the Civil War were tumultuous. Although a slave state, Missouri sided with the Union. Flanked on the south by Confederate Arkansas and on the west by Unionist Kansas, southwest Missouri became a scene of conflict. Three major battles bloodied its soil, and in the closing months of the war, so-called raiders and bush-whackers flooded in from the south.

When Mary and her baby were kidnapped and carried into Arkansas, Moses and Susan Carver at once set out to get them back.

This was not, on their part, an effort simply to retrieve stolen "property." Abraham Lincoln's Emancipation Proclamation did not apply to slave states loyal to the Union, but the Carvers realized that once the war ended Mary and her children would be free. They wanted Mary and her boy back because they were fond of them. When the man hired to give chase managed to return with the infant George—his mother could not be located—the Carvers took him and his brother Jim into their home and raised them as if they were their own children.

A strong and husky boy, Jim was soon in a position to pay them back by helping with the unending chores on a prosperous farm. Not so George. He was frail and sickly, and the Carvers demanded no heavy work of him.

Free to fill most of the hours as he wished, he became a collector of rocks, displaying at an early age a passionate interest in nature. To a "nursery" laid out in the woods he transplanted almost every plant native to the area. Over the years of his childhood he developed a keen eye for growths that were in trouble, along with developing the ability to restore them to health. Neighboring farmers called him the "plant doctor."

Brought up by whites, he had reached his tenth or eleventh year before an event connected with the local church brought home the significance of the color of his skin. To the church, standing about a mile from the Carver farm, George and his brother were welcomed every Sunday. When, however, the two of them tried to enroll in the school held in the same building on weekdays, they were told that no blacks could be admitted.

To George this incident was a double shock. For one thing, it was his first brush with discrimination. For another, it was a blow to what had become the central dream of his boyhood: a determination to obtain an education far beyond the ability of his kind but limited foster parents to provide.

In 1876 he bade good-bye to the Carvers and walked the eight miles to the town of Neosho, Missouri. There, in return for helping with the housework, he found a home with a black couple. And there he began the search for an education that would keep him on the move for the next fifteen years.

The recently opened one-room school for blacks that had drawn him to Neosho proved a disappointment. It was soon clear that the teacher knew little more than he did.

He hitched a ride to Fort Scott, Kansas, seventy-five miles away. In that frontier community the schooling was better, but on March 26, 1879, a tragedy ended his stay there. That night a black man accused of rape was seized by a group of whites, lynched, and burned. Appalled by this outburst of racial animosity, young Carver moved on to other places.

In some of these towns he found a home with a black family. In others he supported himself in a variety of ways—sometimes by operating a laundry, sometimes by clerking at a hotel or railroad station. Once, during a stay in western Kansas, he acquired 160 acres of land and erected a sod house for himself.

The year 1890 found him enrolled at a Methodist institution called Simpson College in Indianola, Iowa. By this time Carver had noted in himself a talent for painting pictures. He was considering a career in that field when one day his art teacher, Miss Etta Budd, discovered in him still another aptitude.

He had brought her some plants that he had cross-fertilized, or grafted. For some time Miss Budd had worried about his future. Even for whites, art was a difficult way to make a living. For a black it would be even more so. Impressed by what Carver had done with the plants, she suggested that he study botany at the Iowa State College of Agriculture and Mechanic Arts at Ames, Iowa, where her father, J. L. Budd, was a professor of horticulture.

Carver gave her proposal some thought. He was fond of painting, but, in the words of his biographer McMurry, he "had already begun to believe that his God-given talents were meant to be used in the elevation of 'his people.'" In the closing years of the nineteenth century most American blacks were farm workers. "By becoming a trained agriculturist, he could obviously be of tremendous service to them." In the fall of 1891 he entered Iowa State.

For a while the going was tough, as he was the only black on campus. At first he was lodged in an abandoned office and compelled to eat with the staff in the basement under the college dining room. He wrote of these humiliations to Mrs. W. A. Liston, one of the closest of the white friends he had made in Indianola.

We have Mrs. Liston's response to his letter in her own words. "I immediately put on my best dress and hat and took the train for Ames," she related later. After eating with Carver in the basement, she "walked all over the campus with him . . . and stayed with him all evening." As he subsequently informed her, "The next day everything was different, the ice was broken, and from that time on, things went very much easier."

Easier indeed. Within a few months Carver had become one of the most popular figures on campus. When the menial jobs on which he depended failed to meet his expenses, the other students found unembarrassing ways of helping him out. Members of the fac-

George Washington Carver and his students in the laboratory. *The Bettmann Archive.*

ulty, impressed by his skills as a nurturer of plants, called him the "green thumb boy." One of them—Professor James Wilson, destined to serve three American presidents as secretary of agriculture—pronounced him "the ablest student we have here."

In 1894, having received his bachelor of science degree, Carver was named to the Iowa State faculty as an assistant in botany. The spring of 1896 found him completing the studies required for his second degree, that of master of science. It also found him pondering

what to do about a challenging proposition from Booker T. Washington, founder and principal of a school for blacks in Alabama known as Tuskegee Normal and Industrial Institute.

Booker T. Washington had become well known throughout America, partly for making Tuskegee Institute outstanding among schools for the training of black teachers and industrial workers, partly because of a speech he had delivered in Atlanta, Georgia, in 1895. In that speech Washington suggested a solution for the racial strife of his era by setting forth what soon came to be known as the "doctrine of accommodation."

He called on his fellow blacks to give up their seemingly doomed efforts to enjoy political and social equality in a society ruled by whites. He urged them instead to cooperate with whites by becoming more efficient workers and to concentrate on attaining economic independence. He suggested that they use vocational education as a ladder to prosperity. He predicted that once they had become a substantial part of their country's economy, political rights would follow.

In a letter inviting Carver to join the teaching staff at Tuskegee, Washington revealed his plans to establish a school of agriculture there. He wanted Carver to direct it. "You perhaps know," he wrote, "that at present all of our teachers are of the colored race." Washington wanted to keep the faculty all black, but "if we cannot secure you we shall be forced perhaps to put in a white man." To avoid this he stood ready to pay Carver a thousand dollars a year, plus board and certain other expenses.

Again, as when he had abandoned a career in art for botany, Carver faced a difficult decision. Iowa State wanted him to remain on its faculty, and he was content in this position. As many who knew him were heard to observe,

he always seemed more comfortable with whites than with blacks. After all, he had been brought up largely by whites and had adopted many of their values and viewpoints.

Still, as he told Professor James Wilson, Tuskegee offered a situation he had been longing for: an opportunity to be helpful to his people. He accepted the job. This was in May, 1896, and in October, having meanwhile received his master of science degree, he took up his duties at Tuskegee.

Here for the rest of his life—forty-seven years in all—he taught and experimented and helped improve the lot of southern farmers, white as well as black. Among his first achievements at Tuskegee was his establishment and conduct of conferences for black farmers. He taught them better ways of tilling the soil and the importance of a balanced diet. With money provided by a New York philanthropist he introduced the "movable school." A wagon bearing equipment, seeds, and an instructor carried new agricultural ideas directly to the farmers' homes.

His talks with southern growers convinced him that their problems were largely the result of their dependence on a single crop, usually cotton. He called on them to plant a variety of crops—peanuts, sweet potatoes, and cowpeas, for example—instead of one.

George Washington Carver at his desk about a year before his death. *UPI / Bettmann Newsphotos.*

To encourage this crop diversification, he labored for long hours in a laboratory where, since Tuskegee's finances were meager, most of his apparatus had been built with scraps of material collected from piles of trash. Here, from peanuts alone, he succeeded in extracting 325 different products, ranging from beverages and pickles to ink and synthetic rubber. He discovered 118 new uses for sweet potatoes and almost as many for cowpeas. He created a process for obtaining paint pigments from clay—a development important to the South, with its extensive clay deposits.

In 1896 when Carver began his work at Tuskegee, peanuts and sweet potatoes, if planted at all in the South, were for private consumption by their growers. By the early 1920s, thanks largely to Carver, they had taken their place among the leading commercial crops of the region.

By this time, too, high-paying jobs away from Tuskegee were being dangled before him. Thomas Edison, the famous inventor, offered him a position in his research laboratory. Several industries requested his services. Carver declined these invitations, convinced that Tuskegee was the place from which he could do the most for what he often referred to as "the man farthest down."

Many honors came to him. The Royal Society of Arts in London elected him a fellow of that famous organization. The National Association for the Advancement of Colored People awarded him its Springarn Medal in recognition of his achievements in agricultural chemistry. Two universities bestowed on him the doctor of science degree. This action was pleasing to those whites among his admirers who were reluctant to address any black man as *Mister*. Now they could address him as *Doctor* Carver.

Notwithstanding his high-pitched voice and his practice of wearing his clothes until they became shiny and threadbare, he was in great demand as a speaker. Again and again, in talks at many colleges, both black and white, he touched on matters that are still of interest to people struggling to clean up a planet threatened by ever-increasing pollution.

His biographer McMurry has pronounced Carver's message to modern environmentalists the most important of his contributions to his country.

What was his message? He believed that nothing in this world exists alone and in isolation. It is connected to ev-

erything else, and to ignore "that fact can have disastrous effects." Any action, Carver contended, "must be considered in the light of its overall long-term consequences, not just its immediate benefits."

One of his frequently reiterated assertions was that "nature produces no waste," that whatever is consumed is "returned to the whole in another usable form." Waste, he insisted, is "man-made." It is the result of man's failure to understand the oneness and unity of the universe. A profoundly religious man, he was given to saying that God has provided all that human beings need, and that the shortages found in so many parts of the world are the result of "man's failure to utilize appropriately the bounty of nature and to work with the forces of the universe."

McMurry concedes that these ideas were not original and that they were "almost as old as man himself." Still, Carver expressed them with such verve and clarity that one can be forgiven for thinking of him as the father of today's environmentalist movement.

His private life, taken as a whole, appears to have been uneventful. For a time he showed some interest in a young woman on the Tuskegee staff. He never married, however, and as his brother Jim had died many years earlier, there were no known survivors at the time of his death on January 5, 1943.

Although money had never interested him—he even rejected salary increases at Tuskegee—he had somehow accumulated an estate amounting to about sixty thousand dollars. This he left to a research foundation, organized in his name at Tuskegee in 1920, which sought to furnish opportunity for advanced study by black youths in chemistry, botany, and agronomy.

George Eastman

1854–1932   American industrialist and philanthropist; inventor of the first camera that large numbers of people could afford and use, as well as most of the machines and processes that went into its making

The third child and only son of George W. Eastman and Maria Kilbourn Eastman, George Eastman was born on July 12, 1854, in Waterville, New York. He was six when the family moved to nearby Rochester, New York, where eighteen years earlier his father had established that city's first business college.

He was eight when his father died and his mother, forced to eke out a living by taking in boarders, began the struggle for survival that created in her son a dread of poverty and a determination to become rich. He was attending a public school in Rochester when one winter he and another boy hammered out some walnut bookcases and sold them. With the five dollars earned in this manner, George opened his first bank account.

Leaving school in 1868, he spent the next thirteen years working first as a clerk in two insurance agencies and then as a bookkeeper in a Rochester bank. By 1877 he was making enough money to take care of his mother's expenses and could point to $3,600 in the bank or in investments.

In his mother's eyes, her twenty-three-year-old son was already a financial success. In his own view, however, he was nothing of the sort. Insurance and banking, his two careers to date, struck him as belonging "to the age of the covered wagon." Eager to carve a niche for himself in the "advancing age of machinery," he began looking into photography, a field concerned with the forming and fixing of an image on a surface so treated with chemicals that it has become sensitive to light.

At one and the same time an art and a science, photography traces its remote beginnings to the fifteenth century, when the Italian master of numerous arts and sciences Leonardo da Vinci illustrated in one of his notebooks what came to be known as the camera obscura. As Leonardo explained, a small hole in the side of a closed box permitted on the side facing the hole the formation of an inverted image of an illuminated scene or object outside the box.

Leonardo had been dead for three hundred years when Joseph Niépce, a French chemist, inaugurated photography as we now know it by finding a way to fix an image created inside a camera obscura.

Niépce took his first picture in 1826, and the next fifty years saw two significant improvements in the process by which pictures are produced. A way was found of making more than one print from a single exposure, and exposure time was reduced thanks to the discovery of a chemical mixture commonly known as hypo. When dipped in hypo, a very faint image, quickly impressed on a plate, could be made into a strong image —a procedure now known as developing.

By 1877 when George Eastman entered the field, photography had advanced considerably, but, as Eastman quickly realized, it still had a long distance to go.

Eastman began his study of the field by purchasing $94.36 worth of picture-taking paraphernalia and hiring a professional to teach him how to use it all. What he learned first, as he told a magazine reporter years later, was that in those days "it took not only a strong but also a dauntless man to be an outdoor photographer."

Since in 1877 pictures could be made only on wet plates, the photographer working outdoors had to carry with him several items of bulky equipment and a corrosive agent called silver nitrate. Eastman's outfit included a camera "about the size of a soapbox, a tripod . . . heavy enough to support a bungalow," and a large plate holder. It also included a "dark tent," since images registered on wet plates had to be developed immediately after exposure. Each plate was coated with a solution called collodion, and just before the plate was exposed to light this coating had to be sensitized to the light by the insertion of some nitrate of silver.

Early in his picture-taking days, Eastman realized that if he could eliminate much of this labor and equipment, he would be on to something. Indeed, as time would prove, he would be on his way to making one of his country's largest fortunes.

Once the moneymaking possibilities

Photographed aboard ship with camera in hand, George Eastman peers through the viewfinder. *International Museum of Photography at George Eastman House.*

of photography had dawned on him, he became a tireless student of the subject. Still working in the bank by day, he spent his nights reading. He devoured books on chemistry and magazines dealing with photographic matters. He took lessons in foreign languages. That way he could read not only scientific books and photographic journals printed in English but also those printed in French and German.

In a British journal one day he chanced upon a formula for the preparation of a light-sensitive emulsion made of gelatin. A series of experiments convinced him that by substituting this gelatinous solution for collodion, pictures could be made on dry—instead of wet—plates. What delighted him about this discovery was that the use of dry plates eliminated the photographer's need for a dark tent when he worked outside, as well as the jar of silver nitrate wherever he worked.

By the fall of 1879 he was not only producing satisfactory dry plates but had invented a machine capable of coating them with the proper emulsion. By early 1881 he had resigned from the bank and, with the aid of a partner, had begun operating in Rochester a company for the manufacture and sale of plates called the Eastman Dry Plate Company.

The business caught on at once, but only a few months after it had opened trouble arose. Photographers everywhere began complaining that the emulsion the company was putting on its plates had a way of losing its sensitivity to light, rendering the plates unusable.

Smart businessman that he was, Eastman at once recalled the defective plates and refunded the money their purchasers had spent on them. Then, retiring to his laboratory, he cooked up a series of different emulsions, trying to find one that would retain its sensitivity to light for an extended period of time.

Three months and 472 experiments later, he came up with the durable emulsion he was looking for. On April 16, 1881, the company resumed business. It ended its first year with a profit of $14,889.88.

Another man finding himself at the head of a fast-growing company might have taken a little time off to have some fun. Not George Eastman. The better the business got, the harder he worked.

He designed all of the machinery used in the plant. "Many were the nights he slept in a hammock at the factory," his biographer Carl W. Ackerman tells us, "and many were the days he cooked his own meals" there. Many, too, were the times that his mother, worried about his health, came to the

George Eastman's original Kodak camera. *International Museum of Photography at George Eastman House.*

factory to talk him into coming home "for a square meal and a good night's rest."

He spent long hours in his laboratory, dreaming up new processes and substances. It was here that he carried on experiments aimed at solving the problems created by the use of glass for photographic plates. Such plates were heavy and subject to breakage.

"What could take the place of glass?" Eastman wondered. Finally, in 1884, after many months of experimentation, he came up with the answer: a sheet or roll of thin, flexible material known as film, made from the chief substance found in the cell walls of plant tissue.

His invention of the first film for use in photography led him, with the help of an employee, to the creation of a mechanism to hold this skinlike stuff in a camera—a lightweight wooden frame called a roll holder. It also led him to change the name of his company to the Eastman Dry Plate and Film Company.

His next step, as his methodical mind told him, was to develop a market for photographic film by constructing the kind of camera in which it could best be used. By 1888 he had invented the first camera that did not have to be supported by a tripod or table. It was a box six and three-quarter inches by three and three-quarter inches in size. Weighing only twenty-two ounces, it could be carried in one hand and held there during exposure. Loaded with film and equipped with a leather case and a shoulder strap, it could be purchased for twenty-five dollars.

Many months of work went into the creation of this device. Many weeks of thought went into Eastman's search for a catchy and easily pronounced name for it. One of his early determinations during this period was to begin the name with the letter *k*. For one thing, *k* had a firm ring to it. For another, it was the first letter of *Kilbourn*, the maiden name of his beloved mother. Along the way he decided that if one *k* was good, two would be better. Hence the name at which he finally arrived: *Kodak*.

With the appearance of the Kodak, photography became a craze in both the United States and England. Soon London theater audiences were laughing at a Gilbert and Sullivan opera in which an ensemble of pretty ladies, all carrying Kodaks and all acting in a very modest manner, tunefully informed their listeners that:

> To diagnose
> Our modest pose
>   The Kodaks do their best.
> If evidence you would possess
> Of what is maiden bashfulness
> You only need a button press—
>   And we will do the rest.

During the closing decade of the nineteenth century, many additional photographic products and processes tumbled from George Eastman's mind.

At first the buyer of a Kodak had to send it to the plant in Rochester to get his pictures: Only there could the exposed film be removed and developed and new film inserted. In 1891 all this bother ceased. That year Eastman brought out a Kodak that could be loaded and unloaded in daylight, thus eliminating the necessity for shipping the camera to Rochester to be serviced.

Other advances followed rapidly. Soon what had become known as the Eastman Kodak Company was turning out thousands of miles of film for the motion-picture camera recently invented by Thomas Alva Edison. Presently, too, the company was operating branch plants in England and France. The year 1895 saw the production of the company's first pocket Kodak; 1896 produced a Kodak that could be bought for only five dollars.

By the opening of the twentieth century, Eastman Kodak was carrying 3,000 people on its payroll. Its operations in Rochester were no longer confined to a building in the center of town. Most of them were taking place in a group of newly built structures collectively known as Kodak Park.

As for Eastman himself, having become one of his country's richest men, he had also become one of its leading philanthropists. His first large donation of $200,000 went to the Rochester Mechanics Institute. This was in 1899, and during the next thirty-three years his gifts to numerous institutions—notably the University of Rochester and the Massachusetts Institute of Technology in Cambridge, Massachusetts—came to $75 million in all.

Although the city of Rochester benefited enormously from Eastman's generosity, something in his makeup, an inner coldness, prevented his ever becoming a popular figure in the hearts

George Eastman (*left*) stands with Thomas Alva Edison behind his movie camera. *The Bettmann Archive.*

of its citizens. Indeed, as Eastman entered his seventies, he was a lonely and less than happy man.

Gone since 1907 was his mother, the only woman in his life and the mistress of the imposing mansion he had built for the two of them on Rochester's elegant East Avenue.

Over the years he had brought in highly capable managers to run every department of his big company. At its offices, consequently, his services were no longer in great demand.

From time to time he dropped in at the company laboratory, only to return to his big house feeling unnecessary. What science his early inventions had required he had taught himself. Now the formally trained scientists he had hired were talking of things that, for the most part, were beyond his comprehension.

It was a man convinced that he was no longer needed who on March 14, 1932, took his own life.

Thomas Alva Edison

1847–1931   American inventor whose innumerable inventions included the electric light bulb, the phonograph, and the motion-picture camera

With his name on 1,093 patents for new devices and processes, Thomas Alva Edison was history's most productive inventor and one of his country's most honored men.

So overwhelming was his success that his biographers have been hard put to identify the personal qualities that made it possible. Was it an outgrowth of talent and hard work, as Matthew Josephson concludes in his *Edison: A Biography*, published in 1959? Or was it a combination of luck, showmanship, and ruthless indifference to the concerns of other people, as Robert Conot contends in his *A Streak of Luck: The Life and Legend of Thomas Alva Edison*, published in 1979? According to Conot, Edison was a self-centered man, interested in little beyond his own ad-

vancement. According to Josephson he was an engineer with a social conscience, bent on providing people with things that would make their lives better.

Born on February 11, 1847 in the frontier town of Milan, Ohio, he was the last of the seven children of Samuel Ogden Edison, Jr., and Nancy Elliott Edison. Both parents had come of age in Canada. Sam Edison was a descendant of New Jersey Tories, who, having supported England during the American War of Independence, had been forced to migrate to Britain's "fourteenth colony" in the New World when that revolution ended. Nancy Edison was the daughter of an American minister who had answered a call from a church in Ontario. When in 1837 she, her husband, and their children fled to the United States, it was because Sam Edison, like his forebears, had taken the losing side in an armed rebellion, this one against the British-controlled government of Canada.

By 1854, when the Edisons left Milan to settle in Port Huron, Michigan, two of Thomas Alva's brothers and one of his sisters had died. One of his surviving sisters had married and left home. The other was about to do so, and the remaining brother, fifteen years his senior, was helping their father with his varying and consistently unprofitable businesses. Consequently, according to his biographer Conot, Thomas Alva was brought up as though he were an only child.

His stern and pious mother, perpetually dressed in black in memory of her lost children, had him reading the Bible at an early age. She hoped that by doing this she could keep him from following in the footsteps of her fun-loving husband. Tall, handsome, and easygoing, Sam Edison was fond of his youngest offspring but puzzled by his behavior. What was one to make of Thomas Alva's bottomless curiosity, his fondness for playing practical jokes on people, his facility for getting into scrapes?

Why does the goose squat on her eggs? he asked his mother. To keep them warm, she replied. Why does the goose want them to be warm? So they'll hatch, he was told. *Hatch* meant what? It meant, said his mother, letting the baby geese come out of the shell. Hours later Sam Edison, alarmed at the long absence of his five-year-old son, found him in a neighbor's barn, sitting on a batch of geese and chicken eggs.

When a year later he took to wondering what a bonfire looked like and burned down the Edisons' barn, his father marched him to the public square. There, before a gang of townspeople, he thrashed him thoroughly. His biographer Josephson sees in Thomas Alva's long recollection of this action—he mentioned it sixty years later—a possible explanation for his lifelong "indifference to physical suffering, whether his own or others."

In his fifth or sixth year he and a playmate went swimming. Suddenly the other boy disappeared under the water. Thomas Alva waited—and waited. Then, with the coming of nightfall, he raced home and went to bed. Later he was awakened by a search party, the word having spread that he'd been seen with the missing boy. Only then did Thomas Alva reveal what had happened and direct the searchers to the stream, where his chum's lifeless body was found.

The incident perplexed his parents. Why hadn't Thomas Alva called for help? He knew what drowning was all about. Why, on his return home, had he said nothing to them? Was this rambunctious child "without feelings," as would be said of him later?

For some years after the family's arrival in Port Huron, Thomas Alva was troubled by fluid in the ears and other symptoms of the recurrent respiratory ills believed responsible for the deafness that thereafter afflicted him in varying degrees. At intervals his mother, a schoolteacher in her earlier years, educated him at home. Instead of giving him primers and simple tales to read, she handed him adult classics: Edward Gibbon's *Decline and Fall of the Roman Empire* for one, and Shakespeare's plays. It's anybody's guess how well he fared with Gibbon. It is a matter of record that later on he showed a wide-ranging familiarity with the works of Shakespeare.

Three times his parents enrolled him in a local school. With his oversized head on a rickety frame, he was an odd-looking child. At the first of these schools the other pupils teased and bullied him, and the teacher pronounced him "addled." Finally he ran home and refused to return. At none of these institutions of learning did he display the brilliance so noticeable in the adult Edison.

When he was nine his parents presented him with a copy of R. G. Parker's *School of Natural Philosophy*, which described a variety of scientific experiments that could be done at home. Thomas Alva was entranced. Soon he had established a laboratory in the basement and was performing the experiments.

But his father's current business was doing badly and laboratory supplies cost money. Here was a problem that, when he was twelve, Thomas Alva solved by creating for himself a job as a vendor of newspapers, sandwiches, and other goods on a train of the Grand Trunk Railway, which ran on weekdays between Port Huron and Detroit, sixty-five miles to the south. Before long he was earning enough to give his mother a dollar a day and to set up another laboratory for himself in the baggage car of the train.

Every weekday morning at seven-fifteen he hopped aboard. During the five-hour layover in Detroit, reached in the late morning, he read books on science and technology at the public library or snoozed on the seats of his train. Thus did he acquire the habit of getting his rest by means of catnaps, a habit that would stay with him for life. Every evening found him at the Port Huron railroad station at eight o'clock with a three-hour journey home by horse and buggy yet to come.

In later times he often referred to his three years on the train as the happiest period of his life, its occasionally hair-raising moments notwithstanding. One day a bottle of phosphorus on the shelf of his baggage-car laboratory caught fire, tipped over, and set the floor ablaze. The baggage master, arriving in time to smother the flames, suffered burned fingers, so he heaved Thomas Alva's collection of chemicals out the door and boxed the young man's ears. A number of largely fictional biographies of him, published later, attributed his deafness to this blow. In fact, though the cuff on the ears may have worsened the condition, the deafness had been with him by this time for at least two years.

The appearance shortly before Edison's birth of the telegraph, invented by Samuel F. B. Morse, had enlivened the commerce of the United States and helped link together the far-flung parts of a growing nation. All over the country young men, fascinated by Morse's invention, began looking for positions as telegraph operators. Thomas Alva himself had mastered the Morse code and had built his own sounder, the instrument used to transmit the dots and dashes of the code.

At the age of fifteen he jumped at a friend's offer to teach him telegraphy on a professional level. Within two months he had learned enough to give up his job on the railroad and get a job as a "plug," or novice operator, at the telegraph office in Port Huron.

During the next three years his new career found him working in almost a dozen places, ranging from Stratford, Ontario, to Memphis, Tennessee. Once he quit his job to take a better paying one and a promotion to first-class telegrapher. More often he was simply fired because of his habit of neglecting his duties to tinker with experiments aimed at improving Morse's still crude and balky apparatus.

During his stay in Louisville, Kentucky, in the winter of 1865–1866, the telegraph operators in New York and Boston staged a contest to determine the fastest sender of messages in the United States. The Louisville office selected as its candidate a man named George Everett. Ever the practical joker, Edison rigged up a gadget that let him send a long and meaningless *brrrrrr* over the wire. "Who in the hell is that?" a startled operator in New York inquired. "That," Edison replied, "is our man Everett."

The years of the Civil War and its aftermath were turbulent ones for the wandering "brethren of the keys." Wherever Edison landed he worked in dilapidated offices and lived in grimy, rat-infested rooming houses. For him the discomforts of the trade were all the greater because of his practice, continued for years to come, of spending practically all his earnings on the equipment his ceaseless experimenting required. One winter he came close to freezing because he lacked the money to purchase an overcoat to supplement his frayed trousers and tobacco-stained linen duster.

"Go west, young man," the famous New York journalist Horace Greeley had advised the ambitious members of Edison's generation. In the autumn of 1867, after a brief visit home, Edison went east instead. In Boston he worked at the Western Union office at night and spent the daylight hours haunting the local bookstores and pursuing his experiments.

One day he chanced upon a copy of Michael Faraday's three-volume *Experimental Researches in Electricity*. This find, Edison said later, was one of the most "decisive events" of his life. Not since his reading of Parker's *School of Natural Philosophy* in his boyhood had anything in print stirred him so profoundly.

He was struck by the similarities between his background and that of the great English scientist: both had been born in poverty, both were self-educated. By his discovery of induction, the means by which mechanical energy can be converted into electrical energy—a find that the physicist Joseph Henry had duplicated in America—Faraday helped lay the foundation for the coming age of electricity. This was the field of endeavor that Edison now resolved to make his own.

In June, 1868, a magazine called *The Journal of the Telegraph* reported that "Mr. Thomas A. Edison of the Western Union Office, Boston," had constructed a duplex telegraph, one capable of sending two messages simultaneously on the same line. A friend had signed the article, but Edison had written it. Like many of his subsequent attempts to publicize himself, this one worked. A little money rolled in from Bostonians interested in investing in promising new devices, and Edison quit his job to become an independent, free-lance inventor.

On January 1, 1869, he received his first patent. It was for a vote recorder, with which the member of a legislature could push a button marked "nay" or one marked "aye" on his desk. At once his vote would show up on an electrified board on the wall.

Today legislatures everywhere use a machine of this sort. But in the mid-nineteenth century, American politicians were not yet ready to expose their votes on a screen. Edison's failure to sell his recorder either to the Massachu-

Thomas Alva Edison sits beside his tinfoil phonograph, April 18, 1878. *U.S. Department of the Interior, National Park Service, Edison National Historic Site.*

setts legislature or the United States Congress moved him to a conclusion that guided his work as an inventor for the rest of his life. There was no point in wasting time making things people didn't want. One should first ascertain what was "commercially feasible," what the movers and shapers of American industry were looking for. Then he should do his inventing accordingly.

But where was the best place for ascertaining what the commercial world was seeking? New York City, of course. And one summer day in 1869, twenty-two-year-old Edison arrived in that clamorous metropolis, his pockets empty as usual and his head as usual full of ideas.

In New York he got in touch with his friend Frank L. Pope, a gifted electrical engineer. Pope was working at a plant headed by Samuel S. Laws, inventor of the gold indicator, a primitive stock ticker used in the offices of the financial district known as Wall Street to keep track of the changing price of gold.

Pope let Edison sleep in a room of the plant and provided him with enough money on which to live until he could find a job. In fact, the job found him. Soon after his arrival in the big city, the main gold indicator in the plant broke down, creating a panic on Wall Street. Neither Pope nor its inventor,

Laws, could figure out what had happened. Edison examined the cumbersome machine, quickly saw what was wrong, and within two hours had put the gold indicators of Wall Street back in business. Next day Laws offered him a job.

Thus began a career in New York and its vicinity that by the winter of 1871 had carried Edison across the Hudson River, where, with a partner, he set up a workshop of his own in Newark, New Jersey. Here, and later in a considerably larger plant, he directed the manufacture of a variety of electrical devices. Most of them were things he himself had developed: an automatic or high-speed telegraph, for example, an improved stock ticker, and the mimeograph machine.

To keep his workshop going he sold the rights to his inventions to Western Union and other large companies. Though in time Edison's financial rewards were substantial, it would appear that over the long run the clever but not always scrupulous leaders of the American communications industry received far more money out of his inventions than he did.

Did this bother him? Not a great deal. "I don't care so much about making my fortune," he said, "as I do for getting ahead of the other fellow." To be the best in his field, to outinvent everybody else—these were Edison's goals, and their achievement provided his greatest pleasure.

It took a critical event indeed to lure him from his labors for more than a few hours. In April 1871 the death of his mother took him home to attend the funeral and to spend time with his sixty-seven-year-old father, who a few months later chose as his second wife a seventeen-year-old dairymaid.

Back in Newark, Edison eyed with approval fifteen-year-old Mary Stilwell, a golden-haired beauty who had come to work in his factory.

"What do you think of me, little girl? Do you like me?" he asked her.

All Mary knew about her pale and high-domed boss was that he was a great man who made many things, though what went into their making she would never remotely comprehend. "Why, Mr. Edison, you frighten me," she stammered. "That is—"

Edison relieved her from any further attempt to answer his abrupt question. "Don't be in a hurry about telling me," he said. "It doesn't matter much unless you would like to marry me."

That he selected Christmas Day of 1871 for the wedding suggests he figured that that was the one holiday when he had no choice but to absent himself from work. His offhand courtship was followed by a reasonably happy marriage, during the course of which he fathered a girl and two boys. None of them ever saw much of him.

In the spring of 1876 the occupants of the half-dozen houses comprising the hamlet of Menlo Park, in the New Jersey countryside, watched the arrival of construction crews and the emergence of a barnlike wooden structure on a hill overlooking the railroad between New York and Philadelphia. It was a hundred feet long and thirty wide, and upon its completion it was surrounded by a picket fence to keep out the pigs and cows. Here Edison established what was to be the best remembered of his private laboratories.

Menlo Park was the world's first factory for the making of nothing but inventions, a forerunner of the private research laboratories now maintained by many large industrial organizations. In an advertisement published at the time of its opening, Edison promised to turn out "a minor invention every ten days and a big thing every six months or so."

He was given to bragging, but rarely did he fail to make good on even his most extravagant boasts. New contraptions poured from his hilltop factory. There were periods when the "Wizard of Menlo Park," as the press dubbed him, found himself working on as many as forty-seven new things at once.

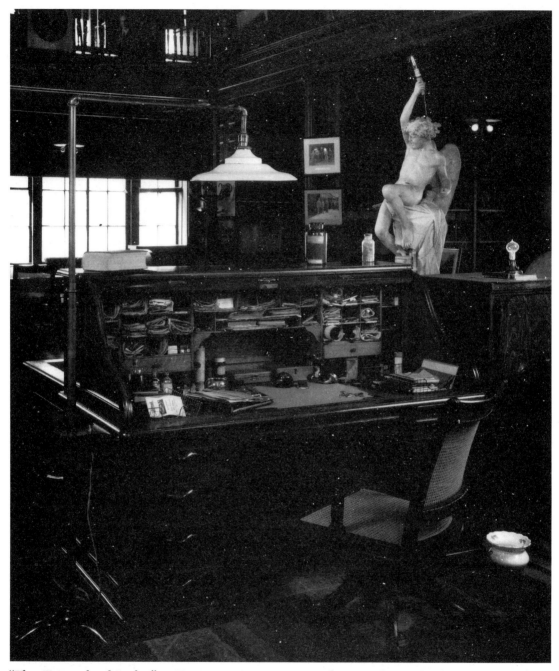

"The Triumph of Light," a European statue converted into a lamp, holds an incandescent bulb above Thomas Alva Edison's desk. *Breton Littlehales / National Park Service, Edison National Historic Site.*

He and his workmen reported in at seven in the morning. Sixteen-hour days were commonplace. When an especially difficult problem arose he would immure himself in the laboratory for days and nights on end, catnapping in his clothes on a table or on the floor under one of his large machines.

As a boy he'd once tried to read a book by England's Isaac Newton, the seventeenth-century's greatest scientist, only to be put off by its mathematics. As an adult he was given to ridiculing mathematicians. He described them as people who put a lot of a's and b's on paper and then came up with the wrong answer. Pure scientists, he said, were people who made discoveries that they were either too lazy or too dumb to convert into things other people could use.

Did he mean any of this? Not a word of it. Edison was as deft as a politician at hiding his true convictions by cracking a joke or by saying what he thought listeners wanted to hear. To join his staff at Menlo Park he brought the best mathematicians and physicists he could afford. He pored for hours over the scientific volumes crowding the shelves of his library. Clearly, one of the qualities contributing to his success was his undying eagerness to learn, his willingness when a question arose in his work to read any number of books and con-

duct any number of experiments to find the answer. He himself would one day make a contribution to pure science with his discovery of the presence in an airless or almost airless enclosure, under certain circumstances, of a free flow of negative electricity, or electrons. Called the "Edison effect," this discovery would help bring about the radio, the television, and many other electronic appliances of our own times.

By 1876, when Menlo Park opened, engineers had been trying for half a century to find a way of using electrical current for illumination. To do so would relieve mankind of its dependence on candles, oil-fueled lamps, and gaslight.

An electricity-powered contrivance called the arc lamp had already been developed. The arc lamp produced illumination by means of a spark that leaped from one of its elements to another. It could be used only in open spaces or in very large and well-ventilated structures. A further drawback was that arc lamps employed a system of wiring "in series," which meant that if one of the sparking units went off, all the others linked to it in the series went off at the same time.

In 1877, at Menlo Park, Edison set out to change all this. By the fall of 1879 he had given the world the devices and processes that were to carry electric lighting into millions of homes and

Thomas Alva Edison's laboratory in West Orange, New Jersey. *Breton Littlehales / National Park Service, Edison National Historic Site.*

workplaces. These new things were the incandescent lamp, a brightly glowing filament inside a transparent globe from which all or most of the oxygen had been removed; a wiring hookup that allowed one or more bulbs to fail or to be turned off without affecting the others; and the plans for the construction of the world's first electric power plant, the Pearl Street Station in New York City, which opened on September 4, 1882.

The electric light bulb was not the only history-changing invention to come out of the Menlo Park laboratory. On December 4, 1877, Edison completed his first phonograph. It was a crude affair, closer to the dictaphone than to the music player produced later after changes by its inventor and others. Still, according to some of its originator's biographers, it was the most remarkable of all his creations. Few important inventions can be called brand new. Most are improvements on previous efforts along the same lines. Not so the phonograph. Edison's sound-reproducing machine seems to have been unlike anything ever attempted before.

He had long since moved to New York to supervise the building and operation of the Pearl Street Station when on August 9, 1884, his wife died in an apartment overlooking Gramercy Square. In the past his relentless work schedule had kept him from all but an occasional social gathering. Now his expanding but still boyish figure became a familiar one at such events. Friends guessed that he was seeking a second wife.

He was. At a party in Boston in the winter of 1885 he was struck by the "rich black hair and great dazzling eyes" of eighteen-year-old Mina Miller, daughter of a wealthy manufacturer of farm tools in Akron, Ohio. On February 24, 1886, they were married at her parents' home. Edison brought his bright and aristocratic bride to the $300,000 chateaulike country house called Glenmont that he had bought for her near West Orange, New Jersey.

To this marriage, as to its predecessor, a girl and two boys were born. And to Mina Edison, as to Mary Edison before her, fell the burden of bringing them up, with little assistance from

From one of Thomas Alva Edison's notebooks, a preliminary sketch of his light bulb. *U.S. Department of the Interior, National Park Service, Edison National Historic Site.*

their busy and chronically absent father. Growing up in the shadow of a great man was not an easy business for any of the six children. Nevertheless all of Mina's children did well, and one of her sons eventually became a respected mathematical physicist.

Edison was rich now, the head of several large companies engaged in selling the things he had made or was in

Thomas Alva Edison with two of his electric light bulbs. *Brown Brothers.*

the process of making. He was also famous, the recipient of many awards from the people of his own and other countries. When in 1888 he established the second of his private laboratories, a sprawling complex of buildings in West Orange, the members of the press were very much on hand.

Reporters were forever seeking interviews with him. They did so partly out of a desire to learn what he was making at the moment, partly because he could be counted on to say something funny or, better yet, outrageous.

"Mr. Edison," a newsman inquired, "if it were possible to hear [on your phonograph] the voice of any man . . . known in the history of the world, whose voice would you prefer to hear?"

"Napoleon's," replied Edison.

When the reporter said that he would rather hear "the voice of our Savior," the great inventor laughed. "Oh well," he said, "you know how *I like a hustler.*"

Soon after the opening of the West Orange laboratory, visiting reporters were barred from a section of one of the buildings. What was going on in that "secret" room? they wondered.

In the fall of 1889 Edison's business affairs took him to Europe for several weeks. On his return home he hastened to the secret room, only to learn that the project begun there had been moved to another building.

There, in a darkened room, he watched as the images of a man walking about and tipping his hat were thrown onto a screen by a machine Edison had conceived. October 6, 1889, saw the creation of the world's first practical motion-picture camera and the birth of the mammoth entertainment industry known as the movies.

New things streamed from the West Orange laboratory. One of them was the fluoroscope, which was manipulated by a surgeon for the first operation in the United States to utilize the recent discovery of X rays by the German physicist Wilhelm Konrad Roentgen. Others took the form of significant improvements in the storage battery developed by France's Gaston Plante in 1859 and

in the telephone invented by Scottish-American Alexander Graham Bell in 1876.

Though, beginning in 1903, Edison was the victim of recurrent ailments, he continued to work steadily. His adoring public saw a man of seemingly unending vigor. It was a legacy, perhaps, from his father, who had retained his youthful zest almost to the moment of his death in 1896, at the age of ninety-two.

During the inventor's last two decades newspapers and magazines regularly hailed him as his country's "greatest" or "most useful" citizen. "This is a hell of a thing," he grumbled during one of the many celebrations to mark his birthdays, "to congratulate a man on the fact that he is getting old."

What did he consider the secret of his success? Reporters were forever asking him that. Was he not a genius? Endlessly quoted in later years was his assertion that "genius is ninety-nine percent perspiration and one percent inspiration."

When in 1914 the First World War broke out in Europe, the members of the press descended on West Orange. By this time the people of the United States wanted to hear the great man's opinions on every subject under the sun. Did he believe this country should help Great Britain and its other allies in Europe by sending its armies across the sea?

Like his close friend Henry Ford, Edison was opposed to the idea. But when his country did enter the war, he served actively on a committee of prominent individuals set up to advise the American military. It was during this period that the man who had scoffed repeatedly at mathematicians and physicists suggested and fought for the establishment of that bastion of pure science, the Naval Research Laboratory, now sited on the outskirts of Washington, D.C.

Startling to those of us who have witnessed the coming of the atom bomb is a statement uttered by Edison during his closing years.

"There will one day spring from the brain of Science," he said, "a machine of force so fearful in its potentiality, so absolutely terrifying that even man, the fighter who will dare torture and death in order to inflict torture and death, will be appalled and will abandon war forever."

When death came at the age of eighty-four, it was the result of a combination of ills. In the early morning hours of Sunday, October 18, 1931, as he lay silent in a room of his New Jersey home, his wife put her lips to one of his deaf ears.

"Are you suffering?" she asked.

"No, just waiting," he replied.

The wait was brief. At 3:24 that morning he was gone.

On the following Wednesday, the day of his funeral, President Herbert Hoover expressed the wish that at ten that evening Americans everywhere would dim the lights that Edison had given them.

Michael Faraday

1791–1867   British chemist; discoverer of the principles that were to make possible the widespread use of electricity and inventor of the dynamo, ancestor of today's electrical generators

Michael Faraday, one of the four children of James Faraday and Margaret Hastwell Faraday, was born on September 22, 1791, in Newington, Surrey, then a country town south of London, now a part of the British capital. His father was a blacksmith who, having fallen on hard times, had only recently moved from the north of England to the London area in search of employment.

Because the elder Faraday's failing health made steady work impossible, Michael's early years were marked by grinding poverty. There were times when he had to make his meals for a week from a single loaf of bread. Still, as he himself subsequently insisted, his childhood was a happy one. This was due partly to the guidance of a wise and loving mother, partly because of his family's membership in a small Christian sect called the Sandemanians, who believed that a cheerful acceptance of one's lot in life was "pleasing to the Lord." We have the word of L. Pearce Williams, one of Michael Faraday's biographers, that behind Faraday's brilliant scientific discoveries lay the Sandemanian-inspired conviction that the noblest thing a person can do with his or her life is to add to mankind's "knowledge of God's universe."

His formal education was limited to learning the "three r's"—writing, reading, and arithmetic—in a church Sunday school. At an early age he was out on the street, delivering newspapers. At fourteen he was apprenticed to a London bookbinder.

Unlike the other apprentices, he read many of the books brought to the shop to be bound and sold—so many that for a time he was utterly uncertain as to which of numerous interesting fields of learning he should pursue. It was only after coming upon an article about electricity in the third edition of the *Encyclopaedia Britannica* that what was to be the dream of his life took form: He was determined to become a scientist.

But how was an almost totally self-educated son of a blacksmith to climb to such heights? That question was at the front of his mind when, in the autumn of 1812, his apprenticeship ended and he was forced to look for work.

It so happened that a few months earlier a friend had given him a ticket to a series of lectures by the famous chemist Sir Humphry Davy at the Royal Institution of Great Britain in London, a center of research and education in the sciences. Fascinated by Sir Humphry's remarks, the young bookbinder's apprentice had taken copious notes on them.

These he now sent to Sir Humphry along with a letter, expressing his approval of Davy's accomplishments as a chemist and his own longing to become one. Where could he learn such a profession better than in the laboratory at the Royal Institution where Sir Hum-

phry conducted his experiments? Was there by any chance a job open at the institution? Some post for which he might apply?

There was none, he was told. But his disappointment at this reply was short-lived. In the late winter of 1813 a young laboratory assistant at the Royal Institution, holder of a position known as "fag and scrub," got into a street brawl and was fired. At this point Sir Humphry Davy, impressed by Faraday's notes on his lectures and flattered by his compliments, sent a messenger to Faraday's lodgings, offering him the newly vacated position.

Thus in March, 1813, began Faraday's fifty-two years with the Royal Institution, a career that saw him move rapidly from fag and scrub to superintendent of apparatus of the laboratory and mineralogical collection to superintendent of the institution as a whole.

In the beginning he was primarily a student, working alongside Sir Humphry Davy, whose achievements included the isolation of several chemical elements, potassium and calcium among them, and the invention of a safety lamp for miners. Davy was plainly delighted with the speed with which his student mastered the many aspects of chemistry. When in the fall of 1813 he and his recently acquired wife decided to tour the scientific cen-

A portrait engraving of Michael Faraday.

ters of continental Europe, they took young Faraday with them.

For the blacksmith's son a jaunt that included stays in Paris and Rome was a useful addition to the learning he had long since set out to acquire. The close and daily contact with Sir Humphry, a brilliant scientist, was an education in itself. It was during this trip, his biographer Williams avers, that Faraday learned from Davy "a way of looking at the activities of matter that was to lead to his great discoveries."

Not that the trip was all bliss. The new Lady Davy was an aristocrat and a snob. She was forever trying to make a servant of Faraday, and when he protested she did not hesitate to remind him of his lower-class beginnings. To her ladyship the high points of the jaunt were the glittering social affairs to which the travelers were invited. Sir Humphry, too, enjoyed these occasions. Not Faraday. Never as long as he lived, he resolved, would he allow the sparkle and gaudery of high society to lure him away from his laboratory.

It is a measure of his devotion to his work that although the events leading to the defeat of Napoleon Bonaparte at Waterloo were underway during his continental tour, Faraday took no interest in them. Politics, he wrote to a friend back home, was a subject he preferred to leave to others.

Back at the Royal Institution in the spring of 1815 he quickly completed his apprenticeship under Sir Humphry Davy. By 1818 he had become a professional chemist on his own. By 1820 his reputation as an analyst was such that several industries hired him to do research for them in the institution laboratory, paying fees that he turned over to the Royal Institution.

During these opening years of Faraday's career he took little time off from his scientific labors for pleasure. His close friends, all men, scolded him. All work and no play, they argued, was a poor sort of life. They urged him to go to parties, to relax in the company of women. His reaction to their plea was to write a poem, beginning:

What is the pest and plague of
human life?
And what the curse that often
brings a wife:
     'tis love.

Among his friends was an Edward Barnard, the son of an elder in the Sandemanian church where Faraday worshiped. Edward showed Faraday's poem to his sister Sarah, who is believed to have reacted to it as any attractive young woman might have. "So Mr. Faraday thinks he can live without a wife," she seems to have said to herself. "Well, we'll see about that."

His biographer Williams points out that a pencil sketch of Sarah Barnard shows a set to her chin "which reveals a certain determination." Michael Faraday, Williams adds, "was a fine-looking man . . . with a respectable place in the world. That Miss Barnard set her cap for him is not to be wondered at and Faraday . . . surrendered absolutely."

Married on June 12, 1821, they set up housekeeping in a suite of rooms in the stately pillar-fronted building of the Royal Institution on London's Albemarle Street.

Sarah knew nothing about science. Nor did she try to learn anything. Friends suggested that since her husband was a chemist she should at least study chemistry. Her reply was that Michael's work was "already so absorbing and exciting to him that it often deprives him of sleep." Her duty, she reasoned, was to try not to discuss with him matters she would never fully comprehend. Her job was to give him a calming and comfortable atmosphere to come home to, "to be the pillow to his mind."

No children were born to their union, but off and on for many years two of Sarah's nieces lived with them. Wrapped up in his research though he was, Faraday managed to do a good deal of fathering. He staged spectacular experiments in the laboratory to entertain the young ladies. He took them riding along the corridors of the Royal Institution on a velocipede he had constructed.

The decade beginning in 1821 saw the discoveries and inventions that were to make him one of the most productive scientists of his era. Fairly late in this period he laid the foundation for today's worldwide use of electricity by setting forth the principles of electromagnetic induction. The term *electromagnetic induction* refers to the generation of an electromotive force on a conductor by an electric current flowing in another conductor near to the one so affected but neither in contact with it nor connected to it. Still later in the same period he constructed the first dynamo, forerunner of the generators now used to convert mechanical energy into electrical energy.

On the heels of these great discoveries and inventions he embarked on a string of experiments aimed at ascertaining the exact nature of electricity and its relationship to other forces. He was unable to complete these investigations. Such results as they produced, however, would help future scientists find the answers to the questions Faraday had raised.

Demanding as his laboratory work was, he found time for other activities.

Michael Faraday's laboratory at the Royal Institution. *Courtesy of the Director of the Royal Institution.*

He published many scientific papers, as well as a book or two for children. He functioned as an elder in the Sandemanian church and as a lecturer at his country's Royal Military Academy, at Woolwich.

In 1825 he helped establish at the institute a course of weekly lectures on science for the public. In 1826 he organized another course of lectures on science, this one open to youngsters only.

Faraday himself delivered many of these lectures, bringing to his appearances on the platform a flare for showmanship rarely present in a scientist. Children enjoyed his talks, finding them at once informative and entertaining. Once, by way of showing them the meaning of the term *center of gravity*, he stood on one leg, simultaneously shifting the bulk of his weight (his center of gravity) so that it was concentrated over the leg on which he was standing, allowing him to stand one-legged for as long as he wanted without falling over.

In 1839 the many years of almost ceaseless labor caught up with him. There was a sudden breakdown in his health marked by a dramatic failure of memory. Though by 1844 he was able to return to the laboratory for a few years, he was never again a wholly well man.

When in 1857 he was offered the presidency of the Royal Society, the most distinguished of England's scientific bodies, he declined, pointing out that he was simply not up to it. In 1855 his mind began to fail, and ten years later, after a number of intermittent mental lapses, he resigned his post at the Royal Institution.

By this time Queen Victoria had offered him a knighthood. This he refused, saying that he wished to leave this world as he had entered it, a plain "mister." The queen had also given him a cottage on the green near Hampton Court, a well-known royal palace standing near the Thames River southwest of London.

Here Faraday passed his final days. Here, as he sat quietly in a chair, he died on August 25, 1867.

"There can be no doubt," writes his biographer Williams, "that, had he so desired, he could have been laid to rest in Westminster Abbey to join the ranks of those whom Great Britain wishes to honor through the centuries."

But this was not his desire. His desire, as expressed to relatives, was for a "strictly private and plain" funeral, with burial in London's Highgate Cemetery, under a simple headstone bearing only his name and the dates of his birth and death.

Philo Taylor Farnsworth

1906–1971   American research engineer and industrial executive; contributor, on a large scale, to the development of modern television

One afternoon in the winter of 1922, a science teacher named Justin Tolman stepped into the study hall of the high school in Rigby, Idaho, to find sixteen-year-old Philo Taylor Farnsworth sketching a large blueprintlike drawing on the blackboard.

Justin Tolman, who was also superintendent of the Rigby schools, was a man who loved to teach. The pale, skinny, underfed-looking freshman at the blackboard was a boy who loved to learn. It was not uncommon, at the end of the school day, for the two of them to get together in this room to talk chemistry, which was Tolman's subject.

But the diagram taking form before him, the middle-aged educator saw, had nothing to do with chemistry. With electricity perhaps; with electrons. Yes,

that's what it appeared to be: a series of electricity-carrying devices, curiously hooked together.

Tolman took a seat and waited for the boy to finish his work. Then: "Well, Phil," he said, "what have we here?"

Phil's answer was to pick up a pointer. One by one he tapped the major elements of his diagram. In the hesitant manner of a person groping for just the right words he identified them. Such terms as *photoelectric cell* and *cathode-ray tube* fell from his lips. What he had put on the board, he announced proudly, was the diagram of a television system—a system that, once it was properly constructed, would bring into people's homes pictures of distant things and events, even as the recently introduced wireless, or radio was beginning to bring in voices and music.

In later years Justin Tolman enjoyed recounting this and other incidents in the life of the most promising of his students.

Born on August 19, 1906, on his parents' farm near Beaver City, Utah, the future inventor of one of the first workable television systems was the oldest of five children of Lewis Farnsworth and Serena Bastian Farnsworth. The Farnsworths were Mormons, members of the Church of Jesus Christ of Latter-day Saints. Both of Phil's grandfathers had come west as part of the 1,300-mile trek of the Mormons from their temporary settlements in the Midwest to what was to be their permanent home in the valley of the Great Salt Lake in north-central Utah. The paternal grandfather after whom Phil was named was for many years the Mormon bishop of Beaver City.

At the age of five Phil declared that he was going to be an inventor when he grew up, and his parents set out to encourage him by subscribing to an array of magazines published for amateur scientists. Soon he was astounding and delighting them by the speed with which he mastered the basics of several sciences, especially mathematics. At twelve years old he entered a contest announced in one of his magazines.

With the twenty-five dollars he received as winner of the first prize he purchased his first pair of long pants.

He was fourteen when the family moved to Rigby, Idaho. There they farmed hay and grain at Bungalow Ranch, a large spread of land on the borders of Yellowstone Park. Here Phil was fascinated by the Delco lighting system that powered appliances both inside and outside the farmhouse. Phil was the only person on the premises who could repair this gadget. So frequently did it break down that the members of the family suspected that he sometimes deliberately put it out of order so as to have the fun of taking it apart and putting it together again. If so, his mother forgave him when he contrived a motor that enabled the lighting system to run her washing machine.

He attended a local grammar school for a year. Then in the fall of 1922, he enrolled at Rigby High School and met Superintendent Tolman. In later years Tolman was fond of recalling the first time young Farnsworth came into his office.

The boy was unhappy with the courses he was taking. He already knew more than the teachers did. He understood that Tolman was giving a good course in chemistry. Why couldn't he join that?

Because, Tolman told him, his chemistry course was for seniors only. Phil would have to wait.

But Phil was not one to wait. A few days later he was back in Tolman's office. This time he suggested that he be permitted to sit in on the superintendent's class. He wouldn't recite; he would just sit there and listen.

To Tolman this seemed a reasonable request. But he quickly discovered that this knowledge-hungry boy was not one to just sit and listen. Presently, when no one else could handle Tolman's questions, Phil was answering them. One day the superintendent arrived late in the classroom and found young Farnsworth at the blackboard, expounding to the other students the theories of relativity recently enunciated by the world-famous scientist Albert Einstein.

In encyclopedias available at the high school Phil found descriptions of the electron theory—how bits of negative electricity called electrons behave and how these tiny charges were being used to transmit sound through the air. If sound could be transmitted electronically, Phil reasoned, surely pictures could be conveyed in the same way. At this moment he began piecing together in his mind the television system that Mr. Tolman found him diagraming on the study-hall blackboard one winter afternoon.

At the heart of Phil's system, as conceived at this time, were two devices, a photoelectric cell and a cathode-ray tube. The photoelectric cell, a major component of his television camera, could change light into electrical energy. The cathode-ray tube, a major element of the receiving set, could change electrical current into glowing fluorescence, thus painting pictures on the television screen.

Optimist that he was, Phil assured Mr. Tolman that it wouldn't take him long to convert his television system into one that could be manufactured on a large scale and sold to the public. Tolman expressed some doubts about this—correctly, as it turned out. It would be many years before Philo T. Farnsworth's television system was ready for commercial production.

Intent though he was on working on his invention, Phil found time to participate in the extracurricular activities at Rigby High. He played violin in the school orchestra. He planned and directed a number of social affairs. He enjoyed the company of the other students, and they enjoyed his. It was a harsh blow when, toward the end of his freshman year, his father's work forced the family to move to a section of Bungalow Ranch too far from Rigby for him to continue his studies there. To make matters worse, the educational offerings at the new location were of no interest to a youngster capable of comprehending the theories of Albert Einstein.

For the next few years, life for young Farnsworth was a string of frustrating starts and stops. To perfect his television system, he needed scientific training that was unavailable in the isolated rural region to which his family had come. His parents were well aware of this. In 1923 his father, giving up his attempt to develop Bungalow Ranch, moved the family to Provo, Utah.

Provo was the seat of Mormon-run Brigham Young University. The plan was for Phil to enter this respected institution as soon as he was ready to do so. It took him only one year to complete his high-school work, but his dream of studying at Brigham Young collapsed when he was unable to find a summer job that paid enough to cover the enrollment fees. Desperate, he joined the navy and served with a unit at San Diego, California. In the back of his mind lay the possibility of someday attending the Naval Academy at Annapolis, Maryland. Nothing came of this dream, either. Shortly before Christmas, 1924, his father died of pneumonia. Soon thereafter the navy, heeding his mother's plea that she now needed her eldest son at home, released him from the service.

Back in Provo there were more starts and stops. Working at odd jobs, Phil somehow kept his widowed mother and his younger brothers and sisters going. Somehow he scraped together enough money to spend a few months at Brigham Young as a part-time student, studying mathematics and other sciences. By the fall of 1925, however, it was clear that he could not earn enough in Provo to keep up with his family's growing needs.

In nearby Salt Lake City, as in many other American cities, a new industry called radio was taking form. Phil's training at Brigham Young had given him a fair idea of how radios worked. He talked the matter over with his mother, and January of 1926 found him in the Utah state capital, looking for work as a radio technician and repairman. Here in the handsome metropolis that the Mormons had erected in the vicinity of the Great Salt Lake, he met a young man named George Everson. For both of them it was a fateful encounter. Out of it came the events that enabled Farnsworth to begin making his significant contributions to the development of modern television.

In the spring of 1926 Everson and an assistant named Leslie Gorrell were in Salt Lake City, organizing a campaign for the collection from private sources of money for that city's Community

Chest, the annually assembled fund used to support a variety of local welfare agencies. One of their first needs was for a six-man crew to survey the city's stores, factories, and other businesses and list those from which contributions could be solicited. Among the applicants for these jobs, sent by the employment office of the city's largest educational institution, the University of Utah, was young Farnsworth.

Unable to find work with a radio-repair shop, Phil had set up his own. Unable to make ends meet this way, he had registered with the university's job-placement office.

Everson and Gorrell, impressed with his brightness and drive, put him in charge of the business survey. Soon the three of them had become friends. The evening hours frequently found them in the office of the Community Chest drive, discussing this and that. In his published recollections of their long and productive association—*The Story of Television: The Life of Philo T. Farnsworth*—Everson describes a series of conversations in the late spring when for the first time Phil began talking about his invention.

And what did Phil call this strange thing on which he was working, Everson and Gorrell wanted to know. "A television system," they were told. The answer drew a blank look from Everson.

He couldn't remember ever hearing of such a thing. What was the purpose of it?

Its purpose, Phil said, was to bring motion pictures of distant people and events into the homes of America. Everson shook his head in disbelief. How in the world, he asked, could that be done? Phil patiently described how pictures taken by a camera can be converted into electrical current and how, at the receiving end of the system, this current can be converted back into images moving on a screen.

Everson agreed that the idea sounded wonderful, but if Philo T. Farnsworth, with nothing behind him but a high-school education and a few college courses, could think up such a contraption, surely better-educated and more experienced individuals could do the same. How about the laboratories of such giant American corporations as Bell Telephone and General Electric? Very likely their scientists and engineers were working on television systems in secret. Any day now they would be putting their first models on the market.

Phil was ready for this challenging assertion. He had done his homework.

At that moment, he informed his new friends, television systems were being developed in four different places: in the Bell laboratories by a team of researchers; in the General Electric laboratories by another such team; in Baltimore, Maryland, by an independent inventor; and in London, England, by another independent.

But none of these experimenters, Phil hastened to add, was going about the work in the right way. For one of the most important components of a television system, a device known as the scanner, every one of them was using a mechanical disk—a moving part. To produce clear pictures a television system must operate at such enormous speed that no mechanical parts can be employed in it. And why, Everson asked at once, did Phil think his arrangement would work fast enough to produce clear images? Because, Phil replied, his system called for no mechanical parts. From camera to screen, his system was wholly electric.

At the start of these conversations Everson was inclined to regard Phil's plans as "little more than the interesting daydreams of an ambitious youngster." But as Farnsworth talked on, the older man changed his mind. Gorrell, Everson's business associate, had some background in science. Everson had little or none and was often hard put to follow Phil's highly technical descriptions. What impressed him in the end was not so much what Phil said about his invention. What impressed him was the

young man's bearing: his earnestness, his obvious confidence in his ability to finish what he started, and his amazing grasp—considering the sparseness of his formal education—of electronics.

One evening Everson asked Phil if he had tried to patent his scheme so as to protect it from the attempts of other inventors to copy it. Phil's answer was that to obtain a patent he must "reduce" his scheme "to practice." In other words, he must first build a working model of his system.

How much, Everson asked, would it cost to do that? Like many an eager inventor before him, Phil mentioned a hopelessly inadequate sum—in this case, one that would prove to be approximately a million dollars short of what the work required. Everson and Gorrell offered to put up the few thousand Phil had requested, and by the completion of the Salt Lake City Community Chest drive the three of them had drafted and signed a formal contract. Under its terms Farnsworth was to devote himself full-time to the building of a model. Everson and Gorrell were to supply the funds needed for this purpose. All three were to share in whatever profits accrued from the sale of finished cameras and receiving sets.

Phil's next step was to select a place in which to begin his experiments. His choice of Hollywood, California, was

Kneeling behind one of his television cabinets, Philo Taylor Farnsworth explains the machine's construction. *UPI / Bettmann Newsphotos.*

dictated by a desire to be as close as possible to the California Institute of Technology, a well-known university for the training of scientists and engineers in nearby Pasadena.

Before heading for California, he attended to a matter that had been on his mind for some time. Prior to his move to Salt Lake City, he had fallen in love. His nickname for the young lady was Pem; her real name was Elma Gardner. On May 27, 1926, at her parents' home in Provo, they were married, and by early June they were living in a four-room furnished apartment in Hollywood, and Phil was filling two of the rooms with scraps of metal and glass. Within a few weeks he had completed what Everson describes as "the first electronic transmitter tube ever built." According to Everson, it was "a strangely shaped vacuum cell, bulbous in formation and with one end considerably larger than the other. It was coated at one end with the photoelectric surface, and there was an electrical lead out of each end." Vastly altered in later years and known as the image dissector tube, it would become the major feature of the Farnsworth television camera.

But by itself a transmitter tube, however cleverly assembled, does not a television system make. As the autumn months approached Phil realized that he was not moving ahead. He needed much more equipment than could be squeezed into a four-room apartment. He needed the help of expert glassblowers and trained engineers. And all these things called for funds greatly in excess of what his friends Everson and Gorrell could supply.

Again Everson came to his rescue. This enterprising Community Chest fund-raiser was well known in the banking circles of California. Within a few months Phil was supported by enough financial backing to continue his experiments in San Francisco, California, in an old workshop known as the Crocker Research Laboratories. This was in the spring of 1927, and from this date on the work proceeded steadily.

But not quickly, for the problems it raised were enormous. Indeed, as Everson tells us in *The Story of Television,* had Farnsworth realized at this time that the task he had set for himself would take another twelve years of hard work, he might have given it up on the spot.

Instead he kept going, and little by little his television system took form. In the fall he connected his transmitting apparatus to his receiving apparatus and invited the bankers who were supporting him to watch a demonstration. What they saw at the receiving end of this primitive arrangement was a slide, a still picture of a dark triangle against a background of glaring light.

The dark triangle was blurry and smudged. To the bankers on hand it was not an impressive sight. These men had put considerable money into Phil's efforts. Understandably, they looked forward to the day when his system would be good enough to be sold so that they could get some of their money back. One of them asked another, "Have you seen [as yet] any dollar signs in Farnsworth's tube?" When a few months later Phil staged a second demonstration, he showed his viewers a still picture of a dollar sign.

At this demonstration the image was sharp and clear, and Phil, greatly encouraged, labored on. Presently he was inviting his supporters to yet another demonstration. At this one he gave them something none of them had seen before. What they saw at the receiving end of his apparatus this time was what appears to have been the first motion picture to be broadcast over a television system—an excerpt from the movie version of Shakespeare's play *The Taming of the Shrew*, starring Mary Pickford and Douglas Fairbanks.

Now the work speeded up. One by one the problems were tackled. To one of the most persistent—the appearance at times of a double (or ghost) image—Phil's answer was his development of

the so-called saw-tooth wave form, an important advance in the science of electronics. Soon he was showing his friends pictures of hockey games and baseball games, of people and cars coming and going in the streets. Soon the magazines he had pored over as a boy were describing his dissector tube and predicting the coming of a time when people, sitting in their homes, could watch what people everywhere else were doing.

In 1931 he moved himself, his family, and his working staff to Philadelphia, Pennsylvania. There he continued his experiments, first in the laboratories of a large radio-making company, and then in his own workshops. In the Pennsylvania metropolis he played host for several days to Vladimir Zworykin, a Russian-born American physicist who for some time had been working on television systems in the laboratories of the Radio Corporation of America. Phil showed the visitor his dissector (or transmitting) tube. Zworykin pronounced it excellent. Zworykin in turn showed Phil a diagram of his version of the same element, a device its maker referred to as an iconoscope. Phil examined the diagrams with interest. It is a measure of his stature as a man that he promptly informed his staff that Zworykin's iconoscope was superior to his dissector tube. Time would prove this judgment sound.

In 1929 Philo Taylor Farnsworth holds a television tube that reproduces the largest image of any machine to date. *UPI / Bettmann Newsphotos.*

Several of the major parts of today's television systems are developments of Zworykin's inventions.

By the time Phil and Pem, as he always called his wife, reached Philadelphia they had become the parents of two boys. Phil junior was born in 1929; Kenneth, shortly before the family's departure from San Francisco. For the infant Kenneth the chill winds of a northern city were more than his small frame could withstand. His death in the closing months of 1931 was a blow from which his father had not yet recovered when, in 1933, another son, to be named Russell Seymour, arrived.

For several years Phil took time from his television experiments to search for ways of adapting the 150 or so electronic instruments he had created to medical use. His hope was that by doing this he could save other infants from premature death.

Over the years he had acquired a large number of financial supporters, including the famous New York investment firm of Kuhn, Loeb and Company. On occasion quarrels erupted between the inventor and his businessmen backers. The backers were forever urging him to pronounce his television system complete so that it could be manufactured in quantity and sold to the public. Phil repeatedly urged them to be patient, insisting that the many components of his system needed additional attention. He was not so much interested in making money as he was in bringing his television system to a state of perfection.

On and on he tinkered. Large scientific and engineering societies invited him to speak to them. More often than not, he avoided these invitations, preferring to spend the time at his workbench. His family saw little of him. When he ate with them he picked at his food. To Pem and the youngsters it was clear that, though physically Papa was with them, mentally he remained in his laboratory. Once in a great while—and then only after much urging by his wife and children—would he accompany them on a vacation.

It was during one of these rare family outings that he and Pem came upon an abandoned ninety-acre farm near Fryeburg, Maine. Both of them fell in love with the place. Soon they were living in this remote rural region. The family occupied the old farmhouse, and Phil carried on his experiments in a nearby barn turned workshop.

In 1937 he sold the rights to a number of his electronic inventions to the Atlantic Telephone and Telegraph Company. As this move put money in his backers' pockets, they were delighted with it. They were even more delighted two years later when Phil, giving in to their pleas, permitted them to establish a company called Farnsworth Television and Radio Corporation, with manufacturing plants in Fort Wayne and Marion, Indiana.

The actual introduction of television to mankind, however, was considerably delayed, owing to the coming of the Second World War. While that conflict lasted, Farnsworth Television and Radio Corporation concentrated on the manufacture of radio parts. It was not until the arrival of the postwar era, in the late 1940s and early 1950s, that the television systems made possible by Farnsworth and Zworykin began operating in gradually increasing numbers around the world.

For some years Phil took little or no active part in the running of the two factories in Indiana. Then in 1947 a forest fire destroyed the buildings on his rural retreat in western Maine. At this point he moved his family to Fort Wayne and began showing up at meetings of his company's board of directors.

His friend George Everson's affectionate account of Farnsworth's career appeared in 1949, and at this moment our knowledge of the remaining years of his life is small. All that can be said with certainty is that at some later date he returned to his Mormon roots, settling himself and his family in Salt Lake City. Here, on March 11, 1971, death came to this brilliant and productive contributor to television as we know it today.

Enrico Fermi

1901–1954   Italian-born American physicist; builder of the first
atomic pile (also known as an atomic reactor), making possible the
controlled release of nuclear energy and its use for military, industrial,
and medical purposes

A few years before the birth of Enrico
Fermi on September 29, 1901, in
Rome, Italy, scientists working in another part of Europe made a significant
discovery. What they learned was that
the atoms of certain chemical elements—uranium, for example—give off
energy in the form of rays.

Today we think of this discovery of
radioactivity as marking the end of an
"old" era of science and the beginning
of the "new" science of our own times.
Whereas the old scientists concentrated
for the most part on an effort to comprehend the world we can see, the new
ones set out to uncover the secrets of
the atom, a world we cannot see, because the atom is so tiny, measuring
only several hundred millionths of an
inch in diameter.

It is the belief of one of Fermi's biographers, Pierre de Latil, that Fermi's
contributions to our understanding of
this invisible world were all the greater
because he and the new science were
born at the same time and grew up
together. Had Enrico begun life a quarter of a century earlier, he would have
had to unlearn the ideas of the old science even as he strove to grasp those
of the new. As it was, by the time he
was ready for one of the Italian universities, its professors were teaching the
new ideas as set forth by such modern
scientists as Henri Becquerel, Pierre
Curie and his wife, Marie S. Curie,
Ernest Rutherford, and Albert Einstein.

Enrico was the last of the three children of Alberto and Ida de Gattis

Fermi. His father was an inspector in the Italian Ministry of Rail Transport, and Enrico grew up in first one and then another of the apartment houses near Rome's main railroad station. Both family flats were spacious—but uncomfortable. There was no heating. In the winter the bathtubs were filled the evening before they were used in the hope that by morning the water would rise to room temperature. In later years Enrico was fond of telling his friends how, as a boy, he read books sitting on his hands to keep them warm while turning pages with his tongue.

It was a lively tongue, for he read endlessly. Works dealing with mechanical matters were his favorites. He and his brother Giulio tinkered with electrical motors and designed airplanes. When in 1916 Giulio died suddenly, following an operation for an abscessed throat, fourteen-year-old Enrico was heartbroken. Quiet and withdrawn by nature, he became for a time less outgoing than ever.

Fortunately for him, he had already found a knowing guide and teacher in one of his father's co-workers, an engineer named A. Amidei. It was Amidei who supplied the boy with the best books available on mathematics and physics. And it was Amidei who solved the problem that arose in the Fermi family in 1918 when Enrico was gradu-

ated from the Umberto I Grammar School.

Where should he go for his higher education? Amidei suggested the university at the Italian city of Pisa, but Enrico's parents objected strenuously. Death had taken one of their two sons. Now Amidei was asking them to send their only remaining boy two hundred miles away. It wasn't "fair," they lamented, pointing out that there was an excellent university in Rome.

Amidei had kind words for the university in Rome. He argued, however, that the new science was being better taught at Pisa. Gradually, as he recorded later, he made Enrico's parents "see that by their sacrifice they would open up a brilliant career for their son."

At Pisa the solemn young man from Rome discovered in himself a hitherto neglected talent for fun. Thanks to his intensive reading under Amidei, he found even his hardest courses easy. There was time to play. And play he did. He joined a group founded by one of his classmates known as the Anti-Neighbor Society. Its members were pledged to make life difficult for everyone around them. When Enrico and other members of the society set off a stink bomb during a lecture, the university authorities threatened to expel them—only to relent at the request of a professor to whom Enrico was giving lessons in the scientific theories of Einstein.

As his mentor, Amidei, had predicted, his doctoral degree in physical science, received at Pisa in July, 1922, was his ticket to a "brilliant career." For varying periods he worked at important physics laboratories in Germany and Holland. For a year he lectured on elementary mathematics at the University of Rome. For several years he directed the studies in mechanics and mathematics at the University of Florence in Italy.

One summer he went to the United States to conduct a course in physics at the University of Michigan. He was impressed by the scientists he encountered in America. Years later pleasant memories of this first of his several visits there would help him make one of the most crucial decisions of his life.

It had long since become clear to the new scientists that the invisible world they were investigating was a strange place. An atom is made up, for the most part, of empty space. Its mass or matter is concentrated at its center, in what is known as the nucleus. The nucleus contains any number of tiny particles called protons and neutrons. Protons have a positive electric charge. Neutrons have no charge; they are electrically neutral. Circling the nucleus, somewhat as the planets of the solar system revolve around the sun, are even tinier particles of negative electricity called electrons.

One of the early findings of the new scientists was that this invisible world does not operate the way the visible world does. Atoms, the combinations of atoms called molecules, electrons, and the various other particles within the atom—all appear to follow laws peculiar to themselves. Soon Fermi was making a name for himself in scientific circles by publishing articles describing his own often original theories as to how these things behave.

Absorbing and time-consuming though these studies were, Fermi did not lose the capacity for fun that had surfaced during his student days at Pisa. Often he and his scientific pals assembled to play games ranging from tiddledywinks to football. It was during one of these get-togethers in Rome in the spring of 1924 that he first laid eyes on Laura Capon, the daughter of a senior officer in the Italian navy.

Laura's book *Atoms in the Family*, published many years later, preserves her first impressions of her future husband. To sixteen-year-old Laura, twenty-two-year-old Enrico was an "odd young man." She described his legs as "short," his shoulders as "bent," his head as "thrust forward." He gave her a "friendly smile," she recalled,

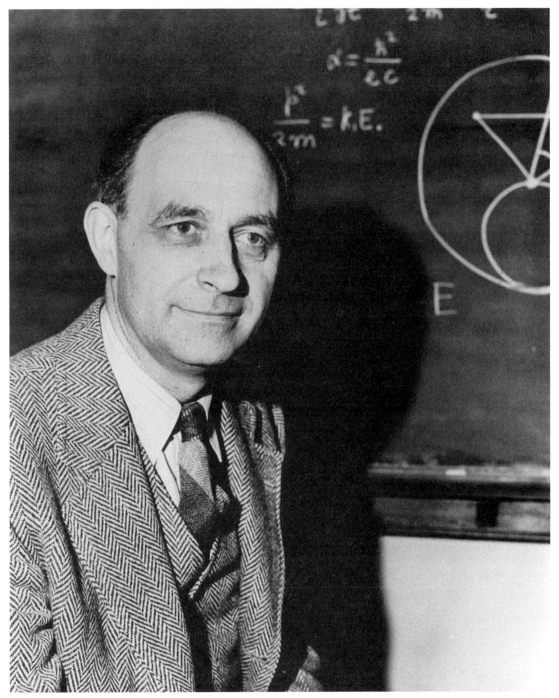

Enrico Fermi in the classroom. *University of Chicago Library*.

adding that it "was hardly a smile for he had very thin lips. But his eyes were laughing; they were set close together, leaving little room for his narrow nose, and in spite of his swarthy complexion they were blue-grey." She noticed that he bossed everyone about. It was he who ruled that they should play football. In selecting her for his team, he implied that he was doing her a favor, as, of course, his team would win. Still, Laura decided, "conceited" was not the word for him. "His self-confidence," she concluded, "was completely without vanity . . . being quite natural and spontaneous."

Love at first sight? Not exactly. During the next few years they were often together. But not until the summer of 1927 did Laura begin hoping that the "odd young man" would say the magic words.

She was visiting a relative near Florence when the mail brought news of Enrico, who was in Rome. The notably thrifty Enrico had recently told her that he intended for once in his life to do something extravagant. She asked what he had in mind. His reply was that he was either going to buy a car. or get married. Now, according to this letter from Rome, he had bought the car, a yellow Baby Peugeot.

Laura's spirits plummeted. Apparently he preferred the car to her. Her despair was premature. Presently the young man and his Peugeot were on hand and the young man was making it clear that he wanted her, too. Their marriage on July 19, 1928, was followed by a honeymoon in the Italian Alps. By fall they had set up housekeeping in an apartment in Rome bought for them by Laura's parents.

Two years earlier Fermi had accepted an invitation to organize and direct a soon-to-be-famous school of physics at the University of Rome. Here, aided by a small band of brilliant young scientists, he began the experiments in radioactivity that were to contribute substantially to the production and use of the terrific power hidden within the atom.

An unforgettable date in this process is January 15, 1934. On that day the French physicists Frédéric Joliot-Curie and his wife, Irène (daughter of the famous Marie Curie), reported that they had compelled an atom to emit radiation by bombarding its nucleus with alpha particles, thus forcing the nucleus to split and give off energy. "For the first time," the Joliot-Curies announced, "it [is] possible to produce by exterior cause the radioactivity of certain atomic nuclei."

To Fermi this development was a call to action. He noted that in their experiment the Joliot-Curies had used electrically charged particles. It occurred to him that some nuclei might repel such a particle and refuse to be split. He decided that the neutron, an electrically neutral particle, would make a far more efficient atom splitter.

This was a leap of faith on his part, a guess that happened to be correct. The vigor with which he acted on it is an example of the important role the guesswork we call imagination plays in the advancement of science. To accomplish in the end, one must dream in the beginning.

One of Fermi's first steps was to find out which of the ninety-two chemical elements known to science in the winter of 1934 would give the longest-lasting spurts of radioactivity. With this goal in mind, he and his associates set out to bombard all of the elements. It was during this long and arduous experiment that Fermi made two great findings. One was that the bombardment of element number 92, uranium, had the effect of bringing to light two previously undetected chemical elements now known as neptunium (number 93) and plutonium (number 94). The other was that the effectiveness of the splitting agent, the neutron, increased noticeably when obstacles were put in its path, thus reducing the speed with which it approached the atom to be split.

When in 1938 Fermi received the Nobel Prize in physics, the scientific body that issues these awards hailed him for "his discovery of new radioactive elements . . . and for his discovery of nuclear reactions affected by slow neutrons."

To Fermi the triumph of winning the most prestigious award in science was tempered by the troubles sweeping Europe in 1938. The German dictator Adolf Hitler and his Nazi followers had seized control of Austria and much of Czechoslovakia. The Italian dictator Benito Mussolini and his Fascist followers had joined forces with Germany, and Mussolini was taking his orders from Hitler. Underway, in short, were the events that a year later would provoke the outbreak of the Second World War.

In Rome life was becoming more and more difficult for scientists and other creative individuals. Members of Fermi's little band of assistants were breaking away. Some had or were about to take posts in other countries. One, as the others would learn later, was preparing to share his knowledge of nuclear physics with the leaders of the Soviet Union.

As for Enrico and Laura, they were planning to emigrate to the United States with their children, seven-year-old Nella and two-year-old Giulio.

Their original intention was to remain where they were for at least a year. Then in August, 1938, Mussolini handed down a collection of laws limiting the rights of Jews. As Laura was Jewish, the Fermis now realized that they should get out of Italy as soon as possible. A few months later word came that Enrico must be in Stockholm, Sweden, on December 10 to accept his prize, and this provided them with a way of carrying out their plans unnoticed. When on December 6 they left Rome for Stockholm, only their closest friends and a few officials at the American embassy in the Italian capital knew that they would not be coming back. Once the ceremonies marking the acceptance of the Nobel Prize were completed in Stockholm, the Fermis boarded a ship bound for America, Enrico having arranged to continue his experiments at Columbia University, in New York City.

Shortly after the arrival of the Fermis in New York on January 2, 1939, a new word, *fission,* entered the vocabulary of the nuclear scientists. A term familiar to us today, fission is the process by which the nucleus of an atom is broken into fragments so as to produce atomic energy.

Put another way, atomic energy comes from the destruction of a tiny amount of matter. If you could weigh the nucleus of a form of uranium called U-235 and then weigh the fragments produced by the fission of that nucleus, you would find that the fragments weighed slightly *less* than the nucleus did before it was fragmented.

Offhand it would seem that as a result of the fission some of the matter has been lost. In fact it has simply been changed into energy, in accordance with Albert Einstein's assertion that energy and matter are different forms of the same thing. This is the theory that Einstein summarized in his now well-known formula $E = mc^2$, meaning that energy equals mass times the speed of light squared.

By the time Fermi began his work at Columbia University, scientists were beginning to see in the discovery of fission a way to produce nuclear energy on a large scale.

On this subject their thinking ran as follows: When a U-235 nucleus is invaded by a neutron it becomes unstable and splits. In addition to releasing energy, this fission of the nucleus produces additional neutrons. These neutrons go on to split other U-235 nuclei, and these in turn produce more neutrons to split still more nuclei. It followed, in the opinion of the new scientists, that if a column of material— a pile—containing a large amount of U-235 could be made big enough to achieve what is called *critical mass,* enough neutrons would be generated within it to split nucleus after nucleus at an ever faster rate. When this happened, a chain reaction would occur, and the energy it released would be enormous.

It was with this goal in mind—the inducement of a chain reaction—that Fermi and his assistants set out in 1939 to build what was to be the first energy-producing atomic pile.

In the world around them historic changes were taking place. On September 1 Hitler invaded Poland and the Second World War erupted in Europe. On October 11 the American president, Franklin D. Roosevelt, was in receipt of a letter personally delivered by Albert Einstein. Einstein informed the president that the "results of recent work by Fermi" and his associates indicated that "in the very near future" the discovery of fission would make possible the construction of "bombs of a new type and immense power." The great scientist pointed out that it was in Germany that the process called fission had been discovered. Even now that country might be trying to fabricate an atom bomb.

Convinced that in the near future the United States would be at war with Germany, Roosevelt took Einstein's words to mean that the work of Fermi and

his team should be subsidized by the federal government. Soon thereafter, in accordance with this decision, the pile-building project at Columbia was being financed by a government agency.

By the fall of 1940 Fermi and his assistants had constructed an eight-foot-square column of uranium and graphite, only to realize within a few months that the ceiling of their laboratory at Columbia was too low to accommodate a structure large enough to induce a chain reaction. At this point, on January 24, 1942, arrangements were made to transfer Fermi and his project to the University of Chicago, on the south side of Chicago, Illinois. Here, in a twenty-five-foot-high squash court under the west stands of Stagg Field, the university stadium, the scientists began their task anew.

In the aftermath of the entry of the United States into the war on December 8, 1941, Fermi's position became a peculiar one. His native Italy was fighting on the side of Germany. Technically, therefore, he was now an "enemy alien." As such he was not allowed to travel on an airplane or to own a shortwave radio. For the frequent journeys his labors necessitated he had to get the permission of the military authorities.

It is a measure of his adopted coun-

"Birth of the Atomic Age," a 1957 painting by Gary Sheahan that illustrates Enrico Fermi and his colleagues overseeing the operation of the first chain-reacting pile in a University of Chicago squash court, December 2, 1942. *Chicago Historical Society.*

try's trust in him, however, that none of his scientific duties were taken from him. He was still the man in charge when, on the afternoon of December 1, 1942, the atomic pile at Stagg Field was pronounced complete and ready for testing.

At 9:45 the next morning, Fermi stationed himself on a platform overlooking a pile containing almost four hundred tons of graphite, six tons of uranium metal, and fifty-eight tons of uranium oxide. On his orders, a member of his team manipulated the control bars inserted in the pile.

At 11:35 all seemed to be going well, and Fermi and his colleagues broke for lunch. Shortly before two they returned, and at 5:25 their instruments showed that a chain reaction was underway and that the pile was capable of releasing nuclear energy in a controlled fashion. Thus ended what two journalists, describing the event many years later, called "the greatest experiment of all time."

At the time of the activation of the first atomic reactor in Chicago, Enrico Fermi was forty-one years old. During the remaining twelve years of his life, he continued to contribute to mankind's slowly growing knowledge of the invisible world of the atom.

For more than a year, beginning in the summer of 1944, he and his family resided in Los Alamos, New Mexico. There, under the direction of nuclear physicist J. Robert Oppenheimer,

Fermi and a number of other scientists and engineers produced the atom bomb. In the summer of 1945 Fermi was a member of the committee of scientists who advised President Harry S. Truman to drop the bomb on two Japanese cities, bringing the Second World War to a close and initiating what we now think of as the nuclear age.

After the war the Fermis made their home near the University of Chicago. Enrico worked as a teacher at the university's Institute of Nuclear Physics, and in the winter of 1946, having become an American citizen, he was awarded the congressional Medal for Merit.

It was during the closing years of Fermi's life that many of the makers of the atom bomb drew back in horror at the terrific power their efforts had unleashed. Banding together in an organization known as the Federation of American Scientists, they called for the establishment of a world authority empowered to control the use of atomic energy.

Fermi did not join this organization, and he himself gave no reasons for this. But his wife, in her book *Atoms in the Family,* published after her husband's death, asserted that "Enrico did not think that for the physicists to stop their work would have been a sensible solution. Nothing is served by trying to halt the progress of science. Whatever the future holds for mankind, however unpleasant . . . we must accept it, for knowledge is always better than ignorance.

"Besides, if the physicists had not made the atom bomb, if they had destroyed all the facts they had discovered . . . other physicists would have appeared in the near future who, in their search for truth, would have progressed along the same path and rediscovered what had been suppressed. And whose hands would the atom bomb have been in then? One can imagine a greater evil than giving it to the Americans."

The summer of 1954 found Fermi in Europe, attending some scientific conferences. Laura was alarmed by his pallor and thinness when he returned home. Doctors, consulted at her insistence, diagnosed a well-advanced cancer of the stomach, and on November 28, two months after his fifty-third birthday, he was dead.

But he is not forgotten. At a meeting of scientists in Geneva, Switzerland, the following summer, the eminent American chemist Glenn T. Seaborg reported his discovery of a hitherto unknown chemical element in the ashes created by the explosion of the first so-called hydrogen bomb. At Seaborg's insistence, the new element, number 100, was named fermium, in honor of Enrico Fermi.

Robert Fulton

1765–1815   American artist and civil engineer; inventor of the double inclined plane and other devices for the improvement of canal navigation; pioneer in the development of the submarine and submarine warfare; maker of the first steamboat to be commercially successful on American rivers; builder of the American navy's first steam-driven ship

Few American inventors have been the subject of more controversy than Robert Fulton.

To this day his admirers consider him a "benefactor of mankind." They claim that by creating a network of steamboats on the Hudson and other rivers in the early 1800s he put his country on the path to its present industrial and technological superiority.

His critics call him a mere adventurer. In his scramble for money and renown, they say, he stole other inventors' notions, told lies, and used rich and politically powerful friends to attain his ends.

And the latest of his biographers, Cynthia Owen Philip, concludes that he was both saint and sinner. The man portrayed in her book *Robert Fulton: A Biography* puts one in mind of the half-angel, half-devil hero of Robert Louis Stevenson's *The Strange Case of Dr. Jekyll and Mr. Hyde*. Like Stevenson's tragically divided protagonist, Fulton exhibited a bright, or Dr. Jekyll side, and a dark, or Mr. Hyde side. He was at one and the same time a man eager to improve the lot of humanity and a self-seeking go-getter.

Both his parents were part of the extensive migration of the Scotch-Irish to the New World shortly before the outbreak of the American War of Independence. Both were Scottish by birth or descent. Both came to America after a considerable stay in Ireland. Both ended up in the swiftly growing frontier settlement of Lancaster, Pennsylvania, where by 1735 Robert Fulton, Sr., was working as a tailor. He was in his forties when he married Mary Smith, a well-educated and well-connected young lady. Soon they became the parents of three girls.

In February, 1765, Robert and Mary Fulton sold their home in Lancaster and used the proceeds to buy at auction a 394-acre farm in Little Britain Township, Pennsylvania, thirty miles to the south. There, on November 14, 1765, their first son was born and named Robert Fulton, after his father. Another boy had arrived by January, 1772, when the elder Robert Fulton, unable to make the mortgage payments, was forced to sell the farm as he had bought it, at a sheriff's sale. Then, with his family, he returned to his tailoring in Lancaster, where he died in 1774.

Robert junior at this time was six, old enough to be deeply affected by the humiliating loss of his home, followed so quickly by the loss of his father. There is reason to believe that the hurt brought on by these misfortunes had the effect of separating Robert emotionally from both parents. Many of the letters penned in his adult years are still around. In none of them does he ever mention his father directly.

Those written to his mother tend to be formal and unfeeling. Still, from boyhood on, he was aware of his duties as the oldest surviving male of the family. Though most of his life was spent apart from its members, he took an interest in their material welfare. He helped them financially whenever his own wildly fluctuating fortunes permitted.

No record of his growing-up years is available, but his biographer Philip sees "a germ of truth" in the legends related by earlier biographers in an effort to explain his creative genius. As a boy he is said to have invented, among other things, an air gun, a skyrocket, and a lead pencil. As he loved fishing but hated the labor of poling a boat up Lancaster's Conestoga Creek, he devised a paddle wheel, easily operated by hand.

He received his earliest education from his mother and then attended a school run by a local Quaker. We do not know what he learned from these sources. We do know that while still very young he owned a copy of Euclid's *Elements*, a classic text on geometry. Apparently he valued this book. Inscribed on its flyleaf in his boyish scrawl are the following words:

I write my name for to Betray
Those that do Steal this Book away

Steal not this Book for fear of Shame
For here you see the owner's name.

During the Revolutionary War, which broke out in his tenth year, Lancaster became an important center for the manufacture of the weapons needed by the soldiers of the newly established United States of America. Fascinated by things mechanical, young Fulton got in touch with the expert gunsmiths pouring into town. By watching them at their work, he quickly became an expert himself. Presently, at their request, he was supplying them with drawings and models of guns.

In his fifteenth year he was apprenticed to a silversmith in Philadelphia, Pennsylvania. But crafting silver utensils and ornaments was not to his liking. He somehow bought himself out of his apprenticeship and set himself up as a painter of miniature portraits. In this action—accomplished we know not how—we see the emergence of the hopes that were to shape the rest of Robert Fulton's life. He had no intention of repeating his father's failures. He was determined not only to succeed but to do so on his own terms and in his own way.

At the painting of miniatures and other artistic work Fulton prospered sufficiently to purchase a small farm for his mother and three building lots for himself. Soon he was preparing to move to London to study under the American-born artist Benjamin West, who in recent years had become historical painter to King George III of England.

England, which he reached in the winter of 1786, was his home for the next eleven years. For seven of them he studied and practiced art. In the spring of 1791 he was writing to his mother that six of his paintings had been accepted for exhibition in important London galleries. Though his work had "rec'd every possible mark of approbation," he wrote, there was "no profit arising from it." It was his guess, however, that in the near future the attention his paintings had attracted would "produce business."

It did. For a year and half, beginning in June of the same year, Fulton resided in a castle in the English countryside, doing a portrait of its titled owner and living on his lordship's payroll. Back in London in 1793, he was again exhibited at a London gallery—four paintings this time. But already his interest in art as a profession was flagging. A longing to return to the joys of invention he had experienced as a boy was taking form. In the years ahead he would continue painting, though now for recreation only. By the end of 1793 he had become what he would remain thereafter, a civil engineer.

An engraving of Robert Fulton, from a painting by Chappel. *The Bettmann Archive*.

For a few years most of his inventions were aimed at helping to solve one of Great Britain's most pressing problems. Of late that nation had entered what historians call the machine age, or the Industrial Revolution. Britain had been an agricultural nation, with most of its people making their livings on farms. Now it was fast becoming a commercial and industrial society, with many of its people making their livings in cities and factories.

Getting the goods produced in these plants to often distant markets was a difficult undertaking. Wagons were used to carry the goods along roads. But inland navigation—boats moving on waterways—provided a cheaper and faster mode of transportation. Hence the growing interest on the part of Britain's industrialists in the development of efficient canal systems.

One of Fulton's many contributions to this effort was a power shovel for cutting canal channels. Another was what he called a double inclined plane, a device for raising and lowering canal boats. With this mechanism—as Fulton explained in his book *A Treatise on the Improvement of Canal Navigation,* published in 1796—boats could be taken from the water and moved by rail across those sections of the terrain that were so rocky that digging ditches through them was prohibitively expensive.

By 1797 his efforts on behalf of inland navigation had earned him substantial sums of money. They had not, however, won him either the great fortune or the worldwide fame he hankered after. It was at this date, or perhaps a little earlier, that he began work on the development of a submarine and a system of submarine warfare—a project he believed would bring him what he wanted and on which he labored, off and on, for the next nine years.

In 1797 France and Britain were at war. France was winning the land battles on the continent of Europe, thanks largely to the military genius of Napoleon Bonaparte. But England still commanded the seas. In this situation Fulton saw an opportunity for himself.

By the fall of 1797 he was living in Paris. In December he was writing to the Directory, the five-person ruling body of France, offering to sell its members the submarine and the method for its use on which he was working. Apparently it did not occur to him that he was offering a potentially deadly weapon of war to a nation whose seagoing cruisers and privateers were even then raiding the ships belonging to his native America. Indeed, the arguments for his submarine that Fulton presented to the Directory are an example of the Jekyll-Hyde halves of his personality. On the one hand he contended that by making all countries equally strong on the seas, the *Nautilus,* as he called his submarine, would end naval warfare forever and in time land warfare as well. On the other hand, he assured the Directory that his invention would enable France to drive the British navy from the oceans of the world.

Fulton was not the first person to construct a machine capable of carrying one or more persons underwater and of firing torpedoes at enemy vessels; but the *Nautilus,* built in the shape of an ellipsoid and twenty-four feet and six inches long, was superior in every way to its predecessors.

At first the members of the Directory agreed to Fulton's proposal that they purchase his invention. Then they changed their minds. The reason they gave for doing so was that the *Nautilus* could sneak up on an enemy ship, under the water and out of sight. It was therefore, they argued, an "immoral" weapon of attack.

This objection to his machine moved Fulton to attempt blackmail. He told the members of the Directory that if they did not buy the *Nautilus* he would offer it to their enemy, Great Britain. His threat worked, but before he and the Directory could arrive at an agreement France was shaken by what historians call the "coup of the 18–19 Brumaire." During this upheaval, in Paris in November, 1799, the Directory was overthrown and replaced by a three-member ruling group headed by Napoleon, with the title of first consul.

Fortunately for Fulton, Napoleon was even more interested in the *Nautilus* than the Directory had been. In the spring of 1800, with funds supplied by France, Fulton put his submarine through its paces in the river Seine at Paris. So impressive was this demonstration that shortly the *Nautilus,* carrying a crew of three men, was operating in the English Channel near the shores of England. Though nothing came of its attempts to blow up British ships, its presence in these waters created a panic among the leaders of the British navy. On March 27, 1802, the treaty known as the Peace of Amiens temporarily halted the conflict between France and England and ended Napoleon's interest in the *Nautilus.*

Meanwhile Fulton had struck up valuable friendships with Americans residing in France. His meeting with Joel and Ruth Barlow, soon after his arrival in Paris, was the beginning of the warmest relationship of his life. Connecticut-born Joel Barlow was a man of many talents. In America he had made his mark as a preacher, a lawyer, and a poet. Coming to France in 1788 for what was to be a stay of almost seventeen years, he speculated in ships and currencies and on occasion ran diplomatic errands for his country. Ruth Barlow, his wife, was the daughter of a New

England blacksmith. Pert and pretty, she was well known for her charm and her witty conversation. The Barlows took to Fulton at once, and he to them. Soon the three of them were sharing a handsome house in Paris, and Joel Barlow was helping to finance Fulton's experiments.

Joel Barlow knew everyone who was anyone in the French capital. It could have been he who in February or March of 1802 introduced Fulton to Robert R. Livingston of New York. Livingston—known as the Chancellor, because of his service as the first head judge of his state—was in France as his country's minister to that nation. Today he is best remembered for his supervision there of the negotiations leading to the Louisiana Purchase. This was the amazing land purchase that in 1803 more than doubled the size of the United States by putting in its possession the vast and formerly French-owned lands lying west of the Mississippi River known as the Louisiana Territory.

Livingston was nineteen years older than Fulton, and in other ways they were miles apart. By birth and rearing the Chancellor was an aristocrat. Owner of Clermont, a huge estate on the eastern banks of the Hudson River forty miles south of Albany, New York, he was a member of one of America's rich-est and most influential families. Fulton's association with titled Englishmen had given him a surface polish, but his manner was still that of a man striving to rise above humble beginnings. Livingston, a brilliant lawyer, exhibited the dignity and reserve one associates with a scholar and a thinker. Fulton—six feet tall, lean, handsome, and high-spirited—tended to be flamboyant. He was forever boasting that he was about to do something spectacular, something that would rock the world back on its heels.

These differences aside, the two men had no sooner met than they realized that they shared a common vision and a common goal. Both were looking forward to the day when the steam engine recently perfected by Scottish-born James Watt could be married to ships and boats, thereby ending mankind's reliance on sails and oars for water travel.

Several steamboats for use on rivers were already in existence. None, however, was efficient enough for regular use. For some years Fulton had been considering possible improvements in such a boat, changes that would make it a reliable and comfortable mode of transportation. Most existing boats used steam-driven oars to push them through the water. Fulton, after trying various methods, concluded that the best way to move a steamboat was to attach paddle wheels to its sides. Existing boats shook and rattled when the engine was turned on. Fulton set out to eliminate these noisy vibrations by designing a better proportioned and more streamlined vessel.

As for Livingston, shortly before his arrival in France, he had persuaded the legislature of New York to give him the sole right to run steamboats on the waterways of that state. Ever since this monopoly had fallen into his hands he had been hunting for an engineer capable of constructing a steamboat that could go up and down the Hudson River, traveling on a regular basis between New York City and Albany, the state capital, a distance of 150 miles each way. Almost at the moment of their first encounter, Livingston sensed that Fulton was the inventor he was seeking. On October 10, 1802, the two men signed an agreement, setting up the partnership that in time would give their country its first commercially successful steamboat line. The agreement called for Fulton to continue his steamboat experiments, for Livingston to finance them, and for both to share in whatever profits their joint venture produced.

Like true love, such partnerships rarely run smooth. Livingston fancied himself as something of an inventor.

He was pleased when Fulton permitted the inclusion in their agreement of a sentence describing both of them as "experimenters." He was not so pleased when Fulton ignored most of the Chancellor's suggestions and let it be known that he meant to carry on the work in his own way and at his own pace. In 1804 he abandoned his steamboat experiments and went back to working on his submarine. By this time the war between France and England had resumed. Napoleon, now the emperor of the French, had assembled a huge fleet of warships at Boulogne, on the French side of the English Channel, and was threatening to invade the British Isles.

Again Fulton saw in a troubled situation a chance to line his own pockets. When Napoleon turned down his latest submarine-warfare ideas as "ridiculous," he moved to England. There, by the end of 1804, he had sold those ideas to the British government. Not wanting Livingston to know that, for the time being, he was doing no work on the steamboat, he conducted his dealings with the British under an assumed name, calling himself Robert Francis. He remained in England three and a half years. He left only after the British admiral Horatio Nelson had defeated a combined French and Spanish fleet off Cape Trafalgar, on the south-

An undated engraving that shows the original plan for Robert Fulton's first steamboat to travel the Seine in 1803. *The Bettmann Archive.*

west coast of Spain, on October 21, 1805. This famous battle, during which Nelson was killed, eliminated Great Britain's fear of an invasion by Napoleon and its need for the submarine-building services of Robert Fulton, alias Robert Francis.

After his return to the United States in 1806, Fulton spent many more months working on a submarine. Only after two demonstrations of this machine in the harbor of New York had ended in failure did he go back to his steamboat.

This was in the summer of 1807, and within a few weeks his frequently remodeled boat was sitting at a Hudson River dock off what is now the Green-

wich Village section of New York City, ready to attempt its first run up the river to Albany. On Monday, August 17, the date set for this trial, hundreds of New Yorkers gathered at the wharf. Two members of the Livingston family were on hand. But Chancellor Livingston himself, alarmed perhaps by the presence of a flu epidemic in the city, was not there.

With its 146-foot-long hull and 13-foot-wide beam flanked by enormous paddle wheels, the boat struck most onlookers as a "crazy," even a "comical," sight. None of them expected it to travel for more than two or three miles at most. Some were certain that the minute smoke drifted from its chimney, Fulton's Folly, as they called it, would explode.

At one o'clock in the afternoon Fulton and a crew went aboard, and the "Folly" took off, followed by the cheers—and jeers—of the crowd. At the insistence of the Chancellor, Fulton had outfitted the boat with square sails, one fore and one aft. But the sails remained furled. Propelled by its coal-fed steam engine, the boat glided steadily northward at four and a half miles an hour. When early the next morning it arrived at Clermont, Livingston's estate on the banks of the Hudson, the Chancellor was on the dock, beaming with pride at this triumphant conclusion of his and Fulton's efforts.

From Clermont on the following morning, the boat cast off for the remaining forty miles of its journey. Traveling this time at five miles an hour, it reached Albany late that afternoon. Two days later it was back in its berth at New York City, and on September 4 it began its twice-weekly trips up and down the Hudson, carrying an average of 140 passengers each way. It continued this schedule until the river froze for the winter and resumed it when spring came. Fulton called his invention the *Clermont*, after his partner's estate. During its years of service on the Hudson, however, no one used that name. Everyone, everywhere spoke of

it simply as "the Steamboat," a tribute to its status, for the time being, as the only such vessel operating on a regular basis in America.

At the time of the Steamboat's first run up the river, Fulton was in his forty-second year. Apparently he thought the time had come to share his life with someone else. On January 7, 1808, he took as his wife Harriet Livingston, a second cousin of the Chancellor and a daughter of Walter Livingston, an attorney of some prominence. Nineteen years younger than Fulton, Harriet had grown up at Teviotdale, her parents' 500-acre estate eight miles northeast of Clermont in upstate New York.

On Fulton's part the marriage cannot be called a love match. His heart remained with Joel and Ruth Barlow, who, having returned to the United States, were now living on an estate called Kalorama on what was then the outskirts of Washington, D.C. Even after his marriage we find him writing what his biographer Philip describes as a "love letter" to Ruth.

Harriet may or may not have realized the depth of her husband's devotion to the Barlows. It is clear, however, that at times she found living with Fulton a trying experience. In a letter to Chancellor Livingston she accused her husband of promising her money that he never delivered. She complained

In this self-portrait, Robert Fulton demonstrates the submarine periscope. *Robert Fulton Papers / Rare Books and Manuscripts Division / The New York Public Library.*

that Fulton, busy building more steamboats and still working on his submarine, often neglected both her and the four children—three girls and a boy—born to their union.

In the years following the success of the Steamboat, Fulton and Livingston were rapidly creating what people spoke of as a "steamboat empire." Soon they were running steamboats not only on the Hudson, but also on the lower reaches of the Mississippi, on the James River in Virginia, on New York's Long Island Sound, and on other waters. Soon, too, both men were spending considerable time in court, defending their empire against the efforts of other steamboat builders to horn in on a profitable enterprise.

Some of these legal controversies

grew out of charges that Fulton had stolen ideas for his boat from others—principally from John Fitch, an American inventor who had built several steamboats and operated them briefly on the Delaware River some twenty years earlier. Some grew out of unsuccessful attempts by rival companies to break the Chancellor's monopoly of the waterways of New York State.

The court battles were still going on when, on February 25, 1813, Robert R. Livingston died in his big manor house at Clermont. Though the partners had had their quarrels, Fulton was grief-stricken. Even more devastating to him was the news, received on the day of the Chancellor's death, that Joel Barlow had died while traveling in Europe on a diplomatic mission for his nation.

During America's second war with Great Britain, the War of 1812, Fulton constructed what was to be his nation's first steam-driven naval vessel, a frigate known as *Fulton I*. The evening of February 4, 1815, found him working on this invention in one of his workshops at Jersey City on the New Jersey side of the Hudson River. When he and the men with him left the shop to return to New York, they discovered that the ferry boats were not running because the river was partly frozen. A small boat

was commandeered to take them home, which carried them as far as the ice mass along the New York banks of the stream.

They walked the remaining distance. Suddenly one of Fulton's companions, a very heavy man, fell through the ice. Fulton went to his rescue. Having pulled the man out with great effort, he reached his house soaked to the skin and so hoarse he could hardly talk.

Hastily summoned doctors managed to keep him in bed for three days. Then, against their advice and the protests of Harriet and the children, he returned to Jersey City to continue work on his seagoing steamship. When he returned home he was sicker than ever, and at 9:30 on the morning of February 23, he died at the age of forty-nine.

His funeral on the following Saturday was the most heavily attended event New York City had yet witnessed. To the many persons lining the streets for the procession and crowding into Trinity Church for the services, he was the genius who had given them a mode of transport far superior to any they had known before. Few among them were aware of the Mr. Hyde side of his nature, and most of those few didn't care. They had come to pay their respects to Dr. Jekyll, to a man who had served both his city and his country well.

Galileo Galilei

1564–1642 Italian mathematician, physicist, and astronomer; improver of the telescope and a major shaper of modern science

Galileo, born in the Italian seaport of Pisa on February 15, 1564, was the first of the three sons and four daughters of Vincenzio and Julia Ammanati Galilei. His father, a lute player by profession, has been described as a man of "independent character and combative" spirit—traits that his eldest son would also display.

Galileo grew up partly in Pisa, partly in the larger Italian city of Florence. His early schooling, some of it at a monastery near Florence, consisted of what today we call the liberal arts. It included none of the technical subjects whose mastery by Galileo at a later date was to give him his place in history as one of the founders of modern science.

In his eighteenth year he enrolled at the University of Pisa as a medical student. This was his father's doing, as the older man had found it hard to support a large family on a musician's income. He wanted to see his son in a moneymaking profession. But medicine was not to Galileo's liking. Already the scientist in him was asserting itself.

We are told that it was during his medical-student days, while sitting in the cathedral at Pisa, that he made the first of his scientific discoveries. A light breeze was blowing through the building. Watching the swings of a lamp, Galileo timed them by the beat of his pulse. What he learned from this experiment was that no matter how wide the swings were or how narrow, each of them took the same time as each of the others. It was on the basis of this finding that, not quite a century later, a Dutch mathematician named Christiaan Huygens would give the world its first pendulum clock. Since, even as a pendulum runs down, each of its swings takes the same amount of time, the mechanism to which the pendulum is attached can be counted on to tick off the minutes accurately.

In 1585 Galileo discontinued his medical studies without having earned his degree. Back home in Florence, he arranged for a friend of the family to introduce him to mathematics. The field fascinated him, and in time he persuaded his father to let him study that and other branches of science on his own.

Fame came quickly. His invention in 1585 of the hydrostatic balance, a tool important to students of the behavior of liquids, attracted the attention of scientists in many parts of Europe. With his publication three years later of a description of the way solids act when they are put in motion, he became known as the Archimedes of his time— a reference to a Greek physicist who, 1,800 years before, had discovered some of the basic principles of geometry and mechanics.

With the death of his father in 1591 Galileo, as the eldest son, became head of the family. On him fell responsibility for the care of his mother, his brothers, and his sisters. By this time his renown had brought him a teaching post at the University of Pisa. But his salary as a lecturer on mathematics was small and the demands of his family large.

Shortly after his father's death his sister Virginia married. It was up to Galileo to raise the dowry—the money every Italian bride was expected to bring to her husband. In 1601 his sister Livia married. Again the problem of the dowry was Galileo's.

This time his brother Michelangelo agreed to bear part of the costs, signing a contract to that effect. But Michelangelo, a talented musician, was a happy-go-lucky fellow. Instead of helping finance his sister's marriage he got married himself and spent every cent he had on an elaborate wedding feast. All of Livia's dowry came out of Galileo's pockets.

An invitation in 1592 to teach at Padua, a center of art and learning in northeast Italy, was therefore especially welcome. During the next nineteen years his earnings as a professor of mathematics at the University of Padua were substantially higher than those he had received at Pisa. Never, however, were they enough to meet the mounting needs of his family.

To supplement his income he took on extra jobs. He taught private students in his home. He opened a small shop for the making of compasses, sur-

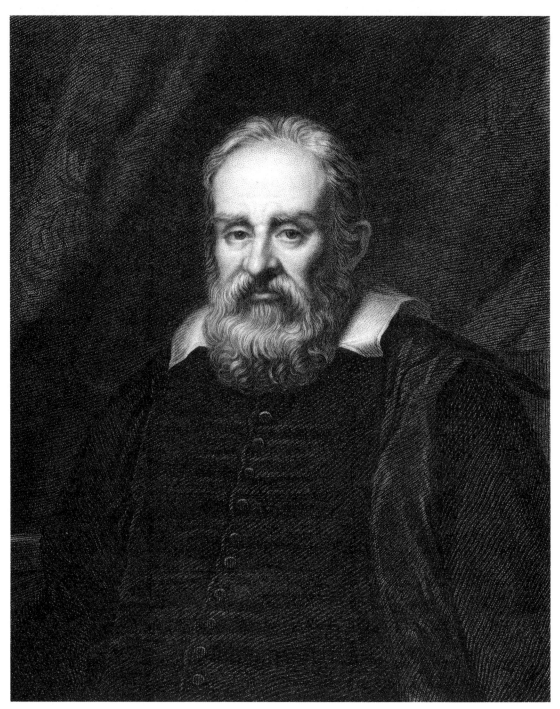

A portrait engraving of Galileo Galilei.

veying instruments, and mathematical apparatus.

It was in this shop in 1609 that he constructed the first of his many telescopes. He is said to have given the impression that he was the inventor of this remarkable instrument. In fact the telescope had many inventors. A knowledge of how to put one together had been around for at least a century. In recent years a Dutch eyeglass-maker named Hans Lippershey had begun making telescopes in quantity and selling them to the armies of Europe.

Lippershey's products were intended for use on land. Galileo trained his much improved telescope on the sky and within a few months had made several startling discoveries.

Aristotle, the great philosopher of ancient Greece, had written that the bright objects in the sky were heavenly spheres. As such they were perfect in shape, unmarred in any way. Not so, according to Galileo's telescopes. The sky visible to man, that vast sea of light by day and of darkness broken by sharp points of light by night, was not at all as Aristotle had pictured it.

The moon was not a smooth and unblemished orb. It had mountains on it. Indeed, in Galileo's telescope its surface appeared to be much like that of planet Earth. Even the sun was blemished with moving patches of darkness

Galileo's telescope. *The Bettmann Archive.*

on its brilliant surface—sunspots, as Galileo and the other astronomers of his day were soon calling them.

Today we know these things to be true. It is hard for us to imagine how upsetting Galileo's revelations were to the people of his time and place. It is not pleasant to learn that the world as you have thought it to be is not that way at all, that it is something so new and strange as to be scary.

For Galileo the splendid uses to which he put his telescope had both a happy and an unhappy result.

The happy outcome was that, thanks to his now increased fame, he was able to return to Florence to serve on the staff of Cosimo II de' Medici. As grand duke of Tuscany, in central Italy, Cosimo II was a man of enormous influence throughout Italy. As Cosimo's mathematician and philosopher, Galileo had no formal teaching duties to distract him. He was free to mull over the discoveries he had made and to draw conclusions from them.

Draw them he did. The unhappy result for him was that some of these conclusions were at odds with the teachings of the Roman Catholic Church to which he belonged.

For centuries the Church had taught its followers that the world was arranged as first Aristotle and later Claudius Ptolemaeus, a Greek astronomer and geographer living in Egypt, had said it was. According to the Ptolemaic system, as this arrangement was known, the Earth stood at the center of the universe, and the sun and all the other heavenly spheres revolved around it.

Over the years a few astronomers had questioned this assumption. Prominent among them was Nicolaus Copernicus. Twenty-one years before Galileo's birth, this Polish scientist and canon of a Catholic cathedral in Germany had published a book setting forth what has come to be known as the Copernican system, or Copernicanism. Destined to become the centerpiece of modern astronomy, Copernicanism asserted that the sun is the center of the universe

(of the solar system, as we say today), and that the Earth and the other planets revolve around it.

It is possible that Galileo's troubles with the Church of Rome would never have come to so tragic an end if he had not been such an earnest follower of his religion. Other Catholic scientists of his day were known to consider the Ptolemaic system dubious and the Copernican system closer to the truth. Some went so far as to publish books saying that, at the very least, Copernicanism should be regarded as a theory worthy of serious consideration.

Had Galileo followed this prudent procedure, who knows? Perhaps he, like some of the other pro-Copernican Catholic scientists of his time, might have been permitted to go on saying and writing what he believed for the rest of his life.

But Galileo went one step farther. Independent and combative like his father, he set out to reform the Church.

He was aware that the Church's respect for the Ptolemaic system rested on certain passages in the Bible. One such passage occurs in the Book of Joshua, where Joshua, leading the Israelites into Canaan, orders the sun to stand still. Another is found in Ecclesiastes: "The sun also riseth, and the sun goeth down, and hasteth to the place where he arose."

The leaders of the Church took these

passages to mean that the sun moved. But only the sun. Nowhere in the Scriptures could they find any indication that the Earth moved. It followed that the Ptolemaic system—the contention that the Earth stood at the center of the universe and that the sun and the other heavenly spheres circled around it— was correct.

During several of his visits to Rome, Galileo discussed these views with the authorities at the Vatican. He urged them to give the biblical references to the sun a second thought. He said that since the Earth did move, as shown by his telescopic observations of the sky, the Church fathers should reinterpret the Bible so as to bring it in line with reality.

Today this seems a reasonable request: an attempt by Galileo to save his Church from being put in the embarrassing position of endorsing ideas contrary to scientifically proven facts. But to many of the Church leaders of his time his arguments were irritating. After all, they asked one another, who was this Galileo? He was a scientist. Let him, therefore, talk about science, which he understood. *They* were theologians, the experts on religious matters. It was for them, not him, to interpret Holy Writ.

In 1615 Galileo published some discussions of sunspots, the blemishes he had observed on the sun. In these works he expressed his approval of Copernicanism, and in 1616 the Church acted.

He was summoned to the Vatican for a talk with Cardinal Robert Bellarmine. Bellarmine was the guiding spirit of the Congregation of the Inquisition, or Holy Office, a body of cardinals set up at the Vatican to see to it that the dogmas of the Church, its sacred beliefs, were accepted unquestioningly by its followers. The powers of the Holy Office were awesome. It could denounce as guilty of heresy those who defied the dogmas in a public way. It could imprison convicted heretics. It could even sentence them to death by burning at the stake.

The meeting between Bellarmine and Galileo took place on the morning of February 26, 1616. It was a friendly session. The seventy-four-year-old cardinal, small and frail with burning bright eyes, respected his visitor as the great scientist he was. Fifty-two-year-old Galileo, tall and squarely built, regarded the aging prince of the Church as one of its ablest administrators.

Also present at this historic meeting was a priest known as the father commissary-general of the Holy Office. It was this official who is said to have drafted a record of the meeting, a memorandum of what was said and done.

Bellarmine, acting on instructions from Pope Paul V, reminded Galileo that in recent days the Church had

An engraving, "Galileo Before the Tribunal."

banned certain books favorable to Copernicanism. None of the works written by Galileo had yet been banned, but the cardinal expressed the hope that their author would regard this action by the Church as a warning and proceed accordingly.

Thousands of words have been written about this famous encounter. But to this day exactly what went on remains unclear. Much of the continuing argument centers on the memorandum prepared by the father commissary-general.

As this document did not come to light until many years later, some students of Galileo's problems contend that it was not written at the time of the meeting, but that it was written later. As such, they see it as a forgery, created by persons who hoped to see Galileo convicted and punished as a heretic.

Most authorities do not go this far. They cite strong evidence that the memorandum was indeed written during the meeting. They assert, however, that its contents do not reflect what actually occurred.

According to the memorandum, Galileo swore that he would stop defending Copernicanism in any way, either orally or in writing. Not true, say most authorities. They note that neither Bellarmine nor Galileo signed the memorandum. They take this to mean that Bellarmine did not insist that Galileo stop talking and writing about Copernicanism. Nor did the scientist promise to do so. His only promise was that he would henceforth present Copernicanism as a scientific theory, as nothing more than his personal opinion as to how the universe was put together.

For the next seventeen years he continued his study of astronomy and related fields, laying the groundwork upon which many scientists coming along after him, have built. In 1621 Cardinal Bellarmine died, thus removing the one person who might have given us an accurate picture of what had actually happened during his memorable conversation with Galileo.

In 1623, in a publication titled *The Assayer*, Galileo again called on his Church to let its scientists explore whatever they wished and report their findings freely. Truth, he wrote, could not be found in the books of Aristotle. Truth could be found only in "the book of nature."

The same year that saw the appearance of *The Assayer* saw the election to the papacy of Galileo's friend Cardinal Maffeo Barberini, who became Pope Urban VIII. Aware that the new pope was interested in science, Galileo arranged for a series of audiences with him. At these interviews at the Vatican—six in all—he urged Urban VIII to have the Church abandon its opposition to the teaching of Copernicanism.

Nothing had come of these efforts when in 1632, in a book called *Dialogue Concerning the Two Chief World Systems*, Galileo reasserted his conviction that the sun, and not the Earth, was the central body of the universe. Though he offered this belief as a personal opinion only, the Holy Office almost immediately banned the book, and the events leading to the trial of Galileo on a charge of heresy began to unfold.

These events, like the meeting with Cardinal Bellarmine, have been much written about. Most of the accounts published prior to 1980 cite Pope Urban VIII as the villain of the drama.

For years, we are told, the pope was one of Galileo's admirers. Then suddenly, annoyed at something the scientist had written, he turned against his old friend. Writing in the 1980s Pietro Redondi, a historian working in Paris, strongly disputes this claim.

Redondi's brilliant book *Galileo Heretic* rests on new evidence, chiefly a hitherto unexamined letter found in the Vatican files. Redondi says that Galileo's downfall was engineered by a group of theologians belonging to the religious order formally known as the Society of Jesus; informally, as the Jesuits. He asserts that the Jesuits wanted Galileo to be tried—not for his defense of Copernicanism but for his often expressed support of what the scientists of his day called "atomism." This is the theory, now universally accepted, that all the matter in the universe consists of atomic particles so tiny as to be invisible to the human eye.

To teach this theory, the Jesuits charged, was to undermine the Catholic belief that at a certain point in the celebration of the Mass the bread and wine brought to the altar become the Body and Blood of Christ. Had Galileo been convicted of this heresy, not even Pope Urban VIII could have saved him from death. It was the pope, according to Redondi, who saw to it that his friend was tried for the lesser crime of teaching Copernicanism.

The trial began on April 12, 1633. On its final day, June 22, Galileo dropped to his knees and solemnly denied his belief in the scientific ideas to the development of which he had devoted his working life. At this point the Holy Office could have sent him to prison. Instead, thanks to the pope, he was placed under house arrest.

For a few weeks he was lodged in the palace of the archbishop in Siena, in central Italy. Then the Holy Office permitted him to move to Arcetri, a suburb of Florence. During his years at the University of Padua Galileo had become the father of a son and two daughters, the children of a woman from Venice, Italy, named Maria Gamba. By 1633 both daughters had long since become nuns and were living in Arcetri at the Convent of San Matteo. Here in a villa near the convent Galileo passed the rest of his life.

He was getting old. For some time he had suffered from arthritis. His handicap notwithstanding, his closing years were productive ones. It was during this period that he wrote a book titled *Discourses Concerning Two New Sciences*, now regarded as the most important of his writings.

Discourses Concerning Two New Sciences was published in Germany in 1637. Its author never saw a copy of it, for in 1638 he was stricken with blindness. Heretofore the Holy Office had forbidden him to receive visitors other than his children. From 1638 on he was allowed to bring into his home two of his brightest students. Both were still on hand at the time of his death, on the night of January 8, 1642.

Robert H. Goddard

1882–1945   American physicist; developer of the liquid-fuel rocket that was to carry his country to the moon and beyond

Robert Goddard once spoke of himself as a "one-dream man." It was an apt description for a man who at an early age decided to spend the rest of his life trying to build a vehicle capable of traveling through space.

Two incidents appear to have been responsible for this resolve. One was his reading, in his seventeenth year, of H. G. Wells's science-fiction masterpiece *The War of the Worlds*. Wells's tale describes the invasion of planet Earth by an army of warriors from planet Mars. What most intrigued young Goddard were the Martians' reasons for undertaking this difficult multimillion-mile journey. Their planet had become overcrowded and its environment was deteriorating.

It occurred to Robert that such troubles could arise on Earth. Then its inhabitants might wish to move to another planet. But how was that to be accomplished? What sort of machine could carry them across millions of miles of space?

He was turning this question over in his mind when one afternoon in his eighteenth year he set out to prune a cherry tree in the backyard of what was then his home in Worcester, Massachusetts.

Saw in hand, he mounted to the lowest limb of the old tree. It was a still autumn afternoon. Below him a creek gurgled, and from above a warm sun edged the leaves with light. He decided to relax a moment before beginning his work. He leaned against the tree trunk,

111

Robert H. Goddard stands beside his first rocket. *Brown Brothers.*

wrapped his long legs around the limb, and closed his eyes.

What happened next was on the order of a dream—a vision so sharp that in later years, writing in his diary, he labeled the date on which it occurred, October 19, "Anniversary Day" and celebrated it as his "scientific birthday."

Suddenly he was aware of the approach of an odd-looking machine. It was shaped like a rod. It moved toward him, seemingly propelled by what is known as centrifugal force. It moved

slowly at first. Then it spun faster and faster and began to lift. Higher and higher it rose in the air. Soon it was out of sight.

When Robert opened his eyes, he was too excited to prune the tree. He ran to his room and began making sketches of the machine he had seen in his vision. For days he labored over these drawings, only to realize that the device he had dreamed of would not do. A machine propelled by centrifugal force could never reach the distant planets. A far stronger force was needed.

It was at this moment that he remembered something he had read in *Principia Mathematica*, a book by the great English scientist Sir Isaac Newton.

Newton had described reactive force: the force that pushes a fireworks rocket into the air. Such rockets had been around for at least a thousand years, but Newton was the first person to describe how they worked.

When the powder at the open rear end of the rocket is ignited, gases form. The gases can't go out through the closed front of the rocket, so they have to go out through the open back end. When they do, the rocket rises.

It *has* to rise, Newton said in what he called his Third Law of Motion. "To every action," he wrote, "there is always opposed an equal reaction." If the gases in the rocket go *down* the rocket itself has to go *up*. The faster the gases go down the faster the rocket goes up. Increase the power of the gases and it will go higher.

Reactive force! That, Robert Goddard concluded, was the answer to his problem. And at once he began designing rockets, one after the other, and dreaming up ways of making them go faster and faster and higher and higher.

The future architect of the age of space spent his growing-up years partly in Worcester, where he had been born in a farmhouse on the outskirts of the city on October 5, 1882, and partly in Roxbury, a suburb of Boston, Massachusetts, where his father, Nahum Danford Goddard, worked first as an employee and then as half owner of a small firm engaged in the manufacture of mechanical knives.

A student of Robert Goddard's career has described him as coming of age in "an atmosphere of machinery and engineering accomplishment." His father, himself an inventor on a small scale, was quick to notice his son's interest in things mechanical and to encourage it. As soon as Robert was old enough to putter about with chemicals and scraps of metal, Nahum bought him a telescope, a microscope, and a subscription to the magazine *Scientific American.*

In his fifth year Robert attempted his first experiment. His father had told him about static electricity. This is the sort of electricity created when you scuff your shoes on a carpet or other hard surface. Robert scuffed his on the gravel sidewalk in front of his Roxbury house. Then, mounting a fence, he hoisted a zinc rod stripped from a battery and jumped. His hope was that the electricity, passing through his body and into the rod, would pull him skyward. In other words, as he explained to his mother when she came out to see what he was up to, he was trying to fly.

But "it might work," Fannie Louise Goddard warned him, "and then you'll go sailing away and might not be able to come back."

Having thought that over, Robert decided to look for a less risky undertaking. One summer he endeavored to create a perpetual motion machine, unaware that scientists had long ago shown that no such device is possible. Another summer he tried to make artificial diamonds out of graphite, only to abandon this project when the blowtorch he himself had assembled exploded and shot innumerable shards of glass into the walls of his attic laboratory. One winter afternoon he folded a sheet of aluminum into a pillow-shaped balloon, filled it with hydrogen, and tried to send it aloft like a kite.

"Aluminum balloon will not go up,"

he recorded in his diary that evening. "Aluminum is too heavy. Failior crowns enterprise." Thus, while still very young, did Robert Goddard learn what sooner or later every inventor discovers: that failure is often one's best teacher. As a rule success comes, if it comes at all, only after long periods of frustrating trial and error.

The same year that saw the failure of Robert's balloon experiment brought disturbing news from physicians called in by Nahum Goddard to examine the boy's ailing mother. Fannie Louise, the doctors announced, had tuberculosis. Informed that the fresher air along the outskirts of Worcester would be good for her, Nahum promptly and uncomplainingly sold his Roxbury house and his share in the small knife-making firm in Boston. By the fall of 1898 he had accepted a run-of-the-mill post in a Worcester knife-making factory, and the Goddards were again living in the farmhouse on Maple Hill where Robert had begun life sixteen years before.

He, too, was unwell. Already recurrent spells of bronchitis and pleurisy had put him two years behind in school, and after the return to Worcester the family doctor saw to it that he stayed at home for still another year.

It was during this period that he climbed into the cherry tree and, having climbed down, began the study of rockets that was to be his life work. It was also during this period that he put Newton's Third Law of Motion to the test, using devices on floats in the brook behind the Maple Hill farm to do so. As he noted in his diary, these tests, showing that the "said law" was correct, made him realize "that if a way to navigate space was to be discovered . . . it would be the result of a knowledge of physics and mathematics."

When in his nineteenth year the doctor permitted him to continue his education, Robert took all the courses in physics and mathematics that Worcester's South High School could offer. From South High School he moved on in 1904 to Worcester Polytechnic Institute and from there in 1909 to Worcester's Clark University, where he obtained his master's degree in 1910 and the highest degree a student can earn, the Ph.D., in 1911.

The following year found him at Princeton University, in New Jersey, working by day as a research fellow in the college laboratories and in the evenings on his own rocket ideas in his room. By this time his mother had become an armchair invalid, and when during a visit home in 1913 her son was prevailed upon to undergo a medical examination, the doctors discovered that he, too, had tuberculosis and pronounced their sentence: Robert Goddard, they said, had only two weeks to live!

It wasn't much time for a young man bent on leading his country into space. Robert took to his bed, but he informed the doctors that he had too much to do to die. A year of rest and exercise did not eliminate the disease. It did, however, quiet it down. So much so that in 1914 he was able to accept a job teaching physics at Clark University and to go on with his rocket investigations. One of his first projects at Clark was to construct an apparatus for firing a rocket in a vacuum. He thus established experimentally what he had already proven on paper: that a rocket could and would operate in the airless regions of space. Having demonstrated this to be the case, his next logical step was to construct one capable of rising to such regions. But this required far more money than he could squeeze out of his salary as a teacher.

His only hope lay in obtaining a grant from some scientific organization. With this in mind, he spent a part of 1916 drafting a summary of his findings to date: a sixty-nine-page manuscript titled "A Method of Reaching Extreme Altitudes" that today is regarded as a classic in the field of astronautical literature.

Anxious days succeeded Goddard's dispatch of this paper to several scientific bodies, a long silence broken shortly before the Christmas holidays by a brief question from the Smithsonian Institution in Washington, D.C. Could the professor, the Smithsonian asked, estimate the cost of building and launching a high-altitude rocket?

The professor could and did. On January 8, 1917, he was writing in his diary: "Got grant for $5,000 . . . from Smithsonian. . . . Read letter to Ma and Pa. . . . Ma said . . . 'Think of it! You send the government some typewritten sheets . . . and they send you $1,000 and tell you they are going to send you [another $4,000 later].' "

Goddard banked the money and made ready to continue his experiments, only to be halted by the First World War. During this conflict, at the request of the military, he designed and built a rocket weapon that was not employed in the field until the Second World War, when it became a familiar sight to American soldiers, who nicknamed it the bazooka.

After the war he resumed his teaching post at Clark and plunged into the many studies and experiments that were to produce the first rocket to be powered not by solid fuel (powder) but by a liquid fuel consisting of a mixture of gasoline and "lox" (liquid oxygen).

Innumerable problems had to be tackled. One, solved early in the process, was the development of a metal covering thin as a dime yet capable of withstanding the intense heat the engine of a high-altitude rocket produces.

Others, solved in later years, had to do with the complicated business of creating reliable steering and stabilizing apparatus.

At Clark, as he finished making each rocket, he static-tested it. He did this by strapping the rocket to a steel rack and firing it. Though the rocket couldn't go anywhere, he could see how it was performing. Then a distant relative, Miss Effie Ward, lent him a portion of her farm some six miles from Worcester. Here Goddard set up a tower, a sixty-foot windmill frame ordered by mail from Sears, Roebuck, and began trying to put his rockets into actual flight.

By this time, the early 1920s, he had met and fallen in love with Worcester-born-and-reared Esther Christine Kisk—tall, stately, blond, and eighteen years his junior. They were married on June 21, 1924, and from then on Esther was an active member of the crew assembled to assist her husband at Miss Effie's farm.

On these acres Goddard tested rocket after rocket. For many months none of them so much as cleared the launching tower. Then on March 16, 1926, he at last managed to send a liquid-propellant rocket for a 184-foot ride in the air, an accomplishment that has been described as the forerunner "of all the 9,000-mile Atlases and Red-stones that will ever fly, all the Sputniks that will ever circle Planet Earth, all the Project Mercury, Saturn and Jupiter capsules that will ever soar to Venus, Moon and Mars."

Another memorable date at the south pasture of Miss Effie's farm was July 17, 1929. That day Goddard succeeded in sending a rocket higher and farther than any preceding one had flown. Unfortunately its parachute failed to open. Smashing to earth, the rocket created an explosion heard by people living as far away as Worcester. Some of them thought the world had come to an end.

As Goddard and his crew were cleaning up the mess, a fire engine clanged down the slope of the pasture. Behind it came two ambulances and a fleet of cars. The county fire marshal, stepping from one of the vehicles, informed Goddard that he had scared people for miles around. If this happened again, Goddard would have to find someplace else to fly his rockets.

"The Big Bang," as the incident came to be known, got into the press. Journalists all over the country poked fun at Goddard. They described him as "crazy enough" to believe that in time one of his rockets would reach the moon. They pointed out that the moon was 240,000 miles from the Earth. One newspaper headline read: MOON ROCKET MISSES TARGET BY 238,799 ½ MILES.

Goddard found this teasing hard to take, but the "bad publicity," as he called it was about to bring him a great deal of good. One afternoon a few weeks later, the telephone rang in his office at Clark University. The man on the other end of the line identified himself as Charles Lindbergh, the famous aviator who only two years before had made the first nonstop solo flight across the Atlantic. Lindbergh had read about "the Big Bang." Could he come to Worcester and talk to Goddard about his experiments?

He came the next day, and the two men talked all afternoon. "Professor Goddard," said Lindbergh as he was leaving, "I have some wealthy friends. I'll tell them about your work. Perhaps one of them will give you the money you need for it."

One of them did. On a June day in 1930, Goddard was in receipt of a letter signed by Daniel Guggenheim.

"Mr. Dan," as friends called him, was the son of a Jewish immigrant from Switzerland. He and his brothers had accumulated a fortune in mining. They had already helped many scientists. Now Mr. Dan stood ready to give Goddard $50,000—enough to permit him to continue his experiments in some wide-open space far from where people lived.

For all but two of the next eleven years, Goddard's "laboratory" was a sandy prairie called Eden Valley, near the county-seat town of Roswell in southeast New Mexico. Here the professor and his wife lived in a clay-walled ranch house. Behind it Goddard built a shop where, over the years, he built most of the 200 parts that engineers still use in the mammoth rockets that today carry scientific payloads to faraway planets and send the manned space vehicle called the Shuttle on its journeys around the globe.

Near his shop Goddard erected an iron windmill frame twenty feet high. On this he static-tested every new rocket. Then he and his crew loaded the rocket on a trailer and towed it to the larger launching tower some ten miles away. During the Eden Valley days there were 103 static tests in all. Of the thirty-one successful flight tests, the most spectacular, occurring on March 26, 1937, saw a sixteen-foot-five-inch-long rocket attain an altitude of almost two miles. Goddard's crew had given the name "Nell" to all of the rockets flown at Eden Valley. This one they nicknamed "Soaring Nell."

In the beginning Mr. Dan supported the experiments in New Mexico out of his own pocket. After his death in 1930, annual grants from a foundation he had established kept the work going. It was still going when, in 1939, the Second

Robert H. Goddard looks through a telescope at his rocket tower in 1940. *Culver Pictures*.

World War broke out in Europe. As German armies marched into France and other countries and threatened England, Goddard, certain that his country would soon be fighting on the side of France and England, traveled to Washington, D.C.

There, for the second time in his life, he offered his rocket to America's armed forces. His thought was that once the rocket was fully developed, the military men could load it with explosives and fire it at enemy forces hundreds of miles away.

But the military men did not want Goddard's rocket. They were unaware that the Germans were already using his ideas. During the last year of the war rockets made by the Germans would fall on England, destroying many buildings and killing thousands of people.

Toward the end of 1941 the United States entered the war, and the military men called Goddard back to Washington. Now they had a job for him. They wanted him to develop a small rocket to be attached to navy fighter planes.

Their name for the device they had in mind was JATO, for Jet-Assisted Takeoff unit.

For three years beginning in the fall of 1942, the Goddards' home was on the banks of the Chesapeake Bay, and every morning Robert drove to nearby Annapolis, Maryland, to work on the JATO. One morning in November, 1942, top naval officers gathered in Annapolis to watch a JATO-equipped plane in action. It streaked into the sky. No airplane had ever taken off so fast before. No one realized it at the time, but a new sort of aircraft had been born. Years later Goddard's JATO would help give birth to the "jet," or jet-propelled airplane.

Toward the end of 1944 Goddard's voice began to weaken and doctors, summoned by his wife, found that his old enemy, tuberculosis, had come back, and he was rushed to a hospital in Baltimore, Maryland. There Goddard, as his wife remarked later, "made his last contribution to science" by dis-

Robert H. Goddard (*left*) and an assistant examine the upper end of a rocket. *Culver Pictures.*

proving the then widely held belief that sufferers from tuberculosis were immune to cancer. The doctors diagnosed a throat cancer as well as tuberculosis. Two operations failed to remedy matters, and on the morning of August 10, 1945, Goddard was dead at the age of sixty-two.

His dream, far from dying with him, came true twenty-four years later on the morning of July 16, 1969.

That morning a million people crowded the sandy beaches of Cape Kennedy, in Florida. On a steel launching pad at Kennedy Space Center stood one of the biggest rockets ever built—the Saturn 5. It was as tall as a thirty-six-story building. It was thirty-eight feet across at its widest. Its cavernous tanks held 6,484,000 pounds of liquid fuel.

At 9:38 A.M. a man sitting three and a half miles away pushed a button that started a computer. The computer fired the rocket, and the Earth quivered as its five giant engines roared into flaming life.

Seated with others on a special platform, Esther Goddard watched the Saturn 5 blast off. She remembered Soaring Nell. She remembered all the other Nells.

How small those rockets were compared to this one. Yet they had made this one possible. Saturn 5 was really just an enormous Nell. Esther's eyes misted as Saturn 5 poked a hole in a distant cloud and disappeared from sight.

In a cabin on top of the huge rocket rode three men in ample spacesuits. Four days later, two of them set foot on the dusty surface of the moon. A special machine had brought them there. It was a strange-looking affair, almost as odd-looking as the machine Robert Goddard had dreamed of in a cherry tree many years before.

Johann Gutenberg

About 1399–1468   Reinventor of printing who gave us the printing press and the modern book

Let us begin our story of Johann Gutenberg with a review of the development of the printing press before he took up that work in the fifteenth century.

Some 1500 years earlier the people of China had started the process by inventing paper. About 900 years later printed books began appearing in that and other Oriental countries.

Some were made from blocks. For this procedure ideograms—the picture-like characters of the Oriental languages—were carved into a page-sized slab of wood. Ink was poured over the slab and paper pressed against it. The result was a printed page.

Some were made from movable type. For this procedure one ideogram at a time was carved in wood inside a matrix, or mold. These many separate pieces were then enclosed in a form, or frame. Ink was poured over the form and paper pressed against it. Again the result was a printed page.

Douglas C. McMurtrie, in his history of printing titled *The Book*, tells us that printed books never caught on in the Orient to any large extent. Whereas in Gutenberg's day most of the languages of Europe used our simple twenty-six-word alphabet, those of the ancient Orient consisted of innumerable ideograms—so many that the printing of books was too difficult and time-consuming to be worthwhile.

In the thirteenth century the making of paper as invented by the Chinese found its way to Europe. There at that time, as had been true for approximately two thousand years, what we now call "books" were handwritten manuscripts.

Carefully, laboriously, monks working in a section of their monastery called the *scriptorium* copied older manuscripts on paper or parchment, a material made from the skins of animals. Using a blunt penlike instrument, a group of monks could produce a manuscript the length of the Bible in a couple of years. Not surprisingly, there weren't many manuscripts around. Only persons in high positions in the Catholic Church or in government ever laid eyes on one.

Then came Gutenberg, and all this changed. What he accomplished can be described as one of the most important events in all history. "It would require an extensive volume," writes McMurtrie "to set forth even in outline the far-reaching effects of [Gutenberg's] invention in every field of human enterprise, or to describe its results in the liberation of the human spirit from the fetters of ignorance and superstition."

Naturally we would like to know a great deal about this remarkable man. But Gutenberg did not want the world to know how he did what he did.

Today the maker of a new thing or process can go to his government and get a patent on it. Under the terms of his patent, the inventor owns all the rights to what he has contrived. For a specified number of years he can do what he wishes with it. He can sell models of it, for example, and pocket the rewards.

In Gutenberg's day there were no patents. When a person created something new, he went out of his way to keep how it was done a secret. Gutenberg not only never revealed much about his work, he also succeeded in keeping nearly everything else about himself a secret. For four hundred years scholars, working like the detectives in mystery stories, have been patiently digging up clues to his life. Alas, the facts have turned out to be few and far between.

When, for example, was he born? The answer to that question, based on other known things about him, is that it was sometime between 1394 and 1399. His place of birth was the German city of Mainz, on the southern banks of the Rhine, where another river called the Mainz flows into that picturesque stream.

His family name was Gensfleisch, but he called himself Gutenberg after the house in which he grew up. His father, known for the same reason as Fiele sum Gutenberg, was a goldsmith associated with the mint operated by the archbishop of Mainz.

A goldsmith's work includes the im-

A frontispiece engraving of Johann Gutenberg.

pressing of figures on metal. Did Johann learn how to do this sort of thing from his father? Perhaps so. Perhaps it was while engaged in this activity that he began forming in his mind the ideas that, later on, enabled him to create the processes and apparatus needed for the casting of movable type and the making of books from it.

Some students of printing assume that, like the making of paper, the art of printing moved over the centuries from the Orient to Europe, where Johann learned about it. Most, however, say there is no evidence for this assumption. They contend that Gutenberg dreamed up his invention independently, which is to say on his own.

His parents were patricians, the name given to the aristocratic rulers of Mainz. During his growing-up years that city was the scene of numerous rebellions. These were usually led by associations composed of skilled workmen known as the guilds.

In 1411 the guilds drove Johann's father out of town. In 1428 they took over the government of Mainz, and Johann fled up the river to the city of Strassburg, in a section of Germany that now belongs to France.

All our knowledge of his fifteen years or so in Strassburg rests on a few legal documents. In 1436 a woman of the city went to court, complaining that Jo-

hann had promised to marry her and had then gone back on his word. How the court ruled in this matter is unknown. All we know is that Gutenberg did not marry the lady—nor, it seems, did he ever marry anyone else.

During the hearings in the courtroom a shoemaker named Claus Schott, speaking on the witness stand, said things that angered Gutenberg. In the high-handed manner of a born aristocrat, he denounced the shoemaker as a "poor creature, leading a life of lies and deceit." Whereupon the shoemaker brought a suit for slander against him and won his case.

Noteworthy is another legal record, dated December 12, 1439, and dealing with a contract between Gutenberg and a group of young men. According to this document, the young men had paid Gutenberg fairly large amounts of money to teach them "the secret of the art."

Of what art? The document speaks of Gutenberg's purchase of lead, other metals, a press, and some "forms." It quotes a witness as saying that he had received money from Gutenberg "only for that which pertains to printing."

All this indicates that during his stay in Strassburg Gutenberg had succeeded in constructing an instrument for the casting of movable type and a printing press. If he produced any books with

Johann Gutenberg examines a page printed by his press. *Culver Pictures.*

these contrivances they are no longer around. Of interest is a comment on this fact by Victor Scholderer in his biography *Johann Gutenberg: The Inventor of Printing.*

Scholderer points out that during Gutenberg's Strassburg days he was struggling to bring the art of printing into existence. Chances are he had not yet perfected his instruments. Nor had he as yet found the best way to use them. Whatever items he printed at this time were probably so crude in appearance that he destroyed them. Indeed, the legal document covering the agreement by Gutenberg to teach the "art" to some

young men describes him as asking one of them to destroy certain "forms"—a term used in his day for both the frame in which type is set and the type itself.

In 1443 or thereabouts, he returned to Mainz. Here he set up a shop and continued his experiments. In time he hired a man named Peter Schoeffer as his foreman and began work on the printing of his masterpiece—the magnificent book that today most of us think of as the Gutenberg Bible. It is also called the forty-two-line Bible, that being the number of lines in each column of its big two-column pages.

Its making took time and money, and

in 1449 or 1450 Gutenberg began his troubled financial association with Johann Fust, a lawyer living in Mainz. First Gutenberg persuaded Fust to lend him 800 guilders, a large sum. None of this money had been returned when, sometime later, he obtained another 800 guilders from Fust.

This time Fust insisted on an agreement, under which he became a part owner of Gutenberg's business. In addition the agreement stated that unless Gutenberg repaid the loans reasonably soon, Fust would take over the entire business.

So matters stood when in 1455 Fust brought suit. The court ordered Gutenberg to pay off the original loan of 800 guilders plus interest at once. Unable to do so, he lost his shop and everything in it, including the forty-two-line Bible or as much of it as had been printed at this time.

At this point Fust took on Gutenberg's foreman as a printer, changed the name of the business to Fust and Schoeffer, and began selling copies of the forty-two-line Bible to the public.

It is in connection with this development that a conflict has arisen between two of the students of the life and work of Johann Gutenberg. Douglas McMurtrie, in his history of printing, contends that Fust and Schoeffer did all the work on the famous Bible and that Gutenberg

had no part at all in its printing. In short, according to McMurtrie, what we call the Gutenberg Bible should be called the Fust and Schoeffer Bible.

More convincing by far, however, are the arguments to the contrary by Scholderer. To be sure, none of the existing copies of the Bible are dated. No one text gives any indication whatsoever as to when the beautiful book was completed, bound, and offered for sale.

It so happens, however, that the date when these things occurred is given in a handwritten note attached to a copy of the Bible owned by the national library in Paris, France, the *Bibliothèque Nationale*. The author of this note is one Heinrich Cremer, the man who drew the lovely designs along the borders of the great book. According to Cremer, the binding of the forty-two-line Bible was completed on August 24, 1456.

The processes that went into this work, Scholderer writes, "would take some time in the case of so large a book (it is bound in two volumes, of 324 and 318 leaves respectively), and if we allow for this we are brought sufficiently close to the date [1455] of Fust's action [his lawsuit against Gutenberg] to be sure that when the case was heard the Bible was already . . . being put on sale or in the last stages of completion." In other words we can go on speaking of the Gutenberg Bible as the Gutenberg Bible.

As for its maker's activities after he lost his shop we have a smattering of information. We know that he eventually opened another shop and ran it for several years. Some authorities believe that he produced another handsomely printed Bible known as the thirty-six-line Bible. Some credit him with the printing of a fine-looking Latin dictionary titled the *Catholicon*.

We also know that toward the end of his days he abandoned printing altogether, and that at the time of his death on February 3, 1468, he was holding a post of some consequence on the staff of the archbishop of his native Mainz.

Jack St. Clair Kilby

1923– American electrical engineer

Robert Norton Noyce

1927–1990 American physicist

Coinventors of the microchip, the "brain" of the modern computer, and of other recently fabricated devices useful in fields ranging from medicine to space exploration

History supplies us with many instances of two or more individuals working independently and coming up with the same new device at about the same time.

At the center of this account of two such American inventors, Jack Kilby and Robert Noyce, is the integrated circuit, more commonly spoken of as the microchip or the chip, and one of the most important products to be brought into existence during the twentieth century.

Micro means "very small," and the microchip is so small—less than a quarter of an inch square and about as thick as a few pages of this book—that it can rest on the tip of one's finger. Tiny though it is, the microchip consists of many thousands of electrical components embedded in a sliver of silicon.

Silicon, one of the most abundant substances in the crust of the Earth, is often used in the making of chips because of its peculiar characteristics. Electricity flows easily through certain materials—copper, gold, and other metals, for example—and these are called *conductors*. Electricity cannot move through certain other materials—rubber and plastic, for example—and these are called insulators.

Silicon is neither a good conductor nor a good insulator. It stands somewhere between the two and is therefore called a *semiconductor*. What makes it so valuable in the manufacture of chips is that, when the silicon is treated with certain chemicals, the movement of electricity through the parts squeezed into it can be controlled.

We are told that when on March 24, 1959, the invention of the microchip was announced at a meeting of the Institute of Radio Engineers in New York City, there was no great excitement. This memory makes us smile today, for no product invented in recent times has altered as many aspects of our everyday living.

The speed with which it has shrunk the size and cost of the computer is a case in point.

The early 1940s saw the construction of the first electronically driven computers. Among them was one built at the University of Pennsylvania and known as the Electronic Numerical Integrator and Calculator, or ENIAC. ENIAC weighed over thirty tons and occupied as much space as a school gymnasium. The price for this monster was a million dollars.

Contained in ENIAC were more than 18,000 glass electronic tubes, each of them about the size of an electric light bulb. So many miles of wire were needed to link the tubes that it took the makers of ENIAC two and a half years to string them. Whenever ENIAC was used, some of the tubes overheated and went out. The wires connecting them and other components sometimes came loose. Engineers, weary of spending hours hunting for faulty tubes and connections, concluded that the computer had no future unless ways could be found of reducing its size and cost.

The first step in this direction occurred in 1947, when three American scientists invented the transistor. Compared with the glass electronic tube, the transistor was small—about the size of an eraser at the end of a pencil. Though it consumed far less electricity than the tube and did not heat up, it could do all the things the tube could do. It could turn weak electrical signals into strong ones. It could direct the flow of electricity through the computer. It could function as an on-off switch, thus enabling the computer to work out intricate mathematical problems.

But the transistor did not end all of the troubles facing computer makers. Like glass electronic tubes, transistors had to be wired to one another and to the other parts of the machine. Today's small and relatively inexpensive computers did not even begin to be a possibility until Kilby and Noyce came along with their tiny chip, its many miniaturized transistors and other parts acti-

The University of Pennsylvania's ENIAC, the world's first all-electric digital computer. *The University of Pennsylvania Archives.*

vated not by means of easily loosened wires but by attachment to the solid circuit board of a computer.

Both inventors of the microchip began life in the American Midwest. Kilby was born to Herbert St. Clair Kilby and Vina Freitag Kilby in Jefferson City, Missouri, on November 8, 1923; Noyce to Ralph B. Noyce and Harriet Norton Noyce in Burlington, Iowa, on December 17, 1927.

Kilby's father, an engineer, worked for a variety of electric-power companies in the Midwest, eventually becoming president of the Kansas Power Company with headquarters at Great Bend in central Kansas. It was in this small city on the shores of the Arkansas River that Jack Kilby passed most of his growing-up years.

He attended the public schools. In the summers he accompanied his father on his trips to the power company's scattered facilities. At these places the two of them examined the works of the generating station, checking out ailing armatures or gauging the capabilities of a transformer.

For Jack the high moment of life in Great Bend came in 1937 when a blizzard, raging across Kansas, toppled telephone lines everywhere and left the roads impassable. To ascertain what was going on at his company's far-flung branches, Jack's father borrowed a ham radio set from a neighbor. He and Jack took turns listening, and in no time Jack had decided that he must have a set of his own.

It so happened that a recently established United States government agency, the Federal Communications Commission, was demanding licenses for radio operators. Jack studied hard, took the examination, got a license that gave him the call letters W9GTY, and constructed a ham set. By the time he started high school he had made up his mind to be an electrical engineer like his father. By the time he finished, his heart was set on getting his college training at one of the country's best schools for engineers, the Massachusetts Institute of Technology, in Cambridge, Massachusetts.

But MIT would never know him as a student. He flunked the entrance ex-

amination. This was in June, 1941, and forty years later the coinventor of the microchip and the inventor of more than fifty other devices could still recall every circumstance surrounding that disappointment. When interviewed by T. R. Reid, author of *The Chip*, a history of how the microchip came into being, Kilby could "remember his score in the test . . . 497, three points short of passing." He could even remember the algebra problems "he thinks he got wrong."

But back in 1941 Jack Kilby had no time to sit around and feel sorry for himself. As he had neglected to apply to any other college, it took fast work on his part to get himself enrolled in the fall at the University of Illinois.

Four months into his freshman year the United States entered the Second World War, and from 1943 to 1945 young Kilby advanced from private to corporal in the army of the United States, serving with an engineering unit in India and Burma. Returning to the university after the war, he acquired his bachelor of science degree in 1947 and by the opening weeks of 1948 was working in Milwaukee, Wisconsin, for an electric-parts firm called Centralab, a division of Globe-Union Corporation.

It was during his years with Centralab that the transistor came into its own. Kilby followed its development with in-

Jack St. Clair Kilby. *Texas Instruments.*

terest. Little by little it dawned on him that only when the transistor was freed of its dependence on connecting wires could it achieve its full usefulness.

He was not the only engineer to recognize the need for creating what in time would become the microchip. Here and there around the country other engineers were endeavoring to do exactly that. Now Kilby joined the effort, only to realize that Centralab, a relatively small firm, did not have the financial resources he needed to accomplish his ends.

Hence his pleasure when he was of-

fered a position at Texas Instruments, a large electric-parts company in Dallas, Texas. Not that the prospect of leaving Milwaukee was a pleasant one. Eight years before Kilby had taken as his wife a young woman named Barbara Annegers. Both Barbara and two girls born to the marriage enjoyed living in Milwaukee. So did Kilby. But in the end the decision was to move, and in May, 1958, he reported for work at Texas Instruments. Not quite four months later, on September 12, a group of Texas Instruments executives gathered in the company laboratory to watch Kilby demonstrate the world's first workable microchip.

Robert Noyce, the coinventor of the chip, did most of his growing up in the pleasant little town of Grinnell, Iowa, where his father, a Congregational minister, had taken over the local parsonage after serving a variety of other churches in the Midwest. Grinnell is the site of a highly reputable college, also known as Grinnell, and when Bob Noyce enrolled there in 1945 he already knew that his favorite subjects were going to be physics and mathematics.

Not that these matters received the whole of his attention. All his life, affable and outgoing Noyce had been a person of multiple interests and multiple enthusiasms. At Grinnell College he

Jack St. Clair Kilby's handwritten diagram, from his lab notebook, of the first integrated circuit, September 12, 1958. *Texas Instruments.*

found time to become the star diver on the swimming team. He sang in choral groups. He played the oboe in a band and a continuing role in a radio soap opera. He even found time to get into trouble.

One night in 1948 a group of Grinnell youths decided to stage a luau, a Hawaiian festival centered around the roasting of a suckling pig. To Noyce and a fellow athlete fell the job of acquiring the piglet—a mission they accomplished by robbing the sty of a nearby farm.

It was a great mistake, for in agricultural Iowa the theft of livestock is considered a heinous offense. Next day, having confessed to the crime, young Noyce was suspended for one semester—after which, returning to his studies midway through his senior year, he somehow managed to graduate with his class, earning high grades and a Phi Beta Kappa key.

Like Jack Kilby, Noyce had watched the coming of the transistor with interest. Like Kilby, he regarded the possibility of crowding innumerable miniaturized transistors and other electrical parts onto a tiny slab of semiconductor material as a dream to be pursued.

From Grinnell he shifted to the Massachusetts Institute of Technology. There he submerged himself in a graduate course in physical electronics. Receiving his doctor of philosophy degree in 1953, he went to work as a researcher for Philco, a firm in Philadelphia, Pennsylvania.

Philco had just embarked on a full-scale effort to develop improved transistors. Soon Noyce was publishing papers on various aspects of this endeavor. One of them caught the eye of William B. Shockley, one of the three inventors of the transistor, and on a day in January, 1956, Noyce received a phone call he would never forget.

The caller was Shockley. He revealed that he was leaving Bell Telephone Laboratories in New Jersey, where the transistor had been developed. He was heading for California to establish a company to be known as the Shockley Semiconductor Laboratories. Would Noyce be interested in interviewing for a job?

"It was like picking up the phone and talking to God," Noyce would later say of this call. "He [Shockley] was absolutely the most important person in semiconductor electronics. Getting that job meant you would definitely be playing in the big leagues."

But soon after getting the job Noyce realized that Shockley, winner of the Nobel Prize for his contribution to the making of the transistor, was not the world's best businessman. "He was continually shifting his researchers from

Robert Norton Noyce. *Steve Allen.*

one job to another," historian T. R. Reid tells us. "He couldn't seem to make up his mind what, if anything, the company was trying to produce."

Frustrated, Noyce and seven other young scientists left Shockley in 1957 to become co-owners of a firm known as the Fairchild Semiconductor Corporation in what is today called Silicon Valley, a section of California at the southern tip of San Francisco Bay occupied by microelectronic and other high-technology industries.

It was at Fairchild Semiconductor on January 23, 1959—four months after Jack Kilby's completion of his microchip at Texas Instruments in Dallas—that Noyce became the second inventor to give the world a workable chip.

No one needs to be told that the development of the microchip is a story that is still unfolding even as these words are written. Already the chip has brought many changes into our lives. As for the future, no doubt it will see chips far smaller and at the same time

Robert Norton Noyce's integrated circuit. *Steve Allen*.

far more powerful than those we now have.

Is the climate of the globe becoming increasingly warmer? Some scientists think the answer to that question is yes. Some think it is no. Many say that only when we produce a much improved chip, one the size of a pinhead but capable of holding at least a billion miniaturized transistors, can scientists produce a computerized model of the earth's environment sufficiently comprehensive to give us an unarguable yes or no.

Hardly a week passes but the media informs us that some new task has been found for the chips that are now on hand.

Medicine has found many uses for them. Chips are the essential components of modern hearing aids and pacemakers for persons with ailing hearts. A chip in a computer can store descriptions of thousands of illnesses. Your doctor can feed your symptoms into the computer and get back both a diagnosis and a treatment.

For many handicapped individuals, chips have provided better lives. Devices tiny enough to be lodged permanently under scalp or skin give at least partial sight and hearing to the formerly blind and deaf. Chips make possible

easily controllable and lifelike limbs for people who have lost legs or arms.

The exploration of space would be impossible without chips. It is these little flecks of transistor-laden material that operate the lightweight computers that guide the space shuttle into orbit and bring it to earth again.

The video games you play employ chips. It is thanks to the chip that some electronic games are so small one can carry them in a pocket.

Many indeed are the uses of microchips. They can be found in devices ranging from microwave ovens to cash registers, from traffic lights to cameras, from calculators to telephones.

No one will be surprised to learn that great wealth and many honors have been the lot of their inventors, Kilby and Noyce. These days Kilby lives with his wife in Dallas, Texas, and works as an independent inventor. Noyce, twice married and the father of four children, was residing in Los Altos, California, and working as a top official of Intel Corporation, the microelectronics company he helped found in 1968, when during a stay in Austin, Texas, on June 3, 1990, he died of a sudden heart attack.

Ernest Orlando Lawrence

1901–1958 American physicist; inventor of the cyclotron, the first particle accelerator or atom smasher to achieve the high energies needed to permit scientists to explore in a comprehensive way the invisible world of the atom

The elder of the two sons of Carl Gustavus Lawrence and Gunda Regina Jacobson Lawrence, Ernest Orlando Lawrence was born on August 8, 1901, in Canton, South Dakota, where his father was the superintendent of schools.

When in Ernest's tenth year the family moved to Pierre, the capital of South Dakota, it was because his father had been elected state superintendent of instruction. When Ernest was thirteen, they returned to Canton so that his father could resume direction of the schools there. "Golly," Ernest was heard to exclaim as he began his year in the eighth grade, "I'd like to go to school sometime where my dad isn't the boss."

Both his parents were of Norwegian descent. Both were devout Lutherans, and Ernie, as he was called by family and friends, grew up in a home in which the guiding rules, in the words of his biographer Herbert Childs, were "absolute honesty, ethical conduct and compassion for others."

He took these teachings to heart. Once during his high-school years a young kinsman who had come to visit the family urged him to get the two of them dates for a dance in a section of town denounced by the pastor of the local church as "hell's corner." Ernie's reaction was to draw himself up to his full height, already slightly more than six feet. He "would not," he said, "go to that dance and did not know the type of girls who would."

Even as an adult the puritan in him

frequently asserted itself. When his fellow scientists told him dirty stories, he laughed loudly. Too loudly, according to longtime friends, who realized that the laugh was forced.

His mother, talking of him long after he had left home to become one of the world's top scientists, remembered him as a boy who "was born grown up." She marveled at his unending cheerfulness and his stubborn independence. "Now Mama," he would say to her, "if you can give me just *one* good reason why you won't let me do this or that . . . I'll not ask for anymore." Nine times out of ten, Gunda Lawrence admitted, the only reason she could come up with was that she was the parent and, therefore, the person in charge.

He was a curious boy, forever plying both parents with questions. His mother was convinced that the tendency to stammer, which became a serious affliction in his ninth or tenth year, was an outgrowth of his practice of asking questions as fast as he could think of them. In his fourteenth year his parents sent him to a summer school in Milwaukee, Wisconsin, where he was taught to control his speech.

From his ninth year on, his passion was electricity. He and a couple of his pals took odd jobs to earn the money needed to purchase apparatus for telegraph and wireless sets. Soon the Lawrence home was littered with spark coils, bells, buzzers, motors, copper switches, and audion tubes.

Curiously enough, when in the fall of 1918 he enrolled at St. Olaf College in Northfield, Minnesota, his plan was to become, not an electrical engineer, but a medical doctor. How he was persuaded to set his sights on a different career altogether is an example of the effect a wise teacher can have on a promising student.

The First World War was raging in Europe, and at St. Olaf College only the Students Army Training Corps was in the hands of capable individuals. To Ernie's disgust, inferior instructors were teaching most of the academic courses, and when his freshman year ended he set out, for the first time in his life, to defy his parents. Both of them had turned down his request to study at the University of South Dakota, his mother arguing that their then seventeen-year-old son was still too young to cope with the "wickedness" bound to prevail at that large institution.

Quietly, when summer came, Ernie got himself a construction job at Vermillion, South Dakota, site of the university. He had earned enough to pay his tuition and entry fees and had been accepted as a student at the university before his parents realized what he was up to.

It was at the University of South Dakota that he encountered Lewis Akeley, dean of the College of Engineering. A trained scientist, Akeley was aware that during the last fifty years or so no branch of science had come up with more exciting discoveries than physics. Had Ernie, he asked the young man, ever considered shifting from medicine to physics?

Ernie's answer was that, having studied some physics under his father, he had decided that the subject was too hard for him. Dean Akeley thought otherwise. Whenever the two of them got together he steered the conversation to physics. Finally, at the end of the school year in 1920, he made young Lawrence a proposition.

"If you come back here and spend the month of August with me," he told him, "I'll interest you in physics. If I can't, I'll never speak of it to you again."

Lawrence took him up on this offer, and in August he not only fell in love with physics but completed all of the physics courses required of students at South Dakota during their sophomore year. After receiving his bachelor of arts degree in 1922, he headed for the University of Minnesota in Minneapolis, having been given a teaching fellowship in physics at that institution.

At Minnesota he found another brilliant guide in the English-born physicist Francis Gray Swann. Here, too, he suffered a temporary setback.

To obtain his master of arts degree he had to go before a committee composed of several professors, all but one of them physicists, and read a thesis he had written on electrodynamic theory. The physics professors present were delighted with his paper, but aging Professor George D. Sheperdson, an electrical engineer whose approval was necessary, refused to accept it.

What in the world, Lawrence mused, could he do about this? Professor Swann had an idea. The problem, he guessed, was that "old Sheperdson" knew next to nothing about electrodynamics. He suggested, therefore, that Lawrence call on the "old boy" and give him enough information on the subject to enable him to understand the young man's thesis.

In Sheperdson's office, Lawrence was momentarily flustered to find a sign on the professor's desk sternly warning visitors not to waste his time. Taking a deep breath, he proceeded to waste enough of it to deliver an abbreviated course in electrodynamics. Profound was his relief on finishing to find the professor nodding his head and assuring Lawrence that his degree would be forthcoming.

As Professor Swann was joining the faculty at the University of Chicago,

Lawrence began work on his doctor of philosophy degree at that institution. This was in the fall of 1923, and when a year later Swann moved again, this time to Yale University in New Haven, Connecticut, Lawrence moved with him. Receiving his Ph.D. at Yale on June 17, 1925, he remained there for another three years, partly as an independent researcher, partly as an assistant professor. When in 1928 he left Yale, it was to join the University of California at Berkeley with the rank of associate professor.

Lawrence carried to Berkeley a long-held desire to meet what he regarded as the greatest challenge confronting the physicists of his day. For centuries scientists had assumed that what we call the atom, that invisible fleck of substance a million times tinier than the breadth of a hair, was the smallest building block of matter and the only one that could not be further divided. Within the last half century, however, a spate of discoveries had shown that this was not the case. Small as the atom was, it contained within itself electrons, protons, and heaven only knew how many other infinitely smaller particles. To examine the interior of this invisible world had become the wish of physicists everywhere.

Lawrence knew, as did all interested scientists, that the accomplishment of this goal called for the invention of a tool that would enable observers to learn the secrets of the atom, even as the telescope had long since permitted them to uncover the secrets of such faraway objects as the sun and its planets.

What was needed was a device capable of generating and controlling energies of such intensity that a stream of atoms or parts of atoms could be put in motion at a speed so terrific that they would break up, thus allowing researchers to examine them in detail.

Many physicists had tried to construct a usable atom smasher, or accelerator, only to find it impossible to contain within the machine the high voltages—which is to say the high energies—required. Indeed, during one such attempt in Germany, one of the three experimenters had lost his life to the dangerously high voltages generated.

Lawrence knew of this and other failures. Still, as he went from experiment to experiment, he never for a moment lost his belief that success would come in time. Sure enough, while reading scientific journals in the Berkeley library one day in 1929, he came across the idea that a short time later enabled him to construct the first cyclotron. What made Lawrence's device practical was that it could make parts of atoms

Ernest Orlando Lawrence adjusts the thirty-seven-inch cyclotron in his Berkeley laboratory, 1934. *The Bancroft Library / University of California, Berkeley.*

whirl faster and faster not by the use of a high-voltage current but by an arrangement that gave the passing stream of matter a series of electrical kicks, much as a person on a swing increases his or her speed by means of a series of small pushes.

In September, 1930, he demonstrated his cyclotron to the members of the American Academy of Science, and a month later the University of California at Berkeley, realizing that Lawrence had given the scientific world a new and invaluable research tool, elevated its twenty-nine-year-old inventor to the rank of full professor.

Lawrence's first cyclotron was so small—only nine inches in diameter—that it could be rested on and operated on the seat of a chair. By July, 1931, however, he had produced one that was slightly larger—eleven inches in diameter—and considerably more effective.

To the scientists summoned to see

this accelerator in action he revealed that he was planning a trip to New York City to raise the $500 he needed to construct a still larger cyclotron. On hearing this announcement, the scientific philanthropist Dr. Frederick Cottrell shook his head. "If you want a large sum, ask for it," he advised. "It is easier to get five thousand dollars than five hundred."

Lawrence kept these words in mind, and soon after his arrival in New York in late July he was in possession of $10,000. Money in hand, he set out to accomplish another mission that had been on his mind for some time.

Back in 1925 while he was still doing research at Yale, he had fallen in love with Mary Blumer, the sixteen-year-old daughter of Dr. George Blumer, a professor of clinical medicine at Yale and a former dean of its medical faculty.

The ensuing courtship did not run smoothly. In the beginning Molly, as she was known to family and friends, thought of Lawrence as "my old Ph.D." She was heard to remark that he was "terribly" thin and "not at all handsome." When he revealed his feelings for her, she said that marriage was not on her agenda. She was planning to study bacteriology at Vassar College and was looking forward to a career in that field.

Lawrence bided his time. He visited her at Vassar and brought her to Yale on occasion for football games and other events. Following his move to Berkeley the two of them corresponded, and by the time of his trip to New York in the summer of 1931 it seemed to him that Molly's letters were growing warmer.

Warm enough, at any rate, to make him hope that the time had come to speak again of marriage. As Mary and her mother were touring in Europe, he arranged to meet their returning ship on the docks of New York and to spend a few days at the Blumers' country home at Haycock Point, Connecticut, on the shores of Long Island Sound.

The ship bringing Molly and her mother home arrived on the second of August, but for most of the next two days Lawrence was unable to get Molly to himself for so much as a minute. Finally, catching her eye from across a crowded room at her parents' country place, he signaled her to join him on the porch outside.

They sat there together in a hammock. "Molly, do you love me?" he asked. "I do," she replied. "Then," said Lawrence, "we ought to get married." Molly's nod brought the long courtship to an end, and on May 14, 1932, in New Haven's historic Trinity Church, the two of them became husband and wife. To their union six children would be born, four girls and two boys.

By the time the newlyweds had settled in at Berkeley, Lawrence had brought into being there a new institution destined to become famous throughout the scientific world as the Radiation Laboratory. Here, over the years, he supervised the construction of a series of atom smashers, each larger and more powerful than its predecessor.

During the Second World War Lawrence, winner of the 1939 Nobel Prize in physics and other awards, contributed in a substantial way to the building of the atomic bomb. After the war he pushed on with his work on cyclotrons.

Housed in the Radiation Laboratory at this point was an enormous accelerator spoken of as the "184-incher." On February 27, 1948, this machine made scientific history by producing *mesons,* strange particles of cosmic radiation that endlessly bombard the Earth and are thought to provide the force that binds nuclear particles together.

The production of the first man-made meson, Herbert Childs has noted, "marked the birth of a new era in science, that of high energy physics." The same year that saw this development saw the beginning of work on an even more powerful atom smasher, a 10,000-ton machine to be known as the Beva-

tron. With his various machines Lawrence brought into existence several substances subsequently used by physicians in the treatment of cancer and other serious ills.

As a researcher, he was orderly and methodical. As a husband and father, his conduct was marked by an often hopeless absentmindedness.

"Let's go to a movie," he'd say to Molly. But once in the car and on their way, he'd suggest, "Let's drop by the laboratory and see how the boys are doing. It'll only take a few minutes." But more often than not it took a few hours, during which Molly entertained herself as best she could in an out-of-the-way corner of the room.

Once, while making a train trip east with their first baby, the two of them arranged to separate at Chicago, Illinois. There Molly, planning a visit at the home of her parents, was to catch a train going directly to New Haven. Lawrence, en route to a scientific conference, was to board one headed for Washington, D.C.

On their arrival in Chicago, Lawrence parked Molly and the baby in the waiting room of the railroad station and went off to purchase the tickets they would need for the remainder of their journeys. He had not yet reached the ticket booths when he encountered a scientist friend, and the two of them

Ernest Orlando Lawrence stands beside the synchrocyclotron, his largest cyclotron. *University of California, Berkeley, Radio Laboratory, U.S. Atomic Energy Commission.*

fell into an animated discussion of mutual interests.

They were thus engaged when Molly, baby in arms, came running to tell them that the train to New Haven was taking off. "Good heavens!" Lawrence exclaimed when she appeared. "What in the world are you doing here?"

To Molly one aspect of her husband's labors was a source of constant worry. Some of the materials he handled gave off dangerous radiation, and his health was far from perfect. There were bouts of pneumonia and other respiratory ailments, and in the summer of 1958 physicians at a hospital in Palo Alto, California, diagnosed the presence of an ulcerated colon and recommended its removal. Performed on August 27, 1958, this operation proved too much for the fifty-seven-year-old Lawrence, who died shortly after its completion.

Leonardo da Vinci

1452–1519   Italian painter, sculptor, architect, musician, engineer, and scientist, whose notebooks abound with designs anticipating many modern devices, including the airplane, the helicopter, the paddle-wheel-propelled boat, the continuous-motion lathe, the army tank, and the submarine

"Pre-imagining," Leonardo wrote in one of his many notebooks, "is the imagining of things that are to be."

The story of Leonardo as an inventor is the story of history's greatest imaginer of things that came into existence after his time.

Four centuries before the American bicycle makers Wilbur and Orville Wright put an airplane into the air, Leonardo was attempting to create one in his workshop.

Four and a half centuries before the Russian-born American engineer Igor Sikorsky constructed a helicopter suitable for human travel, Leonardo was developing one that could be carried aloft by an aerial screw similar to the mechanism devised by the ancient Chinese toymakers to spin a top.

Leonardo's airplane couldn't fly. His helicopter, if it was put in the air at all, couldn't stay there long. Chances are that Leonardo himself understood why. The required knowledge of aerodynamics and engine building that had been accumulated by the time the Wright brothers and Igor Sikorsky came along was not available to Leonardo. Indeed, the amazing thing is not that some of the contrivances described in the 10,000-plus pages of his notebooks could not be used in his time. The amazing thing is that many of them could have been used had Leonardo possessed the technical information accessible to modern engineers. In our own twentieth century, several machines have been constructed in accordance with Leonardo's designs. All of them have been found workable.

Innumerable are the drawings in his notebooks of new things or of things that were to come. He invented the alarm clock, the lamp chimney, the ship's record or log, and a power loom that came close to being operable. He constructed the first parachute—not to get people out of an airplane, although he had ideas about that, too, but as a quick means of traveling from the top of an almost unscalable cliff to the level or only mildly hilly land below. He developed a project for the mass production of workers' houses, a project so much a part of our own times that its appearance in his notebooks rather takes our breath away. He anticipated air-conditioning, devising a method for the air-cooling of rooms. He anticipated the automobile, with his design of a self-propelled wagon. He designed rope and belt drives, paddle-wheel boats, antifriction roller bearings, bevel and spiral gears, link chains, water-shoes, and a continuous-motion lathe.

He hated war, which he called *bestialissima pazzia*, the "most bestial madness." But more than he hated war, he loved liberty. This he called "the chief gift of nature." He wanted the people in the Italian cities where he worked to have the means to defend themselves against enemies bent on robbing them of their freedom. With

this end in mind, he designed a number of military devices and processes. Among them were a gas mask, a covered wagon similar to today's army tanks, and a variety of ways for protecting a fort against invaders. As for the submarine sketched in his notebooks, about that he said nothing to anyone. To be sure, his illustration of the submarine was accompanied by a written description of how it was to be built. But these words were meant for his eyes only.

For this and all other written descriptions in his notebooks, he used what is called mirror writing. Instead of running his sentences from left to right he ran them from right to left, so that they could be read only by holding them up to a mirror. Some students of his notebooks think Leonardo did this because he was left-handed. Others see in these backward-flowing lines a desire to keep his plans to himself until he was ready to reveal them. This characterization of Leonardo as secretive is borne out by what we know of his working habits. Even after he became one of the most famous men in Italy, he kept out of the public eye as much as possible. He preferred to do his work in solitude. His reason for saying nothing about his submarine arose from a conviction that more persons than not are greedy and power hungry. A boat that could travel underwater, he de-

A self-portrait and the only known likeness of Leonardo da Vinci. *Archives of the Biblioteca Reale, Torino, Italy.*

cided, was too "satanic" a weapon of war to be placed in the hands of "unregenerate man."

He was born on April 15, 1452, in the hilltop village of Vinci, a day's ride by mule cart from the large and beautiful city of Florence in the Tuscany section of central Italy. His father's official name was Ser Piero da Vinci. The *Ser* was a title meaning "notary" or "magister." The older da Vinci's work was similar to that of a modern lawyer concerned with civil, as distinct from criminal, problems.

We do not know his mother's last name. Her first was Caterina, and her failure to become his father's wife reflected the social practices of fifteenth-century Italy. Most men, especially those of the upper class, as Piero da Vinci was, took as wives only women able to bring a dowry—a sum of money—to the union. As Caterina could not do this, Leonardo was brought up by a stepmother, a young heiress whom his father married during the year of Leonardo's birth.

All his life Leonardo kept in touch with his natural mother. She and the man she did marry lived near the house in Vinci where Leonardo passed his earliest years. It has been suggested that as a growing boy he may have found it convenient to have a second home to which he could retreat when things got rough in his own.

Perhaps so; but there does not seem to have been much to retreat from. One gathers that, on the whole, his beginning years were tranquil and sunny. Certainly Leonardo was. Courtesy, a consideration for others' feelings, and a tolerance for their foibles—from childhood on these appear to have been major constants of his makeup. A story is told of an incident in his old age when his younger contemporary, the brilliant artist Michelangelo, spoke to him insultingly. According to a witness of this unpleasantness, Leonardo gave no evidence of being offended. He was simply bewildered, unable to comprehend how any human being could speak thus to another.

As a boy he tramped the Tuscan hills in the vicinity of his home. Nature fascinated him, especially the birds. He observed them for hours on end, a study that in time led to his efforts to fashion flying machines. As a man he frequently purchased caged birds with one purpose in mind: to free them. Such was his respect for all living creatures that during the whole of his adult life he was a vegetarian.

By his tenth year, or thereabouts, his father had become a legal adviser to important people in Florence, and Leonardo was living most of the time in that city and working as a student in the studio of Andrea di Michele Gioni, better known as Verrocchio.

Now famous for such splendid statues as *David* and *Boy with the Dolphin*. Verrocchio demanded long hours of hard work and the mastery of many subjects from the boys and the young men who came to him to be trained as painters, sculptors, architects, and engineers. To Leonardo the years with Verrocchio were a joy. He was always happiest when he was hard at work, and a knowledge of everything there was to know was precisely what he wanted to acquire. Not that the routine of his student days was all work and no play. We are told that he was well known as a young man around town— an exceptionally handsome one, if, as some of his biographers believe, it was his features that Verrocchio used in the making of his bronze *David*. It has been said of the young Leonardo that, having toiled all day, he often caroused all night and that he played the lute divinely.

He is often spoken of as the ideal Renaissance man. The term refers to what historians call the Renaissance, or "rebirth," an era that came of age in Italy even as Leonardo came of age. The Renaissance was a period during which the people of Italy, and, in time, of other European regions, started looking at the world in a new way. The wise men of the preceding centuries, the so-called Middle Ages, took the position that to understand the world one needed to study only what appeared to be the laws of God.

Not so, said Leonardo. He thought that one must probe more widely than that. One must study not only nature's God but nature itself. One must endeavor, by means of research and experiment, to discover how the world was put together by its Maker and how it works. With the coming of Leonardo, we see the beginnings of modern science.

From his student days on, he approached every one of his many professions in the spirit of a man who was first of all a scientist.

To create an effective portrait, he reasoned, one must know not only the outside but the inside of a human being. Hence his prolonged study of anatomy, of the structure of human and animal bodies. It was while dissecting the body of a man who had died in his hundredth year that Leonardo discovered the disease now known as arteriosclerosis, or hardening of the arteries. He thus became the father of the modern science of geriatrics, the diagnosis and treatment of the ills of the aged.

In Leonardo's day the success of a portrait depended to a great degree on how the areas of light and shadow were arranged. Hence Leonardo's intensive study of the way light falls on objects and of how the same object seen from a different perspective seems to the beholder to be a different thing.

He endeavored to study everything in nature and everything man was capable of making from nature. He studied the rocks, the flowers, the behavior of liquids, and the workings of machines. The wise men living before him believed that only certain exalted matters, chiefly those connected with religion, were worthy of examination. Not so, said Leonardo. Everything—big or small, gorgeous or ugly—was worthy of it. What counted was not the thing scrutinized but the accuracy of one's observations. Such "is the excellence of truth," he wrote in his notebooks, "that if it praises the smallest things they are made noble."

By his twentieth year he was no longer a student in Verrocchio's studio. He was an assistant and, as such, an artist on his own. We know from his notebooks and from one of his letters that during his many years in Florence he sculpted numerous figures in bronze, terracotta, and marble. But none of his statues of this or any other period seem to have survived. Among the at least seven paintings he completed during his years in Florence is *Ginevra di Benci*. This dazzling portrait of a sixteen-year-old poet, the daughter of a Florentine banker, can be seen today in the National Gallery of Art in Washington, D.C.

In his thirtieth year Leonardo left Florence. For the next seventeen years he lived in or near Milan, in the Lombardy section of northern Italy. By 1488 he had become court painter and engineer to Lodovico Sforza, the duke and ruler of Milan. It was for Lodovico that he began the designs of military things—bridges, a system of canals, and a steam-fired cannon, among them—that occupy so many pages in his notebooks.

It was after his arrival in Milan that Leonardo produced what today are probably the most widely recognized pieces of art in the world: *The Last Supper* and the *Mona Lisa*.

The Last Supper is a mural, a fresco, a painting achieved by the application of watercolors to wet plaster. So frequently has this scene of Christ dining with his disciples been scraped and retouched over the centuries that one of Leonardo's biographers describes what remains of it as "the ghost of a ghost." Now a shrine visited by art lovers from everywhere, it can be seen on the wall of the refectory of the Milanese church and convent Santa Maria delle Grazie.

What we call the *Mona Lisa*, Leonardo called *Portrait of a Lady on a Balcony*. And who was the lady on the balcony? Who sat for this fascinating portrait that now occupies a place of

A model derived from Leonardo's plans for an automotive wagon. *International Business Machine Corporation.*

honor in the museum in Paris known as the Louvre? The guess of the first of Leonardo's biographers was that Mona Lisa (short for Madonna Lisa) was the wife of Francesco del Giocondo, a silk merchant connected with the government of Florence. Others have suggested other names. Leonardo himself, asked to identify her in his old age, said merely that she was "a certain Florentine lady." In short, as Martin Kemp writes in his 1981 book *Leonardo da Vinci: The Marvelous Works of Nature and Man,* "we do not know" who Mona Lisa was, "and anyone who argues to the contrary is building bricks without straw."

As for Leonardo's private life during his years in Milan, we have only scraps of information. We know, for one thing, that in the summer of 1490 he adopted a ten-year-old boy named Gian Giacomo. Gian turned out to be an incurable thief—and Leonardo turned out to be an indulgent father. He nicknamed the lad Salai, meaning "little devil," kept him around for twenty-six years, and gave him half of the small property he owned in the city. We know, too, that in 1495 or 1496 Leonardo's mother, Caterina, died in a Milanese hospital— a circumstance that suggests that at the time of her death she was visiting her son or living with him.

The Italy of Leonardo's time consisted of many small principalities, or city-states. Some, like Florence, were republics. Others, like Milan, were princedoms or duchies. These little states were forever warring with one another; and large European countries like Spain and France, taking advantage of the instability created by these conflicts, were forever trying to seize portions of Italian soil.

On October 6, 1498, a French army conquered Milan, forcing Duke Lodovico Sforza, its ruler and Leonardo's employer, to flee. Not quite a year later Lodovico recaptured the city. But his victory was shortlived. In April of 1500 the French retook it, and Lodovico, seized during a battle at the nearby city of Novara, was marched off to a prison in France, where he died eight years later.

Meanwhile Leonardo, no longer able to make a living in Milan, moved from place to place in Italy. For two years he functioned in a variety of capacities, chiefly as an engineer and mapmaker, for Cesare Borgia, commander of the military forces of the pope, who in those days was both head of the Church and ruler of extensive territories. Early 1506 found Leonardo back in Milan. There, for the next seven years, he worked as an architect and engineer for the French governors of that city.

Frequently, during his second stay in Milan, he spent time in Florence, testifying in the law courts there. His father, who died in 1504, had left no will, and Leonardo's efforts to obtain a share of Piero da Vinci's estate was defeated by the joint efforts of his seven much-younger half brothers.

During these opening years of the sixteenth century his country was embroiled in the turbulence that has come to be known as the Italian Wars. In 1512 Milan changed hands again. The French governors, surprised by an invading army, marched out. Massimiliano Sforza, son of the late Duke Lodovico, marched in. For Leonardo, Massimiliano had no jobs. Fortunately for Leonardo, Pope Leo X did.

In the fall of 1513 Leonardo traveled to Rome, to spend some eighteen months as a member of the papal court. They were not happy months. He was getting old. Younger artists, notably Michelangelo and the equally gifted Raphael, had the ear of the pope. Leonardo did some engineering work on the harbor defenses of Civitavecchio, the port of Rome, but he was given

Leonardo's diagram for hydraulic machinery, designed to raise water to higher levels. *The Bettman Archive.*

few jobs as a painter. He was understandably relieved when Francis I, the king of France, invited him to work and live in that country.

When in the fall of 1516 he headed for France, he took with him a large number of his paintings—an action that explains the presence today of his *Mona Lisa* in a French museum. In France he resided in the town of Amboise, in a small palace called Cloux on the banks of the Loire River.

His household included Francesco Melzi, a young Italian nobleman whom he had adopted as his son and to whom he would leave his notebooks and most of his other possessions. As the king's "premier painter and architect," Leonardo planned a new castle for Francis and supervised its construction. Ever the pre-imaginer, he designed a network of canals that would be dug and put into use three hundred years later.

The king was a frequent visitor at

Cloux. Young and brilliant, Francis delighted in the older man's company. He asserted that Leonardo's knowledge of both the fine arts and philosophy was beyond that "of all mortal men."

Death came on May 2, 1519. It was a peaceful passing, in keeping with one of the backward-flowing sentences long before inscribed in his notebooks: "As a well-spent day brings happy sleep, so a life well used brings happy death."

He was buried, in accordance with his wishes, in a church in Amboise. The building has disappeared, and the exact site of his resting place is unknown. A regrettable loss, yes, but of secondary importance, for in the hearts and minds of thinking people around the world, Leonardo da Vinci lives on. Memorable among the many tributes to him are the words of Umberto Eco and G. B. Zorzoli in their book *The Picture History of Inventions:* "Leonardo's greatness is not that he vaguely foresaw the helicopter or designed submarines which would never have worked; Leonardo was great because he was the initiator of modern scientific methods and in this sense . . . . was the begetter of all of the inventions that came after him."

Cyrus Hall McCormick

1809–1884   American industrialist and philanthropist; inventor of the first widely used reaping machine

First of the eight children of Robert McCormick, Jr., and Mary Ann Hall McCormick, Cyrus Hall McCormick was born on February 15, 1809, on a 1,200-acre farm in the section of Virginia bordered on the east by the Blue Ridge Mountains and on the west by the Appalachian Plateau and known as the Valley of Virginia.

In his fifth year illness struck—an illness so devastating that he survived only because of the prompt efforts of his father, who immersed him in hot steam baths containing bitter herbs and whiskey.

Both parents were strict Presbyterians, and religion dominated the household. Family prayers began and ended the day, and each of the children had to memorize long sections of the Bible and all of the Shorter Catechism.

Cyrus began life in a log cabin, but by his thirteenth year this had been replaced by a brick house. At this time Walnut Grove, as the farm was called, boasted grist mills and sawmills, a blacksmith's shop, a carpenter's shop, a distillery, and the services of nine slaves and eighteen horses.

One can be sure that the distillery was of little import to Cyrus. In a region noted for its hard drinkers and heavy tobacco users, he neither drank nor smoked. Other boys of the area came barefoot to church. Not Cyrus. Not only did he arrive well shod but also well dressed, in elegant broadcloth coat and black beaver hat. While his brothers and sisters played, he preferred to pass the time at the smithy or the workbench.

From such knowledge as we have of

his growing-up years he emerges as a quiet and sobersided youth. From a one-room school in the neighborhood he quickly absorbed reading, writing, and geography, and from a private tutor the elements of mathematics.

He can be described as coming by his interest in making things honestly. His father was an endless tinkerer. The older McCormick was forever trying to bring into existence new agricultural implements, ranging from a blacksmith's bellows to a threshing machine. Few if any of his inventions proved workable. Two different periods, for example, found him completing a horse-powered reaping machine that turned out to be worthless when tested in the fields.

Robert McCormick was not the first person to make this effort. Nor was he the first to fail. Attempts to reduce the grinding drudgery connected with the harvesting of grains by replacing hand-held sickles and scythes with a mechanical reaper went back to the days of the ancient Romans. Probably Robert's oldest son was himself surprised when in the summer of 1831 a reaper he had designed on his own turned out to be a solid success.

One afternoon that summer, Cyrus McCormick's biographer William T. Hutchinson tells us, "a few farmers in the Valley of Virginia watched a strange machine cut ripe wheat on the farm of Robert McCormick." Hutchinson adds that neither Robert nor his son Cyrus, the builder of the machine, realized that in the years ahead this device would greatly improve the agricultural economy of the American West and Midwest, even as Eli Whitney's invention of the cotton gin thirty-eight years before had greatly improved that of the South.

Why did Cyrus's reaper succeed whereas all previously built reapers had failed? Hutchinson's answer to this question is that Cyrus's machine was the first to embody the seven parts the apparatus must have to cut grain without injuring it and to leave its severed stalks so arranged that the person coming along to do the binding can make a neat sheaf without difficulty. Prior to 1831, Hutchinson informs us, other inventors had used anywhere from one to six of the seven essential parts, but Cyrus McCormick "was the first to unite them all into an effective whole."

In 1831 most of the McCormick family's income came from an ironworks in the vicinity of Walnut Grove. Not until the 1837 depression put this enterprise out of business and the family deeply into debt did Cyrus begin to consider his reaper as a possible source of money.

As originally completed, the machine

A portrait of Cyrus Hall McCormick.

had defects. Not the least of these was a clatter so earsplitting that slaves had to walk alongside the moving reaper to soothe the frightened horses. By 1841 Cyrus had rid the machine of this and other faults and was ready to go to market. He sold two reapers that year, seven in 1842, twenty-nine in 1843, and fifty the following year.

From a visit to the prairie states of the Midwest in 1844 he returned to Virginia certain that the future of the world's wheat production—and his reaper—lay not in the hilly East but in the vast and fertile flatlands he had just toured. Hence his decision in 1847 to erect a factory for the construction and sale of his invention in the then-small town of Chicago, Illinois, on the swampy shoreline of Lake Michigan.

The business prospered, and Chicago prospered with it. By 1848 McCormick's company was selling 1,500 reapers a year and Chicago was already on its way to becoming one of the country's biggest cities.

McCormick traveled endlessly. Certain months of nearly every year found him traversing the prairie states, taking orders for his machines. Whether on the road or at his plant in Chicago, he toiled ceaselessly, prompting a friend to remark that every day "Cyrus McCormick works almost two ordinary business days."

Certain portions of nearly every year found him in court, defending himself against what he considered the efforts of other inventors to steal his ideas and profit by them. He enjoyed these appearances in the legal arena. He loved a fight. It was said of him that "he always followed the line of most resistance."

His chief competitor was Obed Hussey, a Maine-born Quaker, developer of a reaper only slightly inferior to McCormick's and the owner of a reaper-building plant in Baltimore, Maryland. From time to time the two inventors entered their machines in contests on the grain-growing fields of the United States or Great Britain. McCormick's machine always won these matches, but Hussey's usually made a good showing.

When McCormick entered his machine in the Great Exhibition of 1851 at the Crystal Palace in London's Hyde Park, the *London Times* scornfully described it as "a cross between a flying machine and a wheel barrow." When soon thereafter the McCormick reaper received the highest awards available, the *Times* changed its tune. McCormick's machine, it decided, would "prove to be worth more to agricultural England than the cost of the entire exhibition." As the *Times* pointed out, whereas a crew of fourteen men, wielding sickles and scythes, could cut two acres of grain in eight hours, a McCor-

McCormick's newly invented reaper is tested in Virginia in 1831. *Chicago Historical Society.*

mick reaper could clear at least fourteen acres in the same length of time.

So frequently was McCormick on the road that when in the summer of 1857 he lingered in Chicago for several weeks, the local gossips exercised their tongues. Could it be that at last the wealthy 48-year-old inventor had found the woman he wished to make his wife?

He had. She was twenty-four-year-old Nancy Fowler—Nettie, to family and friends—a resident of Clayton, New Jersey, who had come west to pass some of the warm months as the house guest of a friend. Though it was in Chicago that McCormick made her acquaintance, he was in New York City on business when in September he proposed to her by mail.

Their marriage at the home of friends in Chicago on January 26, 1858, was followed by a reception for five hundred guests at the Chicago home of one of McCormick's brothers. The *Chicago Daily Press*, in its account of these events, referred to McCormick, whose company was now selling four thousand reapers a year, as the "massive Thor of industry."

In truth, the warlord of American industry was no longer devoting the whole of his time to business. He had become active in the affairs of the Presbyterian Church, his generous financial gifts to the "Old School" or conservative wing of that body making possible, among other things, the establishment in Chicago of the McCormick Theological Seminary.

Politics attracted much of his attention. As the Civil War approached, he sided with the so-called peace Democrats, the northern members of his party sympathetic to the aims of the South. "As a Jeffersonian," Hutchinson notes, "he was not pro-slavery in principle," but he did not want to see the Union split by the demands of Northern abolitionists for immediate emancipation of the slaves.

"If the country had been spared the abolitionists," he said in 1860, "an anti-slavery movement in the South would have been under way by [this time]."

In September, 1864, he ran for Congress on a stop-the-war platform but was unsuccessful. In December of that year, with the armies of Union General Ulysses S. Grant and Confederate General Robert E. Lee confronting one another in lower Virginia, he wrote to President Lincoln, asking to be sent to Richmond, Virginia, as an envoy empowered to bring the conflict to an end. There was no reply from Lincoln, and McCormick was surprised to learn of Lee's surrender to Grant at Appomattox Court House on April 9, 1865.

It was during the closing year of the war that McCormick's love of a fight, along with an unshakable desire to prove himself in the right, brought on a long and costly lawsuit. He, his wife, two of the seven children born to their union, a cousin, and two servants were returning to Chicago by train from Washington, D.C., when some trunks belonging to them were lost in a fire at the Chicago station of the Pennsylvania Central Railroad.

McCormick sued the railroad, estimating his loss at $5,500. The court awarded him that amount, but by the time this judgment came down the inventor had decided that he should have more. After that the case moved from court to court, with McCormick regularly upping his demands. He had been dead for a year when in April, 1885, the suit wound up in the Supreme Court of New York, where McCormick's estate was awarded over $18,000—a trifling sum compared with the legal fees the inventor or his estate had paid during the preceding twenty years.

As this behavior suggests, McCormick kept a close eye on the state of his finances. He once scolded a friend for using writing paper so heavy that the friend had to buy two stamps for every letter he mailed. At home and at work, he questioned the accuracy of practically every bill.

There was no hail-fellow-well-met in his manner. Casual acquaintances, according to his biographer Hutchinson, considered him "cold, imperious, and calculated to inspire awe." Close friends, on the contrary, found him good company, appreciative of a joke, and given to a hearty laugh.

Quick-tempered and demanding, he had trouble keeping secretaries. The prickly aspects of his personality, however, did not seem to have troubled his wife. Notwithstanding the difference in their ages—he was almost twenty-five years her senior—their relationship flourished, fed by such similar interests as a shared religion.

For many years their home in Chicago was a house on the South Side. They were living in a recently built mansion on the Near North, however, when in the spring of 1884 a complex ailment sent McCormick to his bed. His wife was at his side when, in the early hours of May 13, he whispered his last words. "It's all right," he assured her. "It's all right." Soon thereafter, at 7:00 A.M., he was dead.

Two days later a long cortege followed his body to Chicago's Graceland Cemetery. Standing alongside the coffin there, a tribute from the workmen at his factory, were a sheaf of ripe wheat and one of the more popular models of his reaper, with its main wheel missing.

Guglielmo Marconi

1874–1937   Italian physicist; principal inventor of wireless telegraphy, forerunner of radio

Shortly after the birth of Guglielmo Marconi in Bologna, Italy, on April 25, 1874, his family moved to the nearby village of Pontecchio, to live in a manor house on a large estate—the Villa Grifone. His father, Giuseppe, was a landowner of considerable means. Losing his first wife in his thirty-eighth year, Giuseppe had eloped with a seventeen-year-old music student named Annie Jameson, youngest daughter of a wealthy whiskey-making family in Ireland.

If, as this action suggests, the Protestant Jamesons objected to Annie's marriage to a Catholic, it would appear that soon all was forgiven. In Guglielmo's fifth year his mother took him to England. There he met his relatives and began his formal education at a private school. By the time mother and son had returned to Villa Grifone, Guglielmo was speaking English as fluently as Italian. Years later, after he became famous, Britons were given to saying proudly that no matter what language Marconi spoke, he sounded like one of them.

Physically he resembled his Irish mother: blue eyes, light complexion, fair hair, and thin aristocratic features. He was a quiet boy. His older half brother Luigi and his older brother Alonso joined the neighborhood youngsters in their games and sports. Guglielmo rarely did so. He preferred to read in his father's library. Or to go fishing by himself. Or to climb one of the plane trees on the Villa Grifone estate and stretch out for long periods on a lower limb, dreaming about the things that excited him, chiefly chemistry and electricity.

He continued his formal education for a time at home under a tutor. Then for seven years he studied at technical schools in the area. Efforts to enroll at two Italian universities were unsuccessful when he failed to pass the entrance examinations, but a science professor at one of them permitted him to sit in on his classes and conduct laboratory researches.

In his twentieth year an article in an electrical journal caught his attention and started the train of thought that would lead to his invention of wireless telegraphy. Twenty years before, according to the article, the great Scottish physicist James Clerk Maxwell had assumed the existence in the air of what are known as electromagnetic waves, or radio waves.

Such waves travel with the speed of light, 186,000 miles per second. Their behavior can be likened to what happens when a stone is dropped into a pond: Waves ripple away in all directions from where the stone strikes the water. Shortly before his recent death, the article revealed, a great German physicist, Heinrich Hertz, had proven that Maxwell's assumptions were correct. Hertz had done this by using a device called an oscillator to send radio waves through the air for short distances.

What would he have, young Marconi wondered, if he could construct an apparatus capable of sending radio waves to distant places? Histories of science, read in his father's library, provided the answer. Samuel F. B. Morse, the American artist-inventor, had long since given mankind the telegraph. Telegraph messages sped overland by means of electric current running in wires or across the ocean in electricity-carrying cables sunk beneath the waves. With an instrument able to send electomagnetic waves long distances, messages could be sent through the air at a much faster rate and without the use of connecting wires or cables.

Guglielmo was vacationing in the Italian Alps when his eyes fell on the article about Heinrich Hertz and his wave-radiating machine. He spent the rest of the summer filling a notebook with squiggly diagrams. They were comical affairs. He was no artist. But they contained the germs of what in time would be antenna systems capable not only of sending signals around the world but also of picking up the signals and of operating devices that converted them into sounds or printed words.

On his return to Villa Grifone in the fall of 1894 he retreated to his laboratory on the third floor. Here he struggled to transform his ill-drawn diagrams into usable instruments. He rose early. He worked all day and into the night. His mother became alarmed. He had never been robust. Now he was becoming appallingly thin. His face was drawn, his eyes glazed over with fatigue. Finally, to her relief, he announced that his instruments were ready. He invited the family upstairs for a demonstration. Pushing a button on his sending apparatus, he succeeded in ringing a bell on the first floor.

His mother was awestruck. His father shook his head. Unless Guglielmo could find a way of sending signals to a point far more distant than the first floor of the house, the older Marconi grumbled, he would end up with nothing but a parlor game. Giuseppe continued to purchase the expensive equipment his son's labors required, but he kept his fingers crossed.

Guglielmo labored on. Little by little he made significant changes in his sending and receiving circuits, hoping to extend the range of the electromagnetic waves. One day he moved his receiving station to the side of a hill, visible from the laboratory where his sending apparatus stood. He sent his brother Alonso out to the hill. Then, using the telegraph sounder attached to his sender, Guglielmo tapped out the three dots that represent the letter S in the tele-

graphic Morse code. Alonso at once waved a flag to indicate that the hammer on the receiving device had also tapped out the S.

Next Guglielmo moved his receiving paraphernalia to the far side of the hill. Now, from his laboratory window, he could see neither the receiver nor his brother.

Again he tapped out the letter S. This time Alonso fired a gun to let Guglielmo know that the signal had reached him. It was a great moment for the young inventor. Not only had his radio waves traveled three quarters of a mile, but the little hill had not stopped them. What about mountains? Would they block the signals? He thought not, and subsequent tests would prove this guess to be correct.

Summoned to watch a repeat of the over-the-hill test, his father uncrossed his fingers. Businessman that he was, Giuseppe Marconi sensed that his son's invention had commercial possibilities.

Guglielmo thought so, too. He realized, however, that to make his equipment salable he must vastly increase the distance over which it could transmit signals. He tried to persuade the Italian government to finance his efforts to that end. When the government rejected this request, he accepted an invitation from a cousin in London, an engineer named Jameson Davis, to con-

Guglielmo Marconi (*left*) and his assistant operate Marconi station, 1899. *Culver Pictures.*

tinue his experiments there. Perhaps, he told himself, the government of Great Britain would support his endeavors.

He arrived in London in February, 1896. By the end of the year, with Jameson Davis's help, he had demonstrated the capabilities of the apparatus to the government agencies most likely to be interested in a new means of communication: the General Post Office, the War Office, and the Postal Telegraph De-partment. During one of these tests his signals traveled almost two miles. From the government's engineers gathered to witness these performances came lavish praise for what he had accom-plished—but no money.

Unable to obtain funds from the government, Marconi and his cousin pro-ceeded on their own. Raising money among friends, they established the Wireless Telegraph and Signal Company in London. Within a few months, at a town in the English countryside, the new company was operating the world's first factory for the manufacture of wireless paraphernalia.

To Guglielmo's delight, one of the company's earliest customers was the government of his own country. In 1897 the Italian navy began using his devices to transfer messages between its coastal stations and its ships at sea.

Marconi went home to supervise these arrangements. Upon his return to England he traveled widely, installing equipment at various places. Gradually, at the same time, he increased the range of its transmissions. In December, 1897, he erected on England's Isle of Wight a 120-foot mast supporting an antenna made of wire netting. He also placed equipment on two excursion steamers operating in the nearby waters. Soon messages were passing regularly from the Isle of Wight to the steamers and back, a distance of eighteen and a half miles.

The early months of 1899 saw the construction by Marconi of wirless stations on opposite sides of the English Channel. One went up on England's Cliffs of Dover, the other at the town of Wimereux, on the coast of France. The successful exchange of messages across this thirty-two-mile gap attracted the attention of newspapers in Europe and the United States. Wireless, the press declared, had come to stay. In the near future people everywhere would be employing it for business and for many other purposes.

At this point Marconi turned his attention to a long-standing difficulty. As a message flew through the air it could be picked up by any antenna. Here was a problem that had to be solved before wireless could be employed on a wide scale. A government, for example, would hesitate to transmit its secrets by wireless, knowing that every Tom, Dick, and Harry capable of constructing a receiving antenna could listen in on them.

Marconi moved quickly. In a matter of weeks he had worked out a process called syntony, or selective tuning. Using this method and the devices that go with it, an antenna can be restricted to the receipt of signals traveling on one wavelength and on one wavelength only. Reporters descended on Marconi, wanting to know what his new invention was all about. What it was about, he informed them in his succinct manner, was that "messages can be read only when the receiver and transmitter are attuned."

In the fall of 1899 he made his first trip to the United States, where he was invited by James Gordon Bennett, publisher of two newspapers in New York City. With a strong transmitter installed on the shores of New Jersey, Marconi followed that year's America's Cup yacht races and wirelessed reports on them to Bennett's newspapers. The great inventor Thomas Alva Edison watched these proceedings with interest. "That fellow's work," he said of Marconi, "puts him in my class. It's a good thing we caught him young."

So effective was the twenty-five-year-old Marconi's coverage of the races that the American navy began using his wireless apparatus.

Back in England he concentrated on what had long since become the great goal of his life: the installation in England and America of transmitters powerful enough to permit the sending of messages across the Atlantic Ocean.

Hearing of this plan, many scientists dismissed it as a pipe dream. Their research indicated that radio waves did not follow the curvature of the earth. Instead, on reaching the horizon they veered off on a tangent into space. One famous scientist said that because the waves moved in this manner the day was near when the planet Earth could communicate with other planets. Never, he predicted, could England and America communicate with one another by wireless, however.

Marconi stubbornly pushed on with what he called "the big thing." His first step was to erect at Poldhu, at the southernmost tip of England, the most powerful transmitter built to date. It consisted of a circle of antenna-bearing masts, each of them 200 feet high. Most of his earlier transmitters had been powered by batteries. This one utilized a big power plant driven by a thirty-two-horsepower oil engine.

In January, 1901, the Poldhu station went on the air and Marconi hastened to the United States. There, among the sand dunes of South Wellfleet, on Cape Cod, Massachusetts, he constructed an array of antennas similar to the setup at Poldhu.

Watching scientists shook their heads. There was no way, they said, that signals produced at Poldhu could travel the almost 3,000 miles to South Wellfleet.

Today we know that the scientists of Marconi's day were wrong about the behavior of radio waves. These radiations do follow the curvature of the earth. But in the fall of 1901, even nature seemed to be bent on supporting the scientists' side of the argument.

On September 17 a gale described by natives of the region as the "worst in living memory" toppled every one of the twenty masts at Poldhu. The following November 26, a storm that roared up the American coast sent all of the masts at South Wellfleet to the ground.

Members of the board of Marconi's company had never had any faith in his "big thing." Now, once again, they urged him to give it up. But Marconi had not brought a new mode of communication into the world by giving up.

He forged on. He saw to it that a less elaborate transmitting system was constructed at Poldhu. As for the American installation, his decision was to abandon South Wellfleet and set up a station at the nearest landfall, which is to say at the point on the coast of North America where the Atlantic is the narrowest.

This happened to be in Canada. On December 6 Marconi arrived at St. John's, a seaport in Newfoundland. With him came his longtime personal assistant, a British engineer and ex-naval petty officer named George Stephen Kemp.

Next day, after a hasty survey of the area, Marconi and Kemp arranged for their equipment to be toted to the brow of Signal Hill, a 600-foot promontory overlooking the harbor of St. John's. Here they arranged their receiving apparatus on a table in the ground-floor room of a hospital. They fastened some antennas to balloons. These they sent aloft by means of kites.

On December 10 Marconi cabled instructions to his engineers at Poldhu. Beginning on the following day, they were to transmit the three dots of the Morse code S at regular intervals for eight hours. They were to continue these transmissions daily until told to stop.

On the morning of December 11 Marconi and Kemp seated themselves at the instrument table on the first floor of the hospital on Signal Hill. They took turns listening. That day all their single set of earphones picked up was static. From time to time one or more of their balloon-borne antennas broke away, carried off by heavy winds, and had to be replaced.

The opening hours of December 12 told the same story: plenty of static and an occasionally escaping balloon. Then suddenly, at 12:30 P.M., Marconi handed the earpiece to his companion and asked quietly, "Can you hear anything, Mr. Kemp?" Mr. Kemp listened—and heard. Cutting through the static was the unmistakable rhythm of the letter S: the three clicks, followed by a pause.

Marconi had achieved his goal. To this day some scientists doubt that he and Kemp heard the letter S at Signal Hill, given the difficult conditions under which they were working. Whether they did so no longer matters. Not quite a year later, operating from another site in Canada, they not only heard the signals from faraway England but recorded their reception on a printing device.

On April 1, 1902, Marconi and his associates established in New York City the company that today, after several name changes, is known as the Radio Corporation of America. By 1908 regu-

Guglielmo Marconi (*right*) and David Sarnoff (*left*) visit the RCA Communication Transmitting Center at Rocky Point, Long Island, New York, 1933. *The Bettman Archive*.

— Marconi to Father Neptune —
I can beat you out any time
if you will only give me a few more of these life boats —

A period cartoon honors Guglielmo Marconi's invention that helped save *Titanic* passengers stranded in lifeboats on April 14, 1912. *General Electric Company—Marconi Limited, London.*

lar transatlantic wireless service was well underway, and the foundation was being laid for the development of radio broadcasting, an outgrowth of wireless telegraphy.

After Marconi's triumphs in Canada his name was a household word everywhere. Numerous honors came his way. In 1909 he received the Nobel Prize in physics. In 1914 his government gave him a seat in the Italian Senate. In 1929 the king of Italy lifted him to the nobility, with the title of marchese.

By this date he had purchased a 220-foot oceangoing steam yacht to which he had given the name *Elettra*. For the rest of his life the *Elettra* was his main home. It also carried the laboratory in which, almost to the day he died, he continued his study of the behavior of radio waves.

His marriage in 1905 to a young Irish aristocrat named Beatrice O'Brien ended in divorce in 1927. His second marriage, on June 12, 1927, was to a beautiful Italian countess named Maria

Cristina Bezzi-Scali. A boy and two girls were born to the first of these unions, a girl named Elettra to the second.

There were sad moments for Marconi during the First World War. He had always thought that his invention, by giving the countries of the Earth a better means of communication, would further the likelihood of world peace. To see the wireless used for destructive ends in a terrible conflict was disillusioning. In a speech at St. Andrews University in Scotland, he asked, "Have I done the world good, or have I added a menace?"

These were the thoughtful words of a man who has been described as difficult to understand, so oddly contradictory were some of his qualities. He was a creative person, as all inventors are. He was also an excellent businessman, as few inventors are. He got along well with the reporters who were forever dogging his footsteps. He knew how to jolly them into giving his activities favorable press. At the same time, there was about him the aloofness of a born aristocrat. At the building housing his company in London, he would often refuse to ride an elevator with an employee whom he did not personally know.

In 1936 a string of heart attacks incapacitated him for varying intervals. His wife begged him to rest. But the minute he was half recovered, he would return to his studies and experiments. He was in Rome, at a home he kept there, when the final heart attack struck.

This was at five o'clock on the afternoon of July 19, 1937. At 3:45 the next morning, the inventor of the wireless was dead.

Samuel Finley Breese Morse

1791–1872   American artist, inventor, businessman, and politician;
principal developer of the electromagnetic telegraph

Samuel Finley Breese Morse, regularly addressed as Finley by family and friends, crowded four complete careers into his eighty-one years—careers in art, invention, business, and politics. As the American historian Allan Nevins has noted, in three of these careers, "he achieved a distinguished success. Had he never touched a piece of mechanism, he would be remembered as an eminent portrait-painter. . . . Had he never lifted a painter's brush, he would still be famous as the chief figure among the . . . group of Americans who made the electromagnetic telegraph a success."

At Charlestown, Massachusetts, where he began life on April 27, 1791, his father, Jedidiah Morse, was a highly respected figure—pastor of the local Congregational church and author of several books, including the first geography to be printed in America. His mother, Elizabeth Breese Morse, was a granddaughter of Samuel Finley, a president of the College of New Jersey (now Princeton University) and a daughter of a prominent New Jersey jurist.

He was the first of the Morses' children. Ten more followed, but of these only two, both boys, survived beyond infancy.

Finley was the cutup of the family. He was forever on the move, endlessly shifting from one kind of activity to something different. His father urged him to give his attention to one thing at a time. "Hurry, bustle, and agitation," he scolded, "are the never-failing symptoms of a weak and frivolous mind."

Hoping that formal education would tame the lad, his parents sent him, at the age of seven, to the Phillips Academy in nearby Andover, Massachusetts. But Andover would seem to have had little effect on his conduct. The only existing official record of his time there tells us that he received eight demerits for bad spelling and eighteen for whispering in class.

Nor did Yale College in New Haven, Connecticut, succeed in reducing him to the diligent student his parents were looking for. Soon after his enrollment there in his fourteenth year, both the president of the college and Finley's tutor were writing to inform the Morses that their son had an "aversion to study."

Averse to some of his courses he was, but not to all. He was diligent in his attendance at lectures on electricity, thus accumulating some of the scientific knowledge that would stand him in good stead later on. Back in Andover he had found in the painting of pictures a relief from the academic subjects that bored him. At Yale he picked up a fair amount of pocket money by doing portraits of his fellow students. By 1810, when he received his degree, he had made up his mind to be an artist.

His parents would have preferred his becoming a writer of books, like his father. But when two of the best artists in America assured them that Finley had talent, they agreed to send him to England to be trained. There, during the four years beginning in the fall of 1811, he acquired the rudiments of the profession that would dominate his life for about three decades.

It is clear from *The American Leonardo*, Carleton Mabee's biography of Morse, that of all his endeavors art was the one closest to his heart. It was also marked, as were his other careers, by struggle and misfortune.

Even after he had become one of the best-known painters in America and the founder and president of the New York City-based organization now known as the National Academy of Design, he was hard put to make a decent living from his art.

He spent endless hours at his easel. It was not uncommon for him to begin work at the first light of morning. Most days he labored on until darkness, or until the brush dropped from a hand quivering with exhaustion. He traveled ceaselessly, staying for varying intervals wherever there were people interested in getting their portraits made.

On September 29, 1818, he married Lucretia Pickering Walker, a dark beauty from Concord, New Hampshire. Sometimes the two of them and the

Samuel F. B. Morse, photographed by Matthew Brady. *The Bettman Archive*.

children born to their union resided in shabby boardinghouses wherever Finley happened to be working. More often than not he traveled alone, and Lucretia and the children lived with his parents—first at Charlestown and then, after Finley's father had retired from the ministry, in New Haven.

After his marriage, Finley's foremost ambition was to accumulate enough money to purchase a home where he and his family could be together. Though his portraits of many notable Americans, President James Monroe among them, were everywhere acclaimed, he found this a difficult goal to attain. By 1826, when a generous commission from the government of New York City enabled him to rent a house in that city, his wife was dead. So was his father, and Morse's work schedule continued to be so time-consuming that he had to leave the children with their grandmother in New Haven. One can appreciate the bitterness underlying his statement to a friend that to be an artist in America was to live the life of "a beggar."

From time to time he abandoned his studio long enough to engage in activities unconnected with his painting. He helped in the establishment of two long-lasting New York newspapers, the *Observer* and the *Journal of Commerce*. Twice he ran unsuccessfully for mayor of that city, each time as the candidate of a political faction known as the Native American Democratic Association.

The Nativists, as the members of this group were called, wanted the country's immigration laws altered so as to make it difficult for lower-class Europeans to enter the United States and become citizens. Morse's advocacy of this position brought charges from some New Yorkers that he was a bigot. So did his frequently advanced contention that the Roman Catholic Church constituted a "conspiracy" against the democratic way of life. Of his major careers, the venture into politics is the only one that can be described a failure.

A three-year period beginning in 1829 found him again in Europe. On his previous stay there he had confined himself to England. This time he traveled widely.

In Paris he spent time with the Marquis de Lafayette, the Frenchman whose contributions to the winning of the American War of Independence had won him and his direct descendants honorary citizenship in the United States. Back in the mid-1820s, Morse had done a portrait of the French nobleman, and the two had become close friends.

In Italy he haunted the art galleries of Rome and elsewhere, studying the old masters and copying some of them.

Though he was unaware of it at the time, the additional training in art picked up in this manner would be put to little use. En route home aboard the sailing packet *Sully,* Morse encountered information that would inspire the best remembered of his careers—the one that resulted in the first successful electromagnetic telegraph, along with the so-called Morse code, with which telegraphers of the future would send messages speeding over electricity-carrying wires.

On the *Sully* Morse fell in with a group of men interested in finding uses for the mysterious force called electricity. These fellows talked of recent discoveries by scientists having to do with the relationship between magnetism and electricity. These matters had interested Morse since his student days at Yale. He listened carefully to what was being said.

One member of the group posed an interesting question: Did the rate at which electricity passed through a wire become slower as the wire became longer?

Some of the men had looked into this subject. Their answer was no. Even if the wire extended for many miles, the current flowing through it would do so at the same lightninglike speed from beginning to end.

"If this be so," said Morse, "and the presence of electricity can be made visible in any desired part of the circuit, I see no reason why intelligence might not be instantaneously transmitted by electricity to any distance."

Morse was not the first person to express this possibility, but at the time he spoke he thought he was. His biographer Mabee suggests that had he known that he was mouthing an old idea he might have done nothing about it.

Instead, enchanted by the belief that he had dreamed up something new, he began at once sketching in a notebook the elements of the telegraphic system that to this day is being used around the world.

In the system concocted by Morse, an electric current is set up by using only a single overhead wire and employing the Earth as the other conductor to complete the circuit. Signals are sent by making and breaking the current in this circuit with the receiving instrument, activated by an electromagnet.

By November, 1832, when the *Sully* docked at New York, Morse had pictured on paper much of his system and had started work on what would become known as the Morse code. By this time, too, he had decided to start converting his ideas into a working apparatus. "Well," he said to the captain of the vessel as he left it, "should you hear of the telegraph one of these days as the wonder of the world, remember the discovery was made on board the good ship *Sully*."

But planning the telegraph was one thing; constructing the necessary machinery and stringing the necessary wires was something else. For three years his time was occupied by other matters, some connected with his painting, some with his ill-fated political endeavors.

When in 1837 he got down to steady work on his invention, he realized that it required more skills than any one person had. Presently he was taking on partners, eventually acquiring three of them in all.

The year 1838 found him and his partners staging demonstrations, showing how the telegraph functioned, to increasingly larger crowds, in Morristown, New Jersey; Philadelphia, Pennsylvania; New York City; and Washington, D.C.

People coming to watch the new contraption at work at the Capitol building in Washington were awed by what they saw. "Where will improvement and discovery stop?" one of them asked. "Time and space are now annihilated," another exclaimed.

By 1842 Morse and his co-workers had patented their invention in France, England, and America. By this time, too, a committee of the House of Representatives in Washington was considering a bill calling for the United States government to appropriate $30,000 for the construction of a telegraphic circuit capable of flashing messages back and forth between two points some forty or more miles apart.

December, 1842, found Morse in Washington, lobbying for this measure. Day after day he buttonholed his friends in Congress, begging them to see to it that the telegraph bill was brought to the floor of the House and voted on.

When he was not talking to friends he sat in the gallery of the House, waiting—and waiting. He had put all the money he had into this effort to obtain the blessing of the government on his telegraph. If the bill passed all would be well. If not, he would have only a few cents in his pockets after he had paid the bills he had run up during his stay in Washington. With Congress scheduled to adjourn on March 3, 1843, the passing hours grew ever heavier with anxiety.

Not until the last day of the session did the bill come up for final action on the floor of the House. Seventy Congressmen refrained from voting on it, saying that they did not understand what the telegraph was all about. The House vote was eighty-nine for the bill, eighty-three against. That afternoon it went to the Senate, where it passed by a small majority. That evening it was signed by President John Tyler, and Morse gladly took up the work of supervising the erection of a telegraphic system between the national capital and the city of Baltimore, Maryland, forty miles away.

By May 24, 1844, the telegraphic link between Washington and Baltimore was in working order. In Washington that morning Morse sat down before some instruments installed in a chamber of the Capitol building then used by the Supreme Court. In Baltimore two of his assistants manned similar instruments in a railroad warehouse on a downtown street.

Months before Morse had asked Annie Ellsworth, daughter of Henry L. Ellsworth, head of the United States Patent Office, to select the first thought to be transmitted over the world's first intercity telegraphic system.

Going to the Bible, Annie had found a stirring sentence in the Book of Numbers, chapter twenty-three, verse twenty-three: "What hath God wrought!" As Morse sent these words clicking over the wire in the code he had invented, the age of the telegraph began.

For years he had hoped that once his system was perfected, the federal government would take it over. With this in mind, he offered to sell the government his share in the patent for a hundred thousand dollars. Only after it was clear that the government was not interested did Morse and his associates begin setting up the telegraph companies that were to make most of them rich.

On August 10, 1848, Morse took as his second wife a distant cousin named Sarah Elizabeth Griswold. Born and reared in Utica, New York, Sarah was young (twenty-one years her husband's junior), beautiful, and deaf.

As an artist Morse had labored in vain to provide a home where he, his first wife, and their three children could be together. Now, as a successful businessman, no such problem confronted him. For himself and Sarah and the six children born to their marriage there was a town house on Twenty-second Street near Madison Square in New York City and a country home on the banks of the Hudson River a short distance south of Poughkeepsie, New York.

Built in the style of an Italian villa, the country house occupied a hundred-acre estate known as Locust Grove. Here the family passed most of its summers. Here on most mornings Morse rose at six-thirty and was at work in his study by eight o'clock.

Seated at a large oak desk in this half-octagonal room surrounded by a latticed

A photograph of an early telegraph office. *Brown Brothers.*

veranda, he took care of his correspondence. Some of his letters dealt with his telegraphic enterprises, others with his strong political leanings.

He deplored the rise of abolitionism, the movement in some of the Northern states prior to the Civil War aimed at the emancipation of the slaves. Even during the war years he was an active proponent of slavery, a copperhead, as Northerners favorable to the cause of the South were labeled.

Having completed his letters by lunchtime, he usually spent the summer afternoons on the grounds of Lo-cust Grove. He talked with the farmer hired to till the land. Or he played with the flying squirrel he had taught to perch on his shoulder, eat out of his hand, and sleep in his pocket.

If his proslavery views annoyed some of his neighbors, his interest in the rights of women—what today we call feminism—endeared him to others. In 1851 he gave a thousand dollars to a female seminary in the Midwest. In 1865 he was one of the several men responsible for the establishment in Poughkeepsie of Vassar Female College, now known as Vassar College.

Civilian linemen string telegraph wire for the Union Army near Brandy Station, Virginia, 1864. *Brady Collection / The Library of Congress.*

By the close of 1846 almost 1,300 miles of telegraph lines had been strung in the United States, and like many an inventor before him Morse had to go to court in an effort to stop other businessmen from building and selling a telegraphic apparatus similar to the one he had developed. Numerous battles had been fought in numerous courtrooms when in 1854 the Supreme Court of the United States ruled that Morse was indeed the inventor of the system bearing his name.

Few American inventors have been as lavishly honored as Morse. Nor did these honors cease when in 1866, after years of effort, another American, Cyrus W. Field, succeeded in laying wires under the sea and began cable (telegraphic) service between North America and Europe on a regular basis.

Ordinarily, even the greatest of heroes has gone to his grave before his admirers install a statue of him in some public place. Not Morse. He was very much alive when on June 10, 1871, the telegraphers of America, grateful for the employment he had given them, unveiled a statue of him in New York City's Central Park.

To be sure, his days were coming to an end at this time. In March of 1872 an attack of neuralgia followed by pneumonia sent him to his bed in the family home in New York. The pastor of his church in the city came to see him. Said Morse, looking up from his pillows, "The best is yet to come." He was, all his life, a deeply religious man.

The attending doctor tapped him on his chest. "This is how we doctors tele- graph," he said. "Very good," said Morse. These were his last words.

"As he lay on his bed in fever," his biographer Mabee writes, "it seemed to his friends that he was very hand- some," with his waist-length white beard and flowing white hair. The friends thought they saw "the light of heaven" in his eyes.

On April 1 he recognized his wife for a second. All he could do was smile. On April 2, 1872, he was dead.

Isaac Merritt Singer

1811–1875   American actor, inventor, and industrialist; improver of the sewing machine

Isaac Merritt Singer had no desire whatsoever to be an inventor. In his eighteenth year he worked for four months in a machinist's shop in Rochester, New York. There he made a discovery: He had a remarkable pair of hands. He could make almost anything. But making things didn't interest him. He dreamed of one thing only: He wanted to be an actor.

Today some actors make a lot of money, but many do not. In Isaac's day, most did not.

For years he struggled to become a star on the American stage. When he went broke, which was regularly, he picked up a job somewhere, normally at the nearest machine shop. He kept it long enough to catch up with his bills. Then he went back to the stage.

Not until his thirty-eighth year did he give up acting, realizing that he could never make a living at it. It was then that he discovered a useful item that had been around in one form or another for three quarters of a century. It was called a sewing machine. Isaac improved it in many ways. Gradually he made it into something that people wanted.

Most inventors are happiest when they are inventing. Not Isaac. "I don't give a damn for the [sewing] machine," he announced. "The dimes are what I'm after." He got the dimes—so many of them that he became one of the richest men of his era.

In life he was lucky. In death he has been lucky, too. He had his faults, but this enormously talented man has been the subject of only one full-scale biography. But that book—Ruth Brandon's *A Capitalist Romance: Singer and the Sewing Machine*—is as exciting as the man himself.

Soon after Isaac's birth on October 26, 1811, in the village of Schaghticoke, near Troy, New York, his family moved 150 miles west to Oswego, New York, on the shores of Lake Erie. His father, Adam, was an immigrant from Germany and a millwright by trade. His mother, Ruth, was of Dutch descent.

In Oswego Isaac passed his childhood without schooling and probably without much attention, as he was the last of a brood of children. In his tenth year his mother divorced his father and took off. His father soon remarried. This action gave Isaac a stepmother whom he seems to have disliked. At any rate, in his twelfth year he, too, took off. His destination was Rochester, New York, a new but already booming town on the soon-to-be-completed Erie Canal near Lake Ontario.

Years later, talking to a newspaper reporter, Isaac described himself as leaving home "without money, without friends . . . possessed of nothing but a strong constitution and a prolific brain." We know not how he survived in Rochester. Ruth Brandon's guess is that one of his older brothers had moved there and took care of him. We do know

A portrait of Isaac Merritt Singer. *Singer Manufacturing Company.*

that he worked at odd jobs in the summer. In this way he earned enough to attend the so-called common school in the winters.

He was serving as an apprentice at a machine shop when, in 1830, Rochester was visited by a troupe of touring actors headed by one Edwin Dean.

Isaac called on Dean and said he would like to join the troupe. It was a brash move on the part of an eighteen-year-old with no acting experience. But Isaac had looks. He was over six feet tall, brawny and blond. He also had charm. As many persons would learn later, he could talk almost anybody into doing almost anything he wanted them to do.

Dean asked him to list his favorite parts. Isaac named the heroes of some of the dramas by William Shakespeare. Dean asked him to recite a few of the lines spoken by one of them. Isaac did so.

A few nights later he was playing the title role in Shakespeare's *King Richard III*. When he shouted the famous line "A horse! A horse! My kingdom for a horse!" a roar of applause arose from the audience. The same thing happened on subsequent nights. In later years, Singer was fond of telling people that he was "one of the best Richards of his day." One newspaper critic thought otherwise. He described Isaac's performance as "crude and bombastical."

When in the late fall of 1830 Edwin Dean and his strolling players left Rochester, Isaac went with them. Thus began the theatrical career that he followed, off and on, for the next eighteen years. When the Dean troupe no longer needed his services, he joined another company. From town to town he traveled, now with this group of strolling players, now with that.

So deep was his affection for the stage that he took any job a company offered. Sometimes he worked as an actor, sometimes as an advance agent or ticket seller, sometimes as both.

When no theatrical company would

have him, he made his living as a laborer, wood turner, or mechanic. It was while working for a canal-building firm in Chicago that he completed and patented his first invention, a machine for drilling rocks. With the $2,000 he received from the sale of his patent he set up a short-lived company of his own.

In 1830 he married fifteen-year-old Catherine Haley of Palmyra, New York. Five or six years later, following a spate of quarrels with her high-tempered husband, she left him.

Meanwhile Isaac had met and proposed marriage to eighteen-year-old Mary Ann Sponsler of Baltimore, Maryland. This was in the spring of 1836. Not until Mary Ann joined him in New York City a few months later did he reveal that he already had a wife. He said that he had asked Catherine for a divorce and urged Mary Ann to live with him until that happened. Reluctantly she agreed. Until the divorce came through, some years later, the two of them called themselves Mr. and Mrs. Singer.

Catherine had given Isaac two children. Mary Ann brought him ten more.

His biographer, Ruth Brandon, tells us that Isaac saw nothing wrong with having more than one wife at a time. He was indifferent to the laws and morals of his society. He was not indifferent, however, to his children. He was fond of most of them. He saw to it that most of them received proper care.

When in 1849 he quit the stage, it was to work at various printing establishments, first in Fredericksburg, Ohio, then in Pittsburgh, Pennsylvania. Desperate for money to support a growing family, he once again turned to inventing. This time he came up with a machine for the carving of wooden type. In April, having obtained a patent on this idea, he moved to New York City.

There a machine-manufacturing firm gave him space in which to construct a model of his new invention. It was almost ready when, on February 4, 1850, a boiler in the building burst, killing sixty-three persons and wrecking the model.

At this point Singer remembered a visit to his workplace by George B. Zieber, a publisher and bookseller in Philadelphia, Pennsylvania. As Ziebert had expressed admiration for his now destroyed model, he got in touch with him. Would the Philadelphian be willing to finance the construction of a second model? Ziebert, captivated by Singer's persuasive ways, was willing. He went one step farther: He moved to New York. From there, a few months later, he and Singer transferred the now partly built second model to Boston, Massachusetts, where better facilities for its completion were available.

In Boston they rented space on the bottom floor of a machine shop owned and run by Orson C. Phelps. Here Singer finished his model, only to learn that there was no market for it. His machine was designed to carve type from wood. But wooden type was on its way out. All over America printers were beginning to use metal type instead.

What to do? Singer began looking for another idea—for some device that people might buy. He found it on an upper floor of Orson Phelps's machine shop. Here workmen were turning out a sewing machine only recently patented by J. H. Lerow and S. C. Blodgett.

Singer examined the Lerow and Blodgett machine. He saw at once why it was not selling well. It was big and heavy and, therefore, expensive. It was so complicated that only a person with some mechanical ability could operate it.

All that could be changed, Singer announced. Already his "prolific mind" was teeming with ways of doing so. But the change would be costly. Would Ziebert and Phelps put up the money?

They did, simultaneously establishing a three-man partnership to be known as I. M. Singer & Company. Then Singer got busy. Within a matter of months he had made some twenty changes in the machine. One was the

An illustration of a woman demonstrating Singer's first machine. From *American Science and Invention: A Pictorial History*, by Mitchell Wilson. New York: Simon & Schuster, 1954.

addition of a foot treadle for operating the device. Another was his invention of a new and more flexible needle.

The Lerow and Blodgett machine could be sold only to tailor shops and garment makers. The Singer machine could be used by women in their own homes everywhere.

The improvements in the machine notwithstanding, I. M. Singer & Company came close to going broke before it could get started. Phelps, discouraged, sold his share to the other partners. Singer and Ziebert quarreled. Singer, as has been shown, could talk anyone into doing anything. He talked Ziebert into selling his share to him, an action Ziebert would have reason to regret bitterly in later years. In the end, Singer & Company became the property of Singer and a New York lawyer named Edward Clark.

The co-owners never got along well. Both Clark and his wife belonged to old and established New York families. In their aristocratic view, Singer was a "nasty brute." As for Singer, he didn't care what others said about him as long as they were useful to him.

To Singer & Company the Clarks' high standing in the community was very useful. So were Edward Clark's sound business sense and legal expertise. One of the company's early problems was that in the midnineteenth century many Americans believed that a woman who handled any kind of machine was not quite respectable. It was Clark who dreamed up a way of squashing this silliness. He offered sewing machines at half price to American ministers for use by their respectable wives.

When in 1853 Massachusetts-born Elias Howe brought suit, charging that he had invented some of the features of the Singer machine, Clark handled the ensuing court battles as adroitly as anyone could have. The courts ruled, however, that Howe's claims were just. From 1854 on, Singer & Company had to pay him a royalty of twenty-five dollars on every machine it sold.

The turning point in the company's fortunes came in the two-year period beginning in 1858. It was at this time that Singer worked out a process previously used only in the manufacture of guns for the United States Army—a process based on the concept of the interchangeability of parts: The parts fashioned for any machine were exactly like those used in all machines and could therefore be used in any or all machines.

Out of this came a revolution in American industry, the rise of what is called mass production. Some students of American manufacturing consider Singer's contribution to this development his greatest invention.

By 1859 the company was prospering, and Singer and his family were living in New York at 14 Fifth Avenue, near Washington Square, then the most fashionable section of the city. There were servants in the house and carriages in the stables. Mary Ann spent the afternoons leaving her calling card at the houses of the Four Hundred, a term that a fop named Ward McAllister had only recently bestowed on New York's high society. The members of the Four Hundred ignored Mary Ann's cards. There was no place for Mr. and Mrs. I. M. Singer in a group that included old John Jacob Astor, who was still eating his peas and ice cream with a knife.

But if the wealthy Singers were never seen in New York's upper-class homes, they were often seen on its streets. At forty-one, Isaac was still an actor at

Scientific American.

THE ADVOCATE OF INDUSTRY, AND JOURNAL OF SCIENTIFIC, MECHANICAL AND OTHER IMPROVEMENTS.

VOLUME VII.]   NEW-YORK, NOVEMBER 1, 1851.   [NUMBER 7.

THE
Scientific American,
CIRCULATION 16,000.
PUBLISHED WEEKLY
At 128 Fulton street, N. Y. (Sun Buildings.)
BY MUNN & COMPANY.
Hotchkiss & Co., Boston.
Dexter & Bro., New York City.
Stokes & Bro., Philadelphia.
Jno. Thomson, Cincinnati, O.
Cooke & LeCount, San Francisco, Cal.
Courtenay & Wienges, Charleston, S. C.
John Carruthers, Savannah, Ga.
M. Boullemet, Mobile, Ala.
Barlow, Payne & Parken, London.
M. M. Gardissal & Co., Paris.
Responsible Agents may also be found in all the principal cities and towns in the United States.
Terms—$2 a-year—$1 in advance and the remainder in 6 months.

RAIL-ROAD NEWS.

Railroads in Europe.

We have rather been consoling ourselves with the idea that our recent railroad enterprise was greater than that of all other nations together. This seems to be a mistake, for the Continent of Europe, mixed up with despotic governments, appears to be as truly alive to the importance of railroad communication, as the most go ahead of all our States. The London Times has recently been publishing statistics of the progress of the different countries, which exhibit these results :—Belgium has 532 miles of railways, 353 of which have been constructed and worked by the State, the remainder by different private companies. The expense of constructing the whole has been £9,575,000, or £18,000 per mile. The annual expenses are 63 per cent. of the receipts, and the profits three and a half per. cent. on the capital. In France there are 1,818 miles of railway under traffic, 1,178 miles in progress, and 577 miles projected. The cost of construction per mile has been £26,832, and the whole expenditure requisite for the completion of the 3,573 miles is estimated at £95,870,735. The average annual net profit on the capital employed does not exceed two and seven-tenths per cent.

In Germany there are 5,342 miles of railway in actual operation, 700 in progress, and 2,414 miles projected. Of the railways in operation, 1,812 miles were within the Prussian territories, and 771 miles in the Dutch Netherlands, the Danish Duchies, and the ex-German Austrian provinces, and therefore only 4,571 miles can be considered as strictly within the Germanic confederation. Two-fifths of these 4,571 miles were constructed and worked by the State, the remainder by private companies. Those in Prussia, however, are all the result of private enterprise. The expense of construction of the 5,342 miles is estimated at £12,500 per mile, being single track only. The working expenses are about fifty per cent. of the receipts, and the net profits are nearly three per cent. In Russia a railway from Warsaw to Cracow, 168 miles in length, is in operation; one connecting Warsaw with St. Petersburg, 683 miles in length; and one of about 400 miles, from St. Petersburg to Moscow, is in progress. A railway for goods from the Wolga to the Don, 195 miles in length, is also contemplated. In Southern Russia a line of railway between Kief and Odessa has been surveyed. In Italy no extensive system of railway has yet been executed. A few lines, diverging from the principal cities, such as Naples, Milan, Venice, Leghorn, and Florence, are alone in operation. In the kingdoms of Sardinia, Spain, and Portugal, railways are only in prospective.

By multiplying £1 by $4.85 we can arrive at the cost per mile of some of these roads. It will be observed that the French lines—the highest—cost $130,135.20 per mile, or nearly three times as much as those of Massachusetts, the cost of which averages $43,781.00, or about £9,000. If the European lines pay at such an enormous cost, need we be afraid !

SINGER'S SEWING MACHINE.---Fig. 1.

Figure 2.

The accompanying engravings represent a perspective view, figure 1. and a side elevation, figure 2, of Isaac M. Singer's Sewing Machine, which was patented on the 12th of last August. A is the frame, made of cast-iron, and B is a cast-iron standard to support part of the working machinery. C is a large driving wheel, worked by the handle, D. E is a small second wheel, driven by C, and works the shaft that vibrates the needle; E' is another wheel to work the shuttle shaft; a, hung in the bearing straps, b b, fig. 2. F is a round plate on the revolving shaft of E ; it has a small roller stud on its inner face fitting into a plate, G, slotted of a heart-shape, to answer the purpose of a cam. This plate, G, is secured to the vibrating arm, H, to which the needle, I, is fastened. The needle performs three strokes up and down during one revolution of the large wheel, C. The thread, J, of the needle is supplied by a bobbin, K, and goes through an eye in the needle, near its point. The cloth is laid flat on the table on the top of a small rough-faced roller S, with the edge to be sewn under the needle. The cloth is held down by a pad, R, acted upon by a coiled spring. P.

this pad is raised by a pin, O, and kept fixed by a catch bar, N, which presses against a shoulder piece, M. There is another shoulder piece, M, to secure the arm, L. of the pad, R in its place. When the cloth is laid on the table, on the wheel, S, the catch, N, is thrown out, and the pad, R, is pressed on the cloth by the spring, P, and is retained firmly in its place but still allowed to be carried forward as it is stitched. The way in which the stitch is performed is by two threads, one supplied with a shuttle, X, the other by the needle, I. With-

out two threads, no good stitch has yet been made by any sewing machine. X is the shuttle carrying a thread which passes from a pirn inside through a small eye on the side next the needle. Now, to form the stitch, which is just like the lock or link of a chain, the thread in the needle, after having passed through the cloth, opens, and the shuttle passes through this loop, therefore, when the needle is drawn back, and the shuttle also to the end of its raceway, the two threads are drawn tight, forming a link around on the cloth, and thus link after link of these threads form the seam. The drawing of the threads tight, and the forming of the loop on the end of the needle for the shuttle is an essential feature to the successful working of these sewing machines. For this purpose the shuttle, X, has a motion to coincide with that of the needle, I, and it is imparted by the same devices, d, fig. 2, being like plate, F, and Y like cam G, only the shuttle runs horizontally at right angles to the needle : e, fig. 2, is the shuttle arm, and Z is the guide or raceway, in which it runs. Thus the motions of the needle and shuttle are explained. The other lettered devices not explained are those belonging to the cloth-feeding motion. The roller, S, that moves the cloth has a rough face, and, rotates, but moves round slowly, only making its movements forward the length of a stitch for every stitch taken ; this is done by catches or pallets, a well known way to do so. These pallets are vibrated by a rocking shaft, f, having a bar, g, on it, which is moved by a cam, e, on the shaft, a. To the small rocking shaft, f, there is secured a suspended lever, h, having a collar, h surrounding said shaft, near its bearing end, i. This lever has a hook, V, on its lower end, to which is affixed a setting screw, W. The hook, V, catches on the hand of an arm, T, which has pallets or catches in a box, that catch into notches on the shaft of the feed wheel, S ; every time, therefore, the lever, h, is vibrated, the feed wheel, S, moves the cloth the exact length of a stitch forward ; the set screw, W, is for regulating the length of feeding the cloth forward to make short or long stitches.

This machine does good work. The patent claim will be found on page 390, Vol. 6. Sci. Am. The agent of this machine is W. H. Shepard, No. 256 Broadway this city.

Things to be Invented.

Among the things that are wanted by everybody is a substitute for pen and ink. It seems that a single instrument ought to perform the function, and that fluid ink may be dispensed with. Cannot some substance be found, simple or compound, that will make an indelible mark upon paper, being hard enough also to hold a fine point ? Or cannot paper be so prepared, without great addition of expense, as to aid the purpose ?

THE CHRISTIAN HAT.—The improvements of the age have reached almost every thing except the abominable flower-pot hat, that so much needs the kindly attention of reformers. We are glad to notice that attention is being directed by some of our public journals to the unreasonableness of a stiff and perspiration-proof covering for the head. The flower-pot hat cannot pretend to beauty ; it is certainly uncomfortable and unhealthy. Why then shall we not seek a substitute ? The hat should be very light and porous, and by all means soft or elastic ; and if any article of our dress calls for especial ornament, the covering of the head speaks most loudly for something to set off the front that slightly distinguishes one man from another. The Turban is probably most susceptible of such modifications as would be most easily adjusted to the purposes required ; and we think some such change of the head-dress would require little urgency to get into general favor.

heart. He loved to be noticed. In the fall of 1859, he designed and had built an elaborate canary-yellow coach large enough to carry him, Mary Ann, and their eight surviving children. Soon the passage through the streets of Singer's "steamboat on wheels," as a local newspaper called it, had become one of the sights of New York City.

In 1860 the relationship between Singer and Mary Ann began to unravel. Isaac's legal wife, the former Catherine Haley, finally gave him a divorce. Mary Ann, delighted, reminded him of his long-ago promise to marry her when this occurred.

Singer refused, saying that to do so would "put me in your power." Shortly thereafter Mary Ann, riding in her carriage down Fifth Avenue, saw Isaac coming up the avenue in his. With him was a young woman.

At home that evening, Mary Ann demanded an explanation. A row ensued. Singer struck her, and Mary Ann headed for the nearest police station.

His arrest was reported in a newspaper on the following day and Singer left the country, to spend several months in Europe. Soon after his return in the summer of 1861, Mary Ann sued him for a divorce, claiming that her twenty-five years at his side made their association a common-law marriage. The judge agreed, and Mary Ann got her divorce.

The proceedings in the courtroom brought to light the astounding nature of Singer's private life. Mary Ann and the children at 14 Fifth Avenue were not his only family. Elsewhere in the city he was supporting at least two other women and five other children. There were stories in the press—not many, however, for the Civil War was underway and for the time being New Yorkers were not much interested in a domestic scandal.

But if the public was indifferent, Singer's partner, Edward Clark, was not. Clark was horrified. He remembered how hard he had worked to make sewing machines respectable. Now here was his partner turning their company into a laughing stock.

In 1863 Clark persuaded Singer to end their partnership. They then converted their business into a public corporation, to be known as the Singer Manufacturing Company and to be owned by the persons who bought stock in it. On July 13 of the same year, Singer married again. His bride was an attractive young widow named Isabella Eugenia Boyer Summerville. Isabella was the daughter of an English mother and French father. She had grown up in Paris, France. It is not known, however, whether it was there that Singer met her or in America, where they were married.

For two years they lived near Yonkers, New York, in a monstrosity of a house called the Castle, which Singer had built for them. But Yonkers bored Isabella, all the more so as high society in that suburban region, as in New York City, would have nothing to do with the Singers. In 1866 they removed themselves to Europe, never to return.

They lived in Paris until 1870. Then the outbreak of the Franco-Prussian War drove them to England. There, on a hill overlooking the English Channel near the port town of Torquay, Singer began the construction of another monstrosity of a house known as the Wigwam. By this time Isabella had given him three boys and two girls, bringing to eighteen the number of off-spring for whom he held himself responsible.

Portions of the Wigwam were still under construction when the family moved in. The huge house was still not quite finished when on July 23, 1875, Singer died, passing on to his last wife and to fourteen of his children a fortune in the neighborhood of thirteen million dollars.

What, as we bring this brief summary of an eventful life to its close, are we to think of its subject? Obviously we have no reason to regard Isaac Merritt Singer as a character to be imitated. But neither can we overlook the significance of his accomplishments, both as an inventor and an industrialist.

George Stephenson

1781–1848   English engineer; principal inventor of the railroad locomotive

Born on June 9, 1781, in Northumberland, a county in the north of England, George Stephenson was the second of the six children of Robert and Mabel Stephenson. At the time of his birth his father was working at a colliery—a coal mine—in the village of Wylam, on the northern banks of the river Tyne.

Coal pits have a way of petering out. When the one at Wylam could no longer be mined, the Stephensons moved to another mining town. Nor was this the last of such moves. There were several more during George's growing-up years.

Wherever the Stephensons landed, their living conditions were much the same. Home was a one-room cottage with unplastered walls, a clay floor, and open beams under the rafters. Life in the village centered around the pit, with its unsightly fringe of heaped-up ashes, coal dust, and slag. Somewhere in the vicinity, as a rule, the smoking chimney of an iron furnace clouded the sky by day and streaked it with lurid flames by night.

At the colliery, George's father tended one of the engines that pumped water out of the pit. His wages were good, as such things went in the English mining industry of his day. But England was at war with the France of Napoleon. Food was in short supply. The smallest necessities—a loaf of bread or a pound of flour, for example—were expensive. There was no money for schooling, and at an early age the Stephenson boys went out to work.

For a time George herded cows for

neighboring farmers. Next came a series of jobs at the colliery. By his seventeenth year he had become an engine tender like his father. His duties, during his daily twelve-hour shift, were to watch the machine and make certain that the pumps it operated were functioning properly.

The machine fascinated him. In the words of his biographer Samuel Smiles, "it became a sort of pet with him." In his leisure hours he would tear it to pieces to study its parts. Soon his familiarity with them was so great that when one of the other machines broke, its watcher would call on George to fix it. The "engine doctor," the other tenders called him.

He in turn pestered them for whatever information they could give him. In this manner he learned that for many years the steam engines used at the collieries could do nothing but draw water from the pit. Now, thanks to improvements affected by a Scottish instrument maker named James Watt, some of the engines could also bring up the coal in heavy baskets known as corves.

George was tending an engine at a pit near the Northumberland town of Newburn Church when a fellow worker told him that descriptions of Watt's wonderful engines could be found in certain books. It was at this point, in his eighteenth year, that George Stephenson decided that the time had come for him to learn to read.

For two years most of his wages went to schoolmasters in the area. From reading he went on to writing and finally to the calculation of sums. At the colliery, during those periods when the machine was operating as it should, he worked out his arithmetic problems on a slate and carried them to the home of his instructor after the workshift had ended.

Inspired by his reading, he attempted some inventing on his own. He tried to construct a perpetual motion machine. Apparently he had not yet read enough, or he would have known that no such device could be made. Still he was not wasting his time. In later years, the engineering processes learned during this effort to do the impossible would help him to create the world's first successful railroad locomotive.

By his twentieth year he had become a brakeman. This was a post of considerable responsibility in the collieries. It meant that he was making more money than his father—enough, he decided, to support a wife.

On November 28, 1802, he and a servant girl named Fanny Henderson were married, and on October 16, 1803, they became the parents of a child—

their only one, as it turned out, a boy whom they named Robert, after his paternal grandfather. George's delight at the arrival of an offspring was succeeded only a few months later by sorrow over the death of his young wife.

Hitherto Fanny and steam engines had filled his heart. Now Robert replaced them both. From this time on, all of George Stephenson's endeavors were aimed at the achievement of what had become the great dream of his life: to see to it that his son received the education and other advantages he had missed.

To earn money for Robert's schooling, he took what today we call moonlighting jobs, work that could be attended to after he had completed his daily stint at the colliery. From his books and his fellow workers he learned everything he could about footwear and timepieces. Soon he was making shoes for people and repairing their clocks and watches.

In 1812 he was promoted to the position of enginewright at his colliery, with a salary of five hundred dollars a year. This was a good salary in those days. One of his tasks was to assemble the crews required to perform various aspects of the work.

In 1812 his country was fighting another of its wars, this one with the United States. It was also moving slowly

A portrait engraving of George Stephenson.

toward a more democratic society. Britons everywhere were taking their politics seriously. Those who wanted more democracy called themselves Whigs. Those who wanted things to remain as they were called themselves Tories. Obviously, Stephenson understood his countrymen well. When the time came to put together a crew, he laid down a rule. All the members of one crew must be either Whigs or Tories. As he pointed out to the owners of the mine, if some were Whigs and some Tories, no work would get done.

He was functioning as enginewright

at the extensive coal works in the Northumberland town of Killingworth when in 1813 he began considering the possibility of using steam-fired locomotives to replace the horses then pulling freight wagons over his country's primitive railroad lines. He was by no means the first individual to entertain this vision. Nine years earlier the talented English engineer Richard Trevithick had constructed a locomotive and used it for a time on a tramway in Wales.

To function dependably, Trevithick's "iron horse" needed many changes. Trevithick himself was aware of this. But he was one of those restless and adventurous souls who loved to move from project to project. By the time Stephenson had finished his first locomotive in Killingworth, Trevithick was making other things in London. By the time Stephenson had put his second locomotive to work on a line serving the Killingworth colliery, Trevithick was on his way to Peru, hoping to make a fortune in the gold mines of that South American country—a fortune that never materialized.

Between the making of his first and second locomotives, Stephenson perfected what today is regarded as one of his most important inventions. He called it the "steam blast." It consisted of a rearrangement of the pipes so that most of the steam, instead of squirting from the sides of the locomotive, es-

caped up the chimney with the smoke—a change that doubled the power of the engine.

Watching his second locomotive at work, Stephenson made a discovery. Before further improving his machine, he must improve the bed on which it ran. Wheels and rails, as he would remark in later years, must be thought of as "one machine," as "man and wife."

In 1816 he began making changes in the bed. A year later his third and most effective engine to date was ready for its first run. For years to come, Puffing Billy, as it came to be known, pulled long lines of coal-filled wagons from the Killingworth colliery to the shipping docks on the banks of the river Tyne.

In 1819 Stephenson had the pleasure of seeing his son, Robert, graduated from an academy in the coal-shipping city of Newcastle-on-Tyne. For the next two years Robert worked as an apprentice to one of the engineers at the Killingworth colliery, while his father looked around for a university to which he could afford to send him. In 1821 he enrolled his son in a series of science courses at the University of Edinburgh in Scotland. Here Robert took first prize in an important mathematical contest. Here, too, he acquired the education that helped make possible a brilliant career in engineering, crowned some twenty years later by his construction of several of the largest railroad bridges in Great Britain and Canada.

For some time the comings and goings of Puffing Billy attracted little attention. Then the owners of a coal mine at Hetton, in Durham County, hired Stephenson to build a locomotive and install a small railway system for their colliery.

This line, like the one at Killingworth, was limited to the hauling of coal for short distances. Still, according to his biographer Smiles, its opening on November 18, 1822, was a "large step" toward the adoption throughout England of locomotive-using railroads. The year 1825 saw a still larger step, the completion between two Durham-County towns of a much longer line. Designed and built by Stephenson and known as the Stockton and Darlington Railway, this was the first public line in England, the first to use locomotives on a regular basis, and the first to carry not only freight but passengers.

By September 25, 1825, when the Stockton and Darlington opened for traffic, its builder had become part owner of a locomotive-making factory in Newcastle-on-Tyne. His fame as an inventor was spreading rapidly. Two of the best-known railroad promoters in the north of England, Edward Pease and William James, traveled to Killingworth to inspect his Puffing Billy. Both pronounced it the finest machine of its

kind ever made. "Here," said James, "is an engine that will, before long, effect a complete revolution in society."

In other circles the comments on Stephenson were less flattering. Several of England's university-educated engineers questioned his abilities. Nothing useful, they asserted, could come from the hands of a self-taught enginewright who still spoke in the guttural and uncultivated accents of the people of his native Northumberland.

There were grumbles in these quarters when a company organized in part by Pease and James selected Stephenson to plan and build what was to become the famous Liverpool and Manchester Railway.

Liverpool, standing on the river Mersey where that stream flows into the Irish Sea, was one of the great seaports of England. To its crowded docks came the cotton grown in the American South and elsewhere. From Liverpool this raw material moved over a network of canals to the big textile-manufacturing city of Manchester, some thirty miles to the east. In recent years the traffic on the canals had become so heavy that the businessmen of the region were complaining of endless delays. Hence their decision in 1825 to link the two cities by rail.

Like the Stockton and Darlington, the Liverpool and Manchester was to be a public line, hauling both merchan-

An engraving of George Stephenson's "Rocket." *Brown Brothers.*

dise and people. To build a railroad of this sort, its sponsors must obtain the permission of the British Parliament. Accordingly, a bill authorizing the construction of the line was submitted. In the spring of 1825 a committee set up to consider its provisions began holding hearings on the bill in the chamber of the House of Commons in London.

When on April 25 Stephenson took the stand to testify in favor of the bill, he knew that he was in for an ordeal. Opponents of the measure were numerous and vocal.

The owners of the network of canals in the Liverpool-Manchester area were against it. They saw the coming of the railroad as a threat to their pocketbooks.

The owners of the land across which the tracks would be laid were against it. To a man, they were convinced that the churning and hissing of passing locomotives would diminish the value of their fields and endanger the livestock grazing upon them.

"Suppose now," a member of the committee said to Stephenson, "one of these engines to be going along . . . at the rate of nine or ten miles an hour, and that a cow were to stray upon the line and get in the way of the engine. Would not that, think you, be a very awkward circumstance?"

Stephenson's dark eyes were twinkling as he answered the question, pro-nouncing his words, as always, in the Northumberland manner. "Yes," he admitted, "very awkward indeed—*for the coo!*"

For three days on the witness stand, he parried a barrage of questions from lawyers and engineers unfriendly to the bill. Many of their queries dealt with a formidable engineering problem.

Lying between Liverpool and Manchester was a huge bog known as Chat Moss. So soft was the sludge filling this area that the lightest machine sank to the bottom when driven into it. How in the world, Stephenson was asked, was he going to put a railroad across Chat Moss?

He patiently outlined his ideas for doing so. First he would drain the bog. Then he would fill it with rock and dirt. He assured his interrogators that the line he was planning, the Chat Moss section included, would be "perfect."

His statements provoked hoots of laughter among the persons on hand to watch the hearings. His questioners voiced their conviction that this self-educated enginewright from Northumberland was "mad." They dismissed his testimony as so much "trash and confusion."

This first attempt to get a law out of Parliament authorizing the railroad failed, but a few months later a second and somewhat altered bill was passed.

At this point Stephenson moved to Liverpool to be near the offices of the company in charge of the railroad. Work on its construction began at once, and by the end of 1826 Chat Moss was a solid mass, capable of supporting heavy locomotives.

Stephenson made no effort to sell his Puffing Billy to the company. Aware that other inventors were fabricating locomotives, he suggested that the company stage a contest with the understanding that, to at least some extent, the winning engine be used on the line.

On October 7, 1829, this contest began at the Liverpool end of the now-almost-completed railroad. Stephenson's entry was known as the Rocket. Designed by Stephenson and built with the help of his son, this four-ton locomotive was superior in every way to any of its inventor's earlier models. On October 14 it was pronounced the winner, and not quite a year later it made its first run from Liverpool to Manchester and back, pulling a long line of freight wagons and passenger coaches at an average speed of thirty miles an hour. Even at this time, as Stephenson well knew, the Rocket was capable of higher speeds. By the time it was retired from the line five years later, it was averaging sixty miles an hour.

The success of the Liverpool and Manchester Railway, formally opened on September 15, 1830, initiated a flurry of railroad construction in all parts of Great Britain. Landowners, fearful that the value of their holdings would drop, discovered that it was flying up instead. As for the sheep and cattle and horses grazing in the fields, these four-footed creatures soon found the "iron horse" easy to live with. By 1842, when Britain's Queen Victoria began making her frequent trips from London to Windsor by train, well over half a million of her subjects were riding the trains every year. Gloriously underway was that romantic and colorful stretch of time known to history as the Age of the Railroad.

For sixteen years after the opening of the Liverpool and Manchester, Stephenson continued working. He made further improvements in his locomotive. He supervised the construction of a number of railroad systems in England and other countries. He helped develop an extensive coal-mining operation in central England. When he retired in 1846, it was to live at Tapton House on the outskirts of the Derby-County town of Chesterfield.

He shared this comfortable domicile, as he had many previous homes, with the daughter of a Northumberland farmer, Elizabeth Hindmarsh, who had become his second wife in 1819. No children were born to this union, but

George Stephenson, his son Robert, and the "Rocket" appear in William Lucas's painting "George Stephenson and Family," 1861. *The Science Museum, London.*

Stephenson lived long enough to see his son, Robert, become a member of the prestigious Institution of Civil Engineers and the occupant of a seat in the House of Commons.

Famous people visited him now. Among them was the American poet and essayist Ralph Waldo Emerson. Coming away from his brief call at Tapton House, Emerson told a companion that George Stephenson "had the lives of many men in him."

Many men in him there may have been, but every one of them embodied the virtues so admired in the days of Queen Victoria: steadiness, diligence, perseverance, and a respect for his "betters" untouched by envy and accompanied by an equally firm respect for himself. Add a dash of genius, and you have the man who at the time of his death on August 12, 1848, could be described, in the words of his biographer, as responsible for "the grandest application of steam power that yet has been discovered."

Joseph John Thomson

1856–1940   British physicist; discoverer of the electron.

Destined to change the course of scientific history, Joseph John Thomson—J.J. to family and friends—grew up in a largely unscientific atmosphere.

Aside from an uncle who dabbled in meteorology, no one in his immediate family or among his known forebears was interested in such matters. In Cheatham Hill near Manchester, England, where he was born on December 18, 1856, and later in Manchester itself, he attended private schools.

Little of a scientific nature was offered at these places, and when J.J. was free to read what he pleased, he turned as a rule to what in his time were called "yellow books," the forerunners of today's detective stories.

His father, Joseph James Thomson, was a descendant of lowland Scots and a dealer in rare and antique books. His mother, Emma Swindels Thomson, was a native of the Manchester area, a bright-eyed little beauty with almost no liking for literature of any sort. Devoted to J.J. and his older brother, she was untidy about her house and so absentminded that it was not uncommon for her to get lost whenever she strayed from the family hearth.

It was the intention of his father that J.J. should become an engineer. That he became a physicist instead can be described as a happy accident.

"In those days," he tells us in his autobiography, *Recollections and Reflections*, "the way of entering the [engineering] profession was to be apprenticed. . . . It was arranged that I should be apprenticed to [a company that made locomotives] . . . but they told my father they had a long waiting list. . . . My father happened to mention this to a friend, who said 'If I were you . . . I should send him while he is waiting to the Owens College.' "

To Owens, to what is now the University of Manchester, he went. This was in his fourteenth year, and when the Owens authorities were informed of his admission they promptly issued a new rule, considerably raising the age at which students could be accepted.

It was at Owens, under a bevy of inspiring professors, that J.J. discovered in himself a love of physics. That he also had a flare for this demanding subject is shown by his refusal, then or later, to use a slide rule to work out the complicated mathematical problems a physicist constantly encounters. Instead, easily and accurately, he worked them out in his head.

When his father died in 1873, his mother moved to a house near Owens, and J.J. continued his studies there until his twentieth year. At this time, at the urging of an Owens professor, he applied for a scholarship to Trinity, one of the several colleges composing England's ancient Cambridge University. His first application was turned down, but a second try succeeded, and in 1876 he became a student at the institution where he would spend the rest of his life.

Following the receipt of his degree four years later his progress was breathtakingly swift. In 1880 he became a fellow at Trinity, a member of its teaching staff. In 1884 he became the Cavendish Professor of Experimental Physics and as such the director of Cambridge's Cavendish Laboratory, one of the world's greatest centers of scientific instruction and research.

It was during his early years in this post that he conducted the most memorable of his experiments: the study of what are called cathode rays, which led him to conclude, that all matter contains particles smaller than the atoms of which they form a part.

What Thomson found in 1897 is what today we call the electron, one of the particles now known to exist inside the atom. "This was not merely a discovery," Britain's Noble-Prize-winning physicist Owen W. Richardson has written. "This was a revolution." For centuries scientists had assumed that what the ancient Greeks called the atom was the smallest substance in nature—the only one that could not be further divided.

Now, as would be said later, J. J. Thomson had in effect "split the atom," proving by his systematic measurement of the masses and other properties of cathode rays that the atom contains within it particles infinitely smaller than itself. As the significance of this finding

Joseph John Thomson at work in his laboratory. *Cambridge University / Cavendish Laboratory, Cambridge, England.*

became apparent, scientists did indeed find themselves in the midst of a revolution. Everywhere they found themselves working in new fields—in branches of what today we call atomic or nuclear physics.

It is not unusual for a scientist of Thomson's caliber to be so absorbed in his experiments as to be indifferent to everything else. Not J.J.; outgoing and congenial, friendly and talkative, he was curious about everything. Nothing delighted him more than a conversation with someone who, although wholly ignorant of science, knew a lot

about literature or business or any line of endeavor with which J.J. was unacquainted.

Residents of the town of Cambridge smiled at his practice of strolling through the commercial sections, peering for lengthy intervals into the shop windows. Often, on seeing there some unfamiliar object, he would hurry into the shop and insist that the owner or an employee tell him what it was all about.

He loved a joke, even when the laugh was on him. Relating an incident on the golf course to some friends, he claimed to have driven his ball against a wind of such strength that the ball not only rose straight up and very high but then fell back over his head and landed on the ground behind him. When after a moment of stunned silence, one of his listeners squawked, "Is that a fact?" J.J. joined in the laughter that followed.

He also loved a party, and it seems to have been at a Cambridge social gathering that he met and fell in love with attractive Rose Elizabeth Paget. They were married on January 2, 1890, and became the parents of two children, a daughter, named Joan, and a son, George, who became a physicist like his father.

J.J. kept his eye on the politics of his time, on current novels, and on what was going on in the London theater. Plants fascinated him. Demanding as his laboratory labors were, he found time for long hikes in the country. On these he searched for unusual botanical specimens, dug them up, and transferred them to his own extensive gardens. Although golf was his only athletic activity, he was an ardent follower of the Cambridge rugby and cricket teams.

His discovery of the electron was but one of his many contributions to the advancement of science. In a series of lectures delivered at Yale University in the United States, he outlined a new theory of light similar to one Albert Einstein would set forth at a later date. His receipt in 1906 of the Nobel Prize in physics honored his research into the ability of gases to conduct electricity.

During his many years as the director of the Cavendish Laboratory he distinguished himself not only as a scientist but also as an administrator and teacher. Making adroit use of student fees, he financed two additions to the laboratory buildings.

Though scientific research lay at the center of his life, he took his teaching duties seriously. Every school day he lectured to beginning students in the morning and to advanced ones in the afternoon. Of the young men and women who came from around the world to be trained by him, seven went on to become winners of the Nobel Prize, his son, George, among them.

He had his limitations. One of them, his inability to carry a tune, probably had no effect on his scientific career. Another, his inability to make things with his hands, might have hampered him severely had he not discovered in one of his laboratory assistants, Ebeneezer Everett, a workman who could put anything together. During their many years together, Everett constructed over five hundred of the special contraptions Thomson needed to conduct his experiments.

With the onset of the First World War in 1914 he became a scientific adviser to the British military and worried about his son, who, having joined his country's army, had marched off to do battle with the Germans. Learning that George was sloshing about in the trenches that laced the battlefields of France, his father advised him to get himself a pair of wooden shoes such as those worn in Holland.

From time to time he entertained the younger Thomson by sharing with him some of the letters he had received in his capacity as an adviser to the military. Only recently, he revealed in July, 1915, a cleaning woman, having encountered an "awful smell" in the course of her work, had written to suggest that it be "bottled up" and sent to the enemy.

At a large meeting of scientists during the war years, Thomson chided the British government for its practice of financing only what is called "applied science," meaning research aimed at achieving some known and useful end. The government, he argued, should also finance "pure science," research carried on with no useful end in mind but only in an effort to understand better the world in which we live.

As an example of the utility of this science for science's sake, Thomson pointed to the discovery of X rays by a German physicist named Wilhelm Conrad Roentgen. Roentgen was simply trying to figure out the then baffling nature of electricity when accidentally—or, as scientists like to say, serendipitously—he came upon some shortwave rays that could be used to peer inside the human body.

No exercise in applied science, said Thomson, had ever done as much for the practice of medicine and surgery as pure-scientist Roentgen's serendipitous discovery of X rays in 1895.

Today this World War I speech by Thomson can be regarded as one of the opening sallies in a campaign that has long since persuaded Great Britain, the United States, and several other countries to fund pure science to a substantial extent.

Following his discovery of the electron, the Nobel Prize was only one of the numerous honors to come to J.J. In 1908 he was knighted, becoming Sir Joseph John Thomson. In 1915 he was elected to a five-year term as president of the Royal Society, foremost of England's scientific organizations. In 1918 the prime minister of Great Britain offered him the directorship of Trinity College, with the title of master.

His acceptance of this post necessitated his resignation as head of the

Joseph John Thomson (*left*) photographed with F. B. Jewitt of Bell Laboratories. *AT&T Archives*.

Cavendish Laboratory, but during the ensuing years he continued to spend time there, pursuing a variety of experiments.

The mastership of Trinity put him and his family in possession of a handsome house, standing on the banks of the river Cam and known as Trinity Lodge. Here, save for a long stay in the United States for scientific purposes, he spent his remaining years. It was here that he died, on August 30, 1940.

Burial was in Westminster Abbey, in London, close by the graves of other great English scientists, Isaac Newton and Charles Darwin among them. Tributes to him appeared in newspapers around the world. Thomson, wrote the gifted English historian G. M. Trevelyan, "more than any other man, was responsible for the fundamental change in outlook which distinguishes the physics of this [the twentieth] century from that of the last."

James Watt

1736–1819   Scottish instrument maker and self-educated scientist;
improver of the steam engine

Like many great inventions, the steam engine came into existence gradually.

The ancient Greeks, those living shortly before or shortly after the birth of Christ, understood the principle behind such a machine. They saw that the steam created by boiling water occupies far more space than the water it replaces. It followed that this expanding force could serve many purposes, if only a machine could be developed to control and direct it.

One of the ancient Greeks, a mathematician known as Hero of Alexandria, designed several such contrivances. It was the appearance in Europe of a book by Hero illustrating these devices that, in 1575, called the attention of inventors in that part of the world to the possibilities of steam as a source of mechanical energy. By January 10, 1736, when James Watt was born in the seaport town of Greenock, Scotland, a workable steam engine built by an English blacksmith named Thomas Newcomen had been around for twenty-four years.

What was to bring fame and fortune to Watt was his construction many years later of a far superior steam engine. Newcomen's contraption was crude and expensive to operate. It drew water from England's coal mines. But that's all it could do. On the other hand, Watt's engine, as eventually perfected, could run entire factories. It could power automobiles, steamboats, railroad locomotives, and many other devices.

James Watt was the sixth of the eight children born to James Watt, Sr., and

Young James Watt toys with his family's teakettle in Marcus Stone's painting "Watt Discovering Condensation of Steam." *Galerie George, London / The Bridgeman Art Library.*

his wife, the former Agnes Muirhead. Death and illness shadowed James's growing-up years. His four older brothers and one older sister died in infancy. Neither his younger brother nor his younger sister lived to become an adult. James himself was sickly.

Even after his childhood ills had disappeared, thanks to his mother's untiring care, he was often unwell. At any rate, he thought of himself as unwell.

During much of his life the improver of the steam engine was what we call a hypochondriac, frequently complaining of ailments, both real and imaginary.

Kept home by ill health, Jamie, as he was known in the family circle, received his early education from his mother. When in his tenth or eleventh year she enrolled him in a neighborhood school, his clumsiness in the games popular with the other students won him the reputation of being stupid. Sensing that her unathletic boy was in the wrong place, Mrs. Watt transferred him to a school where study came first. Here Jamie's love of reading and his quickness at learning mathematics carried him to the head of his class.

After school and during the holidays, he toiled in one of the several workshops owned by his father, a general merchant, cabinetmaker, and undertaker. Provided with his own workbench and a forge, Jamie repaired ships' compasses and other nautical items. To his labors he brought a fastidiousness that impressed his fellow craftsmen. "Jamie," they said of him, "has gotten a fortune at his fingers' ends."

His mother's death in 1753 was a blow, and another followed when his father's previously prosperous businesses began to crumble. For years the senior James had looked forward to putting Jamie in charge of his mercantile affairs. Now that those affairs were failing, he decided it would be better for his son to learn a trade of his own. With this in mind he sent the boy to the nearby Scottish city of Glasgow to work under an experienced mechanic. By the time young Watt returned home a few months later, he had acquired the rudiments of instrument making.

In 1754 he traveled to London in search of work, only to find on reaching the British capital that he was up against the craft-guild system. Then, as had been the case in Europe for hundreds of years, a craft guild consisted of a number of so-called journeymen—men capable of performing certain kinds of skilled labor—banded together to keep wages and standards high. Only after undergoing a lengthy period of training known as an apprenticeship could one become a journeyman and a guild member. Only a guild member could get a job as an instrument maker in London.

These conditions put Jamie in a desperate fix. On the one hand he did not yet have enough qualifications to be a journeyman and a guild member. On the other hand his age—he was eighteen—made him too old according to guild regulations to sign on as an apprentice.

For weeks he tramped the streets of London, seeking employment. Finally a master clockmaker defied the rules of his guild by accepting him as an apprentice for one year. As apprentices received no wages, Jamie supported himself by taking on extra jobs for pay around the edges of his long working day. It is a measure of his skill and stamina that in twelve months, this killing schedule notwithstanding, he mastered a craft that ordinarily required an apprenticeship of from three to four years.

It was an exhausted young man who

returned to his native Greenock in the summer of 1756. From there, after a few months of rest at his father's home, he headed for Glasgow. He was a journeyman now, and in that large and bustling industrial center on the banks of the river Clyde ample work awaited him.

By August, 1757, he was ensconced in a room at the University of Glasgow with the title of mathematics instrument maker to the university. By the end of 1763 he was owner or part owner of additional workshops, specializing in the repair of musical instruments and mechanical gadgets.

The steam engine entered his life in 1764 when one of Thomas Newcomen's engines was brought to him for repair. In scientific and engineering circles the faults of the Newcomen engine were well known. It worked slowly. It burned an excessive amount of fuel, making it costly to operate. Examining Newcomen's device in one of his shops, Watt quickly saw the reasons for these flaws.

In Newcomen's apparatus, the steam let into the cylinder pushed a piston to one of the cylinder's ends. To drive the piston to the other end, cold water was sprayed into the cylinder. This cooled the steam to water, and as water takes up much less space than steam, the pressure of the air on the other end of the piston drove it back, ready for the next intake of steam.

To perform its work, in other words, Newcomen's engine was first heated and then cooled. Almost at once Watt saw that for a steam engine to work efficiently, the cooling cycle must be eliminated. Somehow the engine must be so reconstructed that its cylinder remained hot all of the time.

But how was this to be done?

The answer to this question came to Watt during a Sunday stroll in one of Glasgow's parks. It was "a fine Sabbath afternoon," he later told a friend. "I had entered the Green by the gate at the foot of Charlotte Street. . . . I was thinking upon the engine . . . and had gone as far as Herd's house when the idea came into my mind, that as steam was an elastic body, it would rush into a vacuum, and if a communication was made between the cylinder and an exhausted vessel [the vacuum], it would rush into it and might there be condensed without cooling the cylinder."

What Watt dreamed up on that "fine Sabbath afternoon" was a way of improving the steam engine by adding to it a new element, a condenser in the form of a vacuum, thus making it possible for the piston to move up and down in its cylinder without the insertion of cooling water.

To get a picture of an improved steam engine in his head was one thing. To build one was something else. It took

A portrait of James Watt. *Culver Pictures.*

him four years, from 1765 to 1769, to bring the engine he had in mind to the point where he could obtain a patent on it. It took him six more years to bring it to the point where models of it could be erected and offered for sale. In all, ten years of labor went into its making, ten years of trial and error, of endless tinkering and experimenting. "Of all things in life," he once said to a good friend, "there is nothing more foolish than inventing."

In the beginning one of his major problems was scientific in nature. Greatly aided by Dr. Joseph Black, a brilliant young chemist at the University of Glasgow, Watt conducted a series of experiments with a kettle, a flask, and a lead pipe.

Out of these exertions came his discovery of what is known as the theory of latent heat. This discovery enabled him to determine with sufficient accuracy the extent to which steam produced by boiling water continues to absorb heat even though no further rise in temperature occurs. Watt's acquisition of this knowledge was crucial to the accomplishment of his ends. We have the word of his able biographer L. T. C. Rolt that without it his steam engine could not have been built.

In Rolt's opinion, what made James Watt so successful as an inventor was that he brought to his labors not only a great dexterity with his hands but also a tireless determination to grasp the scientific principles pertinent to his efforts. In his day he was thought of as a *millwright.* No one called him an *engineer,* because in the eighteenth century that word, as we now employ it, referred only to military engineers, most of them bridge or canal builders. The word *engineer* was then more commonly used to describe a "traitor" or a "con man," meaning one out to get other people's money by illegal means. Today, of course, we think of Watt as a great engineer. He was also a great scientist.

Another difficulty in the beginning was the scarcity of tools precise enough to achieve what he had in mind. Before he could improve the steam engine, he had to improve the tools needed for that purpose. Years went into his search for the sort of packing material that could provide the steam-tight fit that the piston of his engine required. Again and again, confronted by what for a time seemed insurmountable problems, he considered laying down his tools and giving up.

His steam engine might never have come to fruition had it not been for the constant encouragement given him by Joseph Black and other scientists at the University of Glasgow. Like the craftsmen employed by Watt's father,

James Watt's steam engine. *Brown Brothers.*

these men saw the "fortune" at Jamie's "fingers' ends."

The fortune was indeed there, but Watt was often hard put to believe in it. He was given to dismaying shifts of mood. Some days he was confident to the point of being boastful about his abilities. Other days found him convinced that he had no abilities and would never accomplish anything.

Many of the delays that plagued his progress as an inventor were an outgrowth of traits in his own personal makeup. One gathers that he never forgot the decline of his father's once thriving businesses. Much of his life the improver of the steam engine was tormented by the possibility that he, too, might go broke.

His fears on this score grew even greater after July 16, 1764, when he took as his wife a young cousin named Margaret Miller. Shortly thereafter he sold his workshops in Glasgow to accept positions as a land surveyor and canal planner in sections of Scotland and England. So time-consuming were these labors that for months at a time all work on the steam engine ceased. Repeatedly his scientist friends urged him to devote less energy to bread-and-butter jobs and more to his experimental works. Margaret joined in these pleas, but nothing either she or his friends said could persuade Watt to do anything likely to threaten the well-being of his wife and children.

What at first seemed like an answer to his difficulties came in 1765. That year Dr. John Roebuck, a physician practicing in Birmingham, England, agreed to help finance Watt's experiments in return for a share of whatever money his engine brought in after it was perfected. Unfortunately, Roebuck's faith in Watt's ability to complete his invention was shaky. His contributions to Watt were small and tardily delivered. Once a sum of money he had promised never arrived, and Watt had to pay for expensive tools and material out of his own almost empty pockets.

So matters stood with the hard-pressed inventor when, during a trip to Birmingham in the summer of 1768, he was introduced to a forty-year-old industrialist named Matthew Boulton. A man of great wealth and vision, Boulton had erected at Handsforth Heath on the outskirts of Birmingham a large plant known as the Soho Manufactory. It was his intention that this plant should stand as a model to other factory owners in the region. Labor conditions in most Birmingham plants were dismal and dangerous. Not so at the Soho Manufactory. There a thousand men and women worked in safe and comfortable surroundings.

It was Boulton's belief that good conditions made good workers and that good workers turned out good products. Time proved him correct. Soho Manufactory's numerous creations—buttons, buckles, sword hilts, toys, clocks, and ornamental articles in silver of every description—were everywhere in demand.

Boulton and Watt hit it off at once, though no two men could have been more unlike. Boulton was as cheerful as a sunny day. Watt was prone to long spells of depression. To Boulton the recurrent problems of life were simply challenges to be met and conquered by time and patience. To Watt even the smallest problem was a signal that the doom of mankind was at hand.

Boulton listened attentively to Watt's plans for completing his steam engine.

He decided at once that this solemn young Scot was about to give the world a machine of enormous value. He offered to become Watt's financial backer. He realized, as he wrote later, that what Watt needed was "a midwife to ease you of your burthen and to introduce your brat into the world." He said that he stood ready to provide Watt with all the money and tools he needed to carry through the task he had set for himself.

Watt knew that he was talking to a man whose promises could be trusted. But he had signed an agreement with Dr. Roebuck, and it was not in his nature to go back on his word.

He reluctantly turned down Boulton's generous proposition. But Boulton kept after him. From time to time Watt and his wife were guests of Boulton and his wife at their handsome house overlooking the Soho Manufactory. Soon the two men were corresponding regularly. Watt was providing Boulton with step-by-step reports of his progress with the engine when in 1773 Dr. Roebuck's business ventures fell into disarray, making it impossible for him to continue his assistance to Watt. At this point Watt became free to accept Boulton's offer, and the most productive partnership in history between a great inventor and a great businessman got underway.

What remains to be said of James Watt is a success story, blurred now and then by the tragedies from which none of us is exempt. In 1773 he lost his wife. Our knowledge of Margaret Miller is fragmentary. It is clear, however, that Jamie loved her deeply, writing a friend soon after her death that he now dreaded going home because his "welcomer" was no longer there.

It is also clear that his second marriage in 1776 to Ann MacGregor, daughter of a Glasgow dyer, was the action of a man anxious to provide a mother for the children his first wife had given him. To this second union two more children, a boy and a girl, were born.

Ann MacGregor Watt was a relentless housekeeper. So bent was she on keeping the house immaculate that the family dogs were trained to wipe their paws on a mat before coming in. On one occasion Watt moved his workshop from a lower floor to the attic. There, behind closed doors, he could make all the mess he wished and come and go without endlessly changing his clothes.

Watt was thirty-eight when in May, 1774, he and Boulton joined forces, setting up within the Soho Manufactory a company known first as Boulton and Watt and then as Boulton, Watt and Sons, to make and sell models of the steam engine following its completion two years later. Readily appreciated is the statement of an unidentified En-

glish wit that the year 1776 saw the outbreak of two revolutions, one very bad for England and one very good for everyone. The bad one deprived Great Britain of thirteen of her fourteen thriving colonies in the New World and brought into being the United States of America. The good one gave mankind the engine that at long last liberated industry from its dependence on water- or horsepower.

During a five-year period beginning in 1776, almost three hundred models of the improved steam engine were made and sold. So great was the sale to the owners of the tin mines in that strangely beautiful section of England called Cornwall that Boulton built a home there from which he and Watt could supervise the installation and operation of their machines. For some years the two men and their families took turns living in it.

Watt was rich now, but the habit of feeling that everything was about to go wrong persisted. Indeed, the better things got, the more things he found to worry about.

It was Boulton's job to jolly him out of these dark spells. On one occasion his suggestion was that Watt go home and say his prayers, after which he would realize that everything was going to come out all right.

It was Boulton, too, who talked Watt

into improving his improved steam engine. For several years Watt's engine, like Newcomen's engines before them, could do nothing but pump water out of mines. Watt was content with things as they were. But once again Boulton kept after him. It is the bright and genial Birmingham businessman whom we must thank for the changes in the steam engine that after 1781 enabled it to do many, many things, ranging from the driving of all the machinery in a factory to the propulsion of a steamboat.

To Watt home was now no longer a dwelling in Scotland. It was a house he had built in the vicinity of Boulton's home on Birmingham's Handsforth Heath. Here he passed his last years.

One of his sons once said that his father never knew the pleasures of childhood. Now rich and famous and the recipient of many honors in both England and France, he knew the pleasures of old age.

He even became less of a worrier. To be sure, old habits die hard. From time to time he was heard to predict dire happenings. But with the passing years these bouts of dread gradually dwindled away.

Science had always been his great love. Now he had time to read and learn; time to dabble at small inventions that for him were easily achieved; time to attend the meetings of a Birmingham group of scientists known as the Lunar Society and numbering in its ranks some of England's finest minds. To sit down with the "learning lunatics," as the members of the group called themselves—to participate in their discussions—these to the aging inventor from Scotland were the greatest joys life could offer.

We have portraits of him in his late years: tall and spare, with stooping shoulders, a shock of white hair receding from his forehead, heavy brown eyebrows, and keen gray eyes. And we have from the English poet William Wordsworth this summary of his career:

I look upon him considering both the magnitude and the universality of his genius, as perhaps the most extraordinary man that this country ever produced; he never sought display, but was content to work in that quietness and humility, both of spirit and outward circumstances, in which alone all that is truly great and good was ever done.

Almost to the end, his health held up. The summer of 1819 found him on a visit to London. It was on his return to Birmingham that the last illness struck. Death came peacefully on August 19.

The American poet Walt Whitman once remarked that the steam engine, like the stars and stripes, could be a symbol of the United States. What

Whitman had in mind was the amazing growth of manufacturing in his country following the close of the Civil War in 1865. This process began in England a century earlier and then spread to America and other countries. At the start of this hundred years of drastic social and economic change, both England and America were agricultural societies, with most people living on farms and tending the soil. By the end of it, both nations—and several others—were industrial societies with most people living in ever-enlarging cities and working in factories.

Today some historians speak of this development as the Industrial Revolution. Largely responsible for its coming, Watt's steam engine is a striking example of how a single invention can alter the course of history.

Eli Whitney

1765–1825   American mechanical engineer; inventor of the cotton gin, the milling machine, and a prime mover in the development of the tools and methods of mass production that were to make his country a great industrial nation

Eli Whitney grew up in an America struggling with a problem created by its victory over Great Britain in the conflict we think of as the American War of Independence, or the War of the Revolution.

Americans plunged into that war in 1776 with two large hopes in mind. One was a longing to govern themselves. The other was a belief that, once freed from the apron strings of Mother England, they would become overnight citizens of one of the richest nations on earth.

Peace in 1783 brought them the right to govern themselves, but it did not bring them the instant prosperity they had anticipated.

To be sure, the sources of wealth they were counting on could still be seen all around them: endless acres of food-producing land waiting to be farmed; mammoth forests waiting to be converted into lumber and fuel; innumerable waterfalls waiting to be transformed into power for the running of mills and factories; and giant bogs waiting to be relieved of their rich deposits of iron, to say nothing of many other minerals waiting to be discovered.

But to turn these resources into wealth required far more people than the new United States could muster. In the years following the close of the war, the population numbered only some four million persons, thinly scattered over thirteen states.

There were simply not enough people to till large sections of the land, cut down large sections of the forests, dig up enough iron and other minerals, and build and operate a large number of mills and factories.

From the beginning, thoughtful American leaders—Alexander Hamilton prominent among them—realized that to become wealthy America must seek new ways of production, methods that depended less on manpower and more on the creation of labor-saving tools. Eli Whitney, writes his biographer Constance McL. Green, "performed a vital service for his country" by providing it with several of these badly needed tools.

Born on December 8, 1765, on a farm near the town of Westboro in Worcester County, Massachusetts, he was the first of the four children of Eli Whitney and Elizabeth Fay Whitney. He was only five when his mother fell ill, becoming a largely bedridden invalid for the remaining seven and a half years of her life.

On young Eli, as the eldest child, fell much of the burden of bringing up his sister, Elizabeth, and his brothers, Benjamin and Josiah—a burden he carried until his father remarried two years after his mother's death.

Such responsibilities at an early age might have broken another boy. Not Eli. We have the word of his sister that he was not only a good "parent" but a good-natured one. As Elizabeth asserted in later years, her brother's

heavy duties made a man of him in a hurry. By his twelfth year, according to Elizabeth, he had acquired "more general knowledge than men considered of the first standing in the country."

Joined to this swift mental growth was an amazing dexterity with his hands. His father, like many New Englanders, maintained a workshop for the construction and repair of farm gear and household furnishings. It boasted a lathe and a quantity of hand tools. Here, working alongside a 300-pound father whom he deeply loved and respected, young Eli quickly became adept at the making of a variety of useful objects.

In his eleventh year the "shot heard around the world" sounded at Concord, Massachusetts, less than thirty miles from his Worcester County home. The war against England that began officially a year later heaped difficulties on the Whitney household. Supplies that had to be bought for the farm grew scarce. The hard money needed to purchase them all but disappeared.

But to young Eli the hard times brought an opportunity he was quick to seize, displaying at the age of twelve the characteristics that prompted his biographer Green to describe him as closer in attitude to a modern businessman than any other well-membered individual of his time and place. Learning that the war had sent the price of nails sky high, he persuaded his father to install a forge in the workshop and let him make nails there. By his fourteenth year this venture had become so profitable that he had to hire another youth to help him turn out the nails.

In his nineteenth year he startled his family by announcing his intention of going to college. His stepmother opposed the idea. She had assumed that Eli, like his father, would spend his life a farmer, in no need of higher learning. His father approved. But he did so sadly, for he sensed what his son's decision meant. It meant that the younger Eli wanted more out of life than the rather barren soil of Worcester County, Massachusetts, could supply.

He had attended whatever lower schools were available in his neighborhood. These, however, had not prepared him for college. To take care of this matter, he found himself a teaching job and used his modest salary to pay for courses at an academy in Leicester, Massachusetts, set up to prepare young men for Harvard and Yale.

Boys growing up in Massachusetts, if they went to college at all, usually selected Harvard, at Cambridge, Massachusetts. It is not known why in March of 1789 twenty-three-year-old Eli Whitney headed instead for Yale College, in New Haven, Connecticut.

Whatever his reasons for this choice, it turned out to be an excellent one for a young man eager to learn the ways of a world beyond the boundaries of rural Massachusetts and to make a name for himself in some field or other.

He was not yet sure in what field. For a time he considered the law, observing in his letters home that most of America's few rich individuals seemed to be lawyers.

Also attractive to him was "natural philosophy," what today we call science. The Yale of his time was not yet the center of scientific teaching it later became. But there was the museum, with its air pump and its electric machine. There was the library, with among its 3,000 volumes a copy of the *Principia*, by the great English scientist Sir Isaac Newton. There were the classrooms where he could listen to lectures by Ezra Stiles, president of the college and a man experienced in half a dozen professions, law and science among them. And beyond the college gates there was another kind of education to be picked up on the wharves of one of America's busiest seaports and on streets traversed by merchants who had traveled to far parts of the globe and by men important to the public life of the nation.

By September, 1792, when he received his degree at Yale, the farm boy from Massachusetts had become a polished gentleman. He was not, however, a happy one. A teaching job in New

A portrait of Eli Whitney, painted by his friend Samuel F. B. Morse, in 1822. *Yale University Art Gallery / Gift of George Hoadley.*

York City, obtained for him by Yale President Stiles, had fallen through. In its place Whitney reluctantly accepted a post as tutor to the children of a Major Dupont in South Carolina. He was not looking forward to being little more than a servant in a rich man's home. Nor was the prospect of the trip south pleasing to him. It was his understanding, he wrote home, that the climate of South Carolina was "unhealthy and perhaps I shall lose my health and perhaps my life."

His spirits rose somewhat on learning that he would not be making the long journey alone. Arrangements had been made for him to travel with a group headed by Catherine Greene, the widow of Nathanael Greene, onetime quartermaster to George Washington and one of the most fondly remembered generals of the War of the Revolution. Since her husband's death in 1786, Mrs. Greene had been passing her summers in Newport, Rhode Island, and her winters in Mulberry Grove in Georgia, a plantation that state had given the late general for his military services during the war. Accompanying her on the journeys back and forth were her five children and Phineas Miller, the Connecticut-born manager of the estate General Greene had left to his attractive young widow.

The plan was for Whitney to join Mrs. Greene and her party in New York. From there all of them would take ship together for Savannah, Georgia.

For Whitney the journey was beset with difficulties. En route to New York, the packet carrying him across Long Island Sound ran aground, forcing him to cover the remaining six miles in a hired wagon. Less than an hour after reaching the city he met an old friend on the street. They had shaken hands before Whitney realized that the other man, as he wrote home later, "was broke out full with small-Pox."

Catherine Greene, gracious and generous, saw to it that he was inoculated by a good New York doctor. Consequently the ensuing illness was mild, but it held the travelers in New York for two weeks beyond the original departure date.

At Savannah, reached after a week at sea, Whitney spent a day exploring the only southern city he had ever seen. Then he accepted Mrs. Greene's invitation to spend a little time at her plantation. It was his intention, after a brief stay, to move on to South Carolina and take up his duties in the home of Major Dupont.

But he and the major would never see one another. What began as a one-week visit to Mulberry Grove stretched into seven months. During this period Whitney found the answer to a question that had been troubling him for years. What should he do with his life? Should he try to become a lawyer? Or should he look for a career connected with the scientific matters that so appealed to him?

Credit for his decision to become an inventor belongs to Catherine Greene. That bright and high-spirited woman was quick to notice Whitney's amazing manual skills. He made her a tambour, a frame for holding needlework. When neighboring plantation owners, visiting at Mulberry Grove, praised its remarkable workmanship, she let them know that Whitney could create anything with his hands. She predicted that he was the man who was going to rescue the American South from its economic woes.

These woes were an outgrowth of developments in distant England. In recent years scores of cloth-spinning mills had sprung up in that country. These mills stood ready to purchase all the raw cotton that Georgia and the other southern states could grow.

Growing it was no problem. The trouble arose when the pods or bolls of cotton fiber ripened in the middle or late summer. Every such boll contained numerous seeds, and before the fiber could be dried, collected into bales, and sent to market, these had to be separated out. Removing them by hand—

or by an ancient and inefficient device consisting of a couple of wooden rollers run by a crank—was so time-consuming that although many plantations were producing cotton, they were making little or no money out of it.

Whitney, at the time of his arrival at Mulberry Grove in the fall of 1792, had never laid eyes on a boll of cotton. Nor, as a New Englander born and bred, was he interested in the South's economic concerns. But Catherine Greene was interested. Moreover, she had charm, and she knew exactly what to say to her handsome and intelligent but stiff-mannered guest from Worcester County, Massachusetts. When she pointed out that an efficient and fast-acting seed-removing machine would make not only the South rich but its inventor as well, Whitney set out to see what he could come up with.

It took him well into 1793, about six months in all, to construct the first model of what came to be called a cotton gin—a name seemingly derived from the word *engine*. Easily operated by any power available—usually a horse or a waterfall in Whitney's day—the cotton gin consisted essentially of a toothed cylinder revolving against an iron cage holding the cotton bolls and so constructed that the fiber could pass through and onto the cylinder but the seeds could not. A revolving brush re-

Eli Whitney's cotton gin patent, 1794. *The National Archives.*

moved the fiber from the cylinder so that it could be baled and sent to market. Whereas a man could rid fifty bolls of cotton of their seeds in approximately fifty minutes, Whitney's gin could do the same in a minute or less.

During his work on the gin, Mrs. Greene was not his only supporter. Her manager, Phineas Miller, paid whatever expenses arose, and in May he and the inventor signed an agreement under which they became co-owners of a gin-manufacturing company to be known as Miller and Whitney.

In June Whitney left Mulberry Grove and headed for Philadelphia, Pennsylvania, then the home of his country's national government. There he conferred with people in a position to help him obtain a patent giving Miller and Whitney exclusive control of the cotton gin for a period of fourteen years. By March 14, 1794, when the patent came through, Whitney had established a workshop at New Haven, Connecticut, and had constructed the first six cotton gins.

By this time, too, most Americans were aware that Eli Whitney had brought into existence a machine that was about to make the South wealthy. It was also about to put an end to efforts below the Mason-Dixon line to emancipate the slaves.

Prior to the coming of Whitney's gin, the South contained at least as many active opponents of human bondage as did the North. After the gin had arrived and began making the cotton growers of the South rich, no white person in that region dared speak out against slavery. After all, cotton still had to be picked by hand, and the use of black slaves provided the cheapest way of doing so.

Was Whitney bothered by the realization that his machine, as his biographer Green notes, "fastened slavery on the South for three generations"? Apparently not. Nothing he is known to have said or done suggests that he ever gave the matter more than a passing thought.

What did bother him was that in the long pull he and his partner made almost no money out of the cotton gin. Sometimes the inventor of a valuable device contents himself with whatever funds he can get by selling what are called licenses and royalties in it—arrangements under which other individuals purchase the right to make and sell the newly created object. Had Whitney and his partner followed this procedure, who knows? The cotton gin might have enriched them both.

But they did not take this path. Instead they let it be known that only their company, Miller and Whitney, could make and distribute the gin. To the planters of the South, eager to take advantage of the new tool, this situation was intolerable. Unwilling to wait until Miller and Whitney could produce enough gins to go around, they began constructing their own.

For eight years, beginning in 1798, Whitney and his partner spent considerable time in southern courthouses, overseeing over sixty suits brought by them in an effort to stop others from making and using their machine. In the end a judge allotted them a large sum of money. But by the time their lawyers' fees were paid, little of it remained in their pockets.

Never again would Whitney request a patent to protect his rights in a newly created device. Though today we tend to think of him in connection with the cotton gin alone, he was the father of other labor-saving tools and procedures—inventions that have contributed as much to the growth of American industry as a whole as his cotton gin contributed to the growth of southern agriculture.

The year 1798 saw the beginning of his development of the tools and methods by which the thousands of muskets needed by his country's army could be made from interchangeable parts. Prior to this date every component of a gun had to be fashioned by hand. Consequently no two components were alike and no two guns alike.

After 1798, thanks to Whitney, the components of a musket could be made

by machine. With every component precisely the same, every gun was the same. The techniques of mass production that today give us everything from automobiles to Barbie dolls were thus introduced to America by Eli Whitney.

To produce identical muskets in quantity, he established a factory at Mill Rock, on the Mill River in New Haven. Here, in 1818, he built what appears to have been the world's first milling machine.

In this metal-shaping device, as his biographer Green tells us, "a 'chuck' or vise held the work to be shaped upon a plate moved by a power-fed screw driven by a worm gear; the cutting tool, rotating on its own axis and positioned to remove the metal, chip by chip, had a cutting edge irregularly shaped to correspond to the contours the component required. The miller could thus rapidly turn out pieces of intricate form."

Making muskets for the government brought Whitney a fortune. But it did not bring him much fun. The endless labor that went into his many inventions left little time for the ordinary pleasures of life. Writes Green, "His was a completely single-track mind—the only kind of mind, Woodrow Wilson once said, worth having at all."

The year 1796 yielded what to him was startling news. His partner, Phineas Miller, had made Catherine Greene his wife. Whitney's reaction to

An oil painting of Eli Whitney's gun factory on the outskirts of New Haven, Connecticut. *Yale University Art Gallery / Mabel Brady Garvan Collection.*

their marriage, as expressed in his correspondence, was that of a man pricked by the pangs of jealousy.

Was he himself in love with the entrancing Catherine? His subsequent behavior indicates as much. Though he often mentioned a desire for a wife, he did not go courting in earnest until after the fall of 1814, when Catherine died.

His marriage on January 6, 1817, was to Henrietta Edwards, daughter of the Connecticut aristocrat Pierpont Edwards and granddaughter of Jonathan Edwards, world-famous philosopher and one of the first truly creative minds of colonial America.

Marriage had a calming effect on Whitney. Assigning the supervision of his factory to a nephew, he devoted himself to his wife and to the four children, a boy and three girls, born to their union. He had never been in the best of health, and beginning in the fall of 1820 he was the victim of the series of ills that brought him to the end of his days on January 8, 1825.

Wilbur Wright 1867–1912
Orville Wright 1871–1948

American bicycle mechanics; makers of the first powered, manned, heavier-than-air craft to achieve flight

It has been written of Wilbur and Orville Wright that from boyhood on they were "partners in a relationship more binding than most marriages." Wilbur, the brothers' biographer Fred Howard tells us, "was not exaggerating when he wrote the month before he died" that he and Orville had "lived together, played together, worked together, and in fact thought together." It was not uncommon, whenever the two were together, for both "to begin whistling or humming the same tune at the same instant."

Wilbur was born on April 16, 1867; Orville, on August 19, 1871. They were the third and fourth of the five children, four boys and a girl, of Milton Wright and Susan Koerner Wright. Their father was a minister, and from 1878 on, a bishop in the Church of the United Brethren in Christ, a Protestant sect prominent in the American Midwest.

For many years Milton Wright's religious duties kept him and his family on the move. Consequently Wilbur and Orville began life in different localities. Wilbur's birthplace was a farm near Millville, Indiana. Orville's was the small white clapboard house at 7 Hawthorn Street in Dayton, Ohio, to which, after further wandering, the Wrights returned a few years later and which for another twenty-nine years they regarded as home.

From childhood on, mechanical things fascinated Wilbur and Orville. As their father was a believer in encouraging his offsprings' leanings, one of his earliest gifts to them was a toy helicop-

231

ter constructed of cork, bamboo, and paper. Delighted with it, the brothers set out to make a few helicopters on their own. Soon they discovered that the bigger they made them the harder they were to fly. It was their first lesson in the science of "aerial navigation," as what we now call aeronautics was commonly known in those days.

In 1884, the year the Wrights came back to Dayton, Wilbur was seventeen and Orville twelve. At this time the two of them appeared to be much unlike. Orville came close to being a nonstop talker; Wilbur talked little. Orville loved a social gathering; Wilbur was stiff and aloof at such affairs.

Orville was forever trying his hand at this or that moneymaking enterprise. For a time he collected metal scrap and sold it where he could. Next he collected bones. These he sold to a Dayton fertilizer factory. During his summer vacations he worked for a Dayton printer. By the time he finished high school he had become an expert typesetter and the publisher of a short-lived weekly newspaper.

Wilbur was to have completed high school during the year of his family's return to Dayton. But he never got around to doing so. Instead he stayed home a few years, tending to his invalid mother and wrestling with the question of what to do with his life. His father

wanted him to become a preacher like himself. But on matters of faith Wilbur harbored doubts. He had discovered in a book in his father's study the antireligious writings of the famous American lecturer Robert Green Ingersoll. Orville, too, had come upon Ingersoll's writings. On reaching adulthood, both brothers became lifelong nonchurchgoers. Obviously the differences between them were but skin-deep. Underneath they seemed to have almost identical beliefs and interests.

On July 4, 1889, Mrs. Wright died, and a year or so later Wilbur and Orville set themselves up as Wright and Wright, Job Printers. Among the products of their shop was *The Tattler*, a four-page weekly for black readers edited by eighteen-year-old Paul Laurence Dunbar, one of Orville's many friends and the only black student in the Dayton high school Orville had attended. According to one of young Dunbar's early jingles,

Orville Wright is out of sight
In the printing business.
No other mind is half so bright
As his'n is.

In 1892 Dunbar submitted fifty-six of his poems to Orville. As Wright and Wright had no way of binding books, Orville sent them to the publishing house maintained in Dayton by his fa-

Orville (*left*) and Wilbur Wright with their sister, Katherine. From *American Science and Invention: A Pictorial History,* by Mitchell Wilson. New York: Simon & Schuster, 1954.

ther's church. Their publication under the title *Oak and Ivy* launched a four-dollar-a-week elevator operator on what was to be an acclaimed career as a writer of verse and short stories.

By the time *Oak and Ivy* appeared, the Wright brothers had embarked on a new commercial venture. Of late a two-wheeled vehicle called a bicycle had caught the fancy of the American public. With cycling fast becoming a national rage, the brothers put a friend in charge of their printing business and opened a shop for the repair, sale, and rental of bicycles. So successful was this

undertaking that by 1893 they had moved to larger premises. A year later they moved again, this time to even larger quarters on Dayton's West Third Street, and began manufacturing their own bicycles.

Wilbur was twenty-six now, Orville twenty-two. In some ways they were still unlike. Wilbur was calm in a crisis, a hard man to rattle. Orville was easily excited and given to losing his temper. Wilbur was reserved, Orville a fun-lover and player of pranks. Wilbur dressed quietly; Orville was a dandy.

Both had gray-blue eyes, but beyond

that the physical resemblance was minimal. Wilbur was five feet ten inches, tall and slender, Orville was an inch or two shorter and pudgy. With his cleft chin, strong open face, and already deeply receding hairline, Wilbur was a striking-looking man. With his bland features under a cap of thick curly brown hair, Orville was on this score unremarkable.

But if some dissimilarities persisted, the similarities were even more noticeable. Neither man smoked nor drank. Neither showed any marked interest in women. So similar were their high-pitched voices that listeners in an adjoining room were hard put to tell them apart. Both tended to wince when the men around them swore or talked about the configuration of attractive girls.

What each of them had "in about equal amounts," according to their biographer Howard, were mechanical ability and intelligence. "One man with this dual gift," Howard comments, "is exceptional. Two such men whose lives and fortunes are closely linked can raise this combination of qualities to a point where their combined talents are akin to genius."

But, as Howard notes, even genius may languish on nothing but a diet of routine work. To thrive, to assert itself, it must have a goal—some large and daunting thing to do. For the Wright

brothers the challenging goal took form in 1894 when their eyes fell on a magazine article describing the amazing feats of Otto Lilienthal of Germany.

For several years Lilienthal, a mechanical engineer, had been trying to realize man's age-old dream to take to the air like a bird. To this end he had built a number of hang gliders capable of carrying him aloft for varying lengths of time. On August 9, 1896, he and his glider were some fifty feet above the Rhinow Hills near Berlin, when a sudden twist of wind caused the glider to sideslip to earth, breaking Lilienthal's spine and sending him to a hospital, where on the next day he died.

Engraved on his tombstone was a thought he had often expressed. To create a dependable flying machine, "sacrifices must be made." When in 1896, stirred by the report of Lilienthal's death, the Wright brothers resolved to take up the great effort where he had left off, sixteen years of hard thinking, hard work—and sacrifices—lay before them.

They began their new task by following the same methodical procedures that had gone into the development of their bicycle business. First they set out to learn everything they could about aeronautics. On this a couple of encyclopedias in the house on Hawthorn Street and some books from the public

Aviator Wilbur Wright at the controls.

library got them started. A letter to the Smithsonian Institution in Washington, D.C., brought them informative pamphlets and a list of published circulars covering everything discovered to date by other participants in the struggle to achieve human flight.

For more than a hundred years, aviation enthusiasts had been flying balloons, and the day was near when these "gasbags," as some called them, would carry rigid airships equipped with motors and propellers through the skies. In these lighter-than-air contraptions, the Wright brothers took no interest. What they wanted was to send up an engine-driven, propeller-equipped, man-carrying, heavier-than-air flying machine.

By the late summer of 1899, their reading had yielded a discovery that would guide all their forthcoming experiments. It was now clear to them that before a heavier-than-air machine could be launched, they must learn how to control its movements: how, for example, to keep it level when that was desirable; how to ascend and descend, turn and circle. Previous flying-machine makers had given these matters scant attention, but to the brothers, in the words of their biographer Howard, "control was the missing link in the art of flying." Hence their decision to put off for the time being the building of an engine-bearing machine and to begin their experiments with gliders. They began the construction of their first glider in the fall, gradually working into this machine and into others erected later the control system that was to bring their exertions to a successful termination.

Once the first glider was ready, they set out to find a place for testing it. What they needed was a relatively unoccupied area. There should be hills from which they could launch their machine and winds sufficiently strong to lift it. But where in the world could this ideal outdoor laboratory be found?

On May 13, 1900, Wilbur put that question in a letter to Octave Chanute, a French-born industrialist living in Chicago, Illinois, who, like Otto Lilienthal, had been experimenting with gliders for many years. Among the sites suggested by Chanute was the thin 200-mile stretch of sand known as the Outer Banks, which stands as a buffer between the Atlantic Ocean and the mainland of North Carolina.

Here, in the fall of 1900 at the fishing village of Kitty Hawk, Wilbur and Orville began their experiments. Sometimes, holding tight to a guide rope, they flew their big biplane-shaped "soaring machine," as they called it, as though it were a kite. Sometimes

one of the brothers lay on a lower wing, manipulating the controls. Toward the end of September, they moved four miles south to a trio of sand dunes known as Kill Devil Hills. Today the name Kitty Hawk is inextricably linked in our minds to the Wright brothers. In fact, beginning in October, 1900, all their flights on the Outer Banks took place on and in the vicinity of the Kill Devil Hills.

Back in Dayton in late October, Wilbur wrote of his and Orville's first trip to the Outer Banks: "We were much pleased with the general results . . . for setting out as we did, with almost revolutionary theories on many points, and an entirely untried form of machine, we considered it quite a point to be able to return without having our pet theories . . . knocked in the head . . . and our brains dashed out in the bargain."

They spent the ensuing months building another and considerably changed soaring machine. The late summer of 1901 found them again at Kill Devil Hills, testing this glider. Neither man was satisfied with its performance. Back in Dayton they reviewed the notes they had taken on its unsatisfactory flights and concluded that the major trouble lay in the shape of its wings. To find a way of correcting this defect the brothers flew a number of miniature wings in a makeshift wind tunnel.

A wind tunnel, as the name suggests, is an apparatus for studying the effect of an airstream on certain objects. In such a device, depending on the size of the tunnel, entire airplanes or airplane parts or scaled-down models of them are subjected to artificially induced winds. Observers can then determine the path of the air around the objects, the aerodynamic forces exerted upon them, and the reaction of the objects to those forces. The Wrights were not the first to use a wind tunnel, but according to their biographer Howard, theirs were the first tests with one "to yield results of value" in the construction of an airplane. When in the fall of 1902 they conducted their third series of experiments at Kill Devil Hills, flying a newly built glider, the results were so encouraging that they decided the time had come to build their first powered airplane.

They called it the Flyer, and several of its successors would carry the same name. It was a biplane with a total wing area of over four hundred square feet. Their biographer Howard explains its somewhat lopsided appearance by noting that, like "the Venetian gondola, whose right half is wider than the left to counterbalance the weight of the gondolier, who stands on the left, the Flyer's right wing was four inches longer than its left to provide additional lift for the motor and its accessories."

In 1903 the Wright brothers were not the only Americans striving to fabricate an airplane that would fly. So was Samuel Pierpont Langley, an eminent scientist and, since 1887, secretary of the Smithsonian Institution in Washington, D.C. After years of experimenting with models of an airplane, Langley in recent months had constructed a full-sized machine that he referred to as an aerodrome. Twice, in the late fall and early winter of 1903, attempts to launch the aerodrome from a houseboat on the Potomac River south of Washington came to naught.

The last of these failures occurred on December 8. Nine days later, on Thursday, December 17, the Flyer with Orville at the controls glided along a sixty-foot launching track near the Kill Devil Hills on the Outer Banks. Forty feet down the line the Flyer rose on its own power to a height of ten feet. At the time of its abrupt descent twelve seconds later, it had traveled 120 feet in the air, measured from takeoff to landing place. Three more flights followed that Thursday, with the brothers taking turns at the controls. The last of them, with Wilbur aboard, covered 852 feet and remained aloft for fifty-nine seconds.

First Kitty Hawk flight by the Wright brothers on December 17, 1903, with Orville at the controls and Wilbur standing at right. *The Bettmann Archive.*

Everyone in the vicinity of the Kill Devil Hills had been invited to these trials. But only five men, two boys, and a dog showed up to watch the Wright brothers carry mankind into the age of the airplane—into a world so new and strange that for a long while American journalists could not find their way around in it. Nearly everything said in the early newspaper accounts of the December 17 flights was wrong. According to one reporter, for example, all of the 852 feet flown by Wilbur on the fourth and longest flight was straight up in the air!

Seconds after the Flyer landed for the last time, a powerful gust of wind overturned it, severely damaging the machine. Back in Dayton, the brothers stored it in a shed behind their bicycle shop. There it remained for the next thirty-four years. So much for the frequently circulated tale that the original Flyer worked well on the Outer Banks because in that year the winds were right but that when it was brought back to Ohio it never flew again. Indeed, the brothers made no effort to fly it. Instead they built a second Flyer. By the end of 1904, testing it on a dairy farm near Dayton, they had made scores of flights, including two of five minutes each at a speed of thirty-five miles per hour.

For the next seven years, the lives of Wilbur and Orville can be described as a slow ascent to fame and wealth— a process marked by the construction of more Flyers and by a series of demonstration flights in different parts of the world. In 1908, at a racecourse in France, a wildly cheering throng watched as Wilbur, in one of the Flyers, executed a figure eight and other aerial maneuvers never seen before. In 1909, at the big military base known as Fort Myer near Washington, Orville set an endurance record by keeping another Flyer in the air for one hour, twenty minutes, and forty-five seconds at an altitude of 300 feet. By the close of 1909, the brothers were part owners of airplane-making factories in both their own country and France.

By this time, too, aviation enthusiasts from all over the world were coming to Dayton to see them. Entertaining these distinguished visitors in a seven-room house was becoming increasingly difficult. Their older brothers, Reuchlin and Lorin, had married and moved away. But the modest Hawthorn Street house was still home to Wilbur and Orville; to Bishop Wright, their aging father; and to Katharine, their schoolteacher sister.

In the summer of 1911, aided by an architect, Wilbur and Orville planned the construction of a brick mansion to be known as Hawthorn Hill on a seventeen-acre plot in suburban Oakwood. Work on this neoclassical structure began a few months later, but Wilbur would never live in it. The modest clapboard house in Dayton was still home when on Wednesday, May 29, 1912, after a long and wasting illness, death came to the elder of the flying Wright brothers. Twenty-five thousand people visited the Dayton church where his coffin was taken. In his faithfully kept diary, Bishop Wright wrote of his lost son that in "memory and intellect there was none like him. He systemized everything. His wit was quick and keen. He could say or write anything he wanted to . . . but was modest."

Thirty-six years of life remained to Orville, most of them spent in the big house in Oakwood. He saw both world wars come and go. He was appalled by the increasing use of the airplane as an instrument of attack and destruction. Years before he and Wilbur had assumed that, by enabling every nation to keep a close eye on other nations, the airplane would bring an end to warfare. He was grieved at the growing realization that what a great invention does for mankind depends on what mankind does with the invention.

Reporters, coming to interview him at Hawthorn Hill, often came away disappointed. Rarely did he say anything spectacular or even quotable. The complaint uttered by some of them that he was "colorless" suggests that with the death of Wilbur the light that had been Wilbur-and-Orville-together went out.

Almost to the end of his days, Orville maintained a laboratory in Dayton where he experimented with a variety of airplane designs. He was in the office of these premises when on the morning of January 27, 1948, he suffered a heart attack and was rushed to Miami Valley Hospital, where he died, quietly, on the night of January 30. As the funeral procession made its way a few days later to Woodland Cemetery, four jet fighters from Dayton's Wright Field roared overhead in what biographer Howard describes as a "five-plane formation." He adds that the "fifth plane, missing from its slot in the formation, was the equivalent of the riderless horse in a full-dress military funeral."

Eleven years earlier, with Orville's permission, the original Wright Flyer, now known as the Kitty Hawk, was removed from its storage shed in Dayton and sent to England. There for a few years it was exhibited at London's Science Museum. In 1948 it came back to the United States to become the property of the Smithsonian Institution. Today a carefully wrought re-creation of it, with a dummy of Orville on one of the wings, occupies a place of honor in the National Air and Space Museum.

Important Dates in the History of Invention and Technology

By the close of the Before-Christ era, some 2,000 years ago, many inventions were in wide use and many technological discoveries widely known. Among these were the plow, the bow and arrow, the arrowhead, a modeling device for the making of bricks, a scale for weighing, wheels and axles, wooden bearings for use with axles, the water clock, a friction device for pounding grain into flour, river- and ocean-going rafts equipped with sails capable of sailing only before the wind, the art of writing in pictographs (pictures) and in hieroglyphics (signs representing the things or ideas being recorded), the art of irrigation, a method for casting iron, the abacus (ancestor of the computer), awareness of the existence of electricity and some knowledge of how it behaves, knowledge of how to use levers, knowledge of how to drill for oil, an Archimidean screw for raising water, and the waterwheel.

A.D.

100.   Hero or Heron, a Greek living in Alexandria, Egypt, builds a steam engine used to open and close temple doors, a coin-operated vending machine that dispenses holy water, and a windmill. Chang Heng, a Chinese mathematician and astronomer, devises a seismograph for measuring earthquakes.

105.   Ts'ai Lun, official to the court of China, mixes the inner fibers of mulberry bark, hemp, and cloth with water, mashes them to a pulp, presses out the liquid, and hangs the sheets out to dry, thus producing paper. Note, however, that the word *paper* comes from *papyrus*, the ancient Egyptians having found a way to make thin sheets from the papyrus plant. They also used for writing purposes the skin of young sheep or goats. This they called *parchment*. Before parchment and paper came along people wrote and drew pictures on blocks of clay, sheets of metal, and other substances.

300.   Triangular sails capable of sailing into the wind appear on the Arabian Sea.

400.   Printing comes into existence in the Orient.

530.   At his monastery in Italy, St. Ben-

241

edict establishes "the rule," calling for prayers to be recited at set times of the day and night—an action that will lead to the invention of the mechanical clock.

Between 1041 and 1049. A Chinese named Pi Sheng makes the first movable type, using earthenware. Prior to this development printing was done with wooden blocks into which each letter had to be carved by hand. Movable type could be used many times, thus speeding the process.

1100. The first university is established in Bologna, Italy, a cooperative organization of knowledge on an international basis and a great social invention.

ca. 1200. Chinese use kites to carry spies over enemy territory and to punish criminals by sending them aloft.

Late 1300s. Mechanical clocks appear in Europe and gradually replace the sundials, water clocks, and hourglasses previously in use.

1241. A Korean named Yi Kyo-bo brings forth the first movable type to be made of wood.

1320. Berthold Schwarz, a German monk, creates a mixture of saltpetre, charcoal, and sulfur, thus making gunpowder, known in the Far East for centuries, a reliable weapon of war.

1340. The first blast furnace, helpful in the casting of iron, is developed in or around Liege, Belgium.

ca. 1456. Johannes Gutenberg of Mainz, Germany, develops the printing press and produces the first printed Bible.

By 1500. Leonardo da Vinci of Italy has designed all sorts of things that cannot be made until the technology for doing so has been developed. Among his drawings are breechloading cannon, mammoth crossbows, multibarreled machine guns, an armored vehicle foreshadowing the tank of World War

I, various kinds of flying machines, gears, bearings, and a parachute.

1581. The great Italian scientist Galileo discovers the principles responsible for the invention not quite a century later of the pendulum clock.

1589. Sir John Harrington, a British nobleman, invents the flush toilet.

ca. 1590. Zacharias Janssen, a Dutch spectacle maker, creates the microscope. So some authorities say; others credit its invention to Galileo in 1610.

1600. William Gilbert of England ushers in the scientific study of electricity by publishing his treatise *On the Magnet, Magnetic Bodies and the Great Magnet, the Earth.*

1605. Johann Lippersheim, a Dutch optician, invents the telescope. Long before this date, however, the Arabs had discovered that a long tube could be used to isolate a field of stars under observation.

1609. Galileo develops the first telescope for astronomical purposes.

ca. 1616. English mathematician William Oughtred makes the first slide rule.

1617. John Napier, Scottish mathematician, foreshadows the computer by constructing Napier's rods, a device that allows multiplication to be carried out by a series of simple additions.

1631. France's Blaise Pascal, also foreshadowing the computer, invents the adding machine.

1678. English scientist Robert Hooke invents the spiral spring known as a hairspring. Used as a regulator in mechanical watches, it makes portable timepieces possible.

1687. The great English scientist Isaac Newton publishes his *Mathematical Principles of Natural Philosophy.* Two of the ideas contained in this book will help usher in the

Space Age. Newton's law of gravity gave scientists some idea for the first time of the force needed to carry them beyond the pull of the Earth's gravity. Newton's principle that every action produces an equal and opposite reaction suggested the utility of the rocket, the method of propulsion destined to become the key to space travel and exploration.

1698. Thomas Savery, an English military engineer, obtains a patent for a steam pump capable of draining water from mines.

1707. Italy's Bartolomeo Cristofoi invents the piano.

1712. Thomas Newcomen, an English blacksmith, improves on Savery's steam-driven pump.

1719. France's René de Réaumur discovers that paper can be made from wood.

1732. John Key, an impoverished English weaver, discovers how to throw the shuttle back and forth in his loom by pulling a cord. The resulting device, the fly shuttle, greatly increases the amount of cloth that can be woven in a day.

1736. Explorer Charles de la Condamine brings home to France a spongy substance made from the sap of certain trees growing wild in Peru. The day is near when enterprising businessmen will find that this substance, india rubber, can be made into pencil erasers and used in the production of waterproof coats, boots, and hats.

1738. Swiss scientist Daniel Bernoulli discovers the principle behind the airfoil, thus making possible the development of the basic form of the winged aircraft.

1740. America's Benjamin Franklin invents the Franklin stove.

1751. French clockmaker Nicolas Forq invents the planer, an important industrial tool.

1752. Benjamin Franklin, flying a kite in a thunderstorm, discovers electricity in one of a series of risky experiments vital to the progress of electrical science. The same year sees his invention of the lightning rod.

1767. England's James Hargreaves comes up with a spinning machine powered by a hand-operated crank that can spin up to eight strands of thread at the same time. He names it the spinning jenny, after his wife.

1769. France's Nicolas Cugnot makes a steam-driven automobile. Scotland's James Watt invents a steam engine superior to all previous models and the first one capable of driving machinery. England's Richard Arkwright improves on Hargreaves's spinning jenny and powers it with a water wheel. He calls his device the water frame.

1775. Samuel Compton of England combines the best features of the spinning jenny and the water frame into a machine he calls the mule. The mule not only produces the best thread to date but does it faster.

1776. On September 6 the *Turtle*, the world's first submarine, built by America's David Bushnell, is used during the War of the Revolution to attack the British warship *Eagle*. The *Turtle* functions well but the attack fails. During this same year Charles Michael, abbe de l'Epee, a French priest and teacher of deaf-mutes, invents a sign language.

ca. 1779. Nicolas Leblanc, a French chemist, becomes the first person to produce muskets with interchangeable parts.

1780. Alessandro Volta, an Italian physicist, develops the first electric battery, an apparatus in which a continuous flow of electricity is produced not by friction, a long-understood process, but by a chemical reaction.

1781. Watt improves his steam engine and invents the sun-and-planet or epicyclic gear now found in automatic transmissions.

1783. Jacques-Etienne and Joseph Michelle de Montgolfier, French paper makers, construct and fly a balloon. Benjamin Franklin, on hand for a subsequent flight of this new device, is asked by a fellow onlooker, "Of what use is a balloon?" Famous is Franklin's reply: "Of what use is a newborn babe?"

1785. James Rumsey of Virginia makes a small vessel driven by a steam pump. Tested on the Potomac River, his boat achieves a speed of four miles an hour but uses too much fuel to be practical. Ben Franklin invents bifocal spectacles.

1787. English inventor Edmund Cartwright builds the first fully automated spinning machine, driven by a crank at first but shortly thereafter by a steam engine.

ca. 1790. Henry Maudslay and Joseph Bramah, English engineers, perfect the slide rest, a device that eliminates the need for the operator of a lathe to hold metal-cutting tools in his hand while operating the machine. John Fitch of Connecticut, having designed a steamship five years before, operates an improved version of it on the Delaware River. An engineering success, Fitch's invention is a commercial failure.

1793. Eli Whitney invents the cotton gin.

ca. 1800. Whitney produces muskets with interchangeable parts. Maudslay makes the first all-metal screw-cutting lathe.

1803. Richard Trevithick, English engineer, completes the first steam-powered railroad locomotive.

1807. On August 16, the first commercially successful steamship, the work of America's Robert Fulton, begins its frequent traverse of the Hudson River in New York State.

1808. Sir Humphry Davy, an English chemist and physicist, invents the electric arc light, destined to be the only form of electrical illumination until the coming of Thomas Edison's incandescent bulb.

1809. Sir George Cayley, an English baronet, publishes a three-part paper, laying down for the first time the principles of flight by heavier-than-air craft.

1813. George Stephenson, an English engineer, makes the first practical steam-driven railroad locomotive.

1815. England's John Loudon McAdam begins building the first road surface of graded crushed stones, ushering in the use of "macadamized" roads.

1817. Germany's Baron von Drais invents the bicycle. It facilitates his work as an inspector of forests.

1818. Eli Whitney invents the milling machine, a tool used today in any shop in which exact metal parts must be shaped.

1821. English chemist Michael Faraday and American physicist Joseph Henry, working independently, invent the first electric motors.

1823. England's William Sturgeon bends an iron bar into the shape of a horseshoe, wraps thin wire around it, and then, by applying electrical current, produces the first electromagnet—a process soon duplicated by Joseph Henry, working independently.

1826. France's Joseph Niépce makes the world's first photographs.

1831. Michael Faraday builds the first dynamo, forerunner of today's electrical generator. America's Cyrus H. McCormick invents the first practical mechanical reaper.

ca. 1832. America's Walter Hunt invents a lockstitch sewing machine using two threads, but abandons the device for fear it will put tailors and seamstresses out of work.

1834. America's Jacob Perkins invents the first mechanical refrigerator.

1836. America's Samuel Colt invents the revolver that bears his name. Samuel F. B. Morse, American artist, invents the telegraph. John Ericsson in Sweden and Francis Petit Smith in England, working independently, invent the screw propeller for use on steamships, instead of the paddle wheel.

1839. James Naysmith, an English foundry owner, invents the steam hammer and quickly converts it into the pile driver. America's Charles Goodyear gives birth to a vast new industry by his accidental discovery of the secret of vulcanization—that raw rubber mixed with sulfur and then heated becomes durable, staying soft and pliable in any weather.

1840. England's William Talbot advances the art and science of photography by inventing processes that make possible the production of negatives and the development of prints.

ca. 1843. Charles Babbage, an English mathematician, designs the analytical engine, forerunner of the modern computer.

1846. America's Elias Howe patents the first practical sewing machine.

ca. 1850. Alexander Parkes, a metal worker in England, invents the first commercially successful plastic. William Kelly in the United States and Henry Bessemer in Great Britain, working independently, invent the steel converter, making possible the large-scale production of steel from iron.

1851. Isaac Singer, American actor, develops the first commercially successful sewing machine.

1852. America's Elisha Otis invents the modern safety elevator.

1856. William H. Perkin, an eighteen-year-old English youth, discovers how to make synthetic dyes.

1859. Edwin L. Drake, an American army officer, gives birth to the petroleum industry by successfully drilling for oil in Pennsylvania.

1864. George Pullman, American industrialist, designs the railroad sleeping car.

1865. The Massachusetts Institute of Technology opens in Boston, Massachusetts, later moving to nearby Cambridge.

1867. Nikolas August Otto, German engineer, invents the first workable internal combustion engine. Christopher L. Sholes, collector of customs at Milwaukee, Wisconsin, aided by two friends, produces the first practical typewriter. Ives W. McGaffey, American engineer, invents the vacuum cleaner.

1873. Scottish physicist James Clerk Maxwell publishes his theory of electromagnetic waves, thus paving the way for the creation of the wireless telegraph and the radio.

1876. Alexander Graham Bell, Scottish-born American educator, invents the telephone.

1877. Thomas Alva Edison invents the phonograph.

1879. America's Edison and Great Britain's Joseph Swan, working independently, invent the incandescent lamp. Ernest Werner von Siemens, German electrical engineer, invents the electrically powered railroad engine.

1882. Edison opens in New York City the world's first power station and electricity-distribution system.

1884. George Eastman, American industrialist, develops flexible film; and with this invention photography becomes a hobby open to anyone with a small camera instead of just to professional photographers with bulky cameras.

1885. Carl Benz, German engineer, builds the first automobile powered by an internal combustion engine.

1886. Gottlieb Daimler, another German engineer, builds the second such automobile. America's John S. Pemberton, working in his backyard, concocts a formula for a soft drink to be known as Coca Cola. Heinrich Hertz, a German physicist, confirms the existence of radio waves by generating them electrically.

1893. German engineer Rudolph Diesel devises a system of injecting oil into hot, highly compressed air, making possible the diesel engine.

1895. Wilhelm Conrad Roentgen, a German physicist, discovers X rays.

1897. Joseph John Thomson, British physicist, discovers the electron, simultaneously revealing that the atom, long thought to be the smallest substance, contains numerous smaller substances called elementary particles.

1898. Pierre and Marie Curie, scientists working in France, discover that uranium ore is unstable and radiates energy, leading other scientists to conclude that certain atoms can be split and thus made to give off huge amounts of energy.

1903. Wilbur and Orville Wright, American bicycle mechanics, construct and operate the first powered, man-carrying, heavier-than-air craft to achieve flight.

1904. America's King Gillette patents the safety razor.

1906. America's Lee De Forest invents the vacuum, or audion, tube, making possible the talking movie and the transmission of the human voice for great distances without the use of wires.

1908. Henry Ford introduces his Model T in October.

1911. America's Elmer Sperry invents the gyrocompass for use on ships.

1920. Dr. A. A. Griffith of the Royal Aircraft Establishment at Farnborough, England, suggests the idea for what will become the jet airplane.

1926. Robert Goddard, American physicist, having invented the liquid-fuel rocket, flies it 184 feet on March 16.

1930. Ernest Orlando Lawrence, American physicist, invents the cyclotron, the first atom smasher to attain the high energies needed to permit scientists to explore the interior of the atom. Electrical engineer Vannevar Bush invents the differential analyzer, forerunner of the electronic computer.

1931. Vladimir Zworykin, Russian-born American physicist, invents the iconoscope, destined to be a major component of today's television systems.

1934. Philo Taylor Farnsworth, American research engineer, invents the electronic television camera. This and Zworykin's iconoscope make commercial television possible. Irène and Frédéric Joliot-Curie, French scientists, produce artificial radioactivity by bombarding aluminum, thus opening the way to the release and use of nuclear energy.

1935. Robert Watson-Watt, British scientist, invents radar (Radio, Detection and Ranging System). The Eastman Kodak Company of Rochester, New York, ushers in color photography by introducing Kodachrome film.

1937. Grote Reber, an amateur American astronomer, builds the first radio telescope.

1938. America's Chester Carlson invents the photocopier. The Du Pont Company of Wilmington, Delaware, markets nylon stockings.

1939. On April 30, television broadcasting on a scheduled basis begins in the United States. Discontinued during the Second World War, it resumes in 1946.

ca. 1941. Jacques Cousteau, French oceanographer, develops the aqualung for use in exploring the sea bed. Wallace Carothers of the Du Pont Company invents Neoprene, an artificial rubber.

1942. On December 2, Enrico Fermi and his aides produce energy by atomic fission on the squash court under the stadium of the University of Chicago.

1946. The University of Pennsylvania turns out ENIAC, the first practical electronic computer.

1947. Three American scientists—William B. Shockley, John Bardeen, Walter Brattain—invent the transistor.

1949. Harold Ridley, an English surgeon, introduces the first artificial lens and a technique for its insertion in the eye, paving the way for today's operations for the extraction of cataracts and intraocular implants.

America's Edwin Land invents the Polaroid camera, which gives a picture in seconds, without the need of a negative.

1956. The world's first nuclear power station, at Calder Hall in Cumbria, England, begins feeding electricity into the national grid.

1957. The first such plant opens in the United States. The Soviet Union puts the first artificial satellite, *Sputnik I,* into orbit around Earth.

1958. Jack St. Clair Kilby, an American electrical engineer, constructs the first microchip, destined to become the brain of the modern computer and many other devices.

1959. Robert Norton Noyce, American physicist, constructs the second microchip.

1960. T. H. Maiman, an American physicist, builds the first laser (*L*ight *A*mplification by *M*eans of *S*imulated *E*mission of *R*adiation). The principles underlying this remarkable device were established by the Danish physicist Niels Bohr in 1913.

Further Reading

Titles marked by an asterisk are most suitable for young readers.

GENERAL

*Baldwin, Gordon C. *Inventors and Inventions of the Ancient World*. New York: Four Winds Press, 1973.

Boorstin, Daniel J. *The Americans: The Democratic Experience*. New York: Random House, 1973.

_____. *The Discoverers*. New York: Random House, 1983.

*Brown, Kenneth A. *Inventors at Work: Interviews with 16 Notable American Inventors*. Redmond, Wash.: Tempus Books of Microsoft Press, 1988.

Clark, Ronald W. *Works of Man*. New York: Viking, 1985.

*Cooke, David C. *Inventions that Made History*. New York: G. P. Putnam's Sons, 1968.

Dubos, René. *A God Within*. New York: Scribner's, 1972.

Hewlett, Richard G., and Oscar E. Anderson, Jr. *A History of the United States Atomic Energy Commission*. Volume I: *The New World, 1939–1946*. University Park, Pa.: The Pennsylvania State University Press, 1962.

*Hughes, Thomas P. *American Genesis: A Century of Invention and Technological Enthusiasm*. New York: Viking, 1989.

The Inventive Yankee: From Rockets to Roller Skates—200 Years of Yankee Inventors and Inventions. From the publishers of *Yankee* Magazine. Dublin, N.H.: Yankee Books, 1989.

*Kerrod, Robin. *The Way It Works: Man and His Machines*. 2 volumes. London: Octopus Books, 1967–71.

Landes, David S. *Revolution in Time: Clocks and the Making of the Modern World*. Cambridge, Mass.: Harvard University Press, 1983.

*Macaulay, David. *The Way Things Work*. Boston: Houghton Mifflin, 1988.

Men of Science and Invention. By the editors of American Heritage. New York: American Heritage Publishing Company, 1960.

Mumford, Lewis. *Technics and Civilization.* New York: Harcourt, Brace, 1934.

*Pratt, Fletcher. *All about Famous Inventors and their Inventions.* New York: Random House, 1955.

The Smithsonian Book of Invention. Washington, D.C.: The Smithsonian Institution, 1978.

Tocqueville, Alexis de. *Democracy in America.* Volume II, first book, chapter X. New York: Vintage Books, 1945.

*Vase, Ethlie Ann, and Greg Ptacek. *Mothers of Invention. From the Bra to the Bomb: Forgotten Women and Their Unforgettable Ideas.* New York: Morrow, 1988.

Williams, Trevor. *The History of Invention.* New York: Facts on File Publications, 1987.

BABBAGE

Hyman, Anthony. *Charles Babbage: Pioneer of the Computer.* Princeton, N.J.: Princeton University Press, 1982.

*Literrick, Ian. *The Age of Computers: The Story of Computers.* New York: The Bookwright Press, 1984.

*Schneiderman, Ron. *Computers: From Babbage to the Fifth Generation.* New York: Watts, 1986.

BELL

American Telephone and Telegraph Company. *The Bell Telephone.* New York: AT&T, 1908.

Bruce, Robert B. *Bell: Alexander Bell and the Conquest of Solitude.* Boston: Little, Brown, 1973.

BENZ

*Kimes, Beverly Rae. *The Star and the Laurel: The Centennial History of Daimler,* *Mercedes and Benz.* Montvale, N.J.: Mercedes-Benz of North America, 1986.

CARVER

McMurry, Linda O. *George Washington Carver: Scientist and Symbol.* New York: Oxford University Press, 1981.

EASTMAN

Ackerman, Carl W. *George Eastman.* Clifton, N.J.: August M. Kelley, Publishers, 1973.

EDISON

Conot, Robert. *A Streak of Luck: The Life and Legend of Thomas Alva Edison.* New York: Seaview Books, 1979.

Edison, Thomas A. The Papers of Thomas A. Edison. Volume I: *The Making of an Inventor, February 1847–June 1873.* Edited by Reese V. Jenkins and others. Baltimore: The Johns Hopkins University Press, 1989.

Hunt, Inez, and Wanetta W. Draper. *Lightning in His Hand: The Life Story of Nikola Tesla.* Denver: Sage Books, 1964.

Josephson, Matthew. *Edison: A Biography.* New York: McGraw-Hill, 1959.

Lathrop, G. P. "Talks with Edison." *Harper's Magazine.* February 1890.

*Sabin, Louis. *Thomas Alva Edison: Young Inventor.* Mahwah, N.J.: Troll Assocs., 1983.

FARADAY

Williams, L. Pearce. *Michael Faraday.* New York: Basic Books, n.d.

FARNSWORTH

*Everson, George. *The Story of Television: The Life of Philo T. Farnsworth.* New York: Norton, 1949.

*Settel, Irving, and William Laas. *A Pictorial History of Television*. New York: Grosset & Dunlap, 1969.

FERMI

Latil, Pierre de. *Enrico Fermi: The Man and His Theories*. Translated by Len Ortzen. New York: Paul S. Erickson, Inc., 1966.

Segre, Emilio. *Enrico Fermi, Physicist*. Chicago: University of Chicago Press, 1970.

FULTON

Philip, Cynthia Owen. *Robert Fulton: A Biography*. New York: Watts, 1985.

GALILEO

*Fermi, Laura, and Gilberto Bernardini. *Galileo and the Scientific Revolution*. New York: Basic Books, 1961.

Geymonat, Ludovico. *Galileo Galilei: A Biography*. Translated by Stillman Drake. New York: McGraw-Hill, 1965.

Redondi, Pietro. *Galileo Heretic*. Translated by Raymond Rosenthal. Princeton, N.J.: Princeton University Press, 1987.

GODDARD

Goddard, Robert H. *The Papers of Robert H. Goddard*. Edited by Esther C. Goddard and G. Edward Pendray. New York: McGraw-Hill, 1970.

Lehman, Milton. *This High Man: The Life of Robert H. Goddard*. New York: Farrar, Straus & Giroux, 1963.

*Lomask, Milton. *Robert H. Goddard: Space Pioneer*. Champaign, Ill.: Garrard, 1972.

GUTENBERG

McMurtrie, Douglas C. *The Book: The Story of Printing and Bookmaking*. New York: Oxford University Press, 1965.

Scholderer, Victor. *Johann Gutenberg: The Inventor of Printing*. London: The Trustees of the British Museum, 1963.

*Smith, Elwyn A. *Johann Gutenberg*. Evanston, Ill.: Row, Peterson, 1951.

KILBY and NOYCE

*Billings, Charlene W. *Microchip: Small Wonder*. New York: Dodd, Mead, 1984.

*Ledgard, Henry, E. Patrick McQuaid, and Andrew Singer. *From Baker Street to Binary: An Introduction to Computers and Computer Programming with Sherlock Holmes*. New York: McGraw-Hill, 1983.

*Reid, T. R. *The Chip: How Two Americans Invented the Microchip and Launched a Revolution*. New York: Simon & Schuster, 1984.

Rogers, Everett M. and Judith K. *Silicon Valley Fever: Growth of High-Technology Culture*. New York: Basic Books, 1984.

Wolfe, Tom. "The Tinkerings of Robert Noyce." *Esquire*, December 1983.

LAWRENCE

Childs, Herbert. *An American Genius: The Life of Ernest Orlando Lawrence*. New York: Dutton, 1968.

LEONARDO DA VINCI

*Cooper, Margaret. *The Inventions of Leonardo da Vinci*. New York: Macmillan, 1965.

Kemp, Martin. *Leonardo da Vinci: The Marvelous Works of Nature and Man*. Cambridge, Mass.: Harvard University Press, 1981.

Leonardo da Vinci. *The Notebooks of Leonardo da Vinci*. Arranged, rendered into English, and introduced by Edward MacCurdy. Garden City, N.Y.: Garden City Publishing Co., 1941–42.

Payne, Robert. *Leonardo.* Garden City, N.Y.: Doubleday, 1978.

McCORMICK

Hutchinson, William T. *Cyrus Hall McCormick.* 2 vols. New York: Da Capo Press, 1968.

MARCONI

Dunlap, Orrin Elmer. *Marconi.* New York: Arno Press, 1971.
*Morgan, Alfred. *First Book of Radio and Electronics.* New York: Scribner's, 1977.

MORSE

Mabee, Carleton. *The American Leonardo.* New York: Octagon Books, 1969.

SINGER

Brandon, Ruth. *A Capitalist Romance: Singer and the Sewing Machine.* Philadelphia, Pa.: Lippincott, 1977.

STEPHENSON

Smiles, Samuel. *The Life of George Stephenson, Railway Engineer.* London: J. Murray, 1857.

THOMSON

Rayleigh, Robert John Strutt, Baron. *The Life of Sir J. J. Thomson, O.M. Sometime Master of Trinity College, Cambridge.* Cambridge [England] at the University Press, 1942.
Thomson, George. *J. J. Thomson: Discoverer of the Electron.* Garden City, N.Y.: Doubleday. 1966.

WATT

Dickson, H. W., and Rhys Jenkins. *James Watt and the Steam Engine.* Oxford, England: The Clarendon Press, 1927.
Rolt, L.T.C. *James Watt.* New York: Arco Publishing Company, 1963.

WHITNEY

Green, Constance McL. *Eli Whitney and the Birth of American Technology.* Boston: Little, Brown, 1956.

WRIGHT

Crouch, Tom D. *The Bishop's Boys: The Life of Wilbur and Orville Wright.* New York: Norton, 1989.
Howard, Fred. *Wilbur and Orville: A Biography of the Wright Brothers.* New York: Knopf, 1987.

Index

Fast-Talking Dames

Maria DiBattista

PRESS ROOM

Fast-Talking Dames

Yale University Press   New Haven and London

Photographs courtesy the Museum of Modern Art
Film Stills Archive. Page 324: Jean Arthur in
Mr. Deeds Goes To Town

Published with assistance from the foundation
established in memory of Philip Hamilton
McMillan of the Class of 1894, Yale College.

Designed by Sonia L. Shannon.
Set in Adobe Garamond with Shelley Andante
display by Tseng Information Systems, Inc.

Printed in the United States of America by R. R.
Donnelley & Sons.

Library of Congress Cataloguing-in-Publication Data
DiBattista, Maria, 1947–
Fast-talking dames/Maria DiBattista.
p.   cm.
Includes bibliographical references (p.) and index.
ISBN 0-300-08815-9 (alk. paper)
1. Women in motion pictures.   2. Women—United
States—Language.   I. Title.
PN1995.9.W6 D53   2001   00-049946
791.43'65042—dc21

A catalogue record for this book is available from
the British Library.

The paper in this book meets the guidelines for
permanence and durability of the Committee on
Production Guidelines for Book Longevity of the
Council on Library Resources.

10 9 8 7 6 5 4 3

For Dina

Contents

Preface

The origins of this book date to my early teens, when, after school and after hours, I tuned in to the late show and first saw and heard the fast-talking dames celebrated in this book. I had no idea who they were, but I knew I had stumbled onto a unique company of women. Because of them I came to experience the pleasure to be had in words—in the mere *saying* of them—and the gratification in giving a good as well as fair account of yourself. If I had not had their example, I might have passed my adolescence muttering that there was little for me to hope for in a world that paid so much attention to the likes of Marilyn Monroe. Surely I wasn't the only girl, then or now, puzzled and somewhat depressed to learn that Monroe epitomized for so many what was most desirable in my sex. It wasn't that her physical features, breathy voice, and languid movements were inimitable, although I remember several of my friends trying to mimic her speech and walk anyway. It was that she lacked any semblance of ready wit. Even when she said funny lines, which she often did, she never said them as if she knew that a joke was on the way. Even as a teenager I knew that I never wanted to appear that bereft of words and self-confidence, even if it meant that I could never hope to attract, much less entrance, some man.

But on the television screen I encountered a breed of woman, variously shaded in black and white, shimmering with a life more vibrant than that of any garish Technicolor goddess. These women were sexy, but they were sassy, too. Most of all they were sharp and fast with words. They were quick on the uptake and hardly ever downbeat. They seemed to know what to say and when to say it; they were never, except in extreme and exceptional moments, at a loss for words. The American language seemed to be reinventing itself with every word they spoke. They weren't afraid of slang nor shy of the truth. They called things as they saw them, and even if they were wrong—and often they were—

they knew how to correct their mistakes, how to find new words for the changed state of their feelings. In their fast and breezy talk seemed to lie the secret of happiness, but also the key to reality.

Having found them, I never wanted to wander far from their company or stray from their example. I still believe that they offer the most exhilarating and—to use a much abused but in this instance indispensable word—*empowering* model for American womanhood. The young Italo Calvino was equally beguiled by the commanding but lovable presence of these American heroines: "From the cheeky opportunism of Claudette Colbert to the pungent energy of Katharine Hepburn, the most important role model the female personalities of American cinema offered was that of the woman who rivals men in resolve and doggedness, spirit and wit."[1]

It was spirited and witty American womanhood that they distinctly and exuberantly but, alas, not enduringly defined. They were in the public eye at the moment when America was reeling from the Depression and had not yet established its postwar, "modern" identity. The comedy of their self-articulation is thus also a triumphal tale of America coming into its linguistic and cultural estate. The fast-talking dames were as much the daughters in revolt against genteel tradition as were the writers who fled to Paris. Many simply could not afford expatriation, so they stayed home, earning a living. Yet they were equally dismissive of the domestic and sexual pieties of the genteel tradition, especially the doctrine that a woman should marry only for love. They entered the working world rather than the marriage market, fortified by a healthy and sometimes acerbic skepticism that left them determined not to repeat the patterns of their mothers' lives, particularly in the matter of marriage. They believed that love and romance were short-lived, money and security enduring, a conviction nurtured by hard times rather than hard hearts. Since they lived in a comic universe they would come to reconsider their principles, but not without an often tense struggle in which love only barely managed to conquer all. Still, they fell in love with men who seemed quite capable of giving them what they could love and what they could respect. What they gave these men in return was a blithe mastery of words. This was their dowry.

Although they can prosper in gangster and crime melodramas, fast-talking dames thrive primarily in a comic world—marriage, not jail or extinction, is the social fate decreed for them. The marriage with which comedy traditionally concludes satisfies our deepest desire for personal and erotic happiness and also reassures us that the social future is being joyously imagined. Despite the inroads of women in the motion picture industry, the future that these comedies imagined has not been realized. Verbal minimalism, impatient with moral ambiguity and its complex syntax, remains the linguistic fashion of the times. Wisecracks still ricochet off movie soundtracks, but too often they are severed from their roots in actual harsh or bitter experience. They are zingers offered for the sake of the zing, not for the hard truths and obdurate realities that we otherwise could not bear to hear of outright. The smart talkers of today's movies, mimicking the monologism of stand-up comedians or the one-liners of sitcoms, rarely aspire above the level of the put-down. Their gibes are meant to forestall or foreclose conversation, not quicken, complicate, and enliven it.

The marquee value of fast talk is lamentably undervalued at a time when laconic manhood is still rated high as a masculine ideal. The monosyllabic, muscle-proud action heroes who dominate the screen may be resourceful, even morally admirable, but the one thing they are not is talkative. One of the sexual myths that I hope to expose is that a talkative man is a con-man, an intriguer, or not *quite* all man—a prattler too much in touch with his feminine side. Wherever this notion comes from, it apparently receives little support from nature. Recent research suggests that laconic manliness may actually be the result of a low testosterone count. Researchers at the University of Manchester observed "enhanced performance in verbal fluency among the men given testosterone injections." The wag who composed the headline announcing these findings captured the popular conception about the relation of gender to speech: "Testosterone teaches the tongue to trill?"[2] Perhaps, but I like to think that the sex hormones find their natural outlet not just in the trills but in the thrills of speech. There is more than one way to interpret the legal phrase "excitable speech."

Still, the terse action hero who conquers the devils that beset him is less distressing than are the dithering maidens too flustered by life and by men to utter a complete thought, much less a swift one. It has been the sad comic assignment of intelligent, talented actresses like Diane Keaton and Meg Ryan to endear to us the various forms of female inarticulateness, from babbling to stunned, open-mouthed silence. No one has promoted the appeal of such nonplused heroines more ingeniously than Nora Ephron, whose hit *You've Got Mail* (1998) finds comic inspiration in the new verbal intimacy of cyberspace. The movie modernizes a 1940 gem, *The Shop Around the Corner,* translating its enchanting premise—that language can create desire and not just confirm it—into our electronic culture. Ryan's character, Kathleen Kelly, even takes the e-mail handle Shopgirl, but she bears little resemblance to the spirited working girls of decades past. Kathleen owns a book shop that is being driven out of business by the megastore entrepreneur Joe Fox III, played by Tom Hanks. What neither of them knows is that they are beginning to fall in love with each other, sight unseen, over e-mail. However comfortable Kathleen may be in confiding to Joe, her e-mail soulmate, when she finds herself face to face with the actual entrepreneur, she can barely articulate her stupefaction and, even when provoked, can't find the right words to answer back, something the shopgirls of thirties comedies did without blinking. But Kathleen can't think when she's provoked, she confides to Joe in anonymous e-mail messages. Her mind goes blank and she spends "all night tossing and turning trying to figure out what I should have said." "Even now," she confesses, "I can't figure out what to say." Joe reassures her that "when you finally have the pleasure of saying the thing you mean to say the moment you mean to say it, then remorse inevitably follows." Fast-talking dames, who actually knew the pleasure of saying the thing you mean to say the moment you mean to say it, would have treated this advice with the disdain it deserves.

The signs of the times are still too indistinct to interpret. The language of the cineplex continues to be dominated by male ways of speaking, as well as acting. Expletives are displacing the rich vernacular of everyday life; four-letter words are verbal tics triggering laughter among audience members who may never have heard a witty line. Dumb or gross jokes have usurped the prestige of smart talk, and young women, perhaps stunned or baffled by the insistently orgasmic burst of the guffaw, seem hesitant to attempt an available but neglected range of repartee: the retort, the quip, the sally, the well-aimed rather than all-purpose sarcasm.

Thus the obvious topicality of this book: at no time in the past fifty years has what Henry James called the "question of our speech" been more open, troubling, and unresolved. This book is partly a call to lure the young out of the verbal ghettos of what Ruth J. Simmons, president of Brown University, calls mallspeak, a standardized dialect overcrowded by "it's like," "you know," and "whatever." Simmons's denunciation of mallspeak honors her spirited and articulate forebears: "It's minimalist, it's reductionist, it's repetitive, it's imprecise, it's inarticulate, it's vernacular. It drives me crazy." [3]

Certainly there is no lack of both seasoned and youthful talent to enlist in the cause of female articulateness: from Goldie Hawn, Diane Keaton, Susan Sarandon, Holly Hunter, Annette Bening, and Meg Ryan to Lisa Kudrow, Cameron Diaz, Helen Hunt, Laura Dern, Téa Leoni, and Julia Roberts. Black and Hispanic performers like Halle Berry and Jennifer Lopez, women with similar gifts for speaking their minds, might find the fast-talking dame, happily insouciant when it came to class barriers, a model for uninhibited, richly idiomatic speech in multicultural times.

Two caveats to those who pick up this book: You will find little mention of the feminist critique of film as a tool of ideological oppression and the camera as an instrument of the "male gaze," catering to voyeurs and fetishists. Even if this critique were true, which I don't believe it is, it wouldn't seriously affect my argument, since the fast-talking dame doesn't stand or sit or lie still long enough to satisfy such customers. More to the point, my subject is movie talk, and my concern is with the voices, diction, intonation, and the fast, syncopated rhythm that makes the American language distinct. I have been extremely liberal in quoting the lively dialogue and brash speech that once set the standard and pace for the way Americans talked to one another.

This book, then, is meant to introduce fast-talking dames to a new generation of filmgoers and to revive the memories of those who came of age under their spell. These fast-talkers were the verbal muses of a period in American history when the language as well as political institutions of democratic culture were reinventing themselves. They were listened to then by millions of people, and why not again? What they said, and the wit and energy with which they said it, is still worth hearing.

Acknowledgments

This book represents countless hours of fun spent watching and talking about films in the company of amusing and treasured friends. P. Adams Sitney, with whom I taught a course on comedy, encouraged me years ago to think and write about the films I cared most about. His late wife, Marjorie Keller, was the first to suggest that I seriously pursue a study of the comic heroines of classic Hollywood films. David Bromwich offered me invaluable advice as the project neared completion. Between laughs, Cynthia Avila, Julia Ballerini, Suzanne Nash, Deborah Nord, Gaetana Marrone-Puglia, Susan Nanus, Brigitte Peucker, Barbara Rietveld, Barbara Gershen, and Eric Santner provided moral support and timely suggestions. I thank all of them for always being ready to listen to my latest enthusiasm or recitation of my latest comic find. Through his marvelous wit and gift for description, Martin Karlow, who shares my deep enjoyment of these films, always refreshed my sense of what these films still had to say to us. Alan Dale, who was teaching and writing a book on slapstick at the same time as I was writing this one, was generous with both his time and ideas. In particular, I would thank him for our excursions into New York City to catch a rare showing at the Film Forum. Jay Dickson and Lisa Sternlieb, great companions, could always be depended on to watch films with me and chuckle, even guffaw, with unrestrained pleasure.

I have also been fortunate to receive superb professional assistance. The staff at the Museum of Modern Art was particularly generous in offering me advice as well as assistance in researching and illustrating this book. Charles Silver unobtrusively brought files to my attention that enriched my understanding of the actors and films that are featured in this book. Ron Magliozzi was equally attentive. I remember our sharing a moment of pleasure simply thinking about Carole Lombard's performance in *True Confession*. In a stressful time for her,

Terry Geesken helped me sift through files of film stills, and graciously helped me choose, when I felt tormented by indecision, the still that would show off my subjects to their best advantage. The staff at Rockefeller College, especially Pat Heslin and Janée Serio, were as generous in giving me technical help as they were in offering me moral support. Lesley Wheeler, Jay Dickson, and Antonio Garcia were indefatigable and resourceful research assistants who helped dig up facts and root out errors in my presentation of materials.

By her intelligence, sympathy, and superb instincts for what an author needs to hear (not all of it flattering, but all of it sensible and indispensable), my editor at Yale University Press, Lara Heimert, ensured that the publication of this book was the most rewarding experience of my writing life. My agent, Lydia Wills, not only handled the business end of this project with merciful dispatch but gave my confidence a much-needed boost at a time when my reserves were somewhat depleted. Special thanks are reserved for my manuscript editor, Heidi Downey, who saved me from countless solecisms and embarrassing mistakes. More, she caught the rhythm of fast talk and the mood of these films, so that reading over her corrections was more like having a conversation about what mattered, emotionally as well linguistically, about these dames I so admire. Thanks also to Samantha Foster for her scrupulous fact-checking.

Finally, to my splendid sons, Daniel and Matthew, my thanks for indulging their mom's preference for black and white and for coming to share her wonder for fast-talking dames. My beloved mother, who first and last loved to talk, gives this book its major theme—the pleasures of speech. And to my sister, Dina, I hope this book conveys—and not just in the dedication—how much I owe and cherish her.

Fast-Talking Dames

A Comic History of Dames

1 Fast-Talking Dames

Do you not know I am a woman? What I think, I must speak.

—*Rosalind in* As You Like It, *act 3, scene 2*

A girl has the right to talk, doesn't she?

—*Amy Lind (Olivia de Havilland) to T. L. "Biff" Grimes*

(James Cagney) in The Strawberry Blonde

To start with: a curious kind of sexual compliment and come-on that punctuates *It's a Wonderful World* (1939 version), one of those unpretentious gems that gave the thirties, decade of disasters, their distinctive comic glitter. "I don't know, lots of times," confesses Guy Johnson (James Stewart), a gumshoe on the lam, to Edwina Corday (Claudette Colbert), a poet who first avoided Johnson, then invented all manner of reasons to stick with him, "I've thought to myself, 'Well now, this, this just can't be— that all dames are dumb and all men ain't,' but that's the way it seemed to me, until you came along. . . . Yeah, you sort of changed my whole philosophy about women. I don't know, I always figured they all ended at the neck. You sort of begin there." Let us begin, then, where Guy leaves off: reevaluating dames from the neck up. At first Guy, who finds he can't ditch Edwina once she realizes that he is innocent of the murder rap hanging over his head, thinks she is the "worst break I've had in five years." This is saying a lot, given his earlier pronouncement that he had not met a "dame yet who wasn't a nitwit and lunkhead." So this declaration comes as a kind of revelation about a particular kind of woman—a dame—and a dawning masculine awareness of the special charms she holds from the neck up.

We could of course begin by admiring the obvious charms of those luminous female faces that irradiated the screen at that moment in cinema when, as Roland Barthes remembers, "capturing the human face still plunged audiences into the deepest ecstasy."[1] We could start there but we mustn't end there, lest we miss much of what is greeted as really new and wonderful in Guy's recantation. What he's saying is that he now sees a dame—at least this dame—as a brainy marvel. He will change his mind several times on this score, but ultimately he and the movie will vindicate this self-surprising love of brainy womanhood. Stewart, consummate actor that he was, lingers over the phrase "sort of begin there" in a kind of wonderment. His character has had his first glimmer of a new kind of woman being born, seemingly before his eyes. What he sees is no hallucination. There *is* nothing like a dame, as the song tells us in a similar moment of erotic salute. It tells us, too, that in the multicultural world celebrated in *South Pacific* a dame is a specific American creation, one of the things worth fighting for in our culture.

One of the things that makes a dame like nothing else, certainly nothing else you can name, is that nothing talks like a dame—talks fast and talks on and talks in a singularly American way. A momentous, exhilarating yet underappreciated sexual and social revolution occurred when movies acquired the power of speech. The talkies provided the opportunity, quickly exploited, for the representation of emergent social types who spoke, sometimes invented, a language that was to become *the* American idiom. This book is a study of one of the most impressive and influential creations of the talkies—the fast-talking dame. The fast talk isolates the quality that distinguished her life on screen; the dame suggests an unaffected if occasionally uneasy delight in women so swift on the uptake. A pretty or even beautiful face has no particular claim on damehood—that distinction is reserved

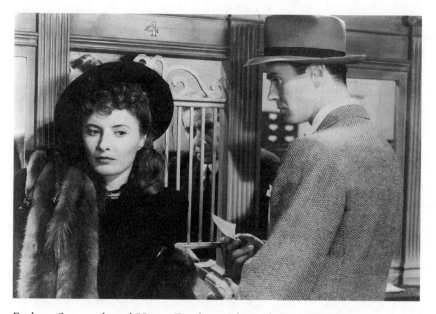

Barbara Stanwyck and Henry Fonda in *The Lady Eve*—"Positively the same dame"

for the quick-witted as well as the attractive. Brains as much as fine facial lines and beguiling eyes account for the unique sexual allure of the fast-talking dame. They also ensure her survival. Anita Loos, the screenwriter who gave many fast-taking dames their snappy lines and who thought of herself as *cérèbrale,* genially drew this moral in remarking on the fate of Madeline Hurlock, the wife of Robert Sherwood: "She is the only known survivor of the Mack Sennett bathing beauties; beauty combined with lack of brains is extremely deleterious to the health."[2] The dames of American comedy possessed lovely, sleek bodies and knew how to show them off to their best advantage, but they captivate us less by how shapely they are below the neck as how sharp they are above it. And nothing gives as much definition to a face or to a dame as her speech—the pace as well as the gist of it.

Her speech as much as her demeanor is, indeed, what defines the fast-talking dame as a female type indigenous to American shores. She exists in ironic and often rebellious relation to British dames, a social as well as linguistic fact that Preston Sturges deliriously embroiders in *The Lady Eve,* which casts Barbara Stanwyck in a dual role as cardsharp

Jean Harrington and aristocrat Lady Eve Sidwich. A running gag has Muggsy (William Demarest), the only character in the film to notice and object to the fact that both women look *exactly* alike, declare to unheeding ears, "Positively the same dame." He is, of course, both right *and* wrong. The American "dame" and the British dame may share the same body, but they are not the same person, as the film goes to extravagant lengths to demonstrate.

In building an entire comedy on this linguistic joke, Sturges was remarking the impatience of Americans—modern, democratic, spiritually and socially mobile—with any suggestion of insuperable class divisions. In calling a woman a dame, then, Americans are rejecting all the genteel associations adhering to the word. Slang has a way of puncturing pretentious usages, but such democratization is not always viewed with good or kindly grace. The sardonic Waldo Lydecker (Clifton Webb) is ready to murder—for the second time!—Laura (Gene Tierney), the heroine-victim of the movie that bears her name, because she has bestowed her affections on the police detective Mark McPherson (Dana Andrews), who refers to her as a dame. Lydecker's villainy, of course, is signaled to us precisely by his refusal to tolerate those who speak the virile common tongue. (He doesn't think highly of Laura and Mark's "disgustingly earthy relationship" either.) His verbal snobbery, like the class snobbery that his starched syntax proclaims, makes him hostile to the jaunty rhythms and salty speech of the American vernacular.

Others are more alert to the comedy of type and behavior that the mere word "dame" can conjure. In *Song of the Thin Man* (1947), for example, Nora Charles, played by the classy (but never snobbish) Myrna Loy, becomes uncharacteristically proper in her diction when her son uses the word "dame" at the breakfast table. She appeals to her husband, Nick, the unflappable William Powell, to correct him. "I never say dame," he instructs his son. "I always say doll or dish." One of the reasons Nora married Nick, we are given to understand from the very first of the Thin Man movies, is that she gets to hear talk, as well as meet characters, as far removed linguistically as they are socially from her Nob Hill crowd. When Nicky is dragooned into paying a family visit in *After the Thin Man* (1936), he cannot help asking of the butler who opens the stately door: "Is this the waxworks?" Once inside, Nora's formidable Aunt Katherine Forrest (Jessie Ralph), looking down while breathing through her nose, at once greets and dismisses him in the snooty locutions typical of her clan: "Hello, Ni-col-ass." In a populist form like the movies, elevated diction, like an overly genteel manner, is often regarded as a sign of the creeping sclerosis that comes from inbreeding. Much of the comedy of *After the Thin Man,* in fact, stems from the comic bout in diction between Nick, who prefers the saloon to the salon, and Nora's high-toned, straitlaced tribe, just as *Song of the Thin Man* derives great fun in having Nora, a quick study, start talking back to jazz musicians in their own stupefying patois.

Still, Nora's discomfort, however bemused, at hearing her son refer to women as dames suggests in the word an undertone of vulgarity, or even vague criminality. This suggestion does not come amiss. Dames are often seen consorting with gangsters, and there is a good reason they do so. They speak the same language. Yet even in their more law-abiding pursuits, American dames may arouse suspicions of moral as well as verbal laxity. Even a slight pre–Production Code class comedy like 1931's *The Hot Heiress* (one of the many films that show us what we missed when Thelma Todd died before she could graduate from delectable comic foil and sidekick to leading comic heroine) pokes knowing fun at the dame's reputation for acting as well as talking fast. A working-class riveter who falls for a "hot" heiress boasts that he knows "a dame so fast she could turn out the lights and jump into bed before the room gets dark." What moralist could hope to catch up, much less keep up, with such high-speed flight? Dames inspire such ambiguous tributes because they tend to ignore, when they do not openly mock, traditional notions of respectable femininity.

These notions were safeguarded to an extent under the censorious Production Code, instituted in 1930 but not effectively enforced until 1934 by Joseph Breen, the "supreme pontiff of motion picture morals."[3] Thomas Doherty, echoing Virginia Woolf's famous pronouncement about the beginning of modern culture, dramatically reports the effect the Code had on classical Hollywood cinema:

On or about July 1934, American cinema changed. During that month, the Production Code Administration, popularly known as the Hays Office, began to regulate, systematically and scrupulously, the content of Hollywood motion pictures. For the next thirty years, cinematic space was a patrolled landscape with secure perimeters and well-defined borders. Adopted under duress at the urging of priests and politicians, Hollywood's in-house policy of self-censorship set the boundaries for what could be seen, heard, even implied on screen.[4]

Banned were "scenes of passion." Adultery, illicit sex, seduction, and rape could not even be alluded to unless they were absolutely essential to the plot and condemned by film's end. One of the commandments of the Code inculcated respect for the sanctity of marriage, an institution that many of the fast-talking dames questioned, often openly. Language necessarily fell under prohibition. By invoking the "dictates of good taste and civilized usage" the Code sought to limit obscenity, seen as "against divine and human law, and hence altogether outside the range of subject matter or treatment" permissible in film, and vulgarity, "the treatment of low, disgusting, unpleasant subjects which decent society considers outlawed from normal conversation."[5] The fast-talking dame was a vulgarian who often flouted the dictates of good taste and civilized usage, hence her often ambiguous reputation in the minds of moviegoers and in the annals of popular culture.

The association between fast talk and loose morals that lurks in the popular imagination is made overt in the conventions of pantomime. In the formulaic characters of pantomime, the Dame, like the villain, is a stock figure, usually a middle-aged woman, who is always impersonated by a man. As a figure of fun as well as authority (the dame initially designated a social superior or ruler), the dame is credited with that power Chaucer's Wife of Bath identified as *maistrie*— mastery over the male, particularly in sexual matters. This wayward pleasure in sexual dominance hovers mischievously and tenaciously on the semantic fringes of a word that in modern usage has mainly been restricted to its aristocratic or colloquial usage. The word "dame" seems to attract, like a magnet, all the free-floating anxieties — as well as erotic interest — inspired by any license with, or reversal of, sexual roles.

There is no question that the fast-talking dames who came of age in thirties comedy were cheeky experimenters who balked at traditional gender roles and were insistent on self-rule. In exposing "The Big Lie" on which she believes Western patriarchy and its modern propaganda organ, Hollywood movies, are founded, Molly Haskell pays tribute to "the proud ones, the unconventional ones, the uppity ones . . . bucking the tide of an industry that, like the human race generally, preferred its women malleable and pleasing to the eye; and that, like men the world over, felt deep down that women should be seen but not heard. Like animals or silent comics (Harpo Marx, Keaton, the silent Chaplin), women are more lovable without the disputatious, ego-defining dimension of speech."[6]

This is a just and shrewd tribute to the uppity ones, but it must be said that the last half of Haskell's comment departs from its first half, turning acclaim into a jeremiad. The crucial fact, as Haskell herself recognizes, indeed celebrates, is that uppity women did speak up and never so smartly nor so insistently as with the birth of sound. They did so partly because, as the studio bosses came to recognize, "those wonderful people out there in the dark" (as *Sunset Boulevard's* Norma Desmond [Gloria Swanson] describes her audience) wanted to hear what they had to say. But there was a more primary, compelling *existential* motive that urged them to speak as quickly and as distinctly as they could. Speech is, as Haskell says, ego-defining, a psychological as well as social fact known to the articulate women of dramatic comedy from Shakespeare to Wilde and Shaw. The classic American comic heroine — the dame who attained her majority with the birth of sound — became a fast-talker not just to keep up with the times, but to run ahead of them. She paved a way for a new class or sort of woman who finally would answer to no one but herself.

This, at least, is the claim of this book — that when film found its human voice, it simultaneously gave to the American woman, as performer and heroine, a chance to speak her mind, to have a real, not just a presumptive, say in her own destiny. It was a chance that women of the silent screen, intertitles notwithstanding, were effectively denied. Recall Gloria Swanson's famous line about the splendor of silent films in *Sunset Boulevard*—the line that sums up her career, her character, and the silent movies in one megalomaniacal statement: "And no dialogue. We didn't need dialogue. We had faces then." Norma Desmond's lament at the advent of talkies records a truth about women in silents. They were limited as well as immortalized by the mesmerizing prestige of their status as stunning visual icons. A comedienne of the thirties and early forties could say with equal authority and conviction: "We had voices then." She captured and held attention with her verbal fluency and improvisational genius as much as with her looks, which were as ravishing as any that graced the screen before or after her heyday.

The female voice has never been recorded in so many expressive registers: the merriment that stitched together Lombard's comic wails and droll sighs, the not unpleasant shrieks and dips in Harlow's sexual yelps, the unladylike sounds made by these reckless, even silly dames unafraid of *being,* as well as appearing, game for anything; the cadences that gave a heart-grabbing lilt to the speech of Claudette Colbert, Myrna Loy, and Irene Dunne, comic actresses with voices that could be petulant or confiding, childish or maternal, erotically curious or sexually knowing; the sharp sophistication in the way Constance Bennett could articulate vowels, making them sound as svelte as her art deco body; Ginger Rogers's way of savoring her repartee, either to make sure her verbal sallies hit their mark or to give herself time to prepare her next one; Rosalind Russell's crisp and supremely confident intonations, which gave her comic delivery the assuredness of a large woman who knows she is taking up room and is enjoying the space allotted her; the husky pitch of Jean Arthur's voice, with that hint of a sexual catch at the back of the throat that suggests her readiness, despite the big-city veneer of cynicism, to be thrilled back to her small-town idealism; the self-assured diction of Katharine Hepburn and Bette Davis, suggesting years of elocution lessons in Yankee finishing schools, years that have never fully erased the undertone that whispers, "I'm a good sport, too."

And then there is Barbara Stanwyck's voice, modulated and enriched by all the under- as well as overtones of a young woman already burdened with a full, often checkered past. Her voice in *The Lady Eve* is that of a young woman who has been around, but one whom experience has not made cheap. Jean Harrington may be crooked, but as her father insists as a point of honor, "never common." On the contrary, the whiff of past affairs is the source of her enticing "perfume," to use Sturges's own metaphor for the aura of worldliness that so intoxicates her mark, Charles Pike (Henry Fonda). Stanwyck, whose Jean is so immersed in the world where getting and spending is accomplished by charming and gulling, is just as comfortable in film noir, the world of *Double Indemnity* (1944), as she is in the menacing, visibly corrupt yet "comic" world of *Meet John Doe* (1941). The expressiveness of Stanwyck's voice is used, with stunning effect, to link the unhappy end of Jean's shipboard romance to the creation of that female revenger, the Lady Eve. Jean is informed that her father has actually pocketed the money that Charles lost in a card game. Jean, satisfied by this turn of events, approvingly remarks, "I feel a lot better already." Stanwyck delivers this line not in breezy repartee but in the dark and determined tone taken by the femmes fatales of film noir. I'll have more to say later about this sudden translatability—and convergence—of comedy and the dark revenge melodrama of crime films and film noir. For now, let us remark the astonishing variety with which female performers amplified the sounds and quickened the senses of the early talkies.

Fast-talking dames were major figures in what Robert Benchley lampooned as the "voice culture" that sprang up with the advent of sound. (Benchley, a humorist, would make a fine living playing to this voice culture, contributing his bon mots and mordant asides not only to his secondary roles, usually as the tippling sidekick to the working girl, but to a series of MGM shorts in which he offered his own woeful but hilarious commentary on the minor hazards and major indignities of ordinary life.) Benchley reported to his *New Yorker* audiences, those sophisticates accustomed to the verbal aplomb of voices trained for the stage, on the droll aspects of the panic that set in when Hollywood needed actors who could speak.[7] The panic was not just commercial, however. The philosopher and movie lover Stanley Cavell has written most perceptively about the existential, indeed ontological, challenge posed by a technology that could capture the human voice in all its registers from the birth wail to the death rattle. "With talkies we got back the clumsiness of speech, the dumbness and duplicities and concealments of assertion, the bafflement of soul and body by their inarticulateness and by their terror of articulateness. Technical improvements will not overcome these ontological facts: they only magnify them." [8]

But not everyone felt terror. Women could feel tremors of excitement, the counterpart of terror, when confronted with the chance to speak and to attest to their own experience of the world. Female daring before the terror of articulateness was observed a century earlier by Alexis de Tocqueville, another philosophical observer of democratic manners. Tocqueville, approaching the end of his study of American personal and political culture, concluded that "if I were asked . . . to what the singular prosperity and growing strength of that people ought mainly to be attributed, I should reply: To the superiority of their women." To what did he ascribe their superiority? To the "happy boldness with which young women in America contrive to manage their thoughts and their language amid all the difficulties of free conversation; a philosopher would have stumbled at every step along the narrow path which they trod without accident and without effort." [9]

In certain cases, such as the ones we're considering in this book, American women can astonish by the sheer speed of their verbal courses. We can gauge the quickness as well as length of their strides by considering the justly admired speaking pace of *His Girl Friday* (1940), certainly the fastest of the talky comedies. So quickly do words come flying out of mouths that it is difficult to follow what is being said, a predicament hilariously dramatized in a scene in which Rosalind Russell (Hildy Johnson) and her former husband, Cary Grant (Walter Burns), are trying to meet a deadline and get an exclusive on a prison break. In a comic oratorio that is played *molto vivace,* they bark orders and telegraph copy to their editor on the phone, hurl words back and forth to each other without any apparent intake of breath, all the while plugging their ears to screen out the noise they themselves are making. Their talk is so furiously fast that it becomes a challenge to sort out from the rapid buzz of words what these two characters are saying to each other, and since they so often speak at the same time, to decide whom to listen to.

This sexual competition for attention is very much the verbal motive for comedy. Howard Hawks, who conceded to women in comedy their dominant part, resorted to a code term to direct Cary Grant in his moments of comic opportunity. Hawks recalls of his collaboration with Grant: "We finally got so that I'd say, 'Cary, this is a good chance to do Number Seven.' Number Seven was trying to talk to a woman who was doing a lot of talking."[10] Number Seven is shorthand for the challenge comedy puts to men: they must try to do what women apparently do so effortlessly—talk a lot.

In issuing this challenge to men, comedy also presents a dramatic and certainly literate alternative to that distinctly American film genre concerned with masculine codes: the Western. In the Western, incorruptible and heroic manhood is associated primarily with the laconic —the "yup" and "nope" that impersonators invariably mimic when they "do" Gary Cooper as the quintessential Western hero. (Cooper good-naturedly mocked himself doing a cameo for the genial Hollywood spoof *It's a Great Feeling*. The glibly narcissistic Jack Carson finds, like many a down-and-out cowpoke before him, that he cannot elicit more than a yup and nope as he relates his woes to the star in the studio commissary.) The recognizably American actors who figure as naifs in American comedies of the thirties and forties—Gary Cooper, James Stewart, and Henry Fonda—also gave us our most memorable screen portraits of the Westerner, the archetypal role that idolized the plain-speaking eloquence of the American male. The Western identified the laconic, even the inarticulate, as the very sign of the manly. That iconic Western figure John Wayne perfected the image of the "quiet man" who conserves his strength for things too important to put into words. The American male of heroic character is often portrayed as either shy of words or suspicious of them. Cary Grant and William Powell, the most articulate as well as debonair of comic actors, would never convince in a Western; they are too cosmopolitan in demeanor, their relation to words too gratifying for them to abide by the Western code of taciturnity. James Cagney and Edward G. Robinson, reveling in their gangster roles, spit out their words like so many bullets; but their exuberance in ranting is never regarded as anything but hooligan self-display, a symptom of their sociopathy. Clark Gable, who began playing gangster and irresistible bad boy roles, soon displayed a gift for comic tomfoolery that absorbed rather than compromised his renegade manliness. Still, his Western roles depend on our considering him essentially an *adventurer,* not, as Stewart or Fonda or Cooper can impersonate so believably and so likeably, the quiet but hardy defender of American values. (In the Westerns he made with Anthony Mann, Stewart tries on the roles of demonic crusader or penitent marauder.[11])

Romantic and screwball comedies of this era redeem us from this culturally endemic paranoia about words. In doing so they provide us with another version of the manly. For Rudolph Valentino and John Gilbert, the stars who defined the erotic style of silent film, the eyes were the sexual organ that transfixed and captivated their female quarry. With the advent of sound, the voice became an erotic instrument on which to play, with infinite more subtlety, the sexual game of give and take, advance and retreat, flight and pursuit. The talkies gave birth to a new kind of woman who needed a new kind of man to fantasize over and, equally important, to *play* with (playing verbal games was especially fun). Thelma Todd's Lola in *The Hot Heiress* has been around, so when her society pal Juliette Hunter (Ona Munson) falls for a riveter she can appraise him without laying eyes—or hands—on him: "I know that type—ungrammatical but strong." Never has the reputed sexiness of the "strong, silent type" been more breezily dispatched. Even in the subdued precincts of a family comedy–turned drama like *Four Daughters* (1938), we can see female impatience with male inarticulateness when one of the daughters, pursued by a shy and virtually wordless suitor, sets the comic terms of her submission: "If he ever finishes a sentence, I'll marry him."

Such attitudes define a new masculine ideal, one that prizes verbal fluency as well as physical or moral charisma. Romantic and screwball comedies rejoice in the giddy energy of human speech, in invective, in repartee, in drop-dead one-liners, and reserve their highest delights— and kudos—for those most adept at verbal sparring. These comedies do not exalt the laconic but reward the quick-witted and outspoken. In Westerns you survive if you draw fast and shoot straight, and talk, if you must, much later and then as little as possible. In comedy you triumph—morally as well sexually—if you think fast and talk even faster. Men must be found—or formed—to answer to such demands. Even if the desired male is initially slow of speech or stunned, like Gary Cooper's Longfellow Deeds in *Mr. Deeds Goes to Town* (1936) into an emotionally burdened silence, he must be made to speak his mind. Such films taught a generation how to talk about the things that meant the most to them. But they also taught the ways that language itself could create desire rather than lamely stumble after it. Fast talk may occasion panic or even terror in quieter, more contemplative souls, but it also offers unparalleled moments of happy astonishment at the creative power of bold and unhesitating speech.

Astonishment, but at some deep unreachable level of national reserve, dismay. Suspicion of fast talk still haunts our culture, especially our movie culture. This suspicion tends to surface and express itself in two major worries. The first is that fast talk is loose or dishonest, especially as practiced by those vaguely amoral, manipulative characters of whom we should beware—this is a psychological and moral objection that mobilizes a great deal of gender suspicion already at large, at any given moment, in the popular culture. Indeed, the misgivings attached to fast-talking dames represent America's contribution to an ancient and venerable misogynistic tradition directed against *mulier loquax* (the talkative woman), as she was called in the eponymous diatribe against her by the Greek rhetorician Libanius of Antioch (A.D. 314–c. 393) and as she was lampooned in Juvenal's Satire, VI. We shall consider this distrust shortly. But let us first attend to the disquiet surrounding fast talk, or any prolonged or virtuoso act of human speech. The disquiet takes the form of a concern that fast talk may privilege pace over meaning, facility over substance.

This is at once an aesthetic and philosophical worry that Cavell has acknowledged as one of his own. While appreciating that the advent of sound made it possible for films to "discover the poetry in speech," Cavell questions the kind of poetry that talkies could ever be expected or be likely to produce. Such poetry, he assures us,

> will not be the poetry of poetry. It seemed at first as if it ought to have been, as if when the filmed world expressed itself in speech it would have the same absolute intelligibility as its ex-

hibition to sight. . . . The best film dialogue has so far been the witty and hard-nosed, apparently because the lines are fast, or laconic. But wit and clip are in themselves not always of the highest interest. They work, I think, because they provided natural occasions on which silence is broken, and in which words do not go beyond their moment of saying; occasions on which silence naturally reasserts itself.[12]

In the talkative world of comedy, however, silence is not something that is broken, or that we subside back into, but something that is *achieved*. We are not born into a noiseless world, nor may we even hope to die into one.

There is no better example of how an eloquent silence struggles for a foothold in the clamorous human world than the comedy that set the standard and style for fast talk—*His Girl Friday*. According to one account, the film reproduces speech at 240 words per minute, compared to the average pace of 100 to 150 words.[13] The evidence comes in the form of an anecdote related by Todd McCarthy in his biography of Howard Hawks. "At one point," he writes, "Roz Russell became concerned that the unvarying torrent of dialogue would prove too much for audiences to take, but Hawks, with great insight, reassured her: 'You're forgetting the scene you're gonna play with the criminal. It's gonna be quiet, so silent. You'll just whisper to him, you'll whisper, Did you kill that guy? And your whispering will change the rhythm. But when you're with Grant, we don't change it. You just rivet in on him all the time.' "[14] Hawks understood that silence is a dramatic complement of speech. In *His Girl Friday*, silence functions powerfully as a form of moral registration. When people are rendered speechless in Hawks's comedies, it is usually because they have run out of words, not out of gall. Silence gives us a chance to glimpse the moral vista of shame. As Manny Farber has noted, it is Hildy's singular reproach of her heartlessly gabby colleagues, "Gentleman of the Press," that calls forth all the sardonic irony lurking in "gentleman." Her rebuke also represents the quietest moment in that film.

But not the longest nor the last. That belongs to the last word, always of supreme importance in any form, but especially in the talking comedy, which equates vitality with quick, witty, and seemingly unstoppable speech. Although wit and clip are in themselves not always of the highest interest, the dialectical relation between them attracts and rewards our attention. The "depths" of silence in comedy do not preexist the characters but collectively form as the talk goes on. Silence is the pool—or bog—into which the sinners and scapegoats of comedy are destined to plunge to expiate their sins of talking to no, or to bad, purpose. The heroines of comedy know that silence is not a natural state but a moral and emotional one reached *through* speech. The heroines of comedy also know the difference between a silence pregnant with emotional or moral meaning and a silence born of or burdened by inarticulateness. The silence that struggles to make itself heard in fast-talking comedies is a silence that, as the saying goes, speaks volumes. Comedy is the talkative form that makes that paradox real, rather than merely a clever contradiction.

Yet having reassured ourselves, however provisionally, that fast talk and silence, hence fluency and depth, are not so estranged as we might think, we immediately confront the moral uneasiness aroused by fast-talking dames. In comedy, happiness is sexual success, the reward of that artfulness which, especially in American culture, is predominantly a female craft. The mating games improvised by the artful female (a designing Eve) to amuse and beguile the ostensibly artless male (an innocent and all too American Adam) constitute one of the standard plots of American comedy. But for the game to conclude in happy as well as holy matrimony, the guileless Adam must be exposed to the questionable pleasures of play and imposture, to the delights in acting, however temporarily, a person other than oneself. One of the enduring aspects of Cary Grant's charm is how good-naturedly he falls in with the woman's instinct to play, nowhere more gallantly than when he refuses to expose his wife's masquerade as a boozy vulgarian in *The Awful Truth* (1937 version).

The laughs are great in this scene, but so are the stakes—the rescue of a marriage. Sometimes the stakes are even higher, compromising as they do the woman's integrity and leaving her open to the charge that she is working a con—which she often is. Love will either exculpate or reform the fast-talking dame but will never ask her to renounce her desire to play, her desire *for* play. Comic literacy revives and establishes the theatrical authority of American women as command performers and moral agents, an authority that the silent movie had eroded, if not abolished altogether.

Jazz Babies and Somnambules

It was an authority, as Tocqueville discerned, emanating from the American woman's enviable confidence and "happy boldness" in the arts of conversation.[15] Tocqueville attributed her facility and fluency to a sensible educational regime that does not shelter the growing girl from the moral facts of life but, removing her from direct maternal supervision, inculcates sturdy habits of moral reflection and self-trust. "Long before an American girl arrives at the marriageable age," he wrote, "her emancipation from maternal control begins: she has scarcely ceased to be a child when she already thinks for herself, speaks with freedom, and acts on her own impulse." Tocqueville was perfectly sensible of the moral "irregularities" and corruptions "inseparable from democratic society," yet he commended Americans for deciding that the best way to inoculate a young woman against bad manners was not to instill a "mistrust of herself" but to enhance her "confidence in her own strength of character."[16]

Moral choice for women in comedy most often presents itself in the form of sexual choice—who she marries and on what grounds may be taken as index of her character as well as her sexual taste. Leaving the staid bridegroom at the altar, as Ellie Andrews (Claudette Colbert) does in the elating comic climax to *It Happened One Night,* represents more than a mad dash for sexual joy.[17] We are thrilled by such acts of public desertion not just because they represent the triumph of renegade Eros over the programmatic machinery of social rituals, but because, morally speaking, we recognize that the heroine's sexual choice is also the decent one. The heart, according to this comic wisdom, should be the final arbiter of what is right and wrong. Ellie starts the film as an emotional disaster but is in danger of concluding it with a moral catastrophe. Her desperate resolve to marry King

Claudette Colbert and Clark Gable in *It Happened One Night*

Westley, the professional escort, out of pique and self-loathing is as close as this comedy comes to losing faith in Ellie as a heroine. Marriage to the "wrong" man is the original sin of the comic world, because it is through marriage that comedy signals its commitment to a social future populated by happy, compatible, and, it is hoped, fruitful human beings. Comedies often flirt with the "bad marriage" to show us the difference between irreversible moral collapse and the happy fall of comedy, by which young lovers lose a false pride in themselves to gain a true sense of what they are worth to each other.

Ellie demonstrates as hilariously as any of the madcap heroines of the period that a girl's early, even premature, separation from the mother might leave her on the brink of a comic fall, whirling drearily on a merry-go-round. (Bette Davis's Joan Winfield in *The Bride Came C.O.D.* [1941] suffers from the same unfocused willfulness.) Such a possibility has obviously occurred to Cavell, who notes the absence of mothers, either literally or as strong role models, in what he calls comedies of remarriage, among which he includes *It Happened One*

Night. He offers some guesses as to why mothers are either absent or inconsequential in the comedies of the period:

> Mythically, the absence of the mother continues the idea that the creation of the woman is the business of men; even, paradoxically, when the creation is that of the so-called new woman, the woman of equality. Here we seem to be telling ourselves that while there is, and is going to be, a new woman, as in the Renaissance there was a new man, nobody knows where she is to come from. The place she is to arrive is a mythological locale called America. Socially, it seems to me, the absence of the woman's mother in these films of the thirties betokens a guilt, or anyway, puzzlement, toward the generation of women preceding the generation of the central women of our films — the generation that won the right to vote without at the same time winning the issues in terms of which voting mattered enough. They compromised to the verge of forgetting themselves. Their legacy is that their daughters will not have to settle. The legacy may be exhilarating, but it is also threatening.[18]

This sociological explanation is both credible and discerning, although I would press Cavell to explain more fully what he means in referring to a generation of women compromised to the point of self-forgetfulness. What vital part of themselves are they prone to forget that their daughters dutifully remember?

Yet it is with the mythical reading Cavell offers that I, and I believe the films themselves, differ. The motherless girl as she comes of age in these vintage screen comedies is never the creation of anyone but herself. Her being motherless indicates a spiritual state that is not to be confused with being orphaned nor having need of male guidance. The business of creating woman lies primarily with herself. In any case, male creation, given the physical as well as moral facts of nature, is never actually an act of creation but takes the form of a makeover in the tradition of Shaw's *Pygmalion*. As we shall see in the next chapter, the Pygmalion myth is at the heart of these comic fantasies. When translated to American shores, however, Pygmalion undergoes a sex change. The woman assumes the role of creator, which, as in *Pygmalion,* means the one who wields—or bestows—the power of speech.

This power may be wielded in sheer fun and high spirits, as in the madcap heiress comedies like *It Happened One Night* or *Bringing Up Baby* (1938), but very often the comic heroine is a working girl who literally makes her living out of words. She is a reporter (Jean Arthur in *Mr. Deeds Goes to Town,* Rosalind Russell in *His Girl Friday,* Barbara Stanwyck in *Meet John Doe,* Katharine Hepburn in *Woman of the Year* [1942]) or a writer (Irene Dunne in *Theodora Goes Wild* [1936], Claudette Colbert in *It's a Wonderful World* and *Without Reservations* [1946]) or an actress (Carole Lombard in *Twentieth Century* [1934] and *To Be or Not to Be* [1942], Jean Harlow in *Bombshell* [1933]). The comic task for these films, which ponder the social future of the fast-talking dame, is to imagine the ways that this new woman may go about creating a life and a man worthy of her. The business of woman is, then, first to create herself; second to bring the male of her choosing and delight into her sphere of life by making him a fit—which foremost means an articulate—companion for her. That she is equal to both tasks is already implied in Tocqueville's admiring characterization of the women who come from that mythical locale called America: "An American woman is always mistress of herself; she indulges in all permitted pleasures without yielding herself up to any of them, and her reason never allows the reins of self-guidance to drop, though it often seems to hold them loosely." [19]

The habits of self-command are ripe for comic elaborations, of course. This is the primary cultural and moral function of the heiress as comic heroine, to whom all pleasures are socially as well as financially permitted. The "spoiled brat" is, after all, a figure of fun and comic endearment rather than satiric derision. The action of these spoiled heiress comedies is to make the woman truly mistress of herself by relying on her own heart rather on than the dictates of her upbringing. That is why the heiress is well advised to marry down—it's the best way for her to pick up the reins of self-guidance that she has allowed to drop.[20] Self-guidance is to be distinguished from willfulness, however. Often the two cannot be properly distinguished until the strong-willed heroine, like Ellie Andrews (Colbert) or like Joan Winfield (Bette Davis) in *The Bride Came C.O.D.*, renounces her decision, arrived at through boredom, willfulness, or sheer spite, to go through with marriage to the wrong man. Comedy is a conservative form that respectfully celebrates matrimony as a blessed state, but only if the bride knows who she is and what she wants. The runaway bride is in flight not so much from authority as from a real knowledge of her self. In the course of her comic adventures she becomes acquainted with, then loyal to, her strongest (which is distinct from her most willful) character. By acknowledging the desire born out of a deep and often newly awakened knowledge of who she is, she becomes, in effect, not only mistress but creator of herself. It might be said of many of the heroines of these comedies what Benedick sardonically noted of Beatrice in *Much Ado About Nothing*: "Truly, the lady fathers herself." It is this woman, born, when all is said and done, of and for herself, who marries at the end of comedy.

Women in talking pictures continue and cultivate this freedom, this Emersonian license for self-creation. Indeed, I would claim that the fast-talking dame, with her capacity for original action, represents a distinct social mutation. Like all mutations, she at once fulfilled and rendered obsolete preexisting female types whose sexual and social manners seemed less adapted to the rapidly changing conditions of modern American life. We have spoken of fast-talking dames as predominantly a motherless tribe, and for the most part they were. Still, everyone, even the most self-reliant, are the offspring of their times. The fast-talking dame came of age in the early thirties and reached maturity in the early forties. She bore the era's imprint, particularly its linguistic imprint, when, in fact, she did not outright create the signature speaking style of the time. But there was also an entrenched culture of gender roles and expectations with which she had to contend, sometimes to the point of mutiny, more often in tongue-in-cheek rebellion.

The cultural import of the fast-talking dame as an iconoclast should be celebrated. Most impressively (and hysterically), she was the early talkie's comic retort to James Thurber's hilariously beleaguered protest against the phenomenon he called pedestalism. The term is to be found in Thurber's learned inquiry *Is Sex Necessary? Or, Why You Feel the Way You Do*, a work that may be read most profitably, I insist, as a prologue to this comic history of dames. In this best of sexual self-help manuals, Thurber lamented that in "no other civilized nation are the biological aspects of love so distorted and transcended by emphasis upon its sacredness as they are in the United States of America." "In China," Thurber wryly observed, "it's all biology. In France it's a mixture of biology and humor. In America, it's half or two-thirds psyche."[21] The American mentalization of sex, a regrettable "advance" on Oriental sensualism and Gallic esprit, witty and carnal, is a recent (hence possibly reversible?) development. Thurber claims that it dates only as far back as the beginning of the century, when the American male first found himself sure enough of his economic livelihood to pursue pleasure for its own sake. But he had difficulty adapting to a life based not on economic striving but on the pursuit of sexual and emotional happiness.

The nineteenth century, Thurber insisted, knew nothing like pedestalism and its compensatory behaviors, as evidenced by the fact that there "was not a single case of nervous breakdown, or neurosis, arising from amatory troubles, in the whole cycle from 1800 to 1900, barring a slight flare-up just before the Mexican and Civil Wars."[22] But once the American male had the leisure to take up the pursuit of women, he found the female to be "equipped with a Defense far superior in polymorphous ingenuities to the rather simple Attack of the male."[23] Repeated injuries to his sexual self-esteem caused the American male "in a sort of divine discontent, . . . to draw apart by himself. This produced that separation of the physical and the psychic which causes the adult to remain in a state of suspended love, as if he were holding a goldfish bowl and had nowhere to put it."[24]

The dire result of this separation of psychic and physical is indicated by the title of Thurber's satire and elaborated in its epigraph, which comically quotes Major General Briggs at Shiloh, "Things look pretty bad right now." The droll epigraph sardonically reminds us that the battle between the sexes is, properly speaking, a civil war. We might wonder whether it weren't time to call a halt to the hostilities, even if it meant calling a halt to sex. Preston Sturges, a veteran chronicler as well as combatant of the war—but never, it seems, to the verge of battle-weariness—visually alludes to Thurber's dyspeptic inquiry in *The Lady Eve* when he has his comic naif, Charles Pike, a victim of pedestalism if there ever was one, reading what might be a spin-off work, *Are Snakes Necessary?* while being ogled by lubricious females as he sits dining, the sole eligible male aboard a cruise ship. The joke, with its sneaky phallic pun, is as telling as any of Thurber's sadsack cartoons—women are no longer creatures to be put on a pedestal but desirous creatures eager to rejoin the psychic and physical. They expect and often demand a real existence, not an ideal one.

In her hunger for reality and her rejection of pedestalism, the fast-talking dame appears in striking opposition to her most immediate and visible precursors on the screen: the vampire and the somnambule, the erotic predator and the sexually compliant woman. This is how Parker Tyler categorized the reigning female types of the silent era, singling them out as the original female interpretations of the silent film. "The somnambules, or the hypnotized ladies," he wrote, "were rendered almost rigid, or at least incapable of very articulate movement. This was precisely the effect produced in the unfortunate males who came within the enchanted zone of the vampire. We have to conclude that nature has provided a poetical antinomy in the sexual struggle."[25] A reasonable enough conclusion, although we might also want to suggest that human culture supplies what nature may have neglected to provide—a woman who is morally articulate and physically graceful, even in the heat of sexual struggle. Whereas the somnambule, as Tyler remarks, "is merely an instrument of the sexual excess of the male,"[26] a dream-figure of compliance, the fast-talking dame is her own sexual agent. She is not afraid of openly pursuing the man she fancies, nor does she hesitate, in contrary instances, to reject any erotic or romantic alliance that does not suit her interests or appeal to her heart. This is one of the more socially unnerving consequences of allowing women to retain the reins of self-guidance. Unnerving for men, who must share the world, at least the erotic world, with equals; unnerving for women, because independence may jeopardize their social future—they must face the possibility that being so independent-minded might scare away mates. This, too, is part of the antinomy that marks the sexual struggle.

The fast-talking dame, who hardly blinked at the "terror of inarticulateness" that Cavell detects in the early talkies, was equally unfazed by the specter of inarticulate movement. Her physical grace and nimbleness are often on display in the balletic tumbles and agile falls of her slapstick clowning. Exhibit A: Claudette Colbert's demonstration of hitchhiking technique in *It Happened One Night,* in which she elegantly extends her leg in marked—and of course funny—contrast to Gable's increasingly frenzied manual hails, proving that the limb is not only mightier than the thumb, but more eye-catching and therefore effective. Exhibit B: Carole Lombard as Hazel Flagg shadowboxing with Fredric March's Wally Cook in *Nothing Sacred* (1937), eventually landing a sucker punch right on the kisser and, noting that he has not yet keeled over, expelling just the right amount of breath to puff him into slaphappy obliviousness. Exhibit C: Myrna Loy's entrance into comic heaven as Nora Charles via a perfectly executed pratfall on the polished floor of Nick's favorite New York bar.

That the fast-talking dame proves such a resilient as well as good-tempered foe in the sexual struggle is due at least in part to her comic ancestry in silent slapstick rather than somnambulism. The fast-talking dame invariably *moves* to the same lively rhythm that regulates her speech. In her limber movements we witness, as Pauline Kael noted, one of the great triumphs and transformations of the slapstick tradition. "The screwball movies," Kael writes, "brought back the slapstick tradition of vaudeville and the two-reelers, and blended it into those brittle Broadway comedies. When it was joined to a marital farce or a slightly daring society romance, slapstick no longer seemed like kid stuff: it was no longer innocent and was no longer regarded as 'low' comedy."[27] The screwball or virtuoso elements in these talky comedies no longer appear innocent because, in fact, they aren't innocent. Their moments of slapstick (pratfall, frenetic chase, or—a Lombard specialty—sexual sparring) are exquisitely timed to coincide with moments of sexual bafflement, moments that remind us that when we scramble after a mate or take a fall, we also acquire knowledge about our bodily limits and susceptibility to more emotional hurt.

The heroines of slapstick comedies were not so much impertinent dames (as the heroines of talkies clearly are) as rambunctious hoydens,

Gilbert Seldes's affectionate name for them. Alan S. Dale, in his exuberant history of slapstick, dedicates a chapter to those irrepressible "girl heroes" who defied social and movie conventions to brave and conquer the world of physical comedy.[28] Dale's admiring term (borrowed from Beatrice Lillie) not only gives a vivid sense of how their celluloid existence depended on their physical expressiveness, but also reminds us how much of their physical heroisim was motivated as much by mischief and sheer high physical spirits, as by a kind of stubborn, admittedly adolescent determination to have fun or to have their way. Often the slapstick heroines formed a cohort of merrymakers. The Sennett Girls formed just such a comic chorus, which specialized in sending up the maenadic group behavior of young, flighty females. The hijinks and zany rituals of closed female societies barely survived early talkies, although the giggly, hormonally overheated culture of adolescent girls has enjoyed a kind of revival in Amy Heckerling's *Clueless* and in the hysterical comedy of Gothic slasher movies like *Scream*. With few exceptions, the comic heroine goes it alone, attended (or assisted) only by a maternal aunt or an avuncular coworker.

The exceptions, however, are worth noting. Even George Cukor's sympathetic direction cannot detoxify the acrid misogyny of Clare Boothe's *The Women,* but the film is fortunately not representative of the giddy camaraderie that typically obtains when high-spirited females unite. In one of her few young debutante roles, Barbara Stanwyck weds the slapstick tradition of wacky group behavior to the more individualistic folktype of the madcap heiress in her portrayal of Melsa Manton in *The Mad Miss Manton* (1938), a comedy–murder mystery that teams her with Henry Fonda. Stanwyck plays the ringleader of a group of society debutantes who are surprisingly and amusingly individualized: there is the compulsive eater, the chronic objector to any hint of enforced solidarity (when one of the girls tries to fend off the killer by reminding him "what you do to her you will do to all of us" she quickly objects, "That's communism").

In the Sennett silents, comic individuality is generally submerged in the female tribe. The focus is on group antics that center around a boisterous ringleader. The irrepressibly playful Carole Lombard delights in taking on this role for the pillow-fighting co-eds at Sunnydale

School whose hijinks are the subject of Sennett's *Campus Carmen* and *Swim Princess* (story by Jane J. Tynan and Frank Capra). Sennett's *Girl from Everywhere,* however, with its enticingly allegorical title, is perhaps the best example of the loosely episodic structure of most Sennett comedies. Comic literacy is confined to pratfalls and chases, although *The Campus Carmen* does feature a hilarious sendup of Bizet's *Carmen,* reminding us of how much even "low" physical comedy is energized by the irreverent force of high-toned parody.

The opening shots of *The Girl from Everywhere* can, in fact serve as a kind of visual primer to the iconography of the female body in slapstick comedy. We first see a silhouette of a nubile female body, then an intertitle that poses a tantalizing question: "Where does the bathing girl come from?" The answer is pictured in a series of "leg" shots. The first is a back view of shapely legs set off by glossy, straight-seamed stockings, a visual, almost tactile delight over which the camera appreciatively lingers, until a hamburger unceremoniously interrupts this pin-up pose; a quick cut gives us a less enthralled view of the short-order cook, a female centaur of the diner whose upper half seems genetically grafted onto her lovely stems. The next shot is a side view of crossed limbs; a quick pan upward discloses, not surprisingly, that they are attached to the body of a typist; the third shot is of comely pair of slender horse legs, a hilarious visual gag in itself, but one that has a bonus shot when the camera pans upward to reveal Carole Lombard perched magnificently on the horse's back. The comic logic of the gag is completed when the visual association between sexy gams and legs made for running yields a final shot of girls on an athletic field in a wild dash toward a goal just outside camera range. The next shot discloses their finish line and finally answers the initial question put to us: the girls are racing toward Mack Sennett's Studio Wardrobe, a "fitting place," as the titles punningly inform us, to start a career as a bathing beauty and screen star. Before Ellie Andrews demonstrated her peerless hitchhiking method in *It Happened One Night,* Sennett was having fun with the cinematic license to fetishize the female leg, both for its sexual enticements and for its motor powers.

The eponymous Girl from Everywhere is not yet a dame, but a precursor to her. The girls or hoydens of slapstick developed a versatile and eloquent grammar of movement distinctly opposed to the hieratic or drugged motions of the somnambule. The fast-talking dame is deeply indebted to the repertoire of the agile, comical gesture that they improvised. In Carole Lombard we can see how the slapstick training carries over into her dynamic physical performances in *Twentieth Century* and *Nothing Sacred*. *Twentieth Century* may have a madcap plot, but its choreography of physical movements is impeccable, especially in the physical orchestration of Lombard's performance as Mildred Plotka, the timid Polish shopgirl who metamorphoses into the histrionic screen queen Lily Garland. In fact, the entire emotional history of Mildred/Lily's relation to her mentor-director-lover-husband Oscar Jaffe (John Barrymore) can be read in the series of diagrammed movements that Oscar scrawls on the stage where he first meets, directs, and falls in love with her. His effort to dictate the scope and form of her movements, her feints, dodges, and finally counterpunches to elude his strict direction, becomes the leitmotif of their professional and marital partnership. When Mildred, who has become the Broadway star Lily Garland, eventually leaves Oscar, the ham-genius, she does so because of his jealous possessiveness.[29]

Lily has every right to protest the physical and emotional constraints that Oscar imposes on her, but it also must be admitted that under his tutelage she learned how to occupy and command center stage. Her canny mobility becomes ripe for comic intensification when she finds herself on the Twentieth Century with Oscar. Lily, cornered in her cabin by the insistent solicitations of a desperate Oscar, contracts her body in order to concentrate her energy, then lets go with a barrage of leg punches. Her kinetic outburst displays all the cunning grace of a genetic adaptation. If you watch the scene attending only to the unique rhythm of Lombard's stationary kick-boxing, you will note how carefully Lombard's kicks are orchestrated. Each kick seems exquisitely timed to punctuate her exasperated retorts to Oscar's histrionic rant, but also to register certain hesitancies in her reaction—at some level, she *likes* listening to the preposterous ravings of this appalling but oh-so-amusing man. Lombard's slapstick girlhood has conditioned those limbs to work in uproarious concert with her mouth, itself energetically employed in dousing Oscar with a stream of protest and abuse.

Physical agility and verbal quickness, then, are allied powers in the fast-talking dame's quest for unfettered movement. With the advent of sound, a new "literacy" was introduced into the silent's portrayal of energetic and resilient life. The slapstick hoydens were great comics who nevertheless lacked the distinct individuality conferred by the speaking voice. For inspiration and ease in the use of words, the comic heroines of the talkies looked to the talkative women of stage comedy, from Shakespeare through the Restoration playwrights to Wilde, Shaw, and Coward (the latter's plays being converted to the screen while their authors were still alive).[30] Fast-talking dames can thus legitimately claim descent from the line of the witty heroines of English stage comedy. Their traits were first observable, some would say perfected, to a degree that their descendants can only hope to aspire to, in Shakespeare's peerless comic heroines—Rosalind, Viola, Portia, and Beatrice. In the witty women of Restoration comedy is a further refinement of the line, in accordance with Restoration's high estimation of the power of wit to secure personal happiness as well as to procure or preserve social status. The paragon of this generation is Millamant in William Congreve's *Way of the World;* she refuses marriage unless the provisos she enumerates are fulfilled by her suitor (whom she loves madly), Mirabell. The Irish playwrights from the eighteenth to the twentieth centuries, Sheridan and Wilde and Shaw, ensured that the Shakespearean line of clever women survived changes in social mores, styles of courtship, and mating habits to achieve the "happy boldness" of the American comic heroine.

We can confirm the Shakespearean lineage of the fast-talking dame's rhetorical virtuosity by remarking her skill in the "seven degrees" of dramatic reply catalogued by Touchstone in *As You Like It:* Retort Courteous, Quip Modest, Reply Churlish, Reply Valiant, Counterattack Quarrelsome, Lie Circumstantial, and Lie Direct. We might discern and admire specializations according to the disposition of player and perfection of type: Retort courteous—Myrna Loy; quip modest, Irene Dunne and Claudette Colbert; reply churlish, Ginger

Rogers, who also scores with reply valiant; counterattack quarrelsome, Katharine Hepburn, beginning with *Bringing Up Baby* and becoming downright litigious in *Adam's Rib;* lie circumstantial, Carole Lombard, the most genial fabricator and fantasist among the fast-talking dames of thirties comedy; and lie direct, the specialty of the great female con artist, Barbara Stanwyck, whose comic heroines in *Remember the Night* (1940) and *The Lady Eve,* both scripted by Preston Sturges, conduct us briefly into the actual precincts of crime melodrama. So good is Stanwyck at her cons that she often ends up deceiving herself, so that she is hardest to read when she seems to be concealing nothing. The conclusion? That the lie direct is to be approached, but never consummated, on the premises of comedy.

Because this Shakespearean lineage has proved so hardy and entertaining, we might forget how much that other genotype—the soft-spoken woman, taken to its misogynistic extreme in Ben Jonson's *Epicoene; or, the Silent Woman*—might have easily attained cultural ascendancy as the desirable, mateable female. Luckily, comedy and comic talkies in particular have little real patience for those who cannot verbally fend for themselves. Those who are taciturn or reticent must either learn to speak their mind or lose out in the comic bounty. In comedy, the reluctance to speak betokens a nature suspicious of if not hostile to the courtship rituals and sexual festivities, especially the marriage feast, with its all-important wedding vows, that comedy yearns to celebrate. It is this yearning that justifies whatever license the fast-talking dame might take—with truth as with language—since without her the human prospect for happiness might vanish in words unspoken, vows untaken. Woman's strategic role in effecting the comic resolution is the subject of the Epilogue to Sheridan's *The Rivals,* in which we meet one of the most talkative—and hilarious—misspeaking comic characters, Mrs. Malaprop. But the last word goes to Mrs. Bulkey, who took the part of Julia, the sagest of the play's female characters:

Ladies for you—I heard our poet say—
He'd try to coax some moral from his play;
"One moral's plain"—cried I—"without more fuss;
Man's social happiness all rests on us—

Through all the drama—whether damned or not—
Love gilds the scene, and women guide the plot."

No trace of erotic predator here. Shakespearean comedy and its grand tradition through the dramatists Sheridan and Wilde celebrate the designing woman as the guide and guardian of the comic plot, the architect and custodian of man's social happiness.

But when the comic heroine was transported and reproduced on American soil she attained a distinctive and spectacular coloration. She stopped being aristocratic and, though she may have dressed as elegantly as any continental dame, felt more at home in a nightclub than in a ballroom. Even the moneyed heiresses of screwball comedy know that their family fortunes are too new and often too precarious (as in *My Man Godfrey* [1936] and *5th Ave. Girl* [1934], both directed by Gregory La Cava) to affect the haughtiness that is the natural bearing of *real* class (which is a European social invention). The American comic heroine is radically democratic, which means that she is given the social latitude to gratify a craving for physical fun that the heroines of Old World comedy simply never had the opportunity, much less the inclination, to indulge. The fast-taking dame is the true child of democratic manners and speech. In listening to her words, then, Americans were not just hearing the terms, newly fashioned, by which women and men agree to love and live together. America was hearing articulated through her, in a distinctive and irrepressible voice, the very genius of the American idiom.

This is a large claim, but it is, to resort to the irresistible pun, a sound one. The pun, however obvious, even execrable, is one that no less an authority than the "master" of the language, Henry James, resorted to in his own remarks on the relation of women to speech, delivered as the Graduation Address for the Bryn Mawr Class of 1905 (nearly twenty years before Katharine Hepburn matriculated there). For James, the "question of our speech" was the supreme question we should ask ourselves as a people and as a nation. It was a question whose answer comprehends our personal identity, gender politics, social status, our "culture" in all its private and public forms, indeed our very life. On this last point, James was insistent. "All life," he held

. . . comes back to the question of our speech, the medium through which we communicate with each other; for all life comes back to the question of our relations with each other. These relations are made possible, are registered, are verily constituted, by our speech, and are successful . . . in proportion as our speech is worthy of its great human and social function; is developed, delicate, flexible, rich—an adequate accomplished fact. The more it suggests and expresses the more we live by it—the more it promotes and enhances life. Its quality, its authenticity, its security are hence supremely important for the general multifold opportunity, for the dignity and integrity of our existence.[31]

In a paternal irony that verges on rebuke James advises the young women before him not to take the complacent view that "the question of whether we are heirs and mistresses of the art of making ourselves satisfactorily heard, conveniently listened to, comfortably and agreeable understood" has been permanently settled in their favor.[32] Rather, he would impress upon them, as I would upon you, the absolute importance and value of the speaking voice in the fashioning of identity. Let James, then, dictate the closing thoughts for this opening chapter and let us heed his admonition that there is no such thing as a voice, pure and simple: "There is only, for any business of appreciation, the voice *plus* the way it is employed; an employment determined here by a greater number of influences than we can now go into—affirming at least, that when such influences, in general, have acted for a long time we think of them as having made not only the history of the voice, but positively the history of the national character, almost the history of the people." [33]

It is positively the history of the national character—almost the history of the people—that this book aims to recount and celebrate in capturing the speech of the fast-talking dame. We live in a culture in which the question of our speech is very much alive, but primarily as a negative demonstration of the power of words to inflict harm or take unfair advantage of those less articulate or well spoken than ourselves. Hate speech is a national shibboleth that has driven out of public consciousness the simple fact that words can do more than give offense. Perhaps the time has come to rephrase the question of our speech and address ourselves to how the American language might work the same positive magic on the national character as it did when the movies first learned to talk. If we take the time to revisit that cultural moment when the fast-talking dame was in her heyday, we will find women to instruct us in the happy boldness of their speech. At the very least we might be thrilled, even heartened, by those animated visions of irrepressible life racing past us in a torrent of words.

2 Female Pygmalions

We have really everything in common with America nowadays,

except, of course, language.

— *Oscar Wilde*

We have a great desire to be supremely American.

— *Calvin Coolidge*

N o one talks like a dame, certainly not like the fast-talking dame of vintage American comedy. Prospering at a time when sexual tastes ran unin-hibitedly toward "high-class mama[s] that can snap 'em back at ya," she is the direct heir of that free-spoken woman whom Tocqueville admired nearly a century before: self-reliant, gazing upon the bustling theater of the world without illusion, responding to it without fear. Her talk was sexy and smart and high-spirited, yet the pungency and energy of her speech made her an exemplary rather than anomalous figure for democratic culture. She was at home in reality and spoke its language, a vivid vernacular. When she passed her comic judgment on the world, she could be bemused or indignant, but never sanctimonious. In assessing her legacy, we should first appreciate, as the film critic André Bazin did, that American comedy "was the most serious genre in Hollywood—in the sense that it reflected . . . the deepest moral and social beliefs of American life."[1] No one could articulate the nature of those beliefs and their moral claim upon us better than the fast-talking dame. For that distinction she deserves to be celebrated not just as a sexual ideal but as an icon of American individualism, bold and imaginative in her pursuit of happiness.

Hers, of course, was a comic pursuit, which means that her success, though predicted by the form itself, was nevertheless contingent on her understanding, perhaps as no other screen type before or since, the deep and abiding connection between language and life. "It is," as Henry James advised, in a remark that gives this chapter its happy theme and humorous variations, "very largely by saying, all the while, that we live and play our parts."[2] Speech, James is reminding us, is the primary and continual means by which we represent ourselves to the world and even to ourselves (hence the therapeutic power of Freud's famed talking cure). Our way of "saying" what is on our minds and in our hearts is the most personalized signature of who we are, which is why the degradation or loss of speech is always felt as a diminution of life, a sad erosion of whatever is distinctive about us. Our words literally "bespeak" our characters. The question of our speech is fraught with anxiety and excitement precisely because our speech has the power to betray us, show us up as either merely playing our parts, or playing them quite badly. Life on the stage and in the talking film presents an inescapable analogy to the way "we live and play our parts" off-stage and off-screen. Being social creatures, James advises us, we gain—or lose—our deepest sense of life *through,* not despite, the speaking parts we choose as our own.

We shall take James at his expert word, then, that the human voice, the instrument of our "saying," is "not a separate, lonely, lost thing." It is what James proclaimed it to be—a builder of character. Not every voice, of course, realizes this destiny. Only those possessed of a certain kind of know-how can be assured of achieving a commanding and not merely vociferous character. I mean this literally—the knowing *how* as well as when and what to speak. This, too, was part of the lesson imparted by James to those articulate young women about to make their voices heard in the public world. "You don't speak soundly and agreeably," James counseled them, "you don't speak neatly and consistently, unless you *know* how you speak, how you may, how you should, how you shall speak . . ."[3] As true now as it was in 1905, and decidedly true in that golden age of speaking voices that spanned the early thirties to the mid-forties, a time when America's image both at home and abroad was being refashioned and then tested in the loud theater of an economically unsettled, politically boisterous, and finally bellicose world.

For the novelist, screenwriter, and reviewer Penelope Gilliatt, who holds that the "reviving comedy of homo sapiens rests in love of language, and knowledge of its freight," the verbal universe of thirties comedy qualifies as a linguistic marvel. She hails these films for developing a comic language that was "instantly accurate and serious." Americans not only knew how to speak, but they did so with a quickness, an alertness, a spirited intelligence that remains a wonder. "When one sees the American romantic comedies of the thirties in a run," she writes in her splendid dissection of the "skin and bones" of modern comedy, *To Wit,* "it is their utterance and their estimate of the audience's intelligence of it that is constantly a wonder. The dialogue comes out like grapeshot, instead of at the speed of a railway announcement, and the laughs and plot points go by in a flash; if you miss them, too bad."[4] Too bad is right, for you had to keep up if you wanted to survive in the thirties. It was not a time favorable to stragglers or dreamy contemplatives who missed what was rapidly passing before their eyes. Gilliatt also notes that "in the dialogue there is a note of last-ditch reliance that keeps recurring and seems special to the time. 'I can take care of myself.' 'Nobody can push me around.' In the Depression people were on their own, and there wasn't much more damage the world could do."[5]

It is difficult, and perhaps needless, to determine how much the talkies reflected the new fashion for fast talk and how much they dictated it. The sheer speed of this talk induced in audiences a general alertness to something new and infectious in social attitudes and behavior. As the words flashed by, audiences recognized the familiar vigor and directness, the semantic impatience that increasingly differentiated American speech from its English counterpart. American movies projected a new national *manner* of speech, faster and more stubbornly, stunningly idiomatic than ever before. The indolent drawl of the Southerner and the laconic intonations of the Westerner remained peculiar and recognizably American creations, but they lacked the distinctive modern note—speed. Everything was accelerated about modern life: the pace of change, the tempo of daily life, the modes of transportation. The American language proved a supple medium for a forward-moving, often jittery modernity. No one spoke this language with greater ease, confidence, and quickness than the fast-talking dame. The story of her impressive adaptation to modern conditions is preserved in celluloid, most immediately and engagingly in those comedies of the thirties and early forties noted for their fantastical acts of verbal self-display. Aside from their appeal as entertainment, these films offer vivid, historically valuable testimony to the self-reliant spirit of the times and to the character of the American vernacular: snappy, inventive, and very up to date.

In the decade before the advent of sound, the American aptitude for pungent idioms and neologisms was increasingly recognized as constituting the very genius of our native tongue. Colloquialisms were revitalizing the literary language of the day, but they were also enlivening the life represented on the screen. The newborn talkies were hungry for words after the long fast imposed by the silents. Hollywood scrambled to find writers to satisfy moviegoers who sought to hear how modern men and women did or *should* sound. The fashioning of a language suited to American realities was not just the business of studios eager to create and keep mass audiences. It was a job that engaged highbrow culture as well. The postwar generation of American writers was famously intent on capturing the lively rhythms and vivid slang of their native speech. The American vernacular was the moral ballast for Hemingway's taut sentences and Fitzgerald's romantic paragraphs; it anchored the demotic repetitions of Stein's weirdly "natural" sentences and the hallucinogenic rhapsodies that rippled through Faulkner's prose. Hollywood grasped this fact early on and recruited the high-class literary talents of the day to provide scripts as well as lend their prestige and aura of high-mindedness.

The results, predictably, were mixed. The common reader and moviegoer probably remembers hearing that Fitzgerald and Faulkner worked for the movies, neither of them all that happily or productively (although Fitzgerald's Pat Hobby stories and *The Last Tycoon* are as richly comic, shrewdly observed tales of the culture of moviedom as we are likely to get). Ian Hamilton, in his detailed and sympathetic study *Writers in Hollywood, 1915–1951,* fairly and, when appropriate, amusingly tells their story. One of the most sardonic stories that he relates is of Theodore Dreiser's unsuccessfully suing Paramount over the film "treatment" of *An American Tragedy.*[6] But Hamilton reminds us of the gallery of talented writers who fared somewhat better in Hollywood—Nathanael West, Dorothy Parker, Lillian Hellman, Dashiell Hammett, and Raymond Chandler, not to mention P. G. Wodehouse. He only glances at the celebrated career of Anita Loos, whose *Gentlemen Prefer Blondes* made her an international celebrity.

Among the most successful and influential writers who set the brisk pace and wiseacre tone of the talkies in their heyday was Ben Hecht, whose scripts include *Twentieth Century, Nothing Sacred,* and *It's a Wonderful World,* to name only my favorites. Hecht, like W. R. Burnett, the novelist and screenwriter responsible for such gangster classics as *Little Caesar, Scarface,* and *High Sierra,* hailed from Chicago, a city whose colorful urban dialect translated easily to the screen and gave the early talkies much of their verbal kick. In his evocation of this period, Samuel Putnam recalls Hecht's prominence in the "prairie Renaissance" of the early to mid-nineteen-twenties, singling out his role in founding the Dadaist *Chicago Literary Times.* The *Times,* Putnam remembers, was "without a doubt the most extraordinary 'literary' magazine ever published in America, one of the rules being that no headline must have anything whatsoever to do with the article that followed."[7] Knowing this about the Dadaist proclivities of Hecht's early writings, listen again, with a more informed ear, to this nearly perfect absurdist exchange between a newspaper editor (Stone) and his star reporter (Wally) in *Nothing Sacred.* Wally has discovered that his boss has eavesdropped on the boxing match he has just staged to exhaust Hazel, who is supposedly dying of radium poisoning, in order to make her appear sick and spent when doctors examine her.

WALLY: You mean to say you stood there and let me beat up a defenseless woman?

STONE: I did, Mr. Cook.

WALLY: Where's your sense of chivalry?

STONE: My chivalry? Aren't you a little confused, Mr. Cook? You hit her.

WALLY: That's entirely different. I love her.

Swarming with non sequiturs, casually irreverent in its sexual attitudes and social codes, quick in defense of its own Dadaistic illogic—this is what screen dialogue could sound like when written by those with a good and, let it be said, educated ear for the delectable comedy of human speech. (In her memoirs, Anita Loos drops the names Voltaire and Molière with the same affectionate familiarity as those of Jean Harlow and Clark Gable.)

We can best measure the astounding rapidity with which Americans were responding to the question of our speech by citing Edmund Wilson at two different moments in the evolution of post–World War I American popular culture. In 1926, reviewing a lackluster performance of Wedekind's *The Loves of Lulu,* Wilson lamented the bad acting and miserable translation, but what distressed him most was how the production was all too representative of the "vagueness and lack of energy" afflicting the American theater. "Foreigners visiting the United States," he went on, "are struck by the slowness of American speech, as we are likely to get the impression that all Europeans—including the English—speak with excessive rapidity. And the truth is that Americans still drawl—in the city as well as in the country: not even New York, unlike Paris or London, has a language of the quick intelligence." To bring New York up to cosmopolitan standards, Wilson advised, American theater needed to provide its performers with "training in precision and speed in the delivery of lines." [8]

But the language of quick intelligence was gestating even as Wilson lodged his complaint, although it may not have become generally audible until the advent of the talkies, just three short years and a Wall

Street collapse away. Wilson had no way of anticipating such a development, yet once it became discernible he immediately responded to the giddy inventiveness of popular speech. Only a year after his critical remarks about the American drawl Wilson relished the astounding range of slang terms spawned by that peculiarly American phenomenon — Prohibition. With mock-scholarly soberness, Wilson compiled a partial lexicon of those expressions "denoting drunkenness now in common use arranged . . . in order of the degrees of intensity of the conditions they represent, beginning with the mildest stages and progressing to the more disastrous." Wilson never staggered, but marched methodically through a verbal plain littered with such terms as lit, squiffy, lathered, plastered, soused, bloated, polluted; he discovered along the way the syncopated poetry of alcoholic affliction: to have the heebie-jeebies, the screaming meemies, the whoops and jingles. Wilson concluded his loquacious bender on a note of lyrical minimalism: the last expression he recorded is "to burn with a low blue flame." [9]

Wilson had heard something brewing in the fast times and easy money of the Jazz Age — an intoxication with words and phrase-making. F. Scott Fitzgerald noticed it, too, and linked it to a growing confidence and pride in the American way of doing — and saying — things. "We were the most powerful nation," Fitzgerald remarked in that first intelligent retrospective of the decade just past, "Echoes of the Jazz Age": "Who could tell us any longer what was fashionable and what was fun? Isolated during the European War, we had begun combing the unknown South and West for folkways and pastimes, and there were more ready to hand." [10] Among the native resources that were both fashionable and fun was, of course, the language itself. H. L. Mencken's *American Language,* whose title alone seems a linguistic declaration of independence from the mother tongue, dates to this period. The first edition was published in 1919. America had just emerged triumphantly from the Great War and was about to embark on the decade of the Big Money. In this first edition Mencken took note of a growing divergence between British and American English, and by the fourth and definitive edition he had unapologetically embraced a triumphalist

narrative in which American speech had eclipsed its English parentage. Posing what had for him become the purely rhetorical question—
"English or American?"—Mencken claimed to have offered his readers
"sufficient evidence that the American of today is much more honestly
English, in any sense that Shakespeare would have understood, than
the so-called Standard English of England." The reference to Shakespeare is a particularly crafty bit—appropriating the national icons of
the soon-to-be-superseded mother culture for one's own camp, even if
the community is only a linguistic one.

Even cannier are the reasons that Mencken presents to explain to
those either puzzled or outraged to learn that "Standard English must
always strike an American as a bit stilted and precious. Its vocabulary is
less abundant than his own, it has lost to an appreciable extent its old
capacity for bold metaphor and in pronunciation and spelling it seems
to him to be extremely uncomfortable and not a little ridiculous. . . .
He believes, on very plausible grounds, that American is better on all
counts—clearer, more rational, and above all, more charming."[11]

Mencken's view may be chauvinistic, but it should not be dismissed outright as lacking foundation.[12] Or English adherents. Virginia
Woolf, for one, conceded that the verbal genius of English had historically gravitated to American shores. Americans, not the English, she
admitted, were keeping the language fresh and vital by inventing new
words. "For the Americans," she wrote with something like grudging
admiration,

> are doing what the Elizabethans did—they are coining new
> words. They are instinctively making the language adapt itself
> to their needs. In England, save for the impetus given by the
> war, the word-coining power has lapsed; our writers vary the
> metres of their poetry, remodel the rhythms of prose, but one
> may search English fiction in vain for a single new word. It is
> significant that when we want to freshen our speech we borrow
> from America—poppycock, rambunctious, flip-flop, booster,
> good-fixer—all the expressive ugly vigorous slang which creeps
> into use among us first in talk, later in writing, comes from
> across the Atlantic.[13]

The American language's forcefulness—was it a harbinger of the cultural imperialism of which many European cultural pundits now complain?—is sardonically honored in Somerset Maugham's *Cakes and Ale* (1930), in which the narrator notes:

> The wise always use a number of ready-made phrases (at the moment I write "nobody's business" is the most common), popular adjectives (like "divine" or "shy-making") and verbs that you only know the meaning of if you live in the right set (like "dunch") which give a homely sparkle to small talk and avoid the necessity of thought. The Americans, who are the most efficient people on the earth, have carried this device to such a height of perfection and have invented so wide a range of pithy and hackneyed phrases that they can carry on an amusing and animated conversation without giving a moment's reflection to what they are saying and so leave their minds free to consider the more important matters of big business and fornication.[14]

Maugham, who in fact went on to work in Hollywood, pays ironic tribute to the American attitude toward slang as a labor-saving device. The people who love "ready-mades" can be expected to prefer standardized behavior in their love as well as business dealings.

Of course there is nothing natural nor even inevitable in efficiency taking the form of linguistic proficiency. Historical and social forces were at work between Mencken's first and fourth edition that took America from the Jazz Age, with its jubilant spirits and eloquent silent films, into the Depression-ridden thirties, with their dampened spirits and manic talkies. A growing nativism in speech was one way that America was struggling to forge a postwar identity, to become, in the terse phrase of Calvin Coolidge, "supremely American." America under Coolidge was flush with newfound wealth, social ebullience, and sexual as well as economic adventurism. Echoing Dickens on a similar revolutionary moment, Fitzgerald proclaimed that postwar America was "an age of miracles, it was an age of art, it was an age of excess, and it was an age of satire." Yet what really marked the age as a decisive one in the formation of our "modern" national character was that "we had our way at last."[15] Words had to be found to express this newly won freedom and to satirize the stodgy institutions and enervated instincts of the old, restrictive orders of life.

Satiric irreverence was quickly taken up as a dominant style of early talkies. The age of satire marks the reign of the city-slickers, habitués of pressrooms and saloons, of nightclubs and watering holes like the legendary Algonquin Hotel. Pauline Kael has written exuberantly—and gratefully—about what happened when the irreverent New York journalist-literary gang of the twenties (whose seat of government was the Algonquin) moved west to help the talkies find a voice. "Hollywood destroyed them, but they did wonders for the movies. In New York, they may have valued their own urbanity too highly; faced with the target Hollywood presented, they became cruder and tougher, less tidy, less stylistically elegant, and more iconoclastic, and in the eyes of Hollywood they were slaphappy cynics, they were 'crazies.' . . . Though their style was often flippant and their attitude toward form casual to the point of contempt, they brought the movies the subversive gift of sanity. They changed movies by raking the old moralistic muck with derision."[16]

They may have been crazies in the eyes of Hollywood, but Kael is right to hear sanity in their language. And when sanity spoke, it assumed the voice of the living moment, of topical satire, of the latest slang. The advent of sound allowed the New York wits and Chicago wordsmiths to extend their cultural reach and influence, to leave their flippant, cynical, but undeniably witty imprint on the national character. By bringing their irreverent and exuberantly vernacular style to the movies, they championed the national claim of the American language as the standard-bearer of a cocksure, exultant modernity.

The subversive sanity of the early talkies ministered, at a time of deep skepticism, to the national ideology of self-advancement and self-invention. The language of the times was fast and pungent, and to survive you had to learn how to speak it. If you were a fast talker you could create your own reality, just as Barbara Stanwyck "creates" John Doe in a newspaper column and then makes sure he doesn't expire on the page. You could even create or re-create yourself by the same means—through language. This is shown to be literally true in the comedies, and even the melodramas, of the time. Heroines study the language in order to become the women they want to be, playing, one might say, Pygmalion to themselves. In *Shopworn,* Kitty Lane (Barbara Stanwyck) systematically sets out to memorize the words in the dictionary to facilitate her rise up the social scale. She is making impressive strides until she is stumped by the word "eleemosynary." The joke is erudite, but apposite. As an impoverished, proletarian heroine, she must stumble against the hard irony of learning a word whose charitable reach probably does not extend to her.[17] *Shopworn,* as the title openly advertises, was a movie made to order for the day, yet it is hard to imagine any routine "programmer" released today that would hinge its social satire on such a literate, bitter joke. Of course, even in the early thirties it was not in parroting the multisyllabic and often laughably precious diction of the educated elite that the screen heroines could realistically hope to make their way. Their prospects depended on their articulating, with the precision and speed that Wilson complained had eluded even the most accomplished Broadway actors, a new idiom— snappy, knowing, and above all relentlessly modern. What wonder, then, that the words they uttered seemed to have been invented even as they spoke.

The talkies, which ransacked "classic" nineteenth-century fiction and Broadway plays for material, found the most exhilarating timbre for its newly acquired voice in slang. As Mencken understood, even celebrated, American slang was the product of a "kind of linguistic exuberance, an excess of word-making energy." We should also remember that talkies, in learning how to reproduce the human voice, cleverly converted this energy into what Stanley Cavell calls "wit and clip," which meant, among other things, that there was little leeway among the word-spouters for the ill-said any more than there was for the slow or soft-spoken. Ian Hamilton credits Warner Brothers with making the important discovery that "dialogue didn't have to sound like dialogue; it didn't have to be Broadway posh or particularly intelligent." But then Hamilton mars his point by slipping into a rare moment of condescension: " 'Yeah, yeah, awright, you guys, yeah, yeah' was verse drama to the ears of 1930's groundlings."[18] Maybe it did strike some as verse drama, but what the groundlings were hearing was a more syncopated as well as more savvy (if not well-schooled) speech than Hamilton allows. Watch any of the snappy comedies from this time and see how quickly the performers rattle off what was on their minds. There was little time and less tolerance for those actors backwardly stuttering out yeah, yeah, yeahs (and even *that* phrase has a poetry of its own, as the Beatles showed some thirty years later).

Partly this was simply a technical bonus derived from the use of fast-stock film, in which everybody's speech sounded speeded up. But it also soon became apparent that the talkies had a special affinity for subjects and milieus where fast talk and energetic slang was rife: proletarian heroes scrambling out of the working-class slums; adventurers like Gable, and adventuresses like Harlow, prowling the China Seas, speaking a slapdash lingo and picking up rough trade; heiresses whiling away the hours in nightclubs; songbirds from the slums or the hinterlands looking for the big break on Broadway; and, of course, colorful, strong-willed, and tough-talking mobsters pursuing their fortunes in an underworld that suddenly, and scarily, became *our* world.

It is the nature of slang to change with the times, to migrate from one milieu or subculture to another. Reality, unvoiced by the mainstream, verbally erupts in strange and often exciting, if baffling, coinages that spring up in the economic perimeters and criminal margins of well-heeled, tight-lipped society. When movies first learned to talk they drew much of their slang from what was being said on the Broadway stage, but soon they preferred the cruder but more vivid lingo of another, less reputable, institution — gangland.

Fitzgerald, with his characteristic sociological prescience and fine ear for the vernacular, noted in 1931 how the characteristic words of the Jazz Age had "since yielded in vividness to the coinages of the underworld." [19] And Mencken, in an editorial supplement to the 1936 edition of *The American Language,* noted how much our slang is born in the criminal hinterlands of society: "Today," he reflected,

> we know that much if not most slang is argot, which emerges from or is discarded from the subcultures of the professional criminal on many levels and in many different specialties. The

"wit of Broadway," while still the immediate source of much slang, always was—and still is—closely attuned to the underworld for new and salty terms. For example, Damon Runyon studied the fringes of criminal cultures closely. Wilson Mizner spent many years as a professional grifter before he became a writer and went right on writing just the way he talked, and S. J. Perelman has long been a discerning observer of the criminal world and its idiom. . . . Invention of slang words by the literati of the dominant culture appears to be meager; most of them, it seems, are borrowed from underworld sources.

It is from this quarter that most American slang comes, a large part of it invented by gag writers, newspaper columnists and press agents, and the rest borrowed from the vocabularies of criminals, prostitutes and the lower orders of showfolk.[20]

The language of gangsters takes up residence in the comedies of the era, feeling very much at home amid the hectic, madcap proceedings. There is, besides, the undeniable allure of the gangster as a peculiarly American, irreducibly twentieth-century creation. He is the creature of the modern neighborhoods and their mean streets. He is often a fascinating hybrid, at once bootlegger and ladies' man. Frequently he affects to be a dandy, a pretension reflected not only in his dress, but in the monikers assigned him, like "Joe Lilac" in *Ball of Fire*. Whatever his sartorial style, the mobster is a fervid sponsor of the popular culture of speakeasies, of anything goes. The gangster is a figure of social protest, but also of impressive self-invention, a maker—and enforcer—of his own rules. Little Caesar (Edward G. Robinson) begins life as the impoverished Rico and attracts a lurid respect for converting the sad pun of his name into the imperial power accorded a Napoleon of crime. James Cagney's Tom Powers is a public enemy who shares Rico's energetic criminality, while Howard Hawks's Scarface (Paul Muni) covets his sister as much as he does the power and prestige of running a gang.

For Roland Barthes the gangster's "gestural vocabulary" and its "few festoons of slang" epitomize the stylistics of "cool"; the gangster world, he maintains, "is above all a world of *sang-froid*." [21] Fitzgerald recognized the insidious, often irresistible glamor of the gangster and made it a part of the allure surrounding that quintessential American figure, the Great Gatsby. The Jimmy Gatz who becomes Jay Gatsby is either a romantic idealist or a gangster-entrepreneur, possibly both. That he could equally or plausibly *be* both hints at the affinity, even the moral kinship, between the idealist and the pragmatist, renegade strains so oddly combined in the American national character. The same steady purpose that makes a man pursue a woman no matter what the obstacles also gives psychological credence to the rumor that Gatsby once killed a man.

Some Like It Hot

Great gangster films, from *Scarface* and *Public Enemy* to *White Heat, Force of Evil,* Francis Ford Coppola's *The Godfather* and *The Godfather, Part II,* and Martin Scorsese's *GoodFellas* and *Casino,* entice us with the lurid glamor of gangster culture. For this reason the gangster film, more than the Western, is the great American epic of contemporary life. The world of the Western, with its easy-to-spot good guys and bad guys, showdowns, and morally clear challenges, tends to be a mythic world, hence distant from the world of economic and moral desperation where gangsters flourish, a world still with us. The "code" of the Western is laconic for a reason—it is a genre that grubs at the roots of our linguistic being, as befits its morally stark, primordial heroes. The language of the West cuts through the verbal layers that time and civilization have encrusted over our primal selves, sometimes brutally stripping the human voice of any cultured intonations it might have acquired. The epigrammatic style would never do in a Western. Puns and double meanings elude the man with a gun, whose retorts tend to be as blunt as his pistol shots. Westerns are literate, and they can sparkle with crude barroom ridicule, but derision only reinforces the clear division between good guys and bad guys.

We come closer to psychological and moral portraiture of men struggling with a morally mixed world in "revisionist" Westerns like John Ford's *The Searchers,* any of Anthony Mann's fifties Westerns with James Stewart, and Sam Peckinpah's luminous *Ride the High Coun-*

try, whose tone is from first to last elegiac and the greater for it—that, and the stoic performances of two cowboy veterans, Randolph Scott and Joel McCrea. When it comes to targeting the dark places in our national psyche, it is the gangster whose story hits us, morally and historically, closer to home.

We might not expect such nefarious characters to make themselves at home in a vintage comedy, yet they do, and in fact they seem to belong there. Comedy extends them a welcome, knowing that the thrill of violence has its own kinetic charge. Billy Wilder's *Some Like It Hot* (1959) builds an entire sex comedy around the intersecting cultures of loose-living showfolk, gangsters, and robber baron millionaires who operate "off shore," presumably beyond the reach of the law. Wilder, as *Sunset Blvd.* (1950) and later *The Fortune Cookie* (1966) grimly confirmed, had a knack for finding black-comic inspiration in the ghastly accidents of life, but nothing he wrote or directed approached the ghoulish ingenuity of making the notorious gangland murder, the St. Valentine's Day Massacre, the trigger for a transvestite romp through the playgrounds of the rich. George Raft, in a reprise of the famous bit of business from *Scarface*—the repeated coin tosses that set the style for gangster aplomb—strides into the film as Spats Colombo, a visiting dignitary from another genre. The camera, in comic obeisance, pays its (visual) respect to his spats.

Usually the in-jokes and send-ups of rival genres are less intricate and the cross-breeding of genres less ornate than in Wilder's film. In *The Bride Came C.O.D.,* the pilot Steve Collins (played by James Cagney, the public enemy of 1931) presents himself to Joan Winfield (Bette Davis), the heiress he has contracted to return to her father, as a gangster. Intrigued, as heiresses often are, with the criminal orders, she asks him if he belongs to a gang. Ever the individualist, Collins informs her that he always works alone, hence his moniker, the Solo Kid. Both stars are at their peak in this perky comedy, sending up the screen roles that launched them into the empyrean, Davis more good-humoredly, since she endures a crash landing, parachuting into a cactus patch, and (so she thinks) a mine cave-in. Remy Marco (Edward G. Robinson), with the canny and devoted assistance of his clean-speaking consort, Ruth Marco (played by the unfailingly droll Ruth Donnelly), entertains us with the comedy of reform in *A Slight Case of Murder* (1938; the "slight" in the title a tip-off to the verbal savvy of the screwball-gangster tale to follow). The world represented in *It's a Wonderful World* is as wonderful as it is partially because we get to hear not only the argot of gangsters and detectives but also the banter of theaterfolk, since detective Guy Johnson (James Stewart) leads himself and Edwina Corday (Claudette Colbert) to a provincial theater where the bumbling cast of *What Price Glory?* is shielding a killer. Then there are screwball comedies, like *Bringing Up Baby* (1938) that impersonate gangster culture when they can't round up actual gangsters. When the wacky, tirelessly inventive Susan Vance (Katharine Hepburn) lands in jail for impersonating herself, she concocts her most outrageous alter-ego—Swinging Door Susie, moll of the Leopard gang.

Susan obviously loves the way gangsters talk. Dr. David Huxley (Cary Grant), her unwitting "accomplice" in crime, can't get a word in edgewise during her jailhouse riff. He is reduced to spluttering amazement that *anyone* would listen to, much less speak, such nonsense. Susan likes gangsterese not just because it is amusing, although it is fun to poke fun at constables, as every self-respecting, law-breaking comedy can tell you. She also likes this talk because it allows her, through language (which is the safest way) to try on an identity or to flirt with an existence beyond, or rather beneath, her usual range of acquaintance.

One of the reasons heiresses are runaways in the thirties is that they yearn to defect from their class. Outlaw life excites and entices them, even if the only social renegades they encounter are the gigolos and randy habitués of nightclubs of the type so ably impersonated by Jack Carson in films like *The Bride Came C.O.D.*[22] The heiress is a madcap, and we need to feel in these comedies her proximity to danger, to irrecoverable loss of dignity, loss of status, and finally loss of self. Only then can we fully appreciate the wit and cunning that saves her from herself. Most of the time the danger is a symbolic or fantasized element in the plot, as in *The Bride Came C.O.D.* and *Bringing Up Baby*, or in Clark Gable's pretending he is the muscle for a kidnaping ring in *It Happened One Night*.

All this risky fantasy-flirtation with hooliganism calls for comment, if not moral reproof. At the very least, the odd companionability of gangsters and fast-talking dames suggests the need for psychological counseling. Comedies of this era may recognize the need, but they prefer laughs to therapy, or rather they present therapy as a laugh. Psychiatrists, like gangsters, are familiar presences in vintage American film comedy. Like gangsters, they inspire all manner of topical jokes. They, too, have their own professional argot ripe for comic treatment. Indeed, entire comedies can be built around psychiatric humor, like the efforts of shrink Tony Flagg (Fred Astaire) to "cure" Amanda Cooper (Ginger Rogers) of her aversion to marriage in the aptly named musical comedy *Carefree* (1938). More typically, the jargon of psychiatry is treated joco-seriously, as when Hepburn's Susan Vance listens respectfully to Dr. Fritz Lehmann (Fritz Feld) informing her that the love impulse in men frequently takes the form of conflict. The movie itself gives more credence to the language of loons, which at least has the voice of nature behind it. But Dr. Lehmann gets off rather lightly, all things considered. Consider the fate of court-appointed psychiatrist Dr. Egelhoffer (Edwin Maxwell), hired to certify that the patsy Earl Williams (John Qualen) is sane and worthy of execution in *His Girl Friday*—he ends up being shot in the "classified ads, no ad." [23]

The indignity inflicted upon Dr. Egelhoffer is not especially severe, nor even uncommon, for comedies of the time. Never has a psychiatrist—indeed, the entire profession of psychiatry and its high-falutin jargon—been exposed with more satiric relish than in the sanity hearing that concludes *Mr. Deeds Goes to Town*. Longfellow Deeds (Gary Cooper), schooled in the crackerbarrel philosophy of small-town America, has a field day with Dr. Emil Von Hallor (Gustav von Seyffertitz), the psychiatrist who proclaims him insane. The estimable and visibly self-satisfied Dr. Hallor regales the court with his fancy talk about manic-depressives, illustrating his diagnosis with a chart purportedly tracking the highs and lows of Deeds's "diseased mind." But Hallor gets his comeuppance (we can hardly call it a second opinion) once Deeds gives his own homespun explanation for his idiosyncratic behavior. People tend to behave oddly, he reasonably observes, during times of stress or in states of distraction. Deeds may not know the clinical term for behavioral compulsive disorders, but, having had plenty of time to observe his accusers and judges, he can spot an "o-filler" (the judge presiding over his sanity hearing, as a matter of fact), a nose-twitcher, and a knuckle-cracker in the crowded courtroom. Most impressive, having observed Hallor idly drawing his own Rorschach tests as he listens to other witnesses, Deeds donates a new word to the American language: doodler.

That a sanity hearing should come down to a dispute over words is a comic idea of the first order. In fact, the case against Deeds dramatically as well as juridically finally comes down to a single word—pixilated. That is how the genteel spinsters, seemingly speaking for everyone who knows Deeds in his hometown, describe his general, indeed congenital, mental state. Their testimony seems damning until Deeds gently extracts from them the exculpatory information that everyone in Mandrake Falls is, in the estimation of these venerable ladies, pixilated, an aberration, they gladly testify, that obviously afflicts the presiding judge.[24]

But nowhere are the lexical fancy of comedy, the unlicensed appetites of gangsterism, and the Freudian language of unconscious association more happily united than in Howard Hawks's *Ball of Fire* (1941), an odd-couple romance that pairs a linguist (Gary Cooper as Professor Bertram Potts) and a fast-talking, slang-spouting showgirl (Barbara Stanwyck as Sugarpuss O'Shea). Sugarpuss represents for Potts the untold (but not unheard!) glories of colloquial, living speech. When the film opens, Potts, assisted by a cohort of mild-mannered, genial pedants, is busily working to complete an encyclopedia. When a garbage man intrudes on the professorial sanctum to get some answers for a radio show "quizzola," Potts, who has just finished a twenty-three-page article on slang—in which he diligently compiles eight hundred examples, including pejorative uses of zig-zag and the root of skidoo in skedaddle—realizes that his work is outmoded. To Potts's credit, he does not treat the trash man's language as so much verbal refuse. He appreciates the linguistic and social fact that the garbage man speaks a language that needs to be translated, not scrapped. He talks about his mouse and the need for moolah so he can have his share of hoi toi toi ("And if you want that one explained," he tells the baffled Potts and company, "you go ask your pops!"). Professor Potts, ever the conscientious scholar, determines that the garbage man "talked the living language; I embalmed some dead phrases." So he sets out to make the rounds of the town, tracking down contemporary slang to its living sources.

A montage that is a lexicographer's dream shows us Potts canvassing the modern city, dutifully recording the slang he overhears: a newsboy barking tabloid headlines ("Dogs dunked in cement"); a woman on a subway ("plenty gestanko" and "just a jerk"); fans at a ball game ("two-ply poke" and "bop the apple"); coeds on campus ("oolie droolie" and "solid sender"); sharks in a pool room ("clip the mooch" and "slap happy"). He ends up in a nightclub, where he is captivated by a jive-talking dame singing "Drum Boogie" to the beat of Gene Krupa's drums.[25] She is Miss Sugarpuss O'Shea—a tantalizing name, so sweetly promising of verbal as well as sexual riches! Following her backstage after her knockout performance, Potts becomes even more entranced when he hears what comes out of Sugarpuss's puss:

POTTS: I hate to intrude like this, but . . .

SUGARPUSS: Cut the chorus . . .

POTTS: What? Well, this inquiry is one of considerable importance.

SUGARPUSS: Stop beating up with the gums.

POTTS: What was that?

SUGARPUSS: Get this. I don't know from nothing.

POTTS: Oh, but you do. Every word you say proves as much. Well, where's that paper . . .

SUGARPUSS: Suppeeny? [*Her rendering of "subpoena."*] Suppose you tell that D. A. to take a nice running jump for himself.

POTTS: Bewildering. And you want to tell me that you're not the person I'm looking for.

When Sugarpuss asks about the others on the job and is told that they are asleep, she begins to get suspicious.

SUGARPUSS: Say, are you a bull or aren't you?

POTTS: Well, if bull is a slang word for professor, then I'm a bull.

Potts then invites her to assist him in his study, but she tells him to "shove in your clutch." "Exactly the kind of thing I want," he assures her, but she persists, giving him the royal brush-off—in slang, of course:

SUGARPUSS: Okay. Scrow, scram, scraw.

POTTS [*delightedly*]: A complete conjugation!

The minute she opens her mouth he is a goner. He confesses on returning to his colleagues that he didn't notice her face but that the language she spoke was so bizarre that his mouth watered. Linguistically, he is in love. The carnal variety will soon follow.

The fun, of course, is seeing how Potts learns to speak her language and, in the process, develop some unsuspected lyric capacities of his own. But he has a rival for her time and ultimately for her affections: her gangster boyfriend, the dandified killer Joe Lilac (Dana Andrews). To protect him Sugarpuss agrees to "help" Potts in his inquiry, providing she can share his professorial quarters (where the police would hardly dream of looking for her). The arrangement allows screenwriters Billy Wilder and Charles Brackett and director Howard Hawks to work a clever and blessedly unsentimental turn on Snow White and the Seven Dwarfs.

But cleverer still is Sugarpuss's finding her metier—and her finer self—in playing Shaw's Pygmalion in reverse. Rather than having the professor teach her the King's English, as Higgins does Eliza Doolittle, she instructs him in the latest slang. Taking the job first as a ruse, then as a lark (finding unexpected fun in teaching the bashful and gawky professorate the conga), she eventually becomes quite adept in giving Potts instant etymologies. When Potts asks her to leave because her presence is having a disruptive effect on the scholarly regimen, she, like a Scheherazade of slang, immediately diverts him and thereby puts off the moment of expulsion. Does he know, she teasingly asks, what an ameche is (current slang for telephone, after the actor Don Ameche, who played the inventor of the device in *The Story of Alexander Graham Bell*)? When Potts remains adamant about her leaving, she dissuades him with the sweetest word she knows—yum yum (lip-smacking slang for kiss)—and promptly demonstrates its meaning. That Potts's strictly professional interest in learning slang was destined to take just such a romantic turn is hinted at in the elaborate lexical tree he reconstructs around the various colloquial permutations of the word corn, whose meaning migrates from nutritious substance (succotash) to sappy sentiment: off the cob, hick, corny, cornball.[26] What is more American than the American appetite for corn in both its comestible and comic variety? And is there a sneaky pun lurking in "cans of corn," the screenwriters' judgment on the movie reels of glossy romances and weepy melodramas of the period?

Hawks, Wilder, and Brackett, whether working individually or in comic collaboration, pose a serious threat to cornball sentiment. But they are not so cynical as to deny the power of Sugarpuss's tutelage. At the beginning of the film Potts confesses to being barely articulate in the presence of the opposite sex. He has to be prodded by his associates even to get his tongue around the provocative vowels in "woman" (he gets as far as "woo" and completes the word only because one of his cohorts slides a pipe down his back). Thanks to Sugarpuss he will cease to require artificial stimulus to send sexual tingles down his spine. More to our immediate and important point, he will find the words to talk to a woman when he needs them. He will even begin to have fun twisting or inventing words or word combinations that make their own kind of sense. When Potts and company are held hostage by Duke Pastrami (Dan Duryea) and Asthma Anderson (Ralph Peters), Lilac's henchmen, Potts diverts the captors with a hilarious mumbo-jumbo explanation for their chins "convecting into the cataclysmic protoplasm," describing how the "totalitarian mastoid" of their earlobes seems to be "prematurely extricated from the paranoid agriculture"—nothing to be alarmed about, though, according to the "latest centrifugal research"! Cooper was reportedly upset at having to memorize and speak such gibberish, but the rest of us, especially those who endure jargon in their chosen field, should be grateful for the spoof.

Perhaps only a comedy that takes such pleasure in parodying academic jargon and sending up the latest street lingo could unpretentiously admire a literary language of feeling that never seems to go out of date. Certainly this is the case with *Ball of Fire*. When Potts gives Sugarpuss a ring, he inscribes it with Shakespeare's words rather than his own:

> Look how this ring encompasseth thy finger,
> Even so thy breast encloseth my poor heart:
> Wear both of them, for both of them are thine.
> (*Richard III*, act 1, scene 2)

We might wonder why Potts chose to declare his love with the same words with which Richard III (a Fascist "gangster" type, as Ian Mc-Kellen played him in 1995) wooed the widow Anne as she was departing from her husband's funeral. It certainly makes me wonder how deep might go the verbal jokes in this movie about lovers who speak different languages. Far enough, at any rate, to translate these lines out of the realm of cynical masquerade and into the domain of sweet corn. Shakespeare provides the words for the love that Potts, the grammarian, has yet to articulate on his own. Still, Sugarpuss knows what he means, even if she doesn't yet understand his words.

Indeed, Potts's words, however incomprehensible, are resonant enough to turn her affections and loyalty from Lilac to him, despite his lamentable, yet to her adorable, lack of standard masculine attributes. When Sugarpuss is being pressured by Lilac to marry him (more out of legal than amorous urgency), she refuses. She then lists her reasons for loving the improbable Bertram Potts: "I love those hick shirts he wears with the boiled cuffs, the way he always has his vest buttoned wrong. He looks like a giraffe and I love him. I love him because he's the kind of a guy who gets drunk on a glass of buttermilk, and I love the way he blushes right up over his ears. I love him because he doesn't know how to kiss, the jerk." That Gary Cooper, in private life an elegant dresser and womanizer, could fit this ungainly description is testament to his powers of impersonation. But it is also a testament to Stanwyck that she could make these reasons convincing to us, not only as an indication of Potts's boyish charms, but of her change from "tramp"—her own word for herself—to a "dizzy dame" who prefers a man wearing hick shirts to a man partial to monogrammed silk purple pajamas.

The change in Potts is equally dramatic. Because of Sugarpuss, he comes to understand more than the jazzy parlance of the day. He begins to comprehend what his heart, muted by discipline and disuse, is trying to tell him. The first visible sign of the rush of feeling that brings this male Galatea to life is a negative one—he begins to lose control over his speech until he literally is at a loss for words. It happens like this: On the night of his "betrothal" to Sugarpuss (who up to this point is reluctantly playing along with him in order to hook up with Lilac across the state line in New Jersey), Potts wanders into the motel room he thinks belongs to Professor Oddly, the one professor who has been married and so can believably profess some unacademic knowledge, however meager, of women. At Potts's bachelor dinner, Oddly, a botanist, cautions the eager bridegroom about the fragility of brides, whose delicacy he likens to the anemone nemerosa, a wildflower whose bloom will be destroyed by any impetuous embrace.

Potts, first pondering and then doubting the analogy, has entered what he thinks is Oddly's room partly to argue but mostly to plead with him to reconsider his sexual analogy. He confesses his inability to be so courtly and, more to the point, so patient. But it is Sugarpuss's room into which he has mistakenly stumbled, and it is to her eyes, glowing preternaturally in the darkened room, that he speaks of the sexual urgency that has mastered him. He allows for the "beauty and delicacy" of the relationship Oddly describes but protests that as a man in love he wants to take his bride in his arms. Becoming more agitated as he speaks, he indignantly but politely disputes the very idea that he should dampen his ardor because his bride bears a remote resemblance to a flower from the buttercup family! "Why, if this marriage had been delayed," he splutters, "I mean should have been delayed, I mean should be . . . " Potts the esteemed grammarian yields to Pottsy the tongue-tied lover who can't finish the sentence because he can't bear either the thought or the syntax of deferred sexual gratification. He's got it so bad, he admits, "Oddly, I don't know my tenses anymore. I've gone goofy, completely goofy, bimbuggy, slaphappy." As if

Barbara Stanwyck, Gary Cooper, and company in Howard Hawks's *Ball of Fire*

Oddly would know the meaning of these words, much less comprehend the giddy condition to which they refer! But Sugarpuss knows
what he's talking about and she takes him at his word. She puts an end
to her inadvertent deception and throws herself in her Pottsy's arms,
undeterred by his protest: "To say such things to a woman!"

For talking that way, and before a woman, is just what she—and
we—want to hear. Pottsy now speaks her language because it is the
only language he can use to describe the way his love for her affects
him. He has learned, we might say, not just what it means, but how it
feels to be goofy, bimbuggy, slaphappy. But he has to learn a lot more;
he must learn who she is, how she has deceived him, how to read her
heart. At first he is not really ready for this additional knowledge. When
Lilac shows up to claim his "fiancée," the disillusioned Potts sends her
on her way. He vows never to think of her again. But she has sent
him a coded message, undecipherable even to herself. Before she (unwillingly and unhappily) departs with the thuggish Lilac, Sugarpuss

returns Pottsy's engagement ring but "mistakenly" gives him Lilac's ring instead. Potts thinks the substitution inconsequential, but Professor Gurkakoff (Oskar Homolka), citing Dr. Freud, pedantically insists that the subconscious mind makes no mistakes. In returning Lilac's ring, he tells Potts, she was giving back the ring she didn't want and keeping the one she did. "She loves you," is his incontrovertible verdict. Potts, true to form, prefers linguistic proof to the sign language of the unconscious, and he gets it when he learns from Pastrami about "a little trouble with Sugarpuss's vocal chords. Wouldn't say yes."

To rescue Sugarpuss calls for a concerted effort from Prince Potts and his seven loyal retainers, who are more than up to the job. They as well as Potts begin to caper with comic life after Sugarpuss blows away the dust that has gathered about their hearts. She may regard the professors as "squirrely cherubs" — which they are — but they become formidable opponents of Lilac and his gang. Using their brains (since their brawn is frankly negligible), they bring the gangsters down. This is literally the case. Held hostage by Pastrami and Asthma Anderson, they ingeniously adapt Archimedes' method for starting a fire with reflected light to bring a picture crashing down over Pastrami's head. Their stunt also provides a singularly funny illustration of what is meant by the Sword of Damocles, a question posed by the garbage man, who unwittingly wanders into the hostage situation in search of an answer to the latest radio quizzola.

Ball of Fire is smart enough to poke fun at academic insularity without really doubting the superior power of brains over "muscle." In fact, Potts will prove superior even in that department, as he takes on Lilac in a fist fight — and wins. Having soundly pummeled Lilac, Potts encounters one last obstacle: Sugarpuss's own reluctance to wed. Hers is a feeble but necessary protest. She gallantly reminds him of his own rule of "no women aboard." "And now above all women," she chides him, "you want to take a dizzy dame like me." The word dame functions like a linguistic and erotic trigger. As a grammarian, Potts knows when words cease to be of use. There remains but one argument, he declares to all concerned, and proceeds to make it. He grabs a pair of books, not to read, but to elevate Sugarpuss to his level (a symbolic elevation that the comedy cannot do without, given how beneath him Sugarpuss once was). He then plants on her pretty puss that silencing kiss which is often comedy's last word—in this instance a lip-smacking yum yum. In a kind of coda, the attending professors, like a well-schooled chorus, give the telltale click of knowingness that Sugarpuss had taught them.

The gangsterism that Potts and company so handily defeat is not always so easily routed, especially when it takes the form of political racketeering with a distinctly Fascist cast, as it does in Frank Capra's *Meet John Doe* (1941). In such cases, the comic protagonists have a rougher time stemming the tide of corruption or making the right moral, as well as sexual, choice. Capra's fast-talking dames—they are invariably reporters who earn their keep by marketing their words—are a breed apart. The world they set out to conquer through the power of their speech is as dark and repressive as any entertained in the gangster and domestic melodramas of the time. The imposing Edward Arnold is one of the reigning figures of this demonic comic world, just as Walter Connolly and Eugene Pallette share honors for the irresistibly irascible fathers of the great heiress comedies, *It Happened One Night* (Connolly) and *The Lady Eve* (Pallette). Arnold, however, reigns supreme as the great Nobodaddy of America's (certainly Capra's) political unconscious during the thirties and forties. His D. B. Norton has presidential ambitions, backed up by a private, militarized "motor corps" in *Meet John Doe,* and in *Mr. Smith Goes to Washington* he plays Jim Taylor, a news baron who controls a distribution system that can deliver newspapers as efficiently and ruthlessly as bootleggers.

Stanley Cavell first paid serious attention to the absence of mothers in thirties comedies, but equally salient and generically more predictable is the "bad" presence, either ineffectual or actively maleficent, of fathers. Casting the father or his symbolic delegate as antagonistic to the comic hero or heroine's desire is a standard comic device, a way of dramatizing the inevitable clash between generations, a clash that often escalates into a conflict between an established society and one restless under prevailing erotic or social constraints.

This formula can take many devious or upsetting turns and has from the days of Plautus and Menander. Wilder and Brackett, with their usual comic intuition about how to update classic comic plots and stock characters, suggest the baleful forms that paternity can take when they have Lilac pretend to be Sugarpuss's "daddy." When Potts finally understands that he has been duped, he says, as if in amazement, "You're not her father." Lilac's retort is coarse and on the money: "You're getting warm. I'm her daddy." The joke, which evokes an appreciative chortle from Pastrami, is funny, but it is also devastating, because it brings out into the open what kind of life Sugarpuss has been leading. Fathers are figures of identification; daddies, for women of full age, are targets of infantile fixation or crass—and mutual—exploitation.

If we are alert to this distinction, then the moment Sugarpuss calls *herself* a tramp won't seem as startling as it does on first hearing. When Potts walks out of her motel room, leaving her with a blank page on which she had tried to represent herself, he leaves her to find the word that sums up who and what she has been before she found her vocation as a female Pygmalion to his tongue-tied Galatea. She does, and even though she is not a tramp, at least not now, she needs to be this hard on herself so that she can finally accept the truth not so much of what she is but of what Lilac is—a killer. (This fact, by the way, is forgotten by everyone until Sugarpuss reminds us in her final showdown with Lilac, in which she says won't marry him even if he ties a piece of cement around her neck and tosses her into the East River like he has all the others who have opposed his will.) Sugarpuss's self-disgust at having given her heart to her "daddy" is as bleak a moment of self-judgment as one is likely to get in comedy.

Sometimes such moral perceptions are not confined to those solitary moments in which the heroine pitilessly confronts herself. When the comic vision of corruption is sustained from scene to scene, building momentum, then we have something like Capra's political comedies, which give us yet another astonishing variation on the odd and sometimes overtly "bad" parenting explored in these vintage works. The very act of fathering takes on a new social meaning in Capra's "problem" comedies, and not just because the traditional father has either abdicated his role or been superannuated. In these morally unsettled and unsettling comedies, the heroine graduates from linguistic and emotional "instructor" and assumes the weightier role of symbolic progenitor. She is typically the working girl who "fathers" the man whom she will eventually love. She works this existential and romantic magic by adapting to her needs and purposes the Pygmalion formula— giving the man the language that brings him to life.

Mr. Smith Goes to Washington, the most histrionic of Capra's political comedies, is also the most sanguine in suggesting how we can dispense with fathers in engendering our comic heroes. Much of its optimism can be ascribed to faith in the incorruptible nature of its all-American boy hero, Jefferson Smith (James Stewart), the country lad who travels to the city and loses his innocence, if not his character. That he manages to lose one and preserve the other is largely due to the intercession of a smart-talking senatorial aide, Clarissa Saunders (Jean Arthur), a superlative foil for Capra's wide-eyed hero.

Capra has a special fondness for this stock comic figure, the *agrikos,* or rustic whose rough manners and countrified ways prove unfailingly amusing to urbane wits and power brokers (be they Shakespeare's dukes or Capra's media moguls). But only a democratic country steeped in agrarian values would think that such a stock figure could serve as a *romantic* hero. The very possibility that the rustic could be at the center of the comic doings is unthinkable in Shakespearean, Restoration, Wildean, or even Shavian comedy. The populist Capra boldly brings the marginal, even buffoonish, figure (like Mr. Deeds in certain attitudes) center stage.

The proverbial naivete of the agrikos trying to negotiate the urban cultural maze provides Capra with all the leeway he needs to mount his social satire. His comic, romantic hero in the political comedies after *It Happened One Night* is a "simple" and plainspoken man who proves to be the sexual as well as moral superior to the urban sophisticates who initially mock or gull him. Capra thus can have it both ways, playing up the homespun virtues of the country-bred hero while gently reprimanding his audiences, who, whatever their place of birth or habitation, are always assumed to be better informed about the ways of the world.

No one suffers this irony with more pained disillusionment than Jefferson Smith (Cooper's Mr. Deeds and John Doe are laconic and stoic when their moment of personal—and civic—trial arrives). Unlike Longfellow Deeds or John Doe, Jefferson Smith is initially provided with an apparent "good father" to teach him how to negotiate that most devious of American cities, Washington, D.C. His mentor is senior Senator Joseph Harrison Paine (expertly played by Claude Rains, who holds the patent for powerful yet curiously abject males, as portrayed in this film and, more stunningly, in Hitchcock's *Notorious* and Vincent Sherman's *Mr. Skeffington*). The senator is at once a family friend and second father to Smith. He means to be kind to the junior senator, and he even encourages him to pursue his pet project of a boys' summer camp. But then he finds out that Smith wants to locate the camp on the land that has been earmarked by Jim Taylor (Edward Arnold), the only political power he really answers to, for a dam project. So the senator works to dissuade Smith from presenting his bill. When his initial efforts fail, the senator, owned lock, stock, and barrel by Taylor's machine, reluctantly but skillfully repudiates and humiliates Smith in the open Senate. Against such political thuggery the comic naif, stranded in his institutional ignorance of the rules and the rulers of modern government, is helpless.

The ordeal that this naive Jeffersonian hero endures is not altogether negative. Comedy sensibly prefers to educate its heroes and heroines rather than ratify an innocence that may be dangerous to themselves and others. Experience *should* enlighten us to the nature of the world, whatever that world happens to be at the moment of our awakening into it. In Jefferson Smith's case, his great awakening is not religious, nor is it particularly sexual, however smitten he may be with his mentor's classy but cold daughter; nor is it genuinely social, since his vision of American community remains agrarian and federalist, like that of his namesake. Jefferson's great awakening is first and foremost rhetorical. He realizes that his only effective weapon is his senatorial power of speech.

It is not a realization this American Adam comes to alone. There is also an Eve in this drama of political innocence despoiled. She is Arthur's Clarissa Saunders, the legislative aide who has already sampled the tempting apple of political knowledge. Saunders teaches her charge how to beat the devil at his own game by outtalking him. Under her instruction Smith begins to see how he can take up arms against those with more money, more votes, more guile, but not more determination. He triumphs over his adversaries by conducting a one-man campaign — the filibuster. Smith's filibuster is a piece of grand political oratory, and as impressive as he is in this role, we should remember that it is a woman who prepared and emboldened him for his greatest part.

Saunders conceives, scripts, coaches, and directs his debut in the Senate chamber, that great theater of democratic government. She prompts him from the observers' gallery when he is in danger of losing the floor. Jefferson will temporarily lose his voice during the course of the filibuster, but not before he has learned how language itself can be an instrument of the will, used for good as well as evil. Capra's fast-talking political comedy is built on this insight, as is one of the more splendid specimens of the genre, George Cukor's *Born Yesterday.* In Cukor's 1950 comedy senators are still up for sale, only this time they are being bought by garbage kingpins. But in this comedy there is no need to filibuster. A single word — "Cartel!" — shouted by the vocally irrepressible Billie Dawn (Judy Holliday) is enough to shut up and shut down all venal conspirators.

The sexual politics of what we might call Capra's boy-mister comedies are fascinating to chart. They begin with the erotic and professional promotion of a strong, sassy, and independent-minded heroine out for herself, build to a point where a man falls for this dame, who in many cases literally puts words into his mouth, then collapses, as Barbara Stanwyck does in the final scene of *Meet John Doe,* into the traditional sexual postures: man, the strong upholder of the moral order (and of the female body); woman, delighted onlooker or appalled spectator of his public fate.

Given this weird arc, which brings emotionally as well as professionally robust heroines to the point of hysterical collapse, we should give Capra's sexual idealism a much harder look. *Mr. Smith Goes to Washington* is the most comforting of these films, in large part because Capra so disarmingly invokes the major icons of democratic society — the presidential memorials, imposing political institutions like the Senate, and the free if cynical press. But the greater, more searching political comedies, *Mr. Deeds Goes to Town* and *Meet John Doe,* imaginatively spring from the seeds of an authentic social nightmare. In these comedies it is a woman reporter who gives the male hero his public identity, but in a more compromised, even derisive way than Saunders does in *Mr. Smith Goes to Washington,* a film that for all its fulminations is really a gentle, even genteel satire on American political institutions. In both cases the hero is played by that blushing marvel of slow yet seductive speech, Gary Cooper.

In *Mr. Deeds Goes to Town,* Jean Arthur plays Babe Bennett, the reporter who gives the name Cinderella Man to the newly made millionaire from Mandrake Falls. The name carries a double comic sting. It's a joke, a devastating one as it turns out, about Deeds's fairy-tale fate — becoming a millionaire overnight, an economic fantasy that survives relatively unmolested in the American psyche (where it now takes the form of lottery mania and an unshakable confidence in a bull market). But, as the Cinderella tag snidely hints, the transformation from small-town rube into big-city celebrity takes a toll on his manhood. Riches *unman* Deeds. His manhood as well as his values become inactive and inert, albeit temporarily, in the finery and foolery of his new life in rich (if not smart) society. A sartorial makeover is the first sign that his homespun virility may be in jeopardy. Deeds, stripped of his trousers, is flustered trying on the emasculating attire of big-city high life, like tails and morning coats (a fine in-joke, given the masculine elegance of Cooper's studio portraits from the early thirties).

Cooper's capacity for disarming boyishness seems to have enchanted thirties audiences. I find it affected, even obtrusive, but it is the telling element in his performance as Mr. Deeds, because it suggests how distracting Capra found sexuality to be when he wanted to prove his credentials for "serious" social comedy. Never has Cooper's sexuality been made to appear more gawky and adolescent in its sudden craving for impulsive and uninhibited movement, like sliding down a banister or running down fire engines racing to a fire. The Longfellow name seems to jest not just at his poetic aspirations but at his unwieldy height, an impressive attribute that he has not yet learned to command. Capra gives us a long fellow whose limbs are imperfectly wired to his brain. His gangliness thwarts even as it accentuates his hormonal urges. The one love scene he plays with Arthur, who masquerades as the proletarian waif Mary, concludes with his hurrying *away* rather than toward her after having declared his love, crashing into garbage cans. How one yearns in this false moment for the languorous Cooper who gave Dietrich the eye in *Morocco* (1930) or proved equal to her sexual guile in *Desire* (1936).[27] It's important to remember Cooper's sexual charisma lest we lose sight of his apparent ability to *turn down* his sexual wattage in order to let a different kind of luminosity irradiate his monumental face. Cooper portrays Deeds in a way that confirms Babe's description of him as a Cinderella Man awaiting metamorphosis.

Deeds's sexual immaturity is reflected in his amatory ideals, corny even by vintage Capra standards. Deeds confesses that his sexual fancy (of course he doesn't see it as that, but that's what it is just the same) is aroused by the prospect of rescuing a damsel in distress. Knowing this, the smart Babe Bennett, who is as defenseless as a wolf, insinuates herself into his life, into his confidence, and finally into his heart by feigning weakness from starvation after a day of futile job-seeking. She plays the gag to the hilt, but in a searingly contemporary way. Deeds, true to the letter as well as spirit of his name, takes action. He treats her to a nutritious—and sumptuous!—dinner at Tullio's Café, where the literati gather (and where it is hard not to pick up a gibe at the Algonquin Round Table).

Their first night together may begin as fairy tale, but it concludes in fisticuffs. Deeds, finding himself in the same restaurant as a poet whom he greatly admires, seeks an introduction. It is not long before even the ingenuous Deeds realizes that he is being mocked rather than applauded for writing his greeting-card poetry on order. Capra wants us to side with Deeds, the bard of greeting cards, against such high cultural snootiness, and to cheer when Deeds, finally understanding that he is only a joke to these big-city sophisticates, rebukes and then punches out his mocker. Capra shows up these men of words as effete as well as insufferably boorish. We are apparently encouraged to think that Deeds, better looking with a better build and better character, possesses, despite the banality of his doggerel, a more *virile* literary posture than does the urbane poet. (When, in *It's a Wonderful World*, Guy Johnson [James Stewart] scoffs at Edwina Corday [Claudette Colbert] for being a poet, the soft sarcasm of her riposte—"too

Jean Arthur and Gary Cooper in *Mr. Deeds Goes to Town*

manly for poetry, I suppose" — nails the Philistinism that underlies his sneer.)

Deeds may pummel the man of words, but he can't begin to answer back Babe's creation of his public persona. She has built an image of him through the power of words alone. And we sense that Deeds, although he thinks that he is courting a lady in distress, may subconsciously be drawn to a woman as smart as Babe. Like so many of the comedies of this time, the gender reversals that lie behind the physical attraction of the lovers are fun to watch, even if the emotional logic that dictates them can make some viewers uneasy. Still, the coupling of Longfellow and Babe makes excellent linguistic as well as erotic sense: he a small-town boy with an old-fashioned feeling for hackneyed sentiments; she the city girl who is smart to the ways of the world and can speak its fashionable language with just the right amount of irony and distance.

This time, however, the woman educates her Cinderella Man in the negative relation between language and its most practiced, skillful users. Deeds's attitude toward language has already been complicated by his disenchanting encounter with New York's literati, but it is catastrophically impaired when he discovers that his beloved Mary is the news hound who reported his escapades with just enough malicious humor to make his harmless sprees seems heartlessly flighty, even decadent. ("Cinderella Man Fire-Eating Dragon" runs one headline, lampooning his pursuit of a fire engine.) Deception is one of the great themes of comedy, not just how lovers deceive each other but, more profoundly, how they deceive themselves. Treachery is the crevice where comedy mines its darkest insights into human nature. Comedies like *Mr. Deeds Goes to Town* and *Meet John Doe* emotionally transport their hero and heroine to that public hell where all our failings are magnified and disproportionately punished. They are among the finest, which means in this context the direst, examples of ironic comedy in the American film tradition. In ironic comedy, Northrop Frye observes, "the demonic world is never far away," and the comic dramatist, keen to exploit its proximity, "tries to bring his action as close to a catastrophic overthrow of the hero as he can get it, and then reverse the action as quickly as possible."[28] Capra was adept at staging such near-misses, especially in *Meet John Doe*.

For Mr. Deeds, catastrophic overthrow takes the form of his public humiliation by the big-city press and the devastating private realization that his beloved Mary is the Babe—or dame—who made him a laughingstock. "That dame took you for a sleigh ride that New York will laugh about for years," his press agent Cornelius Cobb (Lionel Stander) bluntly tells him. "She's the slickest two-timing, double-crossing . . . Every time you opened your kisser you gave her another story." His desolation at her betrayal brings him to the point of calamitous self-undoing. Deeds prepares to leave New York when he is stopped by a crazed farmer who half-heartedly tries to kill him, supposedly for squandering money in such short supply. Shaken and visibly moved, Mr. Deeds devises a plan to finance deserving farmers to a homestead. Suit is then brought against him by greedy relatives and disgruntled retainers, charging mental incompetence.[29] Only a madman, the litigants contend, would feed doughnuts to a horse in the middle of a depression, and only a madman would decide to give all his money away. Deeds, once in danger of losing his manhood, is now in danger of losing his freedom. Yet he refuses to defend himself. He remains stubbornly silent, apparently no longer trusting speech. His attitude may be understandable, but it is also suicidal. Dr. Hallor might be a fool in diagnosing Deeds's affliction, but he is right in suggesting that Deeds, depressive and mute, has lost his will to live. Only words can reanimate him and legally, if not yet emotionally, give him his life back. An agitated, repentant Babe begs him to speak in his own defense and publicly confesses her love. Without her histrionic pleas, Deeds might be lingering to this day in some underworld inhabited by the mad. Her words, which once disabled his manhood, now work to restore it in the only form that comedy really admires—a manhood that can give a good account of itself.

No one gave a better account of principled American manhood than Cooper in films like *Sergeant York, High Noon,* and *Friendly Persuasion,* in which his characters personify the quiet strength and modest demeanor that underlie all admirable heroic action in the American mode. (Homeric heroes are boastful and genealogy-proud; knights can be vainglorious. Americans prefer their heroes strong, but modest.) Cooper can even bring to the preposterous role of the iron-willed, uncompromising Howard Roark in *The Fountainhead* a sexual intensity that blazes through the romantic kitsch that surrounds but cannot insulate it. Like those other great American originals, Henry Fonda and James Stewart, he locates the soul of American maleness in an integrity as blunt as it is imperturbable, which is why one is always curious about how he will fare in the verbal rough-and-tumble world of comedy.

Given Cooper's sculptural handsomeness and imposing physique, it comes as a kind of surprise to realize that Cooper's most lovable as well as notable comic heroes—Deeds, Long John Willoughby in *Meet John Doe,* and Professor Potts—are the most emotionally brittle and psychically fragile characters in the comic brotherhood brought to life by Fonda, Stewart, William Powell, Melvyn Douglas, and Robert Montgomery. Even Cary Grant, the most protean, sexually playful of the comic actors of the period, never comes as close as Cooper does to that point where his masculinity is not only compromised but shattered.

Cooper may in fact be the most refashioned man in movie history. His good looks combine with a comic pliancy to make him a fascinating and nearly irresistible object of female desire in early films. This often lands his characters in erotic predicaments, of which the most curious is his sexual and moral quandary in *Meet John Doe.* In this film he plays Long John Willoughby, a pitcher with a bum arm who agrees to impersonate the John Doe that Ann Mitchell (Barbara Stanwyck) has literally made up out of words. Having created John Doe, she then personally ensures that Willoughby is suitably dressed, adequately coached, and faultlessly directed to give the performance of his life. As Preston Sturges will do in *The Lady Eve,* Capra seems to have projected onto Stanwyck all the talent and skill that go into the making of a motion picture.

Barbara Stanwyck is Ann Mitchell, a newspaperwoman who envisions the "gag" that sets the comedy going. When she sits down to her typewriter after being sacked in a company takeover and furiously types out her last column, we see only her eyes, burning with indignation and, it turns out, the light of creation. Under the name of John Doe she writes a letter of fiery protest against unemployment and other social ills visited on the common man by crooked politicians and corrupt, unfeeling business. The letter causes a public sensation, and Ann talks her managing editor, Henry Connell (the peerless James Gleason), into hiring her back to run a series of "I protest" columns. To avoid exposure by already suspicious rival papers, Ann and her editor decide to hire someone to pose as John Doe.

True, the story she churns out is an old one, but comedy likes the old gags, the old plots and complications, putting its stock in the wit on which an old story turns and in how the story is played. That is where the casting comes in. When hundreds of no-accounts line up outside the newspaper office looking to be John Doe, Ann takes on the role of director, rejecting candidate after candidate, until she sees Willoughby and, in him, possibilities unsuspected even by himself. It is her gaze that isolates this photogenic, charismatic male, and Willoughby blushingly yields to her appraising eyes. She then patiently goes to work eliciting a credible, and then great, performance from him. She coaches him until his face assumes the look that will instantly signify to any spectator the "I protest" that has become his public mantra. Finally, she writes a speech for him that will make him into a moral prophet, ministering to social hopes. The speech, she tells him, represents the populist vision of her late father, a man people listened to. In his first public broadcast as John Doe, Willoughby initially stumbles over the words written for him, but then he finds his rhythm and begins to enter into her father's language. Soon he is racing through page after page of his prepared text, picking up the pulse of optimism, the energy of good will that the movies identifies with the "good" father.

As his performance takes on definition, John Doe becomes less an impersonation and more an incarnation of the average good man whom Ann comes increasingly to identify as the emotional as well as moral replacement for her beloved father. The movie that begins with a newspaperwoman's stunt to increase circulation (and to revenge herself against the company that fired her), develops into a case study of what we might diagnose as pedestalism in reverse: the woman's idealization of the male. Pedestalism was neurotic enough in Thurber's view, but Ann's pedestalism qualifies as perverse, because she apparently falls in love with a man whom she herself has created in the moral image of her dead father. The erotic transference of her fatherly identification onto a man she has created to embody paternal ideals makes perfect psychological sense, but it necessarily leads to an erotic confusion eventually felt by Long John as his own.

In a scene that should give psychoanalysts plenty of fun, John Willoughby tells Ann of a crazy dream that he had in which he *was* her father as well as himself (*not* John Doe). As her father, he somehow walks through the wall separating his room from hers, and finds her sleeping, but as a little girl rather than a grown woman. She takes flight and he chases her for miles, first as her father, then as himself. As she is running, she gradually grows "up" until she becomes, as it were, herself at this very waking moment, on the threshold of marriage. The dream scenario reconstructs a staple of comic plotting, in which a wedding must be stopped and the heroine restored to her proper mate. The dream also makes good psychoanalytic use of the comic fascination with doubling, only the doubles in this dream—or is it a nightmare, and if so whose?—are not Willoughby and his rival but Willoughby as himself and as the father whom he has been groomed to replace. In the dream, Willoughby puts Ann across his knees and, spanking her for emphasis, declares that he won't allow her "to marry a man that's just rich or that has his secretary send you flowers. The man you marry's gotta swim rivers for you, he's gotta climb high mountains for ya, he's gotta slay dragons for ya, he's gotta perform wonderful deeds for ya."

Cooper is reiterating the same exalted sexual idealism that animated his Mr. Deeds, only here it is banished to the dream world, where such a vision of courtship properly belongs. That does not discourage Willoughby from instilling in his "daughter" the power of such heroic and manly love. Continuing in his role as her "dream-father," he begins to "whack" her. This dream of spanking, with its suggestion of forbidden but delectable sexual play, completes and consummates the perverse longings that have been surreptitiously driving the comedy. The action is brought full circle, with Ann now the helpless object on whom the father makes his loving but forceful impression. This is the dream switch that prepares us for Willoughby's recuperation of his manhood and the restoration of public peace and good will in the restoration of traditional patriarchy. (Edward Arnold's Fascist Nobodaddy D. B. Norton represents a perversion of classical male governance.) But for this miracle to take place (and it is a miracle, given modernity's challenge to traditional sex ideology), John Doe, messiah to the people, must be martyred.

The movie has been moving all along to a climax that, being a comedy, it can't possibly fulfill. Ann had written the words that brought John Doe to life in the public mind, but she knew that he would survive in the public heart only if he were given a limited, dramatic existence. So she had determined that he must "die" for his creed of good will toward men just as his divine model did and that he must do so on the very night of promise and hope, Christmas Eve, by jumping from the roof of City Hall. When this film is shown on television today, the squib in the *New York Times* lauds the film but complains, "We still say he should have jumped." A certain brash realism might have been served by that ending, but not the comic weal, that imaginary state to which we entrust our larger hopes for a social future that is desirable if not always attainable. Capra and his screenwriter, Robert Riskin, were

Barbara Stanwyck and Gary Cooper in *Meet John Doe*

right to have Ann's loss of consciousness at the prospect of having her story played out as originally scripted symbolically stand for loss of life. This ending is content to settle for a diminished version of a fall, Ann's fainting in John's now-capable arms. He had fainted when she rescued him from the ranks of the hungry and unemployed. There is an emotional as well as physical logic that joins these two moments of sudden exhaustion. The first signals Willoughby's emasculation by physical need, his docility and ductility in the hands of Ann's imaginative female force. The second restores him to his life as a man within a traditional community of John Does like himself. In this Christian fairy tale, it is a woman who brings the populist messiah into the world, a woman who finds herself in league with that devil D. B. Norton, who would corrupt the fellowship of commoners into a Fascist cult, and a woman who must surrender her strength to ensure that "John Doe" lives rather than dies by her words.

Meet John Doe is the darkest of the comedies that contemplate the verbal art of female Pygmalions. But even as it takes perverse turns, we know that, according to comic convention, a convention based on human hope, the John Doe whom Ann Mitchell has created will turn out to be, somewhat to her surprise but never to ours, a wonderful person. Certainly a person worth loving and marrying. This marriage would never have been thought possible had not the laconic Willoughby shown an uncanny ability to give voice to a woman's memories of what her father not only did say, but might have said. Never has the voice as an erotic instrument been given such a complicated score. That a man should ventriloquize a woman's fantasy of what her father might say—and say those words to a national audience hungry for words to cheer and inspire and ennoble them—is an event, if only a cinematic one, without obvious precedent. Putting the voice to such complicated erotic as well as rhetorical use makes this film unique in the annals recording the verbal exploits of the fast-talking dame.

More typically, her verbal feats are less politically momentous, more of the amatory variety in which comedy more or less specializes in any age. Parker Tyler, who recognized that speech is a specific form of lovemaking and a powerful element in creating sexual situations, claimed that "Hollywood's psychology of love is that an anterior fact of mutual magnetic attractions exists and this rigid, quasi-bedroom fact results in the act of wooing, regarded in essence as a *legal convention* rather than an eloquent ceremony." [30] The comic partnerships of Tracy and Hepburn, Loy and Powell, Dunne and Grant, each with its own special rhythm, suggest that Tyler wasn't looking for love in the right places. Given how acute his ear and his vision generally are, we can only speculate that Tyler missed the eloquence in these comic partnerships because he understandably but mistakenly believed that the magnetic attraction in American comedy is between clearly defined and opposite sexes. But this is hardly the case. Especially when a fast-talking dame is involved, the mating ritual between man and woman can and often does assume the hilarious form of an interspecies encounter.

Animal Magnetism

Consider, for example, the highly diverting love story of the lion and the squirrel. Their story is the wittiest episode recounted in *Tales of Manhattan* (1942), a film composed of vignettes involving the possession of a tailcoat by a series of owners, each more abject or impoverished than the last. In the second tale, Ginger Rogers plays Diane, whom we encounter on the morning of her marriage. Her girlfriend Ellen (Gail Patrick) comes to call and tearfully relates how she found a comb stained with henna in her husband's tailcoat pocket. Finding Diane fairly unsympathetic to her plight and still determined to go through with her own marriage, she challenges her to perform a similar search of her fiancé's tailcoat. To show Ellen that she trusts her fiancé implicitly, she searches the tailcoat and finds stamps, a hat check, a handkerchief ("not even a trace of any lipstick"), cigarettes, matches, and thirteen cents. Nothing incriminating turns up until she discovers a letter addressed to "My passionate Lion" and signed "Squirrel." This being a comedy and not a melodrama, Diane is more fascinated than distraught as she and Gail read the letter to each other.

Overhearing their exchange is Harry Wilson, the culpable fiancé, played with adroit smarminess by Cesar Romero. In one of the mistaken ownership plots so dear to comedy, Harry induces his friend George (the indispensable Henry Fonda) to pretend the tailcoat is his and that he is the Lion whose romantic exploits are so adoringly remembered by Squirrel. George, who has been pining for Diane all along but has never managed to make the slightest impression on her, now assumes a different character in her eyes. A mere word, a pet name, has done the trick. Diane is a Pygmalion who appreciates the symbolic power of language to transform the persons around us simply by giving them different, more alluring names. Diane's own vision certainly is dramatically changed by the word "lion." She glares at George, fixing him with a quizzical and *very* appraising look. First she revises her low physical opinion of him, noting that though George and Harry are the same size and same build, George's shoulders, she now realizes, are "just a tiny bit broader."

Diane's frank look deserves a moment's consideration, even praise. Much academic critical ink has been spilled on documenting the baleful effects of the "male gaze" in subjecting the female body to a depersonalizing and controlling visual regime, where it remains vulnerable to all sorts of fetishizing operations. But the gaze we observe here is boldly female. (Even bolder is the visual appraisal that Ann [Stanwyck] gives Willoughby [Cooper] when she first sees him in *Meet John Doe*.) George, the object of Diane's sexual regard, is at once puzzled and delighted—hardly offended—by this newly won attention. Still, he wonders why she is looking at him as if she has never seen him before. Diane confesses, in a wondering voice that indicates a genuine discovery, that "no, I don't think I have. At least not in this particular light." Indeed, before the word "lion" had attached itself to him, illuminating all kinds of possibilities she had overlooked, he had struck her as "dim"—we assume in the sexual as well as intellectual sense. But now dim George takes on the resplendent look of an uninhibited lion. Not only has Diane revised her opinion of him; Pygmalion-like, she is also providing him with a magnificently leonine alter-ego—a kingly yet primordial male.

The ensuing five minutes of dialogue between George and Diane provide one of the most enchanting examples of the power of language not just to express love but actually to *create* it. It is Diane who initiates the imaginative re-creation of George. First she visualizes the Lion shaking his mane as he strides with authority toward his awaiting Squirrel. George, excited by this jungle-love fantasy, tries to hurry her but is advised to stop interrupting, he'll get there. Suddenly, Diane's imagination fails her. She can't visualize the attitude he takes outside Squirrel's door. Does he knock? Or ring the bell? George, more and more naturalized to this fantasy-self, becomes, appropriately, farouche. No, he tells her, he smashes the door down. Then comes the crucial question. "Tell me, George, what do you two talk about?" Diane asks. George reverts to his blander self: "We just chat about current events." The chat is disappointing; maybe George is dim after all. "Don't you roar?" demands an incredulous Diane. George falters, excusably I think, this being his first opportunity to exercise the full power of his manly voice. Diane derides him for his feeble effort. She is right, though, to insist on hearing his primal bellow, not just so that she may be sure of him but so that he may be sure of himself. In calling on George to reproduce his virile roar, Diane is calling out to the delectable beast within him. His first effort disappoints, resembling, Diane complains, the cry of a Pekingese. Either because he is now aroused or because he is insulted, George lets out a potent roar. The beast, as it turns out, was there all along!

Henry James, of course, would be thoroughly disapproving of this route to love. "There are plenty of influences round about us that make for an imperfect disengagement of the human side of vocal sound, that make for the confused, the ugly, the flat, the thin, the mean, the helpless, that reduce articulation to an easy and ignoble minimum, and so keep it as little distinct as possible from the grunting, the squealing, the barking or the roaring of animals."[31] But in this instance I think that we are observing something different from the degradation of human speech. We are hearing the gradual sublimation—we might say ennobling—of George's roar and Squirrel's delighted, responsive squeals. (Neither, at least, is reduced to the ignominy of a grunt.) For, of course, Diane is ready to confront the beast she has roused from its lair. Lions can be tamed, she reminds him as she picks up a chair in mock-posture of a determined lion tamer.

Both now are speaking the same language, recognizing in the lion's roar a mating call. All that remains—but it is a big and important all—is to convert animal magnetism into eloquent ceremony. Harry reminds her not only that lions can be tamed but that, biblically, their destiny is to be domesticated: "And the lion shall lie down with the lamb and all that," he reminds her, which inspires her rejoinder, "And the lion shall lie down with the squirrel and all that." Then, suddenly remembering the provenance of the letter, Diane gives the proverb a final twist: "And the squirrel shall lie down with the mink." "This probably goes all the way back to Adam," Diane informs him. "Were there squirrels in the Garden of Eden?" George wonders. It is this question that prompts Diane to complete her revision of the fable: "That's probably why Eve left."

The film delights in this extended play with animal natures and sexual masquerade, but it moves steadily and irresistibly into a more human domain in which Diane and George become collaborators, inventing a language of affection that they are beginning to suspect has been theirs all along. First they begin quoting the letter from Squirrel to Lion, then start improvising lines of their own, "sounding" out the love phrases that occur to them. In a subtle duet, Diane tries out a phrase, and George responds in dulcet counterpoint:

DIANE: Brush your lips across my cheek, my dear.

GEORGE: Is that from the letter?

DIANE: Oh, no, out of my head. I just wanted to hear what it would sound like.

GEORGE: Sounded wonderful. Let's see what this sounds like: I want more than anything in the world to hold you in my arms.

DIANE: Letter?

GEORGE: No, head.

DIANE: There was a darkness for a long, long time, and suddenly the light came and the light was you.

GEORGE: Letter?

DIANE: Head.

GEORGE: Darling, now and from the beginning. Head, Diane.

DIANE: These moments we have [*pause*] are ours forever.

GEORGE: These moments we have . . .

DIANE [*interrupting*]: Head?

GEORGE: No, heart. [*They kiss.*]

This love duet culminates not in the head, but in the heart. This movement from head to heart is the great movement of comedy, a movement whose completion is conventionally signaled by a kiss. George and Diane kiss only after the "heart" is invoked as the source of George's pledge of past fidelity — "Darling, now and from the beginning." It is a pledge and a sentiment that the philandering Harry would never have made, much less emotionally understood. *Tales of Manhattan,* having shown us how head and heart might unite through language, wants finally to test how genuine and lasting that union might be. Thus Diane, having kissed George, asks how people know when they're really in love. He hazards an answer: "Well, first I guess they find out they like to be together and then they find out they kind of think the same things, and I guess after a while they get so they even say the same things at the same time." Having established a test to distinguish animal magnetism from love, George and Diane proceed to pass it. In a perfect and literal moment of synchrony, female and male voice chime together: "It must be wonderful when it happens like that." Comic harmony is rarely this jubilant nor so exquisitely timed.

As George, the lion, decamps with his squirrel, we can appreciate anew how American comedy is never more personally enriching and socially productive than when it dramatizes how an enlivening sexual exchange is contingent on animated verbal exchange. Lovers bequeath to each other the gift of expression, the gift of naming their desire as a prelude to their fulfilling it. This is the function of comic language, the gift that it is uniquely fitted to bestow. The female Pygmalions of the early talkies knew the value of that gift. They created men who incarnated their deepest fantasies of sexual delight and then set out to woo them. In what other form, including fairy tale, could we witness what we do in *Tales of Manhattan*—a squirrel giving birth to a lion! Comic lovers need not speak the same language, nor even be of the same species, but they need to be equal to the task of finding words for their love. The man, as tradition mandates, must speak, and his speech must show him worthy of the woman's articulate love.

Hot Heiresses and Working Girls

Part Two

3 Blonde Bombshells

Jean Harlow, Carole Lombard, and Ginger Rogers

There's a dame — strictly on the level like a flight of stairs.

— Former crony, commenting on Jean Harlow's metamorphosis from

secretary to boss's wife in Red-Headed Woman *(1937)*

*I*n *Nothing Sacred* (1937), Hazel Flagg (Carole Lombard), a supposedly doomed creature from the verbal backwaters of Vermont, visits New York as the guest of a tabloid newspaper determined to wring the last lachrymose drop out of her sob-sister story. She is treated to a night at the Casino Moderne, whose marquee advertises — and welcomes! — "Tootsies of all Nations." There she witnesses a revue celebrating the "Heroines of History": Catherine the Great, applauded for saving Russia ("And she could do it, too," the emcee assures us); Lady Godiva ("She saved her virtue; that's the way those things go, folks"); Lypsinka, who saved Holland by putting her finger in the dike; Pocohantas, who saved Captain John Smith and "later on set him up in the cough drop business." In the show-stopper, Mother Earth herself rises up to salute Hazel, her newest evolutionary wonder. Hazel Flagg — "whose smiles in the face of death have wrung the stone heart of our city" — carries the banner, as her name implies, for modern American womanhood. That Hazel is not really dying and that her gallantry in the face of death is merely a pose make her even more deserving of the tribute. The gift for imposture is one of the Pygmalion talents of the fast-talking dame, part of her repertoire for self-invention. Such things are permitted, even encouraged, in American democratic society, whose ideology boasts endless opportunities for self-advancement.

The fast-talking dame translates this ideology into modern parlance. She not only speaks the language of the times, quick and unforgiving, but she also expresses the fluid, unstable character of American society in an era of drastic change. She comes primarily from the ranks of the working class or the idle rich—the extremes of the social order where fluctuations in fortune and in identity tend to be quite pronounced. She may be born in the country or raised in a small town, but she is a city girl at heart. Her values are urban—eagerness for varied stimuli and myriad company, a love of wit and of her own will, a certain knowingness about how the world works. Speed is the catalyst that quickens these values and brings them to fruition. These values do her credit, although not all to the same degree.

In assessing her character, simply contrast the animated face of the fast-talking dame to the heavy-lidded somnambule or the glittery-eyed jazz baby with nothing on her mind but the pleasures of the moment. How much confidence she had in acting on her values and instincts, even if they took the mercurial form of passing fancies! The very stride of the fast-talking dame proclaims that she knows where she is going and seldom pauses to look back. Determination is announced by every exasperated step that Jean Harlow's Gladys makes into the newsroom of *Libeled Lady* (1936), claiming her rights as a cast-aside bride; Rosalind Russell's Hildy Johnson adopts a jaunty gait on returning to her old haunts in *His Girl Friday*, resuming the brisk rhythm of the newsroom without missing a step—or a comeback. Gladys and Hildy are embarked on entirely different missions, but each walks according to the purposeful tempo of the times. The fast-talking dame, whatever her class or ambition, hurtles into life, apparently ready for anything she might encounter. She is a woman insistent on her rights and ready to do whatever is necessary to secure them. For the working girl, the question of rights often comes down to a living wage and a paid vacation, which are what Clarissa Saunders (Jean Arthur) demands in exchange for turning Mr. Deeds into Cinderella Man. Or she may be biding her time for the chance to "marry up," like Jean Harlow's chorine in *The Girl from Missouri* (1934) and Carole Lombard's manicurist in *Hands Across the Table* (1935).

Hers are the habits and ambitions instilled by hard times, but they can quickly become bad habits, dismaying ambitions. She often explicitly rejects the life and values of her mother, determined to find the job or the man who can satisfy her desire for security. The specter of marriage ruined by poverty haunts the fast-talking dame, who initially seems determined to marry for money, if at all. The comedies that entertain her fate show the collapse of that resolve before the superior arguments of love, but the contest is often so close, the memory of quarreling couples so recent, as to give us a real scare. Close calls, the last-minute holdout of pride or "common sense" over love, trouble the American comic heroine on her way to the altar.

The reactions she inspires are thus not simple—she can take some getting used to. She may seem too aloof or too familiar, too serious or too flighty, all work or all play, and most of all, too much her own woman to accommodate herself easily to any man. She is a vexatious creature, self-reliant in the approved Emersonian way, but also disturbingly unresponsive to traditional codes of compliant or otherwise agreeable femininity. She is either a brusque working girl (there really is no other kind, for no other kind would survive in the Depression) or an heiress determined to have fun in her own way and in the company of her own choice. Getting her to the altar is thus harder and easier than if she were an old-fashioned girl. She will either resist marriage based on love, as Eve Peabody (Claudette Colbert) does in *Midnight* (1939), or do the proposing herself, as Connie Allenbury (Myrna Loy) does in *Libeled Lady.* Whether resistant to or eager for the married state, she is not concerned with the conventional protocols governing wedlock. She is the new-fashioned female who demands a marriage made to her liking or no marriage at all.

In her pursuit of happiness, however she may define it, the fast-talking dame will be assisted, indeed empowered, by her adroit way with words. In fact, she often makes her living by them. The most common incarnation of the fast-talking dame is the reporter. The cocksure girl who will do anything to get a story was a ubiquitous figure in thirties comedy, and, as we have seen in so many Capra films, often a morally ambiguous one. She reports on reality but often goes to unseemly lengths to create it. Both Jean Arthur and Barbara Stanwyck, the most accomplished female Pygmalions working in the genre, worked their verbal magic on Gary Cooper, transforming him into a Cinderella Man or a John Doe who lives in the public mind as a paragon of decency. Yet as sensational and as troubling as their achievements are, they fail to match Hildy Johnson's (Rosalind Russell) potential power to *save* a life by her sympathetic death-row interview in *His Girl Friday* or Tess Harding's (Katharine Hepburn) international influence as a political columnist in *Woman of the Year* (1942). Augusta Nash (Claudette Colbert) in *Arise, My Love* (1940) is a reporter who, in her desire to prove her worth as a foreign news correspondent (as opposed to covering the European fashion beat), contrives to rescue Tom Martin (Ray Milland) from a firing squad in Franco's Spain. She impersonates his wife and secures a reprieve, a feat that earns her the nickname Gusto from the grateful and smitten Martin. Others are wordsmiths who work in the more demanding forms of literature, like Claudette Colbert's poet Edwina Corday in *It's a Wonderful World.* She might count as her literary sister Irene Dunne's bestselling novelist Theodora Lynn in *Theodora Goes Wild* (1936), a comic bauble that predates Grace Metalious's novel *Peyton Place* in describing what passes for "racy" doings in a small town but does so with a droll, sympathetic humor missing from Metalious's glum work.

Even in the often stagnant waters of the secretarial pool, the fast-talking dame manages to aerate the environs. Never nondescript, she is acknowledged to be, like Jean Arthur's Carol Baldwin in the film so titled, *More Than a Secretary* (1936). She may even be called on to marry the boss for business reasons (which coincide, as we knew they would, with long-concealed love), as Rosalind Russell's Kendal Browning does in *Hired Wife* (1940). She can also rise to the top and stay there, like the entrepreneurial Alison Drake (Ruth Chatterton), who runs a factory in *Female* (1933), or like A. M. MacGregor (Rosalind Russell), who heads an ad agency and employs Tom Verney (Fred MacMurray) as her secretary in *Take a Letter, Darling* (1942). The initially

Carole Lombard, peering out at the world from her magic coach, in *My Man Godfrey*

obliging Verney eventually chafes under female management. So does MacMurray's Jim Ryan in *No Time for Love* (1943) when Katherine Grant (Claudette Colbert) hires him as a photographer's assistant. The sex comedy benefits from the role reversal that puts the woman on top, even though we know that the outcome must involve both male and female finding the level where they can meet eye to eye, morally as well as emotionally. Social and professional elevation rather suits Myrna Loy, who puts her commanding way with words to good use as a judge who imposes a comic sentence on Cary Grant's bachelor in *The Bachelor and the Bobby-Soxer* (1947), a late addition to the genre of boss-women comedies.

The working girl or female boss may don madcap as a ruse or a form of release, but madcap is most fetchingly worn by the heiresses who figure in the comedies of the period as women of materially un-fettered lives and indomitable though hardly ferocious wills. Despite the populist, often overtly proletarian sympathies of vintage American comedy, the screwball heiress inspires little moral objection and hardly any class resentment. This may be, as many have ventured, because she possesses the means as well as leisure to pursue a life free of consequences at a time when repercussion, whether for sexual or economic misadventure, was the moral rule of the day. This view, a common one, may account for the comic license permitted her, but it doesn't explain the popular audience's *fondness* for the Park Avenue brat who can, as Irene Bullock (Carole Lombard) does in *My Man Godfrey* (1936), park a horse in the library when they themselves were often crowded into such close quarters that the very idea of a entire room devoted to books was unthinkable.

Such personal and social generosity toward the indulged daughters of the rich seems unique to Depression America. The heiress is likely to be regarded as an object of pity, captive to her own wealth, like a princess in a folktale. Prey to fortune hunters and insulated from the bracing affections of the common folks, she is often portrayed as substantially poorer in the things that really give life its zest, its value. In *It Happened One Night,* Peter Warne's (Clark Gable) sly courtship of Ellie Andrews (Claudette Colbert) largely consists of his cataloguing for her all the inexpensive pleasures—like piggyback rides and dunking doughnuts—that she has missed as the pampered child of the leisure class. *The Richest Girl in the World* (1934) distills this pity into active commiseration. Superlative wealth drives Dorothy Hunter (Miriam Hopkins) to impersonate her own secretary, Silvia, a Fay Wray hardly showing the effects of her liaison with King Kong, in order to ensure that she will be loved for herself alone. She will test the man she loves, Tony Travers (Joel McCrea), with this masquerade, even encouraging him to court and marry Silvia (who in fact is already happily married). The plot is eerily masochistic, but not inexpert. Travers is comically vulnerable to the seductions of wealth and comes close to failing Dorothy's test several times, evidence of how *nearly* right she is in believing that the aphrodisiac properties of a colossal fortune usually overwhelm the milder if more enduring potencies of penniless love.

This democratic tolerance for the love travails of the rich is generally reserved for those whose money is not titled and hereditary but of recent acquisition. The nouveau riche are often forgiven their gauche manners, prodigal habits, and blithe self-absorption because in their life on screen they confirm a ruling fantasy of American democratic culture—the elegant life of ease is potentially open to anyone, but its attainment is not always to be envied, since money can bring more problems than it solves. It is an ideologically effective fantasy and a comic bonanza. Comedies of the era are proficient at mining the disparity between the emotional perplexities of the rich and the superior life-wisdom of the common folk in all serious matters of the heart.

The thirties comedies that tapped into the Depression psyche envisioned the figure of the financial patriarch as Walter Connolly or Eugene Pallette, a hardworking but emotionally harassed father whose portly shape tells the story of his financial fortunes—he is no lean aristocrat of refined appetites. When the imposing Edward Arnold is enlisted to impersonate the gruff banker-father in *Easy Living* (1937), he makes the most of his opportunity to voice down-home American prejudices against haute couture, not to mention continental lingo. When shown a hat that is touted for being "very recherché," his dismissal is as brusque as it is uncomprehending: "That's what's wrong with it." Lewis Stone, who played Judge Hardy in the wildly popular Andy Hardy series, would never convince as the father of a madcap heiress. He is simply too knowing and emotionally temperate; most of all, he is too tall. There is nothing irregular or scrappy about his looks or his voice, much less his diction. He could never bark with the thwarted authority of Connolly, baffled in his quest to locate his errant screen daughter Ellie Andrews; he could never believably mimic Pallette's gruff paternal exasperation as his Alexander Bullock receives yet another police summons issued to his miscreant daughters in *My Man Godfrey* (1936).

But lest we forget who has the greater command over social reality, it is Lewis Stone who, as Judge Hardy, presides over a juvenile vision of America. It is Walter Connolly, in *5th Ave. Girl,* whose Timothy Borden experiences all the ups and downs of capitalist fortune and must accede to the open marriage his wife takes as one of the prerogatives available to women of a certain class—and bank account. It is Connolly, frantic about his daughter's happiness in *It Happened One Night,* who opposes his daughter's marriage to the effete King Westley (Jameson Thomas) and announces that his old man's heart will be made happy if his daughter leaves King at the altar to flee with Gable's Peter Warne, even if it means that she will end up spending her honeymoon in an auto court. Such were the long-suffering, blunt, rough-hewn, endearing characters who sired the willful heiresses of the thirties. There wasn't a blueblood in the lot. It is their daughters who carry themselves with a fashionable elegance and whose svelte figures seem to defy the laws of genetics. *The Bride Came C.O.D.* exploits the comedy of class and sex difference metabolically by treating the runaway heiress (Bette Davis) literally as human cargo, whose weight will determine what her father will be charged on delivery. Cagney's pilot Steve Collins, who proposes to transport her to her father (Eugene Pallette), spends a good deal of time encouraging his high-strung baggage to eat.

Body weight is not, however, a universal measure of female value nor a reliable index of female types. For the sake of economy and to conform to a prevalent category in Hollywood typecasting, we will make hair color our signifying agent. This category is not as trivial as may first appear. It has deep roots in the tradition. To cite Ellen Moers in her wonderfully suggestive book *Literary Women,* hair color can prove "momentous" when expressing a mythology not just of sex, but of culture.[1] Certainly a good actress knows how to make the sexual code of hair color work in a performance. Howard Hawks, when asked to name his favorite actress in all the films he directed, unhesitatingly named Frances Farmer. "She was just fabulous. She was a blonde, a natural, but she just used a dark wig; that's all she put on. No change in make-up, just her face changed. Her whole attitude changed, her whole method of talking."[2] Because this is a book about a "whole method of talking," the matter of hair color and the attitude that comes with it is worth taking seriously. Hawks certainly did. On the first day of shooting *Come and Get It* (1936), Farmer was bold enough to make a suggestion to a "real old trouper," Edward Arnold: "If you'd only speak that line a little quicker I could keep this thing going." According to Hawks, Arnold "looked at her, and he spoke it quicker, and the scene was better."[3]

Perhaps the quickest way to begin defining this select sorority is, as is customary in such cases, with an act of exclusion. Let it be noted that Mae West does not form part of the sisterhood that I celebrate. She may be the mistress of double entendre (as of all else), but she is decidedly slow, even lethargic, in speech and movement. Her hourglass figure, maintained against the remorseless advance of age and changing fashion, is a conscious reversion to an earlier sexual type. Indeed, West never looks more natural than when corseted and encased in the Gilded Age finery that so splendidly displayed her buxom womanhood. Kathleen Rowe emphasizes how much of West's defiance of staid sexual codes, her seductive "unruliness," depends on her "creating and manipulating herself as spectacle" rather than taking control of narrative. Rowe is careful to add that for West "being a spectacle doesn't make her vulnerable to men but ensures her power over them." [4] Parker Tyler, on the other hand, celebrates West as the "most extraordinary and insinuating somnambule of them all." [5] What rendered her exceptional, writes Tyler, was her expert mimicry, "mellowed and reassured," of the "hysterically stylized movements of the female impersonator." Perhaps this explains not only her inimitable sexual style but the uncanny impression she gives that she has no real relation to time, hence no social future that we are eager to see fulfilled. She anticipates no exciting species of womanhood nor envisions any altered or improved relation of the sexes. Marriage is an institution she does not care to reinvent. Her domain is sex, not love, which means that finally she may have no abiding interest in the larger comic world she inhabits. Hence, as Rowe observes, her relative lack of interest in narrative and preference to remain ensconced in the domain of visual spectacle. West seems content to be the first and last of her line, brooking no imitators or successors, except, of course, other "female impersonators." For the "real" thing, for the female originals and originators who look out for themselves, we must set our sights elsewhere.

What follows, then, is a tribute to a select group of blondes and brunettes (and occasional redheads) who peopled the screen with their unforgettable looks, relaxed democratic manners, playful natures, and memorably fast talk. These are women, as I have said, who bequeathed to us an "advanced" style of female being. Katharine Hepburn, Irene Dunne, Rosalind Russell, Greta Garbo, and Barbara Stanwyck are awarded chapters of their own for the performances and the movies that elevated them to the level of Grande Dames. Others might have their candidates. These are mine, along with my reasons for thinking them cynosures of modern American womanhood.

Blonde Bombshells

In the sexual lore of American popular culture, blondes are typically prized as trophies or bombshells, combustible sex their specialty either way. Proverbially, they are favored by fortune, even in the most desperate times. "Never seen a blonde in a breadline yet," chortles lovely (and confident) Sharon Norwood (Constance Bennett) to Jim Branch (Clark Gable) in *After Office Hours* (1935), one of the many comedy–murder mystery melodramas in which the era expressed its complicated attitudes toward social reality and toward the women who didn't behave according to the old rules yet seemed to have no deep spiritual affinity to the hedonistic flapper. Neither respectability nor pleasure in their pure state appealed to the fast-talking dame. She was out to redefine the terms of her life and to secure the happiness that the young expect is their due. And why should we contradict her? Life can do that. Comedy protects us from taking reality too much to heart. It might be said that comedy gives us the heart to face breadlines as well as to confront the more complex hunger within.

Jean Harlow

Harlow was arguably the hungriest dame to eat up the screen. Her appetite for life was conveyed without a trace of the fatal softness, the emotional debility of Marilyn Monroe's film personae — her sole physical rival as the Ultimate Blonde Bombshell. Harlow's fast talk is the brash talk of riffraff. Only Barbara Stanwyck surpassed her in portraying picaresque comic heroines determined to work their way up the social scale. Stanwyck gave the definitive performance of the socially ambitious sexual predator in *Baby Face,* her fresh looks and bright eyes suggesting an innocence in no way hers. But it was Harlow who most often *played* the sexual siren as disingenuous child and who, off-screen, answered to her mother's pet name, "the Baby." She might have been thinking of the uses made of her dramatic talent when she described a female character in her own book, *Today Is Tonight:* "She had the ability to suddenly make herself seem very young and helpless, and her voice small and childlike, without in any sense seeming to pose." [6]

It is an ability Harlow demonstrated hilariously as Kitty Packard in *Dinner at Eight,* slipping into a childish simper when her husband wants to refuse an invitation she has been dying to receive. Baby talk is her secret weapon in her ongoing battle with her husband, a way of deflating his braggadocio, which has all the crude authority of money behind it. The contrast between her infantile blather and his boardroom bluster is what makes their marriage work as a comic partnership. Her manner is part of a sexual style that the movie suggests is nurtured by her lower-class hankering after high-class glamor—she dresses in the latest fashions, but that doesn't make her fashionable, and she knows it. Such knowledge is the key to Harlow's portrayals of Lil Andrews, the randy opportunist of *Red-Headed Woman* (1932), and ambitious Eadie Chapman in *The Girl from Missouri* (1934) (both scripted by Anita Loos, the creator of another low-class bombshell, Lorelei Lee, the gold-digging heroine of *Gentlemen Prefer Blondes*).

But this small-town girl with big-city assets could also be concealing a yearning for respectability beneath the brassy pose. The young Frank Capra combined the sexual heat with the craving for gentility when he cast her as a socialite Anne Schuyler in *Platinum Blonde* (1931). He gave the role of Gallagher, the proletarian girl reporter who is a rival in love, to the delicate Loretta Young, whose looks and manner exude the refinement that Harlow half-heartedly impersonates. Harlow, who in fact came from an upper-class family, looks more in her element taking a bath in a rain barrel, as she does to such striking effect on a rubber plantation in *Red Dust* (1932), than she does in the plush surroundings of a Park Avenue mansion.

Gable (as Eddie) will find her again (as Ruby Adams) soaking in the tub in *Hold Your Man* (1933) when he enters her unlocked apartment to elude the police. There he finds a pillow on which is proclaimed her philosophy of life:

We're here today
Tomorrow we're through.
So let's be gay
It's up to you.

Her sentiments, if such laissez-faire attitudes can be called that, have all the fatalistic humor but little of the harshness of the *carpe diem* attitude learned in the school of hard knocks. *Hold Your Man,* like many of Harlow's star vehicles, veers into crime melodrama. Harlow was the least successful of the fast-talkers in disentangling her character from the gangsterism, the vaguely criminal riffraffdom lurking on the fringes of thirties comedy, threatening to overwhelm it. Her comic presence tended to accent the moral instabilities that shadowed America's fascination with lowlife. Since she became a star in the pre-Code era, her sexual adventurism could be treated frankly, as it is in *Hold Your Man* and *Red-Headed Woman,* a film in which she sets her sights on her boss, who bears the symbolically charged name Legendre. She is out to conquer not just a man, the Frenchified pun insinuates, but the entire sexual system.

Harlow's sexual frankness and opportunism were often succeeded by yearnings for more elevated, even cerebral planes of existence. In 1933's *Dinner at Eight,* scripted by the wickedly literate Herman Mankiewicz, Frances Marion, and Donald Ogden Stewart after George S. Kaufman and Edna Ferber's stage hit, she is caricatured as a nouveau riche joke, but a delectable one who deserves, on artistic grounds alone, to wear all those Adrian body-caressing gowns. The joke develops in a predictable direction when she takes a book to bed with her as a prop in the ongoing seduction of her "doctor," but it takes an unexpected turn when we find at the end of the movie that she seems actually to have read it.[7] The book, as Kitty famously describes it to Carlotta Vance (Marie Dressler) on their way into dinner, "is all about civilization or something, a *nutty* kind of a book. Do you know the guy said that machinery is going to take the place of every profession?" Carlotta, an aging actress trading on her past as stage siren, takes one appraising look at Harlow's semi-draped body and reassures her: "Oh, dear, that's something you need never worry about." The famous quip has all the zing of an unanswerable putdown, but it also comes as a compliment from a fellow professional.

Harlow is so explosive yet disarming in her sexual candor that the only way to restrain her is to yoke her to a sentimental myth that she is at heart a one-woman-man whose greatest desire is to get married and stay married. Marriage constitutes her "ideal" in *The Girl from Missouri*. *Libeled Lady* has great fun sending up this screen ambition. She may be a bombshell, but except for *Platinum Blonde,* she will do anything to find and hold her man. *Hold Your Man,* a psychic template for Harlow's rough charm, is one of those morally confused and psychologically improbable movies so common in the thirties that still grab our attention—and short-circuit our condescension at their overall hokeyness—with a sexual realism that retains the power to confound. Harlow's Ruby Adams is a sexual grifter plying a semi-decent trade fleecing out-of-towners. As she announces to Eddie Hall (Clark Gable), Ruby has two rules when she "goes visiting": "Keep away from couches and stay on your feet." Some of the rules seem improvised, as when she will allow Eddie to take her coat but not her hat. "I'm pretty cool in the head" is the wry explanation she offers. Even if she soon loses her cool to Eddie's sexual heat, the line is enough to earn her early admission into the ranks of fast-talkers with quick comebacks. Wisecracks are her sexual armor, but they are open to counterattack.

Necessity as much as temperament accounts for Harlow's aggressive sexual campaigns, for her bombshell character is surprisingly vulnerable to competition. *Red Dust* gives her a formidable rival in Mary Astor, an actress of subtle witchery who will later triumph as the scheming Brigid O'Shaughnessy in *The Maltese Falcon* (1941). But in *Red Dust,* Astor's Barbara Willis, a newlywed who valiantly accompanies her inexperienced husband into the harsh climes of Indochina, is all honest refinement. Harlow's character Vantine, a call girl in some trouble with the police in Saigon, is clearly outclassed but not outdone when she realizes that Barbara is falling in love with the virile Dennis Carson (Gable). The sexual palette that Moers delineated for Old World cultures is updated and Americanized as their rivalry unfolds. It is the platinum Vantine who enlivens the proceedings with her jocular carnality, the brunette Barbara who radiates a translucent and

Jean Harlow and Clark Gable in *Red Dust*

imperfectly subdued sexuality. (In his remake, *Mogambo* [1953], John Ford reverts to Old World types, giving the luscious Ava Gardner the Harlow role and the coolly elegant Grace Kelly the part of the refined but seducible lady.)

The roles and the mythology are reprised in *China Seas* (1935), again with Gable, in which Harlow will have a similarly delayed triumph over Rosalind Russell (early in her career when she was slotted into genteel roles that wasted her talent for raillery). Both films cast her as a working girl in the slangiest sense of the word, but *Red Dust* takes a more comic attitude toward her unsavory past and credits her with a savviness at once hard-boiled and poignant. No wisecrack in the thirties surpasses Vantine's dry but not unfriendly retort to Barbara after hearing her confess that her attraction to Carson is just "one of those excitement-of-the-moment things." "Well, watch out for the next moment, honey. It's longer than the first." A entire history of hopeless passion is condensed in that aphorism — it should be emblazoned on samplers for generations of women to come.

In winning her man from the desirable but overly cultivated Astor and Russell, Harlow vindicates the superior vitality of the companionable dame over the reputable lady. The reformed or redeemed prostitute is a sentimental idea, but one need only compare *Red Dust* to *Pretty Woman* (1990) or *Mighty Aphrodite* (1995) to see how much more intelligent and gritty is the social Darwinism of the thirties than that of the nineties. In *Pretty Woman,* Julia Roberts's character, for all her working-girl credentials, is a creature of a fairy tale, not the streets, and she has no real competition for the hero's affection. Harlow's Vantine, hanging around the rubber plantation as if she were still loitering in a brothel off-hours, reminds us where a lot of our wisetalk originates. She also reminds us how hard working girls work, at one point sloughing off the inconveniences of the accommodations with, "Guess I'm not used to sleeping nights anyway." Her stamina (so poignant given how fragile a hold on real life hers proved to be) is a point in her favor. In *China Seas,* Russell's Sybil proves unequal to the sheer *strain* of loving Gable's Captain Alan Gaskell and keeping the rough company he likes to keep. In *Red Dust,* Barbara (Astor), who succumbs to Carson (Gable) like one of Tyler's somnambules, is too languid to sustain a life with him. Besides, she's married to the pallid, feverish Gary Willis (Gene Raymond) and won't abandon him. The Old World has its values, some of them admirable, after all.

Still, if it is a question of survival of the fittest, there is no real doubt about whether Harlow, the dame of the tropics with a brash mouth, sumptuous body, and reckless love, will triumph over the plucky but thin-blooded "ladies" who try their luck in the wilderness. Harlow's adventure films, with their strong dose of sexual humor, are unsentimental elegies for the pallid heroines and somnambules who had their day in the twenties and who vied with the vamp and the jazz baby for sexual hegemony in the popular imagination. Harlow, without the vamp's erotic darkness or the flapper's untroubled hedonism, sexually pushed for a comic showdown between vitality and vitiated instinct and, in the final reel, she was rewarded for her patience, her pains, and, of course, her sharp tongue.

Her best post-Code manners are on comic display in *Libeled Lady,* in which competition brings out the best in her, even as it shows up all the disadvantages attaching to the dame's estate. She plays Gladys, a bride-to-be whose wedding day is perpetually being cast aside by her fiancé, reporter Warren Haggerty, played by the waggish Spencer Tracy. No such indignity attends the lady in the picture, Myrna Loy's Connie Allenbury, who is vigilantly pursued at every point—by reporters, gold diggers, and, most assiduously, by Bill Chandler (William Powell), who is trying to compromise her so she will drop her libel suit against Tracy's paper. Gable brought out Harlow's sexual humor and what we might call her emotional tenacity in the face of genteel competition, but Tracy and Powell bring out her sexual soul. It is a soul, the movie tells us, that is often insulted by Chandler or habitually overlooked by Haggerty, the man who one day will promise to cherish it. The deliberate gaiety that was her main attribute in *Hold Your Man* and that earned her the self-adopted moniker Pollyanna, the Glad Girl, in *Red Dust,* is acknowledged in Haggerty's pet name for her, Gladdy. She is the spirited dame to Myrna Loy's vivacious libeled lady.

Loy is stiff competition in any league, yet both actresses are too honest to falsify the class underpinnings of their rivalry. There is a whiff, indeed a bouquet, of the hothouse clinging to Connie Allenbury. Gladys comes into the film screaming for attention, trying not to trip over the profusion of wedding finery accumulated after so many nuptial postponements. Connie is the cool society girl, first seen stripping a sweater over her head as if shedding all the irritating encumbrances that go with her money. She is shown propped on her father's desk, insisting on pursuing a libel suit against a paper that has slandered her with false reports of homewrecking sexual escapades. The sangfroid that Connie has picked up on the Continent seems to have chilled her to the bone. She hardly acknowledges Chandler's chivalry in rescuing her from a press posse that assails her as she is about to board a liner returning to America, but then, maybe she already suspects the truth—that he has arranged the entire incident to insinuate himself into her company. She is too smart to feel obligated, much less grateful, for his intervention. She appears quite wise to the devious ways of the world, which may explain why she never once warms to Chandler's goofy charm. She gets his name wrong and doesn't let him finish answering the pathetically formulaic questions she puts to him.

Her aloofness is comic but disconcerting, especially to American manners. The first phase of their snooty courtship concludes with Chandler giving her a verbal check in the name of democracy. He now is the one to adopt a haughty tone. His is not the hauteur of the spoiled rich, however, but the disdain of the offended plebeian. He accuses her of being so delicate she should be under glass. Unerringly, he has touched a nerve, and her response is indignant, even feral—she slaps him. Later Gladdy will slug him.

As this brief history of two very different experiences of courtship makes clear, Gladdy is the vulnerable member of the comic quartet that comes striding toward us in the film's exuberant opening. All seem to be enjoying the mere fact of being together, but Harlow's is the most gladsome face, convulsed with laughter. This impression proves ironic and even misleading, because it is Gladdy who will be most prone to sound the discordant note. She is always chiming in in the minor key, and having found it, sustaining it like an unresolved chord. "You can't do this to me, Warren Haggerty," is the burden of her comically abject refrain. Or else: "The things I do for that newspaper." Or finally: "If you don't want to marry me, just say so." These are the catchphrases that give her speech the splutter-effect of a broken record, turning her heartfelt plaints into the broad humor of gag lines. Gladdy enters the film as an unadulterated "humor" character with one thing on her mind—to get married and stay married. It is to Harlow's credit that she converts a humorous character in bondage to a singular idea into a complex and even poignant comic personage.

This is how she manages it. The plot requires that Chandler masquerade as her husband, a ploy Gladdy agrees to only out of her love for Haggerty, since she is initially allergic to Chandler. At the conclusion of their faux wedding ceremony, the judge ritually asks to be invited to their silver wedding anniversary. "It'll have to be within the next six weeks," Gladdy retorts, which gives the measure of her impatience and distaste for the whole business. But six weeks come and go, and still Chandler has failed to compromise Connie or otherwise deflect her from pursuing her lawsuit. The marital masquerade must continue long enough, it turns out, for gibes to turn into sweet talk.

It is in the interval between Chandler's first and second attempts to compromise Miss Allenbury that Gladdy has her own change of heart. She succumbs to Chandler on the only grounds on which she is believably vulnerable — his sexual gallantry (to which Connie had proved so impervious). Having to spend the night in the honeymoon suite with Chandler, Gladdy locks her door, only to realize the next morning that he has had the key all along. This is a man, remember, whose fortune depends, literally in the Allenbury case, on his skill in compromising women, but on Gladdy he makes no move. Her face melts into a smile in light of this recognition. The smile communicates volumes about Gladdy's sexual history: she either gets the wrong kind of or too little attention from her men. Gladdy, patently starved for romance in any form, begins to warm to the idea of Chandler as a mate. Her insults turn to endearments, and she begins to take pleasure in the fantasy of being Mrs. William Chandler — the same William Chandler who once suggested that she spend the six weeks' interim between their marriage and divorce learning how to read. But we know she does read. We have seen her poring over Real Love Stories, and now, it seems to her, she has a real love story of her own.

Both Harlow and Loy expertly play women whose initial hostility yields to love, a theme in which the comedies of the day excelled, but Harlow's is the harder part and potentially the more demeaning. Chandler deceives her into thinking that his now *real* romance with Connie is still part of the plan to entrap her, and when Gladdy learns of the deception she is determined to stop their elopement. Harlow's last major role gives her the sad occasion to play a female Malvolio, a sexual dupe and refuser of festivities. Chandler and Connie elope on the mistaken belief that his "fake" marriage to Gladdy is void, because her first marriage was never legally dissolved. They are followed to their hotel suite by Gladdy, who is outraged, and newshound Haggerty, who is elated because the marriage will force Connie to drop her lawsuit. Haggerty, having made sure of the marriage, starts to leave, until Connie points out he has forgotten something. In a vaudevillian turn that is funny on stage but strangely cruel in the last reel of a film, he nods, feebly affects a clownish grin and then reaches for his hat. He has to be reminded that a woman, not a hat, is what he has overlooked, and not just this time alone.

In the spirit if not the exact words of Shaw's Eliza Doolittle when she has been ignored just one time too many by Henry Higgins, Gladdy makes her stand by declaring, "I won't be passed over." She has been left out of their comically self-absorbed calculations, and now she's ready to settle accounts. "You're all building up to a nice little happy ending," she grimly warns them. She will overturn their comic victory with a double reversal: proving that her divorce *was* legal, since she got it *twice*, once in Mexico and then in Reno; refusing to annul her marriage to Chandler, if only to prove that she won't play the sap for any man—or lady.

The best comedies of the time aren't afraid of such harsh moments of truth-telling in which we are given a glimpse of the moral collapse that could just as easily have befallen our comic connivers, however justified their deceptions might seem. In such cases the sexes must separate before they can reunite on a more proper and lasting basis. Connie and Gladdy repair to the bedroom, where Connie, with a kindliness that has been growing on her character, gently consoles Gladdy and suggests that it is not Chandler she loves, but only the attention he lavished on her. Gladdy, however, is deaf to all entreaties. Only the sound of men fighting in the next room and the prospect of her Warren being pummeled by the feebly pugilistic Chandler jolts Gladdy's heart back into its predestined position—aimed toward Warren. The couples finally and happily sorted out, the marriage feast merrily turns to cacophony when Connie's father (Walter Connolly), enters, asks for an explanation, and is assaulted by a din of excited confabulation. Gladdy, devourer of Real Love Stories, gets her Pollyanna ending— one that doesn't make a lick of sense, is hardly intelligible, and is of dubious legality. Emotionally, though, it does the trick.

Carole Lombard

Like Harlow, Carole Lombard is often impatient or unhappy with the way her life is going, but her comic response to her predicaments is more rambunctious than raffish. Her sexual morals are definitely higher, but she is also the more accomplished liar. Or should we say, in a more generous mood, that where Harlow makes candor her comic calling card, Lombard is the great pretender. With the exception (again) of Barbara Stanwyck, there is no actress of the time who approaches her range in comic imposture.[8] Her gallery of characters includes the self-dramatizing heiress Irene Bullock of *My Man Godfrey,* the charming fake Hazel Flagg of *Nothing Sacred,* the pathological liar Helen Bartlett of *True Confession* (1937), the outraged yet still game wife of *Mr. and Mrs. Smith* (1941), Hitchcock's only extended venture into comedy. Finally, there are the two marvelous divas who launched and closed, sadly and prematurely, her career as a fast-talking, quick-acting dame: Mildred Plotka, alias Lily Garland, of *Twentieth Century* and the peerless Maria Tura of *To Be or Not to Be.*

In taking on these diva roles Lombard faces down the tradition of prejudice against women who act. Even in pre-Code days, Lombard, whose manner was happily uninhibited in private life, distanced herself from the actress's proverbially easy morals and loose talk.[9] The only note of conventionality in the wildly iconoclastic *Twentieth Century* is sounded by Lombard's Lily Garland when she "confesses" the awful truth that she was never unfaithful to her husband, mentor, director, and keeper, Oscar Jaffe (John Barrymore), if only because he watched her like a hawk and kept her under virtual house arrest. It is less the actress's sexuality than her practiced duplicity that occasions outrage. The same holds true for her turn as the fatally ill Hazel Flagg in *Nothing Sacred.* Once Walter Connolly, playing the irascible editor Oliver Stone (!), discovers that Hazel is not dying from radium poisoning, he denounces her for possessing "the soul of an eel and the brain of a tarantula." Later he will confer on her the dubious distinction of being the biggest fake of the twentieth century. Though the century was relatively young when this verdict is rendered, Lombard's preeminence in fakery holds up.

All the more remarkable, then, that Lombard's talent for dissembling is never associated, as it is with Stanwyck, with a criminal or treacherous nature. She is never subjected to the exposure and humiliation that await so many deceitful women, like Stanwyck's cardsharp Jean Harrington in *The Lady Eve,* or Jean Arthur's Babe Bennett, the reporter who masquerades as a waif in *Mr. Deeds Goes to Town.* When Wally Cook (Fredric March), the reporter who brings her to New York

Carole Lombard emoting for John Barrymore in *Twentieth Century*

and ends up, as we knew he would, falling in love with the doomed and gallant Hazel, finds out that she is not dying and in fact never was, he is jubilant: "I thank God on my knees that she is a fraud and a fake and that she isn't going to die." He even manages to turn the discovery of her deception into his comic opportunity: "I am going to lie and cheat and swindle right through our golden anniversary," he promises, with a lover's true ardor. Even in *True Confession,* when she confesses to a murder she did not commit, her trial is played strictly as farce. Not for a minute does the comedy entertain the possibility that her confession springs from a hidden guilt or unexpressed darkness in her character. Lombard's characters inhabit a Wildean universe remarkably free of evil; they flourish in that most hilarious but difficult of dramatic forms perfected by Wilde—the trivial comedy for serious people.

In playing out this comedy, Lombard remains professionally aware of how theatricality has penetrated to the core of her being, irradiating it but perhaps also handicapping her for the morally mixed world where the rest of mankind must be content to live. This Wildean self-knowledge is present in her first great comic heroine, Lily Garland. Lily succeeds in giving female histrionics a good name, and never more so than when she is renouncing it. For instance, after throwing a tantrum on finding that she has been given a small compartment on the Twentieth Century Limited, she reacts to her maid's exasperated exit with high-toned hauteur: "I despise temperament," she announces to anyone within earshot, carefully articulating every supercilious vowel—even the "a" that typically struggles to be heard between "per" and "ment." We might be forgiven for suspecting she is trying out a line reading for future use. Her current male companion, a stuffy society "boy," is deaf to the subtleties in her craft. "Go on. Go on. Rave on. I suppose I'm seeing the true you at last." These words are his death knell as far as any claim on her affections or our sympathy is concerned. His impatience with outward show would be enough to disqualify him as a romantic prospect for this most dramatic of women. More objectionable, however, is the sheer effrontery in his presuming that he might see, indeed that *anyone* might ever hope to behold, the "true you at last."

Oscar Jaffe, the director and ex-husband who claims to know her better than anyone, would never make such a mistake. He appreciates the heightened and inspired theatricality of Lily's nature. Watching her dismiss her now less than lovesick escort, Oscar can only applaud the way she chose to play the scene. "That's Sappho," he exults as Lily continues her lovelorn ravings. Oscar, a man of the theater himself, knows that for Lily, as for himself, the very idea of a "true you" is, to use Oscar's favorite word of reprobation, anathema. But whereas his style derives from Sardou, Lily, when she is "on," which is just about always, might have been imagined by Oscar Wilde, had Wilde wanted to represent how Americans, famed for the unaffected "naturalness" of their social manners and verbal style, might take up the pleasures of affectation.

These pleasures, of course, come at a price, and Lily, who before her rebirth in the theater had the unglamorous life and name of Mildred Plotka, salesgirl, knows how to calculate it. In the midst of one of her recurring battles with Oscar, she suddenly stops the action and apparently steps out of character to comment on the scene she has been so expertly playing. "We're not people, we're lithographs; we don't know anything about love unless it's written and rehearsed. We're only real in between curtains." Oscar, momentarily taken in by her honesty, marvels, "Why, Lily. You're crying." Lily refuses to yield her point. "Sure, sure, I turned on the faucet. It's that sort of scene; that's the devil of it." Oscar, recognizing this appeal to his theatrical intelligence, corrects her. "That's the pity of it, you mean." We would be greatly mistaken to think that Oscar is bemoaning any loss of emotional realism. His pity is of the excoriating rather than compassionate kind. He's chastising her for imitating in her off-stage life scenes taken from movies rather than the "legitimate" theater. He returns the discussion to aesthetic grounds, where, of course, Lily meant to keep it all along. Even her lament pays homage to her talent for creating finely etched impressions. She doesn't conceive of herself and Oscar as vain shadows but as lithographs, elegant works of art rather than pitiable illustrations of existential desperation.

Lombard, as comic lithograph, thus distinguishes herself as the least opaque of comic actresses. To sustain the impression of triviality so crucial to the serious business of being whoever and whatever she chooses to be, she avoids, both in her physical manner and her way of speaking, any inappropriate suggestion of unsuspected depths. She keeps your eyes riveted on the surface of her acting, where everything seems to—and in fact does—happen. The quicksilver mobility of her face allows her suddenly to take on a look of intense concentration that is unashamedly transparent, as if you could see the wheels moving inside her brain or glimpse the excited flutters of her heart. Her voice possesses a similar agility, with its quick drops into languor or depression, its leaps and excited yelps of laughter.

Even in a confused and lackluster comedy-gangster-melodrama like *The Gay Bride* (1934), by her own estimation the worst picture she ever made, the Lombard character proudly advertises her technique.[10] She plays a gold-digging chorine named Mary who is determined to marry for money and get out of the chorus for good. Since the only men who come her way are gangsters, she sets her sights on one called Shoots (Nat Pendleton), even though the idea of wedlock has never crossed his admittedly limited mind. She holds out for matrimony, giving Shoots the performance of her life. "Just because I'm in the theater doesn't mean I don't prize decency and real affection," she blubbers. She then insists that "what I want out of life is marriage, yes, and a home and babies." The gangster's factotum, who answers to Office Boy (Chester Morris), is the only real critic in the house. "What a performance," he marvels. "It had everything, heart, tears, and baloney." Office Boy obligingly captures for us the essential components of every great Lombard performance, here tried out, as it were, in the sticks. Heart and tears any good actress can bring off, but to mix in baloney without upsetting the stomach is a feat achievable only by the most accomplished hams.

It is the hamminess of childhood preserved and stored for adult use. Elizabeth Kendall has characterized this aspect of Lombard's comic personae as the "mischievous-child version of the romantic-comedy heroine." [11] But the love of mischief is secondary and subordinate to Lombard's love of make-believe. Like all children, she likes pretending. In the diverting comedy-mystery *The Princess Comes Across,* she pretends to be the Swedish princess Olga, à la Garbo, in order to launch a movie career. Only Marion Davies's impersonation of Garbo in *Blondie of the Follies* is more adroit in caricaturing Garbo's exotic allure. Playing Garbo certainly proves more fun than going through life as Wanda Nash of Brooklyn, although that is the identity she resolves, at the end of the film, to take up again. But in the interim she has enjoyed living out the most enchanting of fantasies—being born again into a fairy-tale life.

Lombard's heroines are often of this born-again variety. Mildred Plotka rebegins the world as Lily Garland. Hazel Flagg, stuck in the boonies of Vermont, is less happy on learning that she will not succumb to radium poisoning. The news reduces her to tears, but for pricelessly comic reasons: "To be brought to life twice," she laments, "and both times in Warsaw!" Hitchcock and his screenwriter Norman Krasna have fun giving Lombard's skill in leading double lives a naughty (by the standards of the day) twist in *Mr. and Mrs. Smith.* The Smiths, Mrs. Smith announces early in the day, have a marriage based on respect, "respect for each other as persons." Lily Garland would scoff at such cant. When her tagalong suitor questions her behavior, she turns on him in a fine comic rage: "Who cares about respect?"

she sneers. "I'm too big to be respected!" Hitchcock, too, gives this bromide the treatment it probably deserves. We see how much respect enters into Mr. Smith's (Robert Montgomery) feelings for Mrs. Smith when, on learning that their marriage is legally void, he schemes to keep the news from her. The doodle on his notepad suggests how much fun he intends to have with the newly restored maiden: "Miss/tress Ann Krausheimer." The diacritical slash cuts through all the pieties about chaste womanhood. Rather than continuing to honor his wife, he would rather enjoy her both as virginal miss and game mistress. The rest of the comedy is devoted to the ridiculous ploys to which both partners resort in trying to remake a marriage that doesn't dissolve the mistress in the Mrs.

Of all her assumed identities, her most endearing is Irene Bullock of *My Man Godfrey*, the society girl who pretends to be that most chimerical of beings—a grownup. Her fast talk is the fast talk of a child who breathlessly wants to get her words out before she is cut off. As the younger child perpetually trying to cut into grown-up conversation, she's not used to completing her sentences, only beginning them. Indeed, the first important personal fact we learn about her is that she is always losing out to her older sister, Cornelia (Gail Patrick). This would explain her anxiety about being heard, but also why, in those pre-Seinfeld days, she believes "Ya, ya, ya" to be the unanswerable comeback to Cornelia's taunts.

But Irene's biggest triumph over her elder sister is in making the man who pushed Cornelia into an ashpile the family butler. She thus establishes her claim to the "my" in the title, even though the movie will make that possessive ambivalent and insecure. She, like the title, claims Godfrey Parke (William Powell) when and where the world has forgotten him, in the city dump. She ventures there at the beginning of the movie in order to find a forgotten man, the last and most elusive item in a scavenger hunt. She will leave with Godfrey in tow, taking with her not only a forgotten man but a dawning awareness of the greater perplexities of life. Why someone might live in a dump when there are so many nicer places to live is the first perplexity that assaults her curious but sheltered mind. Godfrey replies to her questions with the sarcasm they deserve, but he soon will come to appreciate that behind Irene's childish presumption that everyone is free to live as they please—except herself—lie a vitality and generosity that he might do well to make his own. The deep human charm of the movie and of Lombard's comic being will escape you unless you take seriously her claim that Godfrey is indisputably "my man." By this possessive she does not mean to designate his subordinate relation to her as her sexual property or personal servant. In calling him my man she is declaring his exalted status as her protégé.

The word has a charismatic meaning for Irene; she assigns to it all manner of magic. "It makes me feel so mature having a protégé," she enthusiastically confesses to Godfrey on his first morning butling. "It's terribly thrilling. Not only does it occupy my mind, but I think it is character building too." For her part, Irene has a model of patronage in her own mother, Angelica Bullock, played to scatterbrained perfection by Alice Brady, and her protégé Carlo (the hilarious Mischa Auer), whose talents seem to be limited to playing "Otchi tchornia" and imitating, with uncanny accuracy, a housebound ape. With such an example in mind, no wonder Irene anticipates her new identity as a patron with undaunted enthusiasm: "It's really not much work and it gives you something to think about and it's such fun," she informs the astonished Godfrey in one of her many run-on sentences. Then, in a sudden access of vision, she sees it all clearly. "You know what you are? You are my responsibility."

Irene thus shows herself the only person in the film capable of intuiting the moral obligations attaching to the possessive pronoun "my." But on what could this claim be based, if not her childish sense that she and she alone is responsible for this man since she is the one who has given him new life? We have no less an authority than Godfrey himself to authenticate Irene's creative power. When he later revisits his former "home" at the dump, he memorializes it as the "birthplace" of Godfrey Smith. "Where are the ashes of Godfrey Parke?" his boyhood companion asks. "Scattered to the winds." In other films Lombard gives birth to herself; in *My Man Godfrey* she oversees the comic rebirth of another. Lombard's Irene Bullock belongs to our pantheon of female Pygmalions with the power to bring men to life. How does she work this miracle?

Carole Lombard as Irene Bullock, the female Pygmalion about to bring William Powell a new life in *My Man Godfrey*

If, as Godfrey later insists, the only difference between a derelict and a man is a job, then Irene has made a man of him by the simple expedient of employing him. That is the first and perhaps most essential standard of manliness for Depression-era America. But the second standard connects more deeply with the American ideal of democratic fellowship, a fellow-feeling that survives fluctuations in the economy and changes of class fortune. Irene's comradely feeling prompts her to take Godfrey's hand on leaving the dump for the society gala, as if he were not so much a forgotten man as a prodigal son returning home, which, in many ways, he is. She is grateful to him for doing something "I wanted to do . . . ever since I was six years old"—pushing Cornelia into an ashpile. She enjoys more triumph over Cornelia by producing Godfrey to win the scavenger hunt. Godfrey carries the day by telling off the crowd and vowing to return to a "society of really important people," but it is Irene who acts on the principle that makes a good society possible—reciprocity: "I wish I could do something for you," she pleads. "Because you've done something for me, don't you see?" Godfrey, approving of the morality as well as the utility of the principle, suggests that he give her a job. Can you butle? she quickly asks, a sign that she means to stand by what she says.

In resenting the imbalances of power in her own family, Irene embraces reciprocity as the ideal principle of all human contact, extending even to the accidents of life. On the first evening of his employment, Irene giddily notes how just that morning she and Godfrey were sitting on her bed and now they are sitting on his. "We'll overlook that startling coincidence," Godfrey advises, and then, still taken aback by her familiarity, wonders, "Hasn't anyone ever told you about certain proprieties?" Apparently not, so Godfrey feels obliged to. Considering her mental habits, he resorts to a fairy tale to make his point: "Once there was a very sentimental little girl with a very kind heart and she helped out a man who was very grateful. Then she became a nuisance and undid all the fine work she had done."

She doesn't become a nuisance, though. She becomes something hilarious—a lovelorn strolling player, devotedly following Godfrey around as he butles his way into and around the family's madcap routines. When she is falsely informed that he has a wife and five children, she becomes conspicuously disconsolate: "Life is but an empty bubble," she intones to all who will listen (no one does). Only spoilsport Cornelia pays her any mind, and then only so she can pan the performance. She catches Irene in a particularly histrionic attitude, which she identifies as "pose number eight" in her dramatic repertory. "Am I spoiling your act, dear?" she asks, in witchy irony. Irene is not deterred. So intent is she on self-dramatization that she begins to refer to herself and to her inattentive audience in the impersonal third person. "What difference does it make where one puts flowers when one's heart is breaking," she informs Godfrey when flowers arrive for her tea party. When he ignores her, she escalates into ominous, lugubrious prediction: "All I have to say is some people will be sorry someday." "For what?" asks Carlo. "Some people will know for what and then it will be too late." The comic payoff comes when Irene begins to see how reciprocity is a principle that can serve the darker purposes of spite: "Well, if other people can have five children, so can other people," she vows.

Retaliation, however ludicrous, is not in Irene's moral nature. Reciprocity, turnabout, and fair play are the principles she introduces into the film. These are the comic values that motivate her to recall Godfrey, the forgotten man, back to active life, and in return he will rescue her family from economic and moral bankruptcy. In what we might call the first comic ending, Godfrey acts the part of a modern-day magus, converting impending calamity into unexpected blessing. Using the pearls that Cornelia had planted in his room to get him dismissed for theft, Godfrey purchases some stocks that eventually make his fortune—and restore the Bullocks' as well. He views his magical transactions in the marketplace as a form of restitution to the family that worked his own rehabilitation. He has helped them, he explained, because, by their example, they helped him, a spoiled rich kid "never educated to face life." From Mr. Bullock he learned patience, from Cornelia, humility. But it is to Irene that he owes his greatest debt: "You're grateful to me because I helped you to beat Cornelia and I'm grateful to you because you helped me to beat life." Beating Cornelia and beating life are not commensurate acts—Irene gives more than she receives.

It was Ernst Lubitsch who put this gift for beating life to unexpected use in *To Be or Not To Be*. Lombard plays Maria Tura, the diva in a troupe of Polish actors who are mounting an anti-Nazi play on the eve of an invasion. We first see her as she strolls onto a stage and asks the director whether he likes her dress, an exquisite, body-caressing concoction. He absentmindedly answers yes, until he realizes that she plans to wear it in the play about Nazis, where it would be absurdly, even shockingly, out of place. He can't believe, he objects, that an artist could be so inartistic. But the diva's artistic instinct, which unsurprisingly coincides with her histrionic character, is to defend the dress on the grounds that it would present a "tremendous contrast" when the lights go on to reveal a tortured woman being "flogged in the dark." Lombard's practiced insouciance in the art of tremendous contrasts gives her, as the film proceeds to demonstrate with ingenious, often hilarious, invention, a particular and decided advantage in the various occasions for sexual play—and politics—in the film.

At first her sexual charm is directed toward a flirtation with a young Polish flier eager to take her away from the complicated life of the stage and give her the simple life on a farm that she so adores. "By the way, where was that?" he inquires, recalling her pictured behind a plow. "In the *Chronicle,*" she wistfully returns, as if internally admiring the effect of that pose and the publicity that has turned her into the most idolized woman in prewar Poland. Lubitsch has great fun elaborating the premise that the young flier's main attraction for Maria is, delicately put, her fascination with meeting a man "who could drop three tons of dynamite in two minutes," a line Lombard delivers to suggest something between sexual awe and professional delight in the thought of such high-octane performances.

Maria calls on her own thespian, as well as womanly, skills to improvise her own difficult and unscripted part in the Polish resistance. She has been summoned to the Hotel Europski by Professor Alexander Siletsky (Stanley Ridges), the traitor who the next morning will reveal the names of members of the Polish underground to the Gestapo. Siletsky, obviously taken with Maria's beauty, seeks to recruit her to the Nazi cause. First he appeals to her on purely *professional* grounds: success in life, as in the theater, he blandly insinuates, ultimately depends on what role—or side—one takes. Maria, affecting a delectable disingenuousness, asks, "Which side is that?" "The winning side," Siletsky promptly assures her. Lubitsch stages their exchange in fairly close shot-countershot sequence. He wants to bring us as close as he dares to the moral abyss that Siletsky invites her to ease into. Maria, who once played a spy—to rave notices!—is asked to "entertain" for the Nazi cause. The material rewards, he promises, will be considerable. She will be given the proper surroundings; life will made very comfortable again. "Naturally, it all sounds very attractive and tempting," she coyly admits, "but what are we to do with my conscience?" Maria states the question as if it represented an authentic perplexity, yet it is the mark of Maria's abilities as an actress and her decency as a human being that the line hovers over the rest of the scene.

In the diabolic inversions that give their subsequent banter its menacing rhythms, Siletsky, in answer to her question, offers his suave reassurances that all the Nazis want in the final analysis is a "happy world for happy people." Nazism is ingeniously promoted as what we might call "totalitarian comedy," a comedy for those who aspire to create a happy world if happiness is understood etymologically as that which is rooted in "hap," that which is found to be *suitable* or *convenient*. Certainly that is the way Maria, in her comic prescience, understands it. She immediately responds to the eugenic menace implied in the Nazi myth of total happiness: "And those who don't want to be happy have no place in a happy world?"

Lubitsch complicates his vision of the totalitarian eugenics that would create a happy world at the expense of all the "unhappy" people targeted for extinction by maintaining that what renders the Nazis horrifying is that they are not deviants outside the human pale, but very much within it. Lubitsch's insistence that his Nazis must be understood in human terms finds ironic, diabolic confirmation in Siletsky's characterization of the Nazi "race": "We're not brutal. We're not monsters. We love to sing, we love to dance. We admire beautiful women. We're human." Song, dance, and love, the ebullient foundations of comic existence, are summoned as evidence that Nazis have the same "dimensions, senses, affections, passions" as the rest of mankind. Siletsky's appropriation of Shylock's Rialto speech—"Hath not a Jew eyes? Hath not a Jew hands, organs, dimensions . . . "—is both ingenious and sinister.

Maria's disingenuous responses to Siletsky's dark seductions are so lightly given that they seem to evaporate even as they are ventured, but her own talent for recognizing the power of "tremendous contrasts" reemerges at the conclusion of the scene. Noting her present destitute appearance, she asks leave to return home to change, so that she may "present the Polish case in more suitable attire." She initially bids a calm and dramatically unremarkable *au revoir* when she is stopped at the door. Siletsky, with undisguised self-importance, informs her that it is harder to get out of Gestapo headquarters than to enter: "I'm terribly frightened and terribly thrilled. Bye!" Lombard utters the word "thrilled" with a breathlessness only an actress in control of her breath could bring off. The moment is at once much lighter and darker if we remember that both the word and the awe it originally if comically reflected were inspired not by a suave traitor but by a disingenuous patriot who nevertheless could drop three tons of dynamite in two minutes.

For better and, in *To Be or Not To Be,* for worse, life in Lombard's company is thrilling. The histrionic Lily Garland, who knows how to play to her public in *Twentieth Century,* and the dramatic actress who was unaffectedly appealing in *Made for Each Other* (1939) and *Vigil in the Night* (1940) peacefully cohabit the psyche of Lombard's last great incarnation—the diva Maria Tura, transcendent in her narcissism and her decency alike.

Ginger Rogers

Harlow and Lombard may each call on their inner children, Harlow to beguile, Lombard to amuse herself as much as others. But only Ginger Rogers actually impersonates a child in Billy Wilder's pseudo-pedophilic comedy, *The Major and the Minor* (1941), and, well into her prime, regresses to a childhood state in *Monkey Business* (1952). Irene Dunne will be suspected of being an unwed mother in *Theodora Goes Wild,* but it is Rogers who will actually live out the fantasy, bestowing comic legitimacy to a new social type for the self-dependent American woman—the Bachelor Mother. Perhaps it is her physical grace that allows her to dance expertly across the border of sanctioned behavior into rarely visited social and psychological territory. One thing is certain: Rogers can survive on her own wherever she happens to land.

Rogers's promptness in responding to the challenges of her sex marked one of her first film appearances, in *42nd Street* (1933). Her sexual alacrity was publicized in her character's nickname, Anytime

Annie; she was reputed to have "only said no once and then she didn't hear the question." Later she would make headlines as Roxie Hart, the gum-chewing showgirl on trial for murder in the tabloid wonderland of Chicago in the late twenties. *Roxie Hart* (1942), directed by William A. Wellman, who also directed the raucously entertaining *Nothing Sacred,* satirically celebrates that human anomaly—a comic murderess. Only Judy Holliday, in her hilarious turn as the woman who attempts to murder her husband in *Adam's Rib* (1949), would be as successful as Rogers in bringing off such a risky characterization. Roxie is comically feted for advancing the cause of all those "beautiful women who shot their men full of holes out of pique," while Holliday, who would come to embody what little sexual whimsy the fifties produced, plays a housewife so emotionally anesthetized by a postwar ideology of dutiful wifedom that her murder attempt is played out—and legally justified—as robotic farce. Rogers's Roxie is an unreconstructed, high-spirited vulgarian who seems right at home in the carnivalesque world of tabloids, courtroom theatrics, and jailhouse rock (in one jubilant scene, everyone joins Roxie in a rendition of the "Black Bottom," including the deliciously unflappable jailhouse matron, the peerless Sara Allgood).

Headline-grabbing Roxie, who avidly follows her lawyer's instruction to show as much leg as possible when she takes the stand, was a lark for Rogers, though. Indeed, to "fill out" her character, Rogers revealed in her autobiography, she "decided this girl had to have dark hair." [12] This shading of her character, which Rogers insisted was not left to the studio but decided by her according to her understanding of the role, was effective in part because her "initial blonding" had become such a part of her screen image. As her life as a feisty but morally durable blonde took on definition and dignity, Rogers became, in Murray Kempton's crisp phrase, "staunchly if never sternly pure." Perhaps, Kempton speculated, "the Legion of Decency compelled her in that direction less forcibly than her own nature." [13] If Kempton is right, this is because Rogers's purity is less sexual than existential. It's her independence, hard-won, more than her chastity, easily defended after all, that she fights ardently to preserve.

Her integrity, her sense of who she is, takes precedence over conventional notions of female sexual honor. Elizabeth Kendall, for instance, applauds Rogers's Jean Maitland in *Stage Door* (1937) not only for "breaking one of Hollywood's sternest unwritten rules in any genre —that a female must pay for a premarital experiment," but for "challenging the ideology of romantic comedy." *"Stage Door,"* she writes, "lets Jean quietly make her foray into kept womanhood and then come back unscathed, to concentrate on her career. And with that trajectory, the movie takes a romantic-comedy heroine farther in the direction of work and self-realization than any heroine had yet been taken." [14] The foray into kept womanhood is quieter than Kendall's account indicates. When the caddish producer Anthony Powell (Adolphe Menjou) offers to become her Pygmalion, Jean, unsure of the mythological reference, interprets the proposition as a marriage proposal. She is high on champagne when Menjou starts his seductive story of the woman brought to life by a man's ardent love, but, entranced as she is, she has no serious or even drunken intention of becoming a kept woman. Kendall is right, however, in seeing Rogers as a Depression heroine who, whatever the libidinal distractions and social diversions offered her, manages to keep herself pointed in the direction of work and self-realization.

Rogers's determination to meet the world head on lends a special piquancy to her relations with men with money and the acquired culture of their class. It is telling about our cultural memory and the selective perception that informs our sexual ideology that the screwball heiress has been indulged, patronized, and celebrated, but not her male counterpart: the screwball heir. Mr. Deeds's sudden elevation to that status betokens a dream fantasy lurking in the minds of Depression audiences, but there are bona fide rich and fine fellows in many of the major comedies of this period—Henry Fonda's Charles Pike in *The Lady Eve,* Tim Holt's Timothy Borden, Jr., in *5th Ave. Girl,* David Niven's David Merlin in *Bachelor Mother* (1939). The last two feature Ginger Rogers, who also scored in *Kitty Foyle* (1940), the story of a lower-class Irish working girl who falls in love with the scion of a Main Line family (Dennis Morgan). Rogers also gave rich expression to Ellie May Adams, the poor girl determined to rise above her degraded family estate in *Primrose Path* (1940).

This last film, though a melodrama, begins with an epigraph from Menander: "People don't live as they want—but as they can." In the course of the film, Ellie will hear her father, an alcoholic whose love of classics has survived his dissolution, quote the line, which she then translates into modern idiom for her prostitute mother: "People don't live like they wanta, but like they gotta." The observation is comic in the most liberal and humane sense, measuring the distance between one's ideals and one's life, a distance Rogers in her womanly prime could cover with more dexterity and grace than any actress of the day.

She was known, of course, for effortlessly covering great distances with Fred Astaire, a facility commemorated in her first song-and-dance routine in *Swing Time* (1936), "Pick Yourself Up." The lyrics, a paean to American can-do-ism, take on a special authority when Rogers's Penny Carroll, cornered into "teaching" John "Lucky" Garnett (Astaire) how to dance, reassures him that

> Nothing is impossible I have found
> For when my chin is on the ground
> I pick myself up, dust myself off, start all over again.

Rogers's faith in the comic but hard work of rebeginning and self-fashioning will stand her in good stead when, in her movies apart from Astaire, her happiness depends as much on her moral stamina as on her physical and mental agility. This was the Rogers whom Murray Kempton, on the occasion of her death, took pains to remember, the Rogers of his youth "who was of the earth pure and who contended with the world all by herself." [15] In her movies with Astaire she was hardly ever on her own, primarily because the conventions of the dance-romance film favored teamwork over solo acts. Astaire enjoyed the companionable presences of Edward Everett Horton or Victor Moore as his comic foils, but Ginger was equally blessed with funny female sidekicks, like Alice Brady's Aunt Hortense in 1934's *Gay Divorcee* and Helen Broderick in *Top Hat* (1935; as Madge Hardwick) and *Swing Time* (as Mabel Anderson). When Rogers was launched into comic vehicles without Astaire she seemed to steer clear of romantic partnerships that obliged her to follow someone else's lead or take another woman's advice. In

Stage Door her Jean Maitland initially rebuffs the impresario Anthony Powell (Adolphe Menjou), even though she knows it may cost her a job she badly needs. "I didn't like the way he looked at me," she explains to the less fussy—and younger—Annie (Ann Miller). "He wasn't looking for an act. He was putting one on."

Jean, whose been around but never gives the impression of being used up, is genially skeptical of the very idea of sexual cooperation, especially across class boundaries. Of all the comic heroines of the era, Rogers had the most intimate feeling for struggling working women. This sympathy never degenerated into sentimentality about class or feminist ties. Rogers is a working girl who fully appreciates, even expects, that at any moment she might find herself completely on her own. As a proletarian heroine she not only is prepared to contend with the world—solo if need be—but is ready to take on her own sex in defense of working-class values. "Why don't you stick to your ideals," the patrician Terry Randall (Katharine Hepburn) advises her in *Stage Door*. "They're rather crude, but they're all right."

Among her values, contempt of pretense ranks high. Her class feeling can, in fact, erupt into sexual combat with upper-class bluebloods or with those women on the prowl, like Linda Shaw (Gail Patrick) in *Stage Door,* who pretend to a breeding they don't actually possess. Her animus toward Linda is the one dissonant note in *Stage Door* that is never resolved by the film's grander, if percussive, female harmonies. Even the suicide of Kaye Hamilton (Andrea Leeds), the febrile actress who sees the role she cherished go to Hepburn's coolly cerebral Terry, proves redemptive. Her death gives Terry's acting the conviction that had eluded her. Jean's sharp barbs and Linda's icy gibes go beyond sexual or even professional rivalry. These two dames are locked in an irresolvable dispute about how best to face a world that seems intent on ignoring or discarding you, as Kaye, reputedly the most talented of the actresses at the Footlights Club, is overlooked, despite an early critical success. Kaye's inability to accept defeat as something temporary leads her to take her own life, but there are warning signs of her feeble will to survive. She doesn't take meals with the other women and is the only one not given to wisecracks, the verbal defense mechanism all the girls adopt to protect themselves from further injury to their already battered professional egos.

In the battle to survive, Rogers's Jean knows how to mix it up with her kind. She has a worthy antagonist in the underrated Gail Patrick, who excelled in feckless or selfish or simply second-best brunettes. She was the petted and petty Cornelia in *My Man Godfrey,* a role in which she perfectly combined haughtiness and malice. But she could be comically game, as in her hilarious turn in *My Favorite Wife* (1940) as the puzzled, then hurt, then semi-hysterical (and sexually disappointed) bride Bianca Bates, on whom Nick Arden (Cary Grant) can't seem to concentrate once his wife Eve (Irene Dunne), whom he thought dead, returns after being marooned on a desert island. Patrick never plays for sympathy, an admirable discipline for an actress who takes the kind of sexual neglect she suffers in *My Favorite Wife* or the comic abuse she endures in *Stage Door.* (In the last scene she pauses over a staircase just long enough for Rogers to get off one last derisive, high-spirited barb: "Hold on," she advises the guy on the other end of the phone, "gangrene just set in.")

Linda's verbal battle with Jean retains the edge that is eventually blunted in the biting exchanges between Jean and Terry. When Terry first arrives at the Footlights Club, equipped with the hauteur of her class, as well as its material and moral luxuries, she simply refuses to engage with Jean, her roommate and the obvious leader of the Footlights' proletarian brigade, on her own impertinently colloquial level. She repels Jean's wisecracks with a loftiness that tells us she doesn't inhabit the same universe, even if she is sharing the same quarters. "I see that in addition to your other charms, you have that insolence generated by an inferior upbringing," Terry replies to one of Jean's tactless sarcasms, making explicit the class difference between them with a condescension that would make Jane Austen's Lady Catherine De-Burgh purr with approval. Rogers retorts with the upstart's refusal to be impressed by the superiority paraded before her: "Fancy clothes, fancy language, and everything." Not to be put off her high horse, Terry persists: "Unfortunately, I learned to speak English correctly." Jean, however, won't surrender an inch: "That won't be of much use

Working-class Ginger Rogers confronting high-class Katharine Hepburn in
Stage Door

to you here—we all speak pig Latin." Pig Latin is girlish code for the
common tongue, sassy and sarcastic, which unites the members of the
Footlights Club into a spunky sisterhood of hope and struggle.

Terry does not initially nor obviously qualify for this thespian
sorority, not just because of her fancy language but because of her
great good luck. By using that word "unfortunately" Terry ironically
calls attention to her superior fortune. Jean is reacting not only to

Terry's wealth but to the *luck* that accounts for her "fancy" diction and "fancy" dress, which is being unpacked and displayed throughout this sharp exchange (later they will "share" that luxury item coveted by all lower-class girls—an ermine wrap). Jean apparently heeds Terry's words, caustic but useful, for later she will lament, "I wish I'd been born lucky instead of beautiful and hungry." The line, "pure" Rogers in both its unvarnished directness and rueful humor, epitomizes how desirable "advantages" of fortune can seem to the unlucky person who must do without them.

Jean and Linda, on the other hand, belong to the same luckless class, battling against the same "disadvantages"—beauty and hunger. They both seek to get "lucky" with Powell (Menjou), who has the power to make a career—or feed a girl hungry for more than food. Their sexual rivalry has professional as well as moral dimensions that transform the battle of these two seasoned combatants into a kind of ritual combat for the soul of the working girl. Linda is the flavor of the month for Powell, a passing distinction, but one that inspires her to put on airs. She torments the famished girls of the Footlights Club— who are constantly joking about the frequency and questionable contents of the boardinghouse staple, lamb stew—by announcing that she will be dining on pheasant bordelaise. Jean settles their stomachs and evens the score. "Whoa, girls, listen, 'bordelaise' she says!" "Be sure not to eat the bones and give yourself away" is her parting advice to Linda as she exits for her night on the town.

Jean, of course, likes fancy food and finery as much as the next girl, and will even borrow Terry's ermine, but she never dissimulates who she is or where she comes from. She may dream of being Galatea, a woman "brought to life" by a man's transforming touch, but she will not alter her inner nature, not adopt obnoxious airs. Jean will disguise her fears but never allow them to disfigure her.[16] Terry comes to know and appreciate this in her character, and when she suspects Jean might succumb to the blandishments of the other sex is quick to put in her two cents' worth: "Don't be sentimental. Remember, you're a ham at heart." Terry has earned her "equity" card—she has learned not only the values but also the language of the thespian tribe and now can play with the best of them. And Rogers, of course, is the best.

Rogers's combativeness is played down in subsequent films, but there are still victories to be savored. *Vivacious Lady* (1938) gives Rogers a chance to act out the full repertoire of the stinging repartee that is the working girl's most effective weapon in her skirmishes with derisive damsels of the leisure class. Rogers plays a nightclub singer, Frances Brent, who one night meets and marries Peter Morgan (James Stewart), a professor at a small-town college. They return to his home town, their marriage unannounced. They decide to postpone telling his family and his official fiancée, Helen (Frances Mercer), until the proverbial "proper time." When Frances gets her first look at the woman she has displaced she manages to keep her cool: "After all, I can't have my husband engaged to just anybody." Peter's scapegrace brother Keith (the affable James Ellison) "reassures" her that she need have no worry on that account. Helen is pure "quality": "Blue blood, black tongue. A thoroughbred."

This, it turns out, proves an accurate as well as witty characterization. At a school dance Frances decides to go *mano a mano* with Helen after watching her dance disturbingly close to Peter. ("If she gets any closer to him, she'll be behind him," she snorts in disapproval to Keith, her "escort" for the evening.) Their showdown occurs at the worst possible time. Peter has gone to fetch his father and mother, break the news of his marriage, and introduce them to his vivacious bride. Frances, nervously awaiting the interview, sits demurely on the veranda until Helen wanders out from the party and decides to set her straight. "You see," she declares, eying Frances as if she were some kind of deadly microbe, "Peter needs protection against a certain type of woman." When Frances refuses to withdraw from the field of battle, Helen escalates the verbal hostilities. "Now, are you going to mind your own business or must I really give you a piece of my mind?" she huffs. "Oh, I couldn't take the last piece," Frances replies, with a mock courtesy that so infuriates Helen that she rises from her seat to give Frances the back of her hand. A slapping match ensues in which Frances attempts to calm the hysterically irate Helen with a series of expertly time "shhs" that both quiet and disarm her, leaving her comically vulnerable to Frances's counterstrikes. Soon the two are engaged in full-scale gladiatorial combat, kicking and gouging and pulling at each other's hair.

The bout, orchestrated with a comic ferocity that elevates the cat fight into a martial art, is halted by the arrival of Peter, his appalled parents in tow. In her autobiography, Rogers explains how she was shielded from hurt as the scene escalated from verbal to physical combativeness: "Since I was on the receiving end of the kicks, the prop department wrapped my legs with boards. When Frances Mercer slammed her high heels against my shins, I was protected by the padding, though you wouldn't know it by my pained facial reactions." [17]

Rogers's professional pride in producing an effect — in this instance the believable mimicry of pain — belongs to her on-screen character as well. Knowing how good she is is what makes her vivacious lady vivacious. Frances's pride in her talent as a performer becomes the comic glue that attaches her to Peter, who has been "bragging" about his dream of one day becoming a college president (like his father). Bragging is his word for what he fears is his immodest way of making an impression, but Frances matter-of-factly endorses this endearing form of self-pride. "No, I like people who think they're good," she reassures him. She seems to mean it, too, for she immediately seeks to make an impression herself, even though Peter gallantly insists that "you don't have to say anything. You speak for yourself, and very eloquently, too." Charmed as she may be, she still regrets that he hasn't seen her best number. When he asks if she is good in it, she doesn't hesitate a second: "Sure I'm good." Such moments remind us of how *appealing* Rogers made the woman who takes pride in her work and in herself. Her vivacious lady — the epithet signals her life-enhancing attitudes — radiates with the non-narcissistic pleasure to be had in being good at whatever it is one does.

Only a woman so sure of her talents and of herself could afford to play as "innocently" as Rogers did with the social and sexual conventions meant to keep female vivacity within bounds. [18] The year 1939, which some regard as the *annus mirabilis* of Hollywood cinema, marked the stellar appearance of Rogers's most socially adventurous heroines: Polly Parrish, the shopgirl who finds herself forced to take on the role and responsibility of a "bachelor mother"; and Mary Grey, the (barely) working girl employed as a "5th Ave. girl" of questionable duties — and morals. Both roles catapult her from a social and an economic state verging on destitution to a life free of economic but not moral worry. Both are fairy tales, of course, of that distinctly American variety, identified by screenwriter Preston Sturges as the fantasy of *Easy Living* (1937). But Sturges's moneyless heroines—Mary Smith (Jean Arthur) in *Easy Living,* Gerry Jeffers (Claudette Colbert) in *The Palm Beach Story* (1942), the Girl (Veronica Lake) in *Sullivan's Travels* (1941)—leave the world they infiltrate intact. The upper classes seem roomier than they did before—that's all. The real change that interests Sturges is internal, and besides, he is too much of a showman to want to dismantle the class system that inspires his wickedest and truest comedy of manners. Rogers, perhaps unique among her generation in this regard, has the power to transform the world she intrudes or stumbles upon. It isn't just that she recharts social boundaries, showing them to be more permeable than they initially appear. Any number of comedies of the era, some fine, some dreadful, accomplished that bit of social remapping. Rogers explored situations, often quite delicate ones, that tested and finally redefined the very nature of the human bonds that link parents to children, husbands to wives, the working to the leisure or moneyed class.

Of these feats of social engineering, the most daring and modern was her short but consequential stint as a bachelor mother. Unlike our contemporary term "single mother," with its suggestion of a woman bravely or defiantly going it alone, or the outdated colloquialism "bachelor girl," with its insinuation that being unmarried is merely a way station for girls on their way to the womanly state of marriage, "bachelor mother" conjures the image of an unmarried woman whose independence is complemented rather than compromised by her having to care for a child. But it is also an image that arouses all kinds of anxieties about the moral and social status of the unwed mother. *Bachelor Mother* has fun both activating the anxiety and spoofing it. It does so by comically treating the social problem of illegitimacy as a case of mistaken identity. For, of course, even if she weren't so "pure," Rogers could not have a baby out of wedlock and still remain a comic heroine. She would have had to migrate into the precincts of melodrama to join Charlotte Lovell (Bette Davis), glumly looking on while another woman (Miriam Hopkins) raises her child in *The Old*

Maid (1939), or Miss Josephine Norris (Olivia de Havilland), gallantly surrendering her boy in *To Each His Own* (1946). The advantage of being an unwed mother in a comedy is that you are assured of shunting the social stigma of illegitimacy by the last reel, marrying the man you love, and raising your baby yourself.

Still, getting to that last reel is never easy, especially when you have neither the intention nor the funds to raise a child by yourself. Rogers's bachelor mother, unlike Diane Keaton's similarly surprised bachelor mother in the 1987 remake *Baby Boom,* is not a high-paid executive whose primary comic predicament is not being able to find good help. She is a working girl who soon won't even be working. Polly Parish is discharged from Merlin's Department Store on Christmas Eve. On her lunch hour she goes out looking for a job but finds a baby instead. She sees it being left on the steps of an orphanage by a muffled figure whom she first mistakes for the distraught mother but then discovers to be an old woman. This figure strikes an uncanny appearance, as if she were some kindly "good" witch materialized out of folklore onto the disbelieving streets of Manhattan. That it is Christmas time, ritually the season of miraculous birth, contributes to the impression that this baby is no ordinary foundling, that he (for it is a boy) may be possessed of, or protected by, special powers.

Also ministering to this impression of mysterious parentage is the aura of magic attaching to the family name Merlin, the name of Polly's employer and his son, her future suitor. Both father and son will, in fact, live up to their name, experiencing the enchantment of paternity, its mystery and its charms. The younger Merlin, David (David Niven), who "gives" the child to Polly as her "Christmas present," finds himself strangely drawn to the child, calling on Polly to make sure he is fed correctly and provided with the latest toy. So attentive does he become that he is soon suspected (wrongly, of course) of being the father. Meanwhile, the elder Merlin (Charles Coburn) is only too eager to bestow his name on the infant, who "looks just like me." When he decides to claim the child legally, Polly, now grown desperately fond of the baby, pretends that her landlady's son is the father. In the meantime, David Merlin has hired a store clerk to pretend that he is the father, a man secretly convinced that David actually is the real father and is only covering his tracks. In the reproductive melee that ensues, the baby who enters the film without a mother is in danger of having too many fathers. None of these competing and equally bogus claims bothers the elder Merlin, determined on patriarchy. He is so pleased with his "grandson" that he doesn't really care who sired the magical child. "I don't care who's the father," he decisively announces. "I'm the grandfather!"

It's a funny line to say, and a revolutionary one to take. It is one thing to maintain that paternity is a legal fiction, quite another to insist that grandfatherhood is an emotional and unassailable fact. But so, finally, are all the human bonds that the movie succeeds in forging. Polly keeps protesting that she's not the mother, at one point becoming so frustrated that she blurts out to the maddeningly "understanding" functionaries that "there isn't any mother." Indeed there isn't, in the traditional sense. That's the idea the movie dares to toy with—that true motherhood, like genuine fatherhood, is less a biological fact than a moral and an emotional reality. Polly's last name, Parrish, encapsulates this truth. Her very being seems to be a haven for this abandoned baby, who settles happily into her cradling arms. Thus it is to no avail that she protests to David Merlin, "I am *not* the mother of that child." He refuses to consider the possibility that the foundling home had made a mistake. "They know a mother when they see one," he argues, as if this were incontrovertible proof of her biological parentage.

How one knows a mother is the deeper comic question that *Bachelor Mother* dares to put to its audience. It is a question that *Baby Boom* doesn't even think of pursuing, but it is one that Rogers's tact in forging unconventional relationships makes it possible not only to ask but to answer. In *The Major and the Minor* her gift for intimacy will inspire her rival's sister, the hilariously precocious Lucy Hill (Diana Lynn), to declare that "you are more my sister than Pamela." The baby in *Bachelor Mother* seems to feel something like the same thing about Polly. He cries whenever he is taken from her enfolding arms, sufficient proof, the officials at the orphanage agree, that she *is* his mother. And perhaps she is. That maternity—like paternity, like grandfatherhood—transcends biology is an unsettling and socially innovative idea. It is a comic idea of the first order, and one that director Garson Kanin cunningly works out in the otherwise ordinary romance between a shopgirl and her employer's son. Rogers certainly is not put off by the class difference between them. It is the question of her "purity," her status as an unwed mother, that gives her, not to mention him, pause.

The sexual issue keeps intruding into their courtship. Kanin's humane solution is to make the very thing that should keep them apart bring them together—the baby. At first David Merlin displays mildly proprietary feelings toward the child he feels he has restored to his natural mother. But soon his philanthropic interest matures into comically overblown—and endearing—paternal pride in the baby's "unusual" gifts. When Polly gets into a bragging contest with another couple, he not only corroborates her preposterous claims but outdoes them. She has the baby talking at six months. He has him reciting "Gunga Din"! We know that he is destined to be the father—comic convention wills it so—but that knowledge doesn't spoil the wonder of the moment when he "admits" to his own father that "I am the father of that baby." "Those are the first true words you've spoken," the happy grandfather replies. And he is right. The words *are* true, but it took a Christmas miracle to make them so.

To this truth we must attach one more emotional marvel—that Merlin and Son accept Polly and her child into their family not only not caring who the father is, but still believing that she is the mother. The film leaves Polly's future husband and father-in-law in the same ignorance in which it found them. "And you still think I'm the mother of that baby?" Polly asks in comic disbelief when David confesses that he can't live without her, that he loves her and the baby. He merely nods, and she, wisely, refuses to enlighten him. A lovely "ha, ha"—to herself? to us?—is her final comment on the divine comedy of human attachments. That chuckle takes the reality of having and caring for babies out of the realm of conventional morality and deposits it where it probably belonged in the first place: in the realm of everyday miracles.

Rogers works a similar though less magical transformation in Gregory La Cava's underrated satire *5th Ave. Girl*. Rogers's Mary Grey doesn't create a new family so much as restore an old one to its former life and affection. It is a family headed by plumbing magnate Timothy Broder (Walter Connolly). As the movie begins he finds himself harassed by business worries, neglected by his wife, and simultaneously exploited and ignored by his children. Left alone on his birthday, he winds up watching the seals in the park, where he meets Mary, similarly occupied. He enjoins her to keep him company, promising that "we can have lots of fun insulting the rich." Eventually he hires her as his "5th Ave. girl" in a cagey if desperate attempt to get his family's attention.

Rogers comes as close as any modern heroine to reviving and modernizing the part of the tricky slave of Roman comedy in reknitting the frayed threads of the family fabric. First, Mary obligingly goes along with Broder's masquerade that he has suddenly regained his youth, a metamorphosis he celebrates by going dancing every night. (In reality, the chauffeur drives them around until it is time to come home at a disreputable hour.) The ruse is enough to capture his wife's wandering attention, sufficient indeed to make her cook his favorite meal, beef stew, as a counterenticement to Mary's charms. Once the upstairs romance seems well on its way toward recovering marital happiness, Mary goes downstairs, to the kitchen, to be exact, where she stages her own palace revolution. Katherine, the daughter of the house, is madly in love with the revolutionary-minded chauffeur, Michael (James Ellison), a firebrand who is forever condemning his employers' sumptuary excesses. The dazzled daughter of "capitalist scum" ardently embraces his ideology along with his person, professing that she "can't wait until the day . . . " "The day?" her father interrupts her. "You know," she sweetly explains, "when we'll all be comrades. Michael calls it Dialectical Materialism." But things can't wait until that millennial age, so Mary takes matters into her own hands. She pretends to stalk Katherine with a knife when she tries to intervene in her verbal battle with Michael. Michael and Katherine embrace for protection—and solidarity! Leaving the premises well satisfied with her work, she coolly informs the startled but visibly impressed butler to quell the emotional uproar downstairs. "Oh, Higgins. You had better go down to the kitchen. There's a revolution or something going on down there."

As a new marriage is made and old one renewed, Mary finds herself without the motive, or the heart, to stay on. Pretense is not her style, and as physically luxurious as the life of the rich may be, she's had enough. She's tired of pretending, and tired of defending herself against Michael's most stinging charge: "You're a capitalist pawn. . . . You're a renegade to your class." She is set to leave but is finally stopped by the morally rehabilitated son, Timothy (Tim Holt), who now claims her as his own. Such is the comically foreordained ending for the *5th Ave. Girl*—taking up permanent residence in the household she has emotionally enriched. Her installation in the ranks of wealth is not her real achievement, however. That comes elsewhere in the film when Rogers, challenged by Michael's snide question—"Aren't you stepping out of your class?"—gives him a simple but definitive rejoinder: "Me? I haven't any class." To be able to say that about oneself, about life in America, is a day we might all look forward to. As a fast-talking dame intent on making her own place in the world, Rogers brought that day a little closer.

4 My Favorite Brunettes

Myrna Loy, Jean Arthur, and Claudette Colbert

According to Anita Loos's famous formulation of the relation of hair color to sexual destiny, gentleman may prefer blondes, but they marry brunettes. This is not literally true, of course. We are dealing here with a particular kind of comic symbolism that developed in the movies but is by no means confined there. In the color scheme that helps define movie characters, the brunette is the dame who not only enters into marriage, but seems to redefine it.

Marriage for Harlow, as we have seen, is desirable *because* it is an institution associated with respectability and economic security. She wouldn't change it for the world. She wants merely to exploit it according to her needs. For Lombard marriage is a field of play, even license, giving full rein to her highly developed instinct for pretending. Rogers, who incorporated as much of the brunette as the blonde into her screen personality, was existentially receptive to all kinds of experiments with the marriage state. Pioneering as a bachelor mother is her most radical comic challenge to America's social imagination, but she comes close to subverting the cornerstone of marriage—monogamy—in the arch but weirdly impertinent *Tom, Dick and Harry* (1941), which, oddly enough, is one of her most dated films. Rogers plays the hopelessly indecisive Janie, who, having engaged herself to three men within as many days, entertains, if only in dream form, the idea of marrying all three of them, a polygamous fantasy that comes to an end only when her dream husbands begin to disrobe in preparation for the wedding night. Understandably alarmed, she calls the fantasy off.

Hedy Lamarr and Ava Gardner would revive the fatal glamor of the dark and tempestuous screen siren in the forties and early fifties, but these dark charmers, however luscious, were no match for the fast-talking dame, as Lamarr's Karen Vanmeer found out, somewhat to her surprise, when Betsy (Claudette Colbert) wins Big John (Clark Gable) back from her in *Boom Town* (1940). Lamarr is foreign born, but even Gardner, luxuriant bloom of the tobacco fields of North Carolina, knows to stick to film noir, where her smoldering sexuality may excite comment but only limited conversation. The early talkies catered to the sexual taste that Nick Charles (William Powell) admits is behind his craving for his wife, Nora (Myrna Loy). When Loy, in her first appearance as Mrs. Charles, in *The Thin Man* (1934), asks him what is his type, he gallantly but not falsely assures her, "Only you, darling—lanky brunettes with wicked jaws." The wicked jaw of course refers not just to Loy's finely chiseled chin but to her wicked way with repartee.

Myrna Loy

Perhaps no other actress of her refinement has been so encumbered by the stock star epithets meant to promote her than has Myrna Loy. She was touted as the perfect movie wife and eventually crowned queen of the silver screen in 1936, the only actress deemed the charismatic equal to Gable's virile king. Her coronation was a publicity gimmick that nevertheless captured something essential to Loy's screen character: she was the most unaffectedly regal of the women stars of her vintage. Norma Shearer, queen-regent of MGM, worked very hard to live up to her billing, but she lacked Loy's easy charm, as her painfully noble performance in *The Women* attests.

Loy could also convey an unmitigated hauteur, evident in her performance as the exacting, selfish wife in *The Animal Kingdom* (1932). The comedies that paired her with Powell would interpret this hauteur, as Powell's Charlie Lodge does in *Double Wedding* (1937), as a "certain aloofness, a sense of repression." Assuming this demeanor, Loy allows herself the lordly habit of command. Her briskly efficient businesswoman, whom Powell will dub "Margit Incorporated," declares at the outset of the film that men and marriage simply take up too much

Myrna Loy eying William Powell's booty in *The Thin Man*

time when she has so many important things to attend to. What time she has she devotes to planning every detail of her sister's life, as her sister Irene (played by Florence Rice), at once exasperated and compliant, complains to Waldo (John Beal), her mousy fiancé: "Margit picks you out for me, Margit makes you fall in love with me; Margit arranges our wedding. I suppose if I don't make a good wife for you,

Margit will divorce me." And we can be sure that Margit Incorporated might well do so, at least before she herself decides to find time for Powell (time always well spent). Impressively, whether playing perfect wife or controlling career girl, Loy managed to retain her popular appeal while transcending the stereotypes associated with her ebullient personality. A laugh was always lurking in her eyes, the happy product of some distillation of high spirits. Such qualities make Loy the most *companionable* of modern women—witty, unaffectedly but unmistakably intelligent, and reliably good-humored. The "lucid self-possession in confronting their male counterparts" that Italo Calvino so admired in the female personalities of American cinema found "its most intelligent and ironic exponent in Myrna Loy." Accordingly, she became his "prototype of the ideal feminine."[1]

The ideality projected by her intelligence emerged only after a somewhat dim apprenticeship in the silents and very early talkies. Loy began her career as a dancer and bit player. (An early "part" aligned her, gam by gam, with Joan Crawford to form one leg of a human chandelier!) She soon found her singular beauty appropriated for studio exotica, typecast as vamps in roles that later she would recall with chagrin. She even put on blackface to approximate Hollywood's idea of a darkly seductive Senegalese spy, but her most spectacular impersonations were Oriental wantons. Loy brought a fiendish glee to her lurid roles as Ursula Georgi, the half-caste with hypnotic powers out to revenge herself against her white sorority sisters in *Thirteen Women,* and as Fah Lo See, the "sadistic nymphomaniac" (as Loy described her) in *The Mask of Fu Manchu* (both 1932). A supporting role in Rouben Mamoulian's *Love Me Tonight* (1932) uncovered the comic enchantress lurking beneath the woman of sinister charm. Her narcoleptic Countess Valentine revives whenever an eligible male wanders into her vicinity. Asked whether she could go for a doctor when Princess Jeanette (Jeanette MacDonald) has one of her fainting spells, this sleeping beauty responds with an enthusiastic, even grateful, "Could I!" Loy had a way of reading her lines, even the monosyllabic ones, that uncovered unexpected reserves of energy and irony. The lilt of her voice was as distinctive as the captivating tilt in her nose, in which so much of her comic authority was concentrated.

Loy's Valentine, enchanting as she was, could have lived at any time since the eighteenth century—providing she was lodged in a chateau. It was her teaming with William Powell and Clark Gable in *Manhattan Melodrama* that naturalized Loy as a sophisticated woman very much of her own time. As such, her Eleanor Packer was equally drawn to two competing paragons of American manhood. The debonair, crusading Jim Wade (Powell) won out over the criminally rough but generous Edward "Blackie" Gallagher (Gable) in the film, laying the basis for a lasting screen partnership that would reinvent modern marriage. In 1934's *The Thin Man* Loy literally hurled the modern wife, Nora Charles, at the feet of a delighted public by executing a three-point landing on a barroom floor. Hers was a noteworthy feat, since Loy's comic resilience has the least to do with the physical agility possessed by so many of the other madcap heroines—the boisterous Lombard most of all, but also the athletic Hepburn. Loy rose, dignity intact, to assume her place in the popular imagination as the perfect wife, an accolade that would have burdened a lesser woman, but that Loy could shrug off without mussing a hair.

Powell's Nick Charles might be the detective in their screen marriage, but it was Nora who could give men the eye, an evolutionary as well as personal prerogative reserved only for the women most expert at sexual selection. In *The Thin Man* she has already found her man, so her gaze is free to roam over the wide social and human territory denied her as the daughter of an established San Francisco family. She gets the chance when she arrives in New York just in time to observe Christmas—and to participate in a murder investigation. She enjoys both when she and Nick holiday in the city where he spent many happy years sending crooks up the river, many of whom, apparently benefiting from their confinement, remember him fondly. They certainly always seem happy to see him, a social fact that becomes a running gag in the six *Thin Man* films. Nora, amused rather than distressed by the jail birds (and jail bait) that flock around him, is always complimenting her husband on his inordinately wide circle of friends. She first strikes this amiable note at the conclusion of a particularly raucous Christmas Eve party. Listening to a soused company of parolees, grifters and barflies wailing "O Christmas Tree," Nora, taking in the sideshow with a deadpan glance, throws her arms around her husband and declares with droll affection: "Oh, Nicky, I love you because you know such lovely people." Nora, as open-hearted in her articulation as she is populist in her sentiments, doesn't drench the "such lovely people" in viscous irony, but lets the words expire at the end of a knowing but strangely gratified sigh.

No screen wife has teased anyone, ever, with the same caressing tone as Nora teases Nick, especially on this matter of the company he keeps. A woman bred to a certain station, Nora Charles is nevertheless one of the most genial democrats to populate the screen. When high-society dames consort with the lower or under classes, they risk appearing out of place or glad to be away from home, depending on whether they are condescending or slumming. Nora is herself no matter where—or in whose society—she may be. In *After the Thin Man* (1936), a film whose plot as well as incidental comedy derives from the class difference between Nora and Nick, they return to their home in San Francisco to celebrate the New Year. On the way from the train station they are greeted by a series of engaging, vociferous proletarian characters—fighters, newsboys, street hustlers—such as could be depended on to animate the back lots at Warner's. "You do know the nicest people," is Nora's cheerful observation.

But then the joke veers off in a different, higher direction when Nick and Nora find themselves hailed by two bluebloods ensconced in their luxury motorcar. More out of duty than interest, Nick wonders who this well-heeled couple might be. "Oh, you wouldn't know them darling. They're respectable." Nora says the word "respectable" in a way that strips away its veneer of snobbery, and Nicky, playing along, mugs back at her, since he knows this is not only his only possible response, but the one she wanted to elicit all along. She likes making him make faces. Who wouldn't? Later, he will remember the word when both are fleeing the mansion of Nora's Aunt Katherine ("the waxworks," as Nicky wryly calls it): "Let's go some place and take the taste of respectability out of our mouths." It's an invitation Nora has never been able to resist even if—especially if—it means spending the evening with Willie the Weeper and the boys at his "coming out party."

It is an invitation to savor a salty company. It is also, notoriously, an invitation to drink. Even though officially retired from detective work since his marriage, Nick still is a creature of former habits and former haunts. This provides not only the background for *The Thin Man* plots but the foundation of the Charleses' marriage. In their first outing Nora has to track down her husband down after Asta, their frisky if notably cowardly dog, drags her, as she reports, "into every gin mill on the block." Drinking is what the Charleses *do* together.

If in retrospect alcohol no longer seems so innocent a symbol of high spirits and connubial bliss, neither is it without beneficent, magical properties. As a comic emblem, the martini, which Nick insists must be blended to a specific rhythm, is the festal brew that consecrates Nick and Nora's marriage. While theirs is not the divine drunkenness of the Dionysian revels, such as transports Garbo's Ninotchka and Hepburn's Tracy Lord in *The Philadelphia Story*, neither is theirs a sodden, spirit-dulling bacchanalia. Even in the throes of a hangover Nora is bright enough to sport her ice bag as if it were the latest Parisian adornment. Drink is the stimulant that fuels Nick and Nora's gaiety, but it is also the dissolvent of any residue of that sexual distrust on which many a marriage—and marital farce—have foundered.

Nick and Nora have evolved—or drunk—to the point where there is little room for misunderstanding or miscommunication. That they strike us as fun to watch is thus remarkable. The spectacle of human courtship is generally more entertaining when it is played out in those spats and battles of will that give the sexual drama its erotic charge and psychological, even ethical, interest. In *Double Wedding*, Powell's comically sage painter alludes to this theatrical and amatory truism when he informs the coolly virginal Margit that "love is a strange thing. It takes two courses. Two people like each other enormously or they pretend to dislike each other enormously." In *Double Wedding*, Loy and Powell play the pretending sort of lovers, but not, it must be said, to the same enchanting effect as their Nick and Nora, who obviously like each other enormously. Still, it is *Double Wedding* that is truer to the comic tradition, a tradition memorably evoked by the pugnacious John Alexander (John Garfield) in *Flowing Gold* (1940). "When two people come out fighting," he remarks to his love interest, Linda Chalmers (Frances Farmer), "they usually end up in a clinch."

The idiom is distinctly American, but the formula is as old as Roman comedy. The movies were tireless in finding new ways to rekindle that formula in cinematic couplings that trailers perpetually promise will "ignite" the screen. In defiance of most laws of screen chemistry, the charge between Nick and Nora doesn't require any friction to spark it. These two charmers rely on whimsy, not willfulness, to form a more perfect union. What perfection there is in that union is due to Nora, whose womanly charms are evident though never daunting. Still, she is flawless enough to prompt Nicky to wonder whether she has made any New Year's resolutions. "Any complaints or suggestions?" she inquires. "A few," Nicky admits. "Well, you don't scold. You don't nag. You're far too pretty in the morning." As if committing the list to memory, Nora pledges to do better: "Let's see. Must nag. Must scold. Mustn't be too pretty in the morning."

Nora may have temporarily lost her balance making her entrance into the Thin Man series, but after that she never loses her footing—or her sense of humor—when it comes to herself and to her husband. She is so sure of her place in Nicky's heart that when he casually introduces her to some of his cronies only *after* he has done the honors for Asta, the family dog, she mildly protests that Nick "might have mentioned me first on the billing." Less secure women would have insisted on top billing. They probably would have used the imperative "must" or accusatory "should have" in making their preferences known. Nora doesn't need to press her point, since her status is never really in doubt.

Even when Nick pretends that the lovely young girl (Maureen O'Sullivan) she has just met is the long-lost daughter of his reckless, hot-blooded youth, she knows him too well to be taken in or riled up. Instead, she asks him how many drinks he has had (six) and demands equal consideration. With a general's precision she orders five more martinis to be lined up, as if in battle formation, before her. She is not waging war, only playing catch-up, and even if we might squirm in our alcoholically more enlightened time, we can appreciate, as Nick visibly does, her determination to be in every way his equal—drink for drink, quip for quip, but mostly wink for wink. She winks most sublimely, it must be said, at herself. When Nick, in one of his more gallant effusions, enthuses: "Did I ever tell you you are the most fascinating woman this side of the Rockies?" Nora, with consummate aplomb, not only confirms his assessment but promises more: "Wait till you see me on the other side."

In her enchanting equanimity, Nora can afford not only to indulge Nick's friends and his drinking, but to ignore social conventions normally governing the actions and attitudes of married women of her station. In *The Thin Man,* when she opens a door — rapid pan screen right — to find — rapid pan screen left — Nick cradling a distraught Dorothy Wynant (O'Sullivan) in his arms, she merely crinkles her nose. Nick, acknowledging the look, nods back, but Dorothy, once released from Nick's fatherly embrace, begins the customary disclaimers. Nora cuts her short. "Oh, don't be silly," thus dismissing, in one tidy, admirably impudent gesture, an entire tradition of marital and stage farce built around the act of opening a door upon an apparently compromising situation. Instead of throwing the hussy out, she invites the distressed damsel to stay the night. In *After the Thin Man,* Nora's womanly sympathy extends to a sexual generosity with Nicky. When her cousin Selma Landis (Elissa Landi) asks permission to reward Nicky with a kiss, Nora consents, even while issuing a warning: "Go right ahead, but I warn you, it's a hard habit to get out of." Sexual affection has seldom received so droll a tribute. Nora's compliments are as addictive as Nicky's kisses.

When a situation is not innocent, when it is indeed potentially murderous, Nora is just as quick to assert herself. Eager to find out what happened to Dorothy's missing father, Nora decides to have an impromptu bedside chat. "Nicky, you asleep?" she asks after the Christmas revelers have left and they are finally in their (twin) beds. "Yes," Nick mumbles. "Good," Nora, mistress of the non sequitur, replies. "I want to talk to you." What she wants to talk about is Nicky's taking the case, but before she can make her pitch, a gun-toting hood appears at their door. Nick, to protect Nora, lands a right on her wicked jaw, a chivalric if violent gesture that Nora protests once the police have arrived: "You darn fool, you didn't have to knock me out. I knew you'd take him, but I wanted to see you do it." "There's a girl with hair on her chest," the sergeant chuckles appreciatively. But he and Nick are taken aback by her next contribution to their investigation. On finding an unregistered gun in Nora's drawer, the sergeant accuses Nick of violating the Solomon Act. Nora brightly assures him, "Oh, that's all right. We're married." The Production Code might have settled Nick and Nora in twin beds, but it can't keep Nora from publicly confessing to her own (legitimate) sexual traffic over state lines.

Confusing the Solomon Act with the Mann Act doesn't make her sound stupid, for hers is the mistake of a novice, not an inveterate mangler of language. In fact, she relishes the colorful vocabulary as much as she savors the excitement of detective work. She brightens every time she gets to say a word that never would have surfaced in conversations at home. In *After the Thin Man,* when Nora's linguistically uptight Aunt Katherine Forrest (Jessie Ralph) struggles to find the word to describe her nephew-in-law, Nora can't wait to help out. She literally intrudes upon the comic spectacle of Aunt Katherine searching for a respectable way to describe what Nick does. "With your experience as a . . . " "Flatfoot," says Nora, butting into Aunt Katherine's close-up. "I didn't mean to be as blunt as all that," the ruffled dowager protests. Being blunt, of course, is one of the great democratic offices filled by pretension-puncturing slang. Perhaps only a dame so well schooled as Nora could really appreciate the leveling power of colorful lingo.

In the Thin Man series, Loy and Powell established a vogue for mystery-comedies starring husband-and-wife sleuths that were surprisingly egalitarian in their sexual politics, the next-best of which were Robert Montgomery and Rosalind Russell as bibliophile gumshoes in *Fast and Loose* (1939; the movie itself was part of a series). Such partnerships use humor not only to keep the marriage together but to foil the crooks and murderers foolish enough to take them on. When a thuggish nightclub owner menacingly asks Nick, "Ever been thrown out of any place, Mr. Charles?" Nora nonchalantly rephrases and answers the question all at once: "How many places have you been in, Mr. Charles?" Nick will settle the argument about whether he goes or stays by conking the "bad guy" on the head. Nora, however, transforms this clichéd scene into a rare jest when, isolated in an adoring close-up and gazing straight out at the camera, she allows herself to gloat over what her husband has just wrought: "See?" The next shot, showing the

Myrna Loy producing the key to the liquor cabinet in *Another Thin Man*

men energetically mauling each other, makes it clear that Nora could only have been addressing the audience, vindicating Nicky to them as much as to the rowdy men he has just subdued. Nick and Nora are great kidders, but only Nora takes a moment out of mayhem to mock the movie and the genre she happens to find herself in.

As the series progresses, so does Nora's role. Eventually she advances from ironic if fond commentator on Nicky's detective work to a student of crime who promises to surpass her teacher. Nicky usually is the one who dazzles with his deductions, but there are times when Nora is indisputably the main attraction, even when we don't quite see how she does it. Case in point: In *Another Thin Man* (1939), the Charleses, hoping to enjoy a restful weekend on Long Island, are informed by their host that the liquor cabinet has been locked so that Nicky, who now manages Nora's business affairs, can keep a clear head. Nick is doleful but Nora is cagey, busily fussing over her host. For once (but not the last time), Nicky has no idea what Nora is contriving.

My Favorite Brunettes 143

"What was all that business at the door?" he asks, still grumpy at the thought of the dry evening ahead. "I was just picking his pocket," is her mischievous admission. "I haven't been married to you for nothing," she says, delivering the key. As time goes on and the series matures, Nick concedes more and more to Nora's womanly guile. In *Shadow of the Thin Man* (1941), when Nicky, Jr., is old enough to order his father to drink at the table, he gladly obeys and, reaching for his martini, congratulates Nora on the "great kid" she has produced. "I'm much obliged," he croons. "Oh, it was nothing," she acknowledges. "Anytime." So deft is Loy's intonation that she makes that "anytime" at once an ironic dismissal of the labor involved and an open sexual invitation. Nicky can only respond with one of his appreciative, open-mouthed looks. After all, his son, who is only five, is in the room.

Whatever she might have picked up from Nick on the fine arts of sleuthing—and picking pockets—Nora's conduct and speech in domestic as well as criminal matters is normally determined by the human facts before her. What is true of Nora is generally true of Loy's comic heroines. This is particularly evident in her relations to her leading men, which are keyed to something idiosyncratic, and not necessarily exemplary, in their characters. Loy was teamed with the most desirable and/or complex men of her generation, and in each pairing she discovered the emotional compounds that went into their chemistry. Her rapport with Powell revealed her unerring and untroubled instinct for what her screen mates needed and saw in her. She obviously enjoys improvising everything in her screen relationship with Powell, whose masculinity is so relaxed in her presence that he can afford to caricature it. Nick's most dazzling display with a gun, for example, is shooting Christmas ornaments with a popgun while he lies sprawled on the couch. In *Love Crazy* (1941), Powell's Steven Ireland goes to legally if not clinically insane lengths to win back his wife Susan (Loy), including masquerading as his own sister (he keeps misplacing one of his breasts, which, composed of wool balls, soon begins to unravel anyway).

She is not as droll with Gable, who liked his women sassy but not ironic and, of course, would never allow his masculinity to unravel as easily as Powell's. But that doesn't mean that he was any less susceptible to Loy's transforming influence. The canny but caring Loy knew when and how to drop the stoic facade adopted to attract him. Her staunch but giving heart so impresses him that he is ready to compromise his macho code and become gentler than he generally feels he can afford to be, a transformation she works on him in *Test Pilot* and *Too Hot to Handle* (both 1938).

In the first film, Loy's character falls in love with a pilot (Gable's Jim Lane); in the second she is one (Alma Harding). *Too Hot to Handle* gives Loy her only role opposite Gable (playing Chris Hunter) in which her femininity is cause for comic dispute and disputation. When Chris, a newsreel reporter with a camera where his heart should be, first comes across her, he declares her to be a "comic little dame who thinks she's a man flying around the world with grease on her face and her hands in her pockets." Attracted as much by her courage as her game good looks, he volunteers that "maybe I can show her how it feels to be a woman." Making a female feel like a woman is a Gable specialty in the thirties, but Loy, mistress of the sexual turnabout, returns the favor by making Gable's Chris feel like a man—a new kind of man, that is. Chris's virile blunderbuss eventually yields the verbal field to Harding's pert, affectionate irony. At film's end, it is his masculinity that good-naturedly submits to the comic degradation that will, paradoxically, enlarge him into a man. That, at least, is the promise held forth in Harding's last description of him: "He's a comic little guy running around the world with grease on his face and a camera for a heart. But maybe I can show him how it feels to be a man."

Loy's subtle adjustments to the male psyches she is paired with may never be duplicated, since her rapport encompasses so many qualities and values that are difficult to reconcile: a willingness to laugh at human foibles, stemming from her deep appreciation of the comedy of our behavior, an unshakeable confidence in her own nature and in the fact that she is loved. Nothing dislodges that conviction, even in a comedy like *Love Crazy*, which again pairs her with Powell. *Love Crazy* explores the premise, hardly to be countenanced in their screen partnership, that Powell might ever find another woman attractive as long as she is even remotely around.[2] As Nora Charles, she is always catching Nick in semi-compromising positions with other women, yet nothing in her expression nor in her tone suggests that she takes appearances at face value. In *Another Thin Man,* when she comes upon Nick leaning suggestively over a female body (unconscious, as we know but she doesn't), she falls back on her breeding, politely excusing herself with a tactful, "Oh, pardon me." She knows that Nick will recall her and explain, so she can afford to play it cool. Even when she finds herself being grilled by a detective who is dead certain that Nicky's wandering eye is the clue to a murder, Nora remains sublimely nonplussed. "We're trying to show you what you're up against," her interlocutor glowers confidingly. "It ain't in the books that a man that's had that many numbers to settle down with one." "Was he really like that?" Nora openly wonders. "I always thought he was bragging." The cops don't get anything out of her, but Nora does manage to get them to divulge the name of one of the numbers that Nicky had failed to account for—the lighthouse keeper's daughter, Lettie Finhatten. Later in the movie, she will claim that name as her own.

Loy was unusual among the classy dames of her era to survive without migrating into ponderous historical dramas or value-laden movies, like Hepburn; grim melodramas, like Stanwyck; or Grand Guignol horror movies, like Bette Davis and Joan Crawford. Loy persisted in the national psyche as the womanly ideal after the war. In William Wyler's *Best Years of Our Lives* (1946) she suggested how the generosity that in her comic roles manifested itself in good-spirited camaraderie also subsisted in the forbearing wife assisting in her husband's return to civilian life. But Loy was no stranger to the dark side of the happy marriages she continued humanizing in films like *Cheaper by the Dozen* (1950) and *Belles on Their Toes* (1952). Her wrenching portraits as the alcoholic mother in *From the Terrace* (1960) and the sardonic wife in *Lonelyhearts* (1959) offer a bleak counterface to the festive mien she generally presented to the camera. Her later roles played on the knowledge that the qualities she embodied were fast becoming legendary, so that underlying her performances in *April Fools* (1969) and *Just Tell Me What You Want* (1980) is the melancholy suggestion that her wit, womanly tact, and ironic intelligence had indeed transported her to some unreachable yet still visible realm of perfection.

Jean Arthur

Although technically a blonde, Jean Arthur is a brunette at heart. She is the most ambivalent of the fast talkers, a stammer always threatening to dam up the stream of talk. The startle reflex has not been completely bred out of her voice by overexposure to the stimuli of urban living. Despite her successful adaptation to big-city manners and pace, she can still be brought up short, wide-eyed, in stupefaction and dismay. What brings her to a halt is a sudden appeal to the homespun values that are routinely flouted in hard times. She is the working girl whose cynicism is an encrustation surprisingly easy to slough off. Any smart reporter with the snappy style she perfected in *Mr. Deeds Goes to Town* who would really get teary-eyed on hearing herself described as an angel in Longfellow Deeds's lovesick poem is going to have a hard time of it.

And Arthur does, maybe harder than any other working girl heroine, with the exception of Barbara Stanwyck (whose veneer is, however, more shockproof) and Ginger Rogers (whose protective irony is more adept at deflecting sentimental appeals). She did have one whirlwind turn as a madcap socialite whose irrepressible imagination earns her title billing in *The Ex-Mrs. Bradford* (1936). The "ex," however, is expunged in the course of the comedy, which reunites Arthur's mystery writer, who is always imagining mayhem and murder, with William Powell's sleuthing doctor. She arrives unannounced at his apartment with a subpoena in hand to sue him for back alimony payments. She also comes attended by a caravan of luggage that allows her to join her ex in his often seedy investigations dressed as splendidly as any screwball heiress in the land. In the romantic melodrama *History Is Made at Night* (1937) she is fleeing from a rich man and finding happiness with a penurious but attentive headwaiter played by Charles Boyer. Despite the Continental touches in casting and direction, the film is hardly Gallic. Its final insouciance toward class barriers is American all the way.

That in two of her major roles she takes the screen name Mary — "plain as any name can be," as the popular song would have it — is a tip-off to her populist appeal. As Mary Jones, the "angelic" shopgirl heroine in *The Devil and Miss Jones* (1941), she matter-of-factly accepts, even cherishes, her unremarkable character and unexceptional love. When the "devil," business mogul J. P. Merrick (the irresistibly cranky Charles Coburn), reasonably points out that her boyfriend (Robert Cummings), whom he privately regards as an ideological Svengali, is hardly out of the ordinary, she is neither offended nor nonplussed. By her own account, "I'm not the greatest girl in the world, either." She insists, moreover, that love does not depend on what the world sees but on what the lover beholds. "Two people look at each other," she tells him, and "they see something way deep inside that nobody else can and that's it." The feeling, she admits, may not correspond to the blazing love "you hear in those songs you know, about 'the touch of your hand can set me on fire.'" "I guess," she concludes, "I'm not the combustible type." Still, even if the love she has for her boyfriend is "not the advertised seventh heaven," she does know that "if I thought I'd never see him again, I don't think I'd care if I lived or died."

Arthur may not think of herself as the combustible type, but her feelings run deep, and, as she says, her life comes to depend on them. Moviegoers of the time were accustomed to observing a passion this understated but extravagant in the movies of Howard Hawks. Arthur had one go as a Hawksian heroine in *Only Angels Have Wings* (1939), yet she still managed to snag the supreme Hawksian compliment when Geoff Carter (Cary Grant) greets her Bonnie Lee with "Hi, professional." The greeting signals her admission into the Hawksian fraternity of stoics. She has earned her wings, the movie shows us, in the emotionally arch "Who's Joe" scene, in which Carter, the head of a fledgling aviation company, eats, apparently without a flicker of survivor's guilt, a steak intended for a downed (and much loved) pilot. At first Bonnie is outraged. "How can you eat that?" she blurts in moral outrage. Yet in amazingly short order she comes to accept the cold truth that Joe died "because he wasn't good enough."

A less chilling reason for Bonnie's willingness not only to understand but affirm such stoicism is a childhood memory of her father's doing a high-wire act without a net. (Hawks's adventure heroes are often high-wire specialists.) Bonnie Lee, if by bloodline alone, understands what such professionalism entails, and she understands, too, that when high-flying veterans touch ground, they want to be surrounded by their own kind. Manny Farber's description of Hawks, which isolates this cliquishness, is still the best: he dubbed Hawks a "bravado specialist who always makes pictures about a Group." [3] Arthur can join this company of professionals, but she never seems at home there, which may be why Hawks felt that he never got the performance he wanted out of her.

For one thing, the Hawksian code of stoic reserve grates against her moral nature, which wants to yelp in indignation. On screen, Arthur, notoriously nervous and timid before the cameras rolled, seemed most herself letting out a full-throttled shriek rather than repressing it. And since Arthur has the voice for such outcry, it is a shame not to let her use it, as George Stevens does in *The More the Merrier* (1943). Frank Capra, perhaps out of some lingering resentment against Barbara Stanwyck for refusing to marry him, ranked Arthur as the best actress he ever worked with; he particularly marveled at her voice: "Low, husky— at times it broke pleasingly into the higher octaves like a thousand tinkling bells." [4]

But Hawks wasn't especially keen on exploiting her distinctive voice as an emotional and sexual instrument, especially in those upper reaches, where feelings are likely to soar out of control. As his star-making direction of Lauren Bacall in *To Have and Have Not* (1944) shows, Hawks preferred to keep women's voices in the lower registers, where they harmonize more easily and unobtrusively with men's. Still, he allows Bonnie to have the last word in *Only Angels Have Wings,* refusing to let Carter retreat into a nonverbal understanding that she will be his. "I'm hard to get," she tells him with a clef note of finality in her voice. "All's you have to do is ask me." Hawks loved the oblique rather than the explicit declaration, a verbal manner he admired in Hemingway's prose. But he is also a skilled moviemaker who knows when the time has come for the actors to speak their feelings. It is usually his dames who know when the time is right for love to be declared. Woman, creature of words, must be *asked,* not just silently "spoken" for.

One is therefore grateful that George Stevens wanted—and got— Arthur to vocalize a whole range of female cries, wails, moans, and shrieks as Connie Milligan, the patriotic miss who rents out a room in overcrowded wartime Washington, D.C., in *The More the Merrier*. She finds herself contending with the shenanigans of an elderly male roomer—Mr. Dingle (Charles Coburn), who has a penchant for shouting Farragut's "Damn the torpedoes—full speed ahead!"—and fending off the not unwanted advances of Joe Carter, a young inventor off to the front (Joel McCrea). Arthur uses her voice to give nonverbal expression both to Miss Milligan's easily flabbergasted idealism and to her flustered sexuality. Stevens knows just how to play up and off her talent for befuddlement in the love scene he stages with Joe on the steps of Connie's apartment building. On this occasion, at least, she proves highly combustible. As Joe's hands roam sexily over her neck and arms and back to her throat, Miss Milligan, who has been engaged (tepidly) to another man for four years without one peep of frustration, keeps up the talk, but finally ignites. After Joe plants one surprisingly timid kiss on her lips, she takes his face firmly in her hands, giving him the long passionate kiss he has been working for—and earned! Both are so dazed by the result that, forgetting that they occupy the same quarters, they part, then remember and with a mutually embarrassed mumbling enter the building together.

Through the machinations of Dingle, the duo finally do marry, despite their hesitations about the foolhardiness of marriage when not even the nation's future is secure. Wartime morale, the ending seems to suggest, is best served by succumbing to Eros. The film ends with Connie's bride night arietta composed of variously pitched female cries that signal but do not release the orgasmic sexual cry to which they are clearly leading. (The motto, "Damn the torpedoes—full speed ahead!" which has served as a running gag for Dingle's take-charge nature, are the last words of the film. The battle cry clearly gives the lovers the sexual go-ahead, whatever is happening on the war front.)

Connie is last heard from in *The More the Merrier* executing a virtuoso turn on what the female voice can say without words. Some, like myself, would rather hear the Arthur who so engagingly impersonated another Washington working girl, the senatorial aide Clarissa Saunders in *Mr. Smith Goes to Washington*. The admiring Mr. Smith (James Stewart) thinks she is the most intelligent and capable woman he has ever met. Smith, to his credit, appreciates that her job, indeed her life, probably haven't been so easy for her, and then, feeling he might have offended her, quickly corrects himself, "I mean, for a woman you've done very well." This is offered as a gallant, not a patronizing, remark, as the comment that follows confirms: "I've never known anyone so capable and intelligent," the "anyone" suggesting gender-free assessment. There is a gallantry of another kind in Smith's curiosity about her first name, since everyone calls her Saunders. In enlightening him, Arthur puts a delicate emphasis on the first syllable, elongating it into "clair." Such a pronunciation is, of course, self-mocking, excusing herself from any pretensions adhering to the name she bears. Yet it also foreshadows her comic role as illuminator, the woman who will not only initiate Mr. Smith into Washington's dark ways but who will bring ultimate clarity to the procedural and moral murkiness of Congress's working culture.

Arthur was that rare actress who was thoroughly convincing wrestling with political and ideological questions. She made politics palatable as a comic subject ripe for female intervention. Americans coming out of the Depression embraced sophisticated fantasy confections like the Rogers-Astaire musicals and the Loy-Powell comedy-mysteries, but as Capra's *American Madness* (1932) showed, they also responded to the more textured comedy offered by class and national politics. Arthur, with her proletarian savvy and wry, throaty humor, makes a sympathetic heroine for comedies with class politics on their mind. This may explain why she is never thoroughly believable as a Hawksian heroine with elective affinities to a select group of professionals—or dizzy dames. Despite her accomplished professionalism as a newspaperwoman, senatorial aide or, in *Talk of the Town* (1942), general factotum to a future Supreme Court justice, her deepest loyalty is not to the specialized tribe of experts but to the decent and democratic community. Her last worthy comic role was, in fact, as a congresswoman in *A Foreign Affair* (1948), who in one hilarious and oddly poignant moment relates how she, a stalwart Iowa Republican, once resisted the considerable charms of a mint-julep southern Democrat because to succumb to her yearning for him "would have meant betraying my platform and my constituents." So she filibustered instead.

But it is not as a power broker or legislator that Arthur makes her most irresistible appeal to us. Her moral and comic authority are best exercised as the working girl who explores the nooks and crannies of the plutocratic fantasy lurking in the heart of our democratic society—the fantasy of *Easy Living* (1937), one of her loopiest films. The script, by Preston Sturges (from the play by Vera Caspary), crackles with hilarious contradictions and unexpected concordances between public sentiment and our secret fantasies about what it means to live in the lap of luxury. The revels begin when J. B. Ball (Edward Arnold), banker extraordinaire, in a fit of pique at his wife's extravagances, throws her newest purchase, a mink coat, out the penthouse window. The coat lands on the head of Mary Smith, a young woman on her way to her job on the staff of *The Boy's Constant Companion* (which J. B., perhaps remembering some boyhood indiscretion, will repeatedly call *The Boy's Constant Reminder*). She sets out to return the coat to its proper owner but finds herself, at the end of a trying but fulfilling day, outfitted by Ball and housed by Louis Louis (Luis Alberni), the restaurateur and would-be luxury hotelier who, thinking that Mary is Ball's mistress, installs her in the penthouse suite. There may be providence in the fall of a sparrow, but a mink coat descending from the heavens offers a completely different problem in the unfathomable ways of fortune.

This is confirmed for Arthur in *The Devil and Miss Jones,* an economic morality play that satirizes the capitalist as America's indigenous figure of providence. Working undercover in his own store, the tycoon J. P. Merrick (Charles Coburn) scribbles his findings in a notebook that he calls his Domesday Book. When asked by Miss Jones what he means by that term, he boasts that it spells doom to all who are in it and then candidly admits that "I never forget a good deed or an ill one. I consider myself a kind of divine justice." His employees, of course, view him as a devil ruling over a Darwinian world of merciless economic and social predation. And we have reason to believe they are right. "I'll play with them like a cat and a mouse," Merrick exults while devising his plan to ferret out the agitators who burned him in effigy.

Capitalists may be gorging on the labor of the (sometimes starving) working class, but the irony is that it is Merrick who is confined to a dietary regimen of milk and graham crackers. When Merrick infiltrates the ranks of his department store as the hard-up Mr. Higgins, Miss Jones fears that that he is going without food, which, in fact, he is, but not for lack of money. Along with good advice about how to survive in the shoe department, she also gives him fifty cents for lunch, plus a pleasant introduction to Miss Ellis (the sweet-tempered Spring Byington), whose tuna popovers are a gustatory delight. The vagaries of Merrick's growing appetite assume an especially hearty form when, in an act of solidarity with his newfound community of friends, he joins Mary in eating a paper with the names of 400 "mice" targeted for extermination from his employment rolls. Nourishment is also an issue when Labor and Capital finally sit down at the bargaining table. Miss Ellis, whom the by-now-enamored Merrick-Higgins commends for bringing a "woman's point of view" to negotiations, insists that the canaries be given fresh water to see them through the weekend hours when the store is closed.

But it is Higgins's spiritual rather than physical well-being that inspires Miss Jones's most impassioned and public speech. Innocently taking Merrick, the man whom she had helped burn in effigy, to a clandestine meeting to organize store workers, she finds herself urged to speak out on his behalf. Rising to her feet and gently urging Merrick-Higgins to stand quietly as her prime exhibit, Mary delivers an impromptu speech urging her coworkers to reflect how his desperate condition might one day mirror their own. She presents him as a "picture of you and me at fifty-five years of age" and goes on to envision the sad decline awaiting the "bright, alert" man still in possession of all his faculties who came to work at Neely's department store "without the few cents in his pocket he needed to buy lunch." Though no one can equal Arthur for stammering confusion, she rarely falters when she knows what needs to be said. In this somber and affecting instance, she castigates the managerial providence that will use a man like Mr. Higgins and when he is used up "throw him aside for a younger man, leaving him insecure, friendless, homeless, with no one to turn to but charity and the poor house." Miss Jones has given the devil his due by showing up his own work—himself.

Turning the enemy's best weapons against himself may be a time-worn strategy, but it serves her equally well in her most impressive achievement as a reluctant crusader, in *Mr. Smith Goes to Washington*. As an experienced senatorial aide she is given the thankless task of keeping tabs on a newly elected senator who can quote Lincoln and Jefferson but hasn't got a clue about how to talk in the nation's modern capital. Mr. Smith brings to Washington the words as well as the callowness of the newspaper he founded, whose title, *Boy's Stuff*, says it all. He certainly doesn't know the official language of power. Even before starting the job he finds himself groping for words. "What time does the Senate . . . ," he starts to ask Saunders, but finds he is missing the right word. She immediately supplies it: "convene?"[5]

Saunders will be asked to supply much else before this prairie flower can blossom. First she must get him to adjust to the pace of the city. "Things sure happen fast around here," he casually remarks. His handler advises, "Yes, you'll have to get yourself out of low gear." It's Saunders's job, of course, to make sure that he stays in neutral long enough to ensure that a corrupt efficiency bill passes the Senate. Saunders finds the assignment demeaning but is willing to talk terms with Smith's sponsor, Senator Joseph Paine (Claude Rains). "Look, Senator, I wasn't given a brain just to tell a Boy Ranger what time it is," she complains. "Look, when I came here my eyes were big blue question marks. Now they're big green dollar marks." That she owns up to having her price impresses the senator. "Smart girl, heh?" he says, sealing their bargain.

Clarissa seems willing to abide by their agreement, as distasteful as she finds it, despite her dawning love for the wide-eyed Boy Ranger. She will even come to appreciate the irony of her mission to keep him busy when she discovers that he intends to introduce a bill for a national boy's camp on the very site selected for Paine's graft-ridden water project. She balks only when asked to conspire "woman to woman" with Paine's snooty daughter, Susan-Paine-in-the-Neck (Astrid Allwyn), to decoy Smith from the Senate on the day the efficiency bill is up for a vote. In a drunken scene that both Hawks and Capra singled out as a triumph of "oblique" storytelling, Saunders and her loyal suitor, Diz Moore (Thomas Mitchell), share drinks and dismay over the lamentable facts that, as Diz says, "the dopes are going to inherit the earth anyway." Still, Saunders wonders if the dopes—well, one dope in particular—haven't "got the jump on all of us." She even goes so far as to wonder "if it isn't a curse going through life wised up like you and me." She confesses that there are limits to what she will do—murder, for instance, not of the material but the spiritual kind, the kind that turns Don Quixote Smith into a stooge. She proclaims herself too "squeamish" to watch them "drop the lead balloon" on the unsuspecting rube. Then, mentally staggering from murder to marriage, she proposes to Diz. When he obligingly asks when, she gives the less than urgent answer, "Anytime."

Hawks and Capra delighted in the comic indirectness by which Saunders declares her love for Smith by proposing to Diz. A similar moment occurs in *The More the Merrier* when Arthur's Connie, moved by a traveling case that McCrea's Joe has given her as a farewell present, decides she can't accept it, "since it wouldn't be right to take one man's case on another man's honeymoon." Arthur delivers the line with such earnest but pining intonations that its Freudian meaning, like some kind of sexual contraband, slips into the comedy under the guise of moral rather than sexual qualms.

The sexual transference accomplished in the line—"You're a good egg, Diz"—is of a different order. There is more lyrical than erotic feeling in her love for Smith, as she herself implies in comparing her love to a "mother sending her kid off to school for the first time, watching the little fella toddling off in his best bib and tucker hoping he can stand up to the other kids." Clarissa pronounces "bib and tucker" with just the right amount of drunken mushiness, another clue to how deep and self-patrolling is the ironic intelligence governing her use of words. Saunders senses, too, that Smith has fathered something in her as well. As in all creative relationships, we may say that they give birth to each other, she giving him the knowledge he will need to survive in the "whole new world" he has abruptly entered, he giving her a sense of America as an uncorrupted space. Prompted by Smith's rhapsodic evocation of a landscape filled with such "wonders" as meadows threaded by lazy streams, campfires, and snow drifts, she proposes a fantasy elopement with Diz that will leave them feeling "like people . . . like we just got out of a tunnel." Diz, considerate but skeptical city boy, is struck (as much as he can be in his drunken torpor) by the image of wind leaning against the grass and asks in genuine wonderment: "Does the wind get tired out there?" Had Capra stuck to the genius of that line he might not have fallen prey to the sentimentalism lurking at the edge of his better comedies.

The wistful but world-weary tone of this proposal scene helps make it the best scene, if not the most spectacular one, in the film. Hardly departing from a two-shot, the scene has an emotional rhythm that summons the pastoral idealism of the film, only to convert it into a uniquely modern, urban vision of light coming out of a tunnel, much like the stream of light in which film itself is projected. It is this counter-pastoral vision of a world too complicated to be contained by rhapsodies about the "wonders" of nature that finally prompts Diz, ever obliging but plainly unenthusiastic, to balk at actually seeking a route into Smith's bucolic world: "Do we have to?" Saunders's reply is prompt, final, and satisfying. "No, I can't think of anything more sappy."

Sappiness has its place, one might even say its pride of place, in Capra's comedies, but moments like these, and they are unforgettable as well as formative, remind us of the moral savvy that women bring to his comic world. Mr. Smith will find himself in need of that savvy when he finally learns of Paine's personal and political treachery. Patriarchy, embodied for him in the benign paternalism of Senator Paine and in the wise system of government ordained by the Founding Fathers, has failed him. Not only failed him, but turned against him, turning the "honorary stooge" into a political fall guy. Smith's charges of graft are turned against him with exquisite precision. ("A beautiful thing to watch, that Taylor machine," says Diz in world-weary admiration as the juggernaut run by Jim Taylor [Edward Arnold] goes into high gear.)

Mr. Smith, like Mr. Deeds in an equally dark moment, becomes speechless when what he has loved proves faithless. Called before a special investigation committee on charges of graft, he, again like Deeds, refuses to mount a defense. As Babe Bennett, Arthur has to provoke Deeds (Gary Cooper) into speech by hysterically confessing her love. But hysteria is not in the repertoire of the supremely competent, emotionally controlled Saunders. She tries a gentler approach to reinstill in Smith his idealistic fervor for lost causes. She finds him sitting glumly on the steps of the Lincoln Memorial, where he had come to castigate his own foolish belief in Washington.

It had, of course, been a Washington composed almost exclusively of words and monuments, and now he renounces them. The American mistrust of words reasserts itself in the most sacred precincts of the Republic as Smith repudiates the "fancy words around this town. Some of them are carved in stone. Some of them I guess the Taylors and Paines put 'em up there so that suckers like me can read them." The tradition, and equally important the *rhetoric,* of the Republic has been defaced by Taylors and the Paines—tellingly well-spoken men—and in his verbal as well as moral disgust Smith declares that "I'm getting out of this town so fast and away from all the words and the monuments and the whole rotten show." His ideals have been shown up as "boy's stuff"—although Smith doesn't make the connection, the movie makes it for him.

But having made it, it then introduces Saunders's more mature vision. She poses the first objection to his plan to spread his newfound gospel of disillusion. "I don't think they'll believe you." Then with the slightest but most effective of pauses, she utters the thrillingly personal name, "Jeff." This casual but nevertheless precious sign of human intimacy unites them in a shared ideological purpose. It is the prelude to Clarissa's own lyrical tribute to Lincoln, that fine American who didn't distrust words but put them to use, saving them from corruption. She reminds Jeff—and us—of another Lincoln, Lincoln the fool, prone to dejection, a man who knew that to be thought a fool was often the initial but not lasting fate of anyone who "tried to lift his thought up off the ground." As expounded by Clarissa, America is the land of lost causes, the moral Eden founded on the belief that "all the good that ever came into this world came from fools with faith like that." She then reverts to Jeff's initial impression that Lincoln was seated on his memorial as if he were waiting for something or someone to come along. Seizing on that fantasy—or inspired perception?—she concludes by giving him a vision of his own manly place in the democratic tradition. "I think he was waiting for you, Jeff. He knows you can do it. So do I." These words seem to anoint Jeff, ordaining the moment of his political coming of age. This making of a political manhood is one of the most consequential Pygmalion acts in American screen comedy.

The use of first names carries a different dramatic charge in *The Talk of the Town*. Arthur here plays Nora Shelley, a schoolteacher who rents a house to the Honorable Michael Lightcap (Ronald Colman), a distinguished jurist who wants to spend the summer in seclusion writing his book. Lightcap, however, arrives a day early, and Leopold Dilg (Cary Grant), an escaped convicted arsonist-murderer arrives un-invited, seeking asylum. (The charges, of course, are trumped up.) The names of the two men suggest the legal and interpretive extremes they represent: Lightcap all disembodied theory; Dilg suggesting the gritty experience that makes Lightcap's pronouncements, for all their marmoreal splendor, seem featherweight. Nora mediates between and assists both men, ministering to Lightcap's household and secretarial needs, providing Dilg the sanctuary and finally the cover he needs to elude the police.

The film charts the men's growing respect and affection for each other as they argue their legal philosophy. Lightcap holds that "my business is with the principles of law. I can't allow myself to get mixed up in these little local affairs. The philosophy behind the deed, that's my field." According to this philosophy, the proper and legitimate aim of lawmakers and law administrators is "to build the law firmly on prin-ciples which are above small emotions, greed, and the loose thinking of everyday life." "Impossible," objects Dilg, who should know. He believes such a philosophy to be quixotic and offers his own stark defi-nition of the law: "a gun pointing at somebody's head." Questions of equal justice before the law, he believes, are settled with similar blunt-ness: "All depends on which end of the gun you stand whether the law is just or not." Dilg's verdict on Lightcap—"an intelligent man but cold; no blood in his thinking"—represents the point of view of the comedy and its humanizing mission: "We must start to thaw him out," he informs Miss Shelley.

The "thawing" of Justice Lightcap is a good concept for a comedy, but it can proceed only as long as Lightcap remains under the impres-sion that Dilg is his gardener, not a fugitive from justice. When he dis-covers the truth, the comedy and its language turn harsh. Such sudden darkening in tone and prospect are never dismissed by the comedies of the day but are absorbed into the rhythm of the character's lives and emotions, giving them a density as well as moral ballast. Nora's great scene with Lightcap comes in answer to his condemnation, his moral demotion of her, we might way, when he learns of Dilg's true identity. "You're a silly, dangerous girl. You had me feed and lodge a notorious fugitive from justice. You endangered a lifetime's career for a stupid gesture. . . . Our association is at an end, Nora." Nora's response, oblique and off-center, is unexpected, but not without force. "That's a tip-off, professor, having you good and sore before you got around to calling me by my first name." "Miss Shelley," he corrects himself, but she is quick to block that emotional retreat. "Nora when you're angry, remember."

Arthur, so expert in the dramatic power of personal address, refuses to abide by his curt and coolly official dismissal. "That will be all." "That will not be all, Mr. Lightcap." She intends to get in her closing argument. Here it is: "Dilg is innocent, regardless of all the reasonable evidence dredged up by lawyers and that holy institution of yours and I'd rather be hated by forty frozen legal giants like you than turn him over to those bloodthirsty idiots in Lochester. You were right to grow a beard. You're an old man all your life. You put on a proper costume as soon as you were able. Don't ever shave it off, Mr. Twilight. Someone might think you were alive. That would be misrepresentation." The "Mr. Twilight" is a particularly unforgiving play on his name, but she feels as if she is talking to a dead man and that this may the only way to revive him. She is right. It does.

Arthur's last great comic burst of life comes in Billy Wilder's *A Foreign Affair,* which casts her as Congresswoman Phoebe Frost, on a fact-finding mission to postwar Berlin. This time Arthur plays the character who must be thawed out, as her name Miss Frost advises. She first appears as a physical cartoon of female rectitude and efficiency, which is to say, this being a Wilder film, a cartoon of sexual repression. Her hair is severely drawn off her face, her features pinched, her speech brisk rather than quick-witted. Now it is clearly her turn to shed her "proper costume," relax her stiff manner and lighten up, revealing the sexual glow promised by her first name, Phoebe (which

Jean Arthur as the reluctant crusader and senatorial aide to James Stewart in *Mr. Smith Goes to Washington*

means "bright one"). Like the radiant Clarissa concealed behind the crusty exterior of Saunders in *Mr. Smith Goes to Washington,* the inner warmth of Phoebe, figure of light, is overcast by the official chill of correct Miss Frost.

When Phoebe decides to come out of hiding she can be luminous, although not as star-spangled as the more garish Erika von Schluetow (Marlene Dietrich), who plays her rival for the attentions of Captain John Pringle (John Lund). Dietrich good-naturedly plays up her role as the "blonde flame-thrower" who suddenly finds herself in competition with her sexual antitype—the congresswoman whom she describes as a "funny little woman with a face like a scrubbed kitchen floor." The sexual ideology of the film is obvious but not without its moments of camp fun. We know that the morally slack and slatternly European must lose to the neat and trim American. Dietrich generously sacrifices her character to this patriotic validation of American womanhood. She doesn't try to win us over but accentuates the physical contrast between her face, her body, and her dress and Arthur's less glamorous but more resplendent moral luminousness. She even allows her character to be shown in newsreel footage consorting with Nazi officers, something that Dietrich famously did not do. Indeed, she was made a captain in the U. S. Army for her valiant service entertaining the troops (three times she was trapped behind enemy lines, twice at significant risk to her life), and in 1945 she was awarded the Medal of Freedom for her wartime contributions.

All the more remarkable, then, that when questioned by Pringle about her own political past, Erika feigns a cynical insouciance: "What does it matter, a woman's politics? Women pick up whatever is in fashion, and change it like spring hats." Pringle interprets the shifting allegiances behind her millinery finery: "Last year it's a little number with a swastika on it. This year it's ostrich feathers in red, white, and blue. Next year it's going to be a hammer, maybe, and a sickle." Dietrich's ideological promiscuity, not her sexual availability to the highest bidder, is what rankles the captain. He finally prefers, as we knew he eventually would, the funny woman with the face like a scrubbed kitchen floor. Of course, the very fact that he pays her sexual attention inspires her to tarnish her principles, if not her reputation, by buying a black-market dress that will show off her own physical charms to best advantage. Still he knows that if he were to put to her the question that Dietrich casually dismissed—What does a woman's politics matter?— she would answer "Everything." She once filibustered to prove it. What, then, *does* a woman's politics matter? It is Jean Arthur's comic gift to us to show us how much and in what way they do.

Claudette Colbert

Claudette Colbert, born in Paris, infuses a dose of Continental magic, the moonlit enchantments of Perrault's fairy tales, into her roles as fast-talking dame. There is something charmed about her existence as an American comic heroine, even when she is down on her luck, like Eve Peabody, the game chorine of *Midnight* (1939) who arrives in Paris penniless but abounding in schemes for enrichment; or like the runaway wife Gerry Jeffers of Preston Sturges's *Palm Beach Story* (1942), seeking her fortune—and financing for her husband's latest invention—in the pleasure grounds of the rich. And then, of course, there is Ellie Andrews, the runaway bride of *It Happened One Night,* trying to make it from Florida to New York on four dollars (she makes it, but just barely).[6] The very titles of these films invite us into a world of fable, where wondrous transformations—in character and in feeling—happen as suddenly and irresistibly as in a dream.

Or nightmare. Sturges famously begins *The Palm Beach Story* with the fairy tale ending that segues into comic misfortune: "And they lived happily after—or did they?" the opening titles inquire, a question that brings the galloping rhythms of the Wedding March to a sudden and ignominious halt. This is a question we might put to Ellie Andrews and Peter Warne (Clark Gable), the cocksure reporter she comes to love, who share a fantasy of running off to an uninhabited Pacific island where "you and the moon and the water all become one." Would *they* live happily after, allowing for a few ecstatic nights of lunar and marine and marital fusion? Even they think better of it and decide to take their marriage license and honeymoon in an auto court in Indiana.

That Colbert is capable of such an extravagant fantasy yet content with such an outcome is a tribute both to her romantic idealism and her pragmatism in realizing it. The combination is distinctly American. Despite the European chic that graces her presence on screen, Colbert was utterly American in the modernity of her look and attitudes. In *Midnight,* she claims to be American Dutch Irish and part Choctaw. The nativist strain in her has been highly refined, however. Her high cheekbones and petite, elegant frame make it clear that she could never come from anywhere but a big city. There is nothing of the country girl about her, and even when she is born to poor parents, like Eve Peabody, no trace of proletarian origins survives in her demeanor or her speech. She has so adapted herself to the manners of the rich that she can impersonate, with utter credibility, a baroness.

Midnight, whose title invokes the legendary hour of bewitchment and transformation, celebrates Colbert as a modern-day Cinderella, the quintessential Perrault heroine of low estate transported into a fantasy world of wealth and luxury. This Cinderella being American, a royal marriage is what she must renounce if she would live happily ever after. As Eve Peabody does when she gives up her sure chance to marry the rich and elegant heir to a champagne fortune (Francis Lederer) for a modest life with a Hungarian taxi driver (Don Ameche). Or as Ellie Andrews does when she annuls her marriage to King Westley in order to marry the commoner who has a method all his own for dunking doughnuts. Earlier, after the first night they spent together, Ellie and Peter had thought of calling the little act they put on for the police searching for the runaway heiress "Cinderella, or a Real Hot Love Story," but they rejected the title, even with the tabloid tag, as "too mushy." Cinderella could appeal as a dream figure for Depression America only if she exemplified the unsuspected blessings of *downward* mobility. Colbert obliged, by showing how a poor little rich girl's "mad flight to happiness" landed her, without complaint, in an auto court.

Ellie's mad flight from her gilded cage teaches her the varieties of social movement possible to an American with heart and spirit enough for the ride. *It Happened One Night* is in many ways a movie *about* locomotion, from Ellie's self-propelled dive off her father's becalmed yacht to the autogiro that is meant to carry off Ellie and King Westley after their posh society wedding. In between, of course, comes a memorable bus trip in cramped but eventually comfy quarters. Ellie and Peter even make part of the journey on foot, improvising a hitchhiker's guide to America on the way. At the start of their journey together, Peter, who has nothing but disdain for the spoiled brat, asks Ellie if she has ever considered getting "off your high horse." But if he eventually manages to get her to dismount, it is not long before he finds himself transporting her on his own strong back. Ellie squeals in delight, remembering the piggyback rides of her childhood, but Peter becomes indignant at the very suggestion that Park Avenue phonies (presumably perched on *their* high horses) know how it's done. "You show me a good piggybacker, I'll show you a real human," Peter declares. "Now you take Abraham Lincoln, for instance. A natural-born piggybacker. Where do you get all of that stuffed-shirts family of yours?" Piggybacking is not so much a form of transport as a true democratic measure of a man.

Yet nothing riles Peter more than the thought that Ellie has taken *him* for a "buggy ride." It is a thought that is hatched when he sees Ellie

Claudette Colbert, vowing to climb on pleasure's merry-go-round, in
It Happened One Night

leaving the auto court in a fleet sedan that outpaces his own spluttering
jalopy. Recalling that ride prompts him to demand restitution from
Ellie's father, even if it amounts to only $39.60. "This is a matter of
principle. Something you probably wouldn't understand. When anybody takes me for a buggy ride, I don't like the idea of having to pay
for the privilege." Accounts settled, he then takes what he believes to
be his final leave of her, just as she is about to mount a merry-go-round
with the intention of never dismounting again. She will dismount in
time. She will even make a mad dash for the car that will take her to
the man who, unlike the aviator King Westley, will keep her firmly on
the ground, happy to be traveling along "life's highway" at full speed.

By the time she makes *Midnight,* five years later, Colbert will have
established herself as an expert in the symbolism of social movement.
Her Eve Peabody is more resourceful in her social transit, although she
is not so much in a hurry that she can't poke fun at herself along the
way. When she steps out of Tibor Czerny's (Don Ameche) taxicab to

accept the meal she could never afford on her own, she takes a moment to relish the Cinderella joke waiting to be made. "Ohhh . . . I know," she chuckles. "This is the pumpkin coach and you're the fairy godmother." Eve is not really looking for a pumpkin coach, of course. A pragmatist, she prefers more modern — and luxurious — forms of transport. Czerny offers his counteropinion that "if you want peace of mind, get yourself a taxicab." Eve isn't buying that. "No woman ever found peace in a taxi. I'm looking for a limousine." "They don't ride any better," he counters, but Eve won't be convinced. "They ride better than a subway." She should know, as she proceeds to tell him: "I've spent most of my life on the Bronx local. I've been squeezed, trampled, stepped on. One day I said to myself — That's enough. You're going to get somewhere."

Colbert's Ellie Andrews travels a rather different route. What she encounters in her mad flight for happiness is nothing less than a social map of America, one of whose most natural wonders is the homegrown male, as indispensable to America's mythology as the buffalo. If there is one figure who incarnates the American ideal of companionable masculinity appealing to both men and women it is Clark Gable. Unlike James Stewart and Henry Fonda and Gary Cooper, Gable, whose comic persona retained much of his earlier gangster traits, never dawdled or drawled or stuttered out the feelings deepest in his heart. When his emotions emerged, they were confidently if hurriedly expressed. This fact of movie history and masculine mores is not as well known as it ought to be. It was screwball comedy that rescued Gable from the psychopathology of his early roles — toughtalking gangsters whose sexual hold over dames, even high-class ones like Norma Shearer's in *A Free Soul* (1931), doesn't last long once they get their fill of his rough-housing. Through his humanizing contact with fast-talking dames, most notably Jean Harlow and Myrna Loy, Gable could moderate some of his hard-boiled cynicism. Which is to say, if you will indulge the paradox, that Gable as a romantic comic hero is one of the finest creations of the fast-talking dame and may, indeed, have been modeled after her.

In *It Happened One Night* we can already see how playful Gable has become with words, how untroubled by the prospect of being thought effeminate just because he likes to have his full and literate, even literary say. Memories of the film, however fond, and criticism of it, however detailed, tend to forget that Gable's Peter Warne is fired for indulging himself in all the verbal mannerisms of high-toned culture. On a bender, he submitted his story in free verse, an artistic license unappreciated, and definitely unsponsored, by the "gashouse palooka" who happens to be his (exasperated) editor. Peter often talks in quotations and resorts to studied archaisms, as when he first sees Ellie occupying the seat that had taken a row with the bus driver to secure. "That upon which you sit is mine."

It will soon be hers. Ellie is one of Colbert's most willful but endearing heroines, who has her heart set not on things but on experience. One of the reasons she is drawn to Peter is her sense that he seems so certain about what real experiences are and so intent on preserving them in ritual forms. He constantly flirts with the idea of codifying these daily ceremonies of the common life, instructing the less fortunate rich in the fine art of dunking a doughnut or hitching a ride. Ellie may have wealth, but, according to her, riches have only deprived her of her will. So strong is her conviction on this point that she challenges, sadly rather than combatively, Peter's characterization of her as spoiled. "Well, perhaps I am, although I don't see how I can be," she insists. "People who are spoiled are accustomed to having their own way. I never have. On the contrary. I've always been told what to do and how to do it and when and with whom." Now on her own, she is determined to have and to make her own way.

Being determined to fend for herself is a sign of her female resolve, but also a sign of Colbert's resourcefulness on the road. She gave grit as well glamor to the otherwise pitiable figure of the American nomad, reassuring us that she is a woman with the ability to make herself at home anywhere. We first see her as Eve in *Midnight* enjoying an untroubled sleep in a second-class compartment; then gamely buying a newspaper to use as a rain hat. No fairy godmother could be more inventive on such limited means. Eve, broke but not dispirited, sets out to find a job as a blues singer. She's a gambler who is due for a lucky streak. She strikes a deal with a taxi driver, the amiable Czerny, to drive her around Paris in search of job, double or nothing. She seems to be on a losing streak until she finally strikes off on her own. It is then that we receive the first sign that Eve is worthy of the fairy tale fate awarded her. Dashing through the rain, in a moment of inspired social magic, she converts a pawn ticket into an invitation to a posh musical evening.

During the interlude offered by the music, Eve quietly finds a seat, seeking invisibility. Nevertheless, she draws the attention of George Flammarion (John Barrymore), seated beside her, who after a few priceless glances that blend appreciation, class snobbery, and sexual suspicion in one arch look, becomes her fairy godfather. He gives her the goods to go with her new name and new title, Baroness Czerny: a suite at the Ritz, plus a wardrobe fit for the fashionable dame she pretends, quite convincingly, to be. He sponsors this charade in the hopes that the baroness will seduce Jacques Picot (Francis Lederer), the man who has infatuated his wife, Helene (Mary Astor). Her target, he wryly informs her, is a young man who enjoys "a very superior income from very inferior champagne." Her masquerade will take her to a splendid country estate and almost lead to a marriage with her princely admirer, but this Cinderella, in the end, prefers her proletarian to her aristocratic suitor. She converts back into a dame and marries the taxi driver she has loved all along. Colbert thus achieves the most difficult, morally speaking, of her metamorphoses—turning back into her original self.

But not before she has made the argument she is bound as a woman and gambler to lose. It is an argument contradicting the taxi driver, the advocate for romantic love, who she believes is "talking like a fool." Her argument takes the form of a story about her earlier self: "Back in New York whenever I managed to crash a party full of luscious, big-hearted millionaires, there was sure to be some snub-faced kid in the orchestra playing traps. So around four in the morning when the wise girls were skipping off to Connecticut to marry those millionaires, I'd be with him in some night spot, learning tricks on the kettledrums. And he always had a nose like yours." "Is there anything wrong with my nose?" he wonders, a little petulantly. "Yes, I like it." But now she's going in a different direction, as she tells the man she takes to calling Skipper, relying on her own guidance to lead the way.

If Colbert appears the most self-reliant of heroines, it may be because she is also the most cerebral, the Gallic love of rationality spurring her determination to take control of her life. At her most independent-minded, Colbert gives the unmistakable impression that she has *No Time for Love* (1943), the title of one of her oddest comedies, one that literally drenches her in mud. Colbert plays Katherine Grant, a successful photographer. That it will be her practiced and appraising eye that determines the initial and final look of things in this film is signaled by the hands, presumably hers, seen developing the photographs that serve as the opening credits. This is our visual cue that she in some way stands, as so many of our fast-talking dames do, for the directorial intelligence behind the film itself.

We may be disheartened then, or simply amused, when we learn that in taking pictures for an assignment "backstage at the Ballet," she developed photographs, as her managing editor complains, with "not a sign of a dancer in sight, not a leg, not even a foot." Photographing animate beauty, especially the beauty of motion, is clearly not her specialty. But this is a Colbert film, so we should not be surprised if sooner or later she will find herself moving in unexpected vehicles into unfamiliar places. This time Colbert descends into the depths of a tunnel, an "interborough vehicular river project," where she begins to show her eye for cheesecake, or rather beefsteak. It is an eye that quickly determines, after only a glimpse of a barechested Jim Ryan (Fred Mac-Murray), that she has encountered something like primordial man (in the argot of his trade, he is a sandhog). And she starts popping flash after flash. When her sister Happy (Ilka Chase) catches sight of the pictures she's taken of him, she squeals delightedly to her refined friends, "Hey, come see what Kate found in a hole!" Confronted with this instinctual fascination, both she and her sister wonder whether a "woman of education" could possibly be attracted to a "mental throwback to the alphabet soup era."

At first, the throwback in question doesn't care whether she is or not. For one thing, she's a dame and dames have the reputation of bringing bad luck to sandhogs. For another, he informs her, "You're just not my type of dame, that's all." He feels it is his duty to set her straight since "you've been on the prowl ever since you met me. Aren't you old enough to know it?" Katherine, who earlier had wondered when it became a "crime to photograph inanimate beauty," can't believe she is being accused of having such a roving eye for animate masculine beauty. "Why, why, you conceited ape," she objects, but before she can work up to a really adequate rebuttal, he decides to concede a small but for him not insignificant point. "Maybe there's something about you I could like, I don't know, but right now I'm booked solid, so I figured I'd wise you up that you're wasting your time."

He may think he's being gallant in wising her up, but Katherine presents him with another explanation for his churlish behavior. "You are living proof," she informs him, "that men can exist without mentality." Being without mentality apparently gives the male ego all the more room to grow. Or so Katherine asserts. "Is it," she asks him, "actually within the limits of your exalted ego to believe that a woman of education and love of the finer graces could fall for you?" When he complains that "I don't get all that," she obliges. "May I put it this way? At home in my bedroom I have an inanimate object, a chair, that has ten times more quality and character than you. A chair, Mr. Groundhog." At once insulted and intrigued, Mr. Ground/Sandhog will soon pay a visit to her bedroom to see the chair, only to break it.

As a matter of fact, it turns out to be a fine chair, with much character but little holding power. However it might appeal to those who love the finer graces, functionally it must be considered a failure, a verdict Mr. Sandhog is quick to pronounce. "A chair is made to hold people up. That one couldn't." But the very thought that strength may not be the total measure of an object, much less a man, is an idea that begins subtly to undermine his own manly bravura. He becomes uncomfortably aware of the social distance between a high-class dame and a man literally working in the underworld, a distance not measured by grit but by something more elusive and intangible (perhaps even breakable) called mentality—something, apparently, he is without. As a sandhog he has tunneled himself into a happy understanding of who he is and the "feeling he knows a little about women, but then along comes something like you and you're right back in short pants." To get back into his long pants, he suddenly kisses her.

That kiss not only refits him in his long pants but divests Katherine of some of her "mentality." The next scene escorts us into the world of what we might call her undermentality, the world of her dreams. There we encounter an enlarged and distorted image of that fine, character-graced chair, an image that suddenly is transformed into a Gothic backdrop, its slats the bars of a prison. Wielding the chair and then smashing it to pieces is Katherine's respectable and moneyed fiancé, who now reveals his dream-identity as a dastardly fiend. He soon hurls her into space, her freefall broken only by the Superman hero (Mac-Murray, the sandhog transfigured into a creature of air), who swoops down to rescue her. Returning her to her lofty place in the clouds, her hero casts his villainous rival into the abyss with a triumphant Tarzan yell. This superhero phantasmagoria is the wet dream of a woman not with too much but rather with too little mentality. And Colbert's Katherine knows it. On waking, she decides to rid her mind of the phantasm who has invaded her thoughts. Confessing her attraction, she declares to her sister that "I've decided to have those dreams when I'm awake and have some control over my mind." But in her waking dream, he is "completely without the glamor he assumes at night. . . . His shoes are dirty. His napkin is tucked under his chin. He goes blank when I mention books or plays, and he's utterly incapable of contributing to an intelligent conversation." When her sister wonders at the scheme, she assures her, "I know what I'm doing. I have faith in my own intelligence."

She not only has faith in her intelligence but also takes pride in it as a sign of her modernity. It is her modern mentality that is speaking when she scoffs at the romantic ideology that has doomed many a woman before her. "Romantic marriage went out with smelling salts," she sensibly confides to her sister after a disastrous night out with her primordial man. "Today it's a commonsense institution, and if you don't have intelligence enough to better your position, you deserve to fall in love and starve to death." "Okay," agrees her sister, "quit poking out your chin at me. I'm on your side. What do you want from me?" "An argument, you dope."

Colbert is intelligent and commonsensical enough to know when "mentality" must yield to the better argument of love. No one made that argument better, for and against, than Colbert herself.

The Grande Dames

Part Three

5 *Missing Links*

Bringing Up Baby

*I*t is by now a truth almost universally acknowledged that it is language that separates man from beast, a phylogenetic leap up the scale of being that every newborn recapitulates with more or less success. No one lives by the light of this truth with more good nature and high spirits than that evolutionary marvel, the fast-talking dame. Sad to say, no fossil or human record survives to mark her first appearance in the evolutionary chain. Facts thus being hard to come by, we might justifiably seek clues to her original nature in a tall but not necessarily untruthful tale, such as the one told by James Thurber: Two protoplasmic forms, "gibbous creatures, who had lived in the sea since time began," are washed up on the shore at roughly the same moment. From the first, however, they exhibit radically different dispositions toward their new environment. The female greets her brave new world by exclaiming, "The light that never was!"[1] The male, skeptical and surly, can only grumble, "You're always seeing things that never were. . . . You're always wanting things that aren't yet." As she begins dreaming of things to come — "rose-point lace and taffeta, sweet perfumes, and jewelry" — and starts "flobbering, almost imperceptibly, toward the scrubby brown growth beyond the sand and toward the sun," the male retreats into the sea. Eons later he reemerges and spies the female, who has evolved into a shapelier form. That one look proves a defining moment in the relation of the sexes. "Hey, Mag," the primal male cries, "flobbering" toward the female. "Wait for baby!"[2]

Bringing up baby, timidly loitering on the primal beachhead, is the first momentous task entrusted to woman, the evolutionary trailblazer who is always seeing things that never were and wanting things that are not yet. This, at least, is how James Thurber envisions the phylogenetic advance from amniotic waters to human shores in the initiatory parable of *Further Fables of Our Time*. Lest there be any doubt about the gist of this tale, Thurber, our American Aesop, pronounces the inescapable moral: "Let us ponder this basic fact about the human: Ahead of every man, not behind him, is a woman."[3] Experience may or may not prove this proposition to be incontrovertibly true in every case, but this in itself presents no serious objection to Thurber's droll intuitions. For the most part, the female as pathfinder is a human fact not so much pondered as conceded in those adventurous screen comedies of the thirties and forties that never tired of replaying the erotic and evolutionary game of follow the leader, although with frequent change of leads.[4]

In *Bringing Up Baby* (1938) this game is played, to something amounting to perfection, by a fast-talking dame named Susan Vance (Katharine Hepburn) and the object of her sexual choice, Dr. David Huxley (Cary Grant), a cerebral paleontologist of halting speech who has spent the past four years reconstructing the skeleton of a brontosaurus. No one to my knowledge has openly wondered why David, who has no profession in Hagar Wilde's story on which the film is based, should be given the character (such as Hollywood understands it to be) of a paleontologist.[5] Nor has much thought been given to how the entire menagerie of human and animal types presented in the film relates to that monitory skeleton of the brontosaurus who visually dominates the film's beginning and its end. Manny Farber, observant as always, called attention to director Howard Hawks's predilection for "professionals," but his *Bringing Up Baby* emphasizes an equally dominant strain in Hawks's imagination and, arguably, the imagination of thirties and forties comedy—a zoomorphic humor that treats human behavior, especially human sexual behavior, not as a divine exception to but a more developed instance of the rampant instincts enlivening the entire animal world.

Such a view of our unreconstructed creatureliness may offend our dignity but seldom our sense of reality. Comparing human to animal life can make both more intelligible than either would be in isolation. In the erotic realm, the resemblances can be startling, even unavoidable. We have seen in *Tales of Manhattan* how the squirrel as well as the lamb might lie down with the lion, and how humans, inspired by the precedent, happily follow suit. When Diane (Ginger Rogers) looks at George (Henry Fonda) more appreciatively once she believes his lovemaking (to another woman) has earned him the epithet of lion, she is succumbing to the power of language to act as a kind of aphrodisiac, creating desire where none existed before.[6] But such animal love insinuates something darker and funnier yet: that Diane, who yearns for the virile love enjoyed by Squirrel, and George, suddenly catapulted to king of beasts, are excited by each other as members not of the same species but of radically distinct ones.

Popular culture seems enamored with the proposition that men are from Mars and women from Venus, but there is no need to go to such extraterrestrial lengths for metaphors illuminating sexual difference. The comedy of a post-Darwinian and post-Freudian age provides us with an explanation closer to home — men and women, whatever their biological classification, emotionally constitute two different species. In *Red Dust,* Vantine (Jean Harlow) pauses in the middle of reading to a bedridden Dennis Carson (Clark Gable) tales of Peter Cottontail when she spots such interspecies foolery afoot: "A chipmunk and a rabbit. Say, I wonder how this comes out!" Hawks goes the distance in literalizing this metaphor of the sex relation in *Bringing Up Baby,* a movie that dares to imagine what might happen should a real leopard take a fancy to a dog. Who could predict what brave new world — or at least new life form — might be called into being through such interspecies encounters?

What the looming figure of David's brontosaurus brings to the film, then — besides a great prop! — is the perspective of what we might call Darwinian comedy. The central theme is the drama, usually played as farce, of sexual selection. In Darwin's succinct and sober formulation, sexual selection depends "on a struggle between the males for possession of the females."[7] Victory is generally reserved for the male who has the most vigor, best weapons, or simply the greatest physical charm. That David begins the film engaged to a Miss Swallow (Virginia Walker) and ends up being dubbed by Susan a regular Don Swan affiliates him with the bird kingdom, where looks usually count for more than brawn in the competition for mates. Instead of the dominance rituals that install, for example, the lion in his pride, sexual rivalry among birds takes the entertaining form of an aesthetic performance in which, according to Darwin, "successive males display their gorgeous plumage and perform strange antics before the females, which, standing by as spectators, at last choose the most attractive partner."[8] Comedy, which favors wit and guile over force, humor over magnificence, prefers to stage the sexual combat according to avian rather than leonine rules of engagement.

In American comic film, no one, with the possible exception of William Powell, performs the rites of courtship with more primal delight and instinctual finesse than Cary Grant. Grant and Powell are expert in the physical comedy of male display, but this should not blind us to the central human fact of Darwinian comedy: that the sexual outcome is determined by the female's preference for the male who strikes her as the most comely. The standard of male comeliness is not handsomeness (although Grant certainly has that) but the ability to amuse, both in the common sense of to entertain and also in the now sadly obsolete sense of astonishing the eye.[9] The jubilant partnership of Myrna Loy and William Powell is American film's tribute to the unassailable wisdom of woman's selecting her mate on such grounds. Indeed, there is nothing more optically exquisite in movie comedy than watching Myrna Loy, arching her brows, take in Powell's droll manner with the bemused and appreciative air of a connoisseur.

No one gives men the eye like Myrna Loy, and she does it without a trace of vulgarity or acquisitiveness. Watching her watching Powell in films like *Love Crazy*, where his Steve Ireland feigns madness and primly adorns himself in dowager-drag to win back his place in her heart, or *Libeled Lady*, where his Bill Chandler gives a hilarious impression of fly-casting, even though he has never been fishing in his life, is to see how much fun a woman might have in exercising her natural right to sexual selection. Myrna Loy's characters—Susan Ireland in *Love Crazy* and Connie Allenbury in *Libeled Lady*—are so far

The Darwinian comedy of courtship lands Cary Grant behind bars, while Katharine Hepburn is still at large in *Bringing Up Baby*

advanced on the evolutionary scale that they can afford to let primitive instinct have its say in making their impeccable judgments. Loy indulges Powell's buffoonery, knowing full well that his antic disposition represents a Darwinian tribute to herself as an object worthy to be wooed and won. Out of such knowledge Darwinian comedy is made.

In *Bringing Up Baby,* the comedy is in danger of being over before it begins. The male seems to have already been chosen by Miss Swallow, a Darwinian spoilsport who refuses the very thought of procreation (both as act and outcome). The only way the comedy can get going is to reverse gears—and roles—and present the sexual struggle as a rivalry between two kinds of women: the rationalist miss, all work and no play, who views marriage as a professional partnership unencumbered by "domestic entanglements of any kind"; and a fast-talking dame with a natural talent for game- and role-playing. This dame may be dizzy, but she is also determined to secure her sexual choice—a man who doesn't want to play with her but whom she insists on having, if for no other reasons than he is so good looking without his glasses. No one else in the film sees in the bespectacled Dr. David Huxley the dreamboat Susan sees, which is the first sign we have of her superior sexual judgment. Her choice must be adjudged *instinctually* right, if socially and psychologically incomprehensible to just about anybody in the film, including David himself, who spends most of the film insisting that he is engaged elsewhere.

We thus cannot fully appreciate, much less endorse, Susan Vance's license as a fast-talking dame who says and acts on any zany idea that pops into her head (many of them of questionable legality) unless we understand her comic and social role as a Mendelian renegade. Her surname immediately alerts us to her vanguard status, encouraging us to regard her not as a prime specimen of her class but as a singular human type. Indeed, as played by Katharine Hepburn, Susan Vance is a particularly fine (and refined) if madcap incarnation of the "Hawksian woman." The Hawksian woman was a female type first identified by Naomi Wise. As Wise described and commended her, the Hawksian woman was a radical screen presence who existed apart or beyond the more stolid conventions of movie womanhood. Unlike her counterparts in standard adventure films, whose characters conformed to flat stereotypes of "good" woman or "bad" girl, she was given consequential roles to play and was "if anything, superior to the heroes": "The good girl and the bad girl are fused into a single, heroic heroine, who is both sexual and valuable." [10] And smart. Experience is not lost on her, nor is she passive in confronting the physical and social facts of her life. The Hawksian woman makes her choices "by personal will rather than by social and economic pressures." However amateurish her pursuits might appear, she in fact exemplifies the "professional human being." [11] If true, this is quite heartening, although one wonders whether this new form of social and screen life—the professional (as opposed to the amateur?) human being—isn't so much a desired synthesis as an improbable oxymoron. Surely becoming a successful human being entails more than professional skills in decision making and emotional self-management. Still, if we take self-reliance to constitute an Emersonian profession of sorts, although not one by which you can reasonably expect to earn a living, this seems as good a way as any of describing what is new in the kind of self-dependence the Hawksian woman exhibits in her working and private life.

Yet neither Wise, who recognized that the Hawksian woman represented an original screen creation, nor Leigh Brackett, who worked with Hawks in films like *The Big Sleep* and *Rio Bravo* and agreed with Wise that the Hawksian woman was a "whole and complete human being in her own right . . . minus the hero's hang-ups,"[12] cast a glance at her most attractive comic avatars, Susan Vance and *His Girl Friday's* Hildy Johnson (Rosalind Russell, herself a cross-sexual mutation on a male original from *The Front Page*). This is a regrettable but easily amended oversight, given that these Hawksian heroines, who could talk faster and in general outperform the men they are paired with, become, unlike their counterparts in the adventure films, more than a fantasy-woman emotionally coded to male specifications. Released into the more libertarian world of comedy, the Hawksian woman enlarges her character into a true mate, contributing not only what is compatible and complementary but missing in the male. Biology since Aristotle and religious tradition since time immemorial have regarded the male form as the image of completeness, but in the sexual logic of Hawksian comedy, which specializes in upending rather than endorsing venerable commonplaces, it is often the woman who represents the possibility of a complete humanity. The Hawksian woman, in flouting traditional gender roles, prepares the way for new modes of sexual organization. In the face of her achievement, the Hawksian man, like Thurber's emotionally backward, gibbous male, is often left pleading with the advancing female, "Wait for baby!"

This is surely one of the meanings lurking in the title, *Bringing Up Baby,* which encapsulates the emotional plot of Hawksian comedy. At the heart of the movie is an extravagantly silly sexual and morphological pun that plays on the various ways that the male of the species may be "brought up" by a female entrusted with his care and development. The first reference to a baby, after the title, is to the brontosaurus that will assume, insists Miss Swallow, the role of symbolic "child" in their union, a substitution that alerts us to how weird, as well as self-defeating, human object choice can be. More positively, it introduces into the comedy the fantastical possibility of cross-species attachments, a possibility that will flower in the midnight frolics of a leopard and a dog. It is to this leopard, in fact, that the actual "character" of Baby is assigned, a leopard so named because he can be cajoled into doing just about anything once he hears the plaintive strains of "I Can't Give You Anything but Love, Baby," a deliciously ironic song in a movie where Baby gets to devour thirty pounds of raw steak, not to mention an assortment of chickens and ducks and a couple of swans, and where the heroine will eventually deliver into the hands of her "baby" a check for a million dollars.

But Hawks is not a director who traffics in the kind of social satire that would make much, way too much, out of such piddling discrepancies between sentimental lyrics and hard facts. What he does respond to is "baby" as a term of endearment, and what particularly endears him about Baby the leopard is that he obligingly serves as a totem for comic humanity — its outsized appetites and general state of emotional underdevelopment. That Baby, prompted by Susan, takes to "following" David suggests all kinds of identifications between leopard and the man who has devoted his life to the study of extinct creatures. It suggests, for example, that Baby is Susan's delegate in her erotic pursuit of David, and so may activate the male's irrational fear of woman's feline sexuality stalking and even devouring him. Certainly David has Baby's fearsome sexuality very much on his mind when he sees Baby cavorting with George, the scrappy family dog who has secreted his precious dinosaur bone, and he openly worries that at any minute Baby's play might take a deadly turn and George be devoured. Should that happen, he worries, his intercostal clavicle will be gone forever! To Susan, of course, such friendly capering is an obvious — and reassuring — sign that they like each other.

Hawks directs the scene as if both are right. The scene is magically prolonged, lasting just a minute or so longer than is comfortable. In this hushed moment of exquisite tension, we may glimpse something of the deep mystery of sexual engagement. With every growl and yap, we become less sure of what we are hearing — the sexual signals of animal foreplay or ominous rumblings of a predator toying with his prey? That we don't see how Baby and George disengage leaves the mystery of their moonlit frolics unresolved — Baby caged is one thing; Baby on the prowl is another. To dramatize rather than resolve the enigma of Baby's nature, the film introduces, as a final complication in Susan's pursuit of David, a preposterous plot about Baby's "double," a bad cat who mauled a man to death. Comic doubling is usually reserved for human players, but here the bad cat and the good Baby dramatize two views of female sexuality on the loose, both safely "caged" at movie's end.

But Baby could also serve as a totemic double not for female sexuality but for the persona assumed by Cary Grant as a Hawksian comic hero, ready to do a woman's bidding for a song.[13] Gary Cooper may be the most refashioned man in vintage Hollywood comedy, but Grant is the one who proved most adaptable to the female demands made on him, the man genially available to "suffer" completion, not just remodeling, at female hands. In *Bringing Up Baby* he is the pondering, ponderous scientist who must add play to his repertoire of successful human adaptations; in *His Girl Friday* he is a thoroughly unprincipled editor who must finally yield to his wife's superior instincts for the "human interest" that makes any story worthy of being told; in *I Was a Male War Bride* (1949) he is a former army officer who dissembles his sex in order to book passage home along with his American wife (Ann Sheridan, in an alarmingly efficient impersonation of a WAC); in *Monkey Business,* the coda, as it were, of Hawks's comic history of the sexes, he again plays a scientist, this time one who experiments, as Grant reportedly did in his private life, with rejuvenation formulae. All these comic roles call on him to tamper with, even deface, his physical image—sometimes to grotesque effect, as in *I Was a Male War Bride,* where he not only cross-dresses but wears a wig made of a horse tail that only enhances the maleness of his features and gives his face the denatured look of a gargoyle. Grant's aptitude for zoomorphic mutations reaches a nadir in *Monkey Business,* which presents the distressing spectacle of Grant capering with and like a chimpanzee.[14]

Atavism always lurks as an evolutionary detour for Hawksian men and woman on their way to a more liberated humanity. If, for example, the Hawksian woman proceeds too far into the hinterlands of human possibility, if she proves too precipitous in bringing baby up to new emotional plateaus, the entire comic venture may collapse, as Grant in fact does in the penultimate scene of *Bringing Up Baby.* There, in the jailhouse where all the comic society has assembled—

sheriff, shrink, family lawyer, circus workers, Susan's aunt and her big game–hunter escort, Susan, and Miss Swallow, not to mention *two* leopards—he suddenly finds himself, chair and whip in hand, defending the "defenseless" Susan against a snarling predator, whom he successfully maneuvers into a jail cell. His newfound consciousness of who he is, what he has shown himself capable of (caging a "bad" leopard, for one thing), and whom he actually loves proves too much for his emotional brain to handle. He consequently faints into the female arms—Susan's, not Miss Swallow's—that are ready, willing, and able to receive him.[15] That those arms are capable of supporting his weight is a physical fact that is reciprocated in the final scene of the film, in which David, dangling Susan by a single arm, pulls her to safety as she is about to plummet to the floor. Yet throughout her ordeal, she, unlike him, never loses consciousness.

That the capacity for sustained consciousness is an important measure of the evolutionary distance we have traveled since Thurber's gibbous creatures is signaled by the first fully fleshed human image that greets us after the titles, themselves composed of stick figures that appear to be the work either of a child or a self-conscious primitivist. It is a seated figure of a man assuming the contemplative pose, as many critics of the film have noted, of Rodin's *The Thinker*. This man is in fact perched on a scaffold that elevates him above the presumably less cerebral creatures below. It is to this sanctuary that this eagle—or fledgling?—of thought will retreat at the end of the film in one last and unavailing attempt to escape the irrational, confused world, populated by leopards, loons, and sundry variety of beast and fowl. For the moment, however, the only clue we have that something might be amiss is that his head, seat of consciousness, is visually aligned with that of the pea-brained dinosaur head decorating the wall behind him, hardly an auspicious omen, but auspicious or not, a true indication of the imminent dethronement of his majesty, the rational ego.

In the course of the next forty-eight hours, David (for it is he, our paleontologist-hero) will descend from his lofty perch, where reason flatters itself that it reigns supreme, don all manner of dress and adopt all manner of gaits. The change of clothes and modifications in gait at once facilitate and symbolize the devolution that will liberate the animal nature held captive within him. We may greet his descent from on high, then, as his first step in a necessary and eventually happy regression, since in lowering himself he begins slowly to shed his inhibitions and then those fretful attitudes—or, as Freud called them, the discontents—that he has acquired on the path to his present state of civilization.

The "molting" of David Huxley, if we can call it that, can be accomplished only in the "wilds" of Connecticut (surely a New Yorker's view of the rustic environs). And we can see that the change of scene is having an invigorating effect. The very drive to the country not only calls on David to revive long-dormant instincts but to exercise his language skills in unexpected, even imaginative ways. After Susan collides with a chicken truck, sending Baby in hot pursuit of a midday snack, David must retrieve the marauding beast, helped only by adrenaline and the instinct of the hunt. We don't see the chase, only the comic results: Baby contentedly returned to the back seat, David covered with feathers, a picture of consternation. What galls him, we soon learn, is not just Susan's erratic driving, but the $150 a farmer extracted in compensation for Baby's devouring a pair of swans. When Susan reminds him that they wouldn't have had to pay if he had run as she had urged, David, with all the somberness required of an absurdist hero, formulates his first Dadaist aphorism: "When a man is wrestling with a leopard in the middle of a pond, he is in no position to run."

While it is doubtful that such a finding might assist him in his routine comings and goings, it might prove useful in surviving the "series of misadventures from beginning to end" that make up, according to David, his life since he met Susan. Certainly the very fact that David could utter such a perfectly absurd yet indisputably self-evident proposition means that he is already adapting to the nonsense world into which he has fallen. Susan remarks the incipient change when they arrive at their destination and she begins picking off swan and chicken feathers from his suit. "You're shedding," she explains when he glowers at her impatiently over her intimate ministrations, which in fact resemble the grooming rituals practiced by apes and baboons. But the real molting takes place within David's cluttered psyche. Soon he will be plucked clean of all rational plumage. All this is as it should be.

By the curious logic of evolution that decrees that *on doit reculer pour mieux sauter,* David must revert to some lower, or, to be less prejudicial, some anterior order of consciousness before he can re-ascend to greet the happier future that awaits him. This man has been working hard for four years but secretly yearning for a honeymoon. He now deserves his holiday.

Not just any holiday, but a "holiday barring out of the pedant Reflection."[16] It was just such a holiday that Charles Lamb sought and found in the "artificial comedy" of the Restoration and eighteenth-century theater whenever he felt the need to "take an airing beyond the diocese of strict conscience" and, "for a dream-while or so, to imagine a world with no meddling restrictions."[17] David would never take such a holiday by himself, although he would clearly like to. One of the first things he wishes for when he learns that the museum's expedition has finally found—after four long years—the intercostal clavicle needed to complete the brontosaurus, is that he and Miss Swallow, scheduled to marry within the next twenty-four hours, will go on a honeymoon. She immediately vetoes the suggestion, reminding him that their union must entail "no domestic entanglements." The word entanglements conjures up all sorts of (lawfully) lascivious images of entwining limbs, as David's feeble mutter of disappointment seems to indicate. He hesitantly seeks to clarify the terms of their contract—"You mean children and all that sort of thing?" he asks. "Exactly. This will be our child," she confirms, gesturing toward the lumbering brontosaurus behind them. Such is the rebuke—one can hardly call it repartee—with which Miss Swallow greets David's efforts to bar out the pedant reflection (whose pose, of course, he had assumed in our first glimpse of him).

It is difficult to find more impressive *negative* proof of our primary axiom—that talk is sexy, female talk especially so. Miss Swallow, whose name befits her clipped way with words, fails the comic loquacity test. She is a perfect foil for Susan, a fast-talking dame who, in an excited moment, improvises a criminal moniker for herself, Swinging Door Susie, and offers to open her puss and shoot the works. By their talk we shall know them. It should thus come as no surprise, once we have grasped the relation between sex and speech, that it is the fast-talking dame, with her freer manners and healthier instincts, that will take

David on the holiday of his life, luring him into a dream world beyond the diocese of conscience (since once in this world, a woman can steal another woman's fiancé with the heedless charm of a headstrong Restoration heroine) if not outside the precincts of the law (Susan and David's escapades do finally land them in jail).[18]

Such holiday diversions, much less the prospect of pleasurable domestic entanglements, are not even remotely in view as David ponders the initial problem preoccupying him—where does the bone he is holding fit in the skeleton he has been reconstructing for four long years? We will never really discover where it does belong, only where it definitely will not fit—in the tail. To find a function as well as a place for the bone is as pressing a piece of comic business as retrieving the intercostal clavicle that Susan and the dog, George, mistook for just any old bone, which, in fact, in many ways it is. This information, however negligible it might appear, is actually quite essential for appreciating the comic doings that follow. First we should remark that David begins the film missing a tail, a significant detail in light of the Darwinian fact that the tail is one of the appendages we have jettisoned on our way up the evolutionary ladder. That David will later take on the alias of Mr. Bone, a name conferred on him by the lovestruck Susan, increases our suspicion that this man is a kind of missing link to the childhood of our race, just as Susan is a link to its liberated future.

This opening allusion to a tail thus initiates a series of double entendres that, as Stanley Cavell tactfully yet never prudishly insists, hover near what Freud would have called "smut," the openly obscene or dirty joke.[19] I cannot afford to be quite so delicate in this instance. This perplexity about where the man should put his bone, the first of many tail jokes, really *is* a laughing matter. The laughs will eventually compose and choreograph themselves into a mating ritual in which David and Susan will try all sorts of positions and angles vis-à-vis each other until their bodies find their final (cinematic) alignment. Indeed, the whole secret of their comic destiny seems to hinge on David's relationship to his bones. For in fact, he has several bones to worry about at the beginning of what he will finally admit was the best day in his entire life.

No wonder, then, that Susan is inspired to bestow on him the hilarious but apt alias of Mr. Bone. Never play on people's names is one of the first interdictions on the child's free play with words, but as Susan already has demonstrated in calling the sober Mr. Peabody "Boopie" (George Irving), this is another law that she blithely ignores. Later, when her hijinks land them both in jail, she will rechristen David, twice within two minutes, Jerry the Nipper and Don Swan. We tolerate, even delight, in such pet names, because they are created out of affection. Derision has no role in their formation. But this should not lull us into overlooking that there is a delinquent element in Susan's verbal freedoms, just as there is in her habit of "borrowing" other people's cars. We might put it negatively and say that Susan's penchant for treating words as toys of thought is a sign that she has yet to complete her course in human development, of which a primary part, Freud maintained, is "the child's education in logical thinking and in distinguishing between what is true and false in reality."[20] Or we could interpret her freedoms positively, as an imaginative means of withdrawing from the "pressure of critical reason" and rebelling against the "compulsion of logic and reality." Obviously, I take the latter view of her fast talk.

David will too, although not at first. David, who comes into the film assuming the pose of critical reason, initially dismisses Susan's logical nonsense. "It never will be clear as long as she's explaining it," he declares when Susan attempts to sort out a mixup of purses (another Freudian joke waiting for a smut-minded interpreter). In fact, her explanation is scrupulously correct, as absurdist statements usually are. David, as he is drawn irresistibly into Susan's comic orbit, shows an unexpected aptitude for the delirious logic of fast talk. We are given an early indication of how contagious Susan's verbal style will be when he reports to Miss Swallow the indecisive outcome of his meeting with Mr. Peabody. "Yes, I did see Mr. Peabody, but I didn't see him. Yes, I spoke to him twice, but I didn't talk to him." Only a modern-language philosopher could be more precise in insisting on the difference between seeing as an act of perception and seeing as an encounter in proximate space; between speech as an acoustic phenomenon and speech as an act of communication. What is someone's nonsense is another's exactitude.

Susan's talk is rich in such constructions that may defy common usage. David has as much need of her verbal wealth as he has of her aunt's million dollars, perhaps more, since Susan's verbal fortune, like the treasure in some Oriental tale, has the power to effect magical transformations. For one thing, Susan's fast talk, like her games and her loose and playful manner, can turn a grown man into a hyperactive child. (David's kinetic energy increases during the course of the film; he begins the film seated, and by the middle of the film he literally cannot sit still in his anxiety to "tail" the dog who may lead him to his bone.) Of course, the childhood to which Susan's imaginative ruses and screwball talk restore him does not reemerge in its original state of innocence and naivete but in the altered form of a regressive fixation.

Fixation seems the right term to describe David's psychological state throughout much of the film as he obsesses about the whereabouts of his bone. It is certainly a concept that captures Susan's attention, then her sexual imagination. Happening to chance upon a psychiatrist, Mr. Lehman (Fritz Feld), at the nightclub where she also has met up with David, she takes advantage of the opportunity to press for an explanation for what seems to her his odd way of fervently approaching her, then coolly shunning her. The obliging doctor doesn't require too many details before he delivers, with the grave pomposity of his tribe, his expert opinion: "The love impulse in man very frequently reveals itself in terms of conflict." Susan slowly repeats the psychiatric mantra, as if committing to memory the latest pronouncement of the Delphic oracle. And so it might as well be, since on this metaphor both Darwinians and Freudians agree: love is a struggle in the Darwinian parlance, a conflicted object choice in the Freudian one. Like a child suspecting that a game is afoot, her whole attitude toward David visibly changes once she is the object of his fixation. The entire last half of the film, in fact, might be read, psychoanalytically that is, as Susan's madcap efforts to get David to switch his fixation from his bone to her.

That he has all the makings of an obsessive compulsive is apparent from his first foray into the larger public world, the golf course where he hopes to plead, between holes, with Mr. Peabody for the million dollars the museum needs if it is to continue sponsoring his work. But he gets diverted, or rather his ball does, by a woman who plays with considerable more skill and sense of purpose. It seems that by mistake she has played his ball, the first of many usurpations of which she can be accused (later she will take his car, then his clothes, and finally, through her canine delegate George, his precious bone). David's repeated attempts to retrieve the hijacked golf ball take on that classic form of comic fixation — the running gag. In determined pursuit of what, after all, is only a ball, he will continually call back to his host: "I'll be with you in a minute, Mr. Peabody!" Fateful name! Whether we take it as a sly reference to the namesake of New Haven's famous Peabody Museum of Natural History or a joke on "baby's" (any baby's) puny stature before he has been "brought up" to his full size — Peabody is a man to be perpetually put off. In the meantime, David pursues this Diana of the links as she haughtily plays through the green, sinks her putt, and takes off in his car without giving his claims the slightest notice. The question is, why does he persist in his pursuit, to the point of jumping on the running board of a moving car? What verbal concession does he hope to extract that is worth putting off Mr. Peabody?

Maybe David is simply acting out a wish to exchange the dour company of Miss Swallow for the rambunctious playfulness of Miss Vance. This switch in female mentors proves not only emotionally invigorating but morally instructive. It is, after all, in his initial bout with Susan Vance that he gets his first lesson in the limits of the first-person possessive pronoun. In David's initial meeting with Susan he vainly attempts to convince her that she has, mistakenly, he is willing to believe, played his golf ball. He soon finds himself talking in (and about) circles:

> DAVID: Oh, my, this is so silly. I never saw such— [*he reaches for the ball in the cup*]. There, you see it, it's a circle.
> SUSAN: Well, of course it is. Do you think it would run if it were square?
> DAVID: No. I have reference to a mark on the ball. That proves it's a Pro-Flight, and that's my ball!

Soon he is making similar claims, equally true but unavailing, about the car she is trying to maneuver out of the parking lot. The woman's charge of bringing up baby morally requires that she point out to this grown man the primary narcissism of the claims he is making. "*Your* ball, *your* car," she repeats with dripping irony. "Is there anything in the world that doesn't belong to you?" "Yes, thank heaven. You!" Only a child would think this a witty rejoinder. A more substantive comic truth is concealed in her irony—that, indeed, it all does belong to him—ball, car, and eventually the woman herself, but only the last is the one he will come to desire.

Not that he is ready to admit to anything but aversion when they next meet in a posh supper club. "You don't think I did that intentionally," she protests after involving David in yet another ownership dispute, this time involving her purse, which she had left in his custody. "If could think, I would have run the minute I saw you." That he didn't run means that the pedant reflection is already in flight and that he is unconsciously primed for his holiday. It begins, however, as holidays often do, on an anxious note. David is eager to run down Mr. Peabody, Susan to run down David. In her insistent effort to get him to listen to her, she pulls at his coattails, and, not unexpectedly, they rip. On the links she refuses to concede him anything. Apparently this holds only while objects remain intact. Once they are torn or broken, they revert to him: "Oh, you've torn your coat," she observes with the all the dispassion of a disinterested bystander. It is a concession of the obvious that leaves him, not for the first time in their young acquaintance, speechless. This bit of verbal impertinence will complete the early phase of their courtship, in which their relation to each other was largely dependent on the various uses they made of possessive pronouns. Now they progress to a second phase, in which they will experiment with the more difficult conjugations of the first person plural. David is the first to test out this possible usage: "Let's play a game," David sarcastically proposes. "Watch. I'll put my hand over my eyes and then you go away. . . . I'll count to ten, and when I take my hand down you'll be gone."

It would be easy to subscribe to the theory that the game David proposes is only an expedient way of getting rid of the woman he regards as a petty thief and now a major nuisance. Yet given that we have just made the acquaintance of a shrink, we shouldn't summarily dismiss the possibility that David may have unconscious motives for suggesting this *particular* game. We might infer, for instance, that David is summoning an ancestral memory of a game the baby learns, indeed often existentially *needs,* to play. This is the game Freud called the "Fort da" game after observing a child whose only way of playing with his toys was to make them disappear. When the object vanished from sight, the child would cry "Fort" ("gone"); when he retrieved the object, he greeted its reappearance with a triumphant "da" ("there"). Freud attached great significance to this game, arguing that it represented the "child's great cultural achievement—the instinctual renunciation . . . which he made in allowing his mother to go away without protesting."[21] This primal version of hide and seek must appeal powerfully to a man like David, whose spends almost the last half of the film in search of a lost—well, hijacked—object.

We should note that Susan, for whom civilization has apparently never inspired the least discontent, is not so much unsympathetic as uncomprehending of the importance that David attaches to his bone. When a distraught David informs Susan that it took five years and three expeditions to find the intercostal clavicle, she responds with a suggestion that is at once inspired and ludicrous: "Well, now that they know where to find it, can't they get another one?" For Susan, as for George, David's rare intercostal clavicle is just another old bone. George, whose name literally means earthworker, treats it as he would any plaything, and instinctively, perhaps a little maliciously, returns it to the ground.[22] After an afternoon spent rummaging the earth with demiurgic George, the yard looks like a pet cemetery pitted with freshly dug graves.

The paleontologist (another earthworker) who rummages in the dirt with a dog is far from the sedate thinker with his bone securely in his possession. Hawks found something profoundly funny about men subjected to such comic degradation. When asked if he intentionally set out to humiliate Grant's character in *Bringing Up Baby,* Hawks, without second-guessing himself, simply admitted that "anything we could do to humiliate him, to put him down and let her sail blithely along, made it what I thought was funny. I think it's fun to have a woman dominant and let the man be funniest."[23] For Hawks himself, the woman is foremost a creature of fun. She not only has fun, but makes those who yield to her powers funny in a way they might never be on their own. (How drab is David in his lab coat, how alluring and lively in Susan's negligee!) Fun is to be had by all, in the Hawksian sexual universe, as long as the female is dominant. She is the blithe Prospero of comic misadventures, and the male assumes the aspect of a risible creature (still, the best part of any comedy is proverbially the clown). There is a dose of cruelty in this comic formula, but it has an astringent, purgative effect. The emotional logic seems to be that to become a full human being necessitates the man's sacrificing his prerogatives as a civilized "superior" male answerable only to himself.

David subsumes these prerogatives under the name of "dignity," of which he claims to possess quite a lot and which he believes to be compromised by his very association with Susan. Dignity is the precise word David supplies to explain his resistance to the life of improvised misadventures to which Susan seems to be calling him. "My future wife," he informs her, "has always regarded me as a man of some dignity. Privately, I'm convinced that I have some dignity. Now it isn't that I don't like you, Susan, because, after all, in moments of quiet, I'm strangely drawn to you, but, well, there haven't been any quiet moments. Our relationship has been a series of misadventures from beginning to end." First, let us note that David makes this declaration at the dawn of what he will later admit to be the happiest day of his life. Second, let us recognize that this thinker either instinctively or rationally opposes his private conviction that he is a man of some dignity to his strange attraction to Susan. Neither David nor the film seem unduly alarmed by the prospect of his sacrificing his dignity if it means having Susan—David because he thinks he still can keep his dignity (which he can't and won't), the film because it wants him to lose it, since he will gain in its place something more vital—a clearer sense of what he is feeling and what he wants.

Herein we confront the great paradox of Darwinian comedy: that man's greatest natural achievement—sexual happiness and procreative power—comes at the cost of his dignity. A false dignity, of course, the kind that men often mistake as their greatest cultural as well as personal achievement, the stiff and starched dignity in which their social self is epitomized and displayed. This great, hard, and unyielding comic truth is spelled out with remorseless clarity in Ingmar Bergman's sublime *Smiles of a Summer Night* (1955). Its heroine and presiding genius is Desiree Armfeldt (Eva Dahlbeck), the actress skilled in the arts and feints of love, in whose power the happiness of three couples of various ages and dispositions rests. On stage she plays a sexual charmer who proclaims that love succeeds only when the dignity of man is uncompromised, a proposition that the actress nightly repeats but that she questions, indeed schemes to refute, in her life off stage. The object of her love, the extremely correct Lawyer Egerman (Fredrik Gunnar Björnstrand), endures a series of affronts to his dignity once he leaves his own doorstep, the most literal and inconsequential being his fall into the muddied waters before Desiree's house, the most spiritually grave his humiliation at the flight of his young wife with his own young son. Egerman attains his full humanity only after he has been publicly humiliated and emotionally mortified.

In *Bringing Up Baby,* David will not undergo such extreme mortification. As his sartorial misadventure in the nightclub shows, the most effective assaults on David's dignity are orchestrated with attacks, in one instance a raid, on his clothes.[24] It is the first of many changes of dress (preliminary to deeper changes of habit that the film envisions for him) that David will have to make in the course of the movie. He will wear, in the course of two days, the scientist's customary lab coat, golfing attire, formal dress, a peignoir, and riding breeches. Although there is undeniably an element of child's play (that is, "dress up") in all these sartorial masquerades, all are outfits that symbolize adult activities, even adult games. Adult attire, like command over language and an upright bearing, is what divides, as Anne Hollander eloquently argues, "self-aware human adults from careless infants and innocent beasts."[25]

The self-awareness that divides human adults from careless infants and innocent beasts is not yet David's. Although he assumes the pose of Rodin's Thinker, he doesn't suggest, either in his facial expressions or subsequent bodily gestures, that his thoughts are turned inward. Emotionally he seems to have somersaulted from the stage of careless infancy across the span of self-aware adulthood into a state of abstracted hypercivilization. When called on to adopt the dress and manner of the adult and worldly male, he appears decidedly ill at ease. His discomposure is obvious from the moment he shows up at a dinner club splendidly but uncomfortably sporting tails. We are asked to forget that this is Cary Grant, for whom, along with Fred Astaire, tails seemed to have been invented. Instead we are invited to enjoy the silly stage business he transacts with the hostess about where to put his hat (he will soon find a place for it). He is attired in formal wear that puts him as far as we have presently come from the nakedness of the creatures who might share many of our instincts, even several of our emotions, but not our need to cover ourselves. Susan is also interestingly attired, although a crucial part of her anatomy will be partially exposed before the evening is out. David's top hat completes its work as a comic prop by going from his head to her tail.

This sartorial cross-identification between man and woman does not come amiss in a comedy whose stars take us tantalizingly near the border where sexual differences dissolve into each other. Cross-dressing is the outward form of this psychic interchange between male and female partners. David, in fact, will be inveigled, when his work-day clothes are pirated by Susan in one of her many efforts to keep him from returning to the city and to Miss Swallow, into wearing a peignoir, one adorned with enough ruffles to qualify as a fetish object. In George Cukor's *Sylvia Scarlett* (1935), which first paired Grant with Hepburn, it was Hepburn's Sylvia who took to cross-dressing. Gender reversals are something these two stars bring out in each other.

But whereas Hepburn's sexual masquerade plays off something deeply androgynous in her looks and temperament, Grant's cross-dressing, both in *Bringing Up Baby* and *I Was a Male War Bride,* never for a moment leaves his fundamental masculinity in doubt. In *I Was a Male War Bride,* the sailor admitting him on board ship punctu-ates the cross-dressing gag by grimacing (somewhat ungallantly) at the very sight of him.[26] In *Bringing Up Baby,* David's only real moment of masculine protest comes when he finds himself answering the door to admit Susan's newly arrived Aunt Elizabeth Carlton Random (May Robson) in his "ridiculous" outfit, as Aunt Random stoutly proclaims it. Grant makes the most of his chance to sneak a line past the Pro-duction Code when Aunt Random asks him why he is wearing clothes that make him look "perfectly idiotic": "Because I just went gay all of a sudden." Later, to punctuate his point and his frustration in this sudden shift (or outing) of identity, he stomps imperiously on Susan's foot and cows Aunt Elizabeth into an uncharacteristic submissiveness. He makes clear his manly wants—he wants his clothes, he wants to go back to town, he wants to get married (although not to Susan). The women seem to comply, at least with his request for regular (manly) clothes. Once back in "sporting" clothes, David is never this loudly assertive again.

The comedy of attire is accentuated by the various human and animal gaits that differentiate David and Susan as a duckling from a swan, or, to put it in David's own scientific language, an embryonic from an advanced life form. On the links, David is all distracted and hapless motion, chasing Susan down the fairway while frantically re-assuring Mr. Peabody that he'll be with him in a minute. Susan's stride, in glorious contrast, is athletic and purposeful, her every movement a graceful uncoiling of directed energy. Hepburn's athleticism is mag-nificently on display in *Pat and Mike* (1952), but the story strips her of the emotional strength that gives her sinewy arms their glisten. The comedy is based on the dreary premise that a woman of her physi-cal talent will become psychically enfeebled, even masochistic, in the presence of her patronizing fiancé. (Spencer Tracy's Mike, a promoter, will rehabilitate her psyche as well as her sports career). Even Cukor, normally so tactful in his direction of Hepburn, doesn't depart from Philip Barry's mean-spirited insinuation in *The Philadelphia Story* that Hepburn's Tracy Lord, a superb swimmer, keeps her body so svelte as part of the ritualized regimen she observes as Virgin Goddess. And George Stevens, in giving Hepburn her comeuppance in *Woman of the Year,* would like us to believe that Hepburn's Tess Harding is so unco-ordinated that she couldn't possibly make toast, brew coffee, and bake waffles without making an unholy mess of the kitchen.

Only Hawks bought out something genuinely fanciful in Hep-burn's superbly conditioned body. Her athleticism is integral to her character here and to the comic mischief she works to keep David within her sights. She skips, ambles, strolls, lopes, ducks, crouches, squats, and in general reproduces the entire repertoire of human pos-tures and gaits, not to mention executing a series of pratfalls that would do the most seasoned farceur proud. But her supreme moment of evo-lutionary madcap arrives when she loses her heel after taking one of the many falls she laughingly endures during the moonlit night she spends searching for David's bone. Unhurt, she springs up ready to resume the chase. Once upright, she discovers the asymmetry of her posture, and, humming a military air, struts delightedly like a noncombatant on parade. Bobbing up and down, she even provides a Darwinian ex-planation for her new gait: "I was born on the side of a hill." For a brief comic moment we seem to be witnessing a new bodily adaptation.

This is only one of the small wonders awaiting us during the magi-cal night to which Hawks's Darwinian comedy has been leading us. Major Horace Applegate (Charles Ruggles), Aunt Elizabeth's guest and a paid-up member of the Explorer's Club, sets the tone and theme of the evening by giving an accomplished imitation of the mating cry of a leopard. To his astonishment, he receives a lovelorn reply, which he mistakenly, though understandably, takes to be that of a loon. Natural law seems to be momentarily suspended as species seem to be calling out to species. Aunt Elizabeth will later confess, to Major Applegate's chagrin, that the mating call of the loon and leopard sound very much the same to her. Mixed signals in the human order are to be expected, but that animals should be prey to the same intemperate, even perverse urges for creatures not of their kind is a grave as well as oddly appeal-ing thought. This thought materializes in the visual marvel of *Bringing Up Baby*—Baby and George entangled in a web of moonlight. Against all the teachings of our science, we are entertained with the wondrous possibility that a leopard might find much to like—besides his sup-per—in a dog. The sight of Baby and George interrupts David and Susan's wild chase like a divine vision of a paradise momentarily re-gained, in which, if the lion would lie down with lamb, so the leopard with the terrier.[27]

Still, David's question, "But how long can it last," lingers in the air, reminding us, in the very heart of enchantment, how vulnerable the love impulse, whether in man or beast, is to the eroding action of time and the sudden eruptions of destructive instinct. Eventually the spirit of carnival (symbolized by the circus being in town) gives way to more sober, Lenten reflections. Such as the following: the sexual embrace, however ecstatic, and the human adventure, however playful, represent but a fugitive, indeed fragile, instant when viewed from the perspective of Darwinian time. This is a perspective that the film itself will ostentatiously take in the closing moments of the film. Suddenly the entire visual vocabulary of the film changes, as if beginning to invent a new cinematic language. The visual naturalism that had kept this Darwinian comedy tethered to reality is abandoned as the camera takes up one strange, startling angle after another, some of them from a point of view that seems hardly human.

The last scene takes place a ritual three days after the lunatic night that transformed David from a thinker into a man of action, the "hero," as Susan proclaims him, who rescued her from a "bad" leopard. Either the encounter or the acclaim went to his head and he fainted into Susan's arms, but when we next see him he is fully restored to consciousness and, apparently, to his former self. There he is in his lab coat, with Miss Swallow, as censorious as ever, briskly dismissing him as just a butterfly. Unaccountably, even disturbingly, neither his face, his demeanor, his clothes, nor his words suggest that he has been altered in the slightest by his misadventures in the company of Susan, Baby, and George. He even resumes his initial pose in the film, head in hand, although this time he seems to imitate and interpret the Thinker as a portrait in dejection rather than cerebration. Nothing else, though, seems to have changed, except perhaps for the worse. Nothing, that is, until Susan enters. We see her from David's peculiar vantage point, framed by the two forelegs of the brontosaurus, as if through an evolutionary gateway. It is the first but not the last genuinely odd shot of the film. Perhaps it is this initial glimpse of Susan, connecting her in some vaguely ominous way with saurian giants long extinct, that sends David scurrying up the scaffold, where, in a final game of hide and seek, he sequesters himself atop and behind the huge dinosaur bones. A low angle countershot shows Susan, stranded below, seeking and quickly finding him among all that ossification. We might conclude that a conservative sexual hierarchy is being restored by these high- and low-angle shots, David now looking down, Susan up, the man on top, the woman beneath and below him.

Such a conclusion would not only be premature but untenable for this couple, this director, and this film. The camera is quickly repositioned to defamiliarize our sense of where these two are located in the hierarchy of things by presenting them in the same frame, but from a side view and at a singular remove. Hawks invites us to view them aslant and from afar, taking up the point of a view of a detached, distanced, and hardly human perspective. The consciousness that looks upon Susan and David belongs to no one, but seems rather to align us as viewers with the perspective afforded by Darwinian time itself, which dwarfs the human figure, making it seem helpless, even pitiful.[28] This is what sexual selection might look like if contemplated by an Olympian observer for whom the entire story of human life might seem to be a series of misadventures that leave the species, like Susan after the brontosaurus skeleton collapses beneath her, dangling in midair.

She has been brought to this crisis by her determination to follow David wherever he may go, even to the summit of his professional life. To this end, she has come to deliver a check for a million dollars, along with the intercostal clavicle that George finally deposited in her shoe. Informing him of all these developments, she asks for forgiveness and, sensing its bestowal, begins to sway in instinctive response to David's counterconfession that he never had such a wonderful time, that it was because she was there that it was such a good time, that yes that means he likes her, but more, he thinks he loves her. The penalty for this liberating avowal is the destruction of the "baby" on which David had lavished four years (hardly an instant in the Darwinian calendar) and, it is to be presumed, his professional affection. The symbol of his arduous sublimation now lies in a heap of rubble at their feet. For the second time David drops the pose of thinker and acts the hero, pulling Susan to safety and into his waiting arms.

There remains little now that these declared lovers can say. To say much would be to open the floodgates of recrimination, but Susan, resuming her verbal dominance, supplies him with a speaking part. "Oh, oh, David, can you ever forgive me? You can and you still love me," she at once pleads and announces. Earlier she had promised that when she would go down she would go down quietly, but it is unlikely that she could ever keep that promise. And who watching the film really cares if she ever keeps her promise? Certainly not David, whose "Oh, dear . . . oh, my . . . hmmm" shows that he is the one who must go down quietly, capitulating to the incontrovertible truth and irresistible flow of her words. His "hmmm" is the last human utterance we hear in the film (one can hardly call it a word). It strikes a note of subsiding resistance to the female energy for love and destruction, but we would be mistaken to take it as a sigh of resignation or moral collapse. It is a sigh signaling his acceptance of the fact that this is the way life with her must be—a life of fun, but one perhaps without dignity and value, especially personal value, as he has understood it.

David's "hmmm" carries over like a benediction on the wreckage at their feet. Without that note of acceptance we might be too disconcerted by the comic mayhem that Susan's erotic energy has wrought. The immense waste of work is staggering, as Hawks insists on reminding us in the last shot of the film, of David and Susan embracing over the dinosaur rubble—not in triumph, but in perplexity. We might read this last view of them as something like a moral epilogue to the Darwinian comedy that we have just seen enacted: that humans may not randomly and freely substitute cultural for natural achievements. A reconstructed brontosaurus, that is, may never be sanctioned as a substitute for a baby. That this parable is visually related to us in a natural history museum reinforces its cultural authority and reassures us that had David followed Miss Swallow's sexual rule, he would have become an old fossil, the least impressive specimen of extinguished life in the collection. I think we need subliminally to feel that this would be David's fate with Miss Swallow, or Susan's madcap pursuit of him would seem demented, lacking the sanction of Nature. Nature, contrary to Miss Swallow's notions, has her own work for us to perform—passing on our genes.

Bringing Up Baby is the only one of the great American comedies of the period that reminds us of what is at stake in the hilarious, often desperate antics of human mating—the survival of the species. The title itself acts as a kind of reminder, but only as a comic whisper, not a satiric blast. Like other movies of the period, it doesn't actually commit its couple at film's end to fulfilling the biblical injunction to multiply. *Bachelor Mother* is a glorious exception, building an entire comedy out of the distinction between parentage and parenting. But in general, children, even among the married madcaps of the period, are hardly in evidence, or when they are, as in George Stevens's *Woman of the Year,* it is to satirize (meanly, in my opinion) the woman's incapacity for motherhood.

The lack of children is not in itself remarkable, nor even regrettable. Comedy is about making marriages and ensuring a social future that fulfills rather than absorbs the individual in the tribe. American comedy in particular, deeply faithful to an ideology of individualism, is about imagining ever more preposterous as well as more perfect (private) unions.[29] The preposterous is the one guarantee that marriage will remain private, an expression of individual rather than collective will. Hawks's comedy wonders how preposterous we are prepared to be in our pursuits of happiness. Hawks later regretted that he never provided for a "normal" character in the film, a kind of Philinte or man of right reason, who would provide a standard of sanity against which to gauge the general lunacy of his comic principals. But I think his comic instincts were right in ushering us into a fantastical world where normalcy is banished, as is the pedant reflection, a world where dogs and leopards could mate and a woman can literally catch a leopard by the tail. Fast-talking dames are the natural denizens of such dreamworlds, wherein they merrily pursue the light that never was and things that are not yet. It is, after all, out of such dreamworlds, barred to normal humanity, that our new life forms may come.

6 *The Lady-Dame*

Irene Dunne and The Awful Truth

*I*rene Dunne is the fast-talking dame most in peril of lapsing into a soft-spoken lady. Elizabeth Kendall, perhaps sensing this hazard, anoints her "the Lady among the Runaway Brides."[1] But Dunne was not a runaway, nor even a bride. She was not even a bona fide lady. She belonged to a different spiritual and social order. A bride is a threshold creature, poised on the brink of a partnership that will either absorb or transfigure her individuality. Dunne was always, morally as well as temperamentally, a wife, a woman deeply settled into couplehood, once without benefit of clergy (*Back Street,* 1932). She is not the woman who takes flight but the one you can count on to return.

My Favorite Wife depends on this premise. It asks us to believe that Ellen Wagstaff Arden (Dunne), can be marooned on a desert isle for seven years, be declared legally dead, and still find her way back into the hearts of her family. Her wifeliness is steadfast and charismatic enough to survive not only the separation of years, but the presumption of death. Nick Arden (Cary Grant) takes one look at her and, even though he is about to embark on a honeymoon with a new wife, Bianca Bates (Gail Patrick), emotionally cancels out the intervening years with all their old sorrows (not to mention new attachments). For her fellow castaway, Stephen J. Burkett (Randolph Scott), who plays Adam to her Eve on their island paradise, she consolidates all the possible relations a man might have to a woman — "No man could ask for a better companion, a truer friend, or a more charming playmate." Even when Dunne is single, as in *Theodora Goes Wild,* her predisposition toward conjugal intimacy is more highly developed than is any maidenly skittishness or reserve.

But if Dunne played women who could be all-in-all to their chosen mates, it was because she was her own good company, sufficient, if need be, unto herself. Dunne asserted this emotional paradox most directly in *My Favorite Wife.* Irked when Nick, who has delayed breaking the news of her return to his "other" wife, finally claims her from Stephen, his rival, "on the basis of seniority," she sets them both straight. "It might surprise you to know that I can get along without either one of you." Whether playing a backstreet mistress who becomes a Main Street fashion entrepreneur in *Back Street,* the social-crusading title character in *Ann Vickers* (1933), or Magnolia Hawks, the dainty and naive riverboat belle in *Show Boat* (1936) who metamorphoses into an international diva, Dunne showed that she could get along spectacularly on her own. If a moral were to be attached to a reissue of her films, it might read something like: She loves best and longest who can live, if need be, a life apart. Romantic melodramas convert this perception into tears; comedy into laughs. Comedy has the harder job, but Dunne was up to the challenge. She developed a repertoire of attitudes and gestures that epitomized ladylike love—devoted, trusting, pure, and enduring—and then proceeded to caricature them. Chief among her parodic routines was the classy lady defying the proprieties of her class, the precepts of her upbringing.[2]

Her subversive sendups of ladyhood rescued her from becoming an icon for social correctness, American-style. In many ways, and not all of them lamentable, she was the actress who seemed groomed to fulfill an American ideal of decorous and companionable womanhood. She sported the elegant yet thoroughly democratic manners that relax those in her company but not necessarily of her class or in her league. Such a paragon would soon become unbearable company were it not for Dunne's superb instinct to spoof the canons of good taste and fine manners that she so graciously exemplified. That instinct produces one of the most delicate and yet hilarious gestures she improvises as Lucy Warriner in *The Awful Truth.* When Jerry Warriner (Cary Grant), her soon-to-be ex-husband, arrives at her apartment to demand his "visitation rights" with their pet dog, Mr. Smith, he finds Lucy in the company of her new suitor, Daniel Leeson (Ralph Bellamy). Hoping to increase the awkwardness of the moment, he presses for an introduction. Lucy formally extends her open hand, palm upward, as she begins, in her best grande dame manner, to make a formal presentation, then, either losing interest or energy, she flips her hand over and, with a limpness that is in itself a masterpiece of dismissal, waves Jerry off as if he were no more consequential, but just as irritating, as a fly. Later, as she takes leave of him she is suddenly inspired to kick her heel back, a gesture of comic uppityness and disdain that Pauline Kael singled out as the quintessential gesture of the screwball heroine.

Dunne also had a talent for social mischief. She may have been a morally unimpeachable, happily wed Catholic woman in private life, but on screen she courted impropriety like a pagan. She made the fallen woman a national rage in *Theodora Goes Wild,* treated bigamy as a waiting game in *My Favorite Wife,* and, in *The Awful Truth,* juggled suitors —a future and about to be ex-husband along with a singing master— with all the logistical bravado of an accomplished (bedroom) farceur. She is the only comic actress working under the strictures of the Production Code who actually ends two of her comedies under the covers, enticing her chosen mate into her bed under the guise of keeping him at bay.

Dunne could play—and inevitably win—all the games that a screwball heroine is obliged to master if she hopes to work her sexual will. However, she played with a campiness that elevated such games out of the realm of childish fun into decidedly adult entertainment. Gaiety is her comic specialty, a word that captures, I think, the dash of Continental laxity—especially her preference for innuendo over direct statement—that spices her conversation and that softens, but never fatally compromises, what Henry James would call her "moral sense." Gaiety also seems the apt word to describe her comic relationship to clothes. The flowing elegance of a Ginger Rogers dress serves as aesthetic enhancement of her art as a dancer. Claudette Colbert, happy to perpetuate the sartorial traditions of her ancestors, gracefully communicates the social meaning of chic. She can even transform a Pullman blanket, as she does as Gerry Jeffers in *The Palm Beach Story,* into a fetching skirt, the company name emblazoned across her derrière de-

Irene Dunne displaying her gay plumage in *Theodora Goes Wild*

cades before designers thought of doing so. Dunne wears her elegant gowns as if she were distinctly and ironically aware of them as feminine plumage. Her attitude is thus the most purely comic of all the screwball heroines, because clothes become the means to experiment with her own nature. What fun to pretend to be a different species, with a gaiety of feathers of one's own!

Two examples, one superb, if slight, the other splendid, illustrate

Dunne's sartorial gaiety. The superb gesture, in *Theodora Goes Wild:* As Theodora, a country girl who gives herself a fashion makeover, Dunne flicks the feathers of her new frock, wickedly appraising its showoff value: "A thing like this is darned expensive!" she reports by way of explanation to her publisher, flabbergasted by this newly hatched creature. The splendid gesture, in *The Awful Truth:* Posing as Lola, the vulgarian "sister" of her refined soon-to-be ex-husband, Jerry Warriner (Grant), Dunne confects a delicious burlesque gag out of that most genteel of feminine accessories — the hand scarf. On entering the well-appointed home of his prospective in-laws, she flaunts her scarf to accent her breezy familiarity with all levels of society, even the stuffiest, while genially remarking her need for a drink. "I had three or four before I got here, but they're beginning to wear off, and you know how that is," she confides to her hostess, Mrs. Vance (Mary Forbes), who knows nothing of the kind. Then she settles in for more lively entertainment. With a floozy's absentmindedness, she sits on the scarf, gets up, moves it over to her other side, arranges for Mrs. Vance to sit on it, and finally changes places. "I guess that could go on and on and on and on," she observes, in what almost amounts to a threat. "I hope not," Mrs. Vance mutters with very little hope in her voice. Clearly, Mrs. Vance is no connoisseur of the running gag or she might have appreciated the virtuoso turns Lola had just wrung out of that wayward piece of silk.

We tend to think of such burlesque routines as goofy and childish, but Dunne's tomfoolery is the sport of grownups. As Elizabeth Kendall has pointed out, Dunne was the oldest of the romantic comedy heroines, a maturity most evident in the knowingness that touched off her facial expressions and complemented her apparel like a comic aureole.[3] Her physical maturity, however, did have the further, less happy consequence of limiting her opportunities for pranks and comic imposture. What we now call the inner child was not a personage she could readily or believably call upon as part of her comedic repertoire. She had simply outgrown, if she had ever been young enough to affect, the tantrums, pouting, crushes, gushy enthusiasms, and juvenile peremptoriness of such younger madcap heroines as Lombard, Hepburn in her tomboyish lark, *Bringing Up Baby,* or Ginger Rogers stranded among four hundred adolescent cadets in *The Major and the Minor*. Rogers, thirteen years younger than Dunne, was thirty-one when that film was made, which further confirms that Dunne made her maturity a comic asset rather than a biological fact to be dissimulated as long as possible.

The comic abandon that can transfigure personalities as different as Lombard, Hepburn, and Rogers never overwhelms Dunne's sense of who she is and what she is doing. Her wanton turns as the headline-seeking Caroline Adams in *Theodora Goes Wild* or the loose-lipped, loose-hipped Lola in *The Awful Truth* are just that—acts. Even if comically cornered, as when, in *The Awful Truth,* she finds herself having to dispose of three men and as many top hats in her apartment, she looks harried but never seriously discomposed. She even has time to fit in a classic vaudeville gesture. When Jerry finds the "wrong" hat she has been spending most of their time together trying to hide, she momentarily halts in her tracks, pumping her raised forearms up and down. So do stage comics signal their comic distress when their best laid plans go awry. Expertly directed by Leo McCarey, who directed the Marx Brothers in *Duck Soup* (1933) and piloted (as producer) Laurel and Hardy in such hilarious shorts as *Big Business* (1929), Dunne pays homage to all the beleaguered damsels of stage farce and movie slapstick who have preceded her in this predicament. Her dress on this occasion is decorated with a bold pattern of mazes, a visual clue that Lucy Warriner, at the center of the labyrinthine twists and turns of what her estranged husband calls a "two-men-in-a-bedroom" farce, will find her way to the center of things—if not in this scene, well, then, in another. Her ex-husband and the music teacher he suspects of being her lover go at each other behind the (closed) bedroom door; she makes a good show of it, accepting her ingenuous suitor's apologies for any suggestion made against her honor until the two men scramble out of their hiding place, Jerry in hot pursuit, the voice teacher in desperate flight. "The face which character wears to me is self-sufficingness," wrote Emerson.[4] Even in the midst of bedlam, Dunne wears this face well.

Not everyone finds this face pleasing. This is the first of many awful truths that Dunne's screen presence brings into public view. The film

Irene Dunne trying to convince Cary Grant that the oversized bowler really is his hat in *The Awful Truth,* laying the groundwork for the "two-men-in-a-bedroom" farce to follow

that confirmed her as a farceur for intellectuals as well as for popular audiences gives us a catchphrase for her power both to charm and to repulse. Writing about *The Awful Truth,* Stanley Cavell makes a surprising claim: "About *It Happened One Night* I said that its appreciation depended on a certain acceptance of Claudette Colbert; but my sense of *The Awful Truth* is that if one is not willing to yield to Irene Dunne's temperament, talents, and reactions, following their detail almost to the loss of one's own identity, one will not know, and will not care, what the film is about."[5]

Cavell is emphatic because he knows others have not only resisted but have been repelled by her temperament and, more to our particular point, her facial expressions. James Agee, without going into detail (thankfully), professed that she made his skin crawl, possibly because, as he grumbled in his review of *Life with Father,* she "would probably keep her tongue in her cheek uttering the Seven Last Words."[6] This reaction seems at once too visceral and too abstruse (few probably care how the Seven Last Words are uttered, as long as they can remember them). It is easier to understand, without necessarily sharing, Pauline Kael's brusque hostility to Dunne's looks: the bemused and merry eyes on the brink of a comic gape, the coy and knowing and to my eye indulgently fond smile, that Kael found objectionably toothy.[7] Graham Greene, equally blunt, found her performances in films like *Roberta* and *Magnificent Obsession* (both 1935) "patient, womanly, and rather smug." But Dunne the comic actress won him over. He would applaud her as "one of the best comedians on the screen" once he had seen her in *Theodora Goes Wild* ("the best light comedy since *Mr. Deeds*").[8]

Creepy, toothy and coy, rather smug—this is not a flattering inventory of those qualities of temperament, talents, and reactions on which our enjoyment and understanding of *The Awful Truth,* to some the most profound as well as spirited American comedy of its decade, are said to depend. We return, then, to the exemplariness of Dunne's comportment, sterling enough to make Agee's skin crawl, and the cagey brightness of her smile, offensive enough to make Kael want to slug her. She may prove *too* self-sufficing for those who prefer their women less ironic and contained. If, as Emerson insisted, "Character is centrality, the impossibility of being displaced or overset," then Dunne has the most character of any fast-talking dame of her time.[9] Stanwyck is tough, but she knows when to give in. Rogers is stubborn, but knows when to give way. Hepburn is snooty and aloof, but knows when to join in. Even the pert but generally proper Claudette Colbert, who like Dunne was usually the observer rather than the observed in scenes of physical comedy, has her bouts of physical waywardness, as when her Augusta Nash bites Ray Milland's nose when he becomes a little too friendly in *Arise, My Love* (1940).

Dunne alone seems above or beyond capitulating to an overmastering feeling or irresistible impulse. Such habits of self-command are of questionable value in the moral universe of comedy, especially of American comedy, which fears fixity more than it dreads inconstancy of character. Large-minded, loose-limbed Emersonian America sees a foolish consistency as the hobgoblin of little minds. It regards the self that cannot be dislodged or discomposed more as a satiric target than as a comic cynosure. Comic characters are made, however unwillingly, to be brought down, lest they obstruct the comic momentum toward new life forms, freer personalities, more liberal social adaptations.

The comedy of the era thus showed little gallantry toward its female stars, not hesitating, if a gag was in sight, to suspend the laws of chivalry for a good laugh. Dunne was one of the few accomplished comic actresses to avoid such rude treatment. You may tickle her, as Grant does in a particularly compromising moment in *The Awful Truth,* but you may never upend her. If she does fall, it isn't because she is unbalanced. The one time she physically slips in *Theodora Goes Wild* she is pulled down by her inebriated escort, whom she is trying to help to his feet. Dunne, alas, was never given a fighting chance to enjoy the slapstick frolics that even such high-toned dames like Katharine Hepburn found to their liking. In her screwball romp *Bringing Up Baby,* Hepburn got the chance not only to display her superb athletic skills, which would be more systematically exploited in *Pat and Mike,* but to show her gift for physical comedy by juggling olives, playing "squat tag," marching to her own offbeat drummer on the side of a hill, losing her footing on a ridge and her balance crossing a "shallow" stream, swinging on a jailhouse door, even wrestling with a leopard. In *Adam's Rib* (1949) she went so far as to allow herself, as did Myrna Loy in *The Thin Man Goes Home* (1944), to endure the ultimate physical indignity of being (lightly) spanked on screen. Of course, only Spencer Tracy would dare presume to inflict such "masculine brutality" (condemned as such by Hepburn in the film). Tracy's Adam protests that he was simply giving her a love pat, but Hepburn's Amanda insists she knows the difference between a pat and a "slap." Such scenes make us wince today — they are uncomfortable reminders of the prerogatives that men took not as lovers but as disciplinarians of what they adjudged to be women's unruly spirits.

But these scenes remind us of something else — that female misrule is a force sufficiently respected by men to provoke them to take up arms — or at least hands — against it.[10] Dunne is quite willing to deploy that force, but she seldom seems physically compromised in exercising it. She is a woman as fully in control of her movements as she is of her tone. To come into her own as that American original, the fast-talking dame, Dunne had to go "wild" in a way that her madcap sisters in thirties comedy did not or could not. Wild, but as her scapegrace uncle in the film approvingly remarks, never silly. Even when she is acting flighty she always keeps her feet on the ground. The wildness turns out to be not in herself but in the world's view of her. What the world—or rather the movie audience—sees is a woman who suddenly has no regard for anyone's opinion except her own. *Theodora Goes Wild*, Dunne's first comic outing, defined the Emersonian nature of Dunne's comic persona—the woman who, against all expectations, steps out of what seems her character and assumes a bolder, freer, and much funnier one.

Theodora is Theodora Lynn, raised by her maiden aunts in Lynnfield, the "biggest little town in Connecticut." But Theodora of the backwater harbors another self, Caroline Adams, the author of a runaway bestseller titled *The Sinner*. These two ladies, and they *are* ladies, may peacefully inhabit the same psyche, but not the same town. When the movie opens, Lynnfield's lovably cantankerous newspaper editor (is there any other kind in American populist comedy?) is castigating the town mothers (Lynnfield appears to be pretty much a matriarchy) for resisting the inroads of "modern" civilization. This invasion takes the form of Theodora's book, which awakens all the righteous wrath of the Lynnfield Literary Circle. Theodora enters the fray—and the movie—protesting the serialization of the novel. Our first glimpse of her is a side view, head only, talking into a phone. The shot is cramped, the first of many views of Theodora's environs that emphasize how small a space she, as a well-brought up female, is socially and morally allotted. The tight shot opens up to include the figures of her aunts, visually cuing us that even if it is her voice, it is not necessarily Theodora who is speaking. She is representing the censorious views of the aunts, who in turn echo the opinion of the city elders that *The Sinner* is "sexy trash." This judgment is explicitly rendered by Rebecca Perry (Spring Byington), who brings a hearty appetite for scandal to her role as Lynnfield's most vociferous custodian of public morals. This being a comedy and not a melodrama à la *Peyton Place,* her public reading of the heroine's seduction by a big-city sophisticate excites even as it incenses her audience. Modern civilization is just as degenerate as Lynnfield had supposed but more engrossing than it imagined. Hearing that his paper will be boycotted if he continues to print such licentious trash, the editor promises to print more copies on the morrow.

Theodora herself is reduced to mortified silence in the presence of such overheated responses. She takes her consternation with her to New York, supposedly to visit her uncle but actually to consult with her publisher. Only to him does she confess that she is suffering from writer's block, so abashed is she by public reaction to her work. He is sympathetic but nonetheless delighted that the book is "sweeping the country." "But not a clean sweep!" she wails. The lame pun doesn't say much for her literary wit, but it does capture how it feels suddenly to find yourself estranged from something—or someone—you thought you knew so well. In this case, the something is her book, the some-one is herself. Theodora doesn't see what others see in her heroine and is genuinely perplexed by what her readers then infer about herself. She prefers to keep her identity a secret and is comically irritated when the publisher's wife and the artist, Michael Grant (Melvyn Douglas), who designed the book jacket, discover who she is. She endures their compliments but does object to the illustrator's racy pictorial inter-pretation of her "glorious" heroine. "She may be glorious," Theodora retorts, "but she's certainly underdressed." She seems little prepared for his rejoinder: "That's the way I found her in your book." In fact, Theodora becomes increasingly perplexed at the discrepancy between what she thought she put into her work and what its readers are getting out of it. Her comic wonderment soon is directed at herself: "Where did Caroline Adams come from?" Hers is *not* a rhetorical question. Dunne says the line as if she were voicing a real enigma. As Caroline Adams, Theodora has become a riddle to herself.

She comes, in fact, from quite a distinguished literary line. She was conceived by Mary McCarthy in a story that Sydney Buchman, cred-ited writer for *Mr. Smith Goes to Washington,* adapted for the screen. We can only speculate on how much of herself McCarthy projected into her portrait of a small-town girl who in her heart longs to be called Baby. But the image of Theodora gone wild surely was born in the satiric glint of McCarthy's keen, unblinking eye. It is an image of innocence despoiled but humanity enriched, an image, theologically inspired, of the happy fall. Michael, a painter of literary subjects and the man Theodora will fall for herself, gives as naked a rendering as the subject permits. He mischievously arranges to "show" Theodora his "latest" work, an etching of Eve and the serpent in the Garden of Eden, whose sexual explicitness we can only guess since we never get to see it. He's having fun testing how liberated her taste and, by implication, her sexual behavior really are. Theodora is taken aback by the picture but tries to pretend she's seen its like and better, which is to say, worse. All pretense to sexual realism or even to the most minimal carnal knowledge is instantly dropped, however, the minute Michael wants to see if Theodora's bold words ever translate into deeds. She runs screeching from the apartment, her virtue, unlike her innocence, very much intact.

Like Theodora herself, female virtue is treated lightly but not allowed to become silly. Theodora becomes, in fact, the first to bridle at her pristine reputation. She is provoked by Michael's assumption that he knows her, presumably because there is so little, and that itself of little interest, to know. "You're still full of peculiar notions about me," she informs him with something like a writer's injured pride. Emptying Michael's mind of such notions—which are not all that peculiar but are, at the moment, fairly accurate—becomes her goal, almost her campaign of their evening out, until of course the fatal test of the bedroom (a test that her fictional alter-ego, the eponymous sinner, passed by passing out).

The charm of the first half of the film, which takes Theodora to New York and back to Lynnfield, is in seeing how no one underestimated Theodora more than she did herself. She not only didn't know where Caroline Adams came from, but she hardly knew what she was capable of. Teased, and then comically hounded by Michael, she is goaded into exploring her own nature. Michael turns out to be less a debaucher than a cultivator of Theodora's nature. He claims indeed to be quite a gardener, offering his services to Theodora's household and threatening to make a public nuisance of himself if his offer is refused. Despite his low parodies of country life—like singing "Farmer in the Dell"—he sees himself primarily as a Thoreauvian liberator. In this character he urges Theodora to lead a "natural life" and to get out of Lynnfield. To stay in Lynnfield is not only a waste of life but, "for a lovely woman with talent, too, it's a sin." It's a sin he will do all in his power to absolve. "Don't worry, lady," he promises her. "I'll break you out of this jail and give you to the world." Michael intends for Theodora to rejoin the world as a "free, happy soul" and no "quaking rabbit"—in other words, to enter it not as a lady but as a dame. To encourage and promote this outcome, he begins speaking in horticultural metaphors, importuning Theodora to "transplant" herself out of the exhausted soil in which she has been bred into more nourishing soil, presumably the rich loam of his own metropolitan culture.

That he succeeds in setting Theodora free is due less to the irresistibility of his instruction than to the indomitableness of Theodora's character. Once she decides that she loves him, she will brook no opposition—not even his. Rather than cower before her maiden aunts and (pleasantly) scandalized neighbors when she is "caught" laughing suggestively in Michael's room and on his bed, she turns on them in unexpected comic fury. "This is a free country," she declares, issuing her own emancipation proclamation. "I'm over twenty-one, and what I choose to do is none of Lynnfield's business." The first article of this comic declaration of independence concerns her plans for herself; the second her plans for Michael.

Her grand speech is split scenically as well. The first part takes place in the family parlor, a decidedly public place; the second, in Michael's quarters. A quick but continuous cut shows us Theodora addressing the shocked Literary Society, then lecturing them on her natural rights under the Constitution while they remained transfixed. The uncharacteristic docility of her audience is quickly explained, however, when the camera pans away, showing them to be framed in a photograph hanging in Michael's room (perhaps for anti-aphrodisiac purposes). We then observe Theodora, still mid-stride in her oration, repeating her words for Michael, like a prize pupil declaiming before her drama coach. She is replaying for him the ultimatum she delivered to Lynnfield: " 'That gardener's going to stay here as long as I want him to,' I said, 'and that's forever, because I love him! What's Lynnfield going to do about *that*? I love him! I always will! And there's nobody in this town who's going to stop me!' " She delivers these lines a bit wildly, her fists punctuating each sharply insistent exclamation of love.

Michael is roused, even proud of the performance, until the declaration of independence veers into a declaration of love. Apparently it's one thing to put her garden in order as a seasonal worker. It's another to be employed full time. In the morning Theodora finds a letter declaring, "You are free, baby." Michael, his mission accomplished, says that he has more "gardens" to set in order. Later we learn the real reason for his flight. Michael, apostle of freedom, is himself held captive by familial pieties even stricter than those that rule Theodora's life. He is married to a woman he hasn't lived with for years, a charade he continues to please his father, a public figure with political ambitions.

The second half of the film takes us back to New York, where Theodora is in full erotic pursuit of her runaway mate. Without sacrificing or overemphasizing her femininity, Theodora becomes the virile half of the comic couple, morally strong enough to break not only her chains, but his. She does so by undertaking a Rousseau-like campaign to force her lover to be free. Her strategy is to involve herself in a whirlwind of publicity that will eventually sweep him into its path, compelling him into a spotlight where he can no longer hide the truth of his marriage or his feelings. Even though she begins her screen life as reticent as any Victorian lady novelist seeking or enduring anonymity, Theodora proves to be very much a creature of the twentieth century and its media revolutions. She not only comes to accept her celebrity but, predating Madonna by half a century, to fashion a public image to suit her own private purposes. Theodora's moral nature is burnished rather than dulled once she decides to become as wanton—and as popular!—as her book, living extravagantly, buying expensive clothes, going out at all hours.

Yet Theodora gone wild is less an ancestor of Madonna than a descendent of Thoreau. She is temperamentally ruled by the same "fear" that worries Thoreau at the conclusion of *Walden*, the fear that "my expression may not be *extravagant* enough, may not wander far enough beyond the narrow limits of my daily experience, so as to be adequate to the truth of which I have been convinced." *"Extra vagance!"* Thoreau whoops out in one of his funnier puns. "It depends on how you are yarded."[11] Theodora, cooped up in Lynnfield, is eager to try living out of bounds. She takes up residence, in fact, in Michael's apartment, scandalizing the sanctimonious gossips who are by no means confined to small towns. Her language also wanders into territory previously off limits to her. "Where's your tool shed?" she eagerly asks on entering Michael's bachelor quarters, showing the first signs of her newfound avidity for sexually charged double entendres. Courting publicity she previously shunned, she seems quite at home in the outlands of noto-riety. "Two in a Row," the tabloids gleefully scream when she is named correspondent in two divorce actions.

The comparison to an athletic feat does not come amiss, especially if we remember Theodora's raised fists daring Lynnfield to try to stop her. Theodora is on a roll, and as she promised, nothing and no one is going to stand in her way, not even the governor, whose annual ball she crashes. Once inside she gracefully straddles the divide between genteel and outrageous conduct.[12] She begins the evening grabbing public at-tention by dancing with the governor and charming him so thoroughly that he renounces his opinion of her as that "notorious woman" and rechristens her his "discovery." She concludes the gala night with a pub-lic discovery of another sort: accompanying Michael into the quieter, presumably more intimate spaces of the terrace, she makes sure to sig-nal the hovering newshounds to follow. When she has maneuvered him into a compromising position, she beckons them with a discreet wave of her hand. Before the term was coined, Theodora appreciated the logic and power of the photo op.

"There is nothing in the world more deadly than innocence on a manhunt," declares the wife of her publisher, who will later name Theodora as corespondent in a divorce action. This is hardly an adage that Lynnfield's civic leaders would endorse, although it might be cor-roborated by the denizens of the Gotham Athletic Club (see below). The fatality of innocence may have been the first lesson of mankind, the "awful truth" learned in Eden, but it is a lesson often lost on those who have known only country gardens. The main charge that Lynn-field's editor hurls at his accusers is that they would deny the presence of evil in the world. It takes a big-city girl to inspire and to appreciate the fatality of innocence, the bitter fruit of experience, not all of it bad, but all of it expensive. Theodora, newly fallen, makes it her mission to compel this human fact into public consciousness. She will teach Lynnfield a new definition of sinner and show her lover the meaning of free will, improvising, we might say, her own comic theodicy. We can measure the distance between her high consciousness of the awful truth and the dimmer understanding of the rest of the world in the last words—of love but also of censure—she utters in the film: "Oh, Michael, you idiot!" In saying them, Theodora seems to be not just addressing a mistaken lover but passing a judgment, fondly rather than harshly made, on an entire benighted culture.

Idiot is hardly a flattering word, but it is the appropriate word and, in its way, an encouraging one. Theodora had once charged Michael with having peculiar notions about her, and now, returning the favor, she exposes what is peculiar—*idios* in its original meaning—about him. (Because she is a writer, let us presume that she is aware of this verbal legacy.) What is most peculiar about idiots, and has remained so since Greek times, is their lack of useful knowledge and common sense, their deficiency, broadly speaking, in moral intelligence. To be without such knowledge is not only to be peculiar but to render peculiar judgments. Idiotic Michael, for example, should know, as part of his professional endowment as a painter, the difference between appearance and reality. But Michael, the commercial artist, has no more insight than Shakespeare's Bottom as he watches Theodora's last (presumably) public performance as a notorious woman. Theodora returns triumphantly to Lynnfield, which welcomes her with open arms.

Theodora has not come home alone, and she waits, a huge grin animating her highly gratified face, to see if their embrace is loving and wide enough to accommodate the baby she cradles in her arms. The baby is not hers, but the town doesn't know that, and neither does Michael. Both come to accept whatever Theodora may bring them, because what she brings, as the baby seems to suggest, is the promise of renewed life. She has freed Lynnfield from the jail its residents had made of their own society, releasing the honest, enlivening affections imprisoned behind its joyless, moralizing facades. In welcoming

Theodora they have let in the modern world and its affable, intelligent women, inviting them to make a home in their midst. Michael longs to live with her in that world, but first he must be taught, and come to share, Theodora's extravagant knowledge of what it really means to be a free and happy soul.[13]

It means, in the most extreme and shining instances, going beyond appointed social limits and venturing into that comic never-neverland that Charles Lamb envisioned as the homeland of the cultivated creatures of Restoration comedy, "the land—what shall I call it—of cuckoldry—the Utopia of gallantry, where pleasure is duty, and the manners perfect freedom. It is altogether a speculative scene of things, which has no reference whatever to the world that is."[14] This is not the world of Lynnfield, nor is it, needless to say, the "home on the range" with which Daniel Leeson (Ralph Bellamy) woos Dunne's Lucy Warriner in *The Awful Truth*. It is what the editor of the Lynnfield *Bugle* would call the "modern world," by which he means a brave new world that has wondrous people in it. Lynnfield, and the Production Code, might see these modern gallants as sinners, but comedy welcomes them as explorers who live in a speculative scene, unconfined and unyarded by the gateposts of conventional thought. Theodora had to drag the seemingly cosmopolitan Michael across the threshold. He could not make the trip, emotionally speaking, until he acknowledged what an idiot he had been. Her traveling companion in *The Awful Truth*, however, is no stranger to the utopia of gallantry. It is his natural habitat.

He is Cary Grant, the most hypercivilized male in classic American film comedy. If any man ever sported the manners of perfect freedom, it is the debonair Grant. (He also had darker and more tortured selves, as Hitchcock was diabolically expert in eliciting.) His advanced state of cultural evolution, however, can take quite disparate if equally risible forms. In *Bringing Up Baby* he is the absentminded professor of paleontology who has forgotten the first lesson of his chosen discipline—that those species survive who have not renounced, as he seems to have done, the life of instinctual gratification. In *The Awful Truth*, Grant is a gallant of completely different persuasions. His Jerry Warriner appears to have shed his superego as if it were as disposable as a supernumerary tail. Thus disencumbered, his mind is fully in the service of his pleasures.

Our first glimpse of him, tanning under the sunlamps of the Gotham Athletic Club, intimates his Jerry Warriner to be a highly specialized creature of modern society — the man of mode, the fashionable gentleman of libertine habits and naughty but not unkind wit. He is putting the final touches on an apparently harmless if hardly innocent marital deception — of what kind, with whom, and even for how long, we are not told. We might indeed suspect that he has been hiding out simply to give the appearance that he is still a habitual philanderer, fulfilling his role as man about Gotham.

Such a man will require — and attract — a different kind of mate. She will be a woman with quite a different sense of play and a less direct rapport with animal nature than Hepburn's Susan Vance. Her dog will not answer to the name of George, nor will he remotely resemble an earthworker. She will give him the more formal name of Mr. Smith and confine his games of fetch to the living room and his howling to singing sessions with his master. Most of all, she will be the kind of woman willing to accompany him not into the green world of golf courses and moonlit woods but into the artificial paradises of the nightclub, the parlor, and the enchanted cabin in the country. The city, with its luxuries, enticements, and diversions, is her milieu, and only in desperation would she ever contemplate setting up a "home on the range." We may hail her as the forerunner and prototype of a peculiarly American hybrid, the lady-dame.

The compound gets at something double, but not divided, in Dunne's comic nature — the Theodora syndrome, we might also call it — in which a lady of inerrant conduct happily yields the stage to the wild, exhibitionist dame dormant within her. In *The Awful Truth*, the lady is named Lucy, a figure of light who enters the film as a vision in resplendent white. We may take her radiant look to betoken the innocence of her night in the country, spent at an inn in the company — but not, presumably, in the bed — of her voice teacher, Armand Duvall (Alexander D'Arcy). The dame goes by the sultry name of Lola, a sassy number of somewhat slatternly dress, questionable talents, and even more dubious reputation. Only a woman endowed with the Emersonian character I have ascribed to Dunne could release the Lola within her without hazarding a major personality disorder. Even so, one would expect that, given their differences in taste and outlook, each would be an embarrassment to the other, but embarrassment is to Lucy what notoriety is to Theodora—her social route to personal happiness.

The truth be told, as of course it is destined to be, it was Lucy's husband's initial intention to spare his wife all embarrassment that is largely responsible for the quarrel that leads to their estrangement. The road to Reno may be "paved by suspicions," as Jerry rather flippantly remarks before he takes to that road himself, but the access routes are crowded with the unsuspecting. Jerry intends to keep his wife among their ranks for as long as he can so as not to "embarrass" her. The movie opens by picturing the stately clock of that male sanctuary, the Gotham Athletic Club. It is eight o'clock, the start of a new day, yet one with some leftover business to take care of. Jerry is in a hurry to do so; he wants to get in a few hours the tan that should have taken him a couple of weeks to acquire. The appreciative chortle of a friend passing by— "pulled a fast one on the little wife"—hints at a history of indiscretions as well as a characteristic haste in Jerry's way of doing things. We never actually find out how Jerry has spent the past two weeks, but we can wonder why he is so careless in devising a cover story to conceal the fact that he hasn't been where he says he was—in Florida. Had he taken the trouble to check the weather reports, he might have learned that Florida had been in the throes of a rainy spell. He has a justification, though, for contriving his deception. The real truth, awful or not, about where he has been and what he's been doing, should not be divulged, he maintains, on the general grounds that "what wives don't know won't hurt them."

This may be true of wives, but it hardly applies to husbands. What they don't know may be quite hazardous to their mental health. At least this seems to be the case with Jerry, who already thinks he knows everything about his wife, even if that knowledge eventually, perhaps inevitably, takes the form of doubting her. Of himself he has no doubts whatsoever, as he confidently strides back into his home, society friends in tow, with his own jaunty version of *Ecce homo:* "Lucy, that man is here!" He may be here, but Lucy, somewhat to his surprise, isn't. While quickly circumnavigating the parlor looking for signs of her recent occupancy, he assures his guests that he should not be counted among that general run of "people [who] are always imagining things." Lucy must be with her Aunt Patsy (Cecil Cunningham) in the country, a possibility immediately annulled when Aunt Patsy herself enters the room. Now *everyone* is waiting for Lucy. Still posing as somewhat expert in marital psychology, Jerry extols the virtues of liberal-mindedness and offers himself as the "broad-minded man from the Rio Grande," a phrase that seems formed more to rhyme man than to indicate any real largeness of spirit.

His broad-mindedness is put to the immediate test when Lucy returns, escorted by the suave Armand, in what is definitely not morning attire. She has been chaperoning a party, she explains, but on the way home the car broke down and Armand and she were forced to spend a night in the country. How innocent a night in the country can be is a question that is not as easily answered as one would think. Much depends, as it usually does with Dunne, on what one means by innocent and how one comes to "know" innocence when it presents itself. For Jerry, unbothered by such moral niceties, it is an open-and-shut case. Despite his valiant efforts to act the broad-minded man admirably equipped, as Armand "innocently" avows, with a "Continental mind," he abandons the light irony that kept him afloat when he first discovered his wife was not where *she* should be. Now every word he directs to Lucy and Armand is coated with heavy sarcasm. Lucy's own tone I find extremely hard to read. She initially responds as if (a BIG "as if") she were only a little less insensible of his irony than the tone-deaf Armand. She blithely corroborates Jerry's claim to being broad-minded, or as she puts it, "free of all mean suspicions." To the assembled company she declares her faith in his faith in her: "He knows it's innocent, why, just as well as he knows that, well, that he just got back from Florida."

Seldom has a declaration of certainty received such a doubtful reception. Given what *we* know, the last half of the sentence inadvertently and hilariously refutes the assertions it was called upon to support. But what we know may not be as interesting as what Jerry knows—that the last half of the statement is false—and what Lucy apparently knows—that it has all been innocent. The two propositions can reinforce each other only if the husband and wife, each of whom holds half the knowledge necessary to give full expression to the truth, really do have faith in each other. Or is this the only way of understanding Lucy's argument? What in fact does Lucy know? Does she know that Jerry has not been in Florida, as she seems to indicate later when she remarks that his tan is something of a marvel, given how the newspapers were "full of" stories about the rain in Florida? Or does she "know" that he has not really been in Florida only when she notices that an orange from the fruit basket he has brought her bears the stamp of its origin—California?

On such small but nagging points Lucy's integrity as a truth-teller seems to founder. Even posing them is enough to make me wonder whether I was too quick to trust her, just as Jerry was too quick to doubt her. She is, it must be said, eloquent in her own defense. "You've come home and caught me in a truth," she tells Jerry, "and it seems there's nothing less logical than the truth." "Oh, a philosopher," he retorts in a tone composed of equal parts disdain and exasperation. The philosopher Stanley Cavell believes that she might creditably join his ranks. I see her rather as adept in the art of true statements, if difficult and apparently illogical ones. In the course of the film Lucy comes to appreciate a different way of arriving at the truth, or at least of demonstrating it irrefutably. Dissimulation rather than disputation becomes her preferred mode of making her case for herself. She becomes, indeed, a skilled fabricator of that special class of lies that we call little and white—that is, innocent.

To accept this view of Lucy as a "white liar" is to begin doubting Lucy precisely when one is most likely to believe her. Much of our "faith" in Lucy derives from our belief, amounting to virtual certainty, that Jerry has been faithless and she has not. It is easy to interpret his rashness in thinking her guilty even when she declares herself innocent as his own best defense of what we know has been, at best, a deceit. We seem to have here a classic case of projection in which the culpable (and in this case the apparently adulterous) husband attributes his own breach of faith to his guiltless wife. Indeed, most critics of the film, I among them, assume that Lucy is telling the truth about her night in the country and that she is innocent. I have come to conclude, however, on many subsequent viewings, that these two assumptions are both correct but that they are by no means equivalent, interchangeable, nor even interdependent. Lucy may be telling the truth, but not innocently, or she may be innocent even as she steers clear of the truth. Perhaps because she realizes there is nothing less logical than the truth, hence nothing more unbelievable, Lucy seems determined to seem a woman of dubious character.

It is this dubious character who will eventually metamorphose into Lola, with many fine gradations of duplicity along the way. From the moment she decides on a divorce, Lucy becomes, to her credit, richer in craft than in honor (that dreary, mirthless virtue, especially for women in comedy). She cheats, for example, to win custody of Mr. Smith. McCarey reserves one of his few close-ups in the film to let us in on her ruse. When the judge, in a Solomon-like ruling, decides to let Mr. Smith "decide" the issue of pet-custody, Lucy lures the dog into her arms by extracting from her sleeves a squeeze toy with a cat face painted on it, another "souvenir" Jerry had brought back from Florida. She had obviously come prepared.

This sleight-of-hand is followed by several other actions of questionable probity. She begins to tell real, if small, falsehoods, like pretending that the man who phones her while Jerry is in the room is her masseuse, not Armand. Then there are outright lies, such as telling Jerry that her engagement to Dan Leeson is still on when she has given him his walking papers—Aunt Patsy calls it his diploma—long ago. Finally, there is her grandest deception, her pretending to be Lola, Jerry's wayward sister, and her greatest moment of dissembling, feigning drunkenness in order to get Jerry to take her to the country, where she says Aunt Patsy is waiting (she isn't). Jerry, who doesn't seem to object to being gulled, doesn't register an iota of surprise when Lucy bounds up the stairs proclaiming how tired she is. "She's all in," he wryly observes to the caretaker. He appreciates her pretenses. They're funny and they're flattering, because he knows Lola is Lucy's way of keeping him for herself, a fact that, being undeniable, she promptly and vociferously denies.

Yet none of these lies is potentially fatal, except the one lie she tells herself. That lie takes the incontrovertible form of a certainty. Predictably, it concerns her feelings for Jerry. "I'm sure I never loved him, and now I hate him," she reports to her skeptical Aunt Patsy when the interlocutory decree is first awarded. However serviceable the word "sure" may be to philosophers (or gamblers), it is the least reliable term for adjudging matters of the heart. This Lucy begins to accept after Jerry barges into a recital expecting to catch Lucy and Armand in an afternoon tryst. Realizing but trying to dissemble his mistake, he takes a seat, promptly capsizing it, himself, and any furniture in his vicinity. The spectacle doesn't discompose Lucy, who is just finishing her song. But it does divert her, and she registers her amusement in the touch of laughter than finishes off the lilting sostenuto of her song.

That unrehearsed laugh, a spontaneous variation on her controlled vocalizations, alerts us to the deep pleasure this man gives her. This pleasure is connected to his feelings for her. "Well, I'm convinced he must care about me or he wouldn't do the funny things he does," she confides to Armand, apologizing for Jerry's antics. That she uses the "must" of probability instead of the "sure" of absolute certainty marks a milestone in her relations not only to Jerry, but to herself. Just moments earlier she had finally admitted to Aunt Patsy what she had denied so vehemently before: "I'm still in love with that crazy lunatic and there is nothing I can do about it." That "nothing" presumably includes reminding herself how sane and considerate Daniel is, compared to Jerry, who is insane and inconsiderate. Still, he is the "crazy lunatic"—loving tautology!—for her. That she will keep the name of Warriner, a lingering pun (war in her?), suggests that once she settles the dispute with herself she will no longer be "confused," as she will later accuse Jerry of being, about whether she feels the same as she always did.

Much depends, then, on acknowledging the truth, illogical but irrefutable, of her feelings. And not only for Lucy. We, too, must face the awful truth that many of our sexual ideals, especially if they are forged in that utopia of gallantry that Lamb celebrated, care little whether a man is fine or not. *The Awful Truth* may show very little piety, Darwinian, Freudian, or otherwise, toward the instinctual life, preferring civilization, with all its discontents, to more "natural" ways of being (such one may find, presumably, in Oklahoma), but that does not mean it is not a movie profoundly attentive to the body, especially the male body, as an erotic object. Grant is so desirable a man because his body is both sexually and comically charged, whether still or in motion.

We get to see him in both bodily attitudes in the witty nightclub scene that brings together the ill-matched foursome of Lucy and Daniel, Jerry and his latest companion, Dixie Belle. Jerry is in especially fine form, surviving the first awkward moments of silence and embarrassed glances to congratulate Lucy on her upcoming marriage to Daniel. He seems especially glad that she will soon find herself comfortably settled in Oklahoma, where she will be "well out of it." The cool elegance of McCarey's direction and the star's expert scrambling from one level of irony to another make this the key moment in Jerry's new determination to embarrass Lucy where before he wanted only to spare her. If he seems abashed by Dixie Belle's interpretation of "My Dreams Are Gone with the Wind," he is soon back to his old form when he manipulates Lucy into taking to the dance floor with Daniel, who boasts of being a prize-winning dancer. As he watches Lucy trying to follow Daniel's high-stepping (or stomping) moves, he leans back his chair in a perfect balance of amused, distanced contemplation, a smile lighting up his face, "the holiday in his eye," in Cavell's unforgettable ticketing of this moment.[15] He will try to assume that same pose when he crashes the recital, but on that occasion he will collapse on the floor. The two moments echo each other to remind us of how the debonair gallant of consummate poise and the acrobatic clown who knows how to take a tumble coexist within a performer who can make his body do anything. For a woman, this agility is nigh irresistible.

Daniel, whether standing or sitting, displays a body that seems sexually demagnetized. He may pride himself on his dancing, but Lucy, who can follow him, clearly would rather not. In *The Thin Man Goes Home*, Nick maneuvers Nora into the arms of a jitter-bugger who proceeds to flip, toss, and throw her about with hilarious disregard for her own center of gravity. Nicky wants to go snooping without her, but he watches, comically shocked and not a little pleased, before he gets on with the job. Jerry has other motives, less honorable and by no means professional, for urging Dan to dance with Lucy and then ensuring that her discomfiture is prolonged by paying the orchestra to keep the number going. Jerry accuses her of "holding out" on Daniel about how good a dancer she is, revealing that his own pet name for her was Twinkle Toes.

She has been holding out, because dancing, like any other way in which bodies meet, is not something she can commit herself to with Daniel. Even when she is about to become engaged to him she can hardly bring herself to kiss him, and when she finally concedes, he not only whoops for joy but gives her a bear hug that is enough to squeeze the breath, not to mention desire, out of her. The contrast between Jerry, observing this tenderfoot moment behind the door, lightly tickling her, knowing every sensitive little area on her body, and Daniel, who can only swing her like a sack of potatoes, leaves no doubt that while Daniel may be the more decent man, it is Jerry who would be the "considerate" one in bed.

Even if Lucy could overcome her physical qualms about bodily union with Daniel, there are graver, emotional impediments to their marriage. One of the principal things that disqualifies Daniel as a mate and boon companion is that he can't tell a good laugh from a guffaw (a form of mirth that he has mastered). Lucy often has to tell him when not to laugh, as she does when he goofily and belatedly laughs at one of Jerry's throwaway jokes. Or he laughs in the wrong way at the wrong time—as, for example, when he finally gets her to give him a kiss and lets out an erotic holler—Oh-ho-ho-ho! Laughter, that convulsion which is minor analogue and sometimes prelude to the sexual spasm, is not something Lucy and Daniel can expect to share *with* each other. With such great expectations the Warriners had made and celebrated their own marriage. Lucy and Jerry in happier days "had some grand laughs together," as Lucy sentimentally reminds him on the eve of the final divorce decree.

One of the grandest laughs that we share with Jerry is over Daniel's poem. Daniel recites his poem with the same exaggerated—and misplaced—pride he took in his dancing and singing:

To you, my little prairie flower
I'm thinkin' of you every hour
Though now you're just a friend to me,

I wonder what the end will be.
Oh, you would make my life divine
If you would change your name to mine.

Mr. Deeds, another country versifier, might have composed this corny poem, but because Mr. Deeds is Gary Cooper we wouldn't laugh as hard—we would be responding not so much to the words as to the sexual presence behind them. Both Daniel and Mr. Deeds reduce language, the most subtle form of human lovemaking, to doggerel, but Deeds brings melting tears to the eyes of the verbally cocksure Babe Bennett (Jean Arthur), while Daniel can at best hope that Lucy will keep a straight face.

Lucy not only keeps a straight face but she actually begins to show signs of real distress when she recites an equally trite love poem that Jerry once composed for her. Critics tend to overlook Jerry's effort at poetry, but Lucy doesn't. When she visits his apartment on the eve of the final divorce decree, she recites the toast he offered to commemorate their first drink together and the future it seemed to promise. Reciting it, Lucy seems to lose heart in her charade, an occasion that Dunne marks with her most educated instrument—her voice, allowing it to crack. That such lame verse could elicit such feeling is due not to its art but to the occasion of its composition—the beginning of their time together.

Lend an ear, I implore you.
This comes from my heart;
I'll always adore you
'Til death do us part.

Jerry's poem may be even a bit worse than Daniel's, since Daniel's poem at least includes some homegrown imagery about prairie flowers, while Jerry's is just one clichéd line after another concluding in the ritual formula for marriage itself. Lucy recites it, however, to make a philosophical point as well as emotional one—to indicate how different the end of their union was from its beginning. This is a theme that she will return to later that night when Jerry finally admits that he has been a fool and that he wants to have things back the way they were, only different.

The reason that Lucy and Jerry can find their way back to each other (where they will encounter the same but different life partner they had in the beginning) is that Lucy, unlike Jerry, will spare her mate no embarrassment. The line between the laughable and the embarrassing is one that Lucy, like Theodora straddling the line between genteel and outrageous conduct, is not afraid to cross. Disguising herself as Lola, she decides to set up camp in the land of social discomfiture. She breezes into the drawing room of Jerry's future bride and in-laws, interrupting a story about Jerry's father's exploits in the Princeton game. Her greeting to her rival, Barbara Vance (Molly Lamont), announces Lola's intention to play image off reality. "Well, it's nice to have the chance to meet you," she gushes in her smarmiest manner as she finally meets her rival face to face. "I've seen your pictures in the papers, and I've wondered what you looked like." Lola's gibe may be the only instance in American comedy in which a sexual put-down approaches the (comic) majesty of a Zen aphorism on the deceptive nature of appearances.

The next person whose public image Lola casually (but not thoughtlessly!) debunks is Jerry's father. Allowed to resume his story, Jerry starts to recount Father's exploits for Princeton, but Lola again interrupts, then disputes the tale. "Pop loved Princeton," she interjects; so much so, she continues, "he was there twenty years. If ever a man loved a place, he did. He just adored it. And he certainly kept it looking beautiful. You've seen the grounds, of course?" Jerry's football hero covering ground becomes Lola's groundskeeper. As to her own employments, she proudly recounts her stint at the Virginia Club and happily offers to show the Vances a sample of her act, apparently unconcerned at the aghast looks with which this suggestion is received.

The Couth meet the Uncouth for the second time in the film, only now it is Lucy-Lola who takes the part of Vulgarity. Earlier in the film Lady Lucy had averted her eyes in embarrassment as she watched Dixie Belle sing "My Dreams Are Gone with the Wind," little gusts of air raising her skirts during the title refrain. "I guess it was easier for her to change her name than for her whole family to change theirs," she remarks when the number is over. Now Lucy, who has found it just as easy to change her name to the sultrier-sounding Lola, claims Dixie's act as her own. In pantomiming the wind effects, Dunne adds a distinctive, self-parodying touch of her own. Dixie Belle sways, but Lola wriggles with the same loose-hipped, rubber-limbed brio that animated Dunne's dance in *Show Boat*. In that number, her Magnolia suddenly takes to her feet as Julie LaVerne (Helen Morgan) sings "Can't Help Loving That Man of Mine." The allusion to that performance suggests the motive for her routine as Lola, even while it offers a good-humored self-parody of a younger, more innocent heroine. Jerry can't help loving the shameless spectacle. He muffles laugh after laugh even as his prospective bride and in-laws look on in disbelief.

Jerry and Lucy had had the same reaction to Dixie's number, but their enjoyment now shouldn't be taken as a sign of their hypocrisy nor "classism." [16] Their mutual enjoyment of Lola's performance shows how broad-minded *both* have become in the course of finding their way back to each other, a course they never would have found unless Lucy had gone to these lengths to shut him off from all other erotic byways. They have left not only snobbery behind, but shame and blame and all similar shibboleths of their class and of their age. They have become, through Lola's performance, unyarded. Like the Millamants and Mira-belles who preceded them into the utopia of gallantry, they "break through no laws or conscientious restraints. They know of none." This is a negative knowledge, to be sure, but all the more awful for that.

Comic delinquency is a Dunne specialty that has not gone sufficiently remarked or appreciated. Dunne, at the peak of her career and comic powers when the Production Code limited what could be said and done on screen, was arguably the most extravagant violator of that Hollywood Bible. Though the statute of limitations may have run out, our retrospective appreciation of Dunne, the justified Sinner, might exonerate her of all charges of that capital offense—at least in comedy—of good breeding. Among the themes subject to specific prohibition in the Code are these:

> Scenes of Passion: Excessive and lustful kissing, lustful embraces, suggestive postures and gestures are not to be shown.

Irene Dunne confronting Cary Grant under the covers in *The Awful Truth*

> The treatment of bedrooms must be governed by good taste and delicacy.

As Theodora, Dunne made the appearance of illicit sex both delightful and daring, something explicitly prohibited by the Code, and wrote herself a bestseller to boot. In both *The Awful Truth* and *My Favorite Wife,* she ends up not only in a bedroom, but in bed, under the covers, and with an unmistakable come-hither look in her eyes. *It Happened One Night* and *The Lady Eve* follow their lovers to the threshold of sexual consummation, but both films leave us, with all the decorum such moments used to call for, just outside the bedroom—or in Capra's case, the cabin door. The endings of both *The Awful Truth* and *My Favorite Wife* take place within the marital chamber, not without. Indeed, in both films Grant, who is in a most ambiguous relation to Dunne, who may or may not be his lawfully wedded wife, repeatedly barges into her bedroom, offering one lame excuse after another for coming into her presence.

To gain admittance, he must, like a knight at the entrance of the chapel perilous, say the magic formula that will renew the human compact that has been broken. His words are awful in that sense, having the power to restore that most fragile of human creations—a marriage. A truth so sacrosanct is not easy to formulate. Often the truth can be approached only through slow, often stumbling speech. Stuttering may even be involved. In *My Favorite Wife,* Grant plays Nick, a lawyer, a man who abides by the contractual power of words, but to make his final marital brief he must resort to wordless pantomime. He has forfeited his right to the marital bed because even when his old and indisputably favorite wife was legally restored to life and his new marriage annulled, he wanted time to think things over. His delay makes no sense psychologically, because there is no doubt that he loves her. His dallying seems a perceived necessity of the comic plot rather than a sign of some real hesitation. The only way to defend it dramatically is to hold that Nick needs to abandon the logic of thought and enact that of the heart. It is not enough that he renounce that logic in words, which he does by confessing that "I can go on thinking about it 'til Doomsday. I'm stuck. I don't care what happens. I don't care what people say. I was always mad about you and I always will be." These words, unequivocal as they are, fail to convince his wife. "You better go on your cruise," she advises, and in sixty days' time, come Christmas, he can say with certainty that he knows his own heart. A downcast but not defeated Nick retreats to the attic where he has been bedded for the night, but, a few strange noises later, reappears as Santa Claus, ringing his sleigh bells in the middle of October. It's his jolly way of signaling that he has emotionally as well as symbolically mastered the mystery of human time, which takes the heartbeat, not the clock and certainly not the calendar, as its measure of how quickly or slowly things may happen.

My Favorite Wife is remembering and reworking the final image of *The Awful Truth,* in which a clockwork figure in lederhosen, a stand-in for Grant's Jerry, follows his liebchen into her solitary alcove within the grandfather's clock. It is a deeply comic and yet disturbing image, whose resonance the successor film never fully captures. *The Awful Truth* gives one last glimpse of sexual desire in which the aroused human being, through a process of comic displacement and diminishment, is reduced to a clockwork mechanism, disappearing into the entrails of time. Henri Bergson's philosophical view of comedy as one response to the spectacle of human automatism has never been so vividly "demonstrated." Sex, the most vital and irresistible impulse of our animal nature, is imaged as a mechanism. The film's opening image of the Gotham clock, with its decisive tolling, proclaimed the imperiousness of the human day, with its work to perform and deceptions to complete. The comic day concludes, however, with a close-up of an old-fashioned timepiece that chimes to a different imperative—nature's merry sexual round, bodies coming together and going apart but insistently coming together again.

This image, however piquant and humorous, is not as remarkable as the moments and the words that lead up to it. Before Lucy and Jerry can unite in laughter and in love, they must agree on what they find funny about themselves. Their final verbal exchange recaptures as it redefines a marriage composed of grand laughs. Stanley Cavell has rightly celebrated the metaphysical wit by which Lucy and Jerry articulate for each other the deep mystery of how time changes things and people and yet somehow leaves them the same.

> JERRY: In half an hour we'll no longer be mister and missus. Funny, isn't it?
>
> LUCY: Yes, it's funny that everything's the way it is on account of the way you feel.
>
> JERRY: Huh?
>
> LUCY: Well, I mean if you didn't feel the way you do, things wouldn't be the way they are, would they? Uh, I mean things would be the same if things were different.
>
> JERRY: But things are the way you made them.
>
> LUCY: Oh, no. No, things are the way you think I made them. I didn't make them that way at all. Things are just the same as they always were, only you're the same as you were, too, so I guess things will never be the same again.

Lucy's words have unexpectedly become elliptical, almost sibyline. She is speaking in sentences that would not be out of place in a Henry James novel. Having delivered herself of this masterpiece of indirection, she gives her first satisfied and rather gnomic "Ah" and then dismisses him with a "Good night." Jerry knows her too well to take her at her word, so he leaves, but he connives with a suddenly forceful wind to make his way back into the bedroom:

LUCY: You're all confused, aren't you?

JERRY: Uh-huh. Aren't you?

LUCY: No.

JERRY: Well, you should be, because you're wrong about things being different because they're not the same. Things are different, except in a different way. You're still the same, only I've been a fool. Well, I'm not now.

LUCY: Oh.

JERRY: So, as long as I'm different, don't you think that . . . well, maybe things could be the same again . . . only a little different, huh?

LUCY: You mean that, Jerry? Are you sure?

JERRY: Hmmm.

LUCY: No more doubts?

JERRY: Hmmm.

LUCY: No more being . . . ?

JERRY: Hmmm. [*Jerry smiles and waves arm in a half-moon arc, as if wiping away all traces of suspicion*].

Jerry is verbally paving his way back from Reno, the terminus of those marital roads paved by suspicion. He now understands and trusts that Lucy's constancy was not only sexual but existential, an abiding yet ever-changing sameness of being. He also admits that he was the one who made things the way they were, since his power of invention was essentially negative while hers was constructive, restoring things to what they were — only, of course, a little different. Lucy responds to this admission with a peal of triumphant but not gloating female laughter. Things are now the way they should be because of what she made them. She justifiably pauses to enjoy her moment of sudden glory, letting us in on one last grand laugh. Only Garbo's laugh is more exultant, and like Lucy's, it too will take us into the depths of time.

7 Garbo's Laugh

*G*arbo laughs! Why was this touted as so remarkable an event in the annals of film? To hail Garbo's laugh as a historic occasion was, of course, a savvy promotional gimmick, one that actually predated the making of *Ninotchka,* the 1939 film that it was publicizing. MGM wanted to make a comedy that it could advertise with "Garbo laughs!" as *Anna Christie* (1930) had been promoted with "Garbo talks."¹ But why did it take nearly a decade to exploit the phenomenon of her laughter, as if her powers of speech were quite distinct from, perhaps even incompatible with, her capacity for laughter? What was it about Garbo, the screen goddess, that seemed to make comedy an unlikely if not inhospitable realm for her divinity?

It surely was not an innate aversion to laughter that explains the general mirthlessness of Garbo's screen existence. In fact, she began her career with a comic turn in a short 1921 publicity film for a department store advising *How Not To Dress,* a lesson that Garbo illustrated by attiring herself in men's clothes at once too ugly and two sizes too large for her.² In her second cinematic outing she shed attire to give a Swedish impersonation of a bathing beauty in *Luffar-Petter (Peter the Tramp),* a Swedish silent comedy in the Sennett tradition.³ She would prematurely end her career in 1941 with a marital farce, *Two-Faced Woman.*⁴ Still, the question of Garbo's speech and her spiritual susceptibility to laughter may seem an eccentric one to pose, much less seriously ponder, in a book on fast-talking dames, since Garbo never spoke at a fast clip and never suggested, except in her last film, that

Garbo laughs at herself in *Ninotchka*

her body was attuned to the quick, syncopated rhythms—in speech as in music—that animate as they define the American idiom. There was nothing hurried in her speech or her movements. She entranced by the stateliness of her carriage, the self-possession in her gait (epitomized in the magnificently confident stride of her *Queen Christina*), the confiding languor in her voice. *Two-Faced Woman* presented audiences with the rather gauche spectacle of another Garbo (Karin Borg Blake/Katherine Borg), a twin with more relaxed manners and questionable morals, whom she invents to lure back her wayward husband.

Barbara Stanwyck's Jean Harrington in *The Lady Eve* similarly concocted a twin (Lady Eve Sidwich) as a sexual decoy, but with a different motive—hers was as much an act of class revenge as of sexual reprisal. No such sophisticated if ruthless plot of sexual instruction and class revenge is contemplated in *Two-Faced Woman*. The two faces of Garbo in this flailing comedy represent crude alter egos of Garbo's own screen personality. The Garbo who first attracts Larry Blake (Melvyn Douglas) represents the allure of robust athleticism. She exudes the freshness and vigor of unpolluted nature. She captures him by her indifference to all material enticements, but to keep him she reverts to the role of worldly temptress, the Garbo who years earlier had shattered the apparently in-dissoluble male bond between comrade-brothers in *Flesh and the Devil* (1926) or who entranced the boyish Lew Ayres in her last silent, *The Kiss* (1929). Audiences apparently were not enthralled by *either* type, and the dispirited Garbo retired from the screen. Leaving aside the inferiority of the material and the story itself, the film's gravest miscal-culation is in portraying the comic side of Garbo's nature as essentially a physical one.

Her rumba in *Two-Faced Woman* may be taken as the most em-barrassing evidence of this miscalculation. Her dancing is an awkward affair, although perhaps it was meant to be, since she dances in the character of her "false" self: a well-traveled woman who is neverthe-less rather common in her worldliness. Yet even if we charitably inter-pret the dance as in character, Garbo seems *existentially* uncomfort-able clapping her hands and swaying her hips, trying to affect the easy abandon common to women of less spiritually taut natures. Unlike her supporting costar, the sprightly Constance Bennett, whose Guinelda Vaughn is the only character in the film to excite real merriment, Garbo appears too emotionally intent to relax into the happy convulsions of laughter or let fly, as Guinelda does time after hilarious time, a pro-phylactic scream protesting the routine repressions imposed by the ex-acting protocols of civilized society.

It is her peculiar intensity that marks Garbo, perhaps the greatest female icon of modern cinema, as anti-modern. She was nothing less than glamorous, but there was never anything strikingly contemporary about her manner, either. This is an impression that holds, irrespec-tive of the "time" when her films are viewed, whether in the thirties or on today's classic movie channels. Contemplating the iconography of her deified face, Roland Barthes concluded that "Garbo still belongs to that moment in cinema when capturing the human face still plunged audiences into the deepest ecstasy." The elegiac temper of Barthes's as-sessment prepares us for his historical verdict on Garbo's face as one that marks a transition between "two iconographic ages" and "assures the passage from awe to charm." [5]

We shall return to the historical significance of Garbo's face, for it is a prospect that director Ernst Lubitsch contemplates with great delicacy in *Ninotchka*. What detains me in Barthes's homage is his re-manding Garbo to an earlier iconographic age—his intimation, that is, of Garbo's pre- or even anti-modernity. I want to explore this possi-bility, but with the essential qualification that is not solely the themat-ics of her face that declare her resistance to the modern, to all that is aggressively and vigorously new, that belongs to the passing, excitable Moment rather than to enduring, meditative Tradition.

It is less how Garbo looks than how she speaks, indeed her unique relation to language, her unsteady command of the idioms of every-day life, that betray her anti-modernity. The talking picture, like the modern novel, found its most resonant as well as popular voice in the plain, often rude speech of the everyday. The colloquial was *the* mod-ern idiom. So invigorating was its relation to social reality that euphe-mism and elevated, haughty diction quickly became fuel for satire or cause for embarrassment. In *It Happened One Night* the runaway but high-toned heiress Ellie Andrews (Claudette Colbert) gets nowhere in rebuffing the advances of Shapely (Roscoe Karns) as long as she main-tains, after the manners of her class, a haughty tone of dismissal: the sardonic hauteur only inflames him. But it is her quickness that really stimulates him; he thinks that he has lucked onto a "high-class mama that can snap 'em back at ya!"

The films knew that talk could be as sexy as breathless silence, but how sexy was the question. Garbo explores the limits of this point where speech and sex fuse and mutually excite each other. It is not that Garbo's screen character might overhear and even hazard to engage in the sexual banter that defines the exuberant lovemaking of the early talkies, nor that she has an innate aversion to the popular idioms of her time. It is rather that she utters words as if they were too full of mean-ing, so laden with consequence, to be so casually tossed off or flung away. She doesn't commit herself too quickly in the realm of words. The wariness that the American comic heroine must acquire through bitter if funny experience is in her inborn.

The "laughing" scene in *Ninotchka* exploits this moral fact to full comic effect. Pursued by the debonair gigolo Count Leon d'Algout (Melvyn Douglas) into a working-class restaurant, Ninotchka, the hu-morless Russian envoy, refuses to respond to his attempts to get her to smile. Even when Leon manages to get off a fairly good joke that sends the rest of the restaurant into fits of laughter, she remains stony faced.[6] Only when the frustrated Leon, expostulating that everyone else found the joke funny, falls off his chair, does she explode into laughter. This is the only slapstick moment of the film, a physical rather than verbal display of human comicality. Lubitsch here pays his respect to the slapstick antecedents of American comic romances. Garbo's laugh is caught, however, in countershot. Though she shares the general hilarity, she doesn't share the frame with the well-heeled Leon and the restaurant's proletarian patrons, their social and ideological differences momentarily canceled by laughter. Melvyn Douglas, her costar, doesn't remember her laughing during the filming, and he assumed that her laughter was shot later on a closed set.

Douglas was also struck by another indication of Garbo's apartness, remarking how unnuanced or unemphatic was her pronunciation when compared to a native speaker's: "Perhaps because English was not her native language, she did not 'underline,' she did not pick out the most important phrases in a speech or color individual words for subtle shades of meaning."[7] Lubitsch seems to have understood and relied on Garbo's idiosyncratic relation to speech in *Ninotchka*. Much of the ideological as well as sexual humor of the film derives from Ninotchka's intonations: her monotonic pronouncements gradually yield to more inflected utterances, culminating in her highly "underlined," if extremely drunken, speech in which she pleads for forgiveness from the "people" she always meant to serve and now fears she is betraying in loving Leon. Around the drama of Garbo's voice Lubitsch explores the potentially hieratic relation between women and their own speech. It is a potential that can be realized only in the iconographic age when a woman could awe as well as charm, when her words had the power to daze as well as beguile.

Moreover, Garbo's incarnation as Ninotchka, the special Russian envoy who succumbs to the allure of the West and, most especially, its ideology of love, represents an instructive example of how America implicated the sexual fate of women in its own historical triumphalism. Garbo was the spiritual vessel in which Hollywood of the thirties decanted its highest ideals of womanhood. She could be gay, even gallant, but her moods were dictated by her mysterious inner life, the life that proceeded undeterred by those material cares and economic worries that imposed on the good humor of less ethereal comic heroines of Depression America. It was to Love, both sacred and profane, that she spoke most urgently and to which her screen life seemed dedicated. Hollywood had difficulty envisioning anything but tragic and, more commonly, melodramatic fates for her, fates that confirmed an exalted if doomed spirituality purged of crass motive and selfish calculation. For this reason, even her most luminous speaking roles, in *Grand Hotel, Queen Christina, Anna Karenina,* and *Camille,* seem terribly dated now, as if the womanhood she represented belonged to another era, some other spiritual constellation, visible to us now only across an unbridgeable historical or astral divide.

To Lubitsch was entrusted the delicate task of transplanting the spiritual fervor of the dramatic Garbo into the more pliant mold of the comic heroine. The result was to make Ninotchka the most timeless of her heroines, even though she is the Garbo heroine most deeply immersed in her historical moment—much more so, certainly, than her Queen Christina, a woman in vain flight from a public identity assigned by an implacable history. The passions of a comic heroine must answer in a different way to the rule of the tribe and the exactions of history. Often the price that the comic heroine pays for being human is to default on her pledge to remain true to herself, since disguise and transformation are keys to survival in comedy, as they are in Nature, as they often are in History. In comedy the Real is not shunned but compromised in the name of life-furthering Fantasy, which expertly (that is, plausibly), imagines for itself a future founded on the most irrational and expensive dreams of happiness.

We tend to forget that falling in love *is* expensive. This is the great moral of *Ninotchka*—to impress us with the exorbitant price of things, the unforeseeable cost of happiness, the improvidence of all great loves. The film does not flinch from making this calculation in monetary as well as spiritual terms, reckoning the price of love not only on ourselves but on the people and things around us who inspire a different kind of love.

It is as an advocate of this secular *caritas* that Ninotchka assumes moral authority. She is an "envoy extraordinary" come to Paris to expedite the business and curtail the extravagances of a Russian delegation consisting of three irresistible wags, Buljanoff, Iranoff, and Kopalski (Felix Bressart, Sig Ruman, and Alexander Granach). Her initial purpose is to recall them not only to their bureaucratic duty but to the historical mission and moral superiority of the new Soviet order. Moralists of a humorless ideological stripe are seldom portrayed sympathetically in comedy. Thus one of the most pointed political jokes in the film is one that the initially humorless Ninotchka inadvertently makes in applauding the results of mass trials: "There are going to be fewer but better Russians."

Our sympathies are much more likely to attach themselves to the company of Buljanoff, Iranoff, and Kopalski, who have succumbed to the sybaritic pleasures of Lubitsch's Paris, the scene of the sexual frolics in *So This Is Paris* (1926) and the sophisticated debauches of *The Merry Widow* (1934); the Paris of champagne and cigarettes, top hats and erotically charged laughter, the Paris of revolving and ornate doors whose opening and shutting seem to dictate the very pulse and rhythm of the modern Saturnalia. They procure palatial quarters to uphold the international "prestige of the Bolsheviks" and to guarantee the safety of the crown jewels they have come to sell, even after they are advised by the hotel manager that the only available room—the Royal Suite—"might suit your convenience, but I doubt that it will fit your convictions." The expense account extravagances of their revelries are simultaneously noted and terminated by Ninotchka when, on seeing the trio of cigarette girls who respond to a room service request for cigarettes, she sardonically remarks to her sheepish comrades: "Comrades, you must have been smoking a lot."

She enters the world of the film, then, as an envoy extraordinary from the world of scarcity, a land threatened by famine. She reminds her comrades of the reasons for their mission—the sale of jewels confiscated from the Grand Duchess Swana to buy tractors to increase agricultural production and so avert a looming threat of mass starvation. Ninotchka dutifully imports into the film the "Russian view" of the West as the realm of calculated Surplus, of decadent Excess. Indeed, the film will derive great fun satirizing the Russian's uncomprehending awe of "capitalist" methods. Thus Buljanoff, on hearing a French jeweler explain that he will be taking a huge loss on the sale of the Grand Duchess's jewels, finally grasps the logic of capitalist acquisition of wealth: "Hmmm. Capitalist methods. They accumulate millions by taking loss after loss."

In the comedies of the early thirties, love was wed, for better or worse, to economics. Either the heroines were heiresses who could afford to marry where they would, or they were working girls who had to be wooed and won against their determination to avoid the shabby afterlife that attended their mothers' love-matches. But whatever their class or financial status, "easy living" was the ideal that motivated the heroine and made her suspicious of romantic ideology. Her subsequent comic involvement with the hero forced her to redefine easy living as entailing emotional much more than material comforts. Ease, according to the more humanly enlightened definition, was the ultimate companionableness of the comic lovers. Often the man as well as the woman must come to embrace this definition, especially when, as in *Hands Across the Table,* the love interest, in this instance Fred MacMurray's Theodore Drew III, is very much identified with the female position in the dilemma confronting him—to marry for money rather than love.

Everything depended, naturally, on what made the living easy. For the screwball heiress, like Susan Vance in *Bringing Up Baby* or Ellie Andrews in *It Happened One Night,* easy living meant having the time and money to indulge the luxury of hunting (not to mention the cost of feeding) leopards in Connecticut, revising a hitchhikers' guide to America, or championing, as Irene Bullock does in *My Man Godfrey,* a forgotten but deserving man. Easy living promised ease in everything, including exemption from regret. Even in those comedies where easy living was something you weren't born with but fell into, like Ginger Rogers in *5th Ave. Girl* or Jean Arthur in *Easy Living,* there was no serious effort to alter, much less overturn, the way goods, services, and even happiness were apportioned in capitalist society. Mobility within the system, not radical subversion from without, was the ideological desideratum in such love versus security comedies as *Hands Across the Table, Bed of Roses* (1933; with Constance Bennett and Joel McCrea as a stalwart but impecunious riverboat captain), and, most hilari-ously, in *The Palm Beach Story* (with Claudette Colbert and, again, the steadfast and pretty much irresistible Joel McCrea, who this time around is an inventor whose projects are at once costly and impracti-cable).

Such struggling, often proletarian, and, in Bennett's case, petty-criminal heroines dreamt of scaling the social ladder, not dismantling it. Even Gregory La Cava, the director most hospitable to radical re-sponses to the Depression, envisions the ultimate integration of radical and anarchist—theoretically opposed to the normalizing conventions of marriage—into the redeemed comic society that emerges at film's end. His most delirious and madcap vision of ideological intermarriage is the union of a debutante and the Marxist chauffeur (James Ellison) in her employ in *5th Ave. Girl.* The heroines of these class-conscious comedies subscribed to the dream of easy living even when advised that the price of their ascent was emotional bankruptcy, a price that they calculated and assented to in advance. Invariably such advance con-tracts were abrogated, for in comedy, if not in life, Eros always prevails over Mammon.

But the god whom Ninotchka serves is neither Eros nor Mammon, but the idol created by political modernity—the masses. Her comic ancestress is Shaw's Major Barbara, another heroine whose first love is the people. Although her dogma is dialectic materialism, not Salvation Armyism, she is driven by the same reformist ardor. The well-being of the masses is the standard by which she reckons the moral as well as monetary value of goods and services. She can instantly compute the exchange rates between royal treasures and heavy machinery, con-vert ceremonial swords into agitprop plowshares. The 2,000 francs a day that Buljanoff, Iranoff, and Kopalski are paying out for the Royal Suite could purchase one cow; a duchess's tiara, to other eyes a valu-able historical relic or personal bauble, is worth twelve cows in hers. The woman who can calculate the number of farms that could be sal-vaged by the sale of a tiara challenges our very notion of how to de-termine the value of human goods, of human arts, of human love. Thus Ninotchka's falling in love—and even more costly, finding hap-piness—with a Parisian gigolo, the most decadent (not to mention expensive) of male sexual types, represents an ideological turnabout of a dramatic, highly modern order.

Of course, it is precisely Ninotchka's messianic, revolutionary sense of the expensiveness of personal happiness that makes her a laughable as well as morally imposing heroine. Henri Bergson noted how profound the comic element was in the utopian cast of mind, and remarked the affinity between "these whimsical wild enthusiasts, these madmen who are so strangely reasonable" and the "victim of a practical joke or the passerby who slips down in the street":

> They, too, are runners who fall and simple souls who are being hoaxed—runners after the ideal who stumble over realities, child-like dreamers for whom life delights to lie in wait. But, above all, they are past-masters in absentmindedness, with this superiority over their fellows—that their absentmindedness is systematic and organized around one central idea, and that their mishaps are also quite coherent, thanks to the inexorable logic which reality applies to the correction of dreams, so that they kindle in those around them, by a series of cumulative effects, a hilarity capable of unlimited expansion.[8]

Garbo's sublime imposture of Soviet enthusiasm seems inspired by this Bergsonian perception linking rigidity of thought with inelasticity of demeanor. Until the enchanted moment when the promised marvel occurs and Garbo laughs, the face that for Roland Barthes betokened the supreme ecstasy afforded by cinema is frozen in inexpressiveness, her countenance animated only in the outburst of ideological fervor that concludes her chastisement of the delinquent delegation. This moment is shot and edited, as William Paul observes, in a full-face closeup that contrasts to the oblique angle and medium shots that capture the chagrin of the miscreants, Iranoff, Buljanoff, and Kopalski. Garbo's closeup, Paul argues, visually confers a "sense of integrity to her feeling that will hover over all the ironies directed toward her through the rest of the film."[9]

But Ninotchka's ideological integrity is also an instance and product of Bergsonian "absentmindedness" that will be corrected by the simplest of correctives—laughter. Garbo's laugh will signal her physical abandon to the realities as well as pleasures of comic existence—the pleasures of food, for instance, which before she regarded as strictly as a matter of caloric intake; of drink, which she will soon experience as a form of divine intoxication; of the pure "silliness" of Leon's joke that nonetheless causes her to burst into giggles and relax into a lingering smile days after it has been told. Silliness can betoken divine as well as imbecilic merriment, as signaled by its root meaning: good, innocent, blessed. To be silly in precapitalist societies meant to be touched by grace. The benign feudalism of the gods is temporarily restored to us in the silliness that makes mock of overly rationalized, aggressively sensible modern regimes.

Ninotchka's laughter has the same revolutionary effect as that which resonates in Milan Kundera's *The Book of Laughter and Forgetting*. There Kundera asserts that laughter is most deeply evoked when "things are deprived suddenly of their supposed meaning, of the place assigned to them in the so-called order of things (a Moscow-trained Marxist believing in horoscopes)." How much more radical an intellectual displacement is Ninotchka's—a Moscow-trained Marxist who comes to believe not in horoscopes but in love, something she had always understood as a matter of chemical attraction. Her devotion to the masses, which has hitherto absorbed her spiritual capacity for love, made her grave, burdened her with the weight of custodial responsibility, a weight that flattened her voice and constricted the range of her motions, limiting them to "serious" and utilitarian rather than pleasurable movements. Laughter lightens this weight but also complicates her feeling about herself, previously so untroubled as to be nonexistent. This doubleness is what makes laughter a demonic as well as enlivening force to contend with. "In origin," Kundera professes, "laughter is . . . of the devil's domain. It has something malicious about it (things suddenly turning out different from what they pretended to be), but to some extent also a beneficent relief (things are less weighty than they appeared to be, letting us live more freely, no longer oppressing us with their austere seriousness)." [10]

Kundera's account of the diabolic origins of laughter derives from Baudelaire's insight that laughter is "intimately connected with the accident of an ancient fall, of a physical and moral degradation."[11] Laughter, Baudelaire proposes, is the expression of a divided and contradictory being. It is

> at one and the same time a sign of infinite greatness and of infinite wretchedness, infinite wretchedness in relation to the absolute being, of whom man has an inkling, infinite greatness in relation to the beasts. It is from the constant clash of these two infinities that laughter flows; the comic, the power of laughter, is in the laugher, not at all in the object of laughter. It is not the man who falls down that laughs at his own fall, unless he is a philosopher, a man who has acquired, by force of habit the power of getting outside himself quickly and watching, as a disinterested spectator, the phenomenon of his ego.[12]

Laughter can emanate only from a divided human nature. The holy one, "the sage of all sages, the Incarnate Word, has never laughed. In the eyes of Him who knows and can do all things, the comic does not exist."[13]

But this is also the case with the totalitarian ego, a demonic parody of the divine agent in never feeling itself split between two infinities. Ninotchka's ego is organized as a totalitarian personality. She even thinks of herself as a tiny cog in the wheel of evolution, an incorporated part of a total system. No sense of self-division disturbs her consciousness, which is completely subsumed in its contemplation of and subservience to the collective. Her "fall" into laughter is thus a happy fall, a sign of her recuperable humanity. This, too, accords with Baudelaire's claim that the "phenomenon produced by the Fall will become the means of redemption."[14] As the ardent disciple of Marxist creed, Ninotchka never laughs; she is the object of the comic, not its bemused spectator. This is the negative side of her awesome integrity, her ideological pride impervious to irony. In Garbo's laugh we hear the first peals of the crumbling totalitarian ego that could serenely contemplate the liquidation of her people for the sake of having fewer but better Russians. Laughter is the saving grace for those, like Ninotchka, who have dedicated themselves to the savage gods of modernity. Her laughter, then, is the most sublime expression of her anti-modernity.

This is why Garbo's laugh still resonates. It is in her comic life as Ninotchka, the ideologue who succumbs to the silliness of love, that Garbo speaks most directly to this age of crumbling ideologies. She speaks to us in two ways: as an ideologue, chastened and reformed by laughter, who still respects the moral claims and human aspiration expressed by her chosen ideology, however harsh its political implementation; and as a sexual being who has not abandoned or compromised her power to convey womanhood as an unsolvable mystery.

Befitting the incongruity of chiding, even while relying on Garbo's spiritually taut nature, the film begins with an egregious pun on her alarming power as screen icon (which Barthes regarded purely as a figure of awe). "This picture," declares the introductory title, "takes place in Paris in those wonderful days when a siren was a brunette and not an alarm . . . and if a Frenchman turned out the light it was not on account of an air raid!" A pun, the most egalitarian of rhetorical figures, provides the homely but reliable vehicle for conveying Garbo, the temptress of *The Flesh and the Devil,* to the precincts of Thalia, Muse of Comedy. A siren, like the Vamp, is one of the screen's most legendary images of predatory womanhood. The once-upon-a-time quality of this preface comically blends historical time with the dream time of sexual idyll. As a dream figure, the siren is a source of arousal rather than alarm, yet the effort to disconnect the idea of eroticism from the idea of danger merely reinforces the association. Once reminded of the two possible meanings of siren, it's hard to detach the bedroom-farce image of a Frenchman's turning off the light from the wails of an air-raid siren.

What justifies this egregious if democratically minded pun uniting two apparently disparate definitions of a siren is the idea of extinction, one through a superhuman pleasure, the other through impersonal and mechanical Force. Either sense, then, is sufficient to convey a threat of sexual and physical peril associated with Ninotchka's existence that is never completely dispelled, but rather insistently if quietly elaborated in otherwise anecdotal moments in the film. There is, for example, the story that Ninotchka relates to the enamored Leon, about her brief encounter with a Polish Lancer, who expired, although less romantically than Romeo, on her blade. In an astonishing gesture, Ninotchka suddenly bares the back of her neck, exposing the scar that memorializes their engagement. Comedy always takes seriously the fatality of love, although few go as far in staging, as Ninotchka and Leon do, a mock-execution that will symbolically atone for the hubris of their loving each other.

Lubitsch will cannily play on Garbo's cinematic image, but he is equally adroit in exploiting her appeal as an allegorical figure linking the suspicious but delirious delights of sexual fable to the alarming historical world of mechanical reproduction—bombs and sirens, five-year plans and war machines. The initial casualty of the militant scientism of the Soviet regime may be the idea of Paris itself, which interests Ninotchka only for its technical achievements. Through her enthusiasms we come to know a different Paris, the Paris of engineering marvels rather than romantic escapades, the Paris whose resplendent modernity is symbolized by the odd inclination of the Eiffel Tower, whose 829 steps she resolutely climbs despite the mitigation, offered by the less energetic Leon, that an elevator ride is included in the price of admission. Ninotchka is alert to the odd inclination of its structure, but Leon is alive primarily to the view it affords of the city's scenic wonders. From its observation platform he evokes the Paris of *names*—the Paris of the Grand Boulevards, the Arc de Triomphe, the Opera, Montparnasse, Montmartre. That Ninotchka could resist these temptations on the mount suggests an indifference to the romance of the past.

This is why her entrance into the world of comedy generates fear as well as excitement. What is there to alarm us as the languorous Swede makes her debut as comic siren? Perhaps the very fact that her first directive to the abject trio of Iranoff, Buljanoff, and Kopalski, understandably solicitous of their female superior, is that an issue *not* be made of her womanhood. Only one so dehumanized or one so enlightened—say the emancipated androgyne of a new Soviet Society—could so easily dismiss the sexual courtesies that regulate so much of the interaction of men and women and indeed so offhandedly but effectively challenge the ontological basis of comedy in sexual differ-ence. Garbo will never be a fast-talking dame at home in the raucous, entrepreneurial comedies of the democratic West. Like many of the heroines of the film considered here, however, she heralds a new muta-tion, the once and future woman, with all the unprecedented delights and complications, not to mention anxieties, that such a mutation en-tails, especially when, like Ninotchka, her very appearance bespeaks the triumph of a revolutionized womankind.

Such a woman will have little patience and less pity for the dream lovers who haunt the sexual imagination of the decadent West. Hence the historical verdict she pronounces on Leon, a "luxury" item of capi-talist sexuality. On first meeting him, she immediately perceives the ideological and economic origins of that most deliberately inconse-quent of Western sexual behaviors—flirtation—in the males' "superior earning power." Then, without a trace of malice or regret, she pre-dicts: "Your type will soon be extinct." It is typical of her prophecies that the future is heralded as an extinction. Leon, the gigolo, is espe-cially vulnerable to the historical purges that seem to lie ahead, since he serves a sexual purpose divorced from any known mode of social utility. He leads an expensive but unproductive existence, so that Ninotchka's later question to him—"And what do you do for mankind?"—strikes us as asking a dodo the purpose of its wings. The film treats such apoca-lyptic fantasies as a joke, a risky move, given the date of the film, but justified in light of the comic tradition. Comedy entertains sensualists and hedonists, bon vivants and gourmands of hilariously finicky appe-tites with fond indulgence, appreciating them as the funniest as well as the hardiest elite of comic society.

Of course the real guarantor of a society's future is less the defeat or elimination of its enemies than its success in biologically and ideo-logically reproducing itself. The ideological battle between the new Russia and the decadent West takes its most comic turn on the sexual front. This confrontation takes the form of an ideological debate on the nature of love. This debate occurs in Leon's apartment, whose most arresting feature is a mural depicting a classical, monumental female form, possibly a caryatid, and two Chagall-like figures locked in an em-brace, floating upward into an ethereal dimension. The classic-archaic style defines a modernity that Leon, in other respects an objectionable if charming parasite feasting at the tables of a displaced nobility, themselves casualties of modern history, can both appreciate and embody.

Against this backdrop Ninotchka, drawn to Leon despite his bleak historical prospects and *ancien régime* manners, declares her attraction to him in the arid language of scientific socialism. Love, she asserts, is a "romantic designation for a most ordinary biological or, shall we say, chemical process." Within these terms, she reassures the lovestruck Leon, she finds that "chemically, we're already quite sympathetic." She admires, apparently on eugenic rather than poetic grounds, the clarity of the white of his eyes, the excellence of his cornea. From a technical standpoint, Leon is certainly serviceable, and what, after all, is she but a tiny cog in the great wheel of evolution.

But then the clock strikes twelve. For Ninotchka it is twelve o'clock; Leon insists that it is midnight, and in those two terms lie all the difference in their comic attitude toward time. Twelve o'clock is a chronological marker, midnight a romantic idea, the witching hour when one half of Paris, Leon rhapsodizes, is making love to the other half. With a lover's—or is it a gigolo's?—canny knowledge of how to "speak" his love, Leon echoes Ninotchka's appeal to the authority of Nature, transposing her image of natural impulses into a symptomology of the "divine passion": "Why do doves bill and coo? Why do snails, the coldest of all creatures, circle interminably around each other? Why do moths fly thousands of miles to find their mates? Why do flowers gently open their petals? Oh, Ninotchka, Ninotchka, surely you have felt some slight symptom of the divine passion: a general warmth in the palms of your hands, a strange heaviness in your limbs, a burning of the lips that isn't thirst but a thousand times more tantalizing, more exulting, than thirst?"

Skeptical Ninotchka merely remarks, "You are very talkative," thus consigning Leon and his poetic sensibility to the feminine position. And indeed what starts as a naturalist's inventory is soon exalted into images that detail, as Sappho had done millennia before, the symptoms of the divine passion: a general warmth in the palms of the hands, a strange heaviness in the limbs, the burning thirst of insatiable and ennobling desire. Leon's finest verbal moment is also his most feminized one. To reinforce and visibly highlight the gender reversals and confusions, Lubitsch shoots their climactic kiss from an oblique and high angle, an "odd inclination" visually inspired, perhaps, by the slight tilt of the Eiffel Tower that Ninotchka had observed earlier in the evening. One kiss begets the desire for another. "Again," she commands him. Leon obligingly leans over the recumbent Ninotchka.

But Lubitsch does not sustain the pose, the inclination, nor the implied conventionality of their sexual positions. He repositions the camera to capture Ninotchka sitting upright, regaining the balance and initiative she had ceded only a few moments ago. She then vigorously descends on him, while the overmastered Leon succumbs to the insistent forcefulness of her "natural" chemical attraction. Lubitsch may be capitalizing on the sexual ambiguity that infused Garbo's screen personality. Certainly, he trusts Garbo to play with gender confusion and subtilize it, intimating that such alterations in female nature are on the order of a transfiguration.

Her first appearance in the film is less on the order of transfiguration, however.

She enters the film a disconcerting vision of sexual oddity. At first we suspect that the envoy for whom Iranoff, Buljanoff, and Kubalski are nervously waiting at the train station is the orthodox professorial type they first approach. They are quickly disabused of his ideological outlook when he raises a "Heil Hitler" salute. (This gag, which so boldly asserts that a Fascist was no different from a Bolshevik, that you couldn't even tell them apart, since both have the uniform and the depersonalized look of the totalitarian character—gained a grim pertinence by the Hitler-Stalin pact, which was concluded after the film was made but before its general release.)

When the camera locates Garbo among the bustle of detraining passengers, she stands eerily isolated in the middle distance. Initially her presence in the frame possesses no more visual significance than would that of an extra. She is erect and unflinching when the camera discloses her face, betraying no hint of the languorous sensuality that in her tragic films suggests that, spiritually speaking, she is finely attuned to vibrations unheard by us more sluggish mortals. She appears equipped rather than dressed, with a unisex (not androgynous) suit typically adopted by totalitarian regimes whose ruthless utopianism entails abolishing all evidence of *gendered* culture, whether in fashion, in daily speech ("comrade" for all manner of human relations and affections), or in manners. A rapid cut to her face then announces that this new Garbo will speak in the voice of a new age—a low, uninflected monotone, in keeping with the drabness of her attire, but devastatingly effective in delivering sardonic commentary on the behavior of her comrades and the appalling mores of the West.

Although given all the elements to create a political lampoon, Garbo nevertheless makes us feel what a real ideologue sounds like without reducing Ninotchka to caricature. Her voice is pitched at just the right timbre for the social criticism and political idealism that are the target of the film's first ideological joke. Who is to say who has the saner view of socioeconomics in the following exchange between Ninotchka and the porter:

NINOTCHKA: Why should you carry other people's bags?

PORTER: Well, that's my business, madam.

NINOTCHKA: That's no business. That's social injustice.

PORTER: That depends on the tip.

The porter tops the joke, but it is Ninotchka who scores the point. She refuses to have anyone carry her bags in the same spirit and for the same reasons that she refuses flowers: "Don't make an issue of my womanhood." In her radical sex-utopianism, she regards the sexual division of labor as antiquated as the sexual gallantries persisting from feudal into capitalist societies. When, on leaving the station, she makes her prediction that because of the mass trials "There are going to be fewer but better Russians," we begin to suspect why an issue should not, indeed cannot, be made of her womanhood. Soviet indoctrination has managed to accomplish what the innately murderous Lady Macbeth could only hope the gods would accomplish. It has unsexed her. The Soviet pogroms of eugenic utopianism—mass exile and executions producing fewer but better Russians—fail to elicit the faintest peep of "womanly" protest at the appalling slaughter, the shameful cost in human life. The moral credit that Ninotchka accrues in reminding us how dear food is and how costly love can be is substantially discounted in advance by this evidence of the human price she is willing to pay to secure the triumph of her beloved "masses."

Despite such chilling endorsement of mass trials, there is no question that in this film we are to make the acquaintance of a new Garbo, one who, however ideologically misguided, does not live in and for herself, but only in and for the company and good of other people. This is confirmed when, on being shown the expanse of the Royal Suite, she asks, in a droll but utterly matter-of-fact tone: "Which part of the room is mine?" They inform her that there is no need to divide up space in the West (oh, no?) as in Russia, and when Iranoff asks whether she wants, in fact, to be alone, her response is a quick and curt no. This reply surely ranks as one of the most succinct and good-natured self-debunkings in screen history. In that unemphatic no, Garbo dispatches her private and public image as brooding solitary at home only in her own society. *Ninotchka* gives us that previously unimaginable creature—a *sociable* Garbo.

But this is the sober, spiritually austere Garbo of whom we speak, sociable on certain terms. Hers must be a society that measures up to her ideological specifications. It must conform to her notion of justice in its distribution of wealth, agree with her vision of productive labor and share her sense of the beautiful. In deciding this last requirement, consider, as Ninotchka does, the matter of hats, that increasingly rare emblem of feminine chic and masculine elegance. Kundera might again assist us here. In his personal dictionary of the sixty-three words that mean the most to him, Kundera finds room for only one precious object: "Hat. Magical object" is the concise notation.[15] The only other object grudingly but necessarily admitted to his private lexicon is "the uniform," abject emblem of the "great systems that quantify and plan life." Part of the value and attraction of a hat, we might conclude, is that it is not a uniform. Western underwear apparently possesses the same antitotalitarian properties, as becomes apparent when Ninotchka, once back in Russia but no longer such a "good Russian," gives lingerie to her comrade in a gesture of sexual rather than political solidarity. Lubitsch's eye is worldly, and since Kracauer's indictment of him in *From*

Caligari to Hitler, he has been regarded by those who revere as well as abjure him as uninterested in the political price that underwrites his sophisticated comedies.[16]

To rebut this charge, let us offer the evidence of his profound understanding of the sexual and ideological significance of the hat, which can simultaneously signal, hilariously but quite accurately, the spiritual disposition of his characters and the moral state of their society. In *Design for Living* (1933), Lubitsch's other great Parisian comedy, Gilda Farrell (Miriam Hopkins) complains that men may change women with the same freedom and frequency as they change hats, but for women, the sexual choice is often lamentably limited to one head-piece. The moral dramaturgy of *Ninotchka* is more promiscuously as well as incisively conveyed by the hats symbolizing the various modes of conversion his characters undergo (all the conversions, however different in their seriousness, are regarded through the same indulgent humor). The first visual conversion joke involves the witty transformation of Iranoff's, Buljanoff's, and Kopalski's Russian hats into top hats. The exchange of native and functional headgear for fashionable attire signals a giddily nonviolent revolution in their inner nature. The joke is as economical as it is effective. Brevity, of course, is always the soul of wit, but economy is especially important in a comedy that dramatizes the inordinate expense of the things we want but whose cost to others we conveniently forget to calculate in advance.

The hat that catches Ninotchka's eye when she first enters a Parisian hotel (and a grand one at that) has an even more crucial significance. Unlike the top hat, this nonstandardized example of the milliner's craft epitomizes the mutable, ephemeral, and nonsensical spirit of fashion. Its very form playfully subverts any pretenses to *dignified* beauty (Garbo's beauty in its purest form). Its base is softly conical but its apex is a comic hybrid between a dunce cap and a smokestack. I hazard to describe it as a hat with disappointed or curtailed phallic aspirations, ending as it does on a jagged rather than majestic peak.

At any rate it is a hat whose comic importance in the film is as much a fetish object as a fashion commodity. My students always laugh at the sight of this hat, perhaps because they have been conditioned to see hats (in movies, that is) as sexual symbols, not by their reading of

Greta Garbo, Melvyn Douglas, and Nintochka's hat in *Ninotchka*

Freud but through their viewing of Charlie Chaplin and Buster Keaton silents. Ninotchka also finds the hat symptomatic. "How can such a civilization survive which permits their women to put things like that on their heads?" Then, shaking her head in disapproval and disbelief, she predicts, "It won't be long now, comrades." The hat speaks to her of the decadence of the West, but to me it is a deliriously precious emblem of the ultimate fate of all transcendental projects before the comic corrective of laughter, which dooms them to incompleteness. Ninotchka's historical judgment on the hat is comic, but more deeply comic is her subsequent need to *wear* it.[17]

Ironically, the hat fulfills its comic purpose when it is superseded by the tiara belonging to the Grand Duchess Swana (Ina Claire). The tiara will complete Ninotchka's transformation from dour bureaucrat into fantasy princess, or, to give her the title Leon bestows on her, Duchess of the People. This climactic transformation scene follows Ninotchka's own initiation into the pleasures of the Parisian night. We know that she is ready for the Dionysian Paris of libations and moonlight, for she has exchanged her sensible suit for an evening gown that itself seems a refugee from an MGM costume drama, drunk champagne, and even managed to incite the restroom attendants into a strike. Now she returns to her suite to celebrate her newfound happiness in private quarters.

But there is no private space for Ninotchka. She is always accompanied by her love for the people. Shadowing her joy is her guilt at enjoying this night of pleasure unavailable to them. She regards her happiness with Leon not as a sign of erotic and emotional fulfillment but of defection. It is the Russian in her who craves confession more than kisses. She needs to admit her betrayal of the masses and pay the penalty reserved for traitors to the Russian ideal—the firing squad. Leon indulges this Dostoyevskian fantasy, propping her against the door sill, blindfolding her, and, before returning to the table to uncork the champagne, giving her a farewell kiss. In a faultlessly choreographed moment, Leon pops the cork and Ninotchka collapses to the floor. A statue of Eros hovers in the background, visually asserting that Love has claimed its victim even as Russia has exacted her price. Ninotchka comes from the Russia of mass trials and five-year plans, but her symbolic expiation is in the tradition of Dostoevsky and Tolstoy, spiritual and messianic, rather than of Lenin and Stalin, ideological and totalitarian. "I've paid my penalty," she declares with obvious relief. The redeemed Ninotchka can now finally delight in love's long-deferred revelries.

Revelries require music, so Ninotchka gaily leads Leon to what she takes to be a radio, since it answers to the description of that latest engineering marvel—a box with a knob, out of whose interior come speech and song. But it is not a radio, it is the room safe. Within it are the contested jewels of the Grand Duchess Swana. Ninotchka and Leon are no longer contending parties in a lawsuit to determine ownership of the jewels. They are no longer even custodians of the historical booty that represent for Ninotchka the "tears of Old Russia" and for Leon the confiscated estate of the duchess. They are intoxicated lovers who gaze into the wall hollow as if peering into a sibyl's—or a pirates'—cave.

Their visual and spiritual absorption is filmed from an "impossible" angle—from inside the safe. Another odd angle, then, in a film otherwise committed to the comic detachment afforded by medium shots. As a point of view realizable only in film, this shot has a disorienting but revelatory effect. It discloses the inner sanctum of that apparatus capable of conferring on human beings and objects a unique aura, a glorious if ultimately shadowy and insubstantial existence. Everything in this climactic love scene leads up to and follows from this intuition about the relation between camera eye and "dream" screen. The camera visually transports us into a fantasy realm where articles like hats have magical properties and can change an apparatchik into a princess.

Even the court jewels, already precious by any economic or cultural estimation, are subject to transvaluation. When Swana's jewels were laid out before a jeweler for appraisal earlier in the film, they possessed for Ninotchka nothing but a cash value. Now they possess the aura of cultic objects. Like all cultic objects, they inspire a hushed awe rather than clamorous greed. "They're terrible things, those jewels," she declares. She lets the word "terrible" tremble with its latent and primal sense of terror before the appalling realities of human life. She takes on the burden of this terror with the same majesty that she wears the tiara with which Leon crowns her Ninotchka the Great. Through Ninotchka's mock execution and resurrection, sanctified by her ritual coronation as Grand Duchess of the People, the court jewels are restored to their "rightful" if not legal owners, who paid for them in blood.

There is as much mockery as sympathy in Ninotchka's confounding of political and sexual feelings. And yet *Ninotchka* is a comedy that manages the extraordinary feat of converting its heroine's ideas about love without compromising her principles. Ninotchka the Great in this respect seems a title that properly belongs to her, a title that acknowledges Ninotchka's (and of course Garbo's) charismatic beauty, as well as her moral grandeur. She neither forgets her political allegiance to the people nor banishes, as Shakespeare's Prince Hal did as he assumed his rule, the silliness that is one of the joys of private life and its affections.

Her coronation thus enacts a restoration as well as a revolution.

What is restored is Garbo's cinematic identity as the screen's greatest advocate of Love before the court of History. Garbo's words now perform what her laughter had earlier affirmed—her human nature. In addressing the phantom masses that Leon imagines attending her royal proclamation, she pleads with them not to relinquish their hopes but to forestall their avidity for a future that is destined to be theirs: "Comrades! People of the world! The Revolution is on the march!... I know ... bombs will fall ... civilization will crumble ... but not yet, please ... wait ... what's the hurry? Give us our moment. Let's be happy.... We are happy, aren't we, Leon? So happy and so tired, oh."

Ninotchka, the functionary whose relation to words and to speech had been purely utilitarian, now issues an importunate lyric cry that would isolate out of the remorseless onrush of history—with its catastrophes, advancements, retrogressions, extinctions, and upheavals—a timeless and perhaps senseless moment. She lingers over the word hurry, as if chiding the impatient masses as one would an obstreperous child. We suddenly hear in her voice what we could not see in her face, how *tired* Ninotchka must have become in her dutiful attempts to keep step with the march of history. Now the meaning of her reaction to Leon's first kiss, which she describes as "restful," becomes suddenly available to us. We might recall, too, that when Ninotchka first met Leon she was standing on a traffic island, timing the interval between the change in signals. The "explorer" interested only in chronometric measures now asks permission to linger in a different temporality, the enchanted interval reserved for lovers. Her vision of history is not so much reversed as expanded and enhanced. As a good Marxist, she never abjures the belief in history as a dialectical sequence of irresistible, impersonal movements, but she now allows that within its unfolding one may encounter grace-filled intervals of happiness.

By virtue of this speech, Ninotchka reveals herself to be not so much a siren as a sibyl. Throughout the film she is given to historical prediction, but now her prophecy seems drawn from deeper life sources than the dogma of dialectical materialism. With this in mind, let us finally return to consider the historical meaning of Garbo's face and the iconographic age to which her words as much as her image give such exalted expression. Her face and her words are opposed by a woman with an equally arresting face whose words and manner of speech betray, as do Ninotchka's, the habit of command. She is Swana, the Grand Duchess, Ninotchka's ideological as well as sexual rival, the woman who can afford Leon and who behaves according to an altogether different mythology of womanhood.

Indeed it is Swana, the casualty of history, who offers us one way to read the face. We first see her as she is awaiting the arrival of Leon, her lover, about the fate of the crown jewels that were given to her by her mother, the very jewels Ninotchka has come to Paris to sell. The camera catches her contemplating her face in a mirror, as if visually suggesting that the two fortunes on which her life has depended and which are now both vanishing, one through expropriation, the other through the inevitable depletions of age. History and mortality vie to inscribe their legends onto her face. Either way, Swana is a victim of time. Ideologues might carp that Lubitsch falsely equates a narcissistic injury (a beautiful woman losing her looks) with a grand historical catastrophe (the liquidation of the material basis of a class and a way of life), yet a great simplicity unites both the emotional and historical verdict that Swana renders on her own reflection: "I guess one gets the face one deserves." This is an unsentimental, morally weary judgment. No one unacquainted with the vicissitudes of history and adversities of life would be capable of rendering it.

But in what way does Ninotchka deserve her face? Certainly she does not inherit its grave beauty from Lenin, her Svengali, or, as the film more sensibly proposes, her "little father," whose picture rests by her bedside, token of those familial affections that ideological fanaticism can redirect if not liquidate. As she drops off to sleep, the lovestruck Ninotchka will appeal to that iconic face to smile, as if in benediction, on her night of love. A prayer that is answered! The little father's fixed pose become animated as his lips and then his entire face relax into a smile. Human love has the power, it would seen, to transfigure the stern and rigid features of an ideological icon, conferring on them the suppleness of lived humanity. That such an affirmation should come in the form of a cinematic "miracle," rendering animate an image frozen in an instant of irrecoverable time, reminds us that in going to the movies we are experiencing anew that phantasmic as well as technological magic that transforms the still photograph into a moving image.[18]

But the film is also conscious of a contrary fate for the fetish-photograph in which a beloved or revered face is consecrated. Such love tokens may, in fact they frequently do, end up as Swana's picture does, hidden away in a drawer. That is where Leon has consigned her photograph after meeting Ninotchka, and Ninotchka, on finding it, fears that the same fate awaits her. She begs him never to ask for her picture, since she couldn't bear the thought of being shut up in a drawer; she couldn't breathe. Lubitsch injects this pathos as a commentary on the fugitive, even furtive nature of human loves, which can so quickly find oblivion once their emotional peak or economic serviceableness subsides (Leon was and for all Ninotchka knows, still is, a gigolo). Garbo's face is never caught, or, as she regards it, entombed, in a photograph. The camera, however transfixed by her beauty, might caress her features, but it will not immobilize her in the frozen moment of a "still."

Swana, the woman whom Leon and history have passed over, is played by Ina Claire, a piece of casting that gives to the antagonism between the Old and New Russia a particularly personal resonance. Claire, one of the reigning stars of Broadway in the twenties, had once been married to John Gilbert, Garbo's most famous screen partner and the man she famously jilted on their wedding day. The Hollywood that could callously cast Jean Harlow in *Reckless* (1935), a film depicting the suicide of a showgirl's husband only a year after the scandalous death of Harlow's own husband, the pitiable Paul Bern, is more tactful in presenting Garbo and Claire as sexual rivals. Or rather Lubitsch is more tactful in staging the confrontation between two "stellar" forms of womanhood, one the creation of the theatrical boards, the other of the movie set.

Claire is an actress who belongs to the classical regime of theater, Garbo to the new arts of celluloid. Her moral reflection that one gets the face one deserves resonates somewhat differently in this context. Hers is the remark of a stage actress whose art is hardly concerned

Garbo confronts Ina Claire in *Ninotchka*

with enhancing the human image through visual sleight-of-hand, cosmetic correction, flattering lighting. The stage is the arena of masks, of passions and attitudes simplified into elemental emotions. The film, the comic film especially, rarely gives us heroines with faces they deserve, but faces created by an artful Nature, beautiful faces, enchanting faces, faces animated and perfected as much as humanly possible by the caressing light of cinema.

All this and much more is implied in the extraordinary confrontation between Swana and Ninotchka that leads to the film's final love complication. Swana appears in Ninotchka's suite the night after she has been "crowned" Duchess of the People. Still in her "Sleeping Beauty" attire, Ninotchka receives Swana with a wariness we have seen before. But she is also confident, as we are confident, that Swana will never win Leon back through the feeble blackmail scheme she proposes. As they exchange words, the camera exchanges shot for countershot, sustaining a visual and dramatic equipoise rarely observed elsewhere in the film. The effect is to suggest the validity of each claimant's right to the booty of war, for what, after all, is at stake but the spoils of war salvaged from a decimated, postrevolutionary, postwar Russia.

It is at this moment that Lubitsch makes us feel the *historical* claim of the New Russia against the Old, the moral superiority of its new women. The dispute between the two women is less over the jewels, which, except for the coronation scene, are a mere pretext for the comic action, but over the fate of a class, of a culture, of a historical era. Their rivalry expands beyond the comic perimeters of sexual competition and enters the ideological domain of warring, adversary cultures: the Old Russia that took to its heart the arts and pleasures of the "enlightened" West, with all the decadence communicated in that embrace, and the New Russia, "barbaric" (as Leon deems it) in its messianic fervor to eliminate the injustices of life, even if it means eradicating all the reasons to live it.

The remainder of the film involves the external complications that will keep Ninotchka and Leon apart. They have already overcome the internal deterrents to their love, and these, not ideological differences, are the supreme obstacles to their comic union. We get to see Ninotchka "at home," sharing her quarters with comrades as idiosyncratic as any that might appear in the humor comedies of the West, sharing quarters and Western undergarments with a female comrade, breaking rationed eggs with Iranoff, Buljanoff, and Kopalski to concoct an omelet. However bleak her material surroundings, we know that Ninotchka remains enriched, having learned to enjoy the pleasures of eating.

It was a lesson she learned in the Parisian restaurant where she first laughed. It, too, was a place where the working classes enjoyed common pleasures, only then Ninotchka's relation to food was alimentary rather than festive. Then it was she who was out of place and out of sympathy with the common people. On ordering raw beets and carrots, she is politely but firmly rebuked by the aggrieved restaurateur Pere Mathieu (Charles Judels): "Madam, this is a restaurant, not a meadow." It is another sign of how right Leon was to regard her as a barbarian, since there is something primitive rather than puritanical in her indifference to pleasure, indicating not her aversion to affordable delights, culinary or otherwise, but her failure to even suspect their existence.

Yet even while satirizing Soviet privations Lubitsch seems quite sympathetic to and even admiring of the Russian character and the values exhibited in the Moscow apartment. These are the values most missed in the West and the least likely to survive transplantation. So much is suggested by the film's droll conclusion. Leon successfully lures Ninotchka and her merry cohorts out of Russia, thus proving his worthiness to possess her. They will form a "new Russia," which will make its first settlement in Constantinople, where they will open a restaurant (instead of reclaiming a meadow!). But the assimilation of capitalist methods to launch a Russian joint enterprise concludes with Kopalski, a one-man picket line, going on strike against his partners, Iranoff and Buljanoff. Against this image we might superimpose the memory of Ninotchka's sharing a room, silk undergarments, and an egg to make an omelet. The future woman is brought out from the cold of history, but Lubitsch's subtle art apprises us of what has been lost as well as gained by bringing Ninotchka into the comic fold.

Ninotchka is thus a film that replays in grand historical and lightly comic manner the reimportation of Garbo-Ninotchka into the dream life of the West. It was to be her last great role, one that made the best and most serious use of her grave and exotic beauty, her spiritual authority, and, finally, the sexual ambiguity that made her womanhood at once so distant and so piquant. Lubitsch understood, appreciated, and uncovered the *lightness* that subtended her moral gravity, and one can only applaud his instinct in pursuing his intuition about the essential comic aspects of her divinity, even as he doubted her capacity for laughter. As he recollects his initial hopes and misgivings about casting Garbo:

> Because she was funny. You couldn't see it? You didn't know how funny she was off screen? . . . And I knew she could be funny on the screen. . . . Most of them are so heavy, heavy! But she was light, light always, and for comedy, nothing matters more. When someone has a light touch, they can play com-

edy, and it doesn't hurt if they're beautiful. There was only one thing that worried me a little. I wondered if she could laugh, because I didn't have a finish if she didn't have a laugh. She had the most beautiful smile. What am I saying? She had a whole collection of smiles . . . warm, motherly, friendly, polite, sexy, amused, mysterious. Beautiful smiles. But a smile is not a laugh. I said to her one day, "Can you laugh?" And she said, "I think so." I said to her, "Do you often laugh?" And she said, "Not often." I said, "Could you laugh right now?" And she said, "Let me come back tomorrow." And then next day she came back and she said, "All right. I'm ready to laugh." So I said, "Go ahead." And she laughed and it was beautiful! And she made me laugh, and there we sat in my office like two loonies laughing for about ten minutes. From that moment on, I knew I had a picture.[19]

Garbo herself seems to have been aware of her affinity for the lightness of comic being. Walter Reisch reports the following conversation with Garbo at a time when it might still have been possible for her to come out of retirement:

"Greta, if you ever wanted to make a comeback, give us one hint of what you would like to do. Do you want to play an actress, a spy, a coquette, a scientist?"
"A clown. A male clown."
"The most desired woman on earth wants to play a clown? Who will buy that?"
"Under the makeup and the silk pants, the clown is a woman. All the admiring girls in the audience who write him letters are wondering why he does not respond. They cannot understand."
"It will never do," I said.[20]

It never did do, but it revealed yet again how deeply tied to tradition was Garbo's interpretation of her own nature. The face that once plunged audiences into deepest ecstasy and the laugh that seemed that of a goddess enjoying a fully achieved human incarnation belonged to that silliest and often saddest of dramatic artists—the clown. And it was in a clown that Garbo could behold and secure the most complex image of her womanhood.

8 Female Rampant

His Girl Friday

The film's title blares out at us from a blur of news-print. Its bold headline gives undisputed prominence to an ascendant female type with a jazzy moniker — His Girl Friday. The subject of this fanfare is Hildy Johnson, surely the fastest of the fast-talking dames of American screen comedy and perhaps the best newspaperman ever portrayed on film. She makes us aware of how "talking pictures" gave women the chance to speak up, speak out, and speak to their own desires, dreams, and ambitions. Presented with this opportunity, they made the most of it. They spoke fast and furiously, as if their survival depended on their doing so.

As, indeed, it did. The main business of comedy, unlike that of tragedy or melodrama, is to show us what makes a successful human being, happy in both work and play, sexually and professionally ful-filled. The comedies of the thirties and early forties teach us nothing if they don't impress upon us that slow-witted, reticent, or inarticulate women had little chance for sexual happiness, still less for professional success. In comedy, quickness is all. Why timing *should* be all is a good question, and this film does not hesitate to ask it. It puts this question to us in a particularly charged way: by showing us the relation between Hildy's work as a reporter, which she wants to abandon; her dream of a home, which she wants to pursue; and the impending execution of a convicted murderer, whose life it is in her power to save.

Yet my initial description of Hildy as regnant, by virtue of her quick wit, over the comic action, is somewhat belied by her apparent status as a girl Friday, a term that may strike us as dated, if not down-right retrograde. Consider, for instance, the masculine presumption of that possessive pronoun "his," which intimates some claim to exclusive rights, a claim that editor Walter Burns (Cary Grant) converts into playful threat when he reminds Hildy (Rosalind Russell), his ace reporter and ex-wife, that he would kill her if she went to work for anyone else. Hildy treats this warning as a backhanded compliment: "Did you hear that, Bruce?" she says to her fiancé, Bruce Baldwin (Ralph Bellamy). "That's my diploma!" She is amused at the notion that she can be "his" and rightly feels that she has graduated to a higher and more self-dependent status. Indeed, she announces at the beginning of the film that she will henceforth belong to herself. More accurately, she proclaims her intention of "going into business for myself."

The business, presumably, of getting married and leading, as Hildy declares, a "halfway normal life." Hildy is disgusted with the work of a newspaperman, a sordid scramble to gather all the news unfit to print. When Walter accuses her of being a traitor to journalism, Hildy retorts: "A journalist? Hell, what does that mean? Peeping through key-holes? Chasing after fire engines? Waking people up in the middle of the night to ask if Hitler is going to start another war? Stealing pictures off old ladies? I know all about reporters, Walter. A lot of daffy buttinskis running around without a nickel in their pockets. And for what? So a million hired girls and motormen's wives'll know what's going on."[1] The class animus and mysogyny of this diatribe, lifted from the film's source, Ben Hecht and Charles MacArthur's play *The Front Page,* where is it is delivered by a man, is given an added sexual twist when spoken by a woman. In the play, the lament about the decline of manly journalism into sensationalist fare is part of the masculinist satire against the coarseness as well as imperiousness of female appetites. When a woman speaks derisively of the tastes of hired girls and motormen's wives, we get a different sense of the routine indignities, inflicted and suffered, of the newspaper trade.

The film will confirm Hildy's sense that the life of a newspaperman is the dramatic equivalent of farce, in which sexual and professional decorum, as well as "dignified" notions of truth, are the primary casualties. But Howard Hawks's comedy will also convince us, as it will Hildy, not to fret unduly about the mutual demise of both dignity and truth. This would be an odd moral, even an unacceptable one, if Hawks did not affirm something new—and newsworthy—in their place: an altered relation between the sexes that is breezily indifferent to, when it is not downright contemptuous of, the decorum that regulates a "halfway normal life."

Hildy has yet to learn that for her marriage will entail more than a move to Albany, where she hopes to spend her time in the company of a different class of women: it will entail a change of nature. In pursuing a halfway normal life, Hildy is working not only against her instincts as a newspaperman but against her destiny as a fast-talking dame. In Lubitsch's *That Uncertain Feeling* (1941), Jill Baker (Merle Oberon) tries to fend off her friends' suggestion that she see a psychiatrist to "cure" her recurrent and apparently psychosomatic hiccoughs by insisting that she's a "perfectly normal woman." "Don't say that about yourself, even in fun," is the friendly but firm rejoinder. Being perfectly normal is no laughing matter.

Hildy, of course, is not a perfectly normal woman, although for reasons she takes pains to explain to Walter, and other reasons that she is perhaps concealing, she aspires to become one. To begin with, Hildy was conceived as a man. She was born Hildebrand "Hildy" Johnson in the 1928 play; moved from stage to film in 1931 in the person of Pat O'Brien; and was reconceived and reborn in 1940, thanks to the maieutic skill of Howard Hawks, as Hildegarde Johnson. Although she retains the surname and some of the lines of her namesake, she avoids the fate of imitated being, sexual mimicry, and masquerade. Hildegarde Johnson is a more original, endearing, and modern being than her male prototype, already identified by Hecht and MacArthur as a "vanishing type—the lusty, hoodlumesque, half-drunken caballero that was the newspaperman of our youth." So the playwrights at once tag and eulogize him, lamenting that "schools of journalism and the advertising business have nearly extirpated the species." [2] Hildegarde Johnson is neither endangered species nor rowdy anachronism: she represents, rather, a new female mutation.

Hawks casts a knowing eye on his own predilection for such outlandish human developments when he concludes the film's prologue with the deliberate whimsy of "Once upon a time . . . " I take Hawks at his word in presenting *His Girl Friday* as a modern fairy tale, but am not willing to concede that his reassurance that "you will see in this picture no resemblance to the men and women of the press today" is transparently ironic. Hildy and Walter, in fact, do *not* resemble the men and women of their day. They resemble only themselves, fantastical creatures whose nature is at once primordial and futuristic. By this curious description I hope to suggest how Hildy and Walter cannot be understood, much less appreciated, unless we see them as occupying and making their own kind of time. It was Manny Farber who first called attention to the way Hawks's romanticism—which "wraps the fliers-reporters-workhands in a patina of period mannerism and attitude"—makes his films appear not so much "dated as removed from reality, like the land of Tolkien's Hobbits."[3] Hildy is a new female type very much of this company, a "once and future" woman, as it were.

Hawks's fascination with fantasies of regression is less indulged here than in his atavistic comedies, *Bringing Up Baby* and *Monkey Business* (1952), both also featuring Cary Grant. Indeed, it was Hawks's comic genius to see Cary Grant, surely the most debonair of romantic screen presences, as an evolutionary marvel who could revert, in the right comic circumstances, to the postures and devices of neolithic man and still retain, even enhance, his appeal as desirable mate. Hawks's complex manipulation of comic *time* as both regressive and visionary contributes to the illusion that what we are witnessing in his screwball courtship plots is, in fact, an exciting and perhaps dangerous sexual adaptation.

In transforming Hildy into a woman, Hawks was making obvious what the play presented as latent: a love affair between two men. He also seemed to have observed that their love affair lacked romance. I invoke romance here not just in its common amorous sense, but romance as an idealized depiction of charismatic individuals whose vitality explodes all the rules of right or even good behavior. No such romance is possible in the play because its sense of sexual difference is at once too complacent and too naive to admit of erotic enthrallment. Here, for example, is Hecht and MacArthur's description of Peggy, Hildy's fiancée:

Peggy, despite her youth and simplicity, seems overwhelmingly mature in comparison to Hildy. As a matter of fact, Peggy belongs to that division of womanhood which dedicates itself to suppressing in its lovers or husbands the spirit of D'Artagnan, Roland, Captain Kidd, Cyrano, Don Quixote, King Arthur or any other type of the male innocent and rampant. In her unconscious and highly noble efforts to make what the female world calls "a man" out of Hildy, Peggy has neither the sympathy nor acclaim of the authors, yet—regarded superficially, she is a very sweet and satisfying heroine.[4]

Peggy is regarded superficially as a sweet and satisfying heroine because she is conceived superficially. The iconoclasm of the play never targets the thoroughly conventional notion that the "female world" dedicates itself to one fundamental activity: domesticating the primal, renegade male. The playwrights, while grudgingly accepting the possible social necessity of this reformation work, clearly prefer the rowdy camaraderie of the pressroom, the last Heminwayesque preserve of "Men without Women," that is, men at once "innocent and rampant." In affixing the heraldic as well as characterological term "rampant" to that generic American type, the male innocent, they endow him with a noble genealogy: Roland, D'Artagnan, Cyrano. Only an American male could fantasize such an ancestry in order to ennoble his arrested emotional development. For all the pungency of its idiomatic dialogue and keen satire on contemporary urban life, *The Front Page* remains oddly quaint, a curious amalgam of social cynicism and sexual sentimentalism that we might call urban pastoral. The play is a nostalgia piece that celebrates the pressroom as a "sort of journalistic Yellowstone Park offering haven to a last herd of fantastic bravos that once roamed the newspaper offices of the country."[5]

The modernity of *His Girl Friday,* then, cannot be attributed to a mechanical updating of an esteemed original. The film is determinedly of its own time and place, at once outlandishly contemporary and knowingly retrograde (as opposed to furtively elegiac) in delightedly reversing traditional sexual roles. The male reversals, by no means as visually spectacular as Hildy's sex-change (which we will consider in a moment), are equally inspired and, indeed, help fuel the comic competition for verbal as well as sexual mastery. Hawks, so expert in exploiting the Hollywood language of "types," enriches his film adaptation by splitting the Hecht-MacArthur "male innocent and rampant" into two competing characters: Hildy's rampant boss and ex-husband, Walter; and her innocent beau, Bruce. Comically speaking, Hawks doubles our sexual fun. Take the casting of Ralph Bellamy as Hildy's suitor. His very presence announces that Hecht and MacArthur's male innocent is no longer rampant but undeniably tamed. Bellamy has made this type so familiar that even within the film he is seen to be *sui generis*. Walter, faltering for a way to describe Bruce to Evangeline, the moll he dispatches to entrap him, resorts to the shorthand of a casting call: "He looks like, uh, that fellow in the movies, you know, uh, Ralph Bellamy." The in-joke carries a comic bonus in reminding us how types in the movies are embodied by actors or actresses with morally readable features that are translated from film to film and part to part. Ralph Bellamy is Ralph Bellamy, a human tautology who can be relied upon to be nothing other than what he appears.

Hawks's other famous in-joke works the opposite charm; it locates the charisma of the chameleon and rampant male, Walter Burns. Near the end of the film Walter Burns darkly warns that the last person to cross him was "Archie Leach a week before he cut his throat." Archie Leach is, of course, Grant's given name. Cary Grant is *never* redundant, although he is always and recognizably the star Cary Grant. The in-joke is in insidious keeping with the feeling, subtly but irresistibly growing in a film that would not seem to permit reflection, that death shadows the action and impels the more creative personalities to outwit death by *acting,* continually trying on new lives, inventing ruses that possess the shimmering radiance, if not the consistency, of truth. Walter fascinates, as truth often does not, because he is never redundant.

The man who esteems himself the lord of the universe (Hildy's phrase but one not disputed by her co-workers) first appears on screen primping before his mirror. Apparently one of the prerogatives of his lordship is enjoying the perks, courtesies, and pleasures traditionally accorded to women without jeopardizing his masculinity, losing his wits, or forfeiting his command. Walter's pleasure in usurping the courtesy normally extended to the fairer sex is hilariously evident in his wacky version of how Hildy "trapped" him into marriage. He claims he was tight on the night he proposed and Hildy acted dishonorably in taking him at his word: "If you'd been a gentleman, you'd have forgotten all about it." It's not important whether the story is true, only that it establishes that Walter is not male innocent and rampant. He is something more imposing: male rampant, reckless with the truth.

We can detect in his feminine preening and ironic vulnerability to Hildy's "ungentlemanly" advances more than a whiff of dandyish effeminacy: there is also a dash of mayhem in his scrambling of gender codes. So much is evident in his reliance on Diamond Louie, an underworld factotum who seems to have a whole repertory company of Runyonesque characters at his disposal to abet Walter's schemes. We may take Walter to be a man who flirts with crime as he flirts with femininity. Passing counterfeit bills and arranging for a kidnaping are two of the criminal offenses that this male rampant passes off as "innocent" maneuvers to keep Hildy from leaving him for Bruce—and Albany, too! Such maneuvers become less innocent when Walter, who mocks Bruce's innocence by warning him that he will depart on his honeymoon with blood on his hands should he prevent Hildy from writing the story that could save a convicted murderer, finds his own potentially stained with the blood of Hildy's future mother-in-law.

That Walter seems to be associated with dead bodies is no small obstacle to his romantic appeal. Take the most disturbing cut in the film, which links Walter to Mollie Malloy (Helen Mack), the Clark Street tart who befriended Earl Williams (John Qualen), the man slated to die at dawn for having shot a policeman. When Earl escapes during a state-mandated psychiatric exam, Mollie acts to distract the police and the press in their pursuit of him by jumping out the pressroom window. She is willing to commit her life to Williams because, it seems, he is the only man who wanted to talk to her, not buy her. As she takes her plunge, the camera cuts from reporters' shocked but professional interest in whether she survives to Walter's arrival on the scene.

Visually and dramatically connecting Mollie's suicidal exit and Burns's entrance is not Hawks's idea; it belongs to the play, with its more obvious moralism. In fact, in the play this is the first we see of

Walter. In their stage directions, Hecht and MacArthur make clear that this dramatic entrance is calculated to impress us with the fact that Walter is at once a boss and a figure of nemesis: "Beneath a dapper and very citizen-like exterior lurks a hobgoblin, perhaps the Devil himself. But if Mr. Burns is the Devil he is a very naive one. He is a Devil with neither point nor purpose to him—an undignified Devil hatched for a bourgeois Halloween. In less hyperbolic language, Mr. Burns is the product of thoughtless, pointless, nerve-drumming unmorality that is the Boss Journalist—the licensed eavesdropper, trouble maker, bombinator and Town Snitch, misnamed The Press." [6]

To reduce grandiloquent Mephistopheles to a scandal-mongering town snitch is one way to contain the menace of Walter's unmorality. You needn't exorcize the devil, only familiarize yourself with the local demon and his typical mischief: "At this moment Mr. Burns, in the discharge of his high calling, stands in the door, nerveless and meditative as a child, his mind open to such troubles as he can find or create." Hawks adapts this characterization, and though he doesn't dispute Walter's devilish mischievousness, he does endow him with thought, point, and purpose beyond the childish motive of finding or creating trouble. To appreciate this complication in his character we need only remember that Hildy earlier had said that she, too, had metaphorically jumped out a window to escape her life with Walter.

Hawks doesn't dwell on Hildy's motives nor on Mollie's impulsiveness, but by connecting Mollie's literal jump and Hildy's metaphorical one he does alert us to the possibility that Walter may pose a real danger for Hildy. Hitchcock, in films like *Suspicion* and *Notorious,* openly elicited the demonic impulses lurking beneath Grant's worldly charm, but Hawks had in this film already begun excavating that dark side.[7] Hawks's undercover work discovers a more comically heartless and potentially more dangerous Walter Burns than Hecht and MacArthur's dapper Mephistopheles.

Yet nowhere is Hawks's comic wizardry in animating and transforming the stock company of sexual types more in evidence than in the ingenuity with which he transforms a girl Friday, a generic figure from the classified ads, into a comic heroine who not only occupies the front page but gets top billing. Presuming that Hildy's "job" and her happiness depend on her remaining Walter's girl Friday, it is odd that, to my knowledge, no one has determined which component is more important to the formula—being a girl or being a manservant. What we can say is that Hildy, as girl Friday, is definitely not a woman, as she herself recognizes, nor do her mannerisms suggest a conventional femininity. This being the case, let us confer upon her a more heraldic identity: female rampant.

The conventions of screwball comedy permit, when they do not outright ordain, the most outlandish postures and unrefined gestures. In her enjoyment of this physical freedom, the screwball heroine is clearly the daughter of the slapstick comediennes, those "hoydens," as the appreciative Gilbert Seldes called them, who abjured the languorous poses favored by those females who sought to make their sexual fortune in the sedate world of parlor romance. Yet there is a qualitative difference between Claudette Colbert, in *It Happened One Night*, displaying her comely legs to illustrate that the limb is mightier than the thumb, and Hildy tackling a man in flight or, in the film's most stunning visual gag, bending over to display her backside, revealing the full breadth of her classified ads. Rosalind Russell carries herself in this role with a peculiar insouciance. Her self-indifferent carriage forms a fascinating contrast to Walter's narcissistic posing. She may be said to possess stature without being statuesque (the demeanor of Katharine Hepburn throughout most of *The Philadelphia Story*). Russell brilliantly conveys how Hildy's bodily reactions are keyed to her habits of attention. She can become instantly mobilized when a story—or a fleeing jailkeeper—crosses her line of vision.

There is as much fatality, then, as casualness in the use of the word girl to refer to Hildy in her role of newspaperman. Girl is a word that enjoys peculiar license in American slang. It entails, in the first and most common instance, an endearment that suggests both the dream of easy companionableness—a girl is a pal—and a reticence in admitting adult sexual feeling. Much of this camaraderie persists in the working relationship of Hildy and her fellow bravos in the pressroom, and it infuses the rhythms of her fast, knowing, and uninhibited exchanges with Walter. But "girl" is also a slang term used in uneasy proximity to the more explicit "tart," someone whose loose morals are a function of her employment. In the play, Hildy joco-seriously holds no illusions about the genealogy of his trade: a newspaperman, he says, is a "cross between a bootlegger and a whore." [8] His being a man limits the sting of the whore analogy and leaves his sexual dignity fairly secure—secure enough that he can even afford to mimic, as he does in a particularly loony moment, the whine of an androgyne. A woman could not say this line or claim such disreputable parentage, even in a comedy, without permanently sullying her moral integrity and, probably more to the point, undermining her physical appeal. In the film, it is through Mollie that journalism and prostitution are provocatively linked. That Mollie is the only other woman with a significant part in this comedy is not without point and pathos. In going into business for herself, Hildy finds a dispirited double in the working girl whose "business," like Hildy's, routinely requires her to subordinate her rights and feelings to those of the man paying for her services.

To this the name Friday may attest. In the popular imagination, Defoe's complex creation is reduced to a "native" who assists Robinson Crusoe in the task of survival. His "nature" and his serviceability are conceived as inextricable, much as Hildy's "instincts" as a newspaperman are deemed indispensable but subordinate to Walter's captainship of the *Morning Post*. Yet how can Hildy be seen as a native of the pressroom? We are shown in those engrossing tracking shots that open the film and disclose its working spaces. The camera retreats before an advancing female figure who, because she is not the Rosalind Russell of the title credits, we know not to be his girl Friday, but a girl Friday nonetheless. A more conventional director might have opened with an impersonal pan of the newsroom in which human figures would pass in and out of the frame, no single figure directing or arresting the camera's vision. But Hawks isn't interested so much in mise-en-scène for its own sake as in the motivated movement within it, the movement that attracts attention and imparts life. His camera tracks the advancing female figure until she is replaced by another worker, and the camera then follows him until he scurries beyond the preserve of the working staff to catch a departing elevator. It is then that Hildy emerges from the elevator at the right of the frame, and the camera reorients itself, drawn perhaps by the bold lines of Hildy's pinstriped suit, coordinated with a neo-stovepipe hat, or by the confiding way she reassures her companion, Bruce, that she will be back in ten minutes (the first of many such promises, none of them precisely kept).

The camera halts before resuming its tracking assignment, arrested by this tender exchange, just on the threshold of the swinging gate. Later the gate will be stilled to reveal a sign of "No Admittance." Its ostensible function is to keep visitors out, but given all the diabolic imagery surrounding Walter, we might be encouraged to read it as a moral advisory: "Abandon all sentiment you who enter here." Bruce cannot cross this barrier and enter Hildy's world of work but must remain outside it, "on the job," as Hildy says, waiting for her to complete one last reportorial errand, dispatching her "news" to Walter. Later, Bruce will tire of waiting for Hildy and enter the proscribed domain, the pressroom of the Criminal Courts Building. It proves to be a mistake. After pleading his case to a preoccupied Hildy, he will leave the room—and the film—as he entered it, unremarked. Now, too, the camera leaves him to follow Hildy back into the busy space it has just left. Only this time, with Hildy as the focus of the shot, we see the newsroom staff happily welcoming her back, and Hildy, returning their greeting, confers on them a fleeting but memorable individuality. "How's the advice to the lovelorn?" she asks one columnist. "Fine. My cat just had kittens again," she replies. "Your own fault," Hildy briskly but not unkindly tells her. In this brief exchange we understand at once the mark and the pathology of a professional: taking one's work home—advising, perhaps not wisely, but too well—confusing, as Bruce never would, business and home front.

The next time the camera traverses this space it will be to track Hildy and Walter as they leave the office to rejoin Bruce, stranded in the antechamber. On their way they enact a blithe parody of the male gallantry that yields the lead to the lady. Walter strides confidently forward, then defers to Hildy, but resumes his pride of place when Hildy opens the gate ("Allow me," she obligingly coos), permitting him to stride into the antechamber and perform his superb burlesque of male bonhomie, mistaking a senior citizen for Bruce, her Rotarian suitor: "You led me to expect you were marrying a much older man," he chides Hildy after learning of his "mistake" and, in mock courtesy, pumping Bruce's umbrella instead of his hand. The newsroom, at first animated background, then, briefly, personalized arena of working relationships, finally becomes properly scenic, the space where the sexual vaudeville of courtship is faultlessly performed. With exhilarating economy Hawks works the comic transformation, converting workplace into comedic theater.

These opening shots suggest the full powers of film to expose and shape reality according to its own lights and conventions. There is no attempt to compose within the frame, adjust the focus, or edit, invisibly or self-consciously, the life unfolding, at times unraveling, before us. That graduation from staged to filmed effects will be accomplished later, in the Criminal Courts pressroom and, most impressively, in the jail where Hildy interviews the condemned man, Earl Williams.

For now, what we observe is how the camera becomes absorbed in recording the scenic wonder of Hildy and Walter's reunion. The rapport between the two is a function of pure momentum; the pace of their repartee accelerates but keeps veering into dead ends. Hildy is exasperated here, as she is not in the more relaxed and expertly timed restaurant scene that follows. There she allows herself to share Walter's version of their mutual past, is entertained by his hastily devised, cockamamie stories, and receptive to his proposal to buy a life insurance policy from Bruce if she will do an exclusive interview with Williams. She seems to relax into the old rhythms and verbal intimacies of their former life together. In the newsroom, her timing, like her aim, is slightly off: while she misses few of Walter's cues, she throws back her lines as she hurls her pocketbook, just missing her target. Even her words seem to fly by and around him, searching to reach their mark. They finally do hit home when, showing him her ring, she blurts out the news of her engagement.

The news produces a stunningly quiet moment, another example that in talking comedies, silence is something not overcome but achieved. We will return to the moral import of such silences later. Here we remark that Hildy and Walter's reunion has played out the old motifs of their partnership without transforming them. She's amused, at times, by his bluster but resolute about her mission and, most important, deaf to his reminiscences: "Walter, I want to show you something. It's here. It's a ring. Take a good look at it. Do you know what it is? It's an engagement ring." He stops short. "I tried to tell you right away, but you would start reminiscing. I'm getting married, Walter, and I'm also getting as far away from this newspaper business as I can get." These reminiscences will resurface to bring them together, but for now they must be returned to silence before they can yield their inner, untheatrical essence.

Although the scene appears to develop improvisationally, it retains, as even a brief survey of its multiple if "invisible" cuts will show, a neat, even crisp, narrative line. Dramatically, the scene seems to hurtle forward toward a startling announcement, but its vector is initially controlled by Walter, who insists on taking us back, as he generously says he will take Hildy back. Back to the old complacency of his assurance that he will know her any time, any place, anywhere, back to the dreams of him he suspects Hildy has had as recently as last night, back to that prehistoric era in Hildy's life when she was only a doll-faced hick and he the Pygmalion who turned her into a first-class newspaperman. His comic rant about her ingratitude fails not only because it lacks real cause, but because it no longer captivates her as male performance. Hildy complains that she can barely get a word in edgewise, but when she does it stops Walter cold. She brings him to a momentary but definitive halt when she caps his tirade with its commercial clincher: "Sold American!"

It is after this line that Hildy makes her show-stopping announcement, cutting Walter off from his memories and, of course, confuting *his* waking dream that he would know her any time, any place, anywhere. It is this line, delivered with an auctioneer's decisiveness, that alerts us to the dark logic of their relationship. It is the truthfulness of this comedy that this darkness will never be dispersed, although it will be lightened by Walter's more tender avowals, brought on by Hildy's tears, at the end of the film. For Stanley Cavell, it is a logic played and replayed throughout the "comedies of remarriage," a logic activated in this film by "the early, summary declaration that this woman has recently been created, and created by this man."[9] Cavell's view of the genre and ritual of remarriage is partly based on a compelling reading of Milton's divorce tracts, but *His Girl Friday,* which mocks city politicians for alarums of the Red Scare, is ideologically closer to the spirit of Engels's *The Origin of the Family, Private Property, and the State.* Which is to say that it entertains, even if it finally does not endorse, the view that modern marriage is less a covenant between the sexes or a civil union honorably contracted than an economic institution that flatters, when it does not directly minister to, man's proprietary feelings.

This film doesn't so much want to dispute as to reimagine the economic nature of marriage. It would do so by eliminating the confusion, typically American, between business and work. This is where the film works in romance, in insisting on the romance of work. The intimacy that unites Hildy and Walter is not an intimacy available to every professional association but seems to be unique to the nature of their trade as newspapermen. It is also an intimacy based on their shared professional sense of time as something urgently passing. Hildy and Walter, in work and in love, are always trying to meet some deadline. This is especially true for Walter in his new role as suitor to his ex-wife. The success of his amatory campaign depends on his first postponing, then stopping, her intended departure for Albany, where she will begin what she hopes to be a respectable, halfway normal (deadline-free?) life. Many love stories play on the anxiety of trains being missed; here the anxiety is that they will be caught. This film, justly celebrated for the breathtaking pace of its dialogue, is fast, fast, fast, not just because quickness as well as brevity is the soul of wit, but because it is also the truth of romantic, as it is of filmic, time. Let us call it rampant time.

The first intimate exchange in the film is between Hildy and Bruce, and it is about the meaning of time. About to enter the frenzied precincts of the pressroom, Hildy off-handedly reassures Bruce that she won't be long, a matter of ten minutes. "Even ten minutes is a long time to be away from you," is his doting rejoinder. Hildy pauses, returns to him, and asks him to repeat what he just said. The viewer accustomed to a "normal" life may find the line corny, but to Hildy, for whom even a halfway normal life has so far proved elusive, this way of marking time holds great emotional appeal. She admits to a need to be doted on in this way. Here again we see how work can influence one's sense of time, hence one's relation to romance. Bruce, who sells insurance, is a reassuring but unadventurous suitor because he regards time as something to be insured against, not enlivened or transformed. When Walter, Hildy, and Bruce share a meal in ostensible celebration of the impending marriage, Bruce earnestly remarks the prudence of insuring one's life, then doubtfully adds, "Of course, we don't help you much while you're alive, but afterwards, that's what counts." "Sure," Walter agrees, then fakes a laugh before conceding, in mock ignorance, "I don't get it."

We miss Walter's irony—and his charm—if we miss the downright literalism of that "it"—it being as much the time he will fail to get if he's too busy insuring it, as well as the concept that Bruce is awkwardly expounding. Walter, and in this Hildy is his spiritual mate, brings to the film the dispensation of a future or fantasized time (Walter's seductive fantasy of Hildy's future as a social crusader) or past time (Walter's early, ineffectual appeals to Hildy to remember the times of their shared life or his reminder of the light still burning in his window). I can't agree with Cavell that Walter doesn't get what Bruce is talking about because he is too much of this world to believe or care about an afterlife. Walter doesn't get it because he can makes no provision for a time that he is not actively creating or reinventing, a time, indeed, when Walter Burns will no longer be, either on or behind the scene, the male rampant working his mischief. Walter lacks the comic feeling for a social future in which he can play no living part.

In this sense the social time of this film belongs to Walter. It is the fleeting time frantically pursued by the daily newspaper, which traffics in events as if they were transient and which treats history as disposable, instantly revisable, or easily edited. Hence the sly disclaimer with which the film opens, advising us that the story we are about to see "all happened in the 'dark ages' of the newspaper game—when a reporter 'getting that story' justified anything short of murder." Here is that word "get" again, only now it suggests that stories are not so much reported as procured. What it means to get something—a story, a joke, or a girl—is what this comedy means us to "get," and all without ever fooling ourselves that we ever possess the real story, know all the references in the joke, or can ever be sure, as Hildy and Walter head off to Albany, that Walter has finally "got" her. To get a story is a task that justifies doing anything, any time, anywhere. That the film moves from the newspaper office to the Criminal Courts Building begins to seem, in light of the film's opening disclaimer, a morally significant fact. Getting a story verges on outright criminality. Indeed, the comic complications of the film will climax in the handcuffing of Hildy and Walter as alleged criminals (for obstructing justice and harboring a fugitive) and reunited couple.

Hildy is torn between Walter and Bruce because she can entertain two different kinds of time and responds deeply to their separate attractions. Bruce's need for Hildy's affecting presence, which makes even ten minutes seem like a long time, evokes the child's endearing but unavailing protest at separation from the mother, no matter for how brief a time. Hawks emphasizes, though hardly credits, Bruce's appeal to Hildy's dormant maternal feelings. But Bruce's "feminine" side, however attractive, seems attached, at the hip as it were, to his own mother. Hawks retains the mother-in-law of the original play, if for no other reason than to give Walter the satisfaction of insulting her and of showing up the kind of man—Bruce Baldwin, for example— who believes that a boy's best friend is his mother. Bruce does believe it, of course, and has even arranged for his mother to accompany Hildy and himself to Albany, where their marriage will not so much institute a new family as extend an old one.

The film has great fun with what it means to be a mama's boy in the sublime comic mischief when Walter, seeking to meet the "paragon" (a woman's man as opposed to a man's man) Hildy has discovered, heartily shakes the hand of a befuddled elderly gentleman while Bruce vainly tries to introduce himself as the actual suitor. Walter quickly reverses the gag, quick to notice that Bruce has been properly attired in rain gear and rubbers. Bruce is at once too old and too young for Hildy. Our last vision of him is as the child-man reunited with his mother as the door of the pressroom, the domain reserved for grown-up antics, closes on their hapless embrace.

The wisdom of this film, then, does not come to us in the form of moral knowledge but in the realization that the choice of a mate or the filing of a story is implicated in one's attitude toward time and how it is to be filled. The Hecht-MacArthur play accelerated time to dramatize the clamor of the newsroom, where events break quickly: the first act is set at 8:30, the second thirty minutes afterward, the third an astounding "few minutes later." The effect is to create a sense of on-rushing time, of events veering recklessly toward a comic catastrophe. This catastrophe is one that threatens not only the action of the comedy but its generic spirit. In this catastrophe, state murder threatens to overshadow the conventional triumph of social time in marriage.

But within the play, the passage of time, while breathtaking, never seems to be anything but a local matter, confined to the newsroom. This is not merely because the play is restricted to the stage, for the film, with its few changes of scene, manages to appear at times even more claustrophobic than the stage. Many of Hawks's medium shots have the effect of intensifying rather than neutralizing the intimacy of close-ups or the impersonality and distance of long shots. The frame seems crowded as the camera focuses on the desk that conceals Earl Williams or the table where Hildy and Walter frantically manage the phones.

Where the play gives us, as it were, local time, the film gives us a *rampant* time, swiftly moving toward a deadline for which there will be no reprieve, no second edition. This is visually as well as emotionally impressed upon us by the first self-conscious cut in the film, a high-angle shot from the pressroom of the Criminal Courts Building onto the prison courtyard below. We do not actually see the gallows going up, only the menacing shadow it casts. This dark image is amplified by the sounds of construction hammering out the last hours of Earl Williams's life. The sights and sounds of death taking on concrete form viscerally remind us that these vintage comedies often locate themselves uncomfortably but honestly in the vicinity of crime melodramas, where the moral licenses of comedy are reinterpreted as socially aberrant behaviors.

Most of the high-angle shots of the film emphasize this potential for sociopathy: the searchlights that scan the prison after Earl Williams's jailbreak seems almost stock footage from one of the crime melodramas of which Hawks was a master; and the interview scene belongs, too, to those quiet, soul-searching interludes of the gangster film when the doomed hooligan (Cagney, most memorably) confesses a stoic and uncharacteristically muted understanding of his "true" nature.

The film itself insists on this by visually linking its hysterical rhythms to the impending execution. The action is dramatically paced by the insertion of two high-angle shots of the gallows under construction that establish, by means of a gruesome visual pun, that the world of *His Girl Friday* is a world of deadlines. We recall here that Hawks took a degree as an engineer; there is a kind of grim professional interest in the gallows as a contraption. A startling shot of the finished gallows completing its test run with a definitive thud punctuates the film with a distinctly professional and moral finality. Those gallows are going up faster than we can catch up with the motive for murder, outpacing even Walter's contagious mania for breaking news.

The shadows cast by the gallows extend the moral reach of Hawks's comedy beyond their immediate use in signaling the imminence of the execution. They seem to be pointing, as they elongate over the course of the film, to a darker relation between the frantic pace of the film and the desperate efforts to secure a reprieve. As they lengthen we seem to be taking the measure of time apportioned by judicial decree. Only two powers can keep time from taking its appointed course: the power of the governor and the power of the press.

In both cases this power is delegated to the two experts in human behavior who can get the real story on Earl Williams and thus decide whether he is sane enough to be executed for murder. One is the court-appointed psychiatrist, and the other is Hildy. Hildy understands something beyond Walter's moral capacity to know—that the truth of a story has consequences not only for one's life, but for one's death. Hildy's greatness as a reporter emerges in comparison to the other press hounds for whom someone's death, perhaps even their own, is a news story, touching on no deeper feeling or reality. Their moral deafness is preserved and counterbalanced by their sensitivity to noise: they yell at the gallows builders to keep the racket down. They can't work when the machinery of death intrudes on their consciousness.

What Hildy understands is time as a dramatic medium. So does Hawks, the storyteller-director in sympathy with Hildy, who finally is, if anyone in the film is, his surrogate.[10] To her he assigns the film's "exclusive," sign of his regard for her professionalism and for her superb instincts for story: its excitements, lulls, surprises, and astonishing culminations. She contributes to the comedy what may be simply called its human interest—an interest not confined to the pursuit of a halfway normal life but somehow and seriously related to it. Human interest visually, as well as ethically, emanates from Hildy in the act of "getting" and writing a story. Walter doesn't know what human interest is; he shows us as much when, in barking frantic directions to Duffy (Frank Orth), his city editor, about the next day's layout, he junks a story on a Chinese earthquake in which a million perished but insists on keeping a story about a rooster: "No, that's human interest!"

Human interest finds its most expressive form in the interview. The interview scene is a kind of interlude that in another comedy would take place in some Arcadian glade. In an uncanny inversion, Hawks makes the prisoner's cell a recess where the truth might be quietly and more honestly told. This scene is the film's only uncynical attempt to "get" at something resembling the truth, the human truth, of what makes us do the things we do so unthinkingly, yet irresistibly. And this attempt belongs to a woman. Many critics have noted the odd and uncharacteristically self-conscious high-angle shot that opens the scene, Hawks's homage to German expressionism and its haunting evocations of the lights and shadows cast by human consciousness. I don't believe it is Hildy's consciousness that is encompassed by the shot, although she possesses the keen yet sympathetic intelligence that makes such consciousness possible. The high-angle shot recalls in the first instance the views down into the courtyard where the gallows were being built and where, minutes later, searchlights scan the walls. Such a shot symbolizes a morally elevated view of dispassion and presumed immunity but does not absolves us of complicity.

This is emphasized by the way the scene is introduced, juxtaposing two short tracking shots, the first of Bruce leaving the newsroom with Diamond Louie, Walter's seedy factotum, tailing him; the second, continuous with the first, of Hildy, who continues Bruce and Louie's trajectory across the screen from right to left. She, like Louie, is on an assignment for Walter, one that involves pursuit and vaguely illegal machinations. This juxtaposition also tells us that there is more than a slight comic resemblance between Earl Williams and Bruce Baldwin, both sexual innocents who can be set up, Williams by the political machinery, Baldwin by Walter's underworld boy Friday, Louie. Hildy finds her "prey," the jail warden Cooley (Pat West), whom she will later tackle when he tries to flee after the jailbreak, and drops a bribe to get her in to see Williams. The succeeding high-angle shot thus breaks the line of that movement toward corruption and entanglement, and in doing so stills the action, interrupts it for a moment, giving us time to separate from the world of bribes and frame-ups and so mentally prepare for the scene to follow.

A tense quiet prevails, one protracted in the one dissolve of the film, in which Hildy moves her chair closer to Earl's cell. This dissolve has the effect of slowing down as well as isolating the action, creating a transition into another order of time, a more *meditative,* certainly less clamorous time than the rest of the film. The mood is one of stillness, and the principal players seem, for once, unrushed. It thus comes as something of a surprise when the guard suddenly announces that Hildy's time is up. We had perhaps forgotten that Hildy's interview, like all her other assignments, was conducted with a heightened awareness of time elapsing, and elapsing perhaps too quickly for any human intentions to be realized, whether those be Walter's desire to stay the execution *and* permanently detain Hildy, or Hildy's intention to get the story that might save Williams and still catch the night train to Albany.

The scene is shot with Hildy dominating the frame, separated from Earl by the grid of cell bars. The basic form of human interchange doesn't change in this scene. There is the same overlap and interruption of lines, but the dramatic and emotional effect achieved here is solemn rather than frenetic. Urgency is now given a human meaning in the quiet insistence with which Hildy coaxes Earl to tell his story before it is too late: What did he do? What did he hear? What was he thinking? She barely permits him to complete a sentence, yet she never seems to rush him or hurriedly extort a confession. And she still has time — and the heart — to notice, before she takes leave of him, the flowers sent by Mollie to cheer him and her picture tacked on the cell bars.

Hildy proves herself to be the film's true, if unaccredited, psychiatrist, out to find an angle, not to work one (like the sheriff and his cohorts, who believe an execution will win them precious votes in the upcoming election). She finds her angle in a phrase picked up and lingering in an aggrieved and distracted mind: production for use. Earl had heard this phrase at a political rally and, Hildy suggests, finding a gun in his hand, put the phrase itself to use.

> HILDY: Now look, Earl, when you found yourself with that gun in your hand, and that policeman coming at you, what did you think about? . . . You must have thought of something. . . . Could it have been, uh, "production for use"? . . . What's a gun for Earl?
>
> WILLIAMS: A gun? . . . Why, to shoot, of course,
>
> HILDY: Oh. Maybe that's why you used it.
>
> WILLIAMS: Maybe.
>
> HILDY: Seems reasonable?
>
> WILLIAMS: Yes, yes it is. You see, I've never had a gun in my hand before. That's what a gun's for, isn't it? Maybe that's why.
>
> HILDY: Sure it is.
>
> WILLIAMS: Yes, that's what I thought of. Production for use. Why, it's simple isn't it?
>
> HILDY: Very simple. [*Hildy sighs rather than asserts her agreement in a way that suggests at once sympathy and world-weariness.*]

Production for use, as Marilyn Campbell notes, was the memorable slogan of Upton Sinclair's run for governor, a campaign satirized in Budd Schulberg's *What Makes Sammy Run.*[11] Campbell rightly stresses the importance of this phrase to the film's cinematic as well as ideological effects. She got the importance right but overlooked, I think, some of the effects. The most important structure produced for use, as Hildy's story dramatically concludes, is the gallows. Unlike other commodities and objects that circulate in the film, causing mischief and making visible hidden relationships—stories, money, cigarettes, even desks (they can be used, as Earl discovers, as a hideout)—the gallows have only one use. Production for use reminds us not only that things are produced, but how they are used, to what ends.

Hildy builds a story around this perception, linking Earl's misguided application of this principle. But then she tears up the story in a fit of rage. She is angry at Walter for reneging on his bargain and for having made use of her. Is this what leads her to disassociate herself from a utilitarian economy in which things are put to what seems inhuman use? It is Hildy's anger that blinds her to the higher human interest that her story might serve—saving Williams's life. We come face to face in this moment with a fury not just beyond words, but at their expense—at the expense, that is, of our power to redeem as well as falsify reality.

In the depressed moral economy of this comedy, where language circulates unattached to any standard of truth or even plausibility, Hawks can only revert to the intrinsic authority of cliché and silence as monitors of human value. To this ingenuity we might ascribe the force of Hildy's parting shot, "Goodbye, Earl, and good luck." We had heard something like this line before, when Hildy, after announcing her engagement, had consoled the stunned Walter: "Better luck to you next time." We will hear this formula once again, spoken not by Hildy but by Walter, as he seems, at last, willing to give her up to Bruce: "Goodbye, dear, and good luck." Neither goodbye is final, of course. Earl will escape and entrust his fate to Hildy. Hildy will discover to her relief that Walter's goodbye to her, unlike hers to Williams, is not an act of heartfelt leave-taking but another ploy to impress on her what it *really* means to leave him. Yet each is rhetorically effective in provoking a necessary breakdown in the frantic clamor of a film that seems demonically intent on banishing the language of real feeling from its precincts.

That even commonplace terms can be produced for moral use is shown when Hildy, by virtue of a single phrase, makes the rabid throng of newspapermen pause for thought, a pause in which something like self-reproach manages to make a brief appearance. It occurs midway in the film after Hildy, in the only moment of female solidarity she displays (in contrast to her superficial deference to her mother-in-law)

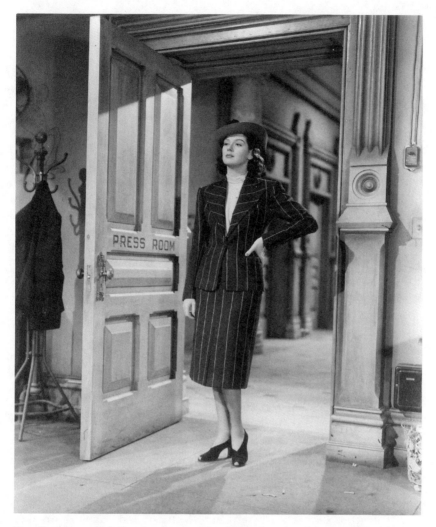

Rosalind Russell delivering her verdict, "Gentlemen of the press," in
His Girl Friday

escorts Mollie out of the pressroom. When Hildy and Mollie exit, they
take any vestige of humanity with them, leaving the newspapermen
oddly and uncharacteristically disconcerted—and silent. They shuffle
around the room, uneasily trying to resume their old rhythms of work,
rhythms by which they hope to regain their composure as nonfunc-
tional human beings. Hildy reenters and delivers her inimitable line:
"Gentlemen of the press." It's a stock phrase, like "goodbye and good

luck," but there is nothing formulaic about the moral impact of that line in the pressroom, filled, for once, with the eerie sound of silence. Those four words reverberate with the unexpressed outrage at the demeaning work of the newspaperman, from peeping through keyholes to harassing kindhearted tarts. Hildy pronounces the word "gentlemen" in a particularly low, grave voice, as if delivering a eulogy for human decency.

All of these silences are full of meanings. Through them we can begin to hear those voices of conscience, remorse, or remonstrance routinely muffled by the sheer din of activity. It is curious how long these moments of morally articulate silence are prolonged in a film justly celebrated for its pace. The truth struggles to be heard in these intervals of quiet but is quickly drowned out by the next onrush of speech, a new burst of sirens.

The self-conscious lighting of the film participates in this moral dramaturgy of the unspoken. As the plot complications intensify, Walter becomes quite busy not only as actor but as stage manager, shutting out lights, pulling down shades. In the determined urbanity of this film, nature is always elsewhere and unreachable—it's where the governor is fishing, it's Niagara Falls, which Hildy, we suspect, will never reach. This is the only comedy I know in which it seems, ironically, entirely *natural* that the romantic lead complains, "Ah, now the moon's out!" Moonlight, of course, signifies the lustrous light of romance, even, as in *Bringing Up Baby,* of the magical mating of species, the leopard and the dog. The filmic apotheosis of moonlight occurs in *It Happened One Night* when Peter Warne (Clark Gable) provokes Ellie Andrews's (Claudette Colbert) declaration of love by describing an island paradise where "you and the moon and the water all become one." In this film, the moon is an obstacle to concealment, and so its glow must be occluded, its light banished.

But if there is no poetic vision of reality, there is the luster of a poetic idea in what Walter offers Hildy: a career as a noble crusader like those honored by statues in the park. There is a grim symmetry in Walter's tempting Hildy with the chance to rise into a completely different class. We recall that when Hildy escorted Mollie Malloy out of reach of the cynical reporters, Mollie cried out, as if in disbelief, "Aren't they inhuman." "I know," Hildy confirms. "They're newspapermen." But Hildy also knows that she is in danger of reverting to something at once more than and yet less than human herself. She finds herself listening, perhaps against her better judgment, to Walter's urging to pursue the "greatest yarn in journalism since Livingstone discovered Stanley." "It's the other way around," Hildy corrects him, but she soon succumbs to his vision of her as a social reformer: "Do you realize what you've done, honey? You've taken a city that's been graft-ridden for forty years under the same old gang. With this yarn, you're kicking 'em out." Walter has turned that doll-faced hick into a first-class news-paperman, and however much we might disapprove of his tutelage, it is clear that Hildy, in accepting the life he offers her, chooses to make a complete break from her past and to renounce any future she might have entertained as a woman leading a halfway normal life.

This break comes in the form of a declaration in the midst of the comic oratorio that gives the film its great concluding set-piece: Wal-ter screaming instructions to Duffy, Hildy trying to rewrite the story of Earl's jailbreak, and Bruce urging Hildy to pay attention and catch that by now emotionally uncatchable nine o'clock train. In the volley of Walter's shouted orders, Hildy's manic rewrites, and Bruce's impor-tuning, she manages to blurt: "I'm no suburban bridge player. I'm a newspaperman." This line, all things considered, is the most amazing kiss-off in movie comedy. It is, first of all, astoundingly casual. Only later will Hildy even remember what she said, just as it will take some time for her to realize that Bruce has indeed left the room, taking with him her chance "to live decent and live like a human being." Though she will complain that Walter has ruined her life, there is little regret and no obvious anguish in the way she bids Bruce goodbye. Yet un-like Tracy Lord's dismissal of her ambitious fiancé, George Kittridge (Katharine Hepburn and John Howard), in *The Philadelphia Story,* Hildy's kiss-off isn't tinged with a "classy" tone of sarcastic triumph. Nor does her brusque, distracted gesture waving Bruce from her side compare to the high romantic kitsch of Ellie Andrews's flight from the high-class altar of emotional immolation to the humble auto cabin

Rosalind Russell back home in the newsroom in *His Girl Friday*

where the walls of Jericho come tumbling down. Tracy and Ellie, of course, are heiresses who may choose either to marry within their class or outside or below it. Hildy is a working girl, and her dismissal of her bourgeois suitor is determined less by her class feeling than by the feeling of belonging to a tribe.

In this case it is the tribe of newspapermen, among whom Hildy decides to make her home. She announces this decision to remain a newspaperman rather than become a suburban bridge player in the midst of composing the greatest story of her life, one that Walter assured her would be the making of her career. But more than raw ambition is blurted here, just as more than a callous repudiation of her patient and by this time much-abused suitor is intended. Hildy is not so much rejecting Bruce as choosing between one way of spending her time and another, between the bridge game of the suburbs and the ritual poker game of the pressroom that, as Hecht and MacArthur describe it, "has been going on now for a generation, presumably with the same deck of cards."[12]

The comedy is decided from that point. What remains is the zany poetry of Walter and Hildy's collaboration and the definitive break with Bruce—a break with all the hopes (or perhaps they were pretenses) that Hildy had for becoming a halfway normal woman. She prefers to work, which means she prefers to spend her time with Walter. Walter's suggestion, made supposedly on noble grounds, that she make herself a life without him desolates her, because for her no such life can really exist.

It is at this crisis point that Hildy shows herself to be all too recognizably a more than halfway normal woman who, when all else fails, cries. Cries to get Walter back, cries to forestall the comic catastrophe of Walter's sudden ennoblement. The comic nerve of this film is in insisting that Walter's reformation would be both a human and romantic calamity. Without his diabolic cunning, death might get his due—on schedule. Walter, deaf to human interest, is the demon who understands nature's dark genius for natural selection. The social time of the film is marked by social and natural catastrophes—rigged elections, mine cave-ins, a strike, a world at war with itself. The film will end with the fast-breaking story of a strike in Albany, ironically fulfilling Walter's smug prediction that Hildy, in marrying Bruce, could look forward to a a "life of adventure," and in Albany, too!

Comedy instructs us what is gained in pursuing a life of adventure, and what is lost. What is lost is easier to describe: the sense of being settled. We are impressed by the magnitude of this loss not so much by Hildy's yearning to have a home as by Earl Williams's inability to find a refuge. Earl, who at one point finds temporary shelter in a desk, is a figure of anti-comedy, a kind of social and emotional black hole that threatens to implode. He's unemployed in a film where everyone is deliriously busy at their job. He complains of being tired, weary of the world, at the point where the comedy is just picking up speed. He's too dimwitted to grasp the comic as well as economic rule of production for use: he meets a tart and talks to her. If the plot didn't give him a reason to stow Williams away in the rolltop desk, Hawks would have had to invent one. Williams is slow, and we never get to see the only quick, smart, and funny thing he does: walking off with the sheriff's gun and shooting the court-appointed psychiatrist in the "classified ads, no ad."

When Hildy heads down the stairs, following Walter and carrying her typewriter, we understand that the female rampant is back in business, clothed in pinstriped suits rather than designer gowns. She has given up the hope of home in her search for a life of adventure, a life whose excitement we might glean from the most piquant memory that Hildy and Walter share in the film, the time they sneaked into the coroner's office and hid out for a week: "We could have gone to jail for that too, you know that," Walter reminds her. Illicit love *would* appeal to Walter, the dapper Mephistopheles, but the film seems more interested not in the legality but in the psychology of their amorous escapades. Love shadowed by death is a keen incitement to action, the more desperate or frenzied the better.

This may be the deeper meaning of the astonishing cut that links Mollie's jump, a futile attempt to rescue Earl from capture, to Walter's entry. I don't mean to imply that Walter is a figure of death. He represents a more fantastical possibility—the evasion of death. An imperturbable belief in his own immunity to mortal accidents may explain why he doesn't "get" life insurance. Or it may be that he simply refuses to bargain with or about death. He stands for life, a life of adventure, not in Albany, but any time, any place, anywhere life presents itself. To accept him is to accept that life and to refuse the notion of a home.

There is, then, something profoundly atavistic as well as exuberantly futuristic in Hawks's new men and women. Hildy Johnson is arguably the most daring of them, going wherever Walter might send her: into caves that might collapse at any moment, into the depths of the Criminal Courts Building, into the bowels of that moral wilderness, the modern pressroom. What Hildy seeks and finds is not a home but a habitat, often gloomy and subterraneous, where she and Walter might reenact their illicit rites of love. The female rampant, uncontrolled in everything but speech, is a natural denizen of that world. The burst of music, conspicuously absent throughout the rest of the film, seems to act as fanfare to her reentry into that strangely erotic underworld, which is wherever Walter happens to be. Musical time, with its formal promise of harmonic resolution, accompanies this dark duo making their way into that night in which the only measure of time is the deadline.

Yet who is to say that this comic ending is not of the most conventional even as it is of the most aberrant kind? Hildy finally gets to go on her honeymoon, to spend her time in the only way that really matters to her—with Walter, who treats her not as a woman but as a newspaperman.

9 The Lady Eve
and the Female Con

The Lady Eve is Preston Sturges's accomplished study of America's finest comic specimen: sucker sapiens. Its heroine, Jean Harrington (Barbara Stanwyck), is a fast-talking dame never at a loss for a word or a palmed card. Its hero, Charles "Hopsie" Pike (Henry Fonda), is an amateur ophiologist of shy demeanor and halting speech, an easy mark for the dexterous charmer who manipulates words and people with enviable finesse. Sturges, who so enjoyed imagining preposterous combinations, presents us with the comedy of the pair's improbable courtship as a fable of routed innocence. This fable concludes in a paradoxical moral: the hero must be swindled in order to be enriched, venturing all chances for happiness on a gambler, a dissembler, and, in her last (false) incarnation, a sexual cheat. Despite the apparent odds, this is not a foolish bet. Comedy is reluctant to award happiness to those deficient in verbal and social guile, the survival skills in which the fast-talking dame excels.

This is not a moral that will appeal to everyone, even when it presents itself in the beguiling form of entertainment. But it is a moral that needs to be impressed on the American character, whose faith in democratic manners is tethered to a transcendental belief in the ultimate superiority of moral innocence over cunning, of the plainspoken over the quick-witted. American film comedy, and Sturges's comedy in particular, exposes the naivete, real or assumed, that authorizes such a disingenuous view of how the world works and how people are

Charles Coburn, Barbara Stanwyck, and Henry Fonda at the card table in
The Lady Eve

formed—for happiness or for disaster—within it. American comedy
entrusts the tricky business of moral enlightenment to the designing
female, who, like Jean Harrington, may admit to being crooked but
never common. The uncommon woman, the artful Eve, is practiced in
the worldly sport of double-dealing, having herself been taught by the
subtlest beast of the field. To *ensure* that the hero takes a fall is Eve's
comic mission on America's Edenic shores.

    The Lady Eve begins at sea, where conventions ordain that two
things are possible: a shipboard romance and piracy (in its more genteel
form of light-fingered card playing). These adventures are not mutually
exclusive. Sturges, with his superb comic instincts, knew that success
in love and gambling requires similar human skills. In either venture it
isn't wise to depend on luck alone in playing out one's hand. Inspired
by this insight, Sturges, more than any other comic artist working in
film, was hospitable to con artists. His evident delight in the art of the
dodge and the deal suggests how deep was his connection to the lit-

erary and popular traditions for whom the sucker sapiens was comic rather than pitiable. His con artists, like Melville's confidence men and Twain's riverboat swindlers—or like their first cousins, the grifters and gold-diggers of Depression culture—instruct as they amuse by playing on the various forms of human gullibility. His skeptics perform an equally important service. They rescue comedy from the mawkish and sentimental (another form of being gulled, this time by fraudulent feeling rather than by fraudulent schemes). In league, his skeptics and con artists can extirpate, with admirable efficiency, the rooted innocence of America's sexual and moral naifs. It is worth remembering that *The Lady Eve* belongs to the same decade that saw the rise of film noir, with its deadly, seductive dames who trouble our assumptions about the survival value of innocence.

Sturges does not ascribe this moral distrust of woman to the disorder and upheavals of modern times. For him, as for many, woman's capacity for double-dealing is the first object lesson in the universal history of mankind. This view is reflected in the movie's title sequence, which stages, in contemporary costume and symbolic shorthand, a return to the Garden of Eden, scene of the first confidence game in history. The titles caricature the misogynist myths that came out of Eden, as if such attitudes are already old jokes for jaded tastes—the tastes, say, represented by a cartoon snake sporting a top hat, slithering along the margin of the frame in lascivious, drunken counterpoint to the titles. He seems to have wandered off, soused and sassy, from a nightclub. Mouth watering with unslaked thirst, he emphasizes his scene-stealing (actually credit-stealing) naughtiness by shaking his rattle-tail, the first of many signs in the movie linking male behavior with childish fetishes and fantasies never quite outgrown nor relinquished. What he wants now is for the show to begin.

To move things along he plucks from the Tree of Knowledge the apples bearing the words that will compose the title, a title that is presented to us in a scrambled, apparently drunken order: first the word Eve, then Lady, and finally the demonstrative, The. Sturges's comic serpent may be a roué, but he is not without a certain intellectual panache for parodying the scientific habit of classifying things by their genera, species, and type. In this instance, the object in need of classification is woman herself. She is first identified in her primal, mythological form (Eve, at once mother and first betrayer of mankind) and then in terms of her class affiliation (a lady as opposed, say, to a dame). The first verbal joke of the film, then, anticipates, in its happily inebriated way, a new speciation, to which it gives, in mock-soberness, a proper phylogenetic designation: Eve, Lady, the.

This approach to reality will prove the undoing of our hero, the scientific explorer and specialist in snakes who exhibits all the mental habits of his trade and class. As the child of both wealth and science, Charles has been educated to impose order on potentially unruly or previously unknown life forms (snakes and dames, for example) by setting up categories and establishing neat systems of classification. This method of dealing with the phenomenal and human world, a habit of mind that the film neurotically elaborates, purports to set unstable or unpredictable things (cards, for instance) or unmanageable people (usually, but not necessarily women) in stable and governable places.

The Lady Eve is primarily about what happens when things threaten and finally succeed in slipping out of their designated categories, things like Charles's pet snake, Emma, who sidles out of her box. These small instances of displacement have an importance out of proportion to their apparent triviality. They show up the futility of trying to organize life into categories resistant to change or the mess of rearrangement. This lesson becomes more pronounced in the physical comedy of the second half of the movie, which shows the disorder that results when Jean Harrington reinvents herself as the British aristocrat Lady Eve—that is, when Jean moves into a social space or class not properly hers.

At first the pandemonium is more physical than psychological. Charles, on meeting the Lady Eve, who is of course the spitting image of Jean, becomes confused by her looks. One of the moral consequences of his disastrous romance with Jean is that he has lost faith in appearances, lacks confidence in truths he once took to be self-evident. His failure to trust in Jean's ultimate goodness has caused him to distrust himself, to disbelieve what is before his eyes. Knocked off his

Barbara Stanwyck as the Lady Eve

perceptual and epistemological pivot, he suddenly finds himself falling over furniture that has been in place for years, because suddenly *he* is out of place.

Muggsy (William Demarest), Charles's bodyguard/nursemaid, is also struck by the resemblance, but he has no problem believing what he is seeing. To prove his point that the Lady Eve and Jean are "positively, the same dame," he takes the place of the servant who normally waits on the table, hoping to get a better and confirming look, to catch her out of character. But he is the one who is asked to explain his presence in the dining room. Servants, after all, have their proper places, and Muggsy is not in his. The order of persons and things and *feelings* that the first half of the comedy almost effortlessly established is overturned by the physical pandemonium and the perceptual confusions of the second half. Sturges's satire on male innocence is cheerfully relentless in mocking the rigid categories of persons (dames versus ladies) by which innocent Adams foolishly hope to defend themselves against designing Eves. But there is both mercy and grace in his comic design to bring the naive hero and the knowing heroine together *twice,* each time with the heroine bent on deception. Only by such devious means can he usher them out of the dark woods of prejudice and resentment into an emotional clearing, the forest glade envisioned in Hopsie's reverie of conjugal happiness.

Such is the grace first experienced in Eden and linked to Adam's gift for calling things by their rightful name. Naming, indeed, is the first human act in the film. Charles is seen departing from the Amazon with a precious charge, a snake, christened with a Latinate name by its "father-founder" and later rechristened, in the language of affection, Emma. The movie title, then, is not innocent; no name in this movie is. Sturges understood that names are never merely ornamental, chosen for their euphony alone. Civilization has its proper names for things—the genus of snakes, the class of women (ladies or dames), for example—and private experience has a whole different set of names. The movie opposes the public title (known and available to all, just as, apparently, Lady Eve was available to all sexual comers) to the intimacy of the nickname or, literally, the pet name, Emma, and the love name, the name Jean adopts from Charles's childhood, Hopsie, to suggest her new relation to him.

The world of social forms and the possible range of personal relationships is represented through this subtle interplay of names and naming: Charles doesn't want Jean, short for Eugenia (from "well-bred," onomastically foreshadowing the high-born Lady Eve she carries in the womb of her imagination), to use his full name, the name he signs his checks with; and of course we are never allowed to forget the archetypal resonance of the name Eve—just plain Eve, as Charles's father says—the name that enraptures the heart, only to betray it. Claudette Colbert's gold-digging chorine in *Midnight* (1939), Eve Peabody, brings off an aristocratic masquerade, posing as Baroness Czerny from Hungary to the Parisian haute monde. This archetypal identification of the beguiling but potentially treacherous woman with the first woman to connive and to fall is perpetuated in the movie *All About Eve* (1950), whose devious schemer, Eve, shares with Eugenia the last name Harrington.

These cinematic Eves, as Stanley Cavell has noted, are rarely attended or chaperoned by wise or sympathetic mothers.[1] Cavell interprets this absence mythically, a sign that the "creation of the woman is the business of men." He bases his mythic analysis on the father-daughter relationship so important to the comic workings of Shakespearean romance. Cavell is shrewd to invoke Shakespearean paradigms in analyzing the comedy, but I believe that he misinterprets the idiosyncratic transpositions of the Edenic myth in this film and in screwball comedies generally. *The Lady Eve* is not a story of man creating woman; it is a story of a woman inventing a bogus identity, playing a role, and manipulating the cards to ensure a happy outcome for herself. Cavell trusts almost exclusively the archetypal association of Jean/Eve with the woman who caused humankind to be expelled from paradise. I think that Sturges's use of the myth of Eden is more parodic and suspicious, more radical in its account of this misogynist myth of sexual relationships. Jean's primal hubris is that she dares to create herself. She gives birth to Lady Eve Sidwich, researches (in the jargon of Method acting) her role, and even dreams up a heraldic crest inscribed with a (grammatically authentic) Latin motto, Sic Erat Fatis ("Thus was it fated").

But the attitude of resignation, even abnegation, implied by this insignia is a pose like any other. Jean is not resigned to what the fates might bring. She tries to bend them to her desire, fashioning a destiny with the same imaginative audacity with which she remakes and renames herself. If women in comedy trusted fate they might never know, much less secure, the happiness within their grasp. As Jean tells

Hopsie, young women must look after themselves—become their own mothers—or be resigned to dying old maids. To be natural (that is, artless), rather than artful, is to risk remaining unmarried, to suffer and to submit to an unhappy sexual destiny. Happiness in comedy is sexual success, and it is the reward of artfulness.

Yet female artfulness cannot always avert the disaster of rejection, and this recognition can embitter. Once crossed, disappointed, or hurt, the woman who enchants, often undergoes a negative transformation. Sturges's comedy enacts this transformation, explains it, and suggests by his title that it is the second female "character" that comedy must redeem. The heroine promised by the movie's title will not appear until the second half of the comedy, the half concerned not with the exhilarating rhythms of courtship and adventure on the high seas but with the darker motives of class revenge and sexual retaliation. Human nature is fallen nature, and the only suspense, for Sturges, is not whether but when innocence meets up with experience and is forced to confront a reality that is no longer morally stable and secure, a reality suddenly brought out of focus.

This sudden slippage of the world off its hinges is one of Sturges's obsessive themes, and the nervous excitability of his characters, primarily males, the human expression of this obsession. His comedies show us what transpires when men find themselves fallen into a world —or a love—that does not conform to their notions of physical and moral order. Men often enter this world without suitable guides, and often without sufficient guile. Guile is an intellectual vice conventionally ascribed to woman, the conniving Eve. Comedy, in its iconoclastic moods, interprets this vice as a virtue and the designing woman our best, if unconventional, teacher.

The movie's opening scenes suggest the imminence of this fall into sexual enchantment. We see Charles Pike leaving the Amazon, a paradise of bachelors where, as Charles says, a young man with scientific inclinations can spend his time in the (exclusive) company of men in the pursuit of knowledge. But there is trouble in paradise, and its name is Emma, a name that suggests that the snake is potentially a substitute sexual object. The dialogue elaborates without belaboring this foolish symbolic substitution when Charles, warned about the predatory nature of women, replies with all the confidence of untested innocence, "You know me . . . nothing but reptiles." The camera that records these scenes, however, seems impatient with such self-assured banalities and pans to a shot of Charles's bodyguard-nurse, garlanded in flowers, saying goodbye to a local maiden with that dogged inexpressiveness that is the signature of William Demarest's character in the work of Preston Sturges. Demarest is usually called on to portray the suspicions and the limitations of the man unimpressed by the presence or company of women.

These two ritual moments of departure reveal that Charles may have discovered a reptile but has lost a chance to discover something in himself. He is leaving paradise much as he entered it. This, of course, may simply be what paradise means to him, a place where things are immune to change. This may constitute the promise and appeal of this womanless Eden, as the scientists who remain behind confirm when they assure Charles: "If you get a chance to come back . . . this is where we'll be." These men belong to a world, to adopt Charles's own language describing the instabilities of the world of love, with no ups and downs, no lights and shadows. They will experience no moments of irritation, but neither will they have moments of unreasoning joy.

At this critical juncture Charles's boat takes off to meet up with a passenger ship, its whistle summoning Pike's little steamer, a kind of mating call between vessels. Sturges is commendably opportunistic in enlisting nonhuman sound or plain noise to tell a story. That whistle later will sound on the honeymoon night when the train whistle blasts its own urgent, shocked response as Eve reveals her "past," each blast representing another lover named, another erotic escapade divulged, until the sound is so insistent and so shrill that it seems to move beyond the range of human hearing, perhaps, indeed, beyond the limits of moral as well as sensory endurance. This whistle, which seems to obliterate any of the finer tones of human interchange and leave only the sensation of aural discomfort and moral pain, contrasts not only to the opening whistle, so full of promise and expectation, but also to one of the movie's most senselessly happy moments. As Charles waits on deck for Jean to appear the morning after their first night of talkative love-making, this abstracted man of science, who previously seemed barely aware of his human surroundings, his head buried in a book even at dinner, looks around, takes interest and even pleasure in the comic passage of life around him, and, casually and unselfconsciously, whistles what we might call the whistle of natural happiness. That whistle is so carefree it seems to signal in itself that this man is about to take a fall.

As a matter of fact, Charles is a man who takes many falls and repeated blows on the head until his stubborn innocence is vanquished. Jean captures his attention by effecting her own symbolic substitution. Watching him, along with countless man-hungry females on board, as he approaches the ship, she takes a bite out of her apple and then, with faultless aim, drops it on his head as he is about to board. Her initial elevation over him visually establishes her position of sexual command, if not of moral superiority. Interestingly, she, too, is part of a paradise of bachelors, which includes her bachelor father (who instructs her, at times amazes her, with the finer virtuoso turns of his trade) and by the family "valet." They form an odd but ultimately loyal and affection-ate family with their own eccentric practices. The father upholds the family tradition of artful seduction, instructing his daughter in the con man's illusionistic craft: sleight of hand and amorous deception. It is a measure of his successful parenting that when the plot actually begins, setting the stage for Charles's fall, it is the daughter who presents us the world of the comedy as firmly within her grasp.

The scene that brings the lovers together opens with a shot of Jean looking into her compact. This conventional gesture, which normally signals an act of feminine preening and self-absorption, a kind of innocent and socially acceptable narcissism, proves to be the feint that conceals Jean's magical manipulations. The image in the compact mirror and the screen image coincide; the camera is steadied, its wayward lens focused by her firm directorial hand. Stanley Cavell writes of this co-incidence of screen and mirror image: "We may take the world she has in her hand as images in her crystal ball, but however we take it, we are informed that this film knows itself to have been written and directed and photographed and edited."[2] Cavell resorts to the reflexive voice, perhaps to avoid stating or conceding the glaringly visible fact that this film knows itself to be in some sense written and directed and edited by a woman, who is a figure of and for the comic artist Preston Sturges, a man. Art is a made thing, and the maker is not Jean as the diviner peering into a crystal ball but Jean as the prestidigitator who manipulates and directs the images on the screen. Cavell rightly notes how she is responsible for supplying dialogue for this otherwise silent farce, blocking the scene and criticizing the clichés of the film's comic stage business ("Holy smoke, the dropped kerchief!").[3]

This woman knows her trade; she's been around, listened and looked, and has seen and heard it all—or most if it, anyway. So complete is her mastery of our attention, so firmly has she established her grip on the staged action that we as viewers forget to notice her feet. The scene concludes with her calculated tripping of Charles as he flees the sexual attention he has excited. In an ingenious and genial reversal of roles and attitudes, she accuses him of breaking her heel, offhandedly and hurriedly makes introductions all around, and, taking him (literally) in hand, spirits him off with a beguiling directness. She never pretends that she doesn't know who he is and why he's garnered so much attention. Like all practiced deceivers, she cloaks her guile in candor's robes. It is this set of double signals, implying both a direct and a hidden motive, that makes the cliché that concludes this scene— "Funny, our meeting like this, isn't it?"—seem both worldly and corny at the same time, a triumph of her directorial finesse in injecting the banal with comic life.

This scene also reveals a defining aspect of Sturges's comic vision of the world. He locates sexual enticement squarely in the world of physical appetites, placing seduction among the acts of eating and drinking. Jean had first claimed Charles as her sexual mark by dropping an apple on his head, apprising him of the gravity of the encounters ahead. Charles is never shown actually biting into an apple (either of knowledge or of discord), but when the con man who impersonates Eve's uncle, "Sir Alfred McGlennan Keith" (Eric Blore) concocts a cockamamie story about Cecilia, the coachman's daughter and Lady Eve's twin, he swallows this explanation, as the con man reports, like a wolf. This sexual comedy is fueled by the awareness that unacknowledged or suppressed appetites, once whetted, may prove at once too easy and impossible to satisfy.

Given how many scenes in this movie revolve around or concern eating, it is comically remarkable that no one is seen eating contentedly or finishing a meal. The only creature who seems to enjoy the satisfactions of regular meals is Emma, whose own favorite foods provide the movie with one of its funniest jokes. While a steward and Gerald, the Harringtons' crony, listen in stupefaction, Muggsy orders Emma's breakfast: "Gimme a spoonful of milk, a raw pigeon's egg, and four house flies. If you can't catch any I'll settle for a cockroach." Gerald (Melville Cooper) must abandon his meal, his appetite for kippers suddenly, violently gone. Jean and Hopsie fare differently, of course, since lovers proverbially do not eat, or they develop strange thirsts (as we saw in *Ninotchka*). Hopsie, in love with Jean, orders Scotch instead of morning coffee, and of course the second part of the film tells and retells the same joke with the same punch line. Every time Hopsie gets near food, he ends up wearing it rather than ingesting it.

Yet Sturges's most comically desperate scene dramatizing how male desires are aroused, only to be frustrated, features Charles's father (Eugene Pallette) sitting down to his morning meal on a beautifully laid table, then finding that the plate, if not his cupboard, is bare. After repeated requests for something to eat he takes to banging the silver dish-covers in a perfectly uncanny parody of a wailing child denied its meals on time. His voice may have deepened into a manly register, but not his response to a world that can't satisfy his hungers and wants.

Indeed, one of the ways that *The Lady Eve* defines its characters, especially its men, is to ask what each is hungry *for*. The answer to that question is often unsettling: they might be starving, Sturges insinuates, for something that does not exist. Loving what does not, nor never can, exist can have dreadful consequences, but then again, it can also be the source of much fun. That seems to be the mood and point of Jean's reminding Charles, at a crucial point in their first love scene, that there is no use in having an ideal that can never be realized. Jean has taken Charles back to her stateroom, where she "allows" him to select slippers from her trunk, packed with what seems the tantalizing garb of a quick-change artist, and place them on her feet. Sturges directs the scene to suggest two images that come from different social and economic contexts, one romantic, even feudal, the knight kneeling in obeisance to his lady; the other farcical, suggesting the somewhat intimate ministrations of a shoe salesman with a leg fetish.[4] After explaining that he is an ophiologist who has been up the Amazon for the year, Charles, whom Jean prefers to call Hopsie, confesses as he glances at her feet, "Now, here's a business I wouldn't mind being in. . . . I never realized before how lovely it could be."

This awareness of a loveliness that previously eluded him induces what we might call a healthy, sexualizing aphasia. Jean's perfume makes him cockeyed, but it also makes him suddenly eager to find words to fit a meaning struggling to emerge. In Hopsie's groping for words we witness what happens inside a mind that never considered such things as girls before. "You see," he brokenly explains to Jean, "where I've been, I mean, up the Amazon, you kind of forget how . . . how . . . I mean when you haven't seen a girl in a long time . . . I mean there's something about that perfume that . . . that . . . " Hopsie, having lost his mind, has also apparently lost his place. But he has also found "something" he was in danger of forgetting. Jean, not ready yet to give him free rein, assigns him to the space previously occupied by Emma: "Why, Hopsie . . . you ought to be kept in a cage." A cage, one suspects, in her keeping, or at least near her bed.

But not too near. Jean is knowing, but not carnally so. Sturges insists on Eugenia's virginity so that we don't conflate moral with sexual purity. The two may coincide, but they are not to be seen as the same thing. Jean may be shady, but she is not tarnished. It is Jean's worldly, grown-up humor, not any sexual deviousness, that prompts her to tease Charles, with more affection than scorn, out of his own unexamined sexual idealism. Her hand is busy during the exchange that follows, running through his hair, entangling him ever more securely with the magic motion of her fingers. Manipulation comes close to dissolving into caress, a sign that Jean is both exercising her power and about to lose it as she and Charles define for each other their own particular "ideal":

CHARLES: What does yours look like?

JEAN: He's a little short guy with lots of money.

CHARLES: Why short?

JEAN: What does it matter, if he's rich enough . . . it's so he'll look up to me . . . so I'll be *his* ideal.

CHARLES: That's a funny way of reasoning.

JEAN: Well, look who's reasoning. And when he takes me out to dinner he won't ever add up the check or smoke greasy cigars . . . and he won't use grease on his hair, either. . . . And he won't do card tricks.

CHARLES: Oh.

JEAN: Oh, I don't mind *your* doing card tricks, Hopsie, I just mean you naturally wouldn't want your *ideal* to do card tricks.

CHARLES: I shouldn't think that kind of an ideal would be very hard to find.

JEAN: Oh, he isn't . . . that's why he's my ideal. . . . What's the use of having an ideal if you can't ever find him any place? Mine is a practical ideal, you can always find two or three in every barber shop . . . getting the works.

CHARLES: Then why don't you marry one of them?

JEAN [*almost indignantly*]: Why should I marry anybody who looked like that? When I marry it's going to be somebody I've never seen before.[5]

As a way of creating—that is, arousing—Charles's own sexual hunger, Jean indulges his moral need to refer to his appetite for women in "ideal" terms, all the while instructing him in the wisdom of practicality. Her description of her ideal is practical because it is so literal: he must be short, so he can look up to her. More important, she knows what he is to be like, down to that detail, pertinent beyond Charles's power of knowing, that her ideal won't do card tricks. Charles's task as suitor is to become similarly knowing, equally articulate in describing and prompt in recognizing his ideal when he sees her.

That he has difficulty performing this task is, of course, the subject of the comedy of identification—Is she the same dame?—that propels the second half of the film. In this comedy about knowledge, the hero must learn to separate useful from irrelevant knowledge. Charles Pike is obliged by heredity and fortune to remember and explain the distinction between ale and beer, but Hopsie is never quite sure of the difference and usually gets it wrong. Besides, in his own words, he doesn't give a hoot about it; it's only information. Hopsie, to succeed, needs a different kind of knowledge to act on, and it is made available to him in this scene in which Jean confides to him her "ideal."

Hopsie is also on the brink of sexual discovery when he finds a cold hot water bottle in her bed. An obvious but good-natured Freudian joke lurks obscenely between the lines of this scene, which begins with Jean screaming hysterically (the first and only time in the film she is really out of control) about a snake on the loose: "Why didn't you tell me you had a slimy . . . ," she splutters, leaving her sentence provocatively unfinished. Charles, reverting to his rationalist mode, seeks to clarify any confusion between his snake and his sex. "But I thought you understood that Emma was a snake," he pleads on his behalf. "How could I understand anything of the kind?" is her panicked reply. "Why should I suspect an apparently civilized man of . . . " Of what? Faced with a Freudian symbol on the loose, she begins to mimic Hopsie's sexual stuttering.

Sturges's canny use of this phallic symbolism is consistent and symptomatic. Jean is unnerved by the sexual presence she has discovered and then aroused in Charles. Jean, it appears, can be manipulated by her own machinations. She has devised a plot that has overcome her as well as Charles. She spends a restless night dreaming of snakes and wakes up screaming. The sound of that scream will be amplified on Eve's honeymoon night, but then the sexual screams will be of the train whistle, each blast a screeching substitute for the names of Lady Eve's lovers. But on this morning, only her father (Charles Coburn) can demystify the terrifying night-magic of sexuality. He rehearses for her the game of fifths, in which phallic aces appear and reappear, suggest-

The Lady Eve and the Female Con   313

ing that he, the elder and wiser, has mastered the game. He has played his hand here, as elsewhere, with what he justifiably calls "virtuosity," a word that cunningly reinforces the connection between physical dexterity and erotic manipulation.

Somewhat later, in a tender scene that reveals to us the intimacy that exists between father and daughter, Jean and her father approach and address each other on this sensitive topic of love through their mirrored reflections. The mirror, prop for Jean's sleight-of-hand in the dining-room scene, now becomes, as Cavell has noted, the filmic space for reciprocity, for seeing through and beyond the magic of projected images.[6] This tender, quiet moment (in a film often punctuated by cacophonous sounds) confirms that behind and beneath all the manipulations, impersonations, masquerades, and prestidigitation of Sturges's comedy abides genuine feeling. The comic art of mirroring human nature at its most laughable gives us real reflections of human emotion, not simply cosmetic and artificially heightened ones.

The affectionate tone of this scene rescues the comedy and its vision of love from the clutches of the merely cunning. Comedy must produce such moments of emotional honesty and tenderness to bring about the desired happy ending. But that ending also requires fantasy, poetry, romance. Sturges, so prodigal in his comic inventiveness, provides us with that poetically satisfying moment when the real and the ideal meet, on shipboard. It is the scene on the moonlit deck when Jean and Hopsie confess their love. This scene is framed and shaped by two shots of the ship cutting through the sea, accompanied by one of the few natural sounds the film permits us to hear. It is as if Sturges wants to distinguish this moment, shot in a heightened romantic light, from all the conning that comes before and after it. A moonlit deck is a woman's business office, Jean claims, and yet what we overhear in this scene is something else, something very much like an idiomatic poetry of "talking" pictures. Here is the prose poem that Hopsie, at once poet and lover and a bit of the cockeyed lunatic newly escaped from the Amazon, improvises on the spot:

> I've just understood something . . . you see, every time I've
> looked at you here on the boat it wasn't only here I saw you;

you seemed to go way back . . . I know that isn't clear, but I saw you here and at the same time further away, and then still further away, and then very small . . . like converging perspective lines . . . no, that isn't it, more like figures following each other in a forest glade. Only way back there you were a little girl in short dresses with your hair falling on your shoulders, in the middle distance your hair is up but you're still gawky like a colt . . . then when you get nearer you look more like you do now, except not so pretty . . . but I've only told you half of it, because way back there a little boy is standing with you, holding your hand, and in the middle distance I'm still with you, not holding your hand any more because is isn't manly, but wanting to. And then still nearer we look terrible: with your legs like a colt and mine like a calf . . . what I'm trying to say, only I'm not a poet, I'm an ophiologist, is that I've always loved you . . . I mean I've never loved anyone but you. I suppose that sounds as dull as a drug store novel, and what I see inside I'll never be able to cast into words . . . but that's what I mean.[7]

Hopsie for the first time finds images for his feelings, even as he admits to the fear that his sentiments sound as if they have been lifted from drugstore novels. But love might never be declared nor lovers ever venture to speak romantic "nothings" if such fears would still their tongue. This, I believe, is Sturges's rather moving point in this love scene—that love can make the dumb speak, make something out of nothing. Charles's love inspires him to give unexpected life to a cliché—"I feel like I've loved you all my life"—in a series of specific moments retrieved from memory. His memories are not of a real past but an ideal one of his heart's creation, a love story in which he sees himself fated (Sic Erat Fatis) for this woman whose image he had unknowingly held and cherished within him since childhood. He may not be as adept at staging effects or scouting locales as Jean, but he shows the latent art of his feeling in the human pictures he summons up and re-creates for her, going back to childhood, where sexuality first asserts itself, through adolescence, the girl of his dreams beside him, but not holding his hand. The fear that public displays of affection are not "manly" originates, this confession informs us, in adolescence, and one of the purposes of the last lingering series of shots as Charles-Hopsie drags Jean along the gangways and kisses her quite publicly—to applause, in fact—is to disabuse us of this ideal of manly reserve.

Hopsie's romantic reverie concludes in a forest glade where perspectives converge in a perfect frame for adult romance—the middle distance. The glade that Hopsie imagines does seem a better version of paradise, a more habitable Eden than the Amazonian wilds. Jean's face, captured in a luminous close-up, is irradiated by Hopsie's stumbling story of maturing, naturally unfolding love, the love that begins in a girlish image and comes to fulfillment in her. Desire itself seems purged and cleansed in this moonlit moment. Jean accepts Hopsie's story of love, and like a good director just given a desirable script, she takes responsibility for materializing his images and dreams. She will think clearly, keep her wits about her, for all may not prove clear sailing. Only she can negotiate this maneuver; Hopsie is too cockeyed, lost in the perfume or aura of his own dream to be trusted to its actualization.

But Jean isn't given a chance to show how she can guide them through the lunacies that imperil their midsummer night's dream. Muggsy's suspicions about her past (so different from Hopsie's romanticized evocations) lead to the first of the film's two "enlightenment" scenes. The first is visually ghastly, the second, on the honeymoon train, shrill and distressful to the ear. The first occurs when Charles is presented with a photograph that identifies Jean and her cohorts as cardsharps prowling the high seas. For the only time in the film, Charles realizes that the woman he loves and the woman in the picture are positively the same dame. If he has any doubts, the identification on the back of the photograph bleakly proclaims who and what she is. This incriminating writing is held up against Charles's face and is blended into his countenance, his complexion paling with the force of sickening illumination. This rare close-up of Charles's morally stricken face contrasts with Jean's emotionally radiant one (when words of love revealed Jean to have a virginal, uncorrupted face). Charles's face approaches a monumental pathos. We are meant, I think, to remember that Fonda is the actor who played, two years earlier, the young Mr. Lincoln, the archetypal figure of probity and plain-dealing.

But Sturges's visual appeal to the moral iconography of Fonda's face does not so much clarify as confuse the ethical judgment rendered against Jean. By this point in the comedy we should know, if Charles does not, that this photograph does not represent the truth of Jean's present feelings, only the official record of her past. We heard her on that moonlit deck, and, more important, we, like Charles, have seen her face. We aren't meant to accede to his quick condemnation of her character. That Charles trusts that photograph is a terrible mistake. He ventures his happiness on the basis of what Jean accurately describes as a rotten likeness. Charles wooed and won Jean with a story about human growth; he made love to her in the language that envisioned a relationship that began in childhood, persisted through adolescence, and culminated in the magical and romantic present, the real time of all comedy. He exulted in a vision of happiness composed of lights and shadows; now he sees only in black and white. The first is the vision of innocent love, the second of disillusioned or experienced love, but it is the latter, in this comedy, that is false.

In her defense, Jean confides to Hopsie that a girl must take care of herself, manage her own destiny, and not leave her fate to the cards. According to Jean, she is an adventuress, but then all women are: "They have to be. If you waited for a man to propose to you from natural causes you'd die of old maidenhood. That's why I let you try my slippers on . . . and then I put my cheek against yours . . . and then I made you put your arms around me and hold me tight . . . and then I fell in love with *you* . . . which wasn't in the cards." This is the only time in the film when the game of chance is not a metaphor for manipulation but represents the real hazards of leaving one's life in the hands of fate. She tries to tell him, too, that "the best women aren't as good you probably think they are and the bad ones not at as bad . . . not nearly as bad." But in his newly acquired knowledge such shadings are lost to him. The film visually punishes him for this moral ignorance, for seeing the world in stark black and white oppositions. Dressed in black (or, at times, in an outfit of contrasting black and white), Jean

Charles oblivious to moral shading

The Lady Eve and the Female Con   317

is more trustworthy and loveable, more protective of Hopsie's interests, even against those of her own father, than the Lady Eve, arrayed in resplendent white. The wedding tableau of the second half of the movie, with the bride dressed in ceremonial white and stepping on a white and black checked floor, completes the picture of deception and treachery composed in answer to Charles's own moral ignorance.

The second half of *The Lady Eve* introduces us to a rather different kind of heroine, created to punish this moral ignorance, and in a sense a product of it. It is this female revenger, the Lady Eve, who vanquishes Charles's moral innocence and educates him in the endemic hypocrisies of his own class. Lady Eve is more "acceptable" to Charles's closed morality, and yet Sturges's darkest point may be his suggestion that ladyhood itself is the creation of revenge. This film is skeptical to the point of cynicism about the ideal of ladyhood and gentlemanliness as the prerogative of the upper classes. Lady Eve is simply not as nice or as appealing as Jean, the "common" adventuress and, need I say, fast-talking, free-wheeling dame. The Lady Eve talks in a shrill and insistent voice; her laugh is too emphatic, and, after she accepts Charles's proposal of marriage (which marks the culmination of her revenge plot), it is almost demonic. She introduces herself into the nouveau riche world of the Connecticut countryside by telling a story about getting lost on the subway and asking the official to "be so good as to let me off at Connect-i-cut." This provokes a little gem of a joke at how the English and the American can speak the same language at cross purposes. "Lady," she reports the conductor telling her, "I don't know where Connect-i-cut is, but this train goes to Harlem." After a wild guffaw from the gentlemen, Lady Eve disingenuously concludes: "I don't know how he knew I was a lady." Proletarian American slang and the nomenclature of the titled British classes use the same word to refer to a different (or is it the same?) class of woman.

The central social and perceptual problem of the class-conscious comedy of the film's second half hinges on this comedy of misidentification and identity. The comedy's double structure is thematically elaborated in its play with second looks, double takes and, of course, taking second chances on the same (or is she a different?) dame. Is

Muggsy right in believing that the Lady is a dame? Eve claims the conductor knew a lady when he saw one. Charles Pike is put to the same test. In trying to confirm or correct his perception that Lady Eve and Jean are, as Muggsy colloquially insists, positively the same dame, Charles takes many falls. This manically timed and farcically staged half of the film is the setting for the most violent juxtapositions and contrasts: Eve's splendid carriage as she is introduced to Connecticut society pointedly contrasts to Charles's gawkiness; her constant upper-class chatter counterpoints his awkward stammering. Incongruity, displacement, dissonance, and cacophony reign in this revenge plot. All these discordant elements in the physical and verbal comedy are condensed in the most cynical love scene in American movie comedy: Charles's second proposal in identical words to the identical woman with a different name whom he may or may not know to be the same dame.

This second proposal scene is imagined, blocked, staged, and directed by Lady Eve, lying like a producer on a casting couch. She seems to be a witch gazing into her crystal ball as she confidently predicts that her sexual trap will be sprung in two weeks. She proceeds to describe to her confederate (and "uncle") the setting of her triumph.[8] She selects as her stage a wooded glen that scenically, indeed cynically, recalls Hopsie's vision of a forest glade. But nature, symbolized by the intrusive presence of the nudging, whinnying horse, works against romance, not with it, as in the earlier, glowing moonlit deck scene. This scene is not the work Jean identifies as woman's business. It is the product of a lady's business, and the difference is important.

As Charles "declares" his love for Eve, hypocrisy, bad faith, pretension, and erotic unease dominate. The language these lovers now speak is not the language of honest, if stumbling, feeling, but the worldly language of double entendre, treacherous double meanings, senseless repetitions, trite and empty endearments. Everything and everyone is nudging each other in this scene in a kind of graceless, dishonest contact. To Charles's banal declaration that he hopes that he deserves her, Lady Eve replies, with all the revenger's delight in concealed irony, "Oh, but you *do,* dear . . . if anybody *ever* deserved me . . . you do . . .

so richly." The word "richly," which she seems to savor for its sardonic taste as it comes off her tongue, betrays the element of class resentment that motivates her sexual plotting. Throughout this scene, then, the clichés of love are not reimagined in the rich tones of the middle distance, but foregrounded (literally) in a comic frame that encompasses horse, man, and woman in one improbable and impossibly cramped space.[9] The horse's final whinny merges and is identified with Eve's final laughter as she accepts Charles's proposal. It is this cacophonous blending of the human and animal that serves as prelude to the most manic sequence in the film, one that carries us through the elaborate preparations of the marriage ceremony and ends with a close-up of the bride, whose "knowing" and satisfied smile signals to us the consummation of her comic revenge.

Eve receives the satisfaction due to her (thief's) honor during the most harrowing honeymoon night in film comedy. Her last is her most distressing and most debauched impersonation—a female Don Juan with lower-class tastes. The Lady Eve plays the role, as Cavell has suggested, of a vulgar Scheherazade, who tells her not-yet-husband the story of what seems to be her 1,001 amorous nights.[10] Charles tries to be manly and sophisticated about Eve's first erotic escapade and pledges to bestow on her his "sweet forgiveness." He repeats this phrase, as if such sweetness is as cloying to his moral as much as to his sexual tastes. Charles's sickly smile as he delivers these words of forgiveness visually works against his chosen text of charity. His idealism is cruelly tested and exposed in taking as his bride a woman morally smaller than he had supposed. But his difficulty in forgiving also suggests that he, too, as bridegroom is disappointing, not "big" enough" to be both loving husband and indulgent father to his bride, the ideal mate the Lady Eve had identified as her manly ideal.

The cramping of characters in roles unsuited to them is reinforced by the claustrophobic train setting, which intensifies the sense of contraction and confinement and, finally, pain. Closeted in a train compartment, with only a window to suggest a world outside, Charles hears the story of Eve's erotic adventures. Lightning flashes and thunder rolls as sexual revelation succeeds sexual revelation, leaving the poor bridegroom speechless. This scene concludes with a fall that transcends slapstick, a fall of the desolated bridegroom into mud, into dirt, into moral devastation. The Lady Eve, in witnessing Charles's physical degradation, no longer keeps up the pretense that her sexual machinations are fitting retribution for his moral failure to trust and love her. She tastes the bitter fruit of her sexual victory and it turns to ashes in her mouth. She closes the blind on the window that looks out onto the dejected and mud-splattered groom. The blind at this moment seems to stand for a blank screen. Jean-Eve simply cannot improve on so complete and final a ruin. Such is Sturges's most profound allusion to the legacy of Eve, the original corrupter of the innocent Adam. His comedy represents her moment of triumph in terms of this bitter and deep misogyny.

The blankness of that drawn shade signals a dangerous exhaustion of the film's comic and moral resourcefulness. The love plot appears beyond recovery, its hero and heroine beyond forgiveness, and, indeed, in the comedy's own terms, they are. Charles is too bitter and will not speak to his bride nor hear any explanation. His refusal to listen forecloses any possibility of a comic ending, which can be accomplished only by talking things through, not blanking them out. The only way the comedy does recover is by beginning again, this time in calculated innocence. The repentant Eve makes this new beginning possible by reassuming her directorial role, stage-managing a reunion with the depressed Charles (on his way back to his paradise of bachelors) on the same boat and in the same manner, through a providential fall that leaves him sprawled at her feet.

We know that it is providential by the urgent manner with which Hopsie drags Jean to his room. He has not only found words; he also has found a confident, eager, purposeful, and manly stride. The result is as exhilarating a picture of two people hurrying to consummate their love as you will find in screen comedy. This sexual haste does not come amiss. Whatever happens, this fall doesn't raise new questions (although it should!) in Charles's mind. He is satisfied with what is useful for him to know—that it is Jean. He kisses her in rapid bursts of instinctive desire. The camera closes in on Jean and Hopsie to hear their first words to each other on the threshold of a private and privileged space that we will not be allowed to enter. Charles forswears a knowledge that is of no use to him (what Jean is doing there, why she is there, only her being there matters now). And Jean gives back to him proof of her love in the language of infatuation—of cockeyedness—that he had used to express his love: "Don't you know I've waited all my life for you and then talked too much, you big mug." Jean doesn't want to pretend or manipulate anymore. She is ready, this female Prospero, to bury her book and close the bedroom door. Her last words are in loving responses to Hopsie's admitting that he is married. "But so am I, darling. So am I." Let my son, Daniel Seidel, pronounce on the significance of her counteradmission: "We do not *see* her pronounce these last words; they are heard from behind the closing door of the bedroom, as though she is back to her old project of directing the action by permitting the consummation of a now-mutual fantasy." [11]

But if the comic victory belongs to the con woman, to the skeptic belongs the spoils. We might expect, when the turning door handle is brought into sharp focus in the film's final frame, that it will either click into place, signaling a more intimate connection that is proceeding within, or that a sign might be hung out advising us not to disturb. Instead, our final view is of Muggsy, the nursemaid, summarily expelled from the room, as if to signal the end of Hopsie's long adolescence. Muggsy doesn't object to this comic piece of legerdemain, or protest his own banishment. He only verifies what has always been deliriously obvious—that Eve and Jean are positively the same dame. His evidential remark is indispensable for bringing together the lovers' opposing worlds and indigenous vocabularies. The last word in the film is his, and it is "dame," a word that amalgamates the nomenclature of the British nobility, the romantic vocabulary of knights and ladies, with the verbal zest of American colloquialisms (and its most vibrant expression in the twentieth century, screwball comedy). The word dame marries the jaunty to the elegant, the experienced to the innocent, the adventuress to the lady and announces them to be positively the same.

In this marriage, the film allays the anxieties that it has itself aroused about the designing woman, the seductive Eve, by assuring us that Jean and Eve, the good (who isn't as good as we want) and the bad (who isn't as bad as we think) are joined in the middle distance. Muggsy's brusque epilogue illustrates, in all its idiomatic pungency, the illusionist wizardry of Preston Sturges in arranging perspectives until they converge in a comic vista where happiness is glimpsed as pure trompe l'oeil.

Conclusion

Blondes Born Yesterday

Oh, she was quick and good and everything.

— Howard Hawks on Ann Sheridan

oward Hawks's praise of Ann Sheridan captures what was existentially thrilling about fast-talking dames: their goodness encompassed not just a mode of behavior but a way of being, a fullness as well as a liveliness of nature. Sadly, Hawks's tribute could serve as an epitaph to the era that gave full rein to such quick and good women who seemingly had and could do everything. By the early 1950s the fast-talking dame was an endangered species. We might attribute her eclipse to the silencing or, more accurately, the slowing and dumbing down of the American comic heroine. Disturbing harbingers of a shift in national mood were already evident in the still snappy but strangely dispirited comedies of the postwar era. Claudette Colbert, who braved Franco's Fascist army in *Arise, My Love* (1940) and served with distinction in the Pacific in *So Proudly We Hail* (1943), finds herself combating the sexual ideology of the home front in *Without Reservations* (1946). We may take her experience as foreshadowing things to come.

Colbert plays Christopher "Kit" Madden, an author who, traveling incognito, has an unscheduled encounter with Rusty Thomas (John

Wayne), a demobilized war veteran. They meet on a train to Los Angeles, where Chris will oversee the filming of her bestseller, *Here Is Tomorrow*. One look at him and she knows that she has found the man to play her hero, Mark Winston, a war-weary but idealistic pilot who yearns for a new world order. The trouble is that Rusty, whose name should tip us off to the weathered but serviceable manhood he represents, has read the book and couldn't wait to trade it to a sick bunkmate for an Afrika Korps helmet with a Rommel insignia (practically a collector's item, his sidekick enthuses). Not knowing, of course, that he is panning the book to its author, he tells Chris, with smug manly conviction, that the book is plain silly in suggesting that its progressive hero would keep saying no to the beautiful woman (to be played by Lana Turner) who has pursued him for four hundred pages just because she happens to be a reactionary.

His sidekick also subscribes to this hormonal school of literary criticism. "But this reactionary is not a fellow," he objects. "She's Lana Turner. What difference does it make what she thinks?" Rusty is quick to agree. In Winston's place, he tells Chris, he would treat Lana Turner as a woman first and argue with her afterward. Leaning forward to emphasize his point, Rusty reduces the sexual relation to a grammatically and existentially simple proposition: "He's a man. . . . She's a woman. . . . That's all." Rusty's abrupt "That's all" reduces the complex verbal and emotional comedy of human courtship back to its primordial elements. Laconic manhood, as sparing of words as it is of feelings, is about to make a comeback. Rusty, an unwitting vanguard in the sexual reaction ahead, proceeds to court Colbert according to these elementary principles, but he finds himself stymied by her desire "to be sure of what's inside of us, our tastes, our interests, our gestures." "Oh, why don't you stop thinking," he objects, the second time in ten minutes that a man dismisses what a woman may be thinking. After kissing her to "prove" that she is wrong, he gives up in peevish exasperation: "I wish I'd met you before you had read that book."

Not only has she read the book, she wrote it. Moreover, she comes into the movie convinced that a "relationship without purpose or mental accord is sterile," a pronouncement lost on the female to whom it is volunteered, a new, somewhat alarming female type that Rusty and his sidekick identify as a "beetle." Beetles are, in GI slang, good-time girls who "make out that everything is all right, that they have no angles, that they just want a good time." This, it transpires, is a fatal illusion. As Rusty explains, apparently from experience, "the first thing you know you find 'em crawling around. They get into your hair, climb in your pocket and they give you mental fatigue." Mental fatigue is to be avoided at all costs, and Rusty spends most of the movie going to great lengths to avoid it.

The beetle, for her part, is adamant that a girl has to look to the future and can't blame anyone but herself if she hasn't mastered the first principle of sexual maneuver: give in to a fella on the unimportant things—like sympathizing with a guy's union work—then get the things you want, like spending a night at the Ritz Club, even if it is frequented by a bunch of reactionaries. The movie doesn't bother to determine whose sexual politics are the most realistic or even whether it is the beetle or Chris who truly represents the "modern" woman. It prefers to take Chris (traveling under the alias of Kitty Klatch), Rusty, and his sidekick, Dink (Don Defore) cross-country, partly by rail, then on the road, to expose them to a "literally uncultivated" American heartland. Rusty, moved by the sight of the Great Plains, begins to tell his own story about the moral dawn of America. He praises the robust pioneers who found a "howling wilderness," and tamed it. Of course, the pioneers also "found some unpleasant little characters who painted their faces." Rusty becomes impassioned recalling the non-cerebral, rugged self-reliance of those first settlers. "Do you think these pioneers filled out form X6227 and sent in a report saying the Indians were a little unreasonable? Did they have insurance for their old age, for their crops, for their homes? They did not. They looked at the land and the forest and the rivers; they looked at their wives, their kids, and their houses, and then they looked up at the sky and said, 'Thanks God, we'll take it from here.'"

Rusty's speech is one that any anti-Roosevelt Republican might have taken pride in delivering. It is full of scorn for the progressivist politics that instituted Social Security, yet never questions the entitlement to a wilderness inconveniently occupied by "unpleasant little characters who painted their faces." *Without Reservations* is saturated by the national politics of its time, and in the argument between Rusty and Kit we can hear the first rumblings of the ideological battles, many of them waged on the sexual front, that will flower into a cold war during the next decade and in some measure persist into our own times.

Chris had anticipated this clash of ideologies in her book. She is still enough of a dame to be entrusted with articulating the social costs and human terms of the future. She, not Rusty, is the prophet of the ideological and sex wars to come, but like many a prophet she is fated to be somewhat discredited in her own land, in her own time. Today Chris's hope for humanity entering a new phase of caring and educated citizenship seems more timely than ever, and one is grateful that, after hearing Rusty's paean to the American settlement, she stubbornly but amiably refuses to concede the argument, insisting that they are talking about two different things. Which they are. She is right in claiming that she speaks for the future, he for a past which itself will be subject to revision (particularly, though she does not say so, when it comes to seeing that the Indians had real reasons for being unreasonable).

The ideological dispute between them is never resolved, as perhaps it never could be. But the sexual quarrel is provisionally settled on a warm afternoon spent with a recently immigrated Mexican family, the Ortegas. While Rusty finds himself fussed over and eventually serenaded by Ortega's lonely, buxom teenage daughter, Chris is consigned to kitchen duty. It is while washing dishes that she hears the family patriarch blissfully recall his passionate love for his tempestuous, and, given the number of children at the table, obviously fertile wife. As the latest comers to America, the Ortegas recall the determined natures that helped settle a frontier without giving much thought to the finer points of sexual selection and propagation.

Chris is not so much drawn to this vision as flummoxed by it, but before she can persuade Rusty to her way of thinking—and loving— her masquerade is exposed. In a kind of comic if not poetic justice, she is jailed for forging a check using her real name, Christopher Madden. We are meant to get a sense of just how important a name hers is when the Hollywood producer who bails her out of jail and clears up the mistaken identity complains of all the negative publicity the incident has generated. But the woman who is "sharing headlines with Hitler and Stalin" gets her biggest dressing-down from Rusty, who declares, with a mixture of hurt and exasperation: "I don't want a woman who is trying to tell the world what to do. I don't even want a woman to tell me what to do. I want a woman who needs me, a Miss Klatch, who's helpless and cute."

Rusty's chagrin at finding "helpless" Miss Klatch to be the supremely competent Miss Madden, eventually gives way, as we know it will and must. Chris manages to woo him back by taking a cue from the beetle's play book. She schemes to make him jealous by gallivanting around with other men, and not just any men, but Hollywood dreamboats like Cary Grant (in a cameo appearance). The devious ploy works, and Rusty apparently resolves to accept the capable Miss Madden. In the last shot, as Chris witnesses Rusty's arrival at her well-furnished home, she looks up and, before joining him, offers *her* thanks to the almighty power who has brought the man she loves—beyond ideology and without any reassuring signs of their "mental accord"—to her door. "Thanks, God, I'll take it from here." Her thanksgiving is eloquent in its homespun American style, but they are Rusty's words, not hers. She may have the last word, but one suspects that it is the last reinterpretation she will offer of Rusty's rugged, manly Americanism. The truth is, Chris's last words are those not of a pioneer but of a throwback.

By the mid-forties, the route to the future had taken Colbert and her audience back to the virtues of yesterday. Once arrived at tomorrow, she might find herself in the company of Joan Fontaine, another female convert to homespun family values in *You Gotta Stay Happy* (1948). Fontaine plays Dee Dee Dillwood, a runaway bride, neurotically averse to marriage, who is rescued on her wedding night by the gallant if wry and standoffish pilot Marvin Payne (James Stewart). They head cross-country, in a plane, but an emergency landing forces them to seek help from a farm family with ten children. In light of these numbers and this exaltation of woman as breeder, we would be excused for thinking that the "gotta" in the title of Fontaine's caper is not so much a wink at the slang that animated the liberated sexual comedies that preceded it as a forecast of the sexual imperatives that are working to strip woman of her feisty modernity and return her to a more sedate, less contrarian womanhood.

Even the indomitable Bette Davis, so terrifically game in *The Bride Came C.O.D.*, begins to lose her timing and verve in *June Bride* (1948). She plays Linda Gilman, the editor of a magazine with the ominous title *Home Life*. In preparing the June issue devoted traditionally to weddings, she is paired up with Carey Jackson (Robert Montgomery), a world-traveling foreign correspondent temporarily without an assignment who, as it happens (and it always does in these comedies) is a former beau. She is the boss in the collaboration that ensues, a position that she willingly relinquishes at the end of the movie when she decides to quit her job to marry Carey and follow him wherever his job may take him. Still, she is the one who presses the issue of marriage, reminding him, "We're perfectly mated. We're of opposite sexes."

The argument has all the Dadaist zing of screwball logic—Lombard could have said it, although she would have uttered it with real conviction. Davis, perhaps glimpsing the times ahead, covers the line in a light but detectable coating of irony. Otherwise, how to explain the feeble humor of her wooing the now recalcitrant Carey with the formal logic of sexual differentiation rather than the unanswerable argument of passionate affinity. He, for his part, is strict as to the terms of surrender: "It's become a simple, old-fashioned question of who wears the pants," he tells her. "And I'd look pretty silly without them." So much for the sartorial and psychological sex-reversals that gave the comedies of the early talkies such grand and joyous laughs.

In Carey's staid refusal to "look silly" we can begin to detect the gathering murmur of sexual discontent that will culminate in Joseph Mankiewicz's witty but anxious paean to the grand dames of an earlier age, *All About Eve* (1950). The film, for all its comic grandeur, marks a fatal loss of nerve in American popular culture. What else but a loss of nerve and vision could account for Margo Channing's (Bette Davis) eloquent yet self-annulling "confession" in a stalled car. She confides to her dearest friend (and well-intentioned schemer) Karen Richards (Celeste Holm), that she has been behaving disgracefully because she feels she can never be what she wants to be—young and helpless and feminine—all that she suspects the usurper Eve is for Bill, the man she loves. She admits that even as a grand star of the theater there is "one career" she shares with all of her sex: "being a woman." This is how she understands that moral imperative: "Sooner or later, we've got to work at it, no matter how many other careers we've had or wanted. And in the last analysis nothing is any good unless you look up just before dinner or turn around in bed and there he is. Without that you're not a woman. You're something with a French provincial office or a—a book of clippings, but you're not a woman." She will later renounce her career as a grande dame in favor of the higher calling of being a "four-square, upright, downright, forthright, married lady." Davis says the line with relish, obviously delighting in the strong accents and forti-fied rhythms that energize and challenge her tongue. Her bravura turn makes us feel even at the moment of her abdication of damehood what a talent is going to waste. As to the man she marries? Well, he is a di-rector who will continue to work without once giving a thought to the career of being a man. And if any woman tries to seduce him into that alternate career path, he will set her straight, as he does the conniving Eve (Anne Baxter), who has the temerity to come on to him: "What I go after, I want to go after," he tells her in a sudden access of sexual disgust. "I don't want it to come after me." Perhaps it is his instinct for drama—he is a director, after all—that turns what should have been a rejection of one woman's advances into a declaration of the sexual rights of man. No one, not even the usually unflappable Eve, thinks to ask why he doesn't he want "it" to go after him, assuming that he indeed wants it as much as it wants him. Many of the most enchant-ing comedies of the thirties—*My Man Godfrey, Bringing Up Baby, The Awful Truth*—would have been stillborn ventures or would have ended miserably had the desirable men in those films not yielded to female sexual pursuit.

All About Eve, coming midpoint of the American century, is a witty, savvy, but finally anxious comedy in which we can begin to see how America justified to itself the expatriation of women from that marketplace where words and desires are coined and exchanged. Margo Channing is among the first, and certainly is the most vibrant and volatile, of intelligent, talkative women nudged off screen, invited or cajoled to get back to the business of running and replenishing the household. Increasingly confined to the homestead, where they might huddle with their dreams and their brood of children, women no longer spoke as freely or as well. The dumb blonde came to replace the fast-talking dame as the national archetype for sexual, festive existence. Smart girls, wise girls, bad girls, even silly girls who defined themselves by and through their words became increasingly rare apparitions, and indeed their muting has lasted into the twenty-first century. Two quite different yet in their way spectacular talents oversaw her demise — Judy Holliday and Marilyn Monroe. They bear little in common with their predecessors. The dizzy blondes of the thirties, like Harlow and Lombard, even when befuddled, bewildered, or simply bamboozled by the world, knew how to speak up for themselves. They were certainly not born yesterday.

This, of course, is the ironic title of the 1950 film that gave Judy Holliday her most famous and most endearing role, Billie Dawn. Billie is a small-time showgirl and big-time gangster's moll who is educated *out* of her pungent speech. What does it mean to be born yesterday? As this plot suggests, it means being, like an infant, without a language anywhere near adequate to one's needs. The need is perceived, however, not by Billie but by her gangster boyfriend Harry Brock, played with gruff bravado by Broderick Crawford. No bright light himself, Brock nevertheless is smart enough to know that if he is to succeed in his congressional "lobbying" campaign, Billie, as his consort, must be instructed in the language of civilized society — or rather the language of the Washingtonian elite, which is not necessarily the same thing. He hires newspaperman Paul Verrall (William Holden) to teach her the patois favored by Washingtonian society.

Born Yesterday might as easily be called *Pygmalion Goes to Washington,* with one significant twist: in the tradition of fast-talking dames, Billie is the student who surpasses the teacher. A surprisingly apt pupil, she takes to studying the dictionary and soon begins to question the "papers" she had previously signed without troubling herself about their contents and shady purpose. Eventually she becomes a trustbuster simply by yelling, with hilarious but unequivocal authority, the single word "Cartel!" Her public service migrates to the private sector as her infectious enthusiasm for words and their power to represent vital concepts eventually restores Holden's jaded Higgins to his original political idealism. She gives him the greatest gift a woman can in American comedy—faith in his own words.

In such turnabouts, Holliday displays her subtle comic genius for subverting the dumb blonde prototype she so giddily fulfilled. The dimwitted Holliday persona was born in *Adam's Rib* (1949), the Ruth Gordon–Garson Kanin comedy that presages the gender troubles that were increasingly to preoccupy the last half of the twentieth century. Holliday, as Doris Attinger, is the film's social wildcard, the woman so wedded to the idea of the sanctity of home that she turns murderous. When she finds that her husband has been cheating on her, she buys a gun, follows him to his lover's apartment, and bursts into the room, shooting wildly. Representing her at her trial is Katharine Hepburn's Amanda Bonner, who defends the assault on the purportedly feminist grounds that a woman, endowed with the same rights as man, has an equal right to protect her home against intruders. Prosecuting her is Spencer Tracy's Adam Bonner, a district attorney whose courtroom manner continues the great tradition of noble but tongue-tied American males. Tracy has never been more deft in impersonating the verbal dyslexia of a man who can't help scrambling his words and garbling his sense when excited. He thus can mount no effective objection to the court shenanigans of his fast-talking wife, who, in the film's most carnivalesque moment, parades women of different professions before the court to prove her point that any woman is equal to any man in whatever human enterprise we care to name. Her prime exhibit is a retired circus acrobat who, despite Adam's expostulations, lifts him over her head, suspending him, somewhat precariously, in midair.

Viewers might object to the physical indignity visited on Adam—he feels the insult quite sharply himself. But the scene serves its purpose not so much in making the legal point about woman's equal rights as in giving us a visual demonstration that the relation between the sexes has increasingly come to resemble a balancing act that neither sex can keep up for very long. Hepburn's summation insinuates this anxiety anew when she asks the jury to imagine a gender switch for the principals of the trial. In the transsexual caricatures that result, the husband,

Warren Attinger (Tom Ewell), looks like a bordello hag; Beryl Caighn (Jean Hagen), the other woman, a lounge lizard Lothario. Only Doris's fixed expression radiates an uncanny androgyny that hints at deeper instabilities in her character and in the sexual ideology that has driven her to pick up a gun.

A woman carrying a gun is as much a phallic threat as she is a public menace, one this movie disarms by having Adam, in a moment suspended between melodrama and farce, wave a gun wildly at his wife and their amorous neighbor, Kip Lurie (David Wayne). After reducing them both to hysterics and eliciting from Amanda the admission that no one has a right to take the law into his or her own hands, Adam calmly puts the gun into his mouth. Rather than pull the trigger, though, he matter-of-factly proceeds to eat it. Adam intends to give his wife a timely lesson on renegade appetites. But Doris, who confessed on the stand her predilection for binge eating, is still on the loose, leaving us to wonder what her social fate will be.

One possible future is shown, indeed exhibited, in *It Should Happen to You* (1954). The amusingly prescient Holliday anticipates the semiotics of postmodernist culture in her role as Gladys Glover, the girl who believes in signs. Gladys, who has tried and so far failed to make it in New York, is determined to make a name for herself. She decides to do so in the most immediate and American way—through self-advertising. She rents a billboard to display her name in one last effort to establish her social existence before she gives up on the big city, and, presumably, on herself. Before Andy Warhol, Gladys subscribed to the theory that anyone, even those without visible talent or demonstrable achievement, could become famous, even if it is only for exemplifying that most dreary of fifties ideals—the average American girl.

This is how Gladys markets herself in a series of television ads meant to celebrate what is average rather than spectacular, ordinary rather than exceptional about her. When Peter Sheppard (Jack Lemmon), the free-lance moviemaker who didn't need an ad to see what was special about Gladys, objects to her mania for self-publicity, she stands her ground. "I'm over twenty-one," she reminds him, a legally sufficient if emotionally hollow rationale for persisting in her adolescent dream of fame. "From the neck down, yeah," is his demoralized retort. We have come full circle from James Stewart's admiring salute to women who begin from the neck up. If we believe in signs, or at least if we can pick up the signals, the era of dumb blondes is about to begin.

It is an era also dominated by Marilyn Monroe, a woman whose two famous comic motions celebrated her endowments from the neck down: the subway scene in *The Seven Year Itch* (1955), which recalls Dixie Belle Lee's "Gone with the Wind" number in *The Awful Truth*, and Monroe's famous entrance in which she sashays along the train platform in *Some Like It Hot* (1959). Monroe's straddling the subway grate, waiting for the blast of air that will cool her down—but raise the temperature of any male who catches the moment of impact!— takes us back to Sennett's world of bathing beauties whose limbs were the most fetching thing about them. Ellie Andrews would show some leg, but even as she stopped traffic she insisted that she did so to demonstrate that the limb was mightier than the thumb. Monroe would never be capable of such a witticism.

We get the first but hardly the last display of Marilyn Monroe's unsteady relation to language and to herself in *Monkey Business,* directed by Howard Hawks. She plays Lois Laurel, whose slow-wittedness is the target of the most hilarious malapropism in the movie. When her doting boss nevertheless feels obliged to object to her punctuation, she solemnly promises that from now on she will try to be on time. Given her physical attributes, perhaps Lois doesn't need to get the point of punctuation any more than she feels obliged to keep to appointed time. Her sense of fluency is confined to bodily rather than intellectual movement, a fact that Jerry (Jack Lemmon) acknowledges when he first sees her famous walk in *Some Like It Hot* and wonders what laws of motion could explain the physical marvel of "Jell-O on wheels." The clue to Monroe's linguistic character lies not in the words she says but the breaths she takes and intersperses between utterances. Her words always seem about to expire on the threshold of intelligibility. Often she will stumble on some funny trick of language—like the pun or the malapropism—that others appreciate but which she seldom enjoys or profits from.

The perky exception to the blondes who populated the dream world of fifties comedies was Doris Day. In such a smart, amazingly fairminded movie as the underrated *Teacher's Pet* (1958), in which her Erica Stone holds her own against crusty Jim Gannon (Clark Gable), and in the wildly popular *Pillow Talk* (1959) and *Lover Come Back* (1961) (remembered now primarily for their virginal heroines), Day rescued the blonde from financial and emotional insolvency. Her best comic roles gave her a job that suggested her mastery over seductive images — interior decorating and advertising. The camera, as if responding to her professional interest in projecting delectable but tasteful images, found reason as well as pleasure in capturing the discreet sexiness of her movements. It especially liked to catch Day on the dance floor, focusing its gaze on her backside, which undulated, like Monroe's, but with less abandon, albeit with equal promise of sexual expertness.

The hallmark of Day's physical being on screen, however, was her impeccable posture and the ramrod integrity it signified. A complicated sexual ethics is implied by the exceptional erectness with which she carried herself. Monroe is such a creature of impressionable flesh that she talks, as she moves, as if propelled by spontaneous animal instinct. Day is self-fashioned, and fashionably so. Monroe's gowns cover her body like a second, often transparent, skin. Day as career girl set the style for sophisticated urban couture, the clothes befitting a woman who exemplified an admirable Emersonian self-reliance. Day made her moral posture a sexual turn-on, indeed a special variety of the sexual tease, especially when she adorned herself in those evening gowns that proudly bared the sturdy and unbowed splendor of her straight back.

Still, watching her comedies now, Day may strike us as the most Bergsonian of American working-girl heroines, rigid where life should be adaptable, supple, and elastic. Her mania for virginity suggests that she might not be out of place in a problem comedy like *Measure for Measure.* She was the last holdout before the sexual liberation of the sixties, as if the culture foresaw the casual polymorphous perversities ahead, and that Day, her very name a beacon, was a luminous argument for playing by the old rules. In the war between men and women, she stuck to the rules of engagement, never resorting to subterfuge.

There is no trace of hucksterism in her, a remarkable trait given how often she was cast as a successful denizen of Madison Avenue, whose job it was to stimulate the appetites and fancies of the rich and glamorous. Even as an ad woman she never exhibited a playful attitude toward reality or language or even toward her own womanhood. What she did master was the slow burn, the mouth twisting in chagrin, finally letting out not an intelligible word but a clearly understandable wail of anger and revolt. She always played fair, an attribute that may be admirable in everyday life but is often a liability and, in truth, a drag in comedy. If Doris Day had not been able to sound so many variations on "Oooooooo"—surprise, chagrin, ire, and determination to have her revenge—when she discovers who Hudson's character really is and how he has tricked her, she would have been pitied as a casualty in the sex war between men and women. But she did sound those notes of protest, and so she deserves to be remembered as one of its most worthy combatants in love, fated, as are all who are worth capturing, to lose, but never to be vanquished.

She proved, indeed, to be one of the last of her kind—the career girl who could thrive in the boardroom and bedroom. Even as she prospered, the conditions of her prosperity were quickly being eroded or commandeered. The American comedy that succeeded in usurping the élan and prestige of the fast-talking dame is Billy Wilder's *Some Like It Hot,* a film that certified the comic screen persona of Marilyn Monroe as a woman defined by fantasies and erotic scenarios of male-devising. Monroe began the decade with a vivid walk-on as a hungry starlet in *All About Eve,* ruefully wondering why all influential producers look like unhappy rabbits, a thought that doesn't deter her from squaring her shoulders and entering the sexual fray. She concludes the decade with her wistful performance as Sugar, a woman who seems incapable of putting on an act, incapable, indeed of being other than herself. The trouble lies in what she is—love's plaything and sex's prize. She shows not one glimmer of that comic intelligence, available even to Harlow and Lombard in their ditziest roles, by which a woman takes the initiative in "directing" the comic romance and determining its outcome. *Some Like It Hot* compensates for this loss of a directorial female presence by having its heroes, Jerry/Daphne (Lemmon) and Joe/Josephine

(Tony Curtis), dress and act as women, first for protective camouflage, finally for amatory profit (Joe so that he can continue to woo Sugar, Jerry so that he can exploit Osgood Fielding III [Joe E. Brown]). Wilder turns and returns to the comic potential of these sexual masquerades as techniques of survival and self-promotion. Perhaps as a concession to the sexually parsimonious fifties, he is almost chaste in the economy with which he reverses sexual roles: the woman is now the character who stumbles out her unhappy story of disappointed love to a fast-talking dame, who happens of course, to be a man. *Some Like It Hot* gave us Tony Curtis and Jack Lemmon putting on the clothes, trying out the voices, and enjoying the freedom that comedy designates for women, the freedom to reinvent themselves. They not only begin to appreciate this freedom but to appropriate it. For them it is a life saver.

I think it is a mark of our time that two of the most clever, strangely jubilant comedies of the past several decades, *Tootsie* (1982) and *All of Me* (1984), are films in which we are treated first to the spectacle of a man who impersonates a woman and second to that of a man inspirited by the soul of a woman. In conversing with and about their "inner woman," these transfigured males recapture some of the comic inventiveness and sprightliness of the great screwball romances. If their memory is beginning to fade now, it may be because their joyous experiments in cross-gender identifications are overshadowed by "buddy" comedies, especially those that celebrate the male varieties of being dumb and dumber, and masturbatory farces like *There's Something About Mary* and *American Pie,* which turn ejaculation into a primping ritual, nineties-style. In the last months of the last year of the century, film audiences were invited to contemplate the comic delirium of Spike Jonze's *Being John Malkovich,* perhaps the first comedy ever devoted to the theme of ontological envy (the desire to be, not just understand or love, someone other than oneself).

The terms of the mind-into-mind-body exchange are, however, inordinately if hilariously high. It drives Craig Schwartz (John Cusack) to tape his wife's (Cameron Diaz) mouth and shut her in a cage. Later they will both fall in love with Maxine (Catherine Keener) and try to kiss her at the same time. But for all the gender-bending, bisexuality, and New Age geriatric fantasies about metempsychosis, the most ontologically sublime scene belongs to John Malkovich, envying *himself* and going inside his own head. There he wanders into a lounge, encountering replicas of himself, the most delectable if uncanny being Malkovich in various states of drag—waitress, society girl, and lounge singer. *Being John Malkovich* is just the latest of the great drag comedies in which ontological envy is figured as envy of women who are quick and good and everything. But these films also resonate with a darker view of the relationship between the sexes. Now the dialogue between men and women, in which love is declared, misplaced, misspoken, and finally reclaimed and ritualized, has become primarily a dialogue with (in some cases *within*) oneself.

This book commemorates another kind of dialogue, one paced by the rapid give and take and give again of the fast-talking dame making her way into the world, claiming her rights and yet never losing her wits or her ability to say, at the right time, "oh yes." "Every language," Henry James reminded young women at the beginning of the twentieth century, "has its position, which, with its particular character and genius, is its most precious property—the element in it we are most moved (if we have any feeling in the connection at all) to respect, to confirm, to consecrate. What we least desire to do with these things is to give them, in our happy phrase, 'away.' "[1] There is no immediate nor even real danger, as James feared, of American women simply handing over their most precious property, but they may be lulled into letting it fall into disuse or disrepair. All the more reason to attend to the vigilant women I celebrate in this book. They had a real feeling for the position, and respect for the value of the American language. Their fast talk was their dowry but also their legacy, one that we should take care not give or fritter away. These women were of their time but ahead of it, too. If we are lucky, we can still catch up with them.

Notes

Preface

1. Italo Calvino, "A Cinema-Goer's Autobiography," *The Road to San Giovanni,* trans. Tim Parks (New York: Pantheon, 1993), p. 52. I am grateful to Marshall Heymann for calling my attention to this passage.
2. *Irish Times,* Friday, April 14, 2000 (lead story on the website: www.ireland.com/newspaper/breaking/2000/0414/break11.htm). My thanks to Barry Mc-Crea for alerting me to this article and chuckling with me over the findings.
3. As reported by Kate Zernicke, "Effective Speaking 101: Cleaning up 'mall-speak,'" *Boston Globe,* March 22, 1999.

Chapter One. Fast-Talking Dames

1. Roland Barthes, "The Face of Garbo," *Mythologies,* trans. Annette Lavers (New York: Hill and Wang, 1972), p. 56.
2. Anita Loos, *A Girl Like I* (New York: Viking, 1966), p. 120.
3. Olga J. Martin, *Hollywood's Movie Commandments: A Handbook for Motion Picture Writers and Reviewers* (New Haven: H. W. Wilson, 1937), p. 35.
4. Thomas Doherty, *Pre-Code Hollywood,* (New York: Columbia University Press, 1999), p. 1.
5. "Details of Plot, Episode, and Treatment," *The Motion Picture Production Code of 1930 (Hays Code),* reprinted in ibid., pp. 356–57. The initial version of the Code can be downloaded from artsreformation.com.
6. Molly Haskell, *From Reverence to Rape: The Treatment of Women in the Movies* (Chicago: University of Chicago Press, 1987), p. 9.
7. Here is a sample of Benchley's bemused report of the panic set off by the advent of the "Movietone": "Perceiving the advent of the Film Which Talks Like a Man, hundreds of movie stars who have attained their eminence because of a dimple in the chin or a bovine eye, but whose speaking voices could hardly be counted on to put across the sale of a pack of Fatimas in a nightclub, are now frantically trying to train their larynxes into some sort of gentility.

Voice culture has become the order, even the command, of the day." Robert Benchley, "Came the Movietone," *New Yorker,* July 14, 1928.

8. Stanley Cavell, *The World Viewed: Reflections on the Ontology of Film* (Cambridge: Harvard University Press, 1979), p. 150.

9. Alexis de Toqueville, *Democracy in America,* 2nd ed. (New York: Vintage, 1990), 2: 214, 199.

10. Howard Hawks, *Hawks on Hawks,* ed. Joseph McBride (Berkeley: University of California Press, 1982), p. 70.

11. Clint Eastwood is the inheritor of this tradition, which equates moral probity with reticence. He has complicated the equation in his *Dirty Harry* roles, in which there is something fanatical and demoniac in his renegade policing. But then Dirty Harry is really a master of the one-liner, an inheritance from psychopathic gangsterism. No Western hero ever said anything so quotable as "Make my day."

12. Cavell, *World Viewed,* p. 150.

13. Todd McCarthy, *Howard Hawks: The Grey Fox of Hollywood* (New York: Grove, 1977), p. 283.

14. Ibid., p. 284.

15. Stanley Cavell offers us an indispensable meditation on the Miltonic sublimities as well as social ideals attaching to the human conversation in *Pursuits of Happiness: The Hollywood Comedy of Remarriage* (Cambridge: Harvard University Press, 1981). He remarks especially that Milton, in describing one of the chief ends of marriage as a "meet and happy conversation" means "something more by conversation than just talk . . . he means a mode of association, a form of life" (p. 87). Cavell later contends that what he calls the comedies of remarriage, all of which feature quick-witted and fast-talking dames, are conducting a "meet and cheerful" conversation with their culture (p. 151). Which I think they are.

16. Tocqueville, *Democracy in America,* 2: 198.

17. This climax was imitated more than thirty years later in Mike Nichols's *The Graduate,* but play the two endings side by side and see how much we have lost when the runaway bride is Katharine Ross rather than Claudette Colbert. This is not only a question of the caliber of the actresses but the character of the heroines. Even though Ross's Elaine Robinson attends Berkeley, she doesn't come close to being as smart of Colbert's Ellie Andrews. The only respect that *The Graduate* accords a woman is that given Anne Bancroft's Mrs. Robinson, and that is cruelly taken from us in the last shot of her screaming, distorted face.

18. Cavell, *Pursuits of Happiness,* pp. 57–58.

19. Toqueville, *Democracy in America,* 2: 199.

20. *The Philadelphia Story* is the exception that proves this rule. Katharine Hep-

burn's Tracy Lord calls off her wedding with her contracted groom, only instead of taking flight like Ellie Andrews, she is left at the altar with some explaining to do. Cary Grant's C. K. Dexter Haven, her ex-husband and social equal, steps in to save the day—and renew his marriage. I may be alone in thinking *The Philadelphia Story* a mean-spirited comedy, but I believe it is fairly clear that the film means to chasten Tracy precisely where Tocqueville might have commended her—for having cultivated the habits of self-command. Philip Barry interprets this as female imperiousness of a particularly deadly sort—the kind that takes the form of sanctimoniousness. Everyone is forgiven their foibles, mistakes, and weaknesses in the film, *except* the lower-class arriviste groom. Tracy must be "instructed," to use Cavell's terms, in the human arts of understanding.

21. James Thurber, *Is Sex Necessary? Or, Why You Feel the Way You Do* (New York: Harper, 1929), p. 35.

22. Ibid., p. 36.

23. Ibid., p. 40.

24. Ibid., p. 44.

25. Parker Tyler, *The Hollywood Hallucination* (New York: Creative Age, 1944), p. 75.

26. Ibid., p. 77.

27. Pauline Kael, "The Man from Dream City," *New Yorker,* July 14, 1975. Reprinted in *When the Lights Go Down* (New York: Holt, Rinehart and Winston, 1980), p. 7.

28. Alan S. Dale, *Comedy Is a Man in Trouble: Slapstick in American Movies* (Minneapolis: University of Minnesota Press, 2000).

29. To be joined up with egomaniacal leading men is a comic fate that Carole Lombard endures with great comic aplomb; her last film, the sublime *To Be or Not to Be,* pairs her with Jack Benny, as that "great, great, great Polish actor, Joseph Tura," a ham constantly hoping to upstage his beautiful and scene-stealing wife.

30. Oscar Wilde's *Lady Windermere's Fan* was actually adopted as a *silent* film by Ernst Lubitsch. Wilde's verbal exuberance can be translated into the silent film's repertoire of exaggerated gestures more easily than can *The Importance of Being Earnest,* whose comedy is purely verbal. Shaw wrote the screenplay for *Pygmalion,* and Coward's *Blithe Spirit* and *Design for Living* (with radical license taken) translated merrily to the screen.

31. Henry James, *The Question of Our Speech* (Boston: Houghton Mifflin, 1905), p. 10.

32. Ibid., p. 8.

33. Ibid., p. 34.

1. André Bazin, *The Cinema of Cruelty* (New York: Seaver, 1982), p. 35.
2. Henry James, *The Question of Our Speech* (Boston: Houghton Mifflin, 1905), p. 21.
3. Ibid., p. 15.
4. Penelope Gilliatt, *To Wit: Skin and Bones of Comedy* (New York: Scribner's, 1990), p. 116.
5. Ibid., p. 117.
6. The film's director, Josef von Sternberg, remarked in his autobiography that Dreiser's lawyers "made a mistake not calling on me as a witness for Mr. Dreiser, for I would have agreed with him. Literature cannot be transferred to the screen without a loss to its values; the visual elements completely revalue the written word." Josef von Sternberg, *Fun in a Chinese Laundry* (San Francisco: Mercury House, 1988), p. 259.
7. Samuel Putnam, *Paris Was Our Mistress* (Carbondale: Southern Illinois University Press, 1970), p. 41.
8. Edmund Wilson, "Can New York Stage a Serious Play?" May 27, 1925, in *The American Earthquake: Documentary of the Twenties and Thirties* (New York: Doubleday, 1958), p. 65.
9. Wilson, "The Lexicon of Prohibition," in *American Earthquake,* pp. 89–90.
10. F. Scott Fitzgerald, "Echoes of the Jazz Age," in *The Crack-Up,* ed. Edmund Wilson (New York: New Directions, 1993), p. 14.
11. H. L. Mencken, *The American Language: An Inquiry into the Development of English in the United States,* 4th ed., ed. Raven I. McDavid, Jr. (New York: Knopf, 1977), p. 774.
12. Mencken clinches his argument that the American and not the English language shall prevail by citing the American belief in the sheerly demographic superiority of his dialect: "And he holds not illogically that there is no reason under the sun why a dialect spoken almost uniformly by nearly 180,000,000 people should yield anything to a dialect of a small minority in a nation of 50,000,000." *American Language,* p. 774.
13. Virginia Woolf, "American Fiction," in *The Moment and Other Essays* (New York: Harcourt, 1948), pp. 126–27.
14. Somerset Maugham, *Cakes and Ale* (New York: Penguin, 1948), p. 25.
15. Fitzgerald, "Echoes of the Jazz Age," p. 14.
16. Pauline Kael, "Raising Kane," *The Citizen Kane Book: Raising Kane* (Boston: Little, Brown, 1971), p. 19.
17. Especially if she desires, as she does, to marry the highborn Regis Toomey, in one of his few leading man roles before he subsides in his Capraesque supporting player role as decent, grass-roots, small-town American.

18. Ian Hamilton, *Writers in Hollywood, 1915–1951* (New York: Harper & Row, 1990), p. 49.

19. Fitzgerald, "Echoes of the Jazz Age," p. 13.

20. Mencken, *American Language,* pp. 705–6.

21. Roland Barthes, "Power and 'Cool,'" *The Eiffel Tower and Other Mythologies,* trans. Richard Howard (Berkeley: University of California Press, 1997), p. 43.

22. Carson excelled in the role of male narcissist, a common, fatuous but humorously admonitory presence in many of the comedies of the period, whose purpose, aside from helping to complicate the love plot, is to spoof the self-love that is the most serious obstacle to the marriage of true minds. My favorite is his hyperactive performance as the archery champion who can't help admiring his own physique in *Love Crazy.*

23. The comedy-mystery, that chic hybrid of thirties moviemaking, also loves sending up the pop psychology of the day. The nerdy scion of the murder victim in *The Thin Man* is constantly offering psychoanalytic insights into criminal motives for murder, but Nick and Nora prefer to pursue more mundane clues—like who stands to profit from the murder.

24. The prominence given to this word in the sanity hearing that concludes the film was worthy of being included in the O.E.D., where we find these informative and entertaining entries dating to the first half of this century:

    1936: in Amer. Speech (1941) XVI. 79/2 "Lawyer: Now tell me, what does everybody back home think of Longfellow Deeds? . . . Jane: They think he's pixilated."
    1936: in Amer. Speech 80/1 "The word pixilated is an early American expression—derived from the word 'pixies' meaning elves. They would say, 'The pixies have got him,' as we nowadays would say a man is 'balmy.'"
    1937: N. & Q; 2 Jan. 11/2 "As a native of the state from which 'Mr. Deeds' is reputed to have come permit me to comment on 'pixilated.' To use the word in the sense of 'crazy' is not correct. A Vermonter would not hesitate to use 'crazy' if that conveyed his meaning. A 'pixilated' man is one whose whimseys are not understood by practical-minded people. . . . More nearly a synonym of 'whimsical.'"

25. The O.E.D. cites this informative entry on the social roots of "boogie," whose etymological origin is apparently unknown:

    1976: "G. Oakley Devil's Music 163 When rent day was due, you 'pitched boogie,' inviting the neighbors round and charging an entrance fee of perhaps a quarter and a jug of gin." From "pitching boogie" to "playing boogie" is but a short, syncopated step. This information is offered in honor of the assiduous Professor Potts.

26. Here I don't think we can either overlook or underestimate the importance of Billy Wilder's contribution, along with Charles Brackett's, as screenwriter. Wilder is surely one of the most witty and adept of the screenwriters of that period (or any period, for that matter), but what singles him out is that he is *not* a native speaker. Like Nabokov, who shares his sense of the comedy of American language, Wilder has a keen ear and keener appreciation for the giddy and fatuous pleasures of our idioms. Professor Potts's lexical trees anticipate the verbal play that give *Pale Fire* and *Lolita* their exuberant language.

27. Gerald Weales astutely remarks how in *Desire* Cooper had already perfected his "little-boy bit," although there his boyishness is a feigned rather than genuine part of his screen character. See Gerald Weales, *Canned Goods as Caviar: American Film Comedy of the 1930s* (Chicago: University of Chicago Press, 1985), p. 171.

28. Northrop Frye, *Anatomy of Criticism: Four Essays* (Princeton: Princeton University Press, 1957), p. 178.

29. Gerald Weales points out that "Deeds is about as radical as John Crowe Ransom was when he called for the 'self-subsistent or agrarian economy' in 1932, and the government, its foundations unrocked, had been experimenting with subsistence homesteads since 1933." See *Canned Goods as Caviar*, p. 182.

30. Tyler, *Hollywood Hallucination*, p. 76.

31. James, *Question of Our Speech*, p. 16.

Chapter Three. Blonde Bombshells

1. Ellen Moers, *Literary Women* (New York: Anchor, 1977), p. 266. Moers, speaking of the momentous significance of dark hair and blonde curls in Mme de Staël's *Corinne,* points to the contrast between the "passionate exuberance of dark-haired Latin culture" and the "subdued and inhibited sensibility of Nordic culture." Blonde and brunette stand in slightly different relation to each other in the sexual semiotics of American popular culture.

2. Howard Hawks, *Hawks on Hawks,* ed. Joseph McBride (Berkeley: University of California Press), p. 98.

3. Ibid.

4. Kathleen Rowe, *The Unruly Woman: Gender and the Genres of Laughter* (Austin: University of Texas Press, Texas Film Studies Series, 1995), p. 120.

5. Parker Tyler, *The Hollywood Hallucination* (New York: Creative Press, 1944), p. 97.

6. Jean Harlow, *Today Is Tonight* (New York: Grove, 1965), p. 31.

7. The charge of illiteracy often assails Harlow's screen characters—in *Libeled*

Lady, William Powell's character suggests that she spend her confinement in a hotel room learning to read. There is, apparently, no variant of the Bombshell myth that allows the possibility of a literate blonde, somewhat of a joke in itself, given that Jean Harlow is the only one of our female cavalcade of verbal marvels who actually wrote a novel, *Today Is Tonight.* (Several, of course, wrote autobiographies, but hardly ever on their own.) On screen, Harlow as literary bombshell—like Irene Dunne's Theodora—was inconceivable.

8. Barbara Stanwyck could play a madcap heiress in *The Mad Miss Manton,* soft-boiled con-woman in *The Lady Eve,* hardboiled stripper in *Ball of Fire,* savvy reporter with a touch of idealism in *Meet John Doe,* and, in her last and most uncomplicatedly cheerful comic movie, *Christmas in Connecticut,* a columnist for a woman's magazine without a clue of how to fry an egg, much less run a household.

9. Lombard, of course, was notorious for her uncensored talk, a strategy, attests her biographer, to keep the roaming packs of Hollywood wolves at bay. According to her brother, Fred Peters, who with his brother Stuart gave his sister a crash course on talking dirty, "Carole kicked out the words and phrases she wanted to use as her weapons. . . . Her language never became as blue as some people said, and she was always proper—she never forgot herself. Some words women throw around today—well, Carole would simply never use them. But everything was different then, and a girl could get herself into a lot of trouble just by talking dirt. But she had the style to carry it off." Her biographer follows her brother's account by noting that Lombard "learned every vulgarism for the copulative equipment of both sexes, the intricately obscene terminology of the act itself, all the catchwords that were spinoffs of the perversions." He also confirms Fred Peters's claim that Lombard had the style to carry off her blue talk: "Word of her brazen verbal accomplishments got around the Pathé studio and gave her the aura of personality. Then the word spread around town generally, and that didn't hurt either." Larry Swindell, *Screwball: The Life of Carole Lombard* (New York: Morrow, 1975), pp. 76–77.

10. Ibid., p. 153.

11. Elizabeth Kendall, *The Runaway Bride: Hollywood Romantic Comedy of the 1930s* (New York: Knopf, 1990), p. 155.

12. Ginger Rogers, *Ginger: My Story* (New York: HarperCollins, 1991), p. 287.

13. Murray Kempton, "Working Girl," *New York Review of Books,* June 8, 1995, p. 67.

14. Kendall, *Runaway Bride,* p. 179.

15. Kempton, "Working Girl," p. 67.

16. Elizabeth Kendall gives a splendid account of how the movie differs from the

stage play and how Rogers transformed a cardboard character into the film's most "fully drawn human" in her chapter on *Stage Door.* See her *Runaway Bride,* especially pp. 161–80.

17. Rogers, *Ginger,* p. 228.

18. Kathleen Rowe devotes an entire book to this comic *topos*—the unruly woman. She is particularly concerned with identifying those characteristics, including a "sharp tongue" that are associated with "comedic forms of female transgression," and in showing how the unruly woman of talking pictures both descends and departs from the "wild woman" of the silents. See especially her chapter "Romantic Comedy and the Unruly Virgin in Classical Hollywood Cinema," *Unruly Woman,* pp. 116–44.

Chapter Four. My Favorite Brunettes

1. Italo Calvino, "A Cinema-Goer's Autobiography," *The Road to San Giovanni,* trans. Tim Parks (New York: Pantheon, 1993), p. 52.

2. The only exception is the dreary *Wife vs. Secretary,* which forces Loy to play the "modern" wife who trusts her husband, even if Jean Harlow is her husband's indispensable secretary. The movie eventually will prove she is right, but not before dragging Loy through the sloughs of Faith Baldwin's didactic melodrama.

3. Manny Farber, *Negative Space: Manny Farber on the Movies* (New York: Praeger, 1971), p. 26. In a priceless riff on *Only Angels Have Wings,* Farber has fun pointing out the "intricately silly" situation in which the Group is represented as a "family unit living at the Dutchman's, a combination bar, restaurant, rooming house, and airport run by a benevolent Santa Claus (some airline: the planes take off right next to the kitchen, and some kitchen: a plane crashes, the wreck is cleared and the pilot buried in the time it takes them to cook a steak; and the chief control is a crazy mascot who lives with a pet donkey and serves as a lookout atop a buzzard-and-blizzard infested mountain as sharp as a shark's tooth)" (p. 27).

4. Frank Capra, *The Name Above the Title: An Autobiography* (New York: Macmillan, 1971), p. 184.

5. In *A Foreign Affair,* Arthur's Phoebe Frost, in trying to resist her "yearning" for Pringle (John Lund), makes quite a different show of her knowledge of parliamentary idiom, declaring his advances "way out of order." She is "overruled," as she probably hoped she would be all along.

6. Of course, the film doesn't take place over one magical night, but the three days and nights favored by fairy tales.

1. Thus anticipating, as the more poetic or pedantic of her descendants might recall, the Wordsworth of "Peele Castle."
2. James Thurber, "The Sea and the Shore," *Further Fables for Our Time* (New York: Simon and Schuster, 1956), pp. 1–2.
3. Ibid., p. 3.
4. Stanley Cavell, meditating on the comic byplay between Susan (Katharine Hepburn) and David (Cary Grant) in *Bringing Up Baby*, contends that the "issue of who is following whom presides over their relationship from its inception" and is soon identified with "the matter of whom is behind whom." *Pursuits of Happiness: The Hollywood Comedy of Remarriage* (Cambridge: Harvard University Press, 1981), p. 121.
5. In the story, the heroine is on the verge of breaking her engagement with her fiancé, with whom she has recently quarreled over nothing much. That seems to be the problem—his lackadaisical attitude. She presents him with the challenge of bringing "baby" to the country as a kind of erotic ordeal that will prove the depth of his love for her. See Hagar Wilde, "Bringing Up Baby," *Colliers,* April 10, 1937.
6. Lovers traditionally turn to the animal kingdom in search of metaphors for the promptings and backslidings of amatory instinct: swans are venerated as paragons of monogamy, while ravens and rabbits are castigated as lascivious, promiscuous breeders. As exemplars of sexual misbehavior, animals may even take up the burden of a comic subplot, as in the custody battle over Mr. Smith, the beloved family dog in *The Awful Truth,* or, using the same breed, in the "marital woes" endured by Asta, the totemic terrier signifying the wry marital concord subsisting between Nick and Nora Charles. In *The Return of the Thin Man,* Asta must defend his consort against the sexual predation of a blackguard poodle who burrowed his way into her affections.
7. Charles Darwin, *The Origin of Species* (New York: Penguin, 1968), p. 136.
8. Ibid., p. 137.
9. The O.E.D. elaborates on this root sense as follows: "To cause to 'muse' or stare; to confound, distract, bewilder, puzzle."
10. Naomi Wise, "The Hawksian Woman," *Take One* 3, no. 3 (January–February 1971): 17.
11. Ibid., p. 18.
12. Leigh Brackett, "A Comment on 'The Hawksian Woman,' " *Take One* 3, no. 8 (July–August 1971): 19.
13. In Hawks's *Only Angels Have Wings,* Grant reverts to an adventurer who lacks the emotional suppleness of Grant's comic characters.
14. In *My Man Godfrey,* Mischa Auer, as Carlo, the mother's ravenous "artis-

tic" protégé, gives what should be honored as the definitive film performance of man imitating ape. His uncanny impression of a gorilla, which includes climbing up the parlor drapes, suggests new heights to which Method acting might aspire in cross-species identification. Grant's simian mimicry can't approach Auer's, who plays the ape with a gravity and gusto that eliminate any trace of irony, so deeply has he immersed his human into the gorilla's nature. Grant's imitation never descends into "ape being."

15. Stanley Cavell, for whom *Bringing Up Baby* illustrates the travails of consciousness, has commented suggestively on this moment. He takes it to be a moment of fulfillment. David, who has gone through the film "in a trance of innocence," finally comes to understand that "Baby" has two natures, "call them tame and wild, or call them latent and aroused." He shows "his acquisition of consciousness," Cavell argues, "by summoning up the courage to let it collapse." *Pursuits of Happiness,* p. 128.

16. Charles Lamb, "The Artificial Comedy of the Last Age," *Elia and the Last Essays of Elia* (Oxford: Oxford University Press, 1987), p. 167.

17. Ibid., p. 165.

18. Within the year, in a remake of *Holiday,* also released in 1938, Grant, taking the role of Johnny Case, will return the favor and invite Hepburn's Linda Seton to share his world of play. But in that film he teaches her nothing; indeed, as teacher he is a failure, because his first object choice, Linda's sister Julia (Doris Nolan), is appalled at the prospect of living a life outside the genteel routines of the haute bourgeoisie. Linda *loves* the playhouse of her childhood, where she retreats with her alcoholic brother Ned (Lew Ayres) to escape the spirit-dampening respectabilities paraded in the family parlor. She is waiting to be rescued; certainly she is not averse to exchanging one playpen for another. Linda is a creature of the playhouse. Johnny merely shows her that the world itself is a playhouse. But he works no fundamental change in her nature, as she does in David's in *Bringing Up Baby.*

19. Cavell, *Pursuits of Happiness,* p. 118.

20. Sigmund Freud, *Jokes and Their Relation to the Unconscious,* trans. and ed. James Strachey (New York: W. W. Norton, 1989), p. 155.

21. Sigmund Freud, *Beyond the Pleasure Principle, The Standard Edition of the Complete Psychological Works of Sigmund Freud,* vol. 18 (London: Hogarth, 1955), p. 15.

22. The O.E.D. notes a special Americanism, "Let George do it"—let someone else do the work or take the responsibility, an interesting usage for a comedy in which irresponsibility is highly valued.

    1910 Bookman May 293/2 "What's going to happen when Lovey asks papa to hold Snookums and that hitherto devoted parent replies, 'Let George do it.'"

1942 Wodehouse Money in Bank (1946) xvi. 140 "He was not familiar with the fine old slogan, Let George Do It."

1948 Chicago Tribune (Grafic Mag.) 10 Oct. 8/1 "Producers have a way of saying 'Let George do it' whenever a particularly difficult villain role turns up."

23. Howard Hawks, *Hawks on Hawks,* ed. Joseph McBride (Berkeley: University of California Press, 1981), p. 70.

24. Bergman, too, exploited the high symbolic comedy of clothes. We know that Egerman is on his way to a serious psychic drubbing when, after having wet and muddied his clothes in his fall, he is forced to don a nightshirt and singularly flaccid nightcap. When Desiree's current lover, the militantly phallic officer who arrives in full uniform, sword and bearing ludicrously erect, Egerman's detumescent headgear becomes even more of a liability, and any pretense to dignity is, hilariously if cruelly, quickly dispatched.

25. Anne Hollander regards the primal and often sacred original purpose of dress "as representing in terms of self-imposed and noticeable bodily applications — which may include distortion and disfigurement — the spiritual aspirations, the imaginative projections, and the practical sacrifices" that separate adults from infants and beasts. Anne Hollander, *Sex and Suits* (New York: Knopf, 1994), p. 9.

26. Hawks, who fully appreciated and exploited Cary Grant's genius in sexual disguise, insisted that the cross-dressing not be played mincingly but as a deliberate masquerade. When Grant began practicing tricks to render his character "feminine," Hawks stopped him and directed him to "just act like a man in a woman's clothes." When he came to the scene when Grant must board ship and answer the questions all war brides were asked — had they any "woman trouble" or had they ever been pregnant — he suggested that Grant, who in the script was to act embarrassed, play the scene the opposite way: "Let the sergeant be embarrassed at having to ask you these things. Say, 'Oh, many times, Sergeant. Oh, I have a great deal of trouble.' " Interview by Peter Bogdanavich, *Movie,* no. 5 (December 1962): 16.

27. The cacophony of animal sounds provides the bass harmony of Hawks's comic oratorio. Bruce Babington and Peter William Evans have selected this moment as the film's "paradigm of Screwball" and ingeniously describe how Susan and David's serenade of Baby, sitting on Lehman's roof, becomes "a trio, then a quartet, as the leopard roars a third part and George switches from yapping to yowling in what is by now very elaborate polyphonic motet." They claim that "in the quartet we have for a moment a ridiculous, yet within the context of all the folly, moving version of 'The Peaceable Kingdom,' as for a moment the humans and the animals raise their voices together." I would stop short of their suggestion that we regard this symphonic mo-

ment as a "comic version of Adam and the Lady Eve speaking the original transparent speech with which the mystic philosopher, Jakob Boehme, credited them, a speech closer to the animals' than to the speech of civilization." They are singing, not conversing. See Babington and Evans, *Affairs to Remember: The Hollywood Comedy of the Sexes* (Manchester: St. Martin's, 1989), p. 35.

28. In *His Girl Friday*, Hawks resorts to a similar high-angle distancing shot to signal a moment of expanded and elevated consciousness not available to anyone, with the possible exception of Hildy Johnson, in the film itself. See Chapter Eight.

29. This is Cavell's stunning point in discussing the ending of *Bringing Up Baby*, and the general reticence of American films that fall under the rubric of "comedies of remarriage" to enact for us a final embrace. For Cavell, this inconclusiveness reflects the "underlying perception that marriage requires its own proof, that nothing can show its validity from outside." *Pursuits of Happiness*, p. 127.

Chapter Six. The Lady-Dame

1. Elizabeth Kendall, *The Runaway Bride: Hollywood Romantic Comedy of the 1930s* (New York: Knopf, 1990), p. 185.

2. She could also be less comically defiant of established social conventions, as in her luminous impersonation of the "separated" Ellen Olenska in the 1934 adaptation of Edith Wharton's *Age of Innocence*.

3. Kendall, *Runaway Bride*, p. 185.

4. Ralph Waldo Emerson, "Character," *Essays: First and Second Series* (New York: Library of America, 1990), p. 270.

5. Stanley Cavell, *Pursuits of Happiness: The Hollywood Comedy of Remarriage* (Cambridge: Harvard University Press, 1981), p. 233.

6. James Agee, *Agee on Film* (New York: Putnam, 1983), p. 272.

7. It is mostly in response to Pauline Kael's reaction to Dunne's performance in *The Awful Truth* that Cavell makes his case for Dunne's ontological centrality to the comedy. While admitting that Dunne is often funny, Kael complains that "she overdoes the coy gurgles, and that bright toothy smile of hers—she shows both rows of teeth, prettily held together—can make one want to slug her." *New Yorker*, July 14, 1975. Reprinted in *When the Lights Go Down* (New York: Holt, Rinehart and Winston, 1980), p. 7.

8. Graham Greene, *The Pleasure Dome: The Collected Film Criticism, 1935–40*, ed. John Russell Taylor (Oxford: Oxford University Press, 1980), p. 137.

9. Emerson, "Character," p. 270.

10. Kathleen Rowe assembles and itemizes the "cluster of qualities" that have come to signify "female unruliness." Items three, four, and seven are of particular interest for this discussion of the lady-dames:

3. Her speech is excessive, in quantity, content, or tone.
4. She makes jokes or laughs at herself. . . .
7. Her behavior is associated with looseness and occasionally whorishness, but her sexuality is less narrowly and negatively defined than is that of the femme fatale. She may be pregnant.

See Rowe, *The Unruly Woman: Gender and the Genres of Laughter* (Austin: University of Texas Press, Texas Film Studies Series, 1995), p. 31.
11. Henry David Thoreau, *Walden and Civil Disobedience* (Boston: Houghton Mifflin, 1960), p. 221.
12. See James Harvey's detailed, appreciative account of this culminating scene in Harvey, *Romantic Comedy in Hollywood from Lubitsch to Sturges* (New York: Knopf, 1987), pp. 221–23.
13. Given the somewhat unusual name of her heroine, it may be worth recalling that Theodora's namesake, the Byzantine empress and consort of Justinian, began life as an actress and bore a child out of wedlock. These details are comically reworked in the second half of the film, which have Theodora acting up a storm and appearing, in her last impish public gesture, to be an unwed mother. Theodora's conversion to modernity echoes, again in a comic and lighter key, the empress's conversion to Christianity, the "modern" religion of its time.
14. Charles Lamb, "The Artificial Comedy of the Last Age," *Elia; and Last Essays of Elia* (Oxford: Oxford University Press, 1987), p. 163.
15. Cavell, *Pursuits of Happiness,* frontispiece.
16. This is Kendall's somewhat politically correct reading of the Warriners' embarrassment *for* Dixie Belle. See *Runaway Bride,* pp. 203–4.

Chapter Seven. Garbo's Laugh

1. Barry Paris, *Garbo: A Biography* (New York: Knopf, 1995), p. 361.
2. I have not seen this film, but Paris describes her manner as one of adolescent insouciance. See ibid., p. 24.
3. Norman Zierold, *Garbo* (New York: Stein and Day, 1969), p. 108.
4. Although she considered many properties after her "retirement," including a remake of *Flesh and the Devil* (she was in the 1926 version), a film version of *Tosca* ("I don't want to kill" was reportedly the reason she rejected it), and *Anastasia,* the closest she came to a comeback was the lead in Max Ophüls's

planned production of Balzac's *La Duchesse de Langeais*. See Paris, *Garbo,* p. 416.

5. Roland Barthes, "The Face of Garbo," *Mythologies,* trans. Annette Lavers (New York: Hill and Wang, 1972), p. 56.

6. Here's the joke that Leon shares with the patrons of the restaurant, who seem to appreciate the jest against a waiter's absurdly obliging literalness in filling an order: "A man comes into a restaurant. He sits down at the table and he says, 'Waiter, bring me a cup of coffee without cream.' Five minutes later the waiter comes back and says, 'I'm sorry, sir, we have no cream. Can it be without milk?'"

7. Douglas remarks as well that "her technical abilities for other kinds of scenes (other than love scenes) were not as fully developed, however. In spite of *Ninotchka*'s billing as the film in which 'Garbo laughs,' she was unable to articulate so much as a titter during the shooting of the restaurant scene. I never learned whether her laughter, which must have been added in the dubbing room, was Garbo or not." It was. Melvyn Douglas and Tom Arthur, *See You at the Movies: The Autobiography of Melvyn Douglas* (Lanham, Md.: University Press of America, 1986), p. 89.

8. Henri Bergson, "Laughter" in *Comedy: An Essay on Comedy,* edited and with an introduction by Wylie Sypher (Baltimore: Johns Hopkins University Press, 1994), p. 69.

9. William Paul, *Ernst Lubitsch's American Comedy* (New York: Columbia University Press, 1983), p. 213.

10. Milan Kundera, *The Book of Laughter and Forgetting,* trans. Aaron Asher (New York: HarperPerennial, 1996), p. 86.

11. Charles Baudelaire, "On the Essence of Laughter," *Selected Writings on Art and Literature,* translated and with an introduction by P. E. Charvet (New York: Penguin, 1992), p. 142.

12. Ibid., p. 148.

13. Ibid., p. 142.

14. Ibid., p. 143.

15. Milan Kundera, "Sixty-Three Words," *The Art of the Novel,* trans. Linda Asher (New York: Perennial Library, 1988), p. 131.

16. Siegfried Kracauer, reacting to what he deemed the "intrinsic nihilism" of Lubitsch's silent historical pageants—*Madame du Barry* (a.k.a. *Passion*), *Anna Boleyn* (a.k.a. *Deception*), and *Das Weib des Pharao* (a.k.a. *The Loves of Pharao,* or *Pharaoh's Wife*), censured Lubitsch's films for "representing not so much historic periods as personal appetites and seeming to seize upon history for the sole purpose of removing it thoroughly from the field of vision." Siegfried Kracauer, *From Caligari to Hitler: A Psychological History of the German Film*

(Princeton: Princeton University Press, 1947), p. 52. Leo Braudy has admirably defended Lubitsch against such charges of "facile nihilism about personal relations," arguing that "whatever 'nihilism' implies, it is not sufficient to describe the way Lubitsch tells stories and the implications he wrings from them, far beyond but always through their immediate plots." See Braudy, "The Double Detachment of Ernst Lubitsch," *Native Informant: Essays on Film, Fiction, and Popular Culture* (New York: Oxford University Press, 1991), p. 70.

17. This remarkable hat inspires yet another reaction, this one from the peerless Parker Tyler, who reads it as an emblem and a vehicle of Garbo's comic demystification. Garbo needed, he writes,

mystification no less than mystery. Her large feet and mannish clothes, however, received too much publicity and had a corrosive effect: as the mystery became stereotyped, the mystification became too evident. In that plodding way the public has, movie audiences began to wonder about the meaning of Garbo's "private" assets. They read she was girlish and unaffected off the set. They read that in real life she had lighthearted romances. The moment came when the mystification had to be elucidated, since the mystery had already been liquidated. Hence *Ninotchka*, in which Garbo's private style of dress became transiently her public, or professional, style. The movie's plot followed the pattern of her "private" Hollywood legend of preoccupation and standoffishness. In it she was cold, absorbed in her work, distant from pleasure-loving society, and, oddly enough, she came as an emissary from that home of a new society, Russia. Ah, she was a revised somnambule of a revised steppes! She obeyed a Svengali called Stalin until a realistic American came into her life and awakened "the woman" in her. Now at last the narcissistic appetite of the American public is satisfied: Garbo, paragon of individual exoticism, has been initiated into the national lessons of *Vogue* and *Harper's Bazaar*! She had entered the shopgirl's paradise: *imported chic*. A strange Americanization for a foreign actress: a fall from the true "Paris" model to the original American Paris-emulated model. How timely Hollywood was—connecting its greatest star with the destiny of hats on the eve of a war which isolated Paris from the fashion world! (pp. 85–86)

Parker Tyler, *The Hollywood Hallucination* (New York: Creative Age, 1944), pp. 85–86.

18. Preston Sturges may have been remembering this moment in *Sullivan's Travels*, adapting it for the opposite effect. Lenin smiles indulgently, but the smil-

ing picture is of the dead husband who frowns on wife's lubricious advances toward her handyman and night boarder, Joel McCrea.

19. Paris, *Garbo,* pp. 362–63.
20. Zierold, *Garbo,* p. 67.

Chapter Eight. Female Rampant

1. *The Stage Works of Charles MacArthur,* edited with introduction and notes by Arthur Dorlag and John Irvine (Tallahassee: Florida State University Foundation, 1974), p. 141.
2. Ibid., p. 128.
3. Manny Farber, *Negative Space: Manny Farber on the Movies* (New York: Praeger, 1971), p. 26.
4. *Stage Works of Charles MacArthur,* p. 141.
5. Ibid., p. 128.
6. Ibid., p. 155.
7. A year later, George Stevens would take Grant's matinee-idol face and cast it in the role of an alleged arsonist in *Talk of the Town.* But the sinister face that makes the headlines of the film's opening montage is quickly revealed to be an impostor, and the easy but thoughtful charmer soon establishes his moral appeal as the town's only truthteller.
8. *Stage Works of Charles MacArthur,* p. 131.
9. Stanley Cavell, *Pursuits of Happiness: The Hollywood Comedy of Remarriage* (Cambridge: Harvard University Press, 1981), p. 167.
10. Walter is prone to getting the time wrong. To lure Hildy back to the *Morning Post* and persuade her to cover the Earl Williams case, he fabricates a tale about Sweeney, "the best man . . . on the paper for that sob sister stuff," expecting twins. What he forgets but Hildy soon remembers is that Sweeny has been married for only four months. Given the sexual mores permissible to the screen under the Production Code, this makes the story implausible. Hawks is incomparable in wedding the sexual naivete of this accepted explanation with the knowing cynicism of the newsroom.
11. Marilyn Campbell, "*His Girl Friday:* Production for Use," *Wide Angle* 1, no. 2 (Summer 1976): 27.
12. *Stage Works of Charles MacArthur,* p. 141.

1. Stanley Cavell, *Pursuits of Happiness: The Hollywood Comedy of Remarriage* (Cambridge: Harvard University Press, 1981), p. 57.
2. Ibid., p. 66.
3. Ibid.
4. I think that this attention to Stanwyck's legs, by the way, is echoed in her famous entrance in *Double Indemnity* (1944), when she comes down the stairs to meet the jaded Walter Neff (Fred MacMurray), who seems drawn, like Charles, by her perfume and her ankles.
5. This scene was shot exactly as scripted. See *Five Screenplays by Preston Sturges,* ed. Brian Henderson (Berkeley: University of California Press, 1985), pp. 388–89.
6. Cavell, *Pursuits of Happiness,* p. 67.
7. *Five Screenplays,* pp. 419–20.
8. The arrival of a bouquet of roses leads Jean to accelerate her timetable for bringing her plan for sexual revenge to its conclusion. This seemingly minor detail speaks eloquently to Sturges's attentiveness to his comic design. We first see flowers in the garland that Muggsy receives from the native woman, and the nature of Jean's feelings for Hopsie are visually recorded when she is shown dreamily caressing her face with a single, simple rose.
9. This particular shot may be an allusion to the romantic endings of B-Westerns, when girl and boy and horse all snort their love together.
10. Cavell, *Pursuits of Happiness,* p. 65.
11. Daniel Seidel, unpublished essay, "The Specter of the Infelicitous in Austin, *The Lady Eve,* and *La Traviata.*"

Conclusion

1. Henry James, *The Question of Our Speech* (Boston: Houghton Mifflin, 1905), p. 40.

Index